MAGE'S BLOOD

THE MOONTIDE QUARTET

MAGE'S BLOOD

THE MOONTIDE QUARTET

DAVID HAIR

Jo Fletcher
BOOKS

First published in Great Britain in 2012 by

Jo Fletcher Books
an imprint of Quercus
55 Baker Street
7th Floor, South Block
London
W1U 8EW

ISBN 978 1 78087 194 3 (TPB)
ISBN 978 1 78087 195 0 (HB)

10 9 8 7 6 5 4 3 2 1

Typeset by Ellipsis Digital Limited, Glasgow

Printed and bound in Great Britain by
Clays Ltd, St Ives plc

TABLE OF CONTENTS

Prologue: The Web of Souls   1

1: The Vexations of Emperor Constant (Part 1)   6

2: Wear Your Gems   27

3: The Standards of Noros   43

4: The Price of Your Daughter's Hand   65

5: The Dutiful Daughter   78

6: Words of Fire and Blood   89

7: Hidden Causes   99

8: An Act of Betrayal   115

9: Enriched   142

10: Soldier of the Shihad   171

11: Graduation   177

12: Council of War   196

13: Contact with the Enemy   217

14: The Road North   221

15: Mage's Gambit   243

16: A Piece of Amber   278

17: Desert Storms   296

18. Lady Meiros   320

19: Offered Hands   343

20: This Betrayal   358

21: Missing and Hunted   375

22: Circling Vultures   392

23: Relearning the Heart   398

24: Manifestation   424

25: The Jackals of Ahm   429

26: Patterns Burnt into Air   438

27: A Trail Gone Cold   449

28: Divinations   457

29: Envoy   468

30: Dressed to Steal   476

31: Lovers   498

32: The Ghost of a Dog   530

33: Southpoint   559

34: Revealed   571

35: Souldrinker and Assassin   592

36: Shapeshifter   612

37: Beneath the Surface   630

38: Not Dead   646

39: Mountains at Dawn   651

Epilogue: Endings are Beginnings   662

This book is dedicated to my wife Kerry; Lucky me!
It also goes out with my love to Brendan and Melissa, my children;
to my patient test readers (you know who you are),
and to friends and family everywhere. And hello to Jason Isaacs.

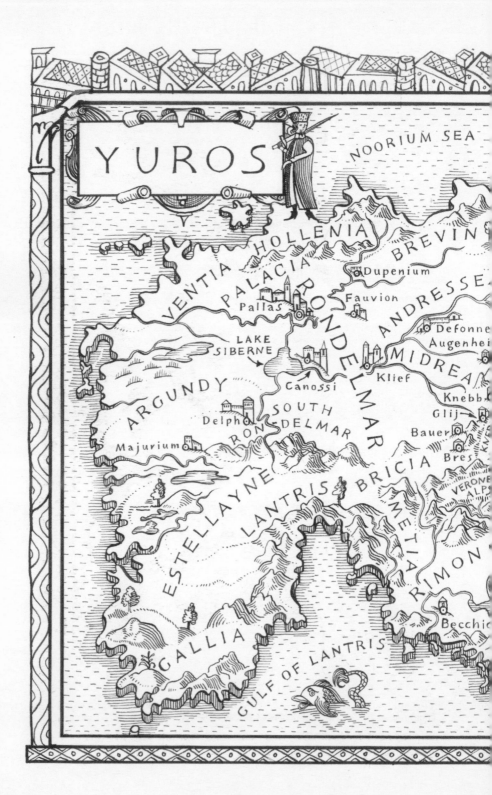

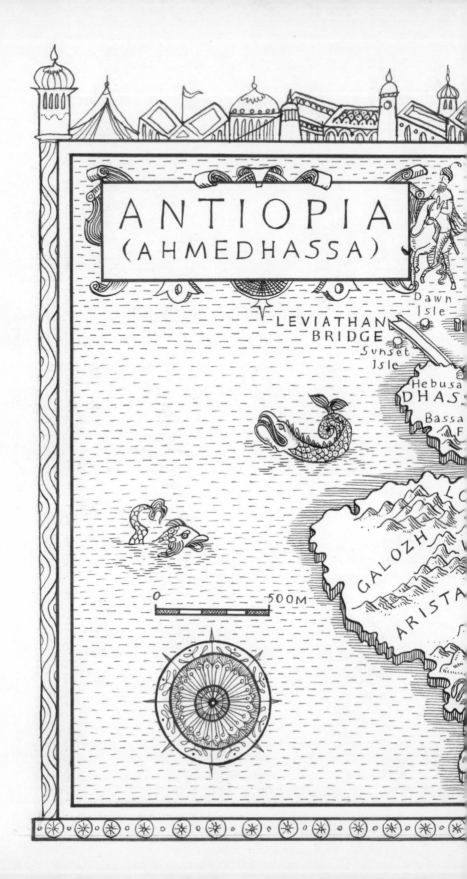

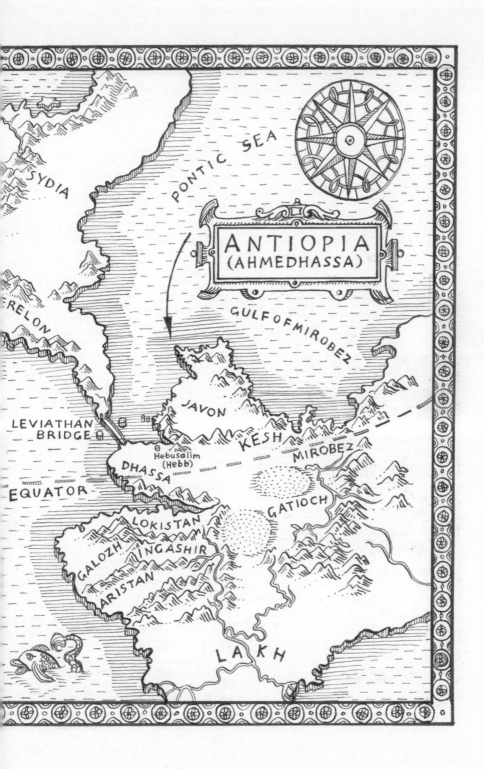

The Web of Souls

The Fate of the Dead

What happens when the soul leaves the body? Paradise or Damnation? Rebirth? Oneness with God? Or Oblivion? The faiths of mankind have made a case for each and many other variants. But we of the Ordo Costruo teach this: that when the soul detaches from the body it remains here on Urte for a time, a disembodied ghost. Whether it eventually dissipates or passes to some other place, we can only speculate. But what we do know is that a mage may commune with such ghosts and gain access to all that those spirits perceive. There are millions of such spirits wandering the lands. By communing with them, it is theoretically possible to be aware of almost everything that is happening on Urte.

ORDO COSTRUO COLLEGIATE, PONTUS

Nimtaya Mountains, Antiopia
Julsept 927
1 Year until the Moontide

As the sun stabbed through a cleft in the eastern mountains, a thin wail lifted from a midden. The refuse heap lay downwind of a ramshackle cluster of mud-brick hovels. The quavering cry hung in the air, an invitation to predators. A lurking jackal soon appeared, sniffing warily. In the distance others of his kind yowled and yapped, but this close to prey, he moved in silence.

There: a bundle of swaddled clothing amidst the waste and filth, jerking spasmodically, tiny brown limbs kicking free. The jackal looked around then trotted forward cautiously. The helpless newborn went still as the beast loomed over it. It did not yet understand that the

1

warm embracing being that had held it would not return. It was thirsty and the cold was beginning to bite.

The beast did not see a child; it saw food. Its jaws opened.

An instant later the jackal was hurled through the air, its hindquarters smashing against a boulder. It writhed agonisingly and tried to run, sliding down the slope it had so gracefully ascended, its eyes flashing about, seeking the danger it had never even sensed. One hind leg was shattered; it didn't get far.

A ragged bulk wrapped in cloth rose and glided towards the beast, which snapped and snarled as an arm holding a rock emerged and rose and fell. There was a muffled crunch and blood splattered. From amidst the filthy cloth a face emerged, a leathery-faced old woman with wiry iron hair. She bent until her lips were almost touching the jackal's muzzle.

She inhaled.

Later that day, the old woman sat cross-legged in a cave high above an arid valley. The land below was stark and jagged, layers of shadow and light playing amongst rocky outcroppings. She lived alone, with none to wrinkle their nose in distaste at her unwashed stench, nor to avert their eyes from her wizened face. Her skin was dark and dry, her tangled hair grey, but she moved with grace as she built up the fire. Smoke was cleverly funnelled up a cleft in the rock and out – one of her many great-nephews had carved the chimney, and though she didn't remember his name, a face floated to mind.

Methodically she spooned water into the tiny puckered mouth of the newborn baby, one of dozens abandoned each year by the villagers, unwanted and doomed from their first breath. All they asked of her was that she saw them on their way to paradise. The villagers revered her as a holy woman and often sought her aid; the Scriptualists tolerated her, turning a blind eye – for they too had needs, their own dead to placate. From time to time a zealot tried to drive away the 'jadugara' – the witch – but they seldom lasted long – condemning her tended to prove unlucky. And if they came in force she was very hard to find.

The villagers wanted her intercessions with the ancestors. She told them what they needed to hear and in return she was given food and drink, clothes and fuel – and their unwanted children. They never asked what became of them – life was harsh here and death came easy. There was never enough for all.

The child in her lap squalled, its mouth questing for sustenance as she looked down at it without emotion. She too was a jackal, of another sort, and great-grandmother of her own pack. When she was younger, she'd had lovers, and conceived once; a girl who became a woman and bred many more. The jadugara still watched over her ancestors, pieces in her unseen game. She had dwelt here longer than any realised, pretending to age, die and be replaced, for centuries. The crypt-cavern in which her predecessors were supposedly buried was empty – at least of her own predecessors; instead she interred the bones of dead strangers. From time to time she would leave to wander the world, wearing scores of faces and names, moving through young woman to old crone like some season-goddess of the Sollan faith.

She did not feed the child, for that would be wasteful and nothing here could be wasted, not in this place and especially not by her, who purchased power so dearly. She tossed a pinch of powder into the flames and watched them change colour from pale orange to a deep emerald. The air temperature fell in seconds, though the flames flared higher. The smoke thickened and the night inhaled watchfully.

The time had come. She picked up a knife from the pile of knick-knacks at her knee and pressed it against the baby's tiny chest. Her eyes met the child's briefly, but she did not reflect or regret. She'd lost those emotions somewhere in her youth. She had done this more than a thousand times in her long life, in dozens of lands, on two continents; for her it was as necessary as food or water.

She pushed the blade through the baby's ribs, silencing the child's brief cry. The little mouth opened and the hag placed her lips to the infant's mouth. She inhaled ... and she was replenished, more than by the jackal. If the child had been older she would have got more, but she would take whatever came her way.

She placed the dead baby to one side, meat for the jackals – she had taken what she needed. She let the smoky energy she had ingested settle inside her. It recharged her as only the swallowed soul of another could. Her vision cleared, her vitality renewed. Replenished, she rekindled her awareness of the spirit world, which took some time – the spirits knew her, and would not approach unless compelled. Some she had bound to her will though, and from these she selected a favourite. She crooned his name; 'Jahanasthami,' as she sent out sticky tendrils of power. She poked at the fire, stirring the embers into flame, and added more powders, making the smoke run thicker. 'Jahanasthami, come!'

It was long minutes before the face of her spirit-guardian formed in the smoke, blank as an unpainted Lantric carnival mask. The eyes were empty, the mouth a blackness. 'Sabele,' it breathed. 'I felt the child die . . . I knew you would call.'

She and Jahanasthami communed, images from the spirit's consciousness streaming into hers: places and faces, memories, questions and answers. When the spirit was confounded by one of her enquiries it consulted others, then passed on the responses. They were a web of souls, connected by uncountable strands, containing so much knowledge that a mind might burst before it could take it all in. But Sabele tried, straining through the endless trivia and minutiae of millions of lives, seeking the nuggets of information that would shape the future. The jadugara shook with the effort.

Hours passed – to her, they were aeons, in which galaxies of information were born, flowered, collapsed and perished. She floated in seas of imagery and sound, immersed in the vast panoply of life, seeing kings and their servants conferring, priests haggling and merchants praying. She saw births and deaths, acts of love and murder. Finally she glimpsed the face she was seeking through the ghost-eyes of a dead Lakh girl haunting a village well – just a tiny instant, when the ghost saw a face revealed by the twitch of a curtain, before a flare of wards buffeted her away. That mere flash was enough, and Sabele moved closer, from spirit to spirit, hunting. She could feel her quarry, the way a spider sensed a distant trembling at the edge of its web, and at last she was certain: Antonin Meiros had finally made his move. He had come south from his haven in Hebusalim, seeking a way to avert war – or at least survive it. How ancient he looked; she remembered him in his youth: a face burning with energy and purpose. She'd barely escaped him then, when he and his order had slaughtered her kindred – her lovers, her bloodline, almost extinguished. *Better you still think me dead, magus.*

She banished Jahanasthami with an irritable gesture. *So, the great Antonin Meiros has decided to act at last.* She had been poking around in the constantly shifting potentials of the future long enough to know what he sought; it only surprised her that he had waited so long to act. Only one year remained until the Moontide and the carnage it would bring. It was late in the game, but Meiros' other options had been torn away.

He and Sabele were Diviners; both had seen the likely futures before them. They had crossed mental blades for centuries, worrying away at the strands of the future. She could hear his questions and felt the answers he got – she had sent him some of those answers herself, lies tangled around suppositions, hooks on gossamer threads.

Yes, Antonin, come south – take the gift I have prepared for you! Taste of life again. Taste of death.

She tried to laugh and found herself weeping instead, in anguish at all that was lost, or some other emotion she had forgotten she could feel. She didn't analyse it, merely tasted it and savoured the novelty.

The sun rose high enough to pierce the cavern and found her still there: an old spider tangled in ancient webs. Beside her the tiny corpse of the child lay cold.

1

The Vexations of Emperor Constant (Part 1)

The World of Urte

Urte is named for Urtih, an earth god of the ancient Yothic people. There are two known continents, Yuros and Antiopia (or Ahmedhassa). Some scholars have speculated that, due to certain similarities in primitive artefacts and some commonality of creatures, they were once joined through the Pontic Peninsula. This is still unproven, but what is certain is that without the power of the magi, there would be no intercourse between the continents now, as they are divided by more than three hundred miles of impassable sea. We surmise a prehistoric cosmic incident which caused Lune, the Moon, to move into a closer orbit, rendering the seas more turbulent, preventing sea-travel and destroying significant landmass.

ORDO COSTRUO COLLEGIATE, PONTUS

Pallas, North Rondelmar, on the continent of Yuros
2 Julsept 927
1 Year until the Moontide

Gurvon Gyle pulled up the hood of his robe like a penitent monk: just another anonymous initiate of the Kore. He turned to his companion, an elegant silver-maned man who was stroking his beard thoughtfully, staring out the grilled window. Shifting light caught on his face, making him look ageless. 'You've still got the governor's ring on, Bel,' Gyle remarked.

The man started out of his reverie and pocketed the easily identifiable ring. 'Listen to the crowds, Gurvon.' His voice wasn't exactly awed, but certainly impressed, which seldom happened. 'There must be more than a hundred thousand citizens in the square alone.'

'I'm told more than three hundred thousand will witness the ceremony,' Gyle said, 'but not all of them will be watching the parade. Pull up your hood.'

Belonius Vult, Governor of Noros, smiled wryly and cowled himself with a soft sigh. Gurvon Gyle had built a career on anonymity, but Vult hated it. Today was not an occasion for display, though.

Heralded by a soft knock at the door, another man slid into the tiny room. He was slender, with the olive skin and curling black hair of a Lantrian, clad in sumptuous red velvets and bearing an ornate crozier. His soft, oval face had full, womanish lips and narrow eyes. Being near him made Gyle's skin crawl at the tingling sensation of gnosis-wardings. Paranoia ruled the Church magi more than most. The bishop flicked back his tangle of black curls and proffered a ring-encrusted hand. 'My lords of Noros, are you ready to witness the Blessed Event?'

Vult kissed the bishop's hand. 'Eagerly ready, my Lord Crozier.' All bishops of the Kore forsook their family and took the surname Crozier, but this man was kin to the Earl of Beaulieu and was accounted one of the rising stars of the Church.

'Call me Adamus, gentlemen.' The bishop leant his crozier against the wall and smiled like a child playing dress-up as he pulled up the hood of his identical grey cloak. 'Shall we go?'

The bishop led them into a darkened passage and up a crumbling stair. With every step the noise grew: the hum and buzz of the people, the blare of trumpets, the rumble of drums, the chanting of the priests and shouting of the soldiers, the tramp of the thousands of boots. They could feel it through the stonework; the air itself seemed to vibrate against their skin. Then they topped the stairs and found themselves on a tiny recessed balcony overlooking the Place d'Accord. The roar became a wall of sound that buffeted their senses.

'Great Kore!' Gyle shouted at Vult, who was smiling in wonder. Neither man was unworldly, but this was something more than either had seen. This was the Place d'Accord, the heart of the city of Pallas, as Pallas was the heart of Rondelmar, which was the heart of Yuros: the Heart of the Empire. This mighty square was the theatre upon which the endless play of politics and power was staged, before a mob whose size was frightening. Giant marble and gold statuary dwarfed the people clustered beneath and on them, like giants come to witness the pageant. Column after column of soldiers marched past, the tramp of the legionaries a drumbeat, a pulse of power. Windships circled above, giant warbirds floating in defiance of gravity, casting massive shadows beneath the noonday sun. Scarlet flags billowed in the soft northerly winds, bearing the Lion of Pallas and the sceptre and star of the Royal House of Sacrecour.

Gyle let his eyes drift to the royal box, some two hundred yards to his left, to where the legionaries directed their straight-armed salutes as they passed. Tiny figures in scarlet and glittering gold presided from above: His Royal Majesty the Emperor Constant Sacrecour and his sickly children. Assorted Dukes and Lords of this and that, Prelates and magi too, all come to witness this never-before-seen event.

Today, a living saint would be inaugurated. Gyle whistled softly, still amazed that someone had the nerve for such blasphemy, but to most here, judging by the joyous and triumphal mood of the crowd, it was deemed right and good.

A cavalry detachment high-stepped past, followed by a dozen elephants, captured on the last Crusade. Then came the Carnian riders, guiding their huge fighting-lizards between the walls of onlookers, ignoring the collective gasps of the crowds. The gaudy reptiles snapped and hissed whilst their riders maintained iron discipline, staring straight ahead except when they too swivelled to salute the emperor.

Gyle remembered what it was like to face such a force in battle and shuddered slightly. The Noros Revolt: a débâcle, a very personal nightmare. It had been the making of him, even as it stripped away both innocence and morality, and for what? Noros was once more part of the Imperial Family of Nations, for all the good it did them. For the empire it had been a blip, a momentary stalling of their conquests, but for Noros, the wounds still festered.

Gyle banished these thoughts. No one outside of Noros cared any more, and certainly no one here. He followed the bishop's pointing finger and dutifully marvelled as the Winged Corps swooped over the Place d'Accord, dozens of flying reptiles in serried ranks coming over the roof of the Sacred Heart Cathedral, battle-magi saddled behind the riders, and dipping before the royal box while the crowds screamed in awe and no little fear. Jaws longer than a man snapped, foot-long teeth gnashed and many of the winged constructs belched fire as they roared: impossible creatures made real by the magi.

How did we ever think we could defeat them?

After that came trumpets and a sudden silence as white flags rose about the royal box – the cue for the populace to still their tongues, for the emperor was to speak. Obedient to a man, the people fell silent as the small, slender shape on the throne rose to his feet and stepped to the front of the royal podium.

'My People,' Emperor Constant began, his high-pitched voice gnostically amplified throughout the square, 'my People, today I am filled with pride and awe. Pride, at the assembled grandeur of we, the Rondian people! Rightly are we acclaimed the greatest nation upon this Urte! Rightly are we known as Kore's Children! Rightly do we sit in judgement on the rest of mankind! Rightly are you, the least of my children, of greater worth to God than all other peoples! And awe, that we have achieved so much in the face of all adversity. Awe, that we have been chosen by Kore himself for his mission!'

Constant went on exalting his people – and by implication himself – cataloguing their glories from the overthrow of the Rimoni Empire and the conquest of Yuros to the Crusades across the Moontide Bridge and the crushing of the infidels of Antiopia.

Gyle felt his attention drift away from the emperor's slant on history. He counted himself fortunate, one of the few who had been educated in something closer to the truth. The Arcanum he'd attended had been more secular and less partisan. The tale he knew was that as recently as five hundred years ago Yuros had been fragmented, its greatest power, the Rimoni Empire, controlling barely a quarter of the landmass, though that encompassed Rimoni, Silacia, Verelon and all of Noros, Argundy and Rondelmar. Wars were constant; dynasties plotted and warred in Rym, the capital. Various faiths, now labelled pagan, struggled for supremacy. Plagues came, famines went. The seas roared, impassable. No one even dreamed that there was another continent beyond the eastern seas.

Then five hundred years ago, everything changed: Corineus came like a blazing comet and set the world alight. Corineus the Saviour, though he was born Johan Corin, son of a noble family of the border province of Rondelmar. He abandoned the savage gentility of the courts for a simpler, rustic life on the road. Johan Corin travelled, preaching of free love and other such idyllic notions, attracting a band of followers that over time burgeoned into nearly a thousand young people. The lost and impressionable swarmed to him and his promises of salvation in the next life and endless debauchery in this one. His people swarmed over the countryside, marked out as troublemakers, until the day when they descended upon one particular township, who panicked and called upon a nearby legion camp for help. The army agreed that the time had come to end the blasphemies of Johan Corin and his followers. That night Corin's camp was surrounded by a full legion, and at midnight, the soldiers closed in to make the arrests.

What happened next passed into legend and became scripture: there were lights and voices, and the legion died, to a man, in a thousand different ways. So did many of Corin's followers, including Corin himself, murdered by his sister-lover Selene. But there were survivors, and they were transfigured: each one had the power of a demi-god, wielding fire and storm, throwing boulders and channelling lightning. They became the Blessed Three Hundred, the first magi.

Abandoning Corin's principles of love and peace to take revenge on the town (now conveniently remembered as a 'wicked place') in an orgy of destruction. Then, realising what they now were, they allied themselves with a Rimoni Senator and formed a new movement that became an army capable of annihilating whole legions without losing a man. They destroyed the Rimoni, razed Rym and made the world anew. They created the Rondian Empire.

The Three Hundred attributed their powers to Johan Corin, claiming he was an Intercessor with God, who had bargained away his own life to gain magical powers for his disciples. They set about claiming the mortal world as their own. Being young and almighty, they slept with whomever they desired, in any land they came to. At first they did not care that the powers diminished in their children the less they bred true, but as their offspring spread throughout Yuros, claiming fiefdoms, and their understanding of their powers grew, they started colleges to teach each other, and they founded a church, and preached of their own divinity to the population.

Now, five centuries later, thousands bore the sacred blood of the Blessed Three Hundred: the magi. Their rule was embodied in the Imperial Dynasty, all descendants of Sertain, who took Corin's place as leader after the transfiguration, and currently vested in Emperor Constant Sacrecour. Gyle himself could trace his ancestry directly to one of those Three Hundred. *I am of this*, he thought. *I am magi, though I am also of Noros.* He glanced at Belonius Vult and then at Adamus Crozier, magi also: rulers of Urte.

Adamus gestured to the lower end of the Place d'Accord as if this were a show he was compering. A massive statue of Corineus stood there, his arms flung wide, just as they had found him the morning after the Transfiguration: dead, with his sister's dagger in his heart. Every one of the Three Hundred claimed to have spoken to and received instruction from Corin after his death. Some said they had seen his sister Selene in their visions, screaming foul words, though she had been nowhere to be found when they came to themselves at dawn with the legion lying dead about them. Their accounts became Scripture: Johan had guided them through the transfiguration, then been murdered by his corrupt sister Selene. He was the son of God and she was the whore-witch of Perdition. He become Corineus, the Saviour, revered everywhere; she became Corinea, the Accursed.

From the breast of the massive statue of Corineus a rose-gold light began to form, shimmering as it grew. The crowd gasped in anticipation and awe as the light became brighter and brighter, casting its brilliance over the square. Gyle could see tears on the faces of many.

Within the rosy light a shape formed, a woman clad in a white gown that looked deceptively simple, until Adamus whispered that it was made entirely of diamonds and pearls. She walked slowly out onto the platform formed by the giant golden dagger piercing the statue's heart: a woman about to be proclaimed a living saint. The entire crowd emitted an awestruck sob, as if all their hopes and dreams rested in her alone. They gasped as she stepped from the golden dagger into the air and floated down the square, some sixty feet above the crowd, towards the royal box. The people cried and cheered at this simple feat that any half-trained mage could accomplish.

Adamus Crozier winked, as if to say 'behold the theatre'. Gyle kept his face guarded.

The woman drifted past them, her palms pressed together in supplication, a sea of faces following her progress as she floated above them. *I hope she's wearing her best underwear*, Gyle found himself thinking, then stilled his mind. Mocking these people, even in the privacy of your mind, was a dangerous habit to fall into. Minds were not inviolate.

The woman floated toward the imperial throne, where Grand Prelate Wurther, Father of the Church, rose stiffly to receive her, his attendants about him. She bent her knees as she landed, hands clasped in humble prayer. The crowd cheered, then fell silent again as the Grand Prelate raised his hand.

Adamus Crozier tugged at Gyle's sleeve. 'Do you need to see more?' he whispered.

Gyle looked at Vult, then shook his head faintly.

'Good,' said Adamus. 'I have a fine scarlo awaiting us below, and we have much to discuss.'

Before they left, Gyle allowed himself to gaze long and hard at the face of the emperor, the young man they would meet in person tomorrow. Using his mage-trained sight he pulled his gaze in closer, carefully studying the man who ruled millions. Constant's face was a study in pride, envy and fear, ill-hidden behind a mask of piety. Gyle almost felt pity for him.

After all, how was one supposed to react when one's living mother had just become a saint?

The following day Gyle found himself whiling away the last few minutes before his audience in the lush palace gardens. As ever, he was the outsider, the interloper in paradise. He turned his collar against the light drizzle and paced a secluded path, his mind elsewhere. He stood out here because he wasn't dressed in vivid finery. This season the fashions were bright, Eastern-inspired, and throughout the gardens were noblemen affecting martial attire. The Third Crusade was approaching, so it was fashionable once more to look like a man of war, but Gyle's weathered leathers made him look like a thrush in a parrot's cage. He wore a sword himself, but his had a razor-sharp blade and a well-worn grip. His lined features, tanned to a deep brown by the desert sun gave him a sinister air amidst these pallid northerners. But still he was careful not to cross the path of any of the young men or women, despite their polished effeminacy and mincing manners: every person in this garden was mage-born, with the power to destroy a squad of soldiers with a thought. He could too, if he needed to, but there was no gain to be had in brawling with a young mage-noble in the emperor's gardens.

Belonius Vult appeared at the entrance to the gardens and gave an impatient wave.

Well then. With small steps, big things begin.

The governor's smooth features crinkled in mild annoyance as he took in Gyle's rough-clad appearance. Vult himself was clad in a silver-blue silken robe, the epitome of the well-dressed magus. Gyle had known him for decades, and had never seen him look less than sumptuously immaculate. Belonius Vult, the Governor of Noros in the name of his Imperial Majesty. Others knew him as the traitor of Lukhazan, the one general of the Noros Revolt who now served the empire in a high post.

'Could you not have at least thrown on a clean tunic, Gurvon?'

Belonius remarked. 'We are appearing before the emperor – and more importantly, his newly sainted mother.'

'It's clean,' Gyle said. 'Well, washed anyway. The dirt is ingrained. It's what they expect of me: an uncouth southerner, fresh from the wilds.'

'Then you look the part. Come, we are expected.' If Vult had any nerves, they were well hidden. Gyle could not remember Magister Belonius Vult looking discomforted very often, not even during the surrender of Lukhazan.

They traversed a tangle of marble courtyards and rosewood-panelled arches, passing statues of emperors and saints, bowing to lords and ladies as they penetrated the Imperial Palace through doors that few were permitted to pass. Strange creatures walked the halls unattended: hybrid creatures, gnosis-constructs from the Imperial bestiary. Some were made to resemble creatures of legend, griffins and pegasi, but others were nameless figments of their makers' imagination.

A final door led to a chamber where Imperial Guardsmen with winged helms stood like statues. A chamberlain bade them set aside their periapts, the channelling gems that enhanced the use of the gnosis. For Belonius, this was the crystal topping his beautiful blackwood and silver staff; for Gyle it was a plain onyx on a leather string tucked inside his shirt. He leant his sword against the wall and hung the gem from its hilt. He shared one final glance with Vult. *Ready?*

Vult nodded, and together, the two Noromen entered the inner sanctum of their conquerors.

Within was a large round chamber with walls of plain white marble, with scenes of the Blessed Three Hundred set in relief. A statue of Corineus ascending to Heaven hung above the table, slowly rotating with no visible support. The Saviour was gazing upward, his face rapt in the moment of death. Lanterns held in either hand illuminated the room. A round table made of heavy oak and polished to mirror-sheen had nine seats set about it, in a nod to the traditions of the north: the Schlessen legend of King Albrett and his Knights. However, Emperor Constant had made something of a mockery of this legendary symbol of equality by seating himself on a carved throne set on a dais above the table, dominating the room. It was decorated with Keshi gold and camel-bone, if Gyle wasn't mistaken: plunder from the last Crusade.

The doorman announced, 'Your Majesties, may I present Magister-General Belonius Vult, Governor of Noros; and Volsai-Magister Gurvon Gyle of Noros.'

His Imperial Majesty Constant Sacrecour looked up from beneath beetled brows and frowned. 'They're Noromen,' he complained in a whining voice. 'Mother, you never said they were Noromen.' He shifted uncomfortably in his heavy ermine-lined crimson robes. He was a thin man in his late twenties, but he acted younger, and his face was permanently pursed into an expression of petulant distrust. His beard had been nervously twisted out of shape and his hair was lank. He gave the impression he would rather be elsewhere, or at least better-amused.

'Of course I did,' replied his mother brightly. The Sainted Mater-Imperia Lucia Fasterius remained seated, but she gave them both a welcoming smile, surprising Gyle, who'd expected a colder woman. She had lines about her eyes and mouth that most mage-women's vanity would not tolerate, and she wore an unpretentious sky-blue dress, her only adornment a golden halo-circlet pushing back her blonde hair. She looked like a favourite aunt.

'You look as radiant today as yesterday, your Holiness,' Belonius Vult said with a deep bow.

It was so obviously untrue that the Empress-Mother cocked an eyebrow. 'I spent enough on that gown yesterday to raise a fresh Crusade,' she remarked drily. 'I hope you aren't going to tell me I should have just worn a peasant's smock, Governor Vult?'

'I meant only that no finery could improve the radiance of your visage, sainted lady,' returned Belonius without missing a beat. Vult could smarm exceedingly well.

Lucia eyed him appraisingly and indicated two seats opposite her. Four men sat at the table, each staring at the newcomers with gazes ranging from neutral to hostile. 'Allow me to offer my congratulations on your sainthood, your Holiness, Vult went on. Never has one so worthy been so justly acclaimed.'

Lucia smiled prettily, more like a girl accepting praise for her looks than a regal saint. But Gyle had heard whispers about what she did to those who displeased her that had chilled his battle-weary soul, so what would he know about saints and how they looked and behaved?

'Welcome to the Inner Council of Rondelmar,' Lucia waved an arm gracefully. 'Do you know these other gentlemen? Allow me to make the introductions.' She indicated a tall, balding man who looked about forty but was probably eighty. 'This is Count Calan Dubrayle, the Imperial Treasurer.' Dubrayle nodded tersely, his ancient eyes distant.

The man beside him had silver hair but youthful features and a heroic build. 'I am Kaltus Korion,' he said coldly. 'I remember you, Vult.' He looked like he wanted to spit. He turned to Lucia. 'I don't see why they need join us – this is the Inner Council, not some market café for travellers to peddle their ideas. I've read the plan. I don't need *them* to sell it to me.'

'The plan we are to implement was devised by these gentlemen, Kaltus, dear. Be nice.'

'I've been as nice as I need to be to Noromen – during their Revolt.' He smirked at Belonius. 'I still have your sword in my trophy room, Vult.'

'You're welcome to it,' replied Vult smoothly. 'I have more potent weapons that are inalienable from my person.'

Careful, Belonius, for Kore's sake, Gyle thought. *That's Kaltus rukking Korion!*

Kaltus Korion sniffed, unimpressed, and looked at Gyle. 'And so this is the notorious Gurvon Gyle? Is it too late to annul the Imperial Pardon and hang him?'

'The Revolt was a long time ago,' Gyle said mildly, meeting the Rondian general's eyes. It was in fact seventeen years since the men of Noros had risen against their Imperial masters, and even appeared victorious, until Lukhazan had been surrendered without a fight by Belonius Vult, and the tide had turned. Gyle had been much younger then, careless of danger in his youth and idealism. Now what was he, a burned-out spymaster? A devious rogue with one last plan to earn a comfortable retirement? Something like that.

'Well said. The Revolt was far too long ago to trouble us now,' agreed a fat man in ornate priestly robes so heavy with gilt and gems it was a divine miracle he could move. Grand Prelate Dominius Wurther looked even more obese up close than he had yesterday when viewed across the Place d'Accord. 'It was long ago, and we have welcomed our Noros-born brothers back into the Imperial bosom. I look forward to the discussion.' He grinned greasily, his jowls wobbling. 'I trust young Adamus entertained you well yesterday?'

The other men in the room glanced at each other. If the Noromen were guests of a bishop, then what did that say about the Church's role in their proposal, or the nature of the hidden agendas?

Gyle had to strain to keep his face expressionless. *Let them speculate.*

The man to the emperor's left half-turned. 'I'm Betillon,' he announced, as if that explained everything. It did, of course: Noromen still called Tomas Betillon 'the Rabid Dog' for what he'd done at Knebb during the Revolt. He had a grizzled, rough-hewn face, untamed whiskers and hooded eyes.

'Do we really need this meeting?' Korion repeated impatiently. 'So Vult has given us a plan – pay him some gold and let him go on his way.' He smirked. 'That's all it took at Lukhazan.'

Lucia tapped the table and everyone stopped and turned to her. 'That's enough introductions, gentlemen.' She fixed Korion with a cold stare, no longer looking like a kindly aunt. 'These gentlemen are crucial to our plans, and they are welcome here. They are attending at my – at *our* – invitation. They have come up with something that has pleased us, and they are vital for the execution.' She waved a hand at the well-padded leather seats. 'Now, please, be seated.'

The emperor looked like he wanted to say something in support of Korion, but he didn't. He pouted a little instead.

Lucia tapped a stack of papers. 'You have all seen the papers and each of you has participated in discrete discussions concerning Magister Vult's plan for the Crusade, but this is the first time we have been able to gather together. Let me emphasise, gentlemen, that we here will decide the fate of millions of people – the fate of *nations*. The course of the Third Crusade will be determined by us, not on the battlefield but here, in this room, by those gathered here at my request.' She looked at her son, the emperor, and added, 'At *our* request.'

Gyle wondered if she outranked him now, being a living saint. *I bet he's wondering that too.*

Lucia looked around the table. 'I will clearly define the situation so that we are all of one understanding. Then we will agree the way ahead.' She got to her feet and began to circle the table. Her voice became clear and emotionless: less saint and more angel of retribution.

'It will not have escaped your notice, gentlemen, that the Golden Age of Rondelmar has begun to dim.' The emperor looked displeased at her words, but didn't interrupt. 'Though outwardly it looks like we were never stronger, the purity at the heart of Rondelmar's rightful dominance of the world has begun to tarnish. *Impurity* has been allowed to enter this realm, by men who care more for gold than for love of Kore. The merchant cabals prosper, whilst we who love Kore and the emperor must struggle for what was once ours by right. A great evil was done, and it *must* be undone. The evil I refer to is, of course, the "Leviathan Bridge" – that cursed creation of Antonin Meiros and his godless cronies.' She slapped the table, suddenly angry. 'When Kore made this land, he made two great continents, separated by vast oceans, and he commanded his sister Luna to make those waters impassable, *so that East should never meet West*. Learned, noble, enlightened West and base, depraved, idolatrous East should never meet, under Sun or Moon – so it was written.

'But Meiros, an Ascendant too craven to join the liberation of Yuros from the Rimoni yoke, left the fellowship of the Three Hundred and built that cursed Bridge, and from that Bridge do all of our woes come! I wonder, does Antonin Meiros even know what he has done?'

He seemed perfectly aware of it last time I saw him, reflected Gyle. He wondered whether Lucia Fasterius truly believed the bigoted dogma she spoke. She seemed intelligent, learned – kindly, even. But in her eyes something fanatic lurked, like a venomous snake.

Lucia came to a halt behind her chair and gripped the wooden back tightly. 'For a century we have seen the Bridge open every twelve years, when the tides drop to levels that permit traverse. We have seen the merchants pour across then return with all manner of addictive Eastern goods – opium and hashish, coffee and tea, even the silks and other luxuries that entrance our people. They can virtually name their prices on return. The bankers extend credit to merchants whilst squeezing the nobility, the magi-protectors who made Rondelmar what it is. Who are the richest men in Rondelmar? *The merchants and bankers!* Fat obsequious slime like Jean Benoit and his merchant cabal. And what have they bought with their ill-gotten gains? Our *homes* – our *belongings* – our *art*, and worse: they have *purchased* our sons and daughters, our *Blood!*' Lucia was shouting now, spittle flecking her lips. 'Those *scum* are *buying* our children and taking them to wife or husband, so that their misbegotten offspring will have *everything*, both gold and gnosis, and as a result, we are seeing a new breed, the mage-merchant, nasty, grasping half-breeds. Make no mistake, gentlemen, there is a war brewing between men of the Purse and men of the Blood. Think about that: lowborn pedlars buying our daughters to breed gnosis-wielding sons and daughters for themselves. And we, the Magi, what are we doing? We. Are. Whoring. Our. *Children*.'

Lucia's eyes narrowed vengefully. 'But the Throne has not been idle, my friends. Two Moontides ago we struck. My lamented husband, the Emperor Magnus Sacrecour, boldly confronted the heretic Meiros – and Meiros backed down. Knowing Meiros would not dare to destroy his own creation we marched our armies into Antiopia, and we *punished* the infidel. We conquered Dhassa and Javon and Kesh and set up new governments to rule in our name and convert the heathen to Kore. But more importantly, we *broke* the traders: We destroyed the trust between the Eastern merchants and Benoit's cabal. Though our people suffered somewhat, we weakened the hold of merchants and bankers.'

'*Suffered somewhat*'? Gyle thought indignantly. *Poverty, destitution and rebellion might have resulted from your actions, but at least you knocked a few percentage points off the profits for the merchants, eh?*

Lucia nodded at Betillon. 'Tomas and his men defend Hebusalim and prepare for the next Crusade, but the Crusades have emptied our Treasury. The people have given, and given generously, yet we still owe millions to those damned merchant bankers – and still they prosper, still they gain in influence – and *still they buy our children.*'

If four-fifths of the wealth plundered in the Crusade had not gone into the private hoards of certain royal personages, perhaps the Imperial Treasury would be better off, Gyle reflected, glancing at Calan Dubrayle, who seemed to be stifling the same thought.

Mater-Imperia Lucia sat again, her face still flushed with passion but her voice colder now. 'Let me be frank, gentlemen: the throne has never before been so weak – not through any weakness in the emperor,' she added hastily, as Constant stirred, 'for though only a child at the time, Constant was both wise and bold, ordering the Second Crusade and strengthening our hold on the Hebb Valley. But the merchants are buying our souls, turning Kore's chosen people into a nation of shopkeepers.'

'We have other enemies too: Duke Echor of Argundy, the former emperor's brother, has made it clear he covets the throne, and all of Argundy marches to his tune. That my son's only uncle plots treachery boils my blood. He too must be destroyed. And' – she looked about to spit – 'another *contamination* has crept into this realm: Antiopian slaves, brought here to do the work of honest men of Yuros. I have no quarrel with slavery – that, after all, is the only thing Sydians are good for – but to permit these *mudskins* into our midst goes too far – they *must* be exterminated!'

Gyle noted Dubrayle suppressing a groan. The Treasurer made a pretty mint from taxes on slave-trading, he recalled. *I bet you won't want that trade closed down . . .*

Lucia looked nothing like a saint now. 'These are our enemies, gentlemen: the merchants, Duke Echor, the mudskins and Meiros. Him above all.' She took a deep breath. 'They must all die.'

She stopped, grim-faced, and the room fell silent. The men at the table nodded agreement, and Gyle felt it prudent to do likewise. *So that is how saints think.*

Lucia gestured at Belonius. 'Our good friend Magister Vult has come to us with a solution to all of these problems. I will now hand over to him, so that we may hear firsthand his plan to save our realm.'

Vult stood instantly and bowed. 'Most Sainted Lady, no one could have summarised our position better. Let me start by properly introducing Gurvon Gyle, my friend and colleague, whose network of informers has enabled us to pull this plan together. Gurvon's eyes and ears are everywhere – he is probably the best-informed man on Urte.'

Gyle resisted the urge to give them his best *I know who you sleep with* look.

Vult breezed on, 'My plan deals with the three main issues Mater-Imperia Lucia has outlined for us: the Merchants, Duke Echor, and the heathens of Kesh. Put simply, we're going to destroy them all, and it starts, as Mater-Imperia has told us, with the Bridge. The Leviathan Span begins at Pontus and runs more than three hundred miles to the Dhassa coast, never deviating an inch. It is a remarkable construction.'

'A demon's device,' muttered Betillon.

Yes, but one you've prospered mightily from, thought Gyle.

Vult continued, unperturbed, 'Twenty-three years ago, in 904, Emperor Magnus marched four legions across the Bridge. Antonin Meiros could have stopped us, and slain tens of thousands of Rondian soldiers and civilians – at the cost of destroying his own construction. Every man would have perished, and in all likelihood the emperor would have fallen in the turmoil that followed. But Meiros and his Ordo Costruo failed to act, allowing Emperor Magnus to seize the Bridge – and Hebusalim.

'When the Bridge closed again we hoped we had done enough. The merchant guilds had lost vast amounts and many were ruined. But our air-fleet has limited resources and the garrison at Hebusalim was eventually massacred by vast hordes of the heathen – our greatest military disaster. In 916 your Majesty' – he bowed to Constant – 'exacted revenge for the massacre and strengthened our hold on Hebusalim, making milord Betillon his governor and bleeding the dark-skinned heathen white.'

Betillon and Korion chuckled at this, and Gyle admitted, *You know how to play them, my friend.*

'Now the Third Crusade is upon us: in one year's time the Leviathan Bridge will rise from the sea and we will march once more. All of Kesh awaits us. The Amteh Convocation in Gatioch has recently declared shihad, Holy War, which obliges every man of the Amteh Faith to take up arms against us. The Third Crusade will be nothing like what has gone before; this will be vast, epoch-shaping.

'We must face the fact that we have had setbacks. In the key kingdom of Javon, the Dorobon dynasty we installed has fallen, supplanted by the Nesti, who are of old Rimoni senatorial stock. Javon, which is peopled by both Rimoni and a branch of the Keshi called the Jhafi, lies to the northeast of Hebusalim and commands the hills above the Zhassi Valley. Control Javon and you have the keys to Hebusalim and to Kesh. To secure our advance, we must secure Javon. It is a complex place, and my colleague knows it well. Gurvon will now reveal our plans for Javon.'

Gyle looked about him, licking his suddenly dry lips. Emperor Constant looked bored, but Lucia was leaning forward, her eyes fixed on him. Korion and Betillon were sullenly defensive and Dubrayle looked as if he'd sat on something spiky. Only Grand Prelate Wurther looked comfortable. *Ah, religion: balm for the soul.*

Gyle cleared his throat and began, 'Your Majesties, when the Javonesi overthrew the Dorobon six years ago, Olfuss Nesti was elected king. You will notice I said "elected": Javon continues the old Rimoni tradition of elected rulers, but there is an added twist. You may be shocked to learn that a man cannot assume the throne unless he has *mixed* blood – Rimoni and Jhafi. This was agreed to forestall civil war when the Rimoni first settled in Javon. Olfuss has mixed parentage, and he has a Jhafi wife, the mother of his two sons and two daughters. Last year I contrived an accident that killed his elder son and heir. His daughters are presently aged seventeen and sixteen and the younger son is seven. There will be no more children. Were Olfuss to die, his eldest daughter would assume the regency until his seven-year-old son comes of age.'

'Son and *heir*?' Lucia asked, looking puzzled. 'Would not a new king be elected?

Gyle shook his head. 'Javon is strange, as I said. If an elected king dies violently, his natural heirs inherit the throne – it is a mechanism intended to deter regicide.'

Korion and Betillon sneered, as did the emperor – Constant had come to the throne after the mysterious deaths of his father and his elder sister.

Gyle waited until he had their attention again. 'In a few months Salim, the Sultan of Kesh, will present Olfuss with an ultimatum, demanding that Javon support the shihad. Olfuss will of course accede to Salim's demands: he is half-Rimoni and half-Jhafi and both halves hate Rondelmar passionately. So we must arrange a coup in Javon and restore the Dorobon.'

'What support do the Dorobon have in Javon?' asked Kaltus Korion.

'The Gorgio family are the second-largest Rimoni clan, and were powerbrokers during the Dorobon regime. They have been ostracised since the Nesti coup. They are well-moneyed, but less interbred with the Jhafi, so they have never been – and will never be – elected kings. They will be our prime allies in restoring the Dorobon.'

'Who is the Dorobon heir?' enquired Calan Dubrayle.

'Francis Dorobon is the heir: he is in fact being schooled in Noros and is a classmate of your own son Seth, General Korion. His mother and sister live in Hebusalim, in the Governor's Palace.'

'Rid me of their harridan dowager and your plan has my blessing,' grumbled Tomas Betillon.

'How many magi have you deployed in Javon, Magister Gyle?' Lucia asked.

'Your Holiness, I run a security company, hiring out magi as protectors to important people. It has operated successfully in Noros, Bricia and Lantris for the past ten years, and in Javon for four, since King Olfuss Nesti commissioned my services. I have three magi openly deployed in the palace to "protect" the family; they are ideally situated to dispose of the Nesti at the drop of a hat – *my* hat, which is at your command.'

'How nice,' chuckled Wurther. 'We have command of a Noroman's hat.'

'Can your agents be relied upon to kill Olfuss and his family? Who are they?' asked Lucia, her eyes gleaming.

'Rutt Sordell is personal bodyguard to the king; Samir Taguine guards the queen—'

'Taguine?' interrupted Korion, 'the Inferno himself?' The general looked impressed.

'The same. And Elena Anborn has charge of Olfuss' children.'

'A woman?' sniffed Tomas Betillon. 'Will she have what it takes to kill her charges?'

'Don't you believe we women capable of doing what Kore demands, Tomas?' Lucia chided gently. 'I'm sure Magister Gyle chooses his agents with due care to their capabilities, do you not, sir?' She gazed frankly at Gyle, her eyes predatory. 'Will this woman kill the children, Magister Gyle?'

'She's a heartless bitch, if you will excuse the term, Holiness,' he replied levelly. *There, Elena, I've made your name known to the Empress-Mother, in the best possible way. Fame at last!*

Lucia smiled gleefully. 'Excellent. I like her already—' She broke off, her brow wrinkling. 'Wait: she's an *Anborn*? Didn't the Anborns whore themselves to the merchants?'

Gyle inclined his head. 'Of course you are correct. Her sister Tesla is married to a merchant, but she is now a burnt-out wreck. Elena hasn't talked to her for years. Elena was one of my Grey Foxes in the Revolt. She has a stone for a heart, your Holiness. She is a killer.'

'I understand she shares your bed,' observed Calan Dubrayle.

'Long ago, my lord. It helped keep her loyal.'

'A woman should no more do her thinking with her fanny than

a man should think with his cock,' Saint Lucia announced, clearly enjoying the way the men winced at her profanity.

'So, Gyle, if your cock no longer holds her, what do you have over her? asked Betillon, ever practical. 'Or indeed any of them, if they decide they have had enough of killing and have enough gold to see out their days?'

'My lord, my assassins well understand that there is no way out. There are no havens secret enough; no one is untouchable. Disobedience to me is tantamount to signing one's own death warrant. Also, I control their life-savings: displease me and they lose everything.'

Betillon grinned wryly. 'That would do it.' He slurped some wine. 'When do we strike? Soon would be good – not a day passes in Hebusalim without that Dorobon hag whining on and on about Javon.'

'Timing is critical. The assassinations will destabilise the realm, so the Dorobon will need time to subdue the kingdom before the Crusade. The plan therefore is to strike in three months' time, in Octen, giving us nine months until the Moontide. We will kill one daughter and marry the other to a Gorgio, giving a semblance of legitimacy to the new regime and enabling an easier transition of power to the Dorobon.' He looked about him, saw them nodding slowly. 'By the time the Leviathan Bridge opens next year, Javon will be in our hands.'

'What emergency resources do you have?' asked Dubrayle. 'Few plans work flawlessly.'

Your plans mightn't, but mine do. Gyle stopped himself from saying it out loud. 'I have access to many other magi who can step in, including shape-masters of unsurpassed skill.' He looked at Mater-Imperia as something flickered in her eyes. *Yes, you know who I mean.* 'Should anything go awry, it will be swiftly corrected.'

The room fell silent. He took a cautious sip of the wine. It was an Augenheim Solvyne, a fine wine. *Too good, unwatered.* He pushed it away regretfully.

After half a minute of quiet, Lucia clapped her hands. 'Thank you,

Magister Gyle. Excellent. Stage one of the plan sounds promising.'
She looked around the table. 'You will all have read the details in
the papers I sent you. Are there any objections to considering the
Javon Question as being dealt with?'

He held his breath, but there were no objections.

'Excellent,' purred Lucia. She reached under the table and rang a
bell. The doorman appeared. 'Ah, Hugo, bring coffee please. We might
as well enjoy the fruits of our conquest while we can.' She smiled
around the table, once more the gentle mother of the people.

As they got up to stretch their legs, sipping thimbles of black
coffee, Empress-Mother Lucia approached Gyle. He bowed, but she
waved the gesture away genially. 'Tell me more of this woman, Elena
Anborn. A woman finds it harder to kill, you know,' she said, almost
apologetically, as though she were not the woman who was rumoured
to have murdered her husband in favour of her son-in-law, despatched
two lovers during the Interregnum and three since, and ordered
both Crusades, each of which had resulted in more than a million
deaths.

'Elena is an altogether selfish creature, Holiness. She is motivated
only by personal gain. She will not hesitate.'

Don't let me down, Elena. Despite everything, don't let me down.

The Mother of the Nation, Saint of the People, smiled benevolently. 'You had better be right, Magister Gyle, or I'll ram a broadsword
up her arse. And yours.' She clapped her hands energetically, evidently
revived by the coffee. 'Gentlemen, to table. Magister Vult has the
second part of his plan to talk us through . . .'

2

Wear Your Gems

Javon / Ja'afar

An arid land, home of a Keshi people known as the 'Jhafi'. Following the opening of the Leviathan Bridge, many Rimoni settled there, finding the climate suited to crops from their homeland. After a civil war in the 820s, a remarkable settlement was brokered by a Lakh guru known as Kishan Dev which saw the monarchy become democratic, with candidates needing both wealth and also, incredibly, mixed Jhafi and Rimoni blood. Remarkably, this agreement has been adhered to for most of Javon's recent history, until the Rondian Dorobon clan usurped power following the First Crusade.

ORDO COSTRUO COLLEGIATE, PONTUS

Brochena, Javon, on the continent of Antiopia
Septinon 927
10 months until the Moontide

The first rays of dawn stabbed across the land and lit up the cloudless skies. Elena Anborn raised a hand to shield her eyes as she gazed out, catching her breath at the stark beauty of light on dark. The mountains were purple, the olive groves shimmering grey like stones on a beach. Beneath her lay the tangled cluster of streets that made up Brochena, the Javon capital. The city was already humming with movement, black-clad women and white-turbaned men making their way to morning prayer. As the first light kissed the dome of the huge Amteh Dom-al'Ahm, the wailing voices of the Godsingers rose to summon the faithful with invocations older than the city itself. She felt an odd impulse to join them, to flutter like a bird down to the streets and be a part of the community gathering in the shadow of the dome – not for any allegiance she held to the Amteh, just a growing desire to belong to something.

Was there any place she truly belonged? Surely not here, where she was a whiteskinned Westerner in the dark-hued East, the antithesis of all a woman was supposed to be. She was unmarried and a warrior, when a woman should be married and confined to her husband's house – and she was magi, here where a mage was regarded as the spawn of Shaitan. In spite of all that, it was here she felt most at home.

She was tall for a woman, and habitually dressed like a man. Her body was all lean muscle and hard planes. Her face was leathered by sun and experience, her sun-bleached hair caught in a pony-tail, her pale blue eyes always moving as she leant from the window of the tower room in the Brochena Palace. The Nesti had given her the room to practise in. *Anywhere with a view*, she had asked, and they had given her views of city, desert, mountain and sky in every direction. It was a hard but generous land, full of hard but generous people.

She wished for a moment that when this was all over she could stay here, though she knew that was impossible. She had loved the desert from the first, the sands calling to an emptiness inside her. *I'm going to miss this place – even the stench of the souks, where men piss against walls and every manner of litter is left to rot, where dung is fuel and bathing is done in a river that looks like a sewage canal.* But coffee hung in the morning air; she could smell it even here, and the colours of the silks and the calls of the traders and the ever-present singing and chanting of the priests . . . these would haunt her for ever.

Sipping a thimble of spiced coffee, she tried to picture her wet, gloomy homeland, but she couldn't. Brochena was too vivid for such fancies. The air was chilly this morning, and a ground mist clogged with campfire smoke hung over much of the desert lands. Winter was approaching, though the days were still hot. The rainy season was over for 927; it would not be until Julsven next year that it rained again, and by then the Moontide would have come, the Leviathan Bridge would have risen from the sea and Urte would be plunged once again into war.

She was about to turn away when a redwing swooped and called brightly before landing on the ledge outside the window. The bird had no concern at her handling it to extract the message from the pouch tied to its leg. She recognised Gurvon Gyle's sigil on the pouch and his face flashed inside her mind: lean, spare, certain. *My lover – can I still call him that when I've not seen him for a year? My boss, anyway. The keeper of my fortune.*

She almost pocketed the message without reading it. She didn't really want to know what it might say. But that would be foolish. She exhaled heavily and unwrapped the note. It was brief and to the point. *Wear your gems.* Little else was needed; those three words said everything. *Wear your gems*: it was Gurvon's pet way of saying, 'Action is imminent: pack your bags and be ready to leave at a second's notice.'

She did a brief mental inventory: her bedchamber was almost empty, save for a small chest for her clothes, a few gifts from the royal family – some Jhafi shawls and a bekira-shroud for going out in public – and her sword. She wore the turquoise periapt that helped her channel the gnosis at her throat. It wasn't a lot, not for a lifetime of struggle. Of course, she also had gold, a career's worth of gold . . . entrusted to Gurvon.

She'd met Gurvon Gyle when she joined the Noros Forest Rangers in 909. She'd been twenty-one. A half-blood daughter of half-blood parents, she had graduated in 906, too late to join the First Crusade when it stormed Hebusalim. Her elder sister Tesla had been there and nearly died. Elena had enlisted with the Volsai, Imperial Intelligence. By 909, when it was clear rebellion was coming, she, like all the Noros-born agents, deserted and joined the Royal Noros Army as scouts. Gurvon Gyle, newly arrived back from the Crusades, was her captain. He had a world-weary, cynical charm that made her smile, and he hadn't mistaken her for a weakling, unlike most. They had bonded sharing missions, and when she finally slipped into his tent one cold wet night somewhere north of Knebb, the horrors another of Betillon's massacres fresh in her eyes, he had appeared to need her as much as she needed him.

The Revolt had been strangely glorious, even in defeat. Despite all she had seen and done – and though it felt terrible to say so now – she had loved it. Magister-General Robler and his army had destroyed Rondelmar's far larger armies in a series of remarkable victories that were now held up as textbook examples of warfare. Gyle's Grey Foxes were heroes, kept hidden and fed by the villagers, and for a while victory had seemed possible, despite the odds. But promised aid from neighbouring kingdoms never came, the mysterious magi who had promised victory vanished, and the Noros legions were gradually isolated and surrounded. Vult's army surrendered at Lukhazan, leaving Robler's forces trapped in the high valleys as winter set in, where they perished in swathes until Robler surrendered.

For Elena the post-Revolt period was traumatic. Normalcy was impossible after two years of danger so she had joined Gyle's new company of mage-spies. Officially they provided protection services to the wealthy, but secretly their work was much dirtier: espionage and assassination. The Rondians wanted to root out the dissidents who had threatened to join the Noros Revolt, and suddenly she found herself on the other side, hunting for the enemies of the empire. For a while it bothered her, but she learned not to care. She went where Gurvon told her, killed the targets he gave her. Her conscience died and her heart became a lump of rock as she slit the throats of good men and murdered innocents who had been unfortunate enough to witness something dangerous. She became a constantly shifting set of lies and illusions; nothing mattered but the gold. Eventually everything led her here to the most lucrative job yet: to protect the Javon king and his family throughout the Crusade. It was just a protection role, and she could even use her own name, for the first time in years.

It had taken time to remember that she was more than a weapon, but the children had broken her down, with their instinctive willingness to trust her, the genuine smiles they shared, the silly games that had reminded her how to laugh. Four years in which to feel alive once more, to realise that life was not just a marking of time. And now this . . .

Wear your gems . . .

Damn! I belong here, *Gurvon . . .*

She sent the redwing on its way, putting its poisonous little message from her mind. She began to limber up for her morning work-out, her movements kicking up motes of dust that glinted in the streaks of light that cut through the otherwise shadowy chamber. The distant call of the Godsingers and the cawing of the crows faded as her concentration deepened. She stretched, spun, kicked and punched the air, working up a sweat as she twirled about the mechanism in the centre of the chamber. Finally she stopped, picked up a wooden sword that leant against the wall and turned to face the machine.

'*Bastido, uno,*' she said both aloud and with the gnosis, and the device came alive. Pale amber light sparked from beneath the helm, its four legs unfolded like a spider's and the gnosis-powered mechanism crept forward with sinister grace. In each of its four 'arms' was a blunted weapon: a sword, a chain flail, a metal-studded mace and a spear-shaft. A small buckler hung beneath a helm that swivelled eerily to face her as she circled. Suddenly sword and spear lunged at once; she parried the blade with gnosis-shielding and the spear with her sword and the bout was on. For forty seconds she darted and lunged, parried and circled until she scored a hit on the helm and the machine lapsed into sullen stillness, though the visor still followed her, glowering like a smacked child.

'Got you, Bastido,' she panted. Most mage-born girls refused to take swordplay, and those who did were usually too delicate and flighty to last through the rigours of the training. But Elena had always been a tomcat, brought up in the country where she'd run wild. She had taken the cuffs and blows as she followed the taxing physical regime, until she'd finally won Blademaster Batto's approval. She was the only girl from Bricia's Arcanum d'Etienne College to graduate with full honours in weaponry. Bastido – The Bastard – was Batto's parting gift to her.

She saluted, readying herself. '*Bastido, duo.*'

This time the machine was more aggressive, its blows subtler, its movements less patterned. The mace joined the fray and now three weapons were always arrayed against her, keeping her constantly leaping, jumping, using Air-gnosis to swoop in and out, bouncing off the walls, parrying with power and precision until she scored another hit. By now she was bathed in perspiration and her breath was coming in gasps. Bastido twitched as if furious with her, itching to lash out. *Go on*, it seemed to be saying, *try me on cinque.*

'I don't think so, Bastido.' She grinned. She'd only tried the fifth once, and the fight had been over in seconds. Three blinding blows had broken her sword-arm and two ribs, and she'd had to be pulled clear by Gurvon. She wouldn't be trying that again – it would always be a step too far at her age. But she did fight another bout, this time on *tre*, scoring half a second before collecting the mace in her left shoulder, which sent her sprawling. 'Hey, that was *after* my touch,' she complained.

The machine almost smirked. Some days it seemed alive.

She took a few deep breaths, bade Bastido return to his place in the corner and deactivated the gnosis-creation. She was parched, and drank deeply from the bucket of water she had hauled up the stairs that morning before tipping the rest over her head. The sodden fabric clung to her, cooling her flushed and sweating frame. She could feel her face burning, pictured the pink glow beneath her freckles and lines. She looked down at her tunic, plastered against her flat chest, her hard belly and muscular thighs. She was no one's idea of beautiful, she knew that, and unlike any other women she knew, even other magi. For a second she felt that wave of loneliness again, and quelled it irritably.

How will I get Bastido out of here? I only brought him because I thought we would actually get to exit this job with dignity . . .

Wear your gems . . . Why? Do we just walk away? What's going on?

She shivered. *Don't think about it. Keep your mind on the money.* She wrapped herself in a Jhafi blanket and left the chamber, seeking the bathing room and some hot water.

*

Half an hour later, washed and clad in the Jhafi smock called a salwar, she accompanied the Nesti children to the Sollan chapel. The relief-carved sandstone walls were soot-stained from torches and the two copper masks behind the altar, Sun above Moon, were in need of a good polish. The old Sollan drui-priest poured the libations, intoning the ritual formulas to invoke the strength of the new day. It all felt very tired – the Sollan faith might be the oldest in Yuros, the religion of the Rimoni and once the dominant belief of the entire western continent, but here in the east, it was a sapling in unfertile soil.

There were just twelve people in the chapel. In the front rank was King Olfuss, his skin dark against his curly white hair and beard, his genial face serious. He was obliged to uphold both faiths of Javon, the Rimoni Sollan and the Amteh worship of the Jhafi, which meant a lot of time on his knees. She couldn't tell if either held his heart. Beside him was his wife Fadah, wrapped in her bekira-shroud. She cared nothing for the Sollan faith, was here by duty only. Behind them were their children, wrapped against the chill: young Timori, the heir, only seven years old, was fidgeting, bored. Every so often he glanced back at Elena and waved, until Solinde noticed and chided him. Solinde was the tallest of the children, though the middle one, with auburn hair and long, graceful limbs. She was considered the family beauty, though Elena preferred Cera's darker, more exotic features. Cera, dutiful eldest daughter, remained deep in prayer.

Elena's colleagues, Rutt Sordell and Samir Taguine, lounged beside the door, neither bothering to look interested. They were Kore-worshippers, and didn't mind who they offended in reminding people. She found both obnoxious and was glad to be apart from them. Three guardsmen were there too, two young men standing at the door while their captain knelt beside Elena, praying softly. Lorenzo di Kestria had a mop of short curls and a roughly handsome face. He'd arrived a few months ago, a younger son of an allied family, and Olfuss had given him a place among his knights. His violet tunic was dishevelled but clean and he smelled of cloves and cinnamon. He met Elena's glance and smiled.

She looked away. She liked Lorenzo, but she did not want – could not afford – entanglements. Especially not now. *Wear your gems . . .*

'Father Sol, we pray unto you,' intoned Drui Prato. 'Sister Luna, we pray unto you. Bring us whole through this festival of Samhain. Ward us these winter nights, harbour the seeds of spring. Light our paths, we pray you.' Elena fidgeted, as bad as Timori. The peaceful phrases, the drui's concerns with the seasons and their cycles, failed to calm her. They were out of place here where the seasons were wrong – praying for protection from winter when here in Javon it was the growing season was just absurd. Even so, she would miss this. No one openly worshipped Sol and Luna back in Yuros any more. The Kore had been imposed everywhere; other faiths were heretical, dangerous.

The little ritual ended with a sip of wine and a dab of ash and water applied to their foreheads by the old drui. Outside the chapel they gathered, Lorenzo hovering solicitously, but Elena knew how to cold-shoulder men without offending them. Cera sidled up and kissed her cheek. 'Buona Samhain, Ella.' Cera's deep brown eyes caught the torchlight. 'Your hair is wet! Have you bathed and exercised already? Don't you know this is a holiday?'

'I exercise every day, Cera. You look lovely this morning. And so do you Solinde,' she added to the younger sister, who simpered, her eyes on Lorenzo. She was growing up too quickly, that one.

'There're going to be lots of dancing tomorrow,' Solinde said eagerly, watching the knight.

Lorenzo smiled at her, but his eyes went back to Elena. 'Do you dance, milady?'

Elena crooked an eyebrow. 'No.'

'I'm going to dance with all the knights,' Solinde announced grandly, piqued at Lorenzo's interest being elsewhere.

'Even the flatfooted, ugly ones?' asked Cera slyly.

'Just the handsome ones,' Solinde replied. 'Like Fernando Tolidi.'

'Ugh,' said Cera, 'you can't dance with him – he's a Gorgio.'

'So? I think he's handsome. And Father said it was time to welcome the Gorgio back to the royal bosom.'

'The royal bosom doesn't mean *your* one,' Cera quipped. 'Anyway, he looks like a horse.'

Timori pushed in between the girls and clutched Elena's leg. As she lifted him effortlessly onto her shoulders she noticed Rutt Sordell whispering some sneering remark in Samir Taguine's ear as they strolled off down the dimly lit hall together. Sordell, the only pure-blood magus on the team, was officially head of this assignment, though Samir, a three-quarter-blood, was the most formidable thanks to his Fire-gnosis affinity. *I wonder what message Gurvon sent them?*

'Donna Elena?' King Olfuss called to her. 'Do you have a moment?'

'At your service, sire,' she said, passing Timori to Lorenzo.

'Don't keep my husband long, Ella,' said Queen Fadah, fondly. 'Breakfast awaits, and we have many guests today.'

The Nesti family twirled about each other in a complicated dance as they followed the two Rondian magi up the hallway. Elena watched them go, a smile playing about her lips, until Olfuss put a hand on her shoulder and drew her back into the chapel. The drui had gone out the back with the rest of the communal wine, so she and the king were alone in the shadowed chamber. He led her to a seat at the back and sat down beside her. His face crinkled warmly. 'It is good to see you smiling, Donna Elena,' he said in his rolling Rimoni tongue. 'You were such a grim woman when you arrived. Perhaps the sun and heat agrees with you?'

'Perhaps, your Majesty.'

'"Milord" is sufficient, between us in private, Donna Elena,' Olfuss said, which usually meant he wanted something. 'Did you know that we placed bets on who could make you smile first? Solinde won, of course. With a foolish jest. Do you remember? "How do you stop a Rimoni from speaking? You tie his hands". Suddenly, you grinned, and then you laughed aloud, and Solinde danced around the room.'

Elena remembered. It had hurt her face, using those muscles again. It had hurt her heart, like placing cold toes too near the fire. 'I hope she won something good.'

'A ruby necklace from Kesh. She did not tell you?'

35

'No, Majesty. I had no idea my demeanour was of such interest.' *Has it really been four years? Four good years though . . . the ones that preceded it were awful, caught between Gurvon and Vedya. It had been a real relief to get out of Yuros.*

Olfuss looked up at the altar. 'It was a big step for us, to take three Rondian magi into our midst, but when the Gorgio employed a Dorobon mage to spy for them, we had no choice but to follow suit, otherwise my every action would have been known to them. Still, magi are not loved here.'

That's the understatement of the century. It's a toss-up who hates us the most – the Rimoni whose empire we destroyed, or the Keshi we invaded and enslaved.

'My children love you, Ella. You are like one of our family. But I wonder, are you happy here? And do you love them in return?' His eyes, serious now, met hers.

She felt a sudden constriction of her throat as she gave a quick nod. 'Of course, milord.' *That's why leaving will hurt so much.*

Olfuss smiled. 'Buona.' He stroked her cheek, his old face crinkling into a grin. 'Maybe we can find you a man, Ella. Then you will settle down with us and I can stop paying your Magister Gyle his exorbitant fee.'

'Olfuss, has the chancellor been nagging you to tighten the purse-strings again?'

He laughed, but didn't look away. 'Ella, we pay a lot of money every month for your services, and those of Sordell and Taguine. The money we spend on you is worthwhile. Those other two . . . I mislike them, and so I wish to employ you directly and dispense with those others. I will double your salary, and we will both win. What do you say?'

She froze in surprise. A part of her leapt inside: to be free, to not have to leave – wasn't that what she wanted? *And damn Gurvon anyway!* But what about Tesla? Her brother-in-law did what he could, but the tuition fees for their son were crippling. She had an immense amount of money awaiting her in Norostein; but if she resigned, she would never see a krone of it, she knew that for certain. And to bodyguard the Nesti on her own might be easy enough in peacetime, but the Moontide was coming . . .

She became aware that she hadn't responded with even a facial expression, that she had frozen solid. She looked apologetically at King Olfuss. 'Milord, I'm honoured. Your offer is flattering, but if Gurvon took this ill . . .' She frowned, calculating. 'He has control of my life-savings, which amount to more than you can afford.'

His eyes wrinkled as he took that in, then he reached out and patted her knee. 'Donna Elena, there are more things in life than gold. We value you, Ella – you are one of us. You are Nesti.' He grinned. 'Or maybe Kestrian, if you'd let young Lorenzo have his way!'

She seized on the change of subject. 'Poor Lorenzo! He's sweet, but I am here to do a job, milord. I'm not tempted.'

'All business, as always, Ella,' Olfuss said, a little sadly. 'What sort of men tempt you, hmmm? Kings, maybe,' he added with a sly smile.

'Fadah would turn you into a castrato if you even looked at me!' Elena laughed. He was not being serious, she knew that, but she appreciated the licence he permitted her.

He grinned in response, looking for a moment like a mischievous teenager, but he sobered quickly. 'Ella, we had news last night that Fadah's sister Homeirah is failing fast. The growths in her belly are killing her, and Fadah must go to her at Forensa. Cera and Timori will accompany her. Solinde insists she must stay here for the ball, and who can deny her when she loves to dance so much? You must go with the children to Forensa, and Taguine will accompany you, to protect Fadah. You will stay until – well, until Homeirah is buried, I expect. I cannot go myself. Salim's emissary has crossed the borders and I must be here to receive him.'

Elena nodded, her mind racing ahead. *What will Olfuss tell the emissary? Surely he will pledge to Salim. Perhaps that is why Gurvon is pulling out? Not doing so would put us on the wrong side of the Crusade. And that's another reason why I can't accept Olfuss' offer . . .*

'I'm sure we can find a way that works for us all,' Olfuss said, as if reading her thoughts. 'We Javonesi have learnt that compromise is the greatest art of all. I will talk with Magister Gyle and we will find a way that benefits both.' Olfuss stood, putting his hand on her shoulder. 'Look after my children in Forensa, Donna Elena.'

She nodded mutely, flushed with a sudden rush of emotion, as if blood were flowing through arteries that had fallen into disuse and filling her with unaccustomed feelings. She didn't know what to say, how to deal with feelings she had long ago cauterised inside herself.

Olfuss seemed to understand, for he limped away and closed the chapel door behind him, leaving her alone in the echoing silence.

The rest of the day was a blur of religious observance as the Rimoni marked Samhain Eve with a court feast that culminated in traditional dances and hymns, then solemn midnight chanting about a bonfire as the drui led the prayers for Father Sol to guide them through the coming winter. Olfuss looked as regal as Sol himself, and Fadah was as darksome and mysterious as Luna, the Moon Goddess. Cera was clad in grey-silver and sang gently, whilst Solinde wore gold and glowed, a trail of besotted young men trailing in her wake. She danced most with Fernando Tolidi, a scion of the Gorgio, one of the few who had unbent enough to leave their northern fastness at Hytel to join the festivities in the capital. Typical Solinde, to chose the partner who would most vex the gathering – though Fernando was an impressive young man, and more personable than most of his clan. Solinde would no doubt scandalise the court by dancing with him again at tomorrow night's grand ball.

All of the important Rimoni families were here, but no Jhafi, who were still fasting on this last day of the Amteh Holy Month. Samhain celebrations were only observed by the Rimoni; the Jhafi's own Eyeed festivities, much more lavish – and popular – would burst onto the streets tomorrow, and the combination of the two would turn the day into one giant party.

Elena had been fascinated by the story of Javon. When the Leviathan Bridge opened, a few Rimoni crossed to trade, and found the climate and terrain in Ja'afar (which they called 'Javon') similar in places to

Rimoni. They purchased land and experimented with olives and grapes and other crops from their home. Over the following years they thrived and their numbers swelled quickly as tens of thousands emigrated before the Crusades, trying to escape Rondian oppression in Yuros. Many compromises had averted war with the native Jhafi, and now the kingdom was a strong one. A guru from Lakh had brokered a peace that averted civil war, and his settlement included a compulsory mixture of blood for any potential rulers. It wasn't popular – on either side – but the desire to avoid war was great, and the guru was deeply respected. In the end the leading families of both races agreed to mixed marriages and legislation to protect both Sollan and Amteh religions. Gradually a new, unique nation had evolved, a place Elena had learnt to love.

Though she seldom danced for pleasure, she would occasionally, just to please the children. She had no desire to be quarrelled over by the single men. Lorenzo was watching her with worshipful eyes, but she left him well alone. As she held hands with Cera and Timori and sang the bonfire hymn at midnight, bidding the full glory of the Sun to return in the spring, she felt a warm glow inside that no liquor could have wrought. It felt suspiciously like happiness.

All the while though she was conscious of Rutt Sordell's sour features as he lounged against the wall, and dark-visaged Samir Taguine, drinking heavily with a scowl on his face. *I'm with you, Olfuss. I can't wait to see the back of that pair either.*

She walked the children and their nursemaid Borsa back to their floor of the keep. The old woman was well gone with Rimoni wine, but her feet were unerring. Solinde looked like she could have danced all night, but Timori was nearly asleep in Elena's arms and Cera was blinking heavily.

'I'm glad I'm staying,' said Solinde. 'I'd hate to miss Eyeed. And the ball tomorrow is going to be the best ever.'

Cera shrugged. 'At least one of us should go with Mother to see Tante Homeirah before she dies,' she said sanctimoniously.

Elena was reminded of her own sister. Tesla had been vivacious like Solinde, while Elena herself was quiet, like Cera. Perhaps it was why Cera was like the daughter she'd never had, though instead of the woodlands and hills she'd explored as a child, Cera explored books and ideas.

'Of course I wish I could come too,' said Solinde quickly, not wanting to appear heartless, 'but, you know . . .'

Cera pulled a face. 'Yes, I know: Fernando Tolidi this, Fernando Tolidi that—'

'That's not fair! I danced with *everyone*.'

'Yes you did,' Elena interjected, 'but now it is time to sleep. Into bed, now!'

She carried Timori to his own room whilst Borsa chased the two girls to theirs. Timori was nearly asleep, so she left him still clothed, pulled the coverlet over and kissed him goodnight. The little prince of Javon looked tiny in the huge bed, but his face was peaceful. Thick maroon candles perfumed the rooms with rose and cinnamon and the flames set the figures in the tapestries to flickering motion.

In the girls' room, Cera hugged her tightly, rolled over and seemed to fall instantly asleep, though the corner of a book could be seen peeking from beneath the bedclothes. Elena left it there. Solinde just waved her away, her mind still on the knights that had crowded about her like moths.

Borsa was waiting in the lobby. She watched as always while Elena walked to the middle of the lobby and commenced resetting her gnostic protections. She lifted her hands in gentle gestures and a web of pale white lines appeared, woven into the walls, the ceiling, the floors, thickest about the door and windows. These were the wards she had created here, and once activated, only she and those people she had authorised could freely come and go. Others would be resisted; they could only enter if they were able to overcome the physical and mental stresses that the wards would bring to bear. It was not an impenetrable defence, but when allied with stone, locks and bars, it was effective against all but an attacker who was both very skilled and very determined.

When she was done, Elena let her Inner Eye close and her powers diffuse. Borsa was looking at her calmly, used to these wonders by now. 'The girls are happy tonight,' the old nurse commented. 'Solinde is growing up so fast.'

'Too fast, maybe?'

'Oh, not in a bad way. It is good that she is eager to marry, and she is a good girl. Cera could take her lead and be a little more open. She will have to marry first, but she hardly notices the young men.' The old servant frowned. 'You feed her too many books, Ella. She thinks too much and feels too little.'

Elena raised an eyebrow. 'That's a little cruel, isn't? She is a princess, and one day she will share the rule of one of the duchies, maybe even the whole kingdom. Far better if she knows how to think and how to reason.'

'Her first duty will be to have children,' Borsa replied, 'and she must also be prepared for the life she *will* lead, not the one she'd *like* to lead.'

Elena exhaled heavily. She'd heard this so many times herself when she was growing up. 'Cera is intelligent, dutiful and courageous. She has a very gentle and caring side, you know that.'

'Si, si, I know.' Borsa pursed her lips. 'I just find her a little cold, sometimes.'

'I've never found her that way.'

'But then, many here would say you are cold also,' Borsa replied. 'You Rondians come from cold places; you carry that in your hearts.'

Elena opened her mouth crossly, then forced herself to close it again. Borsa had been here so long that she had licence to say what she liked, even to Rondian magi. 'At home in Noros I'm considered the merriest soul at any party,' she said lightly.

'Really?' Borsa asked.

'No.' She yawned ostentatiously. 'I'm for bed.'

'Anything to escape a nagging old woman, eh?' Borsa remarked wryly and hugged her. Then she left and Elena was free to go to her own small room.

A turmoil of thought tumbled about her head. *Wear your gems. But I'm not ready to leave, Gurvon. I think this is where I belong.*

She thought about poor Tesla, half-mad, wasting away alone. She thought about Tesla's husband, Vann Mercer, who she had wanted to hate, but liked instead. A courageous, considerate man, soldier-turned- trader, struggling to stay afloat in tough times. He was hoping his son Alaron, a quarter-blood mage, could rebuild the family fortunes. Elena recalled a thin boy with lank reddish hair and an argumentative nature. He would be graduating soon. She recalled her own graduation like yesterday: the handshake from the governor, and the grudging smile of Luc Batto as she took the girl's weaponry prize. It had been an ending and a beginning for her.

Good luck, Alaron. It is all before you.

3

The Standards of Noros

The Magi

Blessed are the Magi, the descendants of Corineus and the Blessed Three Hundred, divinely conceived and given dominion over earth and sky.

THE BOOK OF KORE

Shaitan, what hast thou wrought? Thou hast blighted the earth and sky with djinn and afreet, made demons crawl beneath our feet. Thou hast blasted the soil and poisoned the wells. And worst, thy evil hath been made flesh, in thy spawn the Rondian Magi.

YAMEED UMAFI, CONVOCATION GODSPEAKER, 926

Norostein, Noros, on the continent of Yuros
Octen 927
9 months until the Moontide

Norostein, the capital of Noros, lay on a high mountain plateau north of the Alps, set beside a cold clear lake that covered half the old city, consigned to the depths when the municipal authority dammed the river to improve the water-supply. Some said there were ghosts below, in the flooded graveyards, old revenants that would drag the unwary down to their watery graves. On days when the lake levels were low and no rains had muddied it, you could see the old buildings in the deeps. But it was no such day today: rain had teemed in to spoil the Darklight celebrations, the religious festival that the Kore had put in place of the old Sollan holy day of Samhain. Torrential downpours flooded the plazas and

43

extinguished many of the bonfires. Pitch-smeared torches sizzled sullenly.

The bedraggled populace gathered before the cathedral, damply sweaty and red-eyed, awaiting the midday service. The mage-born would be allowed inside, but the commoners had to keep vigil in the square, praying as much that the rain would hold off as for divine favour. Pickpockets worked the crowds and drunks still reeling from the previous night's celebrations pissed where they stood, usually about the heels of the person in front of them. Young men strutted about, eyeing the girls pretending not to be eyeing them. The crowd was a sea of pale flesh and greasy brown hair, white bonnets and green felt hats. Spontaneous choruses of traditional songs echoed about the plaza, songs of the Revolt, songs of the mountain kingdoms, old folk songs. Some harmless fights kept the Watchmen occupied. The air was laced with perspiration and beer, the smoke of the foodstalls blended with the drizzle, but the throng was in good humour.

Inside the courtyard of the Town Hall, the gentry waited. In a few minutes, the governor would lead them in procession through the crowd to the cathedral. Awaiting him in the courtyard were the landowners, the richest of the merchants, and, first and foremost, the magi families of Norostein, not that there were many; Noros had never attracted many of the descendants of the Blessed, and the Revolt had taken a heavy toll. Now there were just some seventy adult magi gathered under awnings. A few of the young men were showing off, using gnosis-shields to keep off the rain, and one young woman was amusing her friends by conjuring watery creature-forms out of the drizzle. There was laughter in the air, but tension too: young magi were always seeking opportunities to dominate weaker rivals.

A small bony youth with an olive complexion wormed his way through the courtyard, flicking wet black hair from his face. His colouring marked him as an outsider. The babble of voices and the heat of the packed bodies hit him like a wave, but he worked his way past the most boisterous of the young men without attracting

undue attention. He peered into the darkest recesses of the courtyard to where the lightweights among the magi-children skulked
and spotted the person he was looking for. He slid in beside a gangling
figure with a drip of water or snot hanging from a long thin nose.
Lank red-brown hair was plastered to a pale, morose face.

'Alaron,' the swarthy newcomer greeted his fellow, dangling a
small wicker basket full of steaming sweet dumplings under his
friend's dripping nose. They both wore the robes of Turm Zauberin,
the all-male gnostic college of Norostein. 'Three fennik it cost me!
Rukka Hel – festival day prices!' He took a dumpling and swallowed
it whole, then thrust the basket at his friend. 'Bloody merchants,
eh?' he added slyly.

'Thanks, Ramon.' Alaron Mercer grinned despite himself. His father
Vann was a merchant himself; he could see him just a few yards
away, chatting to Jostyn Weber. Alaron wolfed down a dumpling and
looked around. 'What a waste of time. The service will be at least
three hours long, you realise.'

'At least we're inside,' Ramon observed. 'The commoners get stuck
out here in the rain all afternoon – they can't even sit down.' He
glanced around, looking like a ferret peering out from its burrow.
Ramon Sensini was a secretive young man, the son of a Rondian
mage (whose identity he'd never shared) and a Silacian tavern-girl.
The Turm Zauberin gatekeepers had initially refused him entry, even
though he'd funds enough to enrol, but he had shown the Principal
a letter and that had got him in.

As usual, Alaron had a bee in his bonnet over the festival. 'Did
you know that every Sollan festival has had some stupid Kore ritual
put in its place? I mean, could they be more brazen? There isn't even
any evidence that the gnosis has anything to do with the Kore! And
Johan Corin was actually born a Sollan worshipper! Why does no
one remember that? I read in a book that—'

'Alaron, shush! I agree, but it's blasphemy.' Ramon put a finger
to his lips, then pointed at a girl not far away. 'Hey, look, there's
Gina Weber. Aren't you and she going to be betrothed?'

'No!' said Alaron sourly, 'not if I have any say in it, anyway.'

'Which you won't,' put in Ramon unsympathetically.

Alaron peered at the fleshy blonde girl clinging to Jostyn Weber's arm. His father Vann was trying to gesture him over. 'I'm not talking to that boneheaded milkmaid,' he grumbled, pretending not to notice. He looked down at Ramon. 'I can't believe you only got four dumplings for three fennik– that's more than three times the normal price. I thought Silacians knew how to bargain?'

Ramon smirked sourly. 'Of course I bargained! No one else was getting more than one per fennik, so count yourself lucky.'

A blast of trumpetry made further conversation impossible. Governor Belonius Vult appeared at the doors to the town hall, walking down the stairs to the sound of a low, half-hearted cheer. Some twenty more magi, Rondians attached to the occupying army, followed him. Alaron could remember previous years when Governor Vult had been loudly jeered, but dissident voices were rare now the governor had settled into his powerful role. Not that everyone now approved of him, but these days it was neither profitable nor safe to show it.

'Look, it's Lord Craven of Lukhazan,' muttered Alaron to Ramon for old times' sake.

Vult mounted a horse and led the Town Council out of the court-yard. The noise outside in the plaza rose momentarily, then fell as the rain intensified, sending a collective shiver up thirty thousand spines.

Alaron wiped his nose on his sleeve. 'Come on then, let's get this over with.'

After the town leaders, came the magi, the Kore-blessed wielders of the gnosis. Seats were reserved at the front of the cathedral for them, and that included around a hundred students, mostly Noromen, but also from Verelon, Schlessen and, unusually, one Silacian: Ramon. They ranged in age from twelve to eighteen, with just nine or ten students in each year – Turm Zauberin was, after all, both expensive and exclusively male. The magi-girls of the region went to an Arcanum Convent outside of town, and all of them were here today, well-chaperoned, but eyeing the boys with interest – Turm

Zauberin boys were a good catch, more so than those from the poorer provincial Arcanums.

Alaron's year was smaller than usual, a legacy of the Revolt. As well as him and Ramon, there were only five others: Seth Korion, Francis Dorobon, Malevorn Andevarion, Boron Funt and Gron Koll. Only Funt and Koll were actually Noromen, the other three present because their guardians were involved in the Rondian occupying forces. All but Koll were pure-bloods – they referred to themselves as 'The Pure' and treated Alaron and Ramon like dirt.

Malevorn, the most gifted of them, lifted a haughty eyebrow as they approached the procession. 'Look what's crawled from under the flagstones. Where have you been, Mercer, selling oatcakes outside?'

Francis Dorobon grinned and sniggered. 'Yeah, piss off, Mercer. Your place is at the back.' Dorobon was supposedly the rightful king of some place in Antiopia.

They're welcome to him, Alaron thought, *and good luck to the poor heathen bastards*. He could grudgingly admit that Malevorn was both talented and blood-strong; Dorobon was merely the latter, and the same could be said for Seth Korion, son of the famed general. Boron Funt was a portly youth who had 'priest' written all over him, and Koll – well, Koll was just slime personified.

Alaron muttered under his breath and tried to sidle around them, but Malevorn laid a heavy hand on his shoulder. He was strikingly handsome, with a large-boned frame and tanned skin that made him look years older than he was, and he oozed rakish charisma. His black hair curled about his ears and his grey eyes were steely. 'Hey, Mercer, I see that slut Weber is still trying to get your father to agree to a betrothal. Shame she's no longer a virgin. I popped her cherry last year. She cried, you know. It was very touching.'

'Piss off, Malevorn,' Alaron snarled and shoved the bigger boy back. Malevorn went to cuff him, gnosis light flared between them as their shields brushed and the crowd about them started to look interested. Before anything could develop, a hawk-faced Magister with a flowing black hair and beard stepped between them. 'Enough! I've warned you before, Mercer.'

'Sorry, Magister Fyrell.' Alaron bowed his head, seething. *Fyrell always takes Malevorn's side!*

Ramon pulled Alaron away from their smirking classmates, keeping his hand on Alaron's arm as moon-faced Gron Koll spat at him, making sure Alaron didn't attempt to retaliate in front of Fyrell.

What a fine example of the divine magi we are, he thought as he stamped into place in the procession.

The walk across the plaza was fraught with discomfort, the ordinary people peering at them with mixed fear and envy. Girls made eyes at them, knowing that to bear a magi's child was a path to wealth. Young men envious of something they would never have glared sullenly. Citizens who genuinely believed that the magi were beings blessed personally by Kore Himself wanted to kiss their robes, to have their children touched, to give and receive blessings. It all made Alaron's skin crawl.

These poor fools see us as some kind of sacred brotherhood blessed by the Gods. Alaron might have believed that once, but seven years alongside the 'Pure' had destroyed that notion. *What a crock! We're more like a pack of wolves.* He loathed each of the Pure, for different reasons. Malevorn Andevarion was handsome and worldly and far more skilled than Alaron would ever be – and driven, in a way none of his friends were. The Andevarions had fallen on hard times and Malevorn was to be their redemption. He worked as hard as anyone at the college, with a burning competitiveness that meant he couldn't resist stamping down upon all of the others, to make sure they all, even Francis Dorobon, a king-in-waiting and Seth Korion, son of the greatest general of Yuros, knew that he, Malevorn, was the Alpha. But Malevorn's particular delight was bullying Alaron, and so Alaron hated him as much as he envied him. He also despised Dorobon for his self-righteous prating about his destiny, his rights and his privileges. No silver spoon was polished enough for the prince, who complained ceaselessly, until even his friends got impatient with him.

Ramon always called Seth Korion 'The Lesser Son'. Magister Hout, their history teacher, had once commented that great men often had weak sons who failed to live up to their parent's deeds, and

Ramon played on this relentlessly, no matter how often Seth beat him.

Boron Funt was a sanctimonious preacher, always toadying to the religion-master and pulling up the others, especially Alaron, on perceived moral failings. He ate seven meals a day and dressed in pavilion-sized robes. As for Gron Koll – well, he was the sort of boy who practised his fire spells on small animals.

It wasn't a fun group to share seven years of life with, made tolerable only by his friendship with Ramon and weekends at home – but the end was in sight. They were within five weeks of graduation. Next week, the exams began, and in forty days he would be holding his periapt, a fully graduated mage. Then he could join the Crusade and make his fortune.

He brightened at this thought and managed to keep his temper as Funt and Dorobon jostled him as they entered the cathedral. He made it to his seat near the front without being tripped again, where he huddled alongside Ramon. Magister Fyrell appeared and Alaron braced himself to be chastised, but instead Fyrell gestured for the five Pure to follow him. Alaron was puzzled, but at least he and Ramon wouldn't have to share a seat with them.

The next two hours of sermons and hymns were purgatory. Alaron, infected both by his father's apathy towards religion and Ramon's cynical views, had decided the Kore was nothing but a lie told by the magi – he'd certainly never seen an angel, and he felt nothing but his own sweat when he used the gnosis. It had never felt 'divine'. He knew such thoughts were the sort of heresies that could get him expelled if voiced, so he kept them to himself and bowed his head dutifully as the call and response of the prayers echoed through the cathedral:

'Blessed be the Magi, touched by Kore, the Light-bearers. May Holy Kore uphold their might.

'Blessed be Holy Corineus, giver of the Light, wisdom of our Hearts; may his visage light our path to heaven.

'Blessed be the Kore, the Holy Church, guardian of the True Faith, whose light illumines the darkness of the heathen.

'Blessed be the Kirkegarde, Knights of the True Way; may the Amteh blades falter before their charge.

'Cursed be Corinea, sister and betrayer of Corineus. May all women repent of their sinful ways.'

He caught Gina Weber looking at him and wondered if Malevorn had been telling the truth about deflowering her. Probably lying; it wasn't easy to get a girl alone . . . but then again, Malevorn could apparently do anything – and he was quite able to ruin a girl out of spite.

Well, that seals it. I'm not interested in his leavings.

The old bishop wound up his address by announcing Governor Belonius Vult. With a father like Vann and a friend like Ramon, Alaron had always been encouraged to take a keen interest in local politics. Vult was well known to all: a pure-blood magus from an old family, politically appointed as a general during the Revolt, against the famous General Robler's wishes, and then excluded from the legendary general's primary staff. It had been Vult's forces, guarding Robler's rear, that had infamously surrendered without a fight at Lukhazan, precipitating the defeat of Noros. Some said Vult had betrayed the cause, sold out to the Rondians in an act of betrayal. There had been calls for his arrest. Others insisted the war was already lost, that Vult had saved lives and paved the way for peace, even at the cost of his own reputation. Statesman or Traitor? Grateful parents welcoming home their sons from the prison camps after the war gave him respect, but others, especially those who had lost sons in vain, were less forgiving.

Vult had silken silver hair and an elegant beard. He possessed a catlike sleekness of movement and his voice was beguiling as he began, 'People of Noros, the words I speak today are being read aloud in every town and village of this great empire, from Rondelmar, Argundy and Lantris to Verelon and Schlessen and all the way to Pontus. This is a historic address, for it concerns the coming Crusade.'

A low rumble churned through the congregation, then everyone fell silent. Outside, Alaron could hear the rain, carried on a low, moaning wind. Vult's voice echoed about the cathedral and was repeated outside.

'These are the words of His Imperial Majesty, Emperor Constant Sacrecour:

'*My Beloved People. You are my children and I your father, sent to you by our Father in Heaven Above. I am your emperor. I speak with the voice of Kore.*

'*Kore's words are as stars to the navigator and they have steered our great empire these many years. For make no mistake, we are one nation. Though some may look upon the men of Rondelmar, Bricia, Argundy, Noros, Schlessen and elsewhere on the great lands of the empire and see differences, I your father see only similarities. We are one people, despite the differences of language and custom.*

'*For I have looked upon the Dark Continent and seen what we are not.*

'*We are not heathen. We are the children of Kore, the one true God.*

'*We are not dark-skinned as the gutter-born of the East. The whiteness of our skins marks the purity of our souls.*

'*We are not barbarians, who have as many wives as whim takes us, who rule despotically in lavish palaces while nine-tenths of the people must sleep beneath the stars. We are not heathens who dress salaciously and make idols of beast-gods born of dark imaginings. In short, we are not as they.*

'*You all know that we are at war with Antiopia. We have led two Crusades to chastise the heathen, and twice, great victories have been won.*

'*In nine short months comes the Moontide, when the Leviathan Bridge will rise again from the sea. Once more, we will march, and Yuros steel will ring again in Antiopia. Once more the Kirkegarde will raise the banner of Kore in the Dark Lands.*

'*Every morning our brothers in our fortress in Hebusalim scan the skies for windships bringing supplies. Every day they throw back the heathen from their walls. Their need is great. So I say to you, my brothers in Kore: let the Great Muster begin! Let us once more gather and march to Pontus. Let us once more tread the Bridge of the Moontide, the songs of Kore on our lips. Let us bring blessed relief to our sons fighting even now in Hebusalim. Let us give of our blood, our will and our money, to make this Third Crusade the greatest and most glorious of all.*

'Let the Third Crusade begin! This is the will of God!

'Thus speaks our Guide, the God-Emperor of Pallas, Constant Sacrecour.'

Vult paused for applause, at first hesitant, which swelled in fervour as the soldiers about Cathedral Plaza drummed their spears against their shields, then the roar of the people rose above even that clamour. In the pulpit Vult gave a satisfied smile, enjoying the moment. After a minute, as the noise was just beginning to falter, he raised a hand, and silence fell, at least within the cathedral. Outside the noise of the rain-soaked crowd did not subside until he began to speak once more.

'People of Norostein, those are the words of the emperor: a call to arms from the lips of Kore Himself. How can we do otherwise than to heed it?' He leant forward. 'There is one true war on Urte, and it is eternal. It is the war of Good and Evil: the struggle of Kore against the false idols of the heathen. The Bridge was wrought for this – to enable the victory of Kore! And should any of you believe that our war is not just, that friendship with the heathen is possible, let me point out these facts.

'First, it was they, not we, who struck the first blow, massacring traders in Hebusalim. *Our war is just!* Second, it is written in *The Book of Kore*, penned by the Scribes of the Three Hundred themselves, that only those who walk in Kore are worthy of Heaven. Therefore the heathen must perish!

'Third, there is a source of power here in Yuros that brings tyrants, despots and false priests to their knees. The gnosis is that great strength of our people, the gift of Kore, his reward for the sacrifice of Corineus. I speak as one of the descendants of the Blessed Three Hundred: we alone are the wielders of the gnosis. The heathen gods have given no such gift; the heathen have no such shield, and *this* is proof of our rightness, the instrument of our dominion. The gnosis, in the hands of the magi, will light the path to victory and secure our place in Heaven.'

He had to stop, drowned out by the drumming of iron-clad staves on flagstones and weapons on shields. Alaron looked about the old grey cathedral at the other faces around him, all caught up in a fervour of patriotism. He glanced back at his father. Vann Mercer was giving every outward sign of cheering vociferously, but Alaron knew his father better. Watch the eyes, he always said. Now he winked at Alaron, who twitched half a smile and then did some cheering too, in case any of the teachers were watching.

When the tumult quietened enough, Vult told them recruitment for the legions would begin that afternoon in the plaza, to replenish every Noros legion, then raise five new ones. The ceremony seemed to be over, but Vult, like a master showman, had saved his best trick until last. With a wave of his hand, he announced: 'A gift, from The Most Holy Emperor Constant to his beloved people of Noros.' Everyone leant forward as Vult smiled benevolently and gestured again with his right hand.

From behind a pillar emerged Malevorn Andevarion, effortlessly regal, bearing the standard of the Noros IX Legion, the beloved 'Mountain Cats' of Robler's command, one of many lost in the Revolt. The people gasped. Malevorn strode to the front, and the congregation first fell silent, gaping, then let loose the biggest, most genuine cheer of the day. Alaron glanced at his father, and this time his cheers were real: Vann Mercer had fought under that very banner. Behind Malevorn came Francis Dorobon with the 'Silver Hawk' of the Noros VI, Gron Koll with the Noros III's 'Grey Wolf' and Boron Funt bearing the Noros VIII's 'Alpenfleur'. Bringing up the rear, Seth Korion returned to the people of Noros the 'Waystar', the banner of Vult's own Noros II, lost at Lukhazan.

When the five youths bore the standards outside, onto the steps of the cathedral, the rain and cold were forgotten. The pride of Norostein had been restored; the emperor *did* love them, his loyal subjects. Vann Mercer was crying unashamedly now, as were many of the older men – the veterans, Alaron realised. These were *their* banners.

Now Vult could do no wrong. The crowd cheered him to the hilt as he joined the banners on the steps of the cathedral, watching as men fought to be first in line for the recruitment stations. A true festival atmosphere prevailed, though the rain continued to pour down, but no one cared. The five flag-bearing students were caught up in the adulation, and Alaron heard grown-ups calling them 'our pride' and 'the Hope of Noros', though three of them weren't Noros-born. Even he and Ramon became minor celebrities for a time as they walked about the square, young men asking them which Legion they would sign for. They stayed a while, but the attention became tiresome and Ramon was getting waspish about this overwhelming display of patriotism. 'These morons probably got this excited about the Revolt too, and look where that got you,' he muttered. As soon as they found Vann Mercer in the crowd, they persuaded him to leave.

'Da, what did you think of the governor's speech?' Alaron asked as they wound their way home. Tomorrow he and Ramon must be back at college, but tonight they were permitted to stay at home.

Vann Mercer stroked his chin. He was a tall, strong man still, despite a slight broadening around the midriff as he settled into middle-age. 'Well, I know what I think. But what about you, son?'

His father was always telling him to think for himself. Alaron collected his thoughts. 'Well, Vult said that the emperor loves us – but we revolted just a few years ago, so how can he love us?'

'I bet he loves to collect your taxes,' put in Ramon.

'You've been in Kesh, Da – you've always said the people there are a lot like us, and that skin colour has nothing to do with goodness. But Master Fyrell says when two races collide, they fight until one is eradicated. He says it's a law of nature.' He wrinkled his nose with distaste.

'Is that the sort of lessons I'm paying for?' Vann shook his head sadly. 'What do you think?'

Alaron thought for a while. 'Well, even though people say that we got the gnosis from Kore's hand, we all know it's really something bestowed by birth, so I don't know. I've not seen many saintly magi,' he added, thinking of Malevorn and his cronies.

'And gifting the banners back was just a ploy to boost recruitment,' Ramon said, his lively eyes sparkling. 'In the last Crusade virtually no one from Noros joined up.'

'So really,' Alaron decided, 'it was just a big show to boost enlistment numbers. But Da, why did the emperor decide to send his soldiers over the Bridge in 904 anyway? Wasn't he making a fortune from the tolls and taxes from the traders?'

Vann puffed his pipe. 'What do they tell you at college?' he asked, a question for a question again.

Ramon snorted. 'They tell us that Kore sent the emperor a vision that he had to save the world from the heathens.'

Vann half-smiled. 'It's the oldest game in the world: claim your God is the only one and your enemies automatically become evil. I was there that day, in the first windships above Hebusalim. I'll never forget it.'

And he'll not talk of it either, Alaron thought. It was the day his wife, Alaron's mother, was blinded.

But Vann surprised him and continued, 'The windship captains told us the sultan was massing an army of his own to send over the Bridge – they said we were protecting our traders from being slaughtered. We didn't know if this was true or not, but those were the first years that bankrupt magi families started marrying into merchant families in return for sizable dowries. The East had made a lot of traders very much richer, and the traditional order was being threatened. Some people believed the only way to slow or halt that process was to disrupt the eastern trade.'

Alaron waited for more, but his father fell quiet and they walked the rest of the way home in silence, Ramon sucking on a hardboiled sweet, Vann puffing his pipe. Alaron tried to imagine what it would have been like in Kesh, where his father had met his mother, fallen in love and saved her life.

'Mercer! Pay attention!' Fyrell barked.

Alaron blinked. *Damn.* 'Sorry sir, just trying to remember the formula for calculating vectors.' He and Ramon had talked away most of the night, dreaming of their futures after graduation, but now they were back in the grim, moss-walled college. Turm Zauberin was an old castle, four hundred years old at least. Magister Fyrell, his least favourite teacher, had his feet up on his desk and was tossing random questions at the whole class as revision. Alaron hadn't been listening for some time.

'Nice try, Master Mercer,' sneered Fyrell, 'but we reviewed calculus last period. This is Magical Theory.'

Ooops.

'Must I repeat the question?' The five Pure sniggered. Ramon leant back, shaking his head.

Alaron hung his head, flushing. 'Yes sir. Sorry sir.'

Fyrell rolled his eyes and stroked his black goatee. 'Very well. We are revising for the exams – remember them? I asked you to name the four classes of the gnosis and what defines them – a very basic question. Do you think you could manage that for us, Master Mercer?'

Alaron sighed. *Phew, easy.* He stood up. 'There are Four Classes of the Gnosis. First is Thaumaturgy, which is concerned with the tangible and inanimate: the elements. The Four Studies of Thaumaturgy are Fire, Water, Earth and Air. Then there is Hermetic magic: the tangible and animate, which deals with living things, ourselves and others. The Four Hermetic Studies are Healing, Morphism – shapeshifting – Animism and Sylvanism – nature magic. Theurgy is the intangible and animate, using the gnosis to augment unseen forces – like strengthening one's own gnosis, or healing the spirits of the living, curing insanity, calming people, or manipulating them emotionally. The Four Studies of Theurgy are Spiritualism, Mysticism, Mesmerism and Illusion. The last is Sorcery, which deals with the intangible and inanimate, where we use the gnosis to deal with the spirit world – the dead, in other words – to do things like strengthen ourselves, or find out about the past or the future or the now. The Four Studies of Sorcery are Wizardry, Clairvoyance, Divination and Necromancy.'

Fyrell grunted with displeasure and looked at Boron Funt. 'Mercer sounds like he's reciting a textbook. Boron, tell me the omission Mercer made with Sorcery.' He called only the Pure by their first names.

Funt puffed himself up. 'He said that the only spirits are dead spirits, Magister. He omitted the angels of God and the demons of Hel.'

That's because I don't believe in them, Alaron muttered to himself.

'Well done, Boron.' Fyrell smiled. 'Malevorn, tell me of Affinities, using your own as an example.'

Malevorn drew himself to his feet, half-closing his eyes as he spoke. 'Every mage is different: our personalities define the Studies we excel at. Most of us have greater aptitude at one or more of the four Classes of the gnosis. We also usually have one elemental aptitude greater than the others. My element is fire and I am strongest in Thaumaturgy and hermetic-gnosis.'

Fyrell looked approving, as he always did when Malevorn spoke. 'Well done, Malevorn.' He turned to his other favoured pupil. 'Gron, what is Blood-Rank?'

Gron Koll smoothed back his lank greasy hair. 'The Ranks of Blood are numbered First to Sixth. The First Rank are the pure-blooded, those descended directly from an Ascendant or two pure-bloods. The Second Rank are the three-quarter-blooded; the Third are half-blooded, the Fourth are the quarter-blooded, the Fifth Rank the eighth-bloods and the Sixth Rank those with a sixteenth. There are no lower ranks, as anyone with less than a sixteenth of mage's blood does not have the capability to utilise the gnosis.' He paused, then added, 'Above all are the Ascendants, the Three Hundred progenitors of all magi.'

'Excellent,' said Fyrell. 'And what are the degrees of relativity between the Blood-Ranks?'

'Each is roughly the square of the previous, sir. If we use the quarter-blood as a base, a half-blood is twice as powerful, a pure-blood is four times more powerful and an Ascendant sixteen times more.'

'Meaning that we pure-bloods are worth at least four of Mercer,' remarked Malevorn lightly, waving his hand at Alaron, 'and sixteen of Sensini.'

Alaron steamed, but Ramon just shrugged.

'Seth,' invited Fyrell with a lazy gesture, 'what can be done to improve one's powers?'

Seth Korion had a placid face, short blond hair and a solid build. Everyone had expected much of him, the only legitimate son of the famous General Kaltus Korion, but he'd been a plodder: a timid mage and fighter. He had shown none of the strategic and tactical thinking his teachers had expected would come naturally. The only thing he excelled at was healing, which was regarded by the boys as 'girls' magic'. Seth had always been the easiest of the Pure to get at.

'There are varying levels of skill, talent and equipment, sir. An ill-equipped, inept or poorly trained mage is less effective than a well-equipped skilled and well-trained one.'

'Fortunately we have the best in everything, sir,' put in Francis Dorobon, sticking his chest out. His dark hair was slicked back, and he affected a little moustache on his upper lip, making his pale skin even whiter. He wore rings and diamond studs, and he liked to throw little Rimoni phrases into his conversation to remind people that he was rightful King of Javon, nominally a Rimoni country even though it lay in Antiopia. He raised his hand, displaying a large diamond ring on his middle finger. 'This is a *primo* periapt.'

Students could own periapts, but they were not permitted to use them except in class until after they had successfully graduated. Alaron's was a modest crystal, Ramon's even poorer. Alaron knew his father was trying to purchase a better one for him, but quality periapts were rare and expensive.

Fyrell clapped his hands. 'Excellent. Next week, your exams will begin. You will be tested on all aspects of the gnosis, as well as your ordinary academic lessons to decide whether you are to be granted the right to act as a mage and serve the community.' His eyes swept over the Pure. It has been a pleasure to teach most of you.' His gaze flickered disdainfully over Alaron and Ramon and then back to the Pure. 'I wish you well for the coming weeks.'

Malevorn stood up. 'Sir, it has been a privilege to learn from you.' He made a lordly bow. 'For myself, your name and memory will always be on my mind as we strike down the heathen.'

Fyrell puffed up as the other Pure followed his lead, taking turns to praise and thank him.

Alaron and Ramon slipped away, unnoticed.

*

'Malevorn *alwayth* doeth tha'. How do you ge' an ego tha' large into the room? An' Fyrell panderth to him all the time. I am tho thick of thith plathe!' Alaron was nursing a split lip from the fight he'd got into with Malevorn between classes. It stung, but neither he nor Ramon were very good at healing. Three days out from the end of classes and he felt totally miserable – of course he'd totally failed to lay a finger on Malevorn, as always. He was probably the most unsuccessful brawler in the school's history. The younger students, most of them of the same ilk as Malevorn, openly laughed at him.

He sat on the tiny balcony of the room they shared, Ramon beside him, looking glumly over the city as dusk fell. The air was cold, killing the smell of the refuse pits below this side of the building – of course the Pures were on the other side, the sunset side, overlooking the gardens. Each had a room four times the size of Alaron and Ramon's.

Alaron saw the mighty shapes in the sky first, the dark silhouettes in the northeastern quarter, three black dots that grew and grew. He pointed, and Ramon followed his finger.

'Windships,' Ramon breathed. 'Merchant-traders, up from Verelon, maybe, or Pontus.' His eyes shone. All boys dreamt of windships. They watched them grow in the sky, sails billowing as the trade wind swept them up from the Brekaellen Valley, following the river towards Norostein. The enchanted hulls were winged, painted and gilded in fantastical designs, the prows like eagles and serpents, the tall masts hung about with canvas sails. A scarlet flag billowed above. 'From Pontus, I think.'

They watched in silent awe as the ships swung into the Mooring Yards beneath Bekontor Hill. Windships had curved hulls to lessen wind-resistance, and retractable braces for landing. The enchanted hulls and keels kept them airborne, but though Air-gnosis gave the ships life, it was wind that provided propulsion. Air-thaumaturgy could shape the winds, and a ship that was well-guided by a strong Air-thaumaturge could even sail against the wind, but that took real skill and endurance.

All of the trainee magi had learned to fly in small skiffs. Alaron was barely competent, but Ramon had some genuine ability despite his weak mage-blood. Vann Mercer had always hoped that Alaron would be able to build and pilot a trading vessel for him, but Alaron's prime elemental affinity had turned out to be fire and he had proven to be a very poor Air-mage. He was, he'd been told, better suited to a military career. The teachers also told him he had ability in sorcery, but sorcery scared him shitless. Ghosts and spirits . . . ugh!

Ramon looked across at him. 'Shouldn't you be on your way to see Cym tonight? It's your turn.'

Alaron thought about that. His lip was still swollen, his jaw and ribs hurt and he felt totally depressed. But he knew a smile from Cym would lift his mood, though his chances of coaxing one from her would be nigh-on impossible. It was his turn, though . . .

When Ramon had shown up at the college all those years ago he had brought with him a tiny self-possessed gypsy girl with big flashing eyes, cherry-red lips and cinnamon skin. Alaron had taken one look and fallen hopelessly in love. Her name was Cymbellea di Regia, Ramon said; she too was mage-born, but Saint Yvette's, the girl's Arcanum College of Norostein, would not take her in, so she was living in the Rimoni camp outside of town. Without their help she would never learn how to use her powers. Ramon said she'd run away from her mother, who was her mage-parent, which sounded terribly romantic to Alaron, and her plight offended his sense of justice, so it had taken little persuasion to enlist his help in educating her. For the last seven years they had been taking it in turns to slip out after dinner and meet her beside the sally port in the old ruined city wall.

Alaron loved his evenings with her. Even though she gave him nothing more than grief and frustration, he wouldn't have missed their meetings for the world. 'Of courth I'll go. It'th my latht turn.' He thought for a moment. 'You know, after gra'uation you'll return to Thilacia and who knowth where Thym will go? We migh' never meet again. Da wantth me to be a part of his buthineth and get married. I migh' no' even ge' to joi' the Cruthade.'

'And a good thing too,' remarked Ramon. 'You don't want to be a part of that – it's just a bunch of pure-bloods slaughtering loads of Keshi and Dhassans. You're better off out of it.'

'But, *everyone* ith going . . .' He exhaled heavily. 'Everyone *elth*.'

Ramon just shrugged disinterestedly. 'War is overrated, *amici*.'

'Huh.' Alaron got up and stretched. 'I gueth I better go,' he said. 'Thym will be wondering where I am.'

Alaron found Cym in their usual place, a wrecked hovel against the old walls that stank of piss and rot. She was wrapped in a brown blanket, her head cowled in a large shawl. She had lit a fire, small enough to escape the notice of any passing watchman but barely large enough to raise the temperature. She was amusing herself by firing tiny energy-bolts into the city wall, leaving scorch-marks and a strange metallic tang in the air. Such bolts were the mage's most basic weapon, deadly enough against an ordinary human, but easily countered by any other gnosis-wielder.

'You lose another fight?' she asked, eyeing his bloodied lip. 'Here, let me have a look.' It was a sad fact that once she got the hang of it, Cym was actually better than both of them at most of the things they taught her. Alaron suspected that her mysterious mother – Cym never discussed her – had been of considerable power, and Cym herself was a natural. Alaron's frequent scraps with Malevorn meant she got plenty of opportunity to practise her healing.

He closed his eyes, wincing as she poked and prodded, then sent a painful tingle of gnosis-power into his cut that reduced the swelling and sealed the wound.

'There, that should be gone in a few days. Idiot. Hasn't he beaten you up enough for a lifetime already?' It was a rare week that he and Malevorn didn't come to blows, either on the weapons-practice field or in some hall or back room. He just couldn't hold his temper around the Pure.

'Thanks,' he said, running his tongue over the healed cut. He tried to squeeze her hand, but she avoided him deftly, pretending not to notice.

'So,' she said, 'this is it: my last lesson with you. After tomorrow you'll be off doing your exams and I'll have to find other ways to learn.'

'We could continue after the exams,' he offered. 'We'll be graduated then; we could do it openly.'

She shook her head. 'Our caravan leaves on Freyadai – we've got to be in Lantris before the snows.'

'Will you be back in spring?' He found he wasn't able to feign nonchalance.

'Maybe. Who knows.' She leant forward, her face hungry. 'What new things can you show me?'

For the next two hours he taught her the drills he'd learnt since last time and reviewed her progress on earlier lessons, where, as usual, she'd already overtaken him, and ended up helping him as much as he did her. He hoped he might be more than just a rote-mage one day, but he wasn't there yet. He tried to demonstrate shaping fire, but the flames sizzled and went out with a dispiriting pop.

'Let it flow, Alaron,' she scolded. 'You're so tense – you need to relax, let it run through you, like water.'

'I can't!' he groaned. 'I just *can't*.'

'You're a mage – let it come naturally!'

'It's not natural, it's as unnatural as you can get,' he complained dispiritedly. He felt tired and clumsy. Outside, the new moon was up, its great arc covering half the sky. It looked almost touchable – more touchable than Cym, anyway. The Rimoni girl followed his glance, shuddered and pulled up her cowl. She was always leery of the massive weight of the moon hanging in the sky above. 'Off you go. You're too tired for any more. Go home.'

He knew she was right, but to say good night . . . that would be to shut the door on so many dreams. He hesitated, but she'd already stood and ducked under the rotting leather sheet that formed a makeshift door. He had to follow, feeling even more wretched.

Cym turned to him. 'So: after seven years, this is the end, for you and me. I do not know how to thank you for your kindness in teaching me.'

He tried to think of something charming and witty and romantic, but instead he was mute. She put a bony finger to his lips. 'Shh.' She pressed something into his hand and he looked down at it: a copper amulet of a rose. The Rimoni Rose. He gripped it tight, and suddenly realised he was crying.

'Oh, Alaron, you idiot!' Cym stepped into him, pecked his cheek and then she was two feet away, four, ten and then the shadows of the old wall had swallowed her and she was gone. Maybe for ever.

The headmaster addressed them on the last day of the school year. The rest of the students had already gone home, and the usually bustling old keep felt oddly lifeless. Headmaster Lucien Gavius was a political appointment, personally endorsed by Governor Vult himself, elevated out of the classroom where Alaron had always thought of him as a lifeless slug. Gavius waffled about the coming exams, but they already knew what to expect. There were four weeks left in the month of Noveleve, and each would bring a series of tests. Week one was academic: history, theology, calculus, and Rondian, of course, to prove they could read and write. *Calculus is going to be the worst*, Alaron thought, though the most important part was next Freyadai, when they had to present their theses. Recruiters would be there, and scholars too. The thesis was their chance to contribute to the knowledge of the mage community; it was seen by many as the most important part of the exams.

Week two was all about the skills of the battle-mage. They would have to prove their skill with missile weapons and horsemanship, and fight without using the gnosis against soldiers handpicked from the ranks of the Watch, and though using blunted weapons, these men knew what they were doing. The whole week would be demanding, exhausting and dangerous.

During the third and fourth weeks, they would be tested on their use of gnosis: basic energy manipulation and theory, hermetic and theurgic-gnosis, then in the last week Thaumaturgy and Sorcery. All of the teachers would be involved in the testing, and many people would be watching, including recruiters from the Kirkegarde, the

Volsai, the Legions, the Arcanum and the City Watch, and private individuals who hired magi: merchants looking for bodyguards, schools looking for teachers. This was the shop-window; their futures would be made or broken by their display.

Malevorn, Francis and Seth had their future assured by birthright. Gron Koll and Boron Funt were of strong bloodlines too. Ramon, as a foreigner, would only graduate if he pledged himself to a stint in the legions, though he would return to his Silacian village as an important man, probably the only mage in the locality as there weren't many Rimoni-magi.

For Alaron, just another urban mage of no great birth or blood, it would be harder. Quarter-bloods were plentiful, often bastard-born, and tended to end up as front-line battle-magi, the target of every enemy crossbowman and archer and not exactly loved by their own rank and file. Many didn't last long. Vann Mercer wanted his son to eschew the legions altogether; he'd always tried to interest his son in the cut and thrust of trading, but when Alaron dreamed, he dreamed of great deeds and heroism in battle – glory, recognition. He wanted the acclamation of his peers, respect from the Pures . . . and a particular Rimoni girl on his arm.

4

The Price of Your Daughter's Hand

Magi Lineage

The Ascendant Magi of the Blessed Three Hundred were initially concerned with the overthrow of the Rimoni Empire and exploring their new powers. When it came to reproducing, they discovered that the gnosis potential was directly linked to reproduction: magi breed magi, and the quantity of 'mage-blood' directly affected the might of the children. New dynasties were founded, the purer the better – but it was also found the purer the blood, the lower the fertility, in both genders. Therefore the pure-bloods were also compelled to breed with humans to increase the number of magi to meet the numbers the empire required, which has resulted in a few strains of pure-blooded families who dominate the empire, disdaining the 'lesser blooded', yet relying upon them to provide the battle-magi the legions need.

ORDO COSTRUO COLLEGIATE, PONTUS

Aruna Nagar district, Baranasi, Northern Lakh, on the continent of Antiopia
Rami 1381 (Septinon 927 in Yuros)
10 months until the Moontide

Ispal Ankesharan could have been blind and deaf, yet he would still have known exactly where he was by smell alone, here in Aruna Nagar Market. Every aroma was familiar, the spices and coffee and tea and piss and sweat of the largest marketplace in Baranasi, the Jewel of Lakh. It was a place of pilgrimage, a bend in the river where once Gann-Elephant had sprayed water from his sacred trunk to fill the river basin, creating a flow that still ran thickly and slowly across the red-dirt plains to the impassable seas. Here he bought and sold everything that he thought might turn a profit. In this arena he matched wits with buyers and sellers, made friends and enemies, lived and loved. This was the home where he laughed and cried and thanked all of the Thousand Gods of Omali for his beautiful life.

For Ispal Ankesharan had everything: a wonderful community, the love of his gods, a dutiful wife, and many children to carry on his name and pray for him when he was gone. His home was in easy reach of the holy river Imuna. He was not so rich that the mighty were jealous, nor so poor that his family went without. It was a fortunate life, despite having seen war and death at close hand.

He opened his eyes and stared through the hazy light of autumn. The morning's coolness was dissipating fast under the sun's bright glare. He had taken his family to the river that morning with Raz Makani, his blood-brother, though Raz was Amteh. Raz and his two children had watched while Ispal's tribe prayed to Vishnarayan and Sivraman, and of course to Gann-Elephant for good fortune. Luck was Gann's preserve, a less mighty-seeming gift than those of the greater gods, but one you should never be without.

Afterwards his wife Tanuva shepherded the children home while he and Raz shared a pipe and spoke a little of the old days. To those who did not know him, Raz was a nightmare figure, his burns disfiguring still after twenty-two years. He was a man of bitter silences. They had met in 904, when Ispal had travelled north, having heard that great profits could be had by trading with the whiteskinned ferang in Hebusalim. It had been his first time out of Baranasi, let alone Lakh, and what a journey it had been – deserts, mountains, rivers, what an experience! And what a nightmare: for the ferang had sent soldiers instead of traders, and Ispal had lost all of his goods and nearly his life. He, who was a man of peace.

Still, he had survived, and he had saved the life of the fierce Keshi warrior Raz Makani, who was so badly burned it seemed he would not survive. When the war was over he had brought Raz and his woman south, and now they were brothers, men who had looked death in the eye and survived. Raz's woman had stayed with him, though Raz was ravaged by fire, and borne him two children before she died. They had shared much together, Ispal and Raz, and now Raz's son was pledged to Ispal's daughter, to seal their bond in a way that would surely please the gods.

That morning, as usual, he left Raz in his favourite place, watching the river from the shade. He left a wad of tobacco, heavily laced with ganja, and a flask of arak. Other friends would look in on Raz, spend time with him. He might be a fearsome sight, but he was familiar, part of the community.

Ispal walked the market, sniffing out the new produce. Carpets from Lokistan were arriving, bearers unloading them under the watchful gaze of Ramesh Sankar. Ramesh saw him, calling out, 'Ispal, you old rogue, would you like to buy a carpet?'

'Not today, Ram – maybe tomorrow. Good quality, hmm? Safe this time?' They laughed together, for Ram's previous shipment had included a cobra, sleeping inside one of the carpets. A snake charmer had calmed the frightened serpent and kept it, so all was well for everyone.

Together they watched other shipments being unloaded. Neither man had a shop – they dealt in bulk from warehouses nearby – but it was here the deals were cut. More traders gathered, men who knew each other like brothers, to inspect all manner of goods as they arrived, bidding for whatever interested them: spices and tea-leaves from the south, their earthy fragrances wafting through the warm air. Sacks of acrid chillies, cardamom and cinnamon, all laid on blankets on the ground by women with sun-blackened skin. Men roasted peanuts on smoking braziers. One did not stride here, one hopped from space to space. More and more people kept pouring in. This was the cradle of life; its cacophony hung in the air, thicker than the smoke of the cooking-fires. Music played, monkeys performed tricks, out-of-towners gawped: easy marks for the unscrupulous, and there were plenty of those.

The market was busy today; tomorrow was the last day of the Amteh Holy Month and Amteh worshippers – about a quarter of the people here in Baranasi – were making their final obeisance to Ahm on this last day of privation, in which they took neither food not drink whilst the sun was in the sky. But tomorrow night would be insane: drink would flow, food would be consumed by the wagonload, people would sing and dance to celebrate Eyeed, the Feast of Thanksgiving, and the traders would all make small fortunes selling the provender to facilitate this happiness.

'Ispal – Ispal Ankesharan!'

Ispal turned to see Vikash Nooradin making his way towards him, waving a hand. Vikash was slender, with wavy hair and quite pale skin for a Lakh. He was more rival than friend. Ispal patted Ramesh farewell and greeted Vikash cautiously. 'Vikash, how may I help?'

Vikash glanced at Ramesh, then drew Ispal close, his narrow features more animated than Ispal could ever remember seeing them. 'My friend, I have news of a deal that may interest you. An *exclusive* deal.'

Ispal raised his eyebrows in surprise. Vikash Nooradin was not the sort to share knowledge of deals with the likes of him. 'What sort of deal?' he asked curiously.

Vikash met his eyes frankly. 'The deal of a lifetime, Ispal – and only you and I can pull it off.' Vikash put a finger to his lips, and didn't speak more until they were well into the alleys, in a shadowy doorway where they could not be overheard. He huddled closer to Ispal. 'My friend, there is a stranger in town. He is looking for something that only you have.'

Ispal cocked his head, bemused. 'What do I have that no one else has?'

'A wife who produces only twins and triplets, who was daughter and granddaughter of women who produced only twins and triplets.' Vikash leant closer. 'This stranger desires such a wife: he is *very* rich, and he is in urgent need. I have spoken with his agent. His needs are *particular*.'

'Is this a joke?' ' He wasn't sure whether to laugh or not. 'My wife is my wife, and I do not wish to part from her, even if Omali Law allowed divorce, which it does not.'

Vikash shook his head. He was sweating uncharacteristically: Ispal had never seen him look other than cool and debonair. 'No, your *daughter*, Ispal: Ramita – this stranger, this *rich* stranger, may be interested in her. His agent stressed secrecy and urgency. He has promised *vast* sums of money – vast sums!' He mopped his brow.

'But Ramita is betrothed already, to the son of my blood-brother. Perhaps if your stranger were to wait a year or two, one of the younger girls will have bled, and—'

'No, Ispal, it must be your marriageable daughter or you will miss out. He wishes to be wed this month. He cannot afford to wait.'

Ispal shook his head. 'Vikash, this is *insane*. Marriage is sacred: it is a bond before the gods. We do not give our daughters to strangers.' He turned away. 'Thank you for the tip, Vikash, but no.'

Vikash grabbed his arm. 'Ispal, wait – this man is very, *very* rich. Please, at least talk to him—'

'No, Vikash, really, this is becoming ridiculous.'

'*Please*, Ispal – the agent will pay me one thousand rupals just for *introducing* you, much more if a deal is struck. Think what he might pay to you . . .'

Ispal froze, stunned. *One thousand rupals, just for introductions? By Laksimi – what would such a rich and profligate man pay to the people who did the real business?* He wavered, caught in a sudden fantasy of marble palaces and servants galore, with soldiers at his command and a whole caravan of wagons. *By all the gods, think of a whole multi-floor shop full of wares, the Maharaja himself visiting him to make lavish purchases . . .*

Vikash looked at him intently. 'It would not hurt to talk to this man, would it, my friend?'

Their eyes met. Ispal took a deep breath, feeling slightly dizzy, and nodded.

Vikash Nooradin led Ispal to an old haveli with carved wooden gates that were falling apart, and into the dishevelled courtyard beyond. Clumps of incense sticks were burning in braziers to mask the smell of rot. A disused fountain was green with pond-slime, and the verandas were shadowy against the stark sunshine. They sat beneath the shade of a tree on some old chairs, and a servant brought iced tea. Vikash took a sip, then spoke. 'Ispal my friend, this is an opportunity to die for. Inside there is a Rondian called Lowen Graav – you know Rondians, of course, Ispal; you have fought their soldiers, have you not? Well, this man Graav is an agent of a rich ferang. This ferang is seeking a wife – a very fertile wife; a wife guaranteed to bear him twins or more. Like your daughter.' He laughed. 'We all know about your wife's line, Ispal: you are a local legend. Poor Ispal, such a curse, every birthing an army, we say.'

Do you? I have always regarded it as a blessing, he thought.

'The rich ferang is from far to the north.' Vikash smoothed his hair and dropped his voice. 'From Hebusalim,' he whispered.

Ispal rocked back, silenced. Hebusalim: the birth-place of the Amteh Prophet, where he had lost his goods and nearly died. Where he had rescued Raz Makani from certain death. *Vishnarayan protect me.*

His inner turmoil must have shown on his face, for Vikash spoke urgently. 'Ispal, this man has promised a king's ransom for the hand of a daughter such as yours. *A king's ransom* – think of it; is it not what we all dream of? The one massive deal that will change our fortune for ever—'

'But my *daughter*—'

'A daughter is a commodity, Ispal,' said Vikash reprovingly. 'Yes, yes, we talk of love-matches and eternal bliss, but the truth is daughters marry who they must to advance the family.'

'That is true, but she is already betrothed.' He fell silent, struck dumb by visions of influence, a role amongst the powerful of the city, though he knew that sometimes it was best to go safe and unnoticed in this turbulent land. 'Perhaps it will do no harm to talk to him,' he said finally, hating himself.

Vikash went inside, and returned with a whiteskinned man of middle age: a Rondian. His chin was clean-shaven, but he had bushy grey moustaches and was clad in Keshi garb. He was soaked in perspiration, despite the relative coolness of the air – but then, his homeland was far colder than this.

'Master Graav is a mercantile agent from Verelon,' Vikash said, pronouncing the foreign names awkwardly. 'He is based in Hebusalim.'

Graav spoke in Lakh, with a slight rustiness and a Western inflection, but he was easily understandable. He asked about Ispal's family, nodding when Ispal reassured him that every pregnancy that anyone could remember of his wife and her ancestors had resulted in multiple births.

'There must be a lot of you,' Lowen Graav observed, 'many girl-children of the line.'

Ispal frowned. 'Not so many; the trait does not appear to pass down the male line, so my mother-in-law's sons have not fathered such daughters. And bearing successive multiple pregnancies is hard on the women. My wife had six sisters; three are dead. One dwells in a village not far from here, but she married late and has only youngsters. Her daughters will not flower for six or seven years yet. Her other sister bore only sons and is now barren after miscarriage.'

'And what of your own family?'

Ispal wondered a little about the wisdom of telling such things to a stranger, but Vikash smiled reassuringly. 'I married my wife Tanuva when she turned fifteen, after I returned from my first trip to Hebusalim, in what you ferang call the "First Crusade". Our first children together were my eldest son Jai and a stillborn twin – that was the only such mishap we have had. The following year came twin daughters, Jaya and Ramita. Two years later we had twin boys, before I was conscripted into the mughal's army and forced to march north again. That was during what you call the "Second Crusade". What a mess! The mughal and the sultan could not agree, so there was no cooperation. We never even reached Hebusalim before we ran out of food and water. Only my experience and the rank that gave me saved my company. When we got back, people thought we were ghosts, so thin and ragged we were, so blackened by the sun.' He patted his gently rounded belly. 'It has taken me many years to recover my shape.'

'The Second Crusade was in 916,' Lowen ruminated. 'Bad years for traders. And since?'

Ispal finished his tea and looked around for another. Vikash motioned to a servant. 'Whilst I was away, the plague came through – it always follows the wars, you know. Poor Jaya was taken, and both boys, so there were just the four of us, for a time. But Tanuva and I made more: twin boys, then triplets. A fever took one of the triplets two years later. Jai is now seventeen and Ramita has just turned sixteen. The twin boys are ten and the surviving girl triplets are eight – six children in all, and that is enough, I am thinking.' He laughed. 'Poor Tanuva says she has to work too hard!'

Graav leant forward. 'So, this daughter Ramita is the only marriageable daughter you have?'

Clearly Lowen Graav was keen to resolve this deal and return north. *Good. A wise man does not bargain in haste.* 'Clearly, Lowen-*saheeb*,' agreed Ispal. 'She is promised to another, however: the son of my blood-brother. This has been arranged for some time now, and she and the boy are very happy – indeed, they are quite in love.' He smiled benevolently, the caring father who has pleased his daughter in his marriage arrangements.

Vikash Nooridan frowned, clearly wanting Ispal to roll over on this deal, not play hard to get.

Ispal ignored him. 'Who is your client, my good sir?' he asked. 'What is his good name?'

Lowen shook his head. 'My client is an elderly man of great wealth – a man of Yuros. Recently, his only son and heir died. He needs children, he doesn't care what race or creed, but he demands fertility, that above all.' He grinned suddenly. 'He allowed me to say that for a man of his age, every arrow must count. Those are his words. Master Ankesharan, your daughter sounds the most promising girl I have come across. We have travelled far and met no one else with a similar lineage.'

Good, that is another bargaining chip for me. Ispal leant forward, as if mildly interested in something purely academic. 'Let us suppose, just for an instant, that I would break my daughter's heart and break her betrothal to the boy she adores. Let us suppose, for the slightest moment, that I would consider sending her far to the north where

I would never see her again, one of the great lights of my poor existence.' *In truth, before every god, Ramita is a joy, the most dutiful of daughters.* 'Suppose even that I was prepared to risk my own wife's chastisement for destroying her dreams – for what? Do you not know that the Great Convocation has declared shihad? The mughal has spoken: Death to the ferang – death to the Crusaders! Everywhere Amteh and even many Omali are mustering. My blood-brother is a burnt husk through the agency of one of the cursed magi. So why should I wish to deal with you? Why should I not go out in the streets now and call for fifty stout lads who wish to get a head-start in the ferang-killing trade, hmmm? Answer me that?'

Lowen Graav tugged nervously at his moustaches. 'All that is true,' he agreed, 'but my client bids you consider this offer: in return for the totally anonymous marriage, you will receive one crore upfront, plus one lak every year that she lives, and another lak for every child born to them – payable even after your death, to your surviving family.'

Ispal Ankesharan jerked away in shock and the old seat couldn't hold him. He barely noticed as he landed in the dirt, visions of rupals falling like stars about him. One crore: ten *million* rupals! One lak: *one hundred thousand* – every year! *Every. Year. For. Ever*, repeating like the refrain of a song, over and over . . .

Some negotiator you are, Ispal Ankesharan! He let Vikash help him up. Lowen Graav sat there like a big white toad, trying not to laugh. Ispal clambered into another chair, panting. *One crore, and one lak, every year my daughter lives.* One lak alone was more money than he could have dreamed of earning in his lifetime. A crore was beyond those dreams. Such a fortune was enough for diamonds and pearls and gold and silks from Indrabad, and a palace on the river. Enough for finery and servants and a small army of soldiers: riches to outshine all but the princes of Baranasi. *Insane money – this ferang is mad!*

He brushed himself down, desperately trying to think. *This must be either some elaborate hoax . . . or it must be real.*

'May I take it you are a little interested?' enquired Lowen Graav, his voice laced with amusement.

Ispal Ankesharan took a deep, deep breath and closed his eyes. *Think, Ispal, think! Is this offer real? Would you accept if it were? Money is one thing, but people would ask questions. It would have to be managed discreetly – to appear that he had become fortunate, a great commission, a deal with a northern merchant of great wealth, perhaps. Some plausible story – and then it would secure the fortune of his family for ever. I could marry Jai to a princess!*

Ispal knew there would be tears at the sacrifice Ramita would have to make – but that was what dutiful daughters were for, to do what was needful for the family, to be a bargaining chip in profitable alliances. He would need to be careful, breaking it to Raz Makani, and to Raz's fiery son Kazim. Kazim loved Ramita passionately. And Tanuva – she would produce a storm of tears to rival Gann's great trumpeting – she would cry a new river.

But in the end, would it not have all been for the best? Would they not all look back and agree that it had been so? Why, with such wealth they could visit Ramita every year if they so wished. They would not lose her for ever. Graav's client was an old man; surely he could not last too long? Just long enough to father children on Ramita would suffice. He licked his lips, trembling.

Graav smiled and offered his hand. Ispal looked at it and then allowed himself to be hauled to his feet. 'I will need to meet your client before I agree to this. I will need his surety as to the good treatment of my daughter. I will need credible guarantees of his wealth and reliability. I will need to know his name.'

'Of course.' Graav glanced at a rickety door, which twitched open as a tall figure emerged from the haveli. The sunlight caught on a large ruby bound to his brow. Ispal caught his breath. *Surely not . . .*

The newcomer was twig-thin, but very tall, more than six feet tall. *These ferang are all giants.* He was very pale, his beard a dirty ash-grey, his thin hair tangled, but his robes were rich indeed, deep blue bordered with gold braid. It was the ruby at his brow that drew the eye though: the size of a thumbnail, bound there by a circle of filigree gold, impossible to value. It pulsed like a heartbeat: a periapt – which meant this man was a mage.

He bowed very low, suddenly terrified.

The old man's voice was husky and thin, but there were echoes of great authority. He looked beaten down by age, though still a man to be reckoned with. His eyes were ancient, dark-circled, eyes such as a god might have, an old god who has outlived his worshippers. 'Ispal Ankesharan,' he whispered. 'I am the man who would marry your daughter. I am Antonin Meiros.'

His jaw refused to unlock and he couldn't speak. Fear held him immobile, as it had in Hebusalim all those years ago. His heart drummed so violently he thought his ribcage would burst. He thought he might expire with fright. *I should fall to my knees. Or produce a dagger and plunge it into his heart—*

The old man reached out and touched his sleeve. 'Do not be afraid,' he said gently. 'I wish you no harm. My offer is genuine. Please, sit with me.'

Ispal allowed himself to be guided back to his chair. As Meiros sat beside him, Lowen Graav and Vikash Nooridan moved back a little. Meiros spoke the Lakh tongue fluidly – but then, he would, he who had lived so long and done so much. Clearly he'd been listening to the earlier conversation, somehow. *He is a mage, of course he heard us.* 'How—? Why—?'

Meiros understood. 'They killed my son – the light of my life. And I am an old man, very, very old. We magi breed seldom – perhaps it is some kind of punishment for usurping God's powers on Urte . . . But I have so much I must hand on before I die, things a father can trust only his own child with, a child of his own blood. So I need a wife, a fertile wife. I do not care if she is Lakh or Rondian or Rimoni, or the child of some nomadic raider, just that she is fertile.'

Ispal's mind spun. *This could not be happening—* He pinched his arm, but he did not wake. 'My wife's line has always bred multiple births, lord,' he said huskily.

Meiros nodded gravely. 'I will require records – proofs, documents, if such can be had here.'

Vikash Nooradin raised a finger in the air. 'I can speak to this.

Such records do exist, in the prince's archives, and I can show you those. But I vouchsafe that Ispal speaks truly.'

Meiros nodded. 'I can feel the truth of his words,' he said, the light of his periapt twinkling, making Ispal's mouth go dry. The old mage leant forward intently. 'Describe her to me, Ispal Ankesharan, not as a father describing a daughter; I care not for looks or grace. I need to know her character. Describe her as you would were you assessing a businessman with whom you wished to transact.'

Ispal blinked. *Women do not do business.* But he dared not say so to this ferang, whose ways were not his. So he thought of his daughter, and chose his words carefully. 'She is a good girl, lord: honest, but not blindly so. She can negotiate, and she knows when to say no. She does not giggle and gabble as most girls her age do. She is responsible, and can be trusted with money and with children. I have been fortunate in my children.'

'It is as Ispal says, lord,' Vikash put in enthusiastically. 'She is accounted a good catch for any young man of Aruna Nagar. And though you say you care not, she has a sweet face, lord.'

Ispal smiled his thanks. 'But I still do not understand, lord,' he said to Meiros boldly, 'you have lived centuries – surely you have all the time in the world?'

Meiros sighed. 'Would that I had, Master Ankesharan.' Ispal waited for more, but Meiros fell silent.

Then he is mortal after all . . .

'Any children of mine will inherit wealth and power,' Meiros said finally. 'They will be of the Blood; the Mage's Blood, descended from an Ascendant. I am a peaceful man, Ispal Ankesharan, whatever you might have heard to the contrary. If your claims of her are true and you permit me to wed her, I will treat your daughter well. I will honour my promises.'

Here I am, Ispal thought, *Ispal Ankesharan, son of a storekeeper, sharing arak with the most hated man in all of the lands: Antonin Meiros, a name to strike fear and loathing in young and old. The man who joined two continents separated by impassable seas with the greatest bridge ever made, then let the Crusaders pass. A miracle worker, a myth made flesh – and he is here, asking for the hand of my daughter!* It was like a tale from the holy texts, of demon-kings tempting the good man. His hands shook. *Be still my heart, do not explode inside me!*

'Let us assume the records will verify your claims.' Meiros said. 'Do we have a deal? May I wed your daughter?'

Ispal walked shakily home. He had to sit often, overcome with dizziness. Vikash Nooridan was excited, more excited than he. *How much gold have you earned, Vikash?* But he couldn't follow the thought through; there was so much else to think about. How to tell Raz Makani and remain blood-brothers. How to tell Tanuva and remain welcome in his own house. How to tell Jai, who loved his sister. How to tell Kazim and survive.

How to tell Ramita.

It was a pale, shaking Ispal who stumbled into his small, happy house to destroy that happiness. He heard his wife singing with the younger children as she cooked. Jai and Ramita would still be at the market until nightfall. He clutched the door, thanked Vikash in a throaty voice and waved him away. Vikash bounded off, full of energy, but Ispal felt exhausted, as if from crossing the desert again, with but a pittance of food and water, his men dying about him. It was this memory that finally gave him strength. *It was all for a purpose, my cheating of death in two Crusades. It was all for this.*

He took a deep breath and called his wife.

5

The Dutiful Daughter

Lakh

South of the deserts is a vast land filled with the greatest multitude of people.
They call themselves Lakh, based upon their word 'lak', which means one hundred
thousand, but in early days simply meant 'many'. They are the Many . . . and
many there are! There you will see all things: grace and vileness, love and hatred,
piety and despotism. You will see wealth and splendour and the most abject of
poverty: vivid, loud, filling your senses and haunting them for ever.

VIZIER DAMUKH, OF MIROBEZ, 634

Aruna Nagar, Baranasi, Northern Lakh,
on the continent of Antiopia
Rami 1381 (Septinon 927 in Yuros)
10 months until the Moontide

Ramita Ankesharan wore a red string bracelet threaded with spiky
bullnut seeds about her left wrist, a betrothal cord from Kazim
Makani. She sang softly to herself as she worked, roasting pinenuts
for the stall. Her dark skin and flowing black hair were shrouded
from the harsh sun by a fold of her pale yellow dupatta scarf, thin
enough to look through and thick enough to hide her face. Her
salwar smock was yellow too, though stained with ash from the fire.
Her hands were already callused from years of manual labour and
her bare feet hard as the stone of the marketplace. But her face was
still soft, and had lost none of its girlishness. She was barely five
foot when she stood, neither short nor tall by local standards. The
song she sang was a love song, her mind on Kazim.

At the front of the stall her brother Jai was selling their wares: herbs, spices and roasted nuts, paan leaf and seed-cake Mother had baked that morning. They kept a bucket of lemon-scented water on the stall for the thirsty. Father's trading provided sporadic profit, so they used the stall to generate the cash they needed for daily life. There were thousands of people here: buyers, sellers, thieves, workers, soldiers, even a cluster of Amteh women in bekira-shrouds, so they were never still. Jai kept up a constant patter, bargaining for every last seed: 'Hello saheeb, would you like to look? Looking is free!' Banter passed between the stalls. Ramita had a running argument going with a boy from the neighbouring stall about the smoke from her cooking-fire; the boy had already tried to douse it once.

People she knew passed constantly: girls, many with babies bundled in their arms; boys, ostensibly looking for work but really just lazing about. Everyone asked when she would marry. 'Soon! Father promised he would begin to arrange it after Eyeed. Very soon!' Father had promised. She was sixteen now and impatient. Kazim was so handsome and attentive: he filled her world. They stole kisses, but she longed for more.

She gazed skywards, praying for time to speed up, until a furtive movement caught her eye. 'Hey!' she shouted at a little rhesus monkey which had crept onto the corner of her mat. 'Don't you dare!' She waved a fist and the cheeky thing bared its teeth, grabbed a handful of peanuts and was gone. It flashed through the market and launched itself onto the shoulders of an entertainer. 'Hey, control your little thief!' she yelled at the man, who was pulling the nuts from its paws. 'Give those back!' The man just smirked and filled his mouth.

'Hey, sis, more chillies!' called Jai, without looking back. A cloud of old women were all talking to him at once. Ramita hefted a sack and swung it onto the cart that served as their stall. *Gods, it was so hot!* At least they had some awning; the poor folk trying to sell from blankets on the ground looked more and more frazzled as the temperature rose.

'Ramita,' a voice called, and she looked up, her heart leaping.

Kazim leant against the cart, a kalikiti bat in his hand. He flashed his white teeth, brilliant against the short beard and moustache which made him look so rakish and exciting.

She felt her skin go moist and her belly turn just to look at him. 'Kazim.' His eyes were dark, grey-black, beautiful as ebonies.

He hefted the bat. 'I'm off to play this Lakh game you love so much. Can you spare your brother?'

Jai looked at her hopefully.

'Well . . .'

'You've finished the cooking,' Jai burst out, 'now it's just serving up until we run out. It's nearly lunchtime – Huriya will help you.' Huriya was Kazim's sister, her best friend. '*Please*, Sister—'

Kazim leant his support with a hopeful grin that won the day.

'Oh, very well, go – go!' She flapped her hands, her eyes filled with her beloved's face. 'Go, have your fun – men and their stupid games.' But she was laughing as she said it.

Kazim reached out and touched her hand in gratitude, a stolen little intimacy that made her burn and turn liquid at once. The air sang. Then the two youths sauntered off.

'Look at them go,' laughed Huriya, sashaying out of the throng. 'Don't boys ever grow up? Even your father still likes to wave those silly bats around. Did you see, he's gone off with Vikash Nooradin?'

Huriya was taller than Ramita, and more generously rounded. Some of the older boys treated her badly because she was foreign and Amteh and had a sick father, but Kazim looked after her fiercely, and no one stood up to him twice. Huriya's body was hidden beneath her black bekira-shroud. 'Why do we Amteh have to wear these stupid hot tents when you Omali woman can walk around half-naked and no one says anything?' she complained, although today she had the hood pulled back, leaving her sensual face unmasked. She hugged Ramita quickly and then they both turned to face a wall of customers. It was time to get busy.

They worked steadily through the day, dozing when the sun was at its highest and the crowds thinned out, then setting to again as the sun dipped towards evening. The boys had still not returned to help pack up, so cursing them good-naturedly, they loaded up the cart with the remaining stock and stowed the cooking gear. The muddy ground was littered with waste, and every bare wall of the marketplace was wet with piss. Wads of chewed-out paan squelched beneath their toes as they pulled the cart through the streets, heading for home in the darkening, cooling streets. Children swarmed about, caught up in chasing games. An old camel plodded past, pulling a large cart while his driver slept on the back. Soldiers called out rude invitations and Huriya snapped back with feisty bravado. Guttering torches filled the alleys with smoke. Ramita calculated the day's take in her mind: maybe sixty rupals – three times the normal at least. The last days before festivals were always good ones. Father would be delighted. Maybe he was off buying presents from Vikash? He always found little things in the market to amuse them, and no one could bargain like he could.

They pushed their way through the tide of people until they finally reached a small gate into a tiny yard filled with detritus. Father was a hoarder. Above them the Ankesharans' narrow stone apartment towered, three storeys high with a cellar below, but barely ten feet wide, with neighbours on either side. Ispal's father's father had first rented and then bought it and gradually they had settled into it until they were part of the stone, repairing and renewing every season, their sweat and toil part of the mortar. When they married, she and Kazim would take over the second bedroom on the top level until they could complete another level for them alone. They would live their whole lives in this one house, as Ramita's grandfather and father had. At the moment she shared the second room with Huriya, and the boys slept on the roof. There was no room for privacy.

The house was strange tonight. Normally her mother was in the kitchen with the children, gobbling down food and complaining while Ispal and Raz sat in the backyard smoking and drinking. But tonight none of the adults were visible and the children were running amok in the yard. The two young women looked curiously at each other. Ramita went into the kitchen and barked at the young ones, trying to restore order, while Huriya unpacked the cooking gear for cleaning. Then Huriya took over feeding the children while Ramita took a bucket down the alley to the water pump.

When she got back, some semblance of order had been restored. Huriya had charmed the girls into tidying up and the boys were studying the slates they had brought from school, speaking aloud the words etched on them, phrases from an Omali holy book about respect for parents.

Ha! Where are my parents anyway, she wondered. *Upstairs together? And where is Raz? And Jai and Kazim? What is* wrong *with this place today?* She clambered up the narrow stairs and knocked tentatively on the doors to her parent's bedroom. 'Father? Mother? Are you home?' She thought she could hear her mother crying and she clutched her breast suddenly. 'Mother? What is happening?' Ispal opened the door and embraced her in his big soft arms. She looked up at him and at her mother, crying on the bed. 'Father?'

Her father hugged her tight, and then held her at arm's-length, his soft eyes uncertain and his lips moving, as if he were holding some silent argument with himself. She felt a sharp stab of real fear as he said quietly, 'You had best come inside, daughter.'

She staggered from her parents' bedroom an hour later and collapsed on her own bed, almost shrieking through her tears. It was the room she was to have shared with Kazim – but that would never be now. Huriya was shouting at Father, trying to make him change his mind, and neighbours, alarmed at the racket, were shouting at them all. Ispal had stopped trying to explain himself and just held her, wrapping her so tightly to himself she could barely breathe.

Why had Father done this to her? Hadn't she been a good girl? Hadn't Kazim been promised to her? *Promised!* And now, torn away – every dream that they shared with each other, staring at the moon and stars, snatched away, and for what? Didn't they have all the money they could want? What more happiness could all that gold bring them? Even so much gold, more than she could even comprehend . . . Omali girls were supposed to *give* a dowry, not be purchased with one. And to be married to some old man – Father would not even say his name.

She slid off the bed and onto her knees, bombarding the gods with questions, alternately sobbing and whispering in a broken voice. The gods are in the silence, their guru always said. Where were they now? *Is this just selfishness?* a small part of her chided. Would she have felt this way if she'd been told that Huriya had been commanded to make a horrible marriage to make them all rich? Was she being a hypocrite? A dutiful daughter must go obediently into marriage, to bring her family advantage.

But she had dreamt of so much more – a love to last the ages. Father had promised!

Ramita heard Kazim and Jai come home well after dinner-time. She was lying on her pallet, ignoring Huriya's soft snoring, trying to numb her mind. She was wishing she could puff on a hookah full of hashish until the world sank away for ever when she heard the clicking of the latch and the soft laughter.

Ispal was waiting for them. It didn't take long for voices to be raised again. There was no mistaking Kazim when he was angry; he bellowed his fury, careless of whoever heard. She could picture his eyes blazing, his mouth shouting. He had always had a blazing temper, but normally calmed down quickly enough afterwards. She had never heard him like this, though – he had gone berserk, swearing and throwing things. Neighbouring men came around to see what the fuss was and ended up joining the row. She watched from the window as Kazim was thrown out into the alley and bundled away, fists still swinging. It was awful.

There was no sleep afterwards, just shocked, empty hours of disbelief. Just before dawn, there was a soft knock at the door and Guru Dev let himself in. Huriya slunk away, leaving her alone with the old wiseman, their family's mentor and spiritual guide. Despite all the anger she felt inside, she went and knelt at his rough-skinned feet and out of respect heard what he had to say. Guru Dev spoke of sacrifice, of little drops of water that filled oceans, about being a part of the greater whole. The dutiful daughter obeys, he reminded her. He spoke of rewards in the hereafter, of the joy in Paradise at the good deeds of the least girl. He spoke of the labours of her parents and their parents, and how proud they would be looking down upon her as she made secure the futures of her family and elevated them to a place among the great.

'And this old ferang, he cannot have long to live, eh – and then who knows what your life might hold? Imagine a few short years away and then returning, a rich widow, wrapped in silks. Imagine the joyous reunion.'

It sounded so reasonable in the old man's soothing voice. It sounded like something she could do, perhaps even the right thing to do. But she had glimpsed Kazim's stricken eyes, seen the blows of the neighbours bloodying his face. She'd heard his howls, mad with grief. She wondered where he was, alone in the cold darkness, his future shattered.

In the morning, she found she had fallen asleep at Guru Dev's feet as the old man dozed in his chair. Huriya was staring at her. She gave a wan smile as their eyes met. Her belly rumbled and her bladder was demanding relief. Life demanded she go on. She carefully stood, took off the betrothal cord Kazim had given her and put it carefully away. Huriya took her hand silently and they crept downstairs to wash and face the new day.

Two days later, the festivities of Eyeed were still going strong. There were many Amteh-worshippers in northern Lakh, even here in Baranasi on the sacred river, and drums resounded throughout the city. Huriya had gone off to tend her father. Kazim hadn't come home; no one had seen him for two days.

Before dawn the children had been scrubbed under the water pump in the alley. Tanuva had brought out her best soap, and Ramita performed the delicate task of washing in public without showing flesh with practised grace. She rinsed her hair then twisted out the water in bubbly streams. Mother and Auntie Pashinta traced henna patterns onto her feet, her hands and halfway up her arms before dressing her in her best saree. Then the whole family went to the holy Imuna River, to give blessings to the sun as it rose and set marigolds floating in the dark stream. All about them were other townsfolk doing dawn prayer. Jai had on his cleanest white kurta and his head was bound in a turban. He looked tired and was sullen in everything he did. He gave nothing but black looks to his father. Ramita wished he would relent: it couldn't be helped, and he wasn't making anything easier for her. It was hard enough getting through an hour without crying. Her brother's anger just made it worse.

She touched the holy water of Imuna to her forehead and to her lips and to her breast. *I can do this.*

Sometime in the night, she had made peace with this fate she had been handed. It was going to be hard – she still couldn't think of Kazim without crying – but she would endure. She would cast herself upon this pyre as the gods demanded. She would return to Kazim when the old man died. It would not be long. She could endure.

All of the neighbourhood was surreptitiously watching, she knew. Father had told no one the name of her suitor and gossip was flying. The Ankesharans had fought with the Makanis, everyone knew that, and now they had broken the betrothal that was to bind them for ever. Ramita's new husband was coming at midday today, and every goodwife who didn't have a view of their courtyard would be finding an excuse to be in the alleyway outside at the appointed hour. Speculation was rife, expressed loudly and in whispers. Had some prince from the mughal court seen Ramita at market and been entranced? Or was there another boy? Everyone had a theory, but only Ispal, Tanuva and Ramita knew, and the secret burned inside, though in truth the man's name was nothing more to her than a distant legend, less than half-believed.

The noise rose to a babble outside as Jai admitted a soldier from the court of the Raja of Baranasi, who was wondering what this disturbance was. She watched her father placate him and slip him some money before he left. Ispal looked relieved to see him go. All the while the twisting sensation in her belly grew until she had to dash to the slops-drain and vomit up her breakfast. She could imagine what the neighbours made of that: '*Ah, lost her virtue already, the little slut. I knew she would come to no good.*' It was all so unfair. *Kazim, my prince, where are you? Take me away from all this!*

Finally, just as the sun breached the buildings and beamed down upon the courtyard, booted feet tramped up the alley. The babble outside rose, then fell as the marching stopped outside the alleyway. Ispal rose ashen-faced to his feet and waved to Tanuva to marshal the children, while Jai wrestled the gate open. Ramita, the taste of bile stinging her throat, clung to her father's arm, petrified.

A giant of a man strode through the gate. He was more than six foot and wide as a building, helmed and armoured beneath a blue cloak. His face was grim, scarred, but undeniably white. *A ferang!* Ramita felt a quiver of fear. She had never seen a white man before, and he looked . . . *ugly.* Strange. Brutish. He glared about the packed courtyard, took in the overlooking windows filled with watchers, and she could read displeasure on his foreign countenance: a body-guard unhappy with security. He waved four more soldiers inside before turning back to admit Father's friend Vikash Nooridan-saheeb. Then a cowled figure, very tall, but thin and stooped, came in.

Her hands shook as she clung to her father, who was sweating in waves. She stared. *This is he?* He was clad in a cream robe, his features hidden beneath the cowl. Cream and white were funerary colours, yet he wore them to a betrothal – was this some insult, or just ignorance? He used an ebony staff, metal-capped and patterned with burnished silver. Was it magical? Was he really a jadugara, a wizard? Was he really the Antonin Meiros of tales? She felt her fright magnify as the moments passed.

She could feel the eyes of all the neighbours on them as Ispal led her forth. Words were exchanged, beneath her hearing. If the old man said anything to her, she couldn't make it out. A dry hand tugged down her veil and lifted her chin. She found herself looking up into the cowl, where a red gem pulsed like a demon's single eye. She gave a small gasp, wanted to run, nearly fell, but Ispal's hands gripped her arm tight and held her up.

For a few seconds, she had the most frightening sensation, as if her mind were a scroll and this old man was reading it. Her memories, her emotions, the things she cared about, the things she hated, all just patterns on paper, coldly appraised. She wanted desperately to run and hide, but some kind of terrified defiance kept her rooted to the spot.

<Good girl.> The words were spoken into her mind, warm and approving. She almost screamed.

'She has pleasing features,' he said aloud in Lakh. His voice was withered by age. 'Are you willing, girl?'

'Achaa,' she blurted. She could just make out a pallid face, wrinkled skin, a straggly white beard. Ghastly.

The cowl turned towards her father and she managed to breathe. 'Very well, Master Ankesharan. She will do. Let the ceremony begin.' He seemed to think it would all happen now.

Ispal shook his head. 'Oh no, saheeb. There are preparations that must be made. My guru has taken the auspices. It will happen on the day before Holy Day.'

'Out of the question,' snapped the jadugara. 'I must return to the north immediately.'

Ispal put on an expression of apologetic helplessness that Ramita recognised from many a marketplace duel of wits. She marvelled inwardly at his nerve. 'Oh no, saheeb. The ceremony must happen as Guru Dev prescribes. It is tradition.'

Meiros turned that hollow cowl towards Vikash. 'Is this so?'

Vikash waggled his head. 'Oh yes, saheeb.'

Meiros snorted exasperatedly. 'Oh yes, saheeb, oh no, saheeb,' he muttered, then sighed heavily. 'Very well. Master Vikash, make the arrangements. Everything must be cleared with Captain Klein, understood?'

'Oh yes, saheeb.'

He snorted, looking about him. 'Is there some other ritual that must be fulfilled here?'

Ispal looked flustered. He motioned Guru Dev forward and after some muttered debate, a small tray containing an image of Parvasi and a Siv-lingam was brought forth. Guru Dev touched his finger to a bowl of vermillion paste and dabbed a bindu mark on Ramita's forehead, then halted in confusion before Meiros and his ruby-jewelled forehead. 'Enough,' came the sibilant voice. 'I have no patience for this. I consider us betrothed. Do you also consider us so, girl?'

Ramita started, realising she was being addressed. 'Achaa. I mean, yes sir,' she mumbled, afraid to say otherwise.

'We are done here, then?' asked Meiros in a flat, impatient voice.

Ispal bowed. 'Yes, master.' His voice faltered. 'Will you come in, take tea with us? We have cooked—'

'I think not. Good day, Master Ankesharan.'

Then he was gone, as quickly as he had come. Behind him, the street filled with the curious, everyone sharing what they had seen, asking questions: *Who was he? What did he look like? Did you see him? I did, he is a prince from Lokistan, like I told you! Well, I saw . . .*

Ispal stood swaying for a moment, biting his lip. 'Well, I dare say he must be used to better things,' he told Tanuva, who stood aggrieved over her table, weighed down with good food that she, Ramita and Pashinta had laboured over for two days. 'As you soon will be,' he added in a whisper to Ramita.

Ramita trembled, angry that this old man had just marched in, careless of the feelings of her family, ignorant of their labours to prepare for him. Had they no sensitivity, these ferang? How arrogant! She glared at his father. 'I found him rude,' she told him bluntly as he winced, 'rude and ignorant. I don't like him.' She stomped away, seeking her room and solitude.

Where are you, Kazim? Won't you come to me, flying over the rooftops like Hanu-Monkey to rescue me from the evil demon-king? Where are you, Kazim? Why won't you come to me?

6

Words of Fire and Blood

Religion: Amteh

Ahm made the Urte and all things virtuous and good and set man to rule it. All things flow from Ahm. Let these words always be upon our lips: 'All praise to Ahm!'

THE KALISTHAM, HOLY BOOK OF AMTEH

Every evil you perform on this world will be inflicted upon you a thousand times in Hel. But every kindness will be returned one hundred times one thousand in Paradise. And he who dies fighting for Ahm will dwell for ever with Him for ever.

THE KALISTHAM, HOLY BOOK OF AMTEH

Aruna Nagar, Baranasi, Northern Lakh,
on the continent of Antiopia
Shawwal 1381 (Octen 927 in Yuros)
9 months until the Moontide

There was a red-brick Dom-al'Ahm near the edge of Baranasi, deep in the slums, the jhuggis where most Amteh dwelt. How the mughal could be Amteh while his Amteh subjects were mostly impoverished was one of life's riddles to Kazim – but he had bigger problems to deal with: like how and why his life had been turned on its head.

He had spent the last four days at the Dom-al'Ahm for lack of anywhere else to go. He was far from the only one: many homeless came here for a dry place to sleep and some hand-out food. His purse was empty from three days of desperately trying to forget what had happened, to pretend he didn't care. Dancing and singing, and yes, screwing whores. Now he burned with shame. How could he go home now? Not after all those bitter words that had spilled hot from his mouth. How could he look Jai in the face? And how could he face Ispal? And what if he saw Ramita? What could he say to her, after what he'd been doing?

Ispal Ankesharan had been beside his father in battle; he had pulled Raz Makani from the field and kept him alive. He and Huriya would not be alive without him. He owed Ispal his very existence. Ispal had opened his house to them though they were refugees. He had welcomed the birth of Kazim and Huriya, mourned at Mother's funeral. Kazim had come to love him as another father.

And he had come to love Ispal's soft-faced, stubborn, quiet daughter. Ramita was six years his junior, but he had waited, for she was the one. When she turned fourteen, he had asked for her hand in marriage. Everyone had been happy, the street had partied for days. When she turned sixteen, it was agreed, they would marry. That was this autumn. And now she was to be snatched away from him . . .

Who was this man? Why had he been allowed to do this? Money was involved, that was clear, but how much must it be to have Ispal break faith with Raz, his blood-brother? No one would give him answers and it was driving him mad.

A young man sat down beside him on the Dom-al'Ahm floor, cross-legged on the warming stones. It was midmorning. All Kazim had done for the last twenty hours was sleep, curled in a foetal position. Now he was ravenous, and desperately thirsty.

'You are hungry, brother?' said the youth with a friendly smile. He had a small curly bush of a beard and a thin moustache. His kurta was white but grimy and his headdress was a blue chequered Hebb Valley pattern. 'Would you like something to eat?'

Kazim nodded mutely. *Do I look as pathetic as I feel?*

'My name is Haroun. I am a trainee Scriptualist here. We are brothers in faith, Kazim Makani.'

He knows my name. He felt a small quiver of curiosity. Haroun . . .

that was a Dhassan name. He allowed the youth to lead him behind the Dom-al'Ahm to a line of broken, desperate-looking men of all ages, waiting to be fed, too exhausted even to fight their way up the queue.

Haroun found him a chair in the corner, motioning away the man already there with quiet authority. 'Wait here, my friend,' he said, and soon returned with a plate of black daal and a chapatti and some cold chai. Kazim could have wept.

'Kazim Makani, why are you here? What has happened to you?' Haroun asked gently as Kazim wolfed down the food.

His appetite partially satisfied, Kazim regained a little caution. 'Please excuse me, brother, but how do you know my name? I do not recognise you.' Though now he studied him, he did recall seeing him about, watching the kalikiti games, and busying himself at the Dom-al'Ahm.

'I am a son of Ahm and a student of the Holy Book. I strive to be of service to God.' Haroun shrugged. 'That is all there is to know, the whole of the truth of it. I saw your plight, heard of the dishonour done to you, and grieved. I have been looking for you.'

'Why?'

'Is not a good deed reason enough?'

Not in this world, Kazim thought suspiciously.

Haroun smiled. 'We have high hopes of you in our community, Kazim. You are a man of talent, a soul that burns bright among men. I wished to remind you that Ahm loves you. I wish to bring you home.'

'I have no home any more.'

'I am here to bring you home to Ahm.' Haroun pointed skywards. 'Tell me, my friend, what has been done to you?'

Kazim thought about saying nothing. He should be with his father and sister – were they still at home with Ispal's family, or were they on the streets now? He, worthless son that he was, had given them no thought at all in his own mad grief. But he looked at Haroun and felt a desperate need to unburden himself. *It would help to talk of this . . .*

*

He'd been having such a magnificent day. They had set up a game of kalikiti against Sanjay's boys from Koshi Vihar, the smaller market half a mile south. Sanjay was Kazim's age and he was 'raja' of Koshi Vihar, just as Kazim led the Aruna Nagar youths. They had clashed for years, enemies, rivals, almost friends – almost, but never. Sanjay had goaded them into the game, relying on the Amteh boys being weakened by having fasted during the daytime for the last month, but Kazim had wolfed down his food before dawn like it would be his last meal on earth, and the game had been a stunning victory. Then fights had broken out, of course – they always did, but then they made up, as they also always did. They had found a dhaba that sold beer, that most choice of imports from the barbaric Rondians, and got raucous.

Kazim and Jai had been floating in an alcoholic haze by the time they got home, only to find Ispal Ankesharan waiting for them, which he normally never did. They were adults, they could do what they wanted, he always said, but this time he had waited up for them to give Kazim the news that had shattered his life.

'Ramita is to be given to another.'
'We will all be wealthy beyond our dreams.'
'He is an old man and won't last long.'
'No, I cannot tell you who he is.'
'Your father understands.'

Fury had turned him feral. He remembered grabbing Ispal's throat, the man who had given him so much, and shaking him like a dog. He had struck Jai when he tried to separate them. He remembered calling for Ramita, over and over, but only men came, dozens of men, who struck him and bloodied him, who twisted his knife from his hand, who kicked and punched him and left him unconscious in the alleyway a block from the house. He had woken in a puddle of cold cow-piss, bloodied, bruised and filthy.

How could he go home after that?

'You cannot trust these Omali,' said Haroun. 'They are faithless – they understand only money. They cannot be trusted.'

'Ramita is so beautiful – more beautiful than dawn,' he replied.

'She loves me. She is waiting for me.' He made to stand. 'I must go to her.'

Haroun pulled him back down. 'No, it isn't safe. They won't welcome you. They will be afraid of you disrupting things.' He leant forward, his voice dropping. 'Do you know who the ferang is?'

Kazim shook his head. 'No, no name. No one told me anything.'

Haroun seemed a little disappointed and Kazim looked down sullenly, no desire to speak further. He didn't want to tell Haroun how he had spent the three days of Eyeed, inhabiting the lowest places of the jhuggis, drinking and smoking and whoring, spending his last coins. It was too shameful.

Haroun's eyes were knowing. 'Come brother,' he said gently. 'Let us pray together.'

Outside, the Godsingers called, summoning the faithful back to the bosom of Ahm. Kazim, his body replenished but his soul empty, let his new friend guide him to a place where he could abase himself and pray, to beg Ahm that his Ramita be restored to him.

Or to be granted revenge.

A Scriptualist read from *The Kalistham*, from the chapter called 'Words of Fire and Blood'. It had been written by a prophet from Gatioch, where unquestioning faith was instilled at birth. The words were a poetic torrent used since time immemorial to justify and exalt every war ever fought. The Convocation had spoken and the old red stone Dome echoed with the clarion call to arms as shihad was declared on the ferang. Kazim emerged refreshed, no longer alone: he had brothers as angry at the world as he was, though their anger seemed directed at more lofty things than stolen fiancées.

'What did you make of that?' asked Haroun as they shared coffee in a tiny dhaba in the Amteh-dominated Geshanti Souk, watching the rush of people churning past. Here all the men wore white and the women went about in black bekira-shrouds.

'Death to the ferang!' he barked, toasting Haroun with his thimble of thick black Keshi coffee. He had never really thought about the foreigners before, not seriously. Yes, his father was Keshi, and had fled his homeland because of the ferang – but their home was here in Baranasi now. Huriya didn't even pray to Ahm these days but carried on like an Omali girl, all sarees and bindus and Lakh dances.

Haroun shook his head. 'Listen to you, Kazim! You say "death to the ferang", but all you're really thinking about is your girl. Don't you see, your tragedy is but part of a greater wrong? You are a young man of great prowess and fierce determination. Do not waste yourself in despair. Ahm is calling to you, waiting for you to prick up your ears and listen. Ahm wants you.'

'Why me?'

'I've been watching you a long time. You are a natural leader – all the young men follow you. You excel at all manly pastimes: you run like the wind and wrestle like a python. You are a prodigy, Kazim! Were you to put aside your frivolous pastimes and take up a serious pursuit, the other young men would follow you. You are searching for a star. That star is Ahm, if you would but open your heart to him.'

Kazim had heard Scriptualists say things like this before, and always he'd told himself, 'Yes, maybe, but I am going to marry an Omali girl and breed hundreds of children.' That was still his dream – more than a dream: it was destiny. A fortune-teller, an ancient woman who looked older than time, had told him his destiny was to marry Ramita, so how could she be taken away? He was going to be at the wedding, oh yes! And he would look her in the eye and ask her if she loved him and she would say yes. Then he would smite down this stranger and claim his rightful bride. He had come to this decision during the prayers this morning. Love would triumph. He was convinced of it.

Something of this must have conveyed itself because Haroun gave a wry sigh and shook his head. 'Brother, you must join the shihad. You must learn the ways of the sword. You must help us inspire the local boys to march to war. Say you will join us, brother.'

Kazim returned the young Amteh youth's intense gaze. *I should agree to this – but my destiny is Ramita . . .* He bowed his head. 'Let me think about this. My sister – my father – I do not know where they are. I've neglected my duties to them. And Ramita, she still loves me, I know it!'

Haroun's eyes clouded over, but then he shrugged. 'Then let me help you, my friend, and if all works out as you say, well and good. And if not . . . will you then join the shihad, brother?'

Kazim swallowed. *If it came to that, where else could I go?*

Kazim and Haroun searched the ghats, the riverbank steps, seeking Raz Makani. In Baranasi, all life and death flowed from the banks of the Imuna river. The city stood on the west bank of the wide, shallow river flowing north to south, the dark water already filthy from untold uses made of it upstream. In the morning almost the entire city came to the river to pray, to wash, to purify themselves for the coming day. Small coracles took out the wealthier people onto the water to watch the dawn and escape the press of commoners. The prince of the city had a barge upon which he performed the dawn chant on holy occasions, even though he was Amteh, to appease his people who were mostly Omali.

By midmorning the worshippers and bathers were replaced by washerwomen, soaking the clothes, then slapping them against stone slabs before spreading them in the sun to dry. Dung-women rolled cow droppings into patties to dry for fuel. People came and went from the Omali temples all day, chiming the heavy temple bells. Downstream, at the southern end, the funeral fires burned all day, cremating the dead. The ashes were scattered for Imuna to bear away.

The sun beat down hotter and hotter as Kazim and Haroun sought Raz in all his favourite places, but no one had seen his father or sister since before Eyeed. It was Haroun who suggested the temple of Devanshri, where the healer-priests ran an infirmary. He waited outside while Kazim went in, though not a believer inclining his head respectfully to the serene statue of the physician-god. The low moan of the patients droned eerily. He took a deep breath of clean air and pulled his scarf around his mouth before entering the hospital.

The air was incense-laden to chase away noxious vapours and demons of the air. Orange-robed priests and priestesses came and went, and young servants carried water from Imuna to bathe those in their charge. The halls were lined with the sick and injured, the dying, the old. Hands clutched at him as he passed. Two men bore an old woman past as he pressed against the wall, her body arched in rigor, her open eyes gazing sightlessly on the hereafter. He felt nauseous and turned to go.

'Kazim! Kazim!' Huriya raced to his side, hugged him hard, then slapped him. He just stared, his cheek smarting but his mind numb. 'Where have you been, you lazy prick?' she cried. 'I found Father in the sands on the far side of the river. He tried to walk in and drown himself, but the water wasn't deep enough and the opium had him so befuddled he didn't think to lie down.' She wrapped herself around him. 'He's dying! You have to do something!'

He held her close and let her sob, then she drew him towards the silent figure on the pallet in the corner. His father was sleeping, his war-helm cradled in his arms, the one he had brought back from Hebusalim. It was rounded and pointed and had a jackal monogram on the crest. Chain-mail links guarded the cheeks. 'It is yours when you are old enough for it to fit,' Raz had told him when he was a child, but he hadn't pulled it out for years.

'Huriya, there is a Scriptualist outside called Haroun. Tell him I have found my father. Tell him I will seek him when I have done what is needful.'

Huriya looked curious, but bowed her head. She came back shortly afterward to find Kazim stroking his father's face, tears running down his cheeks. 'Did you find Haroun?' he asked without looking up.

'Yes. He asked me if I knew who Ramita was to marry.' Huriya sounded peeved. 'None of his business!'

'He is my friend,' Kazim retorted. 'What do the doctors say about Father?'

Huriya sat cross-legged on the filthy floor in her stained salwar. 'They say he has an ague from lying too long in the cold water. His lungs need to be drained constantly, so they keep turning him onto his stomach and pounding him until he vomits phlegm and blood onto the floor. Then I have to clean it up. And the sores on his back are infected again.' Her eyes were moist. 'I really think he is going to die this time.'

Kazim thought that likely too. 'I'll look after you,' he said automatically.

'What, like you looked after me this time? Well, thanks for nothing, big brother!'

He winced. *I deserve that.* 'I will take care of you, I promise!'

'Ha! I'll look after myself, thank you very much.' She stuck out her chin. 'I'm going to ask to go north with Ramita, to be her companion. I don't need your protection!' She scowled. 'Ispal has been here every day to tend Father, and so have Jai and Ramita and Tanuva. Everyone has come except you.'

He hung his head, put his face in his hands and burned with shame. Though even now, all he could think was, *If I stay here, maybe I will see Ramita.*

He didn't manage even that, though – Ramita stayed away, no doubt because Huriya had reported his presence. Only Jai and Ispal, whom he could not bear even to look at, came. The physicians let Kazim sleep on the floor beside his father's pallet, but he was woken repeatedly to help purge the lungs and change the dressings on the sores, which were purulent and stank. The whole world stank. His sleep was too broken to be any relief or gain to him, and waking and sleeping became one. His father moaned, seldom recognising anyone, and cried aloud of a 'woman of flame' until he had to be sedated. He called for Ispal, many times, until Kazim felt as if he were in a torture cell, never able to satisfy the questioner.

The end was a blessing. His father woke crying for Ispal again, then convulsed, gasping for breath like a fish on dry land. Before they could turn him over, he jerked and went rigid. Kazim held him and cried and sobbed as he had not since he was a child in his long-gone mother's arms.

When he finally awoke he was in a sea of dark faces: Lakh men and women, looking at him, then averting their eyes. The Devanshri priests came, wanting him to move the body as they had other patients needing the pallet. One asked for money, to pay two bearers to take Raz Makani's body to the burning ghats – but Raz was Amteh, so must be buried. Kazim decided that he would carry his father himself. Without a another word or glance at the priests and bearers he took up the burden in his arms. His father was both light as feathers and heavy as the holy mountain. He staggered to the entrance, swayed dazedly and nearly fell.

Haroun was there, waiting for him, looking as tired as Kazim felt: waiting to share his burden, as a true friend would.

7

Hidden Causes

The Ascent of Corineus

Without doubt, the most epoch-changing event in the history of Urte was the Ascent of Corineus. In a backwater village of the Rimoni Empire, a thousand disciples of a disaffected Sollan philosopher had gathered. A legion of Rimoni soldiers was sent to arrest them. What ensued is shrouded in legend. Did Kore himself create the ambrosia that gave Corineus' disciples the gnosis? Or did something more earthly occur? The known truth is that the survivors of that draught, the 'Blessed Three Hundred', destroyed the legion with unearthly powers. Their descendants, the magi, still rule Yuros 500 years later.

ORDO COSTRUO COLLEGIATE, PONTUS

Turm Zauberin, Norostein, Noros, on the continent of Yuros
Octen 927
9 months until the Moontide

The first day of the exams had finally come: the culmination of seven years of Alaron's life. He stared blankly at the wall before him, waiting for the bell to ring out from the old college bell-tower. The hour-long time slots were allocated by alphabetic order, starting with Andevarion; Alaron would be second-last, late in the afternoon.

The first subject was History, which he enjoyed, though his father regarded much the master taught him as dubious; Vann's scepticism and Ramon's acidic reinterpretations had left him somewhat confused, but at least it was interesting.

Finally the bell rang, the door opened and Seth Korion emerged and just stood there, glassy-eyed.

Hard, was it, Seth? Alaron thought. *Perhaps you should have paid more attention, instead of just sitting in class like a zombie, safe in the knowledge no one would ever ask you anything tricky.*

Seth turned around slowly, just becoming aware of Alaron. Alaron prepared himself for some insult or mockery, but to his surprise, Korion said faintly, 'Good luck, Mercer.' It was so unexpectedly *polite* that Alaron could only stare and mumble something at Korion's receding back.

He waited for several hour-like minutes until portly Magister Hout poked his head around the corner. 'Mercer. Come inside.' His voice was disdainful as always.

Alaron got unsteadily to his feet and walked across the unsteady floor and through the door. In front of him was an array of faces, familiar and unfamiliar; it felt like he was being stared at by row upon row of vultures and ravens, all waiting to pick out his eyeballs. In the front was Lucien Gavius, the headmaster, the masters arrayed about him. Fyrell's dark features looked savage in the dim lighting. He peered a little further back and stiffened. Governor Belonius Vult – what on earth? *But then, why not? We're supposed to be the future, aren't we?* There were others, uniforms he recognised rather than faces: a flat-faced Kirkegarde Grandmaster; a bearded legion centurion; a Crozier of the Kore. Alaron felt horribly exposed.

The headmaster rose. 'The student is Alaron Mercer, son of Tesla Anborn, of Berial's line. The father is non-magi. The student is a quarter-blood, born in Norostein.' Alaron noticed that Governor Vult leant forward when his mother's name was read. Perhaps he knew her, or Auntie Elena.

'Are you ready, Mercer?' Gavius enquired.

Alaron's throat went dry, the banks of faces overwhelming. *All those eyes* . . . He swallowed. 'Yes, Headmaster.'

'Good. Then let us begin with a recitation of the Rimoni Conquests. In your own time . . .'

Alaron took a deep breath and began to speak. Initially he felt horribly uncomfortable, but after a while he began to relax and let his words flow. He answered questions about the Rimoni Empire, then about the spread of Kore into Sydia. He spoke confidently about the Bridge and First Crusade. He got his facts wrong a little on the Second Crusade, but nothing disastrous.

When it was over, he felt almost disappointed, but the small rattle of applause lifted him immeasurably. He'd survived. When he walked out, Ramon was in the waiting room, literally shaking in his boots. There was no time for anything but a quick thumbs-up and a: 'Buono fortuna, Ramon!'

It felt like he was off to a good start.

Tydai was calculus, a nightmare. They had to create and solve formulae all day in a series of written tests. Malevorn was confident, but the others were as edgy, even Dorobon. Alaron felt he did passably, but no better than that. Seth Korion threw up outside afterwards. Watching Korion being ill was becoming an exam-week ritual. At first it was off-putting, then amusing, and finally he found himself actually feeling sorry for the wretched general's son.

Wotendai brought Rondian, a welcome relief. *At least it's my native tongue*, he reflected. *Poor Ramon!* The exam itself was largely the recitation of old poems and sagas – a complete waste of time, in his view. *Sadly, it probably came across that way to the markers*, he reflected as he shuffled out of the theatre.

Torsdai was Theology. He squirmed before the half-seen faces and came out of it absolutely hating Fyrell, who seemed determined to prove him a heretic and burn him on the spot. This was the worst day so far. But he banished it from thought quickly. Tomorrow was Freyadai – thesis day; make-or-break day, or so they were all told.

The auditorium was full. Faces loomed out at him: Governor Belonius Vult, come to run his eye over the students again; Jeris Muhren, a hero of the Noros Revolt and now Watch Captain of Norostein; representatives of all the military arms, the regular army, windship commanders, even Volsai and Kirkegarde recruiters. There were many Churchmen hovering about a jaded-looking Crozier, and clouds of grey-robed Arcanum scholars. They all looked bored – Alaron was the sixth presenter, of course. He swallowed nervously. *Don't think about the audience. It's no worse than the other days. You can do this* . . .

Gavius looked up, frowned and then addressed the auditorium. 'This candidate is Alaron Mercer,' he announced and went on to introduce Alaron's lineage for the benefit of those who had not attended previously. He turned to Alaron. 'In your own time, Master Mercer. You have one hour, half of which is reserved for questions. You may begin.'

Alaron bowed, spread out his sheaf of notes and began to speak. Gradually concentration erased his self-consciousness and he forgot the audience. 'Exalted magi, my thesis presentation is entitled "The Hidden Cause of the Noros Revolt".' The title of the thesis caused some interest, he noted. *Good!* He raised his hands and caused a cloud of light-charged dust that he had prepared to billow before him, so that it spread out like a mat of light at waist-height. It was a familiar gnostic technique. 'The histories talk about the Noros Revolt resulting from a combination of excessive imperial taxes, poor harvests and a dissident military. But what I aim to demonstrate is that there was a fourth reason for the Revolt, that has earth-shattering – I repeat: *earth-shattering* – implications.'

He allowed himself to look around and gave a small blink. The faces of the magi audience were intent. He had their undivided attention. Even the governor and the bishop were listening with intensity that surprised him. Any traces of boredom were gone.

'Before I reveal the hidden cause of the Revolt, I want to make a few points about the reasons that are normally cited as the causes. Yes, taxes went up, but, as *this* shows' – he displayed tax records in a visual calculus technique called 'graphing' – 'the tax rises were really not that unaffordable, and they were offset by trading revenue and plunder from the First Crusade. In fact, Noros was better off than pre-Crusade. This has been borne out anecdotally from interviews with townsfolk and officials.'

He risked a look and was struck by the frowning, thoughtful look on the faces. The governor was stroking his beard, while Watch Captain Muhren was chewing his lip. *At least they're listening* . . .

'Secondly, the harvests: the silos were never emptied, and were used to alleviate suffering amongst smallholders.' He cited more sources visually, elaborating on the theme. 'Thirdly, people claim the Noros legions returned from the Crusade in a state of mutiny – however, many of the officers came back rich men. All of them spoke publicly against the poll-tax, but they wanted a peaceful resolution. In memoirs published *after* the Revolt, both General Robler and Governor Vult quoted anti-Revolt speeches they made in 907 and 908 and early 909.' He glanced up at the governor, ready to display the exact texts if he needed to, but Vult nodded abstractly. 'In fact, the military leadership was still anti-revolt in Febreux, but it became dogmatically pro-Revolt *before* the poll-tax was announced in Martrois. Governor Vult's memoir speaks of "an inexplicable yet irresistible swing towards rebellion" in Febreux 909.'

He spread his hands out. 'It could have been that there was a hidden agenda and discreet troop build-ups, but to me, this might well indicate that there was a secret change in opinion among many generals in Febreux 909. It is this change in opinion that I wish to explore.'

He really did have their undivided attention now. Captain Muhren looked like he wanted to interrupt. Vult had a small smile on his lips and he was leaning forward. Alaron felt a flush of pleasure. 'I now wish to highlight four unregarded facts that I believe no one has ever linked before.' He called up an image of three marble busts, fully three-dimensional, and rotated them. He'd spent a long time practising that and he was pleased with how well it came out. 'These three men used to be familiar to every Noros child. There were statues everywhere, and their faces were in every catechism; we used to pray for their blessing. The three canons – saints in waiting – are the only canons in history born in Noros: Fulchius, Keplann and Reiter. All three were Ascendants, given ambrosia by the emperor for their service and virtue. Before the Revolt, they all dwelt in Pallas, all three heroes of the empire. Yet at the end of the Noros Revolt, every statue of them was destroyed and all the catechisms containing their deeds were collected and have not been seen again. They died of age during the Revolt years, we were told. The Church proclaimed the Noros catechisms out of date and withdrew them, and they also proclaimed that in punishment for the Revolt, the images of these three canons would not be displayed any more. It sounds half-credible, but strange. How did three Noros Ascendants all die within a year of each other, when Ascendants can live for centuries? And why are they being erased from public memory?'

Alaron was almost transfixed by the intensity of Vult and by the lip-biting tension on Muhren's face. For a second he faltered, but then he blanked the audience and went on, 'The second thing I wish you to consider is the continued military occupation of Noros. Schlessen and Argundy have revolted several times; Noros has only once, and far less bloodily. Yet the occupation force here in Noros is eight legions. *Eight!* That is larger than the entire Noros armies of the Revolt! Why? Most Noromen have accepted defeat and now regard the Revolt as misjudged and foolish. No one is fermenting rebellion – yet we suffer a closer and more costly occupation than even Argundy, who have revolted five times in the past hundred years!

'And what do all these soldiers do? Eight legions – that's 40,000 men – and the answer is: they dig! They have entirely dug up the manors of every general of the war. The royal palace was taken apart stone by stone, then rebuilt. And still they dig. It is almost as if the Rondians are *looking for something.*'

Alaron became conscious of the utter silence in the auditorium. Captain Muhren caught his eye and gave a small shake of the head. A warning? What did he mean? Alaron blinked and stiffened his resolve. Not far to go now. 'Thirdly, I want to bring up the fate of General Jarius Langstrit and disclose a fact which I believe is almost unknown. General Langstrit was our most decorated general after Robler himself and remains an iconic figure after the Revolt – but where is he now, dead or alive? I had imagined him in retirement on his country estate, but visiting there to try and interview him, I found the manor deserted. One of our most famous generals has vanished.' He brought up an image of a famous painting of a dishevelled but resolute general surrendering his sword to a conquering Rondian commander. 'I'm sure you all know this painting: General

Robler surrendering to Kaltus Korion on the slopes of Mount Tybold. However, any soldier will tell you that Robler was too proud and bitter to surrender, so "Big Jari" did it. Yet ask the people of the Lower Market and they will tell you that Langstrit was found wandering alone and dazed in their market-square the very next day, one hundred miles away. How did General Langstrit end up in Lower Market, Norostein, when he had given his word of honour to remain in camp in the Alps?

'My fourth point: how is it that Robler and his armies defeated the Rondians so often and so frequently, when none of them were more than half-bloods, no match for Rondian Ascendant-Magi? Yet by the time the Revolt was over, eight Rondian Ascendants had fought in Noros, more than joined the Crusade, and somehow our half-blood magi killed four of those Ascendants!'

Alaron raised four fingers. 'Let me reiterate: *one*, three Noromen canons disappear at the time of the Revolt and are now being erased from history. *Two*, Rondian forces continue to occupy Noros and are actively searching for something. *Three*, a general breaks parole, only to wind up dazed and confused in Norostein and then vanish. *Four*, Noromen half-blood magi defeat Rondian Ascendants.' He raised a hand. 'I believe these facts are linked and explainable.' *Here goes . . .*

'This is my hypothesis: the three Noros canons, Fulchius, Keplann and Reiter, did not in fact die in Pallas as we were told. They joined the Revolt – more than that, they *caused* the Revolt. I surmise that they took something very important from Pallas – for why else would eight Ascendants who had not even been interested in the Holy Crusade suddenly want to join the suppression of Noros? And why, after the surrender, did an honourable general break parole – and where is he now? The Rondians are taking our kingdom apart piece by piece, seeking something— What do they seek?'

He let the question hang in the air, feeling a sense of exultation at the stir his words were causing. *I'm going to pass with top marks!*

He displayed a large image of a piece of scroll-work. 'This is what a proclamation of canonisation looks like. Note the words *Raised to the Ascendancy*. Every living saint was raised to the Ascendancy – until the Noros Revolt. Every candidate was taken into the inner chamber at Pallas Cathedral, where the Scytale of Corineus is housed, and they emerged either as an Ascendant – or as a corpse. But since the Revolt, one canon and one living saint have been anointed, and in neither proclamation appear the words "Raised to the Ascendancy", not ever for our beloved Imperia-Mater Lucia!'

There was a mutter about the auditorium. 'Was it just overlooked? Did they *forget* to make Mater-Imperia an Ascendant?'

He had to pause then, to let the buzz swell, then die down. It was exhilarating to have the audience so enthralled. He raised a hand, feeling tremendously powerful, and the auditorium fell silent.

'What if there is another explanation? What if the thing that Fulchius and the others stole, the thing that made our Noros Magi-Generals so powerful, is the thing that the Rondians are still searching for. What if it were the means by which Ascendancy is bestowed? *What if Fulchius stole the Scytale of Corineus?*'

There was a wall of noise, and two faces stood out: Captain Muhren, looking ashen-faced and furious, his face almost enough to make Alaron raise a hand to protect himself. If eyes were daggers, Alaron would be pierced through. And Governor Vult had gone utterly still, with the tiniest hint of a smile on his face.

Alaron belatedly remembered Ramon's words: *It is a dangerous story to tell, amici.* But surely everyone here must be impressed? Most people didn't even know about Langstrit's arrest taking place in Norostein – it wasn't shown in the legion's historical records. He had talked to dozens of veterans to pull this all together. And his mother's library had books most students or even scholars did not have.

'My conclusion fits the facts,' he said, by way of rounding things off. 'The Noros canons stole the Scytale and fermented the revolt. Weak-blooded Noros magi suddenly became powerful. The revolt ended in mysterious circumstances, and the Rondians have been seeking something here ever since. My conclusion fits the facts and explains much that conventional wisdom does not.'

The auditorium buzzed. Headmaster Gavius raised a hand. 'Quiet please, gentlemen. Is your presentation complete, Master Mercer?'

Alaron nodded. His mind was whirling and he suddenly felt exhilarated. He had got their attention and held it. He hadn't screwed up the visuals or the words. He felt drained.

Magister Fyrell raised a hand. 'What evidence have you that the Pallas officials did not simply decide to change the wording on the Ascendancy notices? Or is your whole argument based upon a clerical error, Mercer?'

Alaron suppressed his temper. 'These proclamations are prepared by the Holy Father in Pallas, Magister. They are regarded as the words of Kore and cannot lie. Therefore the omission must be deliberate.'

Governor Vult raised a hand and Alaron felt a nervous flicker. 'If the Noros generals suddenly became so powerful, young sir, how is it that I too am not an Ascendant?' His sycophants laughed dutifully.

Alaron tried to measure the nuances of the question, feeling on uncertain ground. 'My lord, it is possible that none of the Generals ascended and that the miraculous powers displayed by them were in fact secretly the work of Fulchius, Keplann and Reiter, without assistance. But that doesn't explain the continued searching. Possibly – and with total respect, sir – the secret was not extended beyond General Robler's inner circle.' *And we all know what Robler thought of you, your Excellency.*

Vult's eyebrows came together in a coolly appraising look. *He'll remember me*, Alaron thought nervously.

Captain Muhren stood. 'Gentlemen,' he said to the room, 'I want to make something very clear. This thesis, while no doubt diligently and honestly attempted, is of as much use historically as a pile of horse-turds.' Alaron felt something inside himself crumble. The captain went on, his voice strident, 'I fought in the Revolt, and there were no Ascendant canons slinking about the margins – I was a Primus battle-mage; I would have seen them! We won our victories through planning and courage. War is not a board game! Mighty magi can die from a single arrow or sword-stroke. I have no doubt that the Scytale of Corineus is right where it should be, where it *must be*, to preserve our empire: in Pallas Cathedral's vaults.' He looked at Alaron coldly. 'General Robler's victories were based on the courage of our fighting men.' He glared about him, then sat. The auditorium murmured indignantly, swayed by what he said.

Alaron realised he was opening and closing his mouth like a beached fish. He felt his eyes sting, his skin go hot and cold in waves. It was all he could do to remain upright.

The captain's tirade had silenced the questions. Alaron risked a peek at the governor, who was whispering to a man beside him. His silvery eyes seemed to pierce Alaron through, and he had a sudden vision of an iron fist behind that velvet visage.

Headmaster Gavius leant forward. 'Thank you, Master Mercer,' he said. 'The panel will consider your thesis, as it does all examination work. You may go.'

Alaron staggered out, past the waiting Ramon, lurched into a privy and vomited. When he emerged from the foetid chamber all he could manage was to totter to a quiet corner of the courtyard and bury his face in his hands.

It took him a long time to get home, where he found that someone had stolen all of his research notes.

'How's it going, lads?' asked Vann as they dined on Sabbadai, the eve of the second week.

'It's a nightmare, sir,' groaned Ramon. 'The panel hate us. They murder us with questions like knives.'

Vann looked questioningly at Alaron. 'Yeah, what he said, Da.' Alaron pointed at Ramon, nodding. He hadn't told Da all about the thesis, not in detail, nor about the theft – it all hurt too much. Vann had taken pains to tell him to keep his things secure. He'd told Ramon, of course, who was full of theories, but what could they do? The best he could hope for was that maybe if someone had taken it that seriously, perhaps he might scrape a pass-mark. In the meantime, the exams went on.

The second week was for martial tests. On Minasdai Alaron arrived to find Seth Korion slumped in a seat outside the arena, when he should have been inside being tested. It took Alaron a few seconds to realise Korion was actually crying. He had a blackened eye, and a trail of blood and snot was running from his nose. He stared at Alaron like he wasn't sure he was real. The front of his breeches were sodden: Seth had pissed himself during the test.

'Rukka mio! What did they do to you?' Alaron gasped. *What the Hel will they do to me?*

Seth looked up at him miserably. It was clear that all the cushy masters' treatment had left Korion utterly unprepared for the exams. He was failing – unthinkable for anyone, but especially for a Korion.

'I can't do it,' Seth moaned. 'They keep hitting me. I can't take any more.'

'What happened?' Alaron asked hesitantly. He could no more put the boot in to Korion at the moment than he could drown a kitten.

Tears streamed down Korion's face. 'They make you fight one, then two, then three at the same time – just ordinary soldiers, but it's so hard to keep track of them, and then they start hitting you and it just gets worse. They were talking to me, under their breath, so the judges couldn't hear, about what they were going to do to me – how much it would hurt – what a cock-sucking pansy I was . . . I couldn't take it. I can't go on—'

'You've got to go back in there,' Alaron said quietly, 'and if they hit you, you get back up again.' He scowled. 'You liked it plenty watching Malevorn thrashing me all the time.' He grabbed Korion's collar and hauled him up. 'Toughen up, Korion – get back in there!'

'I can't,' Korion whispered. 'I can't . . .'

'Get up, *coward*.'

The word shocked through Korion as if he'd been struck by lightning and he went utterly white, then his eyes glazed over. For a second, Alaron thought he would collapse, but instead he tottered stiffly back into the arena. Through the gates he dimly heard the clatter of wooden blades, and repeated grunts and cries.

Two men carried Korion out on a stretcher ten minutes later. He was unconscious.

Alaron stared after him, then back at the arena doors.

Holy Kore . . .

He limped out an hour later, exhausted. Seth had spoken truly: he'd had to fight trained watchman, in ever-increasing numbers. They may have had blunted swords, but they could still do serious damage if they connected solidly. He was allowed to use the gnosis, but only defensively, not offensively. Parry, shield, leap, lunge if you could – hard work, but he'd managed, with only two touches on him, and those had come right near the end, when he was nearly all in. He'd scored twenty-two. That was pretty good, surely! And as for the verbal abuse, he'd had worse from Malevorn. He'd blanked it out effortlessly.

However Seth hadn't got to the last part of the test, which was facing a battle-mage. Alaron had exhausted himself with the watchman and had little left when the battle-mage emerged for the last bout. That had been humiliating; he'd been given a right kicking. At least there was a decent, sympathetic healer in the infirmary.

Tydai was archery, difficult and exacting, but it wasn't overly tiring. No gnosis was permitted. He'd hit a few, missed a few; it felt like a pass. Wotendai was horsemanship in the stable-yard; that went fine: he was a good rider and knew all the horses well. There was no way they could fail him on that.

Torsdai was equipment: timed dismantling and reassembly of a suit of plate-mail; putting barding on a horse – basic tedious stuff. Freyadai was the worst, because that was back to the theatre for battlefield strategy. Alaron had a nightmare beforehand that he would be asked what Vult should have done at Lukhazan, while the governor himself marked him. It didn't come to that, but he did have trouble explaining Robler's tactics at Geisen. 'He was the best,' he muttered lamely. 'Of course he won.' At least he had the sense not to drag his thesis into it.

'All in all, I think it was a good week,' he ventured cautiously over the Sabbadai dinner table when Vann asked.

'Better than the first week,' agreed Ramon, nodding fiercely.

'But next week we're onto the real stuff: the gnosis. All the other things are just trivia,' said Alaron. 'These next two weeks are the real test.'

'Do you think so?' asked Vann, in his thoughtful questioning manner. 'I would have thought it the other way round.'

'How do you mean, Da?' asked Alaron.

'Well, your gnosis is important, obviously, but I am sure that the real key is what your attitudes are. Are you prepared to follow orders? To kill on command? Have you the courage to face death? That's what I would want to know if I were a recruiter.'

The two students looked at each other uneasily. Neither was exactly the unquestioning type.

The format changed in week three. Now it was two tests, one in the morning and the other in the afternoon, so they had to hang around college all day. On the first morning the Pure took over the common room, so Alaron and Ramon went to the garden. Neither said much. The morning was basic magic skills – combat-gnosis: shielding, warding, blasting targets with mage-fire. They were loaned an amber periapt for the exercises, and both agreed it felt good to be allowed to blast something. Soothing, in a way.

They took lunch in the garden to avoid any contact with the Pure, though their confident laughter echoed through the open windows. In the afternoon, the tests were more exacting. They had to work through the runes, little configurations of energy that performed a variety of effects. The panel of tutors and scholars made Alaron demonstrate every one he had been taught, from runes of enchantment to negation of other magic, runes of hiding and finding, locking and unlocking, making protective circles: all the tiny gnosis-workings the students would be called upon to perform on a daily basis once they graduated. By the time it was over Alaron felt a little dizzy, his skin flushed, the air crackling with energy.

'A bit rough. Clearly only a rote-mage,' he heard Fyrell remark. Alaron felt himself flinch. Rote-mage was the derogatory term for someone who performed the gnosis in a very rudimentary and inefficient manner – he knew he was better than that.

The remainder of that week was spent on Hermetic and Theurgic magic. They were made to perform all the skills they'd been taught of each study, from the least cantrip to the most intricate enchantment. Each of the students had an affinity with one Class of gnosis; Alaron favoured Sorcery while Ramon preferred Hermetic. As Hermetic gnosis was the diametric opposite of Sorcery, Alaron struggled with it, but he was reasonably competent in Theurgy. Though it was scary to be performing with so much at stake, it felt like it was bringing out the best in them both. They managed in the exams feats they had struggled with in class. Alaron tamed a wolf set loose in the arena before it attacked him, something he'd never managed before. The exams were feeling like a vindication of seven years of punishing lessons from sneering teachers who felt that a quarter-blood merchant's son was beneath them.

They slept late on Sabbadai and after persuading Vann that they needed rest more than divine blessing were allowed to skip church. They toasted the last lap of the race, as Ramon put it, at dinner that night.

The final week of exams coincided with cold sleet lashing the city, the fingers of winter stretching its grip from the snow-capped Alps to the south. At least Fire-thaumaturgy could warm their fingers! The magic of the elements was relatively straightforward, though a struggle for a Sorcerer like Alaron. He was a decent Fire-mage and could do a little with earth, but he was weak in air and couldn't manipulate water at all.

His main problem was Sorcery itself. According to his entrance tests, it should have been his strong point, but all four aspects of Sorcery – Necromancy, Wizardry, Divination and Clairvoyance – gave him problems because he was scared rigid of spirits. He could recite the theory, but when he tried to use Wizardry gnosis he failed to summon anything. The same thing happened in Necromancy, when he couldn't manage to summon the spirit of a recently dead young man because he was so unnerved at the corpse before him. All of the teachers were muttering to each other as he exited the arena, head bowed. His efforts at Clairvoyance were just poor; he couldn't identify or find the hidden objects, much to his chagrin. And Divination, the last test, was a bit of a mess too. He'd had to divine his own future, which turned out not to look so good: he'd ended up interpreting a complex vision of stolen notes and hidden snakes as someone conspiring against him. He'd opened his eyes to find them all staring at him with raised eyebrows and sceptical faces.

The headmaster dismissed his half-baked waffling condescendingly. 'Are you saying that the staff of Turm Zauberin have some agenda against you, boy? We are paid by recruiters to produce magi – every failure hurts us as it hurts the community, and I would thank you to remember the years of training we have devoted to you.' He shook his head. 'Really boy, we wish you nothing but success.'

'I think you're failing perfectly well without our help,' remarked Fyrell acidly. 'Now, unless you wish to add any further conspiracy theories to the afternoon's entertainment, you may leave.'

Alaron closed his eyes and wished the ground would swallow him whole.

'So, how was Divination?' Ramon asked him outside. He didn't take Divination at all, so they were both, finally, done.

Alaron groaned. 'I don't want to talk about it. Let's go home.'

Ramon waved a purse. 'No, my friend, tonight, we are going to get drunk, on me.'

'You have money?' Alaron stared.

Ramon grinned. 'I am Rimoni.'

'You *stole* it?'

'Now I'm wounded. You hurt my feelings. Maybe I don't want to drink with you any more.' Ramon eyed Alaron expectantly, eyes sparkling.

Alaron took a deep breath. From somewhere, he heard a fiddle wail. The sun was lowering towards the western hills, casting a reddish glow over the Alpine snow. The air was crisp and bitingly cold. Pass or fail, the exams were over.

'Alaron, relax.' Ramon pocked him in the ribs. 'What's done is done; they'll pass you and whether you get a gold, silver or bronze is irrelevant. What will be will be, amici. Let's go and find some beer!'

Alaron let out his breath slowly. 'Okay, you're right – it's just— No, you're right!'

'Of course I'm right.' Ramon looked around, cupping his ear theatrically. 'I think that music is coming from the Millpond tavern, amici. Let's go!'

8

An Act of Betrayal

The Grey Foxes

The Grey Foxes were a group of magi who aided the Noros Revolt. Declared an irregular force by their enemies, they were branded spies and executed on capture. Post-war, many did not emerge until many years later, after amnesties had been granted by the governor. During the Revolt they were the most feared fighting force operating in the theatre of war, though there were probably fewer than thirty of them. Their commander, Gurvon Gyle, was not pardoned until 915, and then specifically on condition that he join the Second Crusade as a counter-insurgency advisor.

NILS MANNIUS, NOROS: A HISTORY, 921

Brochena, Javon, on the continent of Antiopia
Octen 927
9 months until the Moontide

Elena Anborn trotted beside the caravan of wagons and carriages that rumbled east to Forensa. A blue cotton wrap covered her head, and a gauze shawl over her eyes allowed her to look at the road ahead without becoming dazzled. Heat rose in waves from the baking earth and mirages played on the southern horizon. She thanked the heavens it was winter and the weather so mild – *only half the temperature of Hel, may we be truly thankful.*

They were making good time. It was normally two weeks to Forensa, but with the cooler days they might make it a day or two early; they were probably halfway already. Lorenzo di Kestria was some fifty yards ahead, with one of the scouts. The knight was sweltering in his leather armour. There were a dozen guards arrayed about the six wagons. Timori and Fadah were in the nearest carriage, with Cera following alone in the second carriage, which was festooned with red ribbons warning of a menstruating woman. Amteh men were forbidden to have contact with 'tainted' women. By rights, Elena should have been in there with her, but she had too much to do, so she made do with a red ribbon about her arm and stayed away from the men.

Unfortunately Samir Taguine didn't share the Amteh's superstitions. He jolted towards her, wincing visibly at each movement of his steed. His stirrups were too short; it looked like his knees had locked up, and he had little or no control over the horse. *If I ever have to fight you, Samir, I hope it's on horseback*, she thought wryly.

Samir pulled up alongside her, his bald pate gleaming red in the sun. 'Rukka mio, I hate riding,' he moaned. 'What do you say I sit in there with your pretty little princess?'

'I'd say you should mind your tongue when talking about our royal patrons.'

Samir grunted and stroked his goatee. 'She's a little quiet, that one. I prefer the younger girl – more spunk. I've got my eye on her, I have.'

'You'll stay away from them both,' Elena told him coldly.

He laughed maliciously. 'Oooo, possessive? Why, do you fancy her yourself?'

'You're a sick cur, Samir. Piss off.'

'Make me.' Samir eyed her up insultingly. 'You may think you're in charge here, Elena, but without the boss to take your corner you're just a snivelling little half-blood!'

'Was there something you wanted?' Elena asked stonily.

The mage glanced at her and dropped his voice. 'Yes. Wearing your gems?' He looked eager to burn his bridges and move on. He hated this place as much as Elena loved it.

'Always. And now I'm going to check the northern ridge. Unless you've learnt to ride, it'll be beyond you, so rukk off.' The Rondian magus sniggered behind her as Elena coaxed her horse up the slope.

She knew Samir was dangerous – she had never seen a mage with such a strong fire affinity as Samir the Inferno. *Put up with him*, she told herself. *It's not for much longer . . .*

Later that night, with the new moon a vast crescent in the northern sky, she walked the perimeter, inhaling the clean desert air. From a small rise she overlooked their carriages and tents. A pavilion housed Fadah and Timori, and ordinarily Cera, except that she was menstruating. The men were bustling about the campfires, preparing food. Timori was duelling one of the younger of the guardsmen with a stick, while Lorenzo was erecting the blood-tent for Cera and Elena.

She hunched down and scooped out a small hollow and sealed with a touch of stone-shaping so it would hold water. She emptied her flask into it. *Let's see what Gurvon has to say . . .* He'd been sending mental darts in her direction all day, demanding contact. She wasn't looking forward to it.

She touched the water and let the cool liquid of her gnosis pour into it. The water glowed blue and vapours gave way to a familiar furtive visage.

<Elena, where are you? Sordell tells me you've been sent east with Samir.>

<We're at Khodasha-wadi, about halfway to Forensa. Where are you?>

<North of Brochena. Wearing your gems?>

<Yes.> She bit her lip. *<But . . . >*

<Good. Be ready. Any day now.> His face was taut, careworn. He looked achingly familiar. She'd kissed that face many times – but she couldn't remember what that had felt like now. The last time had been almost a year ago, on one of his infrequent visits. She suspected there was someone else. Vedya, almost certainly.

She pulled together her courage and began to speak. *<Gurvon, Olfuss wants me to stay on – private hire. Just me, not the others.>* There, she'd said it now.

Gurvon scowled. *<Did you tell him you were leaving?>*

<Of course not! He asked of his own volition.>

<Good. He suspects nothing then.> Then Gurvon frowned. *<But why not the others? Are they pissing him off again? Anyway, that's irrelevant*

now. *When I give the word, you and Samir will need to travel northeast and—>*

<Gurvon, you're not listening. I'm going to say yes. I want to stay here.>

He froze, and as she watched his expression went from confusion and annoyance to an impassive, dangerous mask. *<What do you mean, Elena?>*

<I want to stay here. This is the place I want to live – to retire to. I want to leave the Company. I've made up my mind.>

He stared incredulously from the water. *<Then you can damn well unmake it again! That dumb bastard Olfuss is about to make himself an enemy of the empire and you are not going to stay there—>*

<I've decided—>

<You stupid bitch – who do you think you are? Remember, I hold every piece of gold you possess; I own you, woman!> His eyes flashed with fury and the water trembled. For an instant she thought he would launch a gnostic attack, then his face calmed, becoming apologetic . . . a calculated version of apologetic. *<Sorry, Elena – I spoke in anger. Listen, you really need to think this through. What you're proposing just isn't possible. This isn't a game, Elena; it's an Imperial command that we withdraw.>*

<An Imperial command? Since when do we work for the empire? Gurvon, I'm—>

<Hush! Listen, don't talk. You must go away and think again, my dear. Don't make a decision like this so quickly. Talk to me when you reach Forensa. Please, Elena, promise me you'll reconsider – it's for your own good.>

She sucked in her breath, then nodded mutely. What else could she do? She plunged a finger into the pool and it sizzled and evaporated in a flash of blue light. She shuddered slightly, then put her head in her hands and stewed in a mire of confusion.

When she eventually looked down at the campsite, Samir Taguine was peering into the bucket of water, his face illuminated by the light from the surface.

He's talking to Gurvon . . . She saw a flicker of surprise cross Samir's face and he looked up at her.

*

Elena positioned herself in the doorway of the blood-tent so she could see everything. Cera looked up and beamed at her. 'Elena, look, Lorenzo has brought us broth, and he says there will be fried chicken soon.' She looked a little disapproving. 'He fancies you. He keeps looking at you all the time.'

'He's just being friendly. Like a brother.'

'Huh! That's not how it looks to me. Did you know his elder brother wants him to court me? And so does Father.'

'The Kestrians are your family's oldest allies,' Elena remarked. 'It would be a good match.' *And it might stop him flirting with me.*

'He is handsome, I suppose,' Cera mused, 'but I just don't fancy him.'

'But you just said he was handsome,' Elena laughed.

'If you like stubble,' Cera sniffed.

'That's men for you! They're all itchy and scratchy up close.' She peered out of the tent-flap again, trying to keep Samir in her sight. He was over by the well, drinking from a hip-flask. Their eyes met, one hundred yards apart. She could just imagine him waiting until she was asleep and then incinerating her tent. *But no . . . Gurvon wouldn't permit him – surely he wouldn't—*

But Gurvon is a long way away, and what we had was a long time ago.

The desert suddenly looked bleak and empty. It was easy to imagine that the rest of the world had gone away, that there was only this place, these people.

Cera was oblivious to her mood. 'You should ride with me in the carriage. You're bleeding, like me, and I'm bored to death.'

There are worse ways to die than boredom. Now shut up, girl, let me think. 'I've got to keep lookout,' she murmured. 'Anyway, I've nearly stopped. Older women don't bleed so long.'

'I like it when we're in the blood-rooms together. We can really talk then. Like sisters.'

'You've got a sister.' *Will Gurvon release my money if I quit? He'd better!*

'But Solinde and I are so different – all she ever wants to talk about are boys and dancing and clothes. It's not like talking with you. And she's the pretty one,' she added with a touch of envy that made Elena pause.

'You're pretty too, Cera – everyone thinks so. Just a deeper kind of pretty.'

Cera's lips were full, her eyes large, long-lashed. She was not a classic beauty, but she was certainly striking. 'Do you really think so? I just feel plain – I'm too short, too wide. A little *fat*.'

Elena rolled her eyes. 'You're not fat, Cera. You're just not skinny like Solinde, and don't let her tell you otherwise.' Elena was focusing entirely on Samir Taguine, his cocksure gaze staring back at her. 'You're beautiful where it counts, my princessa. I would die before I let anyone hurt you,' she added, almost unthinking.

Cera blinked. 'I know – I mean, that's your job, isn't it? To protect us, I mean.'

'It's more than a job, Cera.' As she looked back at Samir she saw Lorenzo was walking over towards them. *Shit, do I have to protect him too?* 'Hey, here's Lori.'

Lorenzo grinned hesitantly. 'Princess, was the broth pleasing? Pietro has nearly done with the chicken. You'll get the best cuts.'

'So we should, Seir Lorenzo. Our stomachs are screaming!'

Elena rose and met the knight's eye. 'Lorenzo.' She beckoned him closer and whispered, 'Be careful around Samir.'

He looked at her as if he doubted his ears. 'Samir? Is he not loyal?'

'He's a Rondian mage, Lori. He's loyal to his salary.'

Lorenzo looked a little wary. He knew the destruction Samir could wreak, for the mage had frequently shown off in front of the knights, blasting stone until it exploded, or torching a row of archery targets. 'You are magi too,' he said softly.

'But I am Nesti, Lori: you know that.'

'Si, you are Nesti. So what do you want me to do?'

'For now, nothing, just be cautious; see to Fadah and Timi. There is no reason to suspect anything untoward will happen, but be on your guard.' She gave him the easy explanation: 'It's the shihad, you know.'

'You think if the Nesti declare for Salim, Samir might do something?'

'It won't hurt to be vigilant, Lorenzo.'

He grinned nervously. They both knew that if something broke out, Samir could toast him in an eye-blink – unless he was standing behind Elena. He still managed to look nonchalant as he walked away.

Cera was sitting up, her big eyes tinged with unease. 'What was that you were saying to Lori, Ella?'

Elena gave her what she hoped was a reassuring smile. 'Just asking him to keep his eyes open.'

Cera pulled a face. 'I'm not a child any more, Ella. Is something wrong? Something about Samir? I don't like him.'

Nor do I, my girl. She measured the space between her and the Fire-mage. 'Don't worry, Cera. Nothing's going to happen.'

'You look very fierce.' Cera looked up at the little lantern. 'Can you make us a magic light, like you used to on stormy nights?' The ghost of a younger girl seemed to hover within the young princess' eyes, seeking reassurance that all was well.

Elena looked at her indulgently. 'Of course.' She reached out to the water bottle, pulled out the stopper and tipped a little water into her hand. Cera leaned forward as she swirled the water, shaping it, and drew out of herself the gnosis light, gradually working it with the water until it became cohesive, bound together by the gnosis energy. She sealed it with the Rune of Binding and then tossed it, a glowing, rubbery ball of water and light, into Cera's waiting hands. The girl flicked it back and they played a lightning game of catch for a few seconds until Cera dropped the tiny bundle of light onto her blanket and it broke apart.

'You always win now,' she complained. 'You used to let us win when we were younger – you still let Timi win.' She brushed at the water stain. 'And now my blanket is wet.'

'Now you see why I didn't let you win!' Elena waved a hand and caused the water to evaporate.

Cera laughed, then said wistfully, 'I wish I could cast magic spells too.'

'It's not magic, it's gnosis – that's actually a Silacian word meaning

121

"secret knowledge",' replied Elena, watching Samir as he strolled back to his tent. *That's right, Samir, time for sleep.* 'And we don't "cast spells" – we don't need words to direct the energy, just thoughts. Only learners and the less-gifted magi speak words aloud, and that's to help focus their concentration and energy. I only use words if I'm trying something complex.' She watched Samir disappear into his tent and exhaled. She pulled a little bundle of feathers from a pocket, a gift from Gurvon containing beast-gnosis energy. Reaching out, she caught the mind of a night-bird, a desert owl, and set it to watching over their tent. Beast-mastery wasn't her strength, but she could manage something simple like that if a key was provided, even if that key was a gift from her estranged lover.

Are you still seeing Vedya, Gurvon? You promised me that was over, but I don't believe that's true.

Cera rolled onto her stomach and peered at her from behind a curtain of thick black hair. 'What will Father decide, Ella? When he meets with the Keshi about the shihad?'

Elena looked across at her princess, her soft brown face illuminated by the blue light of the water-globe. Cera was asking more and more adult questions these days. She was becoming a woman, with interests that went far beyond childbearing. She wasn't betrothed yet, and that decision was overdue – there had been enquiries from both Rimoni and Jhafi nobles. She was half-Rimoni, half-Jhafi, so she could marry either way without jeopardising the blood-criterion should her children seek the kingship. 'I think your father will try to keep his options open as long as he can. The Jhafi and the Keshi were at war for many years before the Rimoni settled here, and the Keshi have tried to start revolts among the Jhafi before. Our defences are strong in the south, but our armies are small.'

'But surely we won't stay neutral,' Cera said, screwing up her face. 'What the Rondian emperor did was evil – all those poor people in Hebusalim who died! I wish all Rondians were like you, Ella – then there'd be peace like there used to be.'

'Ah, but I'm not a Rondian,' grinned Elena. 'I'm from Noros, and we don't like Rondians any more than you do. We even had a war against them, but we lost.' Faces from the past swelled up in her memory: dead faces, living ones . . . Gurvon . . .

'Is Samir Rondian? And Master Sordell?'

'Samir is. He's pretty typical, except that he's bald – usually they like to have their hair long and curly and wear lacy clothes. Sordell is Argundian, and they're more plain-spoken and earthy. They're stubborn bastards.'

'Rondians, Argy-thingies, Noros . . . they're all the same.'

'So is a Nesti the same as a Gorgio?' Elena said, an eyebrow raised.

'Ugh, no!' Cera cried, 'the Gorgio are *disgusting*.'

'There, you see? You're both Rimoni! Noromen and Rondians aren't even the same nation.'

'Gorgio are a bunch of inbred fellators – we aren't even the same *species*. Can you believe Solinde actually fancies Fernando Tolidi? Yuck!' She rolled her eyes, then went serious again. 'Is Magister Gyle a Rondian? I only met him once. He made me nervous. It was like he was memorising everyone and putting them into little boxes so he could pull them out later and study them.'

How perceptive. He was probably doing exactly that. 'No, he's a Noroman, like me.'

'Was he your, um . . .' Cera's voice became a little uncertain.

'My lover? That's none of your business, my girl.'

'You keep telling me a ruler has to make everything their business, so I'm right to want to know.'

'And when you're ruler, I might even tell you!'

Cera looked at her with calculating eyes. 'You used to speak of him often. You don't any more.'

Elena schooled her face. Sometimes Cera really was just too observant. 'Don't I?'

'No. And Samir said something to Master Sordell, about someone called Vedya? About her being *close* to Master Gyle.'

Elena felt her heart sink. 'You shouldn't be listening to the men talk.'

'You always tell me to keep my eyes and ears open, Ella!'

'So I do – but for now, I'd like you to close them and get some sleep.'

Cera lay back, staring into space. 'I wish I could be like you and go where I want and do what I want. I'll just end up being married to someone and have to live all my life being told what to do.'

'Oh, my life is nowhere like as romantic as you think, Cera. Mostly I just do what I'm told too, which mostly turns out to be dangerous or boring or both.'

'If I'd been born a man, I would have so much more freedom. Men get to do all the fun things.'

Elena remembered making the same arguments to others, years ago. She looked at the princess fondly. *She really is like a little sister.* 'You know I don't disagree, but you should get some sleep.'

'Is it true that Rondian women can marry who they please?'

Elena shook her head. 'No, they have much the same lives as you: no sooner does a girl begin to bleed than her marriage is arranged, even for magi – maybe even more so because the mage's blood is so important. I'm different there too.' She grimaced.

Cera smiled mischievously. 'Will you marry one day?'

Elena blinked. 'Perhaps.'

'Was Master Gyle your only lover?' she teased.

'Cera!'

The princess giggled. 'You can tell me, we're practically sisters.'

Elena gave her an exasperated look. 'Go to sleep!' She turned away while Cera burst out laughing. *Little minx! I bet Solinde put her up to that.*

When Cera spoke again, her voice was softer. 'I'll stop now, Ella. Have you set the wards?'

'Si, Cera, all is well. Have you finished the tea I gave you? It'll help the cramps.'

'All drunk. Buona notte, Ella-amica. I wish I was your real sister and we could travel the world.'

'What do you think we're doing, silly? Sleep well.'

'I love you, Tante Ella.'

'I love you too, princessa. Now for Kore's sake: Go. To. Sleep!'

When she woke in the morning, a dead owl was lying beside the tent-flap, a hole the size of a large coin burnt through its chest where its heart would have been. Samir gazed at her from beside the well, a grim smile on his lips.

Four days later they spotted a party of men on camels approaching from the east. They were clad in white, and their long lances were cradled at rest. A violet banner was unfurled when they spotted the royal party: the king's messengers warning Forensa to expect them had obviously arrived. She glanced across at Lorenzo, who was riding point with her, and gave a relieved sigh. The more men, the safer she would feel. The last four days had been tense and trying, as everyone was aware of the growing rift between the two magi. She could feel their fear that violence would explode and trap them between forces they couldn't possibly survive. Even Fadah had noticed, and asked anxiously if she and Samir had fallen out. Elena had reassured her that it was just a disagreement over politics, while wishing desperately that were true.

The landscape had changed as they travelled, the bracken giving way to tall, sharp piles of rock. The sand was softer underfoot, and at times the horses floundered. The nights were getting colder, the days hotter, and so still that some wind would have been a blessing. But the air didn't move much this far inland except for the occasional massive sandstorm, and they most definitely didn't want one of those.

Elena looked at Lorenzo. The Kestrian knight had been good company on the journey: he was confident and he'd travelled widely before coming to Brochena, which made him an interesting conversationalist. *I will miss these people if I leave*, she thought.

'Wait here,' she told him, and trotted towards the column of majestic camels gaudily festooned in ribbons and bells, their faces imperturbable and disinterested. The lead rider raised a hand in greeting and unwrapped his headscarf, revealing the solemn, hairless skull of Harshal ali-Assam, brother of the Emir of Forensa. His face split into a white-toothed smile. 'Donna Elena! I thank Ahm for your safe arrival.'

'And I, Harshal.' She glanced back. 'We've not arrived safely yet, though.'

Harshal blinked once, like a basking reptile. 'There is a problem, Donna Ella?'

'La, Harshal, don't worry. We're all a little tense, that's all. It is good to see you.' Harshal ali-Assam would be a suitor for Solinde, when she came of age, though the princess wasn't enthusiastic: he was in his late twenties, which was ancient by Solinde's standards. But he was a decent man, and Elena thought he'd make a fine husband for a wayward girl. 'What news, Harsh? How does Fadah's sister fare?'

'Homeirah is not well. Ahm's will be done.' He sighed. 'Had the Keshi envoys arrived before you left Brochena?'

Elena shook her head. She checked behind her and, in a low, confidential voice, said, 'Samir is unsettled by the Keshi embassy. He is Rondian, and King Olfuss' decision affects him more than a Noroman like me.' *Simple and plausible; Gurvon would have approved.* She bit her lip. *I must stop judging my actions by his standards.*

Harsh nodded quietly. 'We will take care. No problem.'

They made good time after that, though Cera insisted she be allowed to ride a camel, and of course Timori immediately wanted to do the same. Elena rode behind Cera and they sang Javonesi folksongs about princes and love affairs and starlit oases. Lorenzo joined in sometimes with his pleasing tenor, until it felt like they were a travelling troupe of musicians riding to their next engagement.

The only black cloud was Samir, brooding and snide, like a vulture waiting for a dying beast to finally expire so he could feed. He goaded Elena whenever she came within earshot, until she had to give him wide birth, lest she explode.

The column entered Forensa from the west, just after midday, three days after meeting Harshal's men. The sun was a distant glowing ball in the sky. The horses and camels became difficult to restrain as they sensed home. They rode more briskly through the reek of endless garbage heaps at the edge of town. Impoverished Jhafi stared at them as they passed and ragged children ran alongside, begging money and food as the party wound through the crowded streets outside the old yellow walls that rose in the middle distance. The children crowded around every wagon and every rider except Elena. They were frightened of her, the foreign witch. It made her feel sad, still.

She was an accomplished healer and had often used her skills in Brochena, healing wounds or cysts or broken bones, but it was exhausting, exacting work and she could never do enough. She asked nothing in return but some new vocabulary. She thought it was appreciated: a tiny victory for communication and understanding. In Yuros people believed a magi's powers were beneficial, gifts of the Kore, but here in Antiopia everyone, even the Rimoni, started with the assumption that she wielded demonic powers.

She sighed and combed her fingers through her filthy hair. Waiting for something to explode was wearing her down: she needed to wash and sleep. *What is Gurvon doing now*, she wondered. *What has he told Samir? What's happening back in Brochena?* The not-knowing gnawed at her.

They wound through the streets to the old market and circled the emir's palace before climbing the hills to the Nesti fortress. Krak al-Farada's tumbledown dome turrets had been replaced with crenelated fighting platforms holding spear-hurling ballistae, and the walls had been thickened and renewed. Armoured men peered down between the violet banners as trumpets greeted the caravan.

Paolo Castellini was awaiting them in the courtyard. He was reckoned the tallest man in Javon. He had broad shoulders, and a lank, grey-streaked moustache and hair framed his mournful face. He opened the carriage doors for the royal family himself, and Fadah, emerging first, accepted Paolo's obeisance graciously before hurrying her children up the stairs, anxious to see her sister Homeirah.

Paolo turned to Elena and nodded formally. *He still doesn't trust me.* She dismounted, her legs aching abominably. Lorenzo was already directing his men towards the stables. Everyone looked pleased to have arrived, even Samir, who tossed his reins to a servant and followed the royal family into the keep. As he vanished, she felt a sudden tremor of apprehension. *Time to move.* She waved at Paolo and hurried up the steps herself, glancing back as she heard someone follow her:

Lorenzo, as anxious as she was. *Always have a plan*, Gurvon said. Well, she had a plan. Magi with a strong Affinity were less versatile than other magi, and she had been observing Samir for four years. Certainly he was formidable in Fire-gnosis, and very capable with Earth and Air, but that was a narrow repertoire. He relied on incinerating his enemies with irresistible flames. If he caught her with a full blast, she would spend her last seconds screaming in agony as the flesh on her bones crisped, even if she presented her strongest shields. If she could avoid that, she might have a chance.

Samir had been gone half a minute, that was all. She hurried past the guards on the front doors with Lorenzo clanking behind her, emerging into the foyer, where twin stairs descended four storeys on either side of a well of space. Walls of carved teak were hung with tapestries and paintings and lined with statues in marble and stone. Opposite, the doors to the great hall were open, the room filled with supplicants and well-wishers, at least one hundred people. She looked around, frightened: she could see neither the Nesti children nor Samir.

A low chuckle sounded above her. Samir was leaning against the balustrade, flexing his fingers, smirking at her. *There will be no warning*, his laughter told her. *No warning at all.*

There was no warning.

Elena rose before dawn, worn out from anxious dreams. She crept softly down through the keep from her small room outside the nursery area, clad only in her nightshift. Her best tunic and breeches were over her arm, but her weapons in the bundle also, something she wouldn't have done back in Brochena. She still felt stiff and battered from the journey, and the thought of a bath before having to get the children ready for morning services was enticing.

She was tiptoeing along the corridor to the bath-house, when she heard Queen Fadah's voice, carrying from the sickroom. Elena had checked on Homeirah last night; she looked nearer to ninety than her actual forty-eight years. She was riddled with cancers, could scarcely breathe, and no longer kept down anything but fluids. She would die soon, nothing was surer.

As Elena glanced down the corridor, a voice, quite distinctly, said <Begin>. It was not in her ears, but in her head, like something over-heard in a dream: a mental call. *Spoken by Gurvon Gyle.*

Begin . . .

Fadah stepped from the sickroom, still talking to someone within. She turned as Elena shrieked a warning. Then the queen was thrown backwards and clamped against the wall by unseen forces. Elena dropped the towel and clothes and grasped her sword and dagger. Her mouth was forming a call for help when a burst of flame blossomed about the queen with lurid, horrible beauty. For a second all Elena could see in the brilliant flash of the explosion were Fadah's bones, visible through translucent flesh, then the concussion of the fire-blast blanketed the entire corridor. A wave of hot force threw her onto her back and her head hammered against the wooden floor. Her vision swam as she fought for purchase on the smooth floor. A liquid rush of flame scorched the air above her and when she looked up, all that remained of the queen was a pile of burning bones.

Samir the Inferno stepped from the sickroom. Behind him, women were crying out in shock, and their cries became agonised screams as he pointed and another gout of flames filled the room. But his eyes were already on Elena. He walked slowly towards her, drawing his sword. He was fully dressed in robes of scarlet, the ruby at his throat gleaming like an ember. She choked back a cry as scarlet gnosis-light gathered in Samir's hands.

'Gurvon said I could screw you before I kill you if I want, but I really can't see the point.' He stabbed a finger at her and flames gushed down the corridor. They were deflected by her shields, but the heat washed through, crisping her feet and singeing her hair and nightclothes. 'You're not my type. I'd rather just watch you burn.' He drew himself erect, gathering a full-powered blast, as she flung up renewed shielding, downward-sloped and anchored to the walls. She could see her feet blistering; they felt like a thousand needles had been rammed into them. She crawled backwards, away from the advancing mage, until her head and shoulders hit the wall: she'd reached the T-junction of the corridor behind her. She had one instant to take in the immensity of the fires playing about Samir's hand, then she dived sideways. A wave of white-hot energy washed over the place where she had stood, but the flames swirled against her shields and were channelled downwards, turning the wooden floor to ash. For a second, she glimpsed Samir's bemused face as his own fires backwashed, disintegrating the floor at his feet, then he was gone, tumbling through the space where the floor had been. She leapt up, wincing with pain as the seared soles of her feet touched the ground, and tore towards the stairs she had just descended, screaming warnings to whoever could hear.

The castle came to panicked life, Rimoni voices calling questions, answered by a roar from below and screaming. With a crash the floor in front of her burst upwards, a geyser of fire blasting through the timbers to incinerate the staircase she was making for. Samir was firing blind through the wooden floor from below.

Her mind raced as he bellowed, 'You can't escape me, Elena!'

She had to get between him and the children: that was her only function. She threw herself off the ground like a diver, and flew the length of the burning corridor on Air-gnosis as another blast shattered the timbers of the floor where she had been standing a second before. Then she heard Paolo Castellini's voice below, calling the guards to him.

'Paolo! The children!' she called as she powered down the smoke-filled corridor, shot like a hawk into the foyer, three flights up, and poised in mid-air to see Samir, below her, facing Paolo Castellini and a guardsman standing beside the main doors. She fired a bolt of blue gnosis-light at Samir and watched it crackle against his shields even as she began her next working. He roared, and his fires flew amiss, blasting apart a stag's head mounted above the door instead of incinerating Paolo as he'd intended. She rolled in the air and conjured images of herself heading in three different directions, each firing a bolt of gnosis-energy.

Samir chose wrong; smoke and flame roared behind her and extinguished one of the images. The Fire-mage laughed mockingly as she soared up to the top level.

Lorenzo di Kestria emerged from a corridor, clad only in breeches, with a buckler over his left arm and holding his broadsword in his right hand. He gaped at Elena, hovering before him in mid-air, but she ignored him as she made a slicing gesture – and severed the ropes holding the chandelier beside her. The glass-and-metal monstrosity plummeted, and she saw Samir's upturned eyes widen as the whole weight smashed against his shields and flew apart. But it left him untouched, shattering around him in a cascade of flying glass and shards of iron. *Rukka mio! How can he be that strong?*

'Lori, the children!' she cried, darting towards the nursery even as Cera emerged, clad only in a white shift, with a pale-faced Timori clinging to her. They took in the burning ceiling and the great plume of smoke pouring upwards.

Cera looked at her desperately. 'Where's Mamma?' Her face was stricken. Elena flashed towards her as Samir flung Paolo aside like a toy and turned his face upwards again.

Timori, his eyes uncomprehending, asked 'What's happening?' and stepped forward to peer through the wooden railings at the scene below, where the echoes of the fallen chandelier were still reverberating.

'Timi!' they all yelled, but Lorenzo was fastest, slamming into the bewildered boy, his buckler interposed an instant before fire engulfed them. The knight howled in agony as the flames washed over him, catching everywhere the balustrade and buckler were not covering: his shoulder, his left leg, the left side of his face.

But Timori had escaped the blast, and now Cera grabbed the boy and dragged him away from the convulsing knight. Elena threw herself towards them, vaulting the burning railing. Crossbows sang below, then two guards roared in agony amidst Samir's laughter.

Cera clutched Timori to her, pouring all her hope and terror into one word: '*Ella!*'

Elena shoved Cera towards the nursery. '*Inside – now!*'

She checked over the railing and quailed: Samir was a devil

unleashed. He was walking horizontally up the stone wall, his feet sinking effortlessly into the brickwork. His face looked carved from lava, glowing ember-red; his beard was a tongue of flame. She pulled Lorenzo to his feet. 'Come on, Lori, we need you,' she cried as he gasped for breath.

The main nursery bedroom, Cera's room, was large, with a bed against the far wall and views through windows north and south. She blasted away the glass from both sets of windows, then wrenched a mirror from the wall and set it on a chair. 'Climb through the window, onto the ledge,' she ordered, then shouted, 'Go!' as Cera, still holding Timori, froze. '*Go*,' she screamed again, and thrust the girl towards the windows. 'Lorenzo, get them out of here—'

She spun and slapped her hands together and gnosis-strands gripped the doors, slammed them shut and locked them.

'What the rukking Hel is happening, Ella?' the knight shouted at her.

'It's Samir – he's after the children!' *I never thought . . . damn you, Gurvon—* She pulled another mirror from the wall, setting it opposite the other one, facing the door. Smoke rolled under the cracks. She looked at herself in both mirrors at once, moved them with subtle finger-movements, aligning them, marked her position, then darted to one side as the door rattled.

Lorenzo pushed the children out onto the window-ledge, then turned, his face resolute: the look of a man who expected the next minute to be his last. She had no time to do anything but scream, 'Hide, Lori!'

There was no calling out this time, no gloating or threats, just a coal-like fist punching a hole in the door just as Elena placed herself on one side. She could only see the door through one of the mirrors, but in the reflection she saw it burst open, then smoke billowed into the room, obscuring everything. She stepped into the shadows and began her next working.

Samir grimaced. Gurvon had warned him that the bitch was quick, and so she was, but she was only a half-blood, and a dried-up prune to boot. *I have absolute Fire-Affinity,* he thought gleefully.

Few on Urte could survive even a single taste of his power, and he'd been preparing all night, building up his powers with meditation. *Just before dawn, be ready,* Gurvon had said. *We're going to kill them all.*

That was an unexpected bonus! *So not just running out on them, Gurvon?*

No, we're killing them all: Sordell and I will do the king; you kill the queen and the children.

What about Elena?

She can't be trusted on this, Samir. She's gone native. Do whatever you need to.

Everyone knew Gurvon was screwing Vedya these days; Elena was nothing to him now. *It'll be my pleasure, Gurvon* – and he'd meant it. He'd been hovering close to that fat dumpling Fadah when the order came. That first burst, the one that crisped the queen to dust, had been *orgasmic.* Then Elena had shown up, and Gurvon had been right: she was damned quick, and cunning – the way she'd angled her shields so that he'd destroyed the floor at his own feet? That'd been clever; he'd remember that trick.

He smashed open the nursery door. *Time to finish this.* He let the first rush of smoke pour into the nursery and held his shields ready, but nothing came at him. She was quick, yes, but she had no firepower, and she was running out of places to hide. Somewhere in the dark he heard Lorenzo di Kestria gasping in pain and he grinned widely. That was the great thing about fire – it didn't just damage, it also left mind-scrambling pain, the sort that made master torturers wet with envy. The sort of pain he was going to visit on that prune-faced Anborn bitch before he started on the children . . .

The smoke rose to the high beams of the nursery, revealing Elena standing before him, between two mirrors, a dagger held in her right hand. She jabbed her left at him and an impotent blue gnosis-bolt dissipated unfelt against his shields. She looked ragged; she must be at the end of her tether.

He smiled, raised his hand and gave her everything he had, crying out in utter bliss as he made the air throb with gushing fire so hot the flames were translucent, warping his vision as they washed over her, through her, and billowed unobstructed to blast the far wall.

She reappeared, right where she had been, twirling two thin blades. *Untouched. How?* He sensed someone behind him, but too late: two numbing blows struck beneath his armpits and jolted through him. There was a metallic grinding noise as the blades rasped against each other, somewhere deep in his chest. He stared, bewildered, as the Elena standing before him winked out.

Numbness flooded through him, and when he reached for his power there was just a void. He tried to speak, but his legs gave way and he felt his own heart stop.

'I'm not left-handed. You should have noticed that,' she whispered in his ear.

Rukka! Mirrors . . . Illusion . . .

The floor pitched up to meet him.

Elena slumped to the floor beside the dead mage. After a moment she pulled herself together and extracted her blades, trembling in relief. He had fallen for her mirror-projected illusion. The analytical part of her brain smirked: she'd targeted his weak spot and scored a direct hit. But damn, it had been close . . . and Fadah was dead.

'Cut off his head,' she whispered to Lorenzo. He looked back at her blank horror. 'I mean it. There are spells that could revive him, even now! We have to make sure he's dead.' She sucked in a rasping, smoke-filled breath and crawled towards the windows. 'Cera? Timi?'

The Nesti children poked their heads above the broken windows. Behind her she heard Lorenzo heft his sword and swing. The *thump* echoed around the room, making Cera cry out. Then she and Timi were clambering over the broken teeth of the shattered window and throwing themselves into Elena's arms. She crushed them to her, and Lorenzo crawled to join them, his face puffy and scalded. Samir Taguine's head lay in a spreading pool of blood, an expression of stunned surprise still on his face.

In seconds violet-clad guardsmen were storming into the room, Paolo Castellini at their head, his craggy face grim and furious. They gently prised the children away, checking they were whole, but Cera wouldn't let Elena go, and Timi clung to Lori, soundlessly wailing.

Elena let the soldiers draw them to their feet, and then she slowly let them lead her away from the destruction, and the headless corpse of the man who had wrought it.

'Is Mother—? And Tante Homeirah?' Cera was in a bed in a room beside the chapel. There were four guards at the door, and physicians and their assistants everywhere. She and Elena were both still in their torn and burnt nightwear. Elena's feet were a mess, though the pain was only now registering.

'I'm sorry,' she murmured, 'I'm so sorry.'

Cera stared out across the room, oblivious to the servants binding her cuts, washing her limbs, numb to everything but the pain inside. Then she put her hand to her mouth as a fresh thought occurred to her. 'Father!'

Elena felt hollow inside. 'I don't know – I've tried to find out, but I can't reach him. I'm so, so sorry.' *This is my fault*, she thought. *I should have killed Samir in his sleep. I should have known that Gurvon would never just pull out, not when there was the chance to make even more money by leaving a pile of corpses behind him. Olfuss, Solinde – who else? The whole Nesti clan? There aren't enough men in Brochena Palace to stop Gurvon Gyle and Rutt Sordell – and who knows if the rest of the gang are there too? I'm an idiot! And now this poor, sweet girl is going to have every blade in the kingdom turned on her. I've failed them all . . .*

The day passed in a hazy mist, faces coming and going to a constant wailing outside the walls. Elena woke from uneasy, nightmares to find she'd fallen asleep on the chair beside Cera's bed, her head on the blankets. A hand was stroking her shoulder.

'Ella,' whispered Cera.

She sat up and bowed her head. 'Cera – I've failed you all.'

'Never! You *saved* us, Ella. We'd *all* be dead without you.' She put a finger to Elena's lips. 'Shhh: you saved us all – me and Timi, Lori, everyone. You are Nesti. You're one of us.' She reached out and pulled

Elena to her, stroking her hair as if she were the child and Cera the elder sister. 'I will give you a medal, and a title, and land. And a new stallion, from our stables. You'll have the freedom of Forensa.' Her face grave and serious, she said, 'I've been thinking. I need to be seen. The people need to know that I am alive. There will be all sorts of rumours until they see me. They need to know there are still Nesti alive here.' She patted Elena's cheek, looking just like her mother. 'You should sleep, Ella. You look terrible.'

Elena looked wonderingly at her young charge. It was as if an adult had overnight supplanted the child. 'How can I sleep when my princessa is working?' she whispered.

'If Father is dead by violence, then no election is required: Timi is his heir, and that makes me regent,' Cera said in a low, astoundingly composed voice. 'I need to take charge.'

'Are you ready for that?' Elena asked her gently. 'The men will try and sideline you – they may not mean to, but they will see you as – well, you know.'

'Yes: "just a girl".' Cera straightened, setting her jaw. 'If I am regent by law, then I intend to be regent in fact. The shihad is coming, and Javon needs a leader, not squabbling factions. I will lead, until Timi is old enough.'

Look at you, child – no, not a child any more. Elena swallowed. *I am proud of you. And I am utterly terrified for you.*

They got up and helped each other dress. Elena belted her sword-belt around her loose-fitting smock. Cera wore regal purple and gold, and her princess-crown, normally only worn for important dinners, was placed on her head. Then Elena followed her out of the castle, through the charred ruins of the reception hall, still littered with blackened timbers and the ruin of the chandelier.

Outside, on the main steps, the sun beat down and the heat rolled in waves off the confined space. The smell of human sweat assailed them as they took in the hundreds crammed into that small area. A ragged cheer broke from the lips of the people, a mix of Jhafi and Rimoni, and Harshal ali-Assam, busy marshalling some workmen, came over. The mourning of the womenfolk gave way to cheers as the crowd realised who had emerged and they surged forward.

Elena hovered beside her charge, nervous of such a crowd, but there was nothing but sorrow and sympathy in the faces of those who pressed close. One girl reverently kissed the hem of Cera's skirts. Elena scanned the walls in case Gurvon had some back-up assassin lurking, but she sensed no one. Would he have even considered that Samir could fail?

Cera raised a hand for silence and everyone pulled back and kneeled. When she spoke, the princess' voice was thin but firm. 'People of Forensa, you know me,' she started. 'I am your princess: I am Cera Nesti, and I have terrible tidings for you. My mother, Fadah Lukidh-Nesti, your queen, the Queen of all Javon, is dead, and so too is her sister, my aunt, Homeirah Lukidh-Ashil. These are bitter losses. But my brother Timori, the heir to the throne of Ja'afar-Javon, is unharmed and well. The casualties were, in the end, minimal. An assassin has struck, his apparent purpose was to slay—' She stopped and swallowed, the first clue to the effort this display was costing her. But she rallied, and went on, 'His purpose was to slay my family, and he would have done so but for the heroism of our valiant guards.'

There was a low cheer, particularly from the Rimoni.

'Foremost in valour and resolution was this woman beside me, Elena Anborn, my bodyguard – my champion. Though injured herself, she fought and slew the assassin, and protected my brother and me. She is my dear friend, and I commend her to you all.'

Elena was suddenly the focus of everyone's attention, and she felt the blood rush to her face as she wrestled with her guilt. Her trembling legs gave way and she slipped wordlessly to her knees and dizzily touched her forehead to Cera's feet. She hadn't meant to, but this public obeisance, the deepest of self-humbling gestures, won a great murmur of approval, and it suddenly struck her that to these people her Noros manner, treating all as equals, was considered arrogance; they saw this accidental homage as a belated acknowledgment of her true station. When Cera raised her to her feet and kissed her cheeks, the affection and trust between them was obvious to all, and first one woman and then many approached Elena and bowed, touching their right hands to their foreheads: *Praise and thanks,* they murmured. *Sal'Ahm. Peace be upon you.*

Even as she accepted this unprecedented acknowledgment, she felt Gurvon Gyle's first attempt to scry her. She forbade the contact. *Gurvon, you murdering bastard: I will make you pay for this.*

That night was full of hideous dreams, when she was eventually able to ignore the pain of her scabbed and blistered feet and calves. The next morning was Minasdai – 13 Octen, she calculated. Cautiously, she checked her wardings, unbroken but tampered with, definitely. She repaired the fraying, 'sniffing' with her gnosis-powers to confirm: Gurvon Gyle had been trying to force contact with her.

What else did Gurvon have planned? She had to presume that Olfuss was dead, and surely Gurvon would have followed that up with a military strike. The Gorgio of Hytel, without a doubt; they alone among the Rimoni had stuck by the Dorobon kings, so they must surely have marched back into Brochena. Gurvon would have informants here in Forensa: she knew how he worked. He built a network, everywhere he went. He had always told her to do the same, but she had grown slack here in Javon: she was a bodyguard, she had reasoned, so why would she need spies? *Wrong again, idiot!* Now she was blind to what was going on elsewhere. She was on her own.

She placed the bowl of water beside the bed into her lap and stared into it, pale light kindling inside it as she sought to scry Olfuss or Solinde. But there was nothing. She replaced the bowl, then hugged her arms about herself and let her grief pour out.

Afterward, she went to the infirmary. Lorenzo was lying there alone. The whole left side of his body was seared red, even his left eye bandaged over, but his right fixed on her as she entered. 'Ella,' he croaked.

'Lori. Did they give you something for the pain?'

He winced. 'Some. More would be good,' he admitted unwillingly.

She looked around her but the physicians were busy elsewhere, so she gently removed the bandages and tended him herself with gnosis-healing; performed in a semi-trance. She let her senses enter the wound and cleanse it, dulling his pain and kindling healing energies: a long gentle outpouring of gnostic balm, and as exhausting as any battle-spell. It took some time, and throughout it all, his handsome-sad face watched her, his big eye soft. Finally she peeled back the covering over his face.

'How bad is it?' he whispered. 'Will it scare the girls away?'

'No more than usual,' she told him, forcing a smile. 'You half-turned at the last instant. Give it a few months and no one will even know.'

'How did you do that? That mirror-trick?'

'Easy: I projected my reflection out from the mirror into the room and let it draw his fire while I came up behind him.'

'A miracle.'

'No, just gnosis. He was a thaumaturge, not good at spotting illusions.' She shrugged, not really wanting to talk about it.

'Do your powers really come from your god?' he asked, his eyes serious.

She shook her head. 'No. They come from me.'

He lifted his hands to her face, grasped her chin and pulled her mouth down onto his. She could have pulled away, but she didn't. His mouth was sweet and tangy, his lips both firm and gentle as they moved on hers. She closed her eyes and enjoyed the moment for a second, and then gently eased away. 'Then you are an angel.' He smiled in beatific triumph, the first of the knights to steal a kiss from the witch, and she scowled, regretting the moment already. Then his face clouded. 'Why did he do it, Ella? Was he acting alone? Or was he under orders?'

Elena shook her head. 'I don't know,' she lied, 'not yet – I'm trying to find out.' He nodded doubtfully and she stood slowly. It was harder than she had thought, to tear herself away. For just an instant, his warm strong arms had felt like a haven, a refuge from the storm that pressed about her. *No. I can't afford this weakness . . .*

'Get some sleep, Lori.' She backed out of the room.

*

Cera and Timori sat at the great table, Timori on a cushion. Elena stood behind Cera, her right hand on her sword-hilt. Her lower legs no longer hurt, but they were scarred. She felt haggard and tired and wracked with guilt. The reverence with which they were treating her was just making the guilt worse.

Harshal ali-Assam and Paolo Castellini were there with a dozen others of both races, local nobles and bureaucrats, holy men and chief citizens. She knew most, though not well. She could see Cera trembling slightly, afraid but determined. She was her father's daughter; he would be proud to see her today. If he were alive. *Who knows, maybe he is? But I doubt that very much*

A young Amteh scriptualist spoke a blessing, followed by a bushy-bearded Sollan drui, then they prayed together for strength and fortitude, asking for God's peace on the fallen and his blessing on the prince and princess. Elena looked at Cera and smiled encouragement. They had laid their plans that morning, then cornered a few of the key men, the opinion leaders, and explained how things would be. The men had all assumed that Cera would step aside and let them deal with the situation, but to Elena's surprise they had readily agreed to Cera taking this stronger role. It was as if they needed someone to plant a banner they could rally to. 'You were the men Olfuss Nesti, my father, trusted above all,' Cera had told them, 'so trust me. I am my father's daughter.' Elena had expected more resistance, but perhaps her presence intimidated them.

Cera addressed the meeting as if she had been doing so all her life: 'My lords, we are gathered here to convene an Emergency Council. I have sent riders to Brochena to ascertain the situation there, but we can expect no word for some time. My champion Elena has used her skills too, but she has been unable to determine whether my father the king is alive. Or my younger sister.'

Several mouths burst open with questions, but she raised a hand to forestall them. *How like a queen she already looks*, Elena thought. *How proud Olfuss would be.*

'I pray the attack here was an isolated act,' Cera went on, 'but I fear that will not be the case. There is strong reason to believe this act was planned for some time, to overthrow Nesti rule and pre-cipitate a coup. I also surmise that this blow has been struck in direct response to my father's decision about the shihad. For now, my hope is that we will soon have word of my father's safety, but in my heart I fear we are alone here, and that we are already at war.'

Enriched

Religion: Omali

And herein is a mystery: that there is but one God and many Gods; but all Gods are Aum and Aum is the sum of all.

THE SAMADHI-SUTRA (THREAD OF ENLIGHTENMENT),
HOLY BOOK OF THE OMALI

*Aruna Nagar, Baranasi, Northern Lakh,
on the continent of Antiopia
Shawwal 1381 (Octen 927 in Yuros)
9 months until the Moontide*

Despite the death and discord tearing at Ramita's family, and Meiros showing no sign of fulfilling his traditional role in a Lakh wedding celebration, there was no way Ispal and Tanuva were going to send off their eldest living daughter without making the right offerings, observances and prayers. To do otherwise would be to invite the anger of the gods on a union that already held many risks. Guru Dev was summoned, together with Pandit Arun, a wispy priest looking like he was made of twigs and hair, to devise a plan for Ramita's spiritual cleansing, for marrying a heathen required special propitiation. Vikash Nooridan ferried messages between Ramita's betrothed and her family, conveying what would and wouldn't be permitted. Fortunately the skilled negotiators of the Aruna Nagar marketplace were more than a match for the old ferang: the final outcome was not too much of a departure from tradition, though it would mean a lot of fasting and prayer.

Ramita remained shut in her room, mostly alone, as Huriya was tending her dying father. She fasted between sunrise and sunset like an Amteh in Holy Month, growing weak with hunger as she was given just curd and chapattis to eat before dawn and after dusk, to purify her body, they told her. Finally, she was summoned downstairs for the two wise men to reveal their plan for her wedding preparations: an array of tasks involving offerings to almost every Omali god in Paradise, as far as she could see.

The sanctifying of Ramita began in earnest a week before the ceremony. A bevy of neighbourhood women clad in bright saffron sarees and led by Mother's best friend, Auntie Pashinta, arrived before dawn to take her to the ghats. They held a makeshift tent made of sheets about her for privacy, and she slipped out of her white shift and immersed herself naked in the cold winter waters of Imuna, repeating it six times: one for Baraman the Creator and the next for his wife Sarisa, goddess of learning and music. Another for Vishnarayan, the Protector, and one for his wife Laksimi, goddess of wealth. One for Sivraman, Lord of Destruction and Rebirth, and the last especially for his dutiful wife Parvasi, who must be her role model for the time ahead. *Enter me, Holy Queen: make me a vessel for your patience and virtue. Infuse me with your obedience and loyalty.* She prayed with a fervour that shocked her, as if something in all the fasting and fear and loneliness of the past few days had brought out some inner being she had never before been aware of. She wondered at this strange overwrought creature she had become, who prayed aloud so vehemently, her words taken up by the women about her. The crowds faded from her consciousness as she was consumed with her quest for the courage to endure.

Once she had bathed, they walked along the banks of Imuna, she wrapped only in a sheet, calling aloud for protection from demons, asking for luck and blessings. The women echoed her cries and sang prayers to Aum, the all-God, as she stumbled barefoot through water and mud and rotting garbage and cow muck without even noticing until they reached the burning ghats. There Guru Dev and Pandit Arun were awaiting them, clad in saffron loincloths with their faces marked by white paste patterns, wardings against evil. The two holy men poured handfuls of ash over her wet hair and smeared it on her face, the ash from the wood of the pyres, and called upon Sivraman to protect 'this benighted girl'. The women twisted her ashy hair into thick knots and rubbed ash over her breasts and belly with their hard callused fingers to aid her fertility. She fell to her knees and bombarded Aum with her prayers, shouted aloud, heedless of the spectacle she made. She felt empty and light-headed, more than a little insane. She shrieked away her fears, purged herself of doubt and sorrow, until she felt some kind of force flow through her, drawing her to her feet and setting her dancing to unheard music. She cared nothing about the filthy sheet that barely covered her, for there was a spirit inside her, moving her limbs. This was real, primal: she felt the eyes of the gods on her.

At last she fell into Pashinta's waiting arms. The women gathered her in, their eyes wide, concerned. *They feel it too*, she thought.

When she had calmed down, Guru Dev touched a sacred tilak to her forehead. Pandit Arun declared her dancing an auspicious sign. *Demons beware, this girl is strong*, he told the gathering. She felt wild and untouchable. *Tremble, Antonin Meiros!*

The remaining days of the week were spent on a pilgrimage to Baranasi's seventy-three temples, her entourage growing as other brides-to-be joined her for luck. She became a kind of celebrity, like one of the many crazy people that lived on the ghats – Baranasi drew such people. Pilgrims touched her dirty sheet to their foreheads: holy madness was powerful magic. The temple priests made approving noises, counting the crowds and asking for donations. Street-vendors hovered at the fringes, selling their wares.

At night she ate like a starved tiger and slept like one of the dead, then rose like a zombie the next morning, only finding clarity in the chilly bite of the river-water. She felt hollowed out, like a coconut that had been carved open and all the milk and flesh removed, waiting to be refilled with something stronger. *This is strengthening me, I feel it*. Kazim didn't seem real any more.

When they took her home two days before the wedding, wet and shivering in the cooling air, her mother was there to welcome her. 'Those old men have finished making you holy,' Tanuva whispered. 'Now we're going to make you into a bride – starting with some food and water. Look at you! I can count your ribs!' She was fed and sent her to bed, and while she slept, the house bustled with labour.

She rose early the next morning and joined in the work. There was so much to do. The courtyard had to be decorated, rangoli patterns of rice-powder dye painted onto the stone work. She helped Jai decorate the piris, the low stools the wedding couple would be seated upon. People came and went, dropping off food, spices and pots of dye. Everyone had a sympathetic word for her, but lost in the work and the bustle and the brittle gaiety, she felt a curious sense of unreality. It was only when she stopped to think that she felt the sting of tears. She would miss all these good people so much!

That morning, Ispal took Jai to bury Raz Makani. They returned with Huriya. Ispal brought the sobbing Keshi girl straight to her and bade her, 'Give comfort to your sister Huriya.'

Huriya threw a shining glance at Ispal: he had named Huriya Ramita's sister, offering Huriya a place in his house for ever – it was not unexpected, but it was confirmation of something she had prayed for. 'Sister,' Ramita whispered in Huriya's ear as the girl sobbed in her arms.

Huriya squeezed her shoulders. 'Take me with you, to the north,' she whispered.

Ramita's throat tightened. She had so wanted to ask, but to drag Huriya to such a terrible place as Hebusalim was selfish and cruel. But now the offer was made, and she could not refuse it. 'Of course! I was afraid to ask.' They cried together while the entire household bustled around them.

They turned the cramped kitchen into a mandap, where the actual vows would be spoken. They dug and rebuilt the cooking pit into a place suitable for the wedding ritual. The strange weight of expectation flowing through all this work, unlike any other wedding she had been part of – and those were many, weddings being the chief entertainment around here. She had not been told the amount, but she knew lots of money was changing hands. The family would be transformed. The community was rallying about, but in her lowest moments she imagined this was only because of the gold – then she chastised herself. The people of Aruna Nagar always pitched in for weddings, or when someone needed help; they were here because they were all one family, first and foremost.

Jai took the cart of gifts for the groom, donated by the friends of the bride. Mostly these were food, primarily fish, which were auspicious for fertility. Ramita was trying not to think too hard about all this fertility symbolism, but it kept intruding, and the thought made her queasy. Nonetheless, she had to bless the cart as it left. The joke was that the fish of Imuna were so bony, weddings that did not have divine favour would be prevented by the groom choking on fish-bones. It had been known to happen.

The cart returned at midday with Jai sitting by the driver and his friends perched all over it. The immense Rondian, Jos Klein, and three of his soldiers led the way. All had suspicious faces. The cart's contents were covered by a dirty brown canvas. Faces appeared at every window and peered over the fences as they guided it into the courtyard. Jai and his friends took the gifts from her betrothed upstairs, to be opened on the morning of the wedding, then he sat down to sip chai, surrounded by the family, and told them, laughing, how the ferang lord had greeted the cart of food and river-fish. 'Most puzzled he was! Vikash had to explain them all. Really, how do they get married where he comes from?'

Though she had dozens of girls about her, sisters and cousins and friends, Ramita's final meal as a maiden was marred by the mystery of the groom's identity. They were unsure whether to celebrate or commiserate with Ramita, and the evening, which should have been a joyous occasion, was awkward. She felt as if she'd already left them.

Late after the feast, Ispal knocked softly on Ramita's door. She and Huriya were awake, sitting with arms about each other staring out of the open window at the huge face of the moon, three-quarters full, which filled the northeastern sky. Its face was gouged, its light harsh. Ispal sat on the end of Ramita's bed. 'I want to tell you both something,' he said in a soft voice. 'It is about what I saw in the north – about my friend Raz Makani, and how we met.'

You've told us a hundred times, Father, Ramita thought, but she nodded mutely.

Ispal gazed at the moon, then closed his eyes. His voice was uncertain at first, but as he spoke it took on the resonance of a scholar reciting an epic. 'Daughters, I have told you before of my journey north, twenty-three years ago. I decided to join the throng of merchants who went every twelve years to trade with the Rondians in Hebusalim. I had a wagonload of Baranasi silks, purchased with all of my savings. The trip north took months, and was a tale all of its own. Eventually though, I reached Hebusalim. The city was full, so I camped outside the walls. Everyone was excited, toasting the Bridge Builders. We dreamt aloud of the fortunes we would make from these foolish white people with purses full of gold.

'It was a chancy time, though. Not all Keshi welcomed the ferang, and there had been trouble already, with both sides guilty, so there were many soldiers. A squad of Keshi was camped near to my site: white-robed Keshi from Istabad with braided beards and hair. They had drink and girls, and discipline was lax. I kept having to shoo them from my wagon – they wanted to use it to bed their women.' He shook his head. 'One of them was Raz. He would apologise when he was done and drop me a coin, then leave me to wash the top layer yet again. Dirty prick!'

Huriya pulled her head from Ramita's shoulder and they exchanged glances. Ispal had never told the tale like this before.

'Ah, my friend Raz . . . he was full of life, and a demon with his scimitar. We used to watch the men sparring, and he was the best. He had powerful shoulders, and his belly was taut and muscular, his thighs solid and toned. He could take them on two or three at a time and still win. We would watch and place wagers, and I always bet on him.' He sighed. 'His woman Falima had hair to her waist and eyes like full moons. She was the most beautiful of the camp-women, and everyone understood that she belonged to Raz alone.'

He looked at Huriya. 'I'm sorry to tell you this about your mother, but this is a night for truth. Falima was a girl they picked up on the march, not the daughter of a merchant as you've been told. These are facts, but they need not leave this room.'

Huriya nodded tensely.

'We had such dreams of the wealth to be made fleecing the ferang traders, and we waited for them with bated breath – but instead, the Emperor of Rondelmar unleashed his legions. All that month, while we were gathering in Hebusalim, he had been marching his men along the Great Bridge. They say Antonin Meiros could have stopped them, but he did not. The emperor secured the complicity of the Ordo Costruo. Meiros let that army through, and the world was plunged into war.'

Ispal paused and took Ramita's hand. 'That is the man you are to marry, Ramita: the man who opened his Great Bridge to the legions. Some say he had no choice, but most revile him for that.'

She said nothing. This was legend, not something real people did. Huriya's eye's were wide. Ispal caught her chin in a firm grip. 'Yes, Huriya-daughter: Ramita is to marry Antonin Meiros, and you must carry this secret. Do you swear?'

Huriya was struck mute, half in amazement, half in disbelief.

Ispal continued his tale. 'I talked to him of this when we spoke of marriage. In my heart I had decided that if he was to marry my beloved daughter, he must answer one question above all. "Why did you do it?" I asked him, looking into his eyes to see his soul. I wanted to know if this was an evil man, a weak man, or a man of honour left with only evil choices.

'What I saw was pain: genuine and still fresh. There was no vindictiveness, no malice, no race-hate, no cunning, just terrible, all-consuming pain. I saw that he suffered as a result of that decision, that he regretted it every day. "I thought I was saving lives," he told me. "To stop them, I would have had to destroy the Bridge, my only option at that juncture. One hundred thousand men would have plummeted into the sea, and the link between Yuros and Antiopia would have been gone, perhaps for ever. Though I received assurances that the soldiers were there to guard the traders, I was doubtful. But what they did – the slaughter, the slavery – truly, I had no idea they would commit such atrocities."'

Ispal ran his fingers through his thinning hair, sighing heavily. 'This he told me, Ramita, and I believe him. I think he was trapped. He is not evil. He told me that he loved Hebusalim and had laboured to make it a paradise on earth. He built huge aqueducts, bringing water from the mountains and turning the landscape green. He built hospitals, where his magi tended the sick. He gifted a palace for the Dhassan Sultan made of golden marble, and built a massive Dom-al'Ahm, the largest in the north. His daughter founded an order of healers and his son created a public library, larger than that of the mughal. His Ordo Costruo were revered, some even believed them to be angels of Ahm. We had only seen their benevolent side. We had never seen a magi in battle. That was about to change.

'The Rondian legions marched over the Bridge, but they were preceded from the air: windships had been massing out over the sea, beyond the horizon. No one even suspected they were there until they moved over the city at dawn on that awful day. Imagine it, daughters, all of those windships, hanging above us in the sky, bristling with men, and magi in flowing robes standing in the bows like figureheads.

'At first people cheered, thinking this was a merchant fleet, the greatest ever, and that our fortunes were made. I thought so too at first – we were standing on our wagons waving to the ships, jumping about like children eager for sweets.

'But Raz looked at me, and he said "Those are warbirds", in a voice I will always remember. "Take care of Falima", he told me and then he was up, pulling his tunic over his head as he ran across the camp calling to his men, "Arm yourselves, you slobs!" At first I didn't understand, or maybe I didn't want to. Then the Rondians struck. Catapults on their decks swung their arms and hurled burning pitch down on us, which exploded all about us. Tents and buildings and wagons alike burst into flames, trapping screaming men inside. As the ships came in lower, archers poured arrows into the crowds and the magi struck down the captains and anyone trying to rally resist-ance, pale-blue bolts of energy stabbing from the skies like light-ning. It was dreadful. We were helpless.

'I remember grabbing Falima to prevent her from following Raz. She fought me like a hellion. Raz entered his pavilion and as he emerged clutching his breastplate, buckler and scimitar, the tent behind him exploded. The concussion threw us against my wagon and when we could see again, there was a crater where the tent had stood. The shadow of a warship hung above us, a young mage at the prow, pouring fire from his hands into the stampeding crowd. As we watched he torched a crowd of traders trying to flee. Then it seemed that he saw me. He raised his hands, and I pulled Falima under the wagon, then all was heat and fire, the air blazing as sand melted to glass right where I had stood a second ago. Falima and I scrambled out the other side, and this time it was Falima pulling me away as I tried in my madness to rescue my silks!

'We found Raz kneeling before the crater where his tent had been, staring at the blackened bodies in the hole. The air throbbed with the cries of dead and living. The warship above swung eastwards, towards the next camp, but others hovered overhead. Every direc-tion seemed wrong, but Raz chose to lead us toward the city. As we ran we fell in with others, swarms of citizens and soldiers fleeing towards the city gates. For some reason we all imagined we would be safe inside the walls.

'Among the large warships were dozens of tiny little windships the Rondians call "skiffs", each with a mage and a few archers. They were faster than the warships, and they swooped over us, attacking randomly. Some came close enough that we could see their faces clearly. They were so young, and almost childishly excited, like hunting quail for the first time. "Is this sport to them?" I remember Raz shouting angrily, waving his sword. The Rondian archers could hardly miss, the lanes were so packed. The noise became deafening as we were swept along, then we came to a sudden jolting halt and I remember an awful convulsion running through the whole crowd as we realised that someone in the city had shut the gates. I heard a roar of terror behind me as a skiff came straight along the lane, out of the rising sun. There was a figure in the prow, silhouetted against the light, arms raised. The lane ran between two- and three-storey stone buildings and we were jammed cheek to cheek. As the skiff came, the magi in the prow did something that made the ground shake and pulled the buildings on both sides of the lane down on top of the people. This mage was a woman, clad in red, and her mouth was open as if she were screaming too, in utter terror of herself. I saw buildings collapse behind her, falling like tiles on a game-board and crushing people by the dozens, as she swept towards us.

'We were swept along by the crowd, everyone frantic to escape this terrible queen of destruction. People fell and were crushed. I clung to Falima as we stumbled over the bodies of the fallen, propelled helplessly towards the closed gates and towering walls of Hebusalim. Raz was carving a way through for us, hurling people aside, his shouts inaudible beneath the dreadful rumble behind us of buildings collapsing and the screams of the dying. Suddenly he darted sideways, yanking Falima and me out of the press and through the doors of a tiny dhaba. The crowd stumbled past, rushing headlong to their deaths.

'Falima had hurt herself, but he had no time for that. "Come!" he roared, pulling her over his shoulder. He led us through the shop, past a frightened family cowering inside. "Out! Out!" he bellowed at them, never pausing as we ran into a back yard where, unbelievably, a donkey was staring at the sky placidly, chewing his feed. Then there came an awful *crack*, as if the earth itself were splitting, and the dhaba collapsed, falling away from us in a deafening smash. A blast of air knocked me sprawling into the donkey, which kicked my left shoulder, and I felt my shoulder-blade break, the most awful pain. The donkey found its feet and was gone, the gods only know where. The tumult moved on to the next building and the next, leaving all the world covered in swirling dust.

'We choked helplessly, until the dust began to settle, showing us the extent of this horror. The whole row of houses were destroyed, collapsed by the woman-magus in the skiff as she soared by. Dreadful new sounds were audible: people trapped beneath rubble. Raz was kneeling, his arms about Falima. He looked at me. "Lakh-man, you live!" he coughed. "Ahm protect us. What have they done?"

'*What indeed!* And *why?* What could possibly justify this carnage? What could they possibly want that they could not get by trading with us as friends? Where was the need for war? Where were Meiros and his Bridge Builders? Where were the gods, to see this dreadful crime and let it happen?

'"We have to move," said Raz, who seemed to me at the moment to be a demigod, so full was he of tenacity and courage. I felt I was in the presence of greatness, and this gave me courage. My shoulder was in agony, but I was determined not to be lacking. We climbed over the rubble, trying not to think of the hundreds, maybe thousands, trapped beneath. Behind us the Rondian skiff was running along the wall of the city, raining down lightning and arrows on the archers on the ramparts. Then it turned away from the wall towards us and headed for another alley, the one we were heading towards. We froze.

'The red-clad mage woman was perhaps one hundred yards away, close enough to see clearly, and approaching fast. Her face was bone-white, her hair the colour of an orange. Behind her a tall, pale-haired man was shouting orders, his face composed. They swung to the mouth of the alleyway, just above the roofs, and the four archers started firing indiscriminately. That alley was as packed as ours had been, and the people were still unaware of what she was going to do – they had not seen the destruction she had already wrought. Raz kissed Falima, told her to wait, and ran towards the alleyway that the skiff was about to destroy. I thought he had gone insane.

'He leapt a fence in a superhuman bound, then made a great leap through the first-floor window of a house. I was *stunned* – I had heard of men and women doing amazing feats when they forgot their limitations, but to *see* it! Raz tore through that building, and still I could not see what he intended. He emerged onto a roof, as another awful *crack!* drew our eyes back to the head of the alley, where the mage-woman had begun to collapse more buildings. Raz had put himself in her path. Falima fought me to go after him, and with my broken shoulder I could scarcely hold her back.

'Raz Makani emerged onto the roof as the skiff surged forwards, buildings falling to either side as it passed. The noise of destruction and the howl of the mob assaulted my senses. Falima clung to me as we watched Raz. He was holding a length of timber and crouching down, and as the building beside his began to fall, he pushed off and began to run towards the skiff as it soared to a point before him. His own roof began to collapse. Falima hid her eyes.

'Raz reached the lip of the building just as it began to topple and propelled himself through the air – it was *impossible*: he was carrying a piece of timber that would take four men to bear! Yet he flew straight at the skiff – I saw him strike it! The heavy spar he carried battered the entire crew, sending them straight into the close-packed mob below. I cried out exultantly, but the witch at the front did not even stagger. She saved the officer beside her too. Raz lost the spar, and sprawled against the mast of their skiff. Just the pale-haired officer and the witch remained aboard. Raz drew his scimitar and they crossed blades, he and the pale man, as the witch tried to regain control of the falling craft, which skewed sideways, veering towards Falima and I as they descended. I will never forget the sight of Raz Makani, raining frenzied blows against the Rondian's straight sword, and the witch-woman shrieking as her skiff struck a high wall on our left and with a crunching sound plummeted to earth. The hull splintered with an almighty crash.

'"Stay here!" I shouted to Falima and then I was clambering through the rubble towards the broken skiff. All about me Dhassan men were pouring through the still-standing buildings, people Raz had saved by his actions, dozens of them, snatching up weapons, spears or swords or knives or pieces of wood, desperate to strike back. My broken shoulder in agony, I clambered onto a shed roof and found the perfect vantage point as the Dhassans reached the mage-woman.

'She was in great pain, but she pulled herself upright against the side of the skiff. I realised with a shock that she was very young, barely twenty. She had an angular face, with tiny freckles scattered over her white skin. Her loose-curled hair was bright gold, and streaked with ash. Beside her, the officer had stumbled to his feet and lifted his sword as the first of the Dhassans tried to leap the wall. The witch raised her hands and blazed a bolt of blue light into his chest. The Dhassan, just a youth with a stick, was flung backwards, but two more came, and again she raised her hands and sent a stream of flames at them, torching them as they came. One fell backwards, howling, but the other came down in the courtyard and the captain stabbed him through the chest. I was terrified, too afraid to move least her dreadful fires be turned on me, but I could not look away. The witch screamed to her gods and wave after wave of fire billowed from her hands as she charred man after man, but still they came, those Dhassans! A madness had taken them, now they had an enemy they could reach. Women joined the charging press, brandishing makeshift staves, and they died too, burned to a crisp. The incinerated dead piled about the walls of the yard. The officer cut down those few who got through. He fought like a cornered lion. And her: I could see every strained line on her face, and it was then that I realised a new thing: she was crying, weeping as she killed. She wasn't even seeing the people she slew now; she was just staring at her hands as if she were appalled at what they were doing. As if they were not hers.

'Then I saw Raz! He was lying inside the skiff like a corpse, but I saw him move. The Dhassans were still coming, climbing the smouldering dead with deliberate steps now, exhausted and impeded by their own dead. Men and women, a few soldiers, all moving like the walking dead of stories, knowing they were doomed, but attacking anyway. The mage-girl kept killing them. I realised one of her legs was injured, and her fires were less now. She was exhausted, using her last energies.

'Raz struck! One second he was lying there, his hand straining towards his fallen scimitar, and then he was up and sweeping his blade at the witch's neck. In that split-second she was helpless. She never even saw the blow coming, so consumed was she with her dreadful labour. But the blow never landed. The straight-sword of the officer interposed as he flung himself between Raz and her. She was batted to one side and I saw her shin snap in two even as the Dhassans broke and fled. Only one remained, a girl-child who had been clinging to her mother as she joined that awful assault. The mother was a blackened corpse now, but the girl walked on, too shocked to comprehend. The witch saw only movement and blasted away, and I could see her eyes widen, saw her desperately trying to retract her spell, but it was too late. The sight of that child broke her concentration – she had flinched when she should not – and the consequences were horrible: her own hands burst into flame.

'She knelt in the sand, staring wide-eyed as her hands became blackened pieces of bone. The child shrieked and fled. All this distracted the officer, and Raz stabbed, his blade piercing the man's mail and thrusting right through his belly and out his back. Raz twisted and wrenched it clear, bellowing in triumph as the man fell. The witch turned, her eyes wild, her hands just stumps. She must have been in agony, but she pulled some last reserve from her very soul. Her hands were useless, but her eyes flashed and fire poured from them, two funnels of awful heat and flame that flung Raz backwards, his robes alight.

'That broke me from my trance. I leapt down and kicked my way through the fences into that dreadful arena. The witch was bent over, her head bowed, her shoulders shaking. Her hair hid her smoking face. The officer was trying to crawl to his fallen sword, clutching his belly. Raz was rolling about, beating the earth. I ran to him, keeping well clear of the officer. The witch heard me and looked up, and I nearly screamed: where her eyes had been, there were now two blackened craters. She had burnt out her own eyes delivering that last dreadful gout of fire. She whimpered a name: *Vann*. Her officer's name, perhaps, for he had found his sword and was dragging himself to her side.

'That sword he pointed in my direction. The threat was clear – but I wanted only to aid Raz. I threw myself onto him, beating at his burning robes, until he went still. When I could look at him, the sight was dreadful, but he was alive, and a hero, had there been any there to acclaim him. I turned him over and looked for something to succour him. There was a water-trough against the wall. I crawled to it, cupped my hands, though the pain of using my left arm was immense, and carried a few drops to him. All the while the officer watched me, one arm around the witch. Her lips were moving and pale light was forming in filigrees around her hands and those blackened pits on her face. I remember feeling utter terror, that she would repair herself and tear me limb from limb, but she didn't. She slumped against the Rondian.

'To my surprise, he spoke in Keshi. "Here," he said, and pulled off his helm and tossed it to me. "Water." I was stunned, but I filled it and bathed Raz's burns. I drank some myself, then on an impulse I filled it again and placed it just within his reach, though I couldn't explain why. He fed it to the girl-witch, who murmured something, looking at Raz strangely. She said a word I didn't know: *Dokken*. I learnt it means "dark" in their tongue. What she meant I have no idea.

'Had I called for aid, they would both have been taken, but I would almost certainly have died, and so would Raz. I am not a hero like him, so I remained quiet as a mouse. The only thing I found courage to do was to ask the officer, "Why?" He just shrugged. "Orders." *Orders*. I felt sickened. They had no more idea why they were killing us than we did. I stared at him, aghast, and he looked back at me, clearly in dreadful pain – his belly wound was one of those that kills over hours and days – And he muttered, "Sorry," finally; "I'm sorry." Then the witch said something, and his attention focused back on her. She was shaking uncontrollably, but a web of light was still crawling over her skin and face, and I could see cuts and scratches vanishing, and the bones in her leg knitting together – it appalled me, somehow. She touched his belly, and the light spread. His breathing became less ragged. Then she sagged and stopped, just her chest rising slowly, her mouth open, her breath hissing.

'The Rondian tossed the helm back to me and said, "More water.

Please." I wanted to fling it away, to hurt him, but instead I filled it and carried it to him. If I had been a hero, maybe I could have snatched away his sword and slain them both – but I didn't. I helped him drink, and we talked a little. His name was Captain Vann Mercer; he was the son of a trader and had come here as a child with his father, selling furs. He asked me of my home. It was surreal, to talk with an enemy about home while all about us the city was being destroyed, but for a time we were alone in the world, the only survivors. He told me the witch was just eighteen and would likely be blind for life. His voice told me he was in love with her, would care for her regardless.

'Finally, a shadow fell over us, another skiff, and before I knew it, there were Rondians all about us, carrying the witch and the captain to safety. I thought they would kill me and finish off Raz, but the captain said something and they left us. Then they were gone, up into the air.'

Ramita and Huriya stared at each other, realised the other was crying. They looked back at Ispal. This was nothing like the story they had been told before; the tale of Raz and Ispal they knew was colourful and funny. But this dreadful story rang true.

Ispal gave them both a measuring look. 'I have told you different versions of that story before, to protect you, but that is the true accounting of how Raz and I became brothers. I brought them south with me, for though he was burned dreadfully, Falima never left his side. She married him, and bore his children: she was as heroic as he, Huriya. Your parents loved each other with a love that towers above we mortals. Be worthy of them.

'Ramita, I tell you this tale to honour my friend, my brother Raz Makani, but also so that you know what your husband-to-be has let loose. I do not believe him evil, but he permitted an evil thing to happen, and he is tormented by this. He seeks to give recompense to the world. You must help him. Respect him, but do not fear him.

'Remember also the reason Captain Vann Mercer gave me for this treacherous assault: "Orders". Daughter, you are going to meet men who give "orders". Beware of them, I beg you. People do the worst evil when they do not have to take responsibility themselves but can blame others.

'And third, I want you to remember that these ferang, for all their power and strangeness, are also *people*. That captain, and others I have met since, have been as much a mix of good and ill as any person I could name here in Baranasi. Condemn an evil deed, but know that few men are fully evil; most just follow "orders".'

He shook his head. 'I hope this tale will help you understand the world a little. It is a muddled, complex place, and anything can happen, with no clear moral or purpose. Sometimes I wonder if all the gods are blind.' He looked up at the moon. 'Maybe the moon has made them all go mad.' Without another word he leant over the girls, blessed them both and left.

The girls were silent, stunned by this new version of family history. They clung to each other for hours, but neither slept for a long time.

When Tanuva shook Ramita awake it was still dark outside, but the moon was on the other side of the sky and dawn was beginning to glimmer in the east. 'Come, daughter. It is your wedding day.' Her voice sounded haunted.

Huriya snored on in the corner, her head thrown back in abandon. Ramita envied her, exhausted from vivid nightmares of witches with burned-out eyes. Ispal was waiting downstairs in the kitchen and together they knelt beside the tiny fire he had kindled. The twins were asleep there, wrapped in blankets, since their room had been taken over for the wedding. Pashinta let herself in the back door. There was water and a bowl of curd into which Tanuva was stirring rice flakes. But first they had to bathe in Imuna one final time. Ramita wrapped herself in a blanket and they walked through the pre-dawn alleys, treading the familiar path to the ghats. In Lakh there were always people around: men stumbling home drunk or servants scurrying about some task while their masters slept. Traders, sleeping in the streets to guard their tiny stalls and shops, from sturdy buildings to holes in a wall, even just space for a blanket on the ground. A lonely cow, mournfully watching them pass. The alleys were smoky and filled with river-mist.

Other women joined them, rising from their doorways as they passed: Tanuva's friends, come to share in the final preparation of the bride. Ramita had known them all her life, but now she loved them, wanted to be one of them, to grow old among them – but the gods wanted her to go north with a strange old man who had doomed the world.

There were ten women, the most auspicious number, clustered about her as she disrobed and walked into the Imuna, letting the cold water stroke her thighs, her belly, her breasts, her face. *Wash me away, Imuna. Wash me away, and leave just a husk to go on. Let my awareness remain here always, whilst an empty shell lives out my mortal life. Hear this prayer, Holy River.* But if Imuna heard, she did not care to grant this wish. Maybe the river was listening only to the women about her praying for her to enjoy a happy and fruitful marriage. Her soul remained firmly in her cold, wet body as she emerged from the river into a warming blanket. The chanting women waited for the sun, which rose golden and burned through the mist, pouring light upon all the other hundreds and thousands of people here, to the left and to the right, all with their hands raised to greet the dawn.

At last there were no more excuses, nothing that remained to be done. She felt numb, in no way ready, despite all the prayers and privations. Her mother and Pashinta took her hands and pulled her erect. Their faces were stony. Time did not wait, even for her.

At home her parents fed her with their own hands, then Ispal led her quietly back to the bedroom, where a fresh nightdress lay, a new one, not even a hand-me-down from Pashinta's daughters. She squeezed his hand, then shooed him away, pulled off her sodden shift and put on the virgin linen. Within a short time she was snoring as deeply as Huriya, who hadn't moved.

When Ramita woke again it was well into the morning and Huriya was lying there waiting for her eyes to open. 'Sal'Ahm,' she murmured.

'Sal'Ahm,' replied Ramita, a lump in her throat. *My wedding day.* Her stomach felt queasy. She would not be able to eat again until the wedding feast. *The next time food passes my lips, I will be married to that dried-out old man with dead eyes.*

'Let's go and see the gifts,' urged Huriya, 'and pick out what you're going to wear.' However sorry Huriya might be for Ramita, she was eager to go north and see the world.

She wouldn't lift a finger to stop this wedding if she could.

Hand in hand they went downstairs, where the kitchen was in full flow. Cakes and biscuits were piling up in heaps as they were swept off the griddle by gap-toothed aunties. Pots of daal were being stirred, perfuming the air with chilli and garlic. Jai and his friends were outside playing cards in between chores. Musicians were tuning their instruments in the yard. Ispal was at the centre of things, giving instructions, paying helpers, but her mother was the one really in command, giving 'hints' to her husband whenever something specific was needed. Everyone was singing or gossiping, the noise so loud she wondered how on earth she had slept so late.

When her parents saw her, they both came and hugged her. 'Every day is a gift,' Ispal whispered, 'but you will remember this one above most others. Cherish it, my dear daughter.'

How can I? Yet she put on her dutiful face as they all went upstairs to the twins' room, a stale little cell with no windows now piled high with mounds of vegetables and piles of bundles, her wedding gifts, unwrapped by her parents. Ispal lit a candle, then lifted a blanket covering a lumpy mound on the bed. Ramita caught her breath as Huriya clapped her hand excitedly. The light of the candle was reflected everywhere, in golden brocade, glittering jewellery, silver chalices and brass statuary.

'Gifts,' Ispal said hoarsely, 'from Antonin Meiros to his wife-to-be.' He wrapped an arm about her. 'You will be the finest bride in Baranasi.'

She gaped, speechless at the sight of more riches than she had ever dreamt of.

'Vikash Nooridan was given money,' Ispal murmured. 'He went with his wife to the finest shops, the ones the princes use – that

bull of a ferang captain went with him. Vikash says that his wife
nearly fainted with the pleasure of it. Come, choose jewellery; you
too, Huriya, you also are my daughter. But remember, Ramita, you
will wear your mother's wedding saree. These others will be for other
occasions. When you are visiting the princes of Hebusalim, perhaps.'
He looked almost happy for a second. Then he turned and left the
room.

Tanuva picked up first one item then another, staring at them
with glassy eyes, then she simply fled, her eyes streaming. Ramita
went to follow, but Huriya caught her sleeve. 'She needs to be alone,
sister.' The Keshi girl picked up a necklace, fondled it greedily, then
thrust it at Ramita. 'Try this on!'

They spent a long time going through it all. Ramita was too
stunned to comprehend that all of this was hers, but she enjoyed
Huriya's almost ecstatic pleasure at the wealth spread about them.
The Keshi girl was in her element, and her boundless enthusiasm
drew Ramita in. They sorted through the earrings, nose-rings and
lip-studs, the bangles, anklets, rings and the necklaces, until rubies
and diamonds and even pearls seemed as common as the chickpeas and lentils in the kitchen below. They caressed the silken saris
and salwars and dupattas, stroking the heavy brocade as they
marvelled at the intricate patterns and vivid colours. Ramita gave
to Huriya the things she most drooled over for the sheer pleasure
of her reactions.

'Isn't this worth it?' Huriya demanded. 'He's just an old man –
he'll die soon, and then we'll be free and rich.' Everything was 'we'
for Huriya now she was permitted to accompany Ramita north, but
Ramita was grateful for that. She needed a 'we' because she couldn't
do this alone.

Late afternoon, the Rondian soldiers arrived, stepping into the
colour and frenzy like steel bugs. Captain Klein tramped through
the gate and his jaw dropped at all the garish ribbons and the brightly
attired women of the ghats. His brutish face loosened into a hint of
a smile as he took it in, though he was clearly still nervous about
the press of people. Everyone stared at him, this outlandish creature

straight out of a story; he certainly looked the part of a ferocious Rondian giant.

Only once all day did she think of Kazim, after a disturbance in the alleys, when she thought she heard him call her name, but nothing happened. Meiros' guardsmen kept everyone away, even the curious street-toughs sent by Chandra-bhai, the local crimelord. Ispal would need to hire guards to stop other men from robbing them – they had never had possessions worth stealing before. For the first time it occurred to her that this new wealth might be a mixed blessing. How would the princes receive a newly rich trader? She began to chew her lip as every new difficulty occurred to her.

No one noticed her silence with so much going on. Some of the older men and women were dancing gently, and the smell of cooking was drawing people of all description. Ragged skin-and-bone children were begging at the gate and whenever she appeared, everyone stared at her. When it became all too uncomfortable she went back inside and slowly, reluctantly, began to prepare in earnest for the evening's ordeal. Time was both frozen and racing past.

She and Huriya washed in the tiny privy with a bucket of hot water. Once they were dry, an army of women crowded into their dressing room, gushing over their saris. Then they saw the jewellery, and were struck dumb. Ramita saw their faces change as it dawned on them that however mysterious this marriage was, there were very material reasons why it was happening. Some of the faces turned envious, peering at Ramita as if wondering: *Why her, why not my daughter?* Others fawned over Tanuva, praising her motherly skills, reminding her of past generosities. Her mother, sensing the change in mood, chased everyone out, declaring that the girls needed time and room to get ready. Only Pashinta was allowed to stay, her tough face sober as she helped clear the room. Tanuva looked on the verge of tears as she called out to Jai to watch over the gifts.

The girls dressed in silence. Only Huriya took pleasure in the riches they hung about themselves. Ramita's handed-down wedding saree was a richly patterned maroon and gold piece, the best – indeed, the only fancy piece of clothing the family had owned before today.

It was a family treasure; this would be its fifth wearing in eighty years. For all that, it was the plainest saree here, outshone by the new ones purchased with Meiros' money.

Ramita felt strange to be hung with gold and gems when all she had worn previously was cheap brass and cut glass. The big looped nose ring piercing her left nostril and fixed to her ear by a chain felt especially uncomfortable, as if it might pull her ear off. The gold and glass bangles on her arm clattered with every movement. Pashinta powdered her face, rouged her cheeks and coloured her eyelids in black kohl. They took a bowl of sandalwood paste and marked her face in a dot pattern sweeping from cheekbone to cheekbone, in the traditional bridal patterns. It took for ever.

Pashinta looked at her critically. 'You are a pretty girl, Ramita. Your groom will be well pleased.' She knew who that groom was, of course. Tanuva trusted her with such secrets. 'Ramita dear, you are doing a brave thing,' she murmured, 'but I don't think this is an auspicious wedding. You are being asked to fly too high. We are simple people. We are not meant to have gold and gems and silks and riches and to walk with princes. Ispal, Vikash and all the other men, they are thinking only about money. I pray you will not be the one who pays the price for their greed.'

'We'll be all right, Auntie,' Ramita said in as firm a voice as she could muster. 'Father has done a good thing.' The assertion sounded hollow, even to herself. *I have to believe I am doing this for the good of my family. I cannot afford to doubt.*

Pashinta looked away. 'You are a good daughter, Ramita. Parvasi watch over you.' They heard a blast of trumpets outside, and everyone froze. Pashinta looked from the window, her face stricken. 'By all the gods, he is here.'

Ramita sat on her piri stool in the kitchen, her henna'd hands clinging to Huriya's so hard her knuckles were pale. She could hear everything and see nothing as Pashinta, in the traditional role as female friend of the house, greeted the groom. Beside her, Father was perspiring thickly. Conch shells blew and the assembled women chanted as they sprinkled rosewater over her groom as he entered the courtyard. She shut her eyes tight and began to pray. This was no dream. Instead of marrying Kazim, as she had prepared her life, she was to be given to a elderly stranger and taken to another land.

'Where is Kazim?' she whispered to Huriya.

Her friend whispered through her veil, 'He's at the Dom-al'Ahm, with Father's body. He told me to tell you that he misses you, that he loves you, that he will be yours for ever.'

She peered through her veil, not fooled. 'What did he really say?' she demanded.

Huriya hung her head. 'Stupid, foolish things,' she said in a flat, unforgiving voice. 'He's angry. He has these new Amteh friends and won't talk to me any more.' Her face hardened. 'If he doesn't need me, then I don't need him.'

Oh Kazim! Don't hate me. I will always be yours, whatever happens.

And suddenly there was no time left. Her mother brushed the back of her hands with trembling fingers, then went upstairs. It was bad luck for mothers to watch their children wed. Huriya handed Ramita two banana leaves, one for each hand. She drew them under her veil, then lifted them to cover her face. She quelled her mounting panic. *I will not disgrace my family.*

Jai and his friend Baghi came in, clad in gleaming white and orange, their faces grim. They bent over her and seized two legs each of her piri stool. 'Ek, do, tin,' Jai muttered, and they straightened. She had to let go of Huriya's hand as they carried her awkwardly into the courtyard to the sound of conches and deafening ululation. She could see the outline of her groom in his pale robes, standing in the middle of the tiny yard, his guards about him. Jai and Baghi bore her around him slowly, the seven turns required by ritual. Meiros, his face hidden deep in his hood, followed her progress. Through the veil, she caught fragments: Father's face, beaded with sweat; Huriya's greedy eyes; a sea of straining faces. Finally the seventh circle was completed and she was held before him. The marigold garland about her shoulders filled her nostrils. She hid behind the two banana leaves and waited.

Meiros raised his arms and pulled back his hood. The entire crowd sucked in their breath, finally able to see the mystery groom. Whoever they had been expecting, it wasn't a whiteskinned old man. She heard gasps of pity and anger as they compared his ancient features to the youth of his bride, and murmurings: how dare Ispal sell his daughter to this old pallid creature? It was an affront to nature. She felt the tension rise about the crowded courtyard.

Pandit Arun stepped through the soldiers and laid a garland of marigolds about Meiros' neck. She cowered behind the banana leaves and closed her eyes. She felt Jai and Baghi lift the front of her veil and settle it over Meiros' head, and the world shrank to a tiny space. The torches and lanterns cast a reddish light through the lace. She could hear his breath, smell his rosewater scent. *He smells old . . .*

Vikash Nooridan's voice intruded, speaking Rondian words to Meiros, explaining the ceremony. 'My lord, this is the unveiling of the bride. You must await her. She will lower the leaves when she is ready and gaze upon you. Then you must exchange garlands.'

She was not obliged to hurry. For a second she thought about remaining motionless for ever.

'Well, girl?' came that dry, rasping voice, speaking in Lakh.

She swallowed. 'My father does not think you are an evil man,' she found the courage to say.

A small chuckle. 'That puts him in a minority. I suppose I should be grateful.'

'Is he right?' she dared to ask.

That made him pause. His eventual reply was reflective. 'I've never believed that a man is good or evil. Deeds might be, but men are a summation of their actions and their intentions, words and thoughts. I have always done what I thought was best.' He laughed bitterly. 'Not everyone agrees.'

She opened her eyes, stared at the trembling leaves. 'Will you treat me well?'

'I will treat you with respect and dignity and honour. I will treat you as a wife. But do not expect love. I have none of that left. Death has claimed those I loved and left that river dry.'

'Father says you had a wife and a son?'

'My wife died many years ago. My daughter is barren. My son . . .
My son was murdered. They bound him so that he could not reach
the gnosis and then tortured him while he was helpless. Then they
butchered him and sent me his head.' His voice lost its flatness. It
was tinged now with loss and anger. Then emotion fled, and the dry
voice said, 'I am sorry to take you from the life you thought to have.
I cannot give you that life, but I can make this one comfortable, and
filled with beautiful things.'

I don't want your beautiful things, she wanted to say, *I just want Kazim.*

'Who is Kazim?' he asked.

Her heart lurched as she finally realised that this man was not
just ferang, but a true jadugara, a magician who could pull thoughts
from her mind. She felt a shuddering jolt of fear. 'The one I was to
marry,' she whispered.

'Ah. I am sorry.' He sounded vaguely regretful. 'You will be bitter,
to have your life so rearranged to be the broodmare of some ghastly
old man. I can't help that. I can only say that this life will have its
rewards also, beyond what you can imagine. But I cannot give you
back your dreams.'

They fell silent. Outside their tiny tent the hushed crowd, held in
suspense, strained to hear the low conversation. Would she refuse him?
What would happen if she did? The moment dragged on and on.

Finally, somewhere inside herself, time ran out. *Kazim, forgive me.*
She slowly lowered the leaves and stared into the watery blue eyes
of the jadugara. They were alien, unreadable. His grey hair and beard
were thin and straggly. His face had none of the traditional Omali
groom-marks. His lips were thin and his demeanour impatient. His
eyes widened slightly as he took her in.

*How do I seem to him, with my dark skin and painted face, my patterned
hands and glittering jewellery? Does he see all the way into my soul with
his jadugara eyes?*

'Why me?' she whispered. 'I'm just a market-girl.'

His eyes never left hers. 'I have great need of children, and you
are highly likely to breed many, quickly. I have divined that the path

of greatest safety lies in siring children swiftly, to a Lakh wife. When I say "safety", I mean not my own, but that of the whole world. There must be children, multiple children of the same birth, to you and I. Those children will be magi, and they will unify the Ordo Costruo and bring about peace. I searched long, but life is perilous here and lineage often uncertain. You are the only one to have the requisite genetic history and race, and I am nearly out of time. You – and our children – represent a chance to stave off disaster, assuming it is not already too late.'

'I am just your broodmare,' she said flatly.

'I am sorry,' he repeated. 'I have no fable of love with which to comfort you. There is only this hard fact: you have the requisite genetic and cultural mix. I will treat you with dignity, but I must also sire children, and that will not be dignified at all. If you must know, it fills me with shame. I never wanted this. I have my pride. I can see the revulsion in your eyes when you look at me. I am no old lecher who craves young girls, but I have no choice. Believe me, I wish I had.' He stopped and half-smiled. 'I think these young men are tiring of holding you, girl.'

It was as if her instincts decided for her paralysed mind. With trembling hands she pulled the garland of orange flowers over her head, reached out and jerkily placed it over his head. He did the same, smoothly and calmly. She heard the sigh of the gathered people, the letting out of anxiously held breath. A few people cheered, but most just stared. Then the veil was pulled away and she was in the middle of a sea of dark faces, white eyes and teeth gleaming in the torch-light. Smoke and incense hung in the air, almost choking. She found her cheeks wet with tears and could not wipe them, for her hands were locked in his garland, shaking wildly.

Meiros was taken into the kitchen where a fire waited, to complete the ritual. Jai and Baghi, panting now, carried her in and placed her before the fire-pit. Huriya, at the door, reached out and stroked Ramita's arm as she passed. Only her father, Vikash, Guru Dev, Pashinta and Pandit Arun were within. 'Now come the vows, Master,' Vikash Nooridan told Meiros.

The jadugara turned and offered her his hands. He pulled her to her feet, surprisingly strong. Her legs felt wobbly, sore from sitting for so long. She shivered as cool, bony fingers tightened around hers: patchy white skin coiled about young dark hands. Her throat was tight, her breath laboured.

She scarcely heard the words spoken, about loyalty, about trust and companionship, about duty. Gods were invoked, blessings made. Then Vikash instructed Meiros to walk about the fire three times. She followed him, stepping on plates and shattering clay pots, kicking over candles and little cups of water, following tradition, as Arun chanted the prayers and propitiations. Then her hand was joined to his again and they slowly promenaded together about the fire. The final circuit. They were wed.

She felt faint and dizzy, and clung to Meiros' arm while people cheered uncertainly. Ispal called Tanuva downstairs, and she embraced her weeping parents. They both looked nervously at Meiros, and then Ispal cautiously extended his hand. Meiros took it briefly and inclined his head slightly to Tanuva. Then Huriya bustled in and kissed Ramita and hugged her. She looked fiercely exultant, as if this wedding was something she had laboured long towards.

You are the only truly happy person here today, Ramita thought.

The Keshi girl curtsied saucily to Meiros and then struck a pose. 'Music!' she called to the drummers and sitar players, and they started a familiar tune. Huriya spun, then stopped, her body arching, breasts straining the fabric, then she danced about that tiny space, graceful, light-footed, nimble. She twirled graceful patterns with her hands and arms, her face alive, expressive. It was a story-dance from Kesh. Ramita saw all the northern soldiers drink in her curvy body and narrow waist, especially the monstrous Klein. The gold ring in her belly-button held a bell that tinkled as she spun and swayed. People clapped, the drumming increased and Jai called out in a loud voice and leapt in beside her, clapping his hands, cavorting about, dancing a fierce male role. She had never seen her brother look so masculine, and she felt a surge of pride. Then everyone was dancing as if this were a wedding like any other, a day of universal joy and celebration.

Food platters appeared before her and she realised just how hungry she was, and dizzy with the stress and strain. Meiros led her to a waiting carpet and settled her on cushions. Up close, she noticed that the air about him shimmered, at times seeming almost to push her away. It gave her a prickling sensation. He noticed her curiosity and leant towards her. 'I am shielded,' he told her. 'From missiles. You will become used to it.'

Shielded: another display of his mysterious magic. She inched away from him, her skin crawling.

Meiros fed her with his hands, as tradition demanded, and she him. He seemed almost human now, laughing at her shaking hands that missed his mouth most of the time, but all she could see in her mind's eye was the way she had imagined this would be with Kazim. *Where are you, my love? Do you know what is going on here? Do you care?* She caught a sober glint in Meiros' eyes and stilled her mind, afraid again. *Will I always have to guard my thoughts around him?*

'No, you won't,' he said, startling her by answering the unspoken question. Then he flinched, as if cursing himself, and added, 'I'm sorry, I should not be listening. I will teach you how to protect your mind. It isn't hard. In the meantime, my apologies.' She shuddered, not in the least consoled.

Her husband – *that old man beside me is my husband!* – looked to be enjoying the occasion, and whenever anyone dared to meet his eye, he nodded graciously. Still no one but she and her family knew his name, for fear of what might occur. Klein still glowered over everything, misliking this chaotic press of people. *Clearly my new husband has dangerous enemies.*

Traditionally there would be singing and dancing until the bridal couple left, then the married women would shepherd their daughters away and the hard drink and ganja leaf would appear. The gamblers would bring out cards. It would be a long and wild night. But Ramita could dance only with her husband tonight, and she did not think him a dancing man. Anyway, she did not want to dance.

The moon, nearly full, sailed over the buildings, bathing the celebration in silvery light, and she whispered a prayer to Parvasi: 'Watch over me, Queen of Light, and watch over my Kazim. Speed him my love.' Then she glanced guiltily at the old magi and let her mind go still.

10

Soldier of the Shihad

The First Crusade

In 904 I was a young soldier. Our generals had told us that the Dhassans were murdering our people in Hebusalim. A letter from the emperor exhorted us to save our brethren. Yet it took all our courage and discipline to set foot on that Bridge. I remember the incredible tension – would Meiros collapse his creation beneath us, sending tens of thousands to a watery grave?

What would Meiros do? Some prayed, others were fatalistic. All were terrified! But Kore was with us, for we travelled safe to Southpoint. I cannot remember kissing my wife as passionately as I kissed the earth the day we set foot in Dhassa, the crossing behind us and Hebusalim already in flames.

JARIUS BALTO, LEGIONNAIRE, PALACIOS V, MEMOIRS 904

*Aruna Nagar, Baranasi, Northern Lakh,
on the continent of Antiopia
Shawwal 1381 (Octen 927 in Yuros)
9 months until the Moontide*

Kazim regretted everything he had said, every insult he had hurled at Huriya, who was so obviously delighted to be going north with Ramita, all the things he'd shouted about Ramita's willingness to marry another.

I was wrong: Ramita has no choice. This is not her fault – and by now Huriya will have told her everything I said and she will think I don't care. She will think I hate her – I never meant to wish her dead. The fortune-teller promised that she was my destiny, so why is this happening?

He *had* said those words, though, pouring out his grief and fury

171

at his self-satisfied little sister. He would have struck her if Haroun had not restrained him and taken him back into the Dom-al'Ahm. He'd stayed with him until he calmed.

Now it was mid-afternoon and Ramita would be sitting in the courtyard, attended by her family, awaiting the nuptials that night. Was she missing him? *I never meant it when I told Huriya that you should slit your own throat before you let that old man touch you. Please believe that!* But he still felt that way, deep inside. *The Kalistham* was full of tales of women who found the courage to end their own lives rather than be shamed – one of the Scriptualists had come and spoken of them after Haroun explained his plight. But he could not bear to think of Ramita taking such a path.

Ispal's greed led her to this – and Huriya is worse! She's going north now. She cares only for her own gain. And she knows who this suitor is and will not tell me, the faithless slattern!

He was determined to interrupt the wedding, though Haroun argued against it. He listened to his new friend out of respect, then as soon as his back was turned, he slipped away. *I cannot do nothing*, he told himself. His imagination was tormenting him with visions of Ramita's eyes, wide in agony and terror as the ferang lowered himself onto her and took what should be his. He stole a bamboo rod from a drover and went striding through the streets, snatching up a flask from a drunk lying in a gutter. Cheap, oily liquor flooded his mouth, unpleasant fuel for his anger. He marched through the neighbourhood until he stopped by a great press of people, a full block from the Ankesharan house, jamming the street as everyone strove to catch a glimpse of the strange goings-on.

One of Chandra-bhai's thugs recognised him and laughed, 'Some other guy's marrying your little slut.'

Kazim bellowed like a bull and swung the rod, smacking the man across the face then kicking him in the belly when he went down. 'Ramita!' he howled, calling out her name over and over as he fought his way through the crowds, swinging his stick with brutal carelessness. An old auntie got knocked aside, children were thrown against walls as he screamed, 'Ramita, I'm coming!'

He staggered into a space and found his way blocked by a huge ferang. Kazim swung at him, but the ferang blocked the rod on his metal-clad forearm. His face was an ugly, broken-nosed block of flesh with narrow eyes beneath a helm of steel. A huge fist swung at Kazim's head.

Kazim arched his back and let the blow pass, hammered a punch into the massive frame before him, right into the belly. His fist met steel and all but broke his knuckles. A blow struck his shoulder and knocked him off-balance. People shouted and clambered aside, clearing a tiny space, too small for dodging. The big Rondian crouched and spread his arms. Kazim grabbed a cooking pan simmering on a brazier, scattering roasted cashews about him and swung, making his foe's helmet ring. *Got you!* He hit him again, but the big man refused to go down, smashing a fist into Kazim's belly. He folded over, air blasting from his mouth as his vision blurred. People cheered and threw him back at the Rondian, stomping their feet. Everyone loved a fight. The big Rondian grinned and opened his arms.

Kazim threw a few punches, but this wasn't like fighting Sanjay. It was liking hitting stone. Then he was caught and borne to the ground, the Rondian landing on him like a falling building. He tried to buck him off, but the weight was too much. The first punch mashed his ear and sound distorted weirdly, then the second crunched sickeningly into his face. He felt his nose break. A third punch left him all but senseless.

The Rondian got off him as he lay whimpering like a child. The crowd had fallen silent. Kazim burned with pain and humiliation. Those huge hands reached down and pulled him upright. 'Don't come back, boy,' the Rondian said softly in Keshi, 'or I'll pulp you. Understood?'

He nodded mutely, nearly passing out at the movement.

'Good. Now piss off, you little fanny. Don't come back.' He shoved him against the wall and buried his fist in Kazim's belly, leaving him vomiting in the gutter. Heavy footfalls receded into the crowd.

When the Rondian had gone, sympathetic hands and faces surrounded him and gently tended him. One man straightened his nose, which had swollen like a kalikiti ball, and they bathed the cuts the man's gauntlets had left on his face. He almost wept with shame and thwarted fury, but everyone patted him and told him he had been brave to face the filthy ferang. *None of you leapt to my defence*, he thought sullenly; *in fact you threw me at him!* But he said nothing. A couple of youths took him back to the Dom-al'Ahm, half-carrying him through the bustle of the market.

There were worshippers everywhere, gathering for the evening prayers. Somehow it was almost dusk. *Even now, Ramita must be— No, don't even think of it!*

Haroun found him after prayers. 'Kazim, my friend – what has happened? Where were you?'

Kazim's head swam. 'I went to a wedding.'

Haroun understood immediately. 'Ah, my foolish friend. I see they were not hospitable to uninvited guests.' He shook his head sympathetically. 'I will bring some water. You look terrible.'

'I'm going to kill the bastard who did this,' Kazim swore.

'Who was he?'

'A massive Rondian pig, built like a bull, with a face like a puckered arse-hole.'

Haroun laughed grimly. 'That's most of them,' he said. 'They are a singularly ugly race.'

They both laughed, a hollow and bitter humour they could not sustain against the oncoming silence.

Kazim sat by the grave of his father, watching the sun rise on the morning after Ramita's wedding. The night had vanished in the flasks of arak he and the young Scriptualist had shared and now Haroun slumbered beside him, childlike in repose. *Ramita, where are you? Did he hurt you? Did you fight him? Did he bloody your beautiful body as he ruined it?*

After scrounging some food they returned to the Dom-al'Ahm for the midday lesson. Jai appeared and knelt beside Kazim just as the Godspeaker began, speaking of the shihad: 'All able-bodied men are summoned,' he said. 'We must slay the infidel and retake Hebusalim.

You are called, my children, all of you, Amteh and Omali alike. Glory awaits, in victory or in death. Ahm has a hundred virgins awaiting each soldier martyred in battle. He is calling each one of you.'

Afterwards, Jai told him that Ispal was house-hunting, and soon they would leave the old house they'd built themselves, the family home of generations, where Jai and Kazim had been born. The world had turned on its head.

'And Ramita?'

'Gone,' Jai replied. 'Father and Mother went to see her this morning. They're gone now.'

His heart lurched. *What is left for me here?*

The Dom-al'Ahm became his home. Behind it were kitchens that fed all-comers, meagre but wholesome fare. He ate there twice a day and slept in a blanket in the lee of the dormitory of the Scriptualists. A new life grew from the ashes of the old.

An old soldier called Ali was teaching swordsmanship in a field outside of town, out of sight of the prince's guards. Even Jai joined in when he could. 'It is a good skill to have,' he would say, one of few Omali among the dozens of Amteh youths present. He wasn't very good, but Kazim kept the others from bullying him. Haroun, being a Scriptualist, did not join them, of course, but he watched intently.

Kazim had always excelled in athletic pursuits, and as the days went by he found he was beating everyone, Ali included. Veteran warriors were watching him, Haroun told him. Kazim felt a grim surge of pleasure when he said, 'They are impressed with you, my friend.'

Ramita was his first thought each morning and his last at night; she was in all of his prayers, the vision that pushed him to run harder, to fight harder. In his memory she grew ever more beautiful.

On the last day of the month, Jai didn't go home. The three of them sat together, swearing blood-brothers, pledging to the shihad. Jai renounced the Omali faith and became Amteh. Haroun sponsored him, Kazim supported him and he didn't even go home to say farewell. 'They are spoiled with greed,' he told them. 'They are no longer my family. Ahm is my father and you are my brothers.'

The next day, they wrapped what little they had in bundles of cloth and joined the small column marching north through the morning mists to join the shihad.

11

Graduation

Magic and Ethics

There are many ways in which the gnosis can be used. As some are unpleasant, harmful, immoral, or bestow unfair commercial or social advantage, there are codes of behaviour required of magi. These are strictly enforced by the Inquisition. The Inquisition resides as part of the Kore and is answerable directly to the emperor.

ORDO COSTRUO COLLEGIATE, PONTUS

Norostein, Noros, on the continent of Yuros
Noveleve 927
8 months until the Moontide

Noveleve brought the first flurries of snow to the streets of Norostein, making the cobbles treacherous. The Alps to the south turned wholly white and the clouds closed in. Buckets of water iced up and fires billowed smoke as frigid wind swirled through cracks and crannies. The watchmen wrapped thick woollen scarves about their helms and huddled around braziers warming their hands and sipping from flasks of brandy. The bitter winds brought illness, streaming noses and hacking coughs. Every day someone else was found dead in the shanties on the northern side, usually a rake-thin homeless child who had given up and lain down to die.

Each morning the recruits for the Crusade marched down to the stableyards on the Lukhazan road, singing hymns. There were thousands of them, practising with spear, sword and bow. Some days Alaron and Ramon went to watch. The young recruits stared at them curiously, but stayed away, their eyes filled with something between resentment and awe. Magi were far above the common soldier.

This morning they had a different errand, visiting Alaron's mother in her country manor. His father had lent them horses. The town woke, summoned to the dawn service by sonorous bells, as they wound their way through the streets. Outside the city walls the ground was white and the hills merged seamlessly with the clouds until it felt like they were moving inside a smoky white bubble. Sound travelled for miles, from the axe-blows of the woodcutters on the high slopes to the calls of the farmhands herding their beasts. Crows cawed as they hunted and squirrels chattered from the branches of ice-encrusted trees.

Ramon puffed warm breath over his hands, sending steamy clouds into the air. 'Mater-Luna, it is *cold*. I should be in bed, not sitting on this bastard horse.' He glared at Alaron. 'It's all your fault.'

'You didn't have to come,' Alaron replied. 'I owe Mother a visit, now the exams are over. And I seem to recall you saying how nice it would be to go for a ride, so how good of me to arrange it for you!'

'Yes, but I was talking about that barmaid last night.' Ramon smirked. 'She was flirting with me, I swear.'

Alaron rolled his eyes. 'Gina Weber is prettier.'

Ramon's mouth twitched. 'Coming round, are you?'

Alaron shrugged. 'Everyone is treating it like a done deal, and I don't appear to have a say in it so I might as well look on the bright side.'

'Welcome to the real world,' said Ramon. 'I've probably already been sold off by my village. I'll arrive home and be married the next day. At least she'll be Rimoni, not some big fat northern milkmaid with a butt like the rear-end of a cow.'

Alaron gave him what he hoped was a steely look. 'Better that than a scrawny Silacian twig.' They glared, then grinned at each other. 'Anyway, Mother's housekeeper Gretchen bakes honey-cakes on Freyadai. We should arrive just as they come out of the oven.'

'Okay, you have my interest again.'

'Do Silacians keep their brains in their belly?' laughed Alaron. 'Hey, listen, Father says the emperor himself is at his Winter Court in Bricia – that's only a few days' ride north of us, isn't it, just across the border. Governor Vult is there too, he said, everyone important – even Empress-Mother Lucia.' He made the sign of Kore.

'They're all thieves and murderers,' sniffed Ramon, who liked to say outrageous things.

'Not the Empress-Mother,' asserted Alaron. 'She's a living saint! Everyone loves her.'

'You're such an innocent! It never ceases to amaze me: it's only a few years since the Revolt, and yet you Noromen still believe such shit. Living saints – ha! We Silacians do not forget that Lucia Fasterius probably murdered her husband, changed the succession so that her favourite son wrongfully became emperor and has been virtual ruler ever since. We Rimoni have not got such short memories!' He tapped the side of his skull. 'Near my village there's this valley where a Fire-mage trapped a Rimoni centurion and his men in the trees and burnt them all alive. The ground is still ash-black. My village might have a Kore church, but there are Sollan drui in the forest who keep the old hallows.'

'It was an amazing feat though,' Alaron mused, 'to conquer all of Yuros with three hundred magi.'

'Three Hundred *Ascendants*,' Ramon corrected him. 'That's enough power to burn the Sun! Don't forget, the Rimoni legions had no cavalry or archers then, they just threw javelins – fat lot of good that would be against a flying Ascendant two hundred feet above. It would've been like a turkey-hunt. These days there's better armour, better weaponry and better tactics, and the Ascendants are all dead or senile and drooling into bibs.'

Alaron threw up his hands and laughed. 'I would just love it if you said these things in class. Can you imagine Mistress Yune if you did? The old battle-axe would turn purple.'

'I didn't want to get thrown out until I had completed,' sniffed Ramon.

'It'll all be over next week,' Alaron said with a grin. 'Graduation – I can't wait!'

'Si, that's the only thing keeping me here. Just give me a periapt and I'll leave gratefully. Even if they don't, I'll get hold of one. You can get anything in Silacia.'

'But if you don't graduate they'll not give you licence to use the gnosis!'

'Who'd know? The Rondians never come to my village. They all live in legion camps, and the nearest is forty miles away from where I live. There are so few Rimoni magi – even if I don't graduate I'll be treated like a king at home.' He looked at Alaron. 'What about you, amici? You going to be a good boy, marry Gina and work for your father?'

Alaron sighed. 'I don't know yet. Maybe I impressed one of the recruiters? My Auntie Elena was a Volsai – perhaps they might want me too.'

Ramon screwed up his nose. 'You don't want to be one of those bastido, Al. There's only one thing we hate more than a legion battle-mage and that's a sneaking Volsai, scrying out secrets and locking up people to torture and blackmail. If those fellators offer you a job, you tell them where to shove it.'

'Aunt Elena isn't like that – she was a Grey Fox.'

'Then she's the only decent Volsai there ever was.'

Presently they entered the woods about Anborn Manor. He'd been born here, lived here the first eight years of his life, tended by a nurse and then a private tutor while his father was off trading. His mother would lie abed, or sit propped in a chair. She was always in pain from badly healed wounds. Her face was drawn, her scarred hands like the claws of a gargoyle. Her ruined eye-sockets were empty, though she could still see by using the gnosis. He'd always found it unsettling, the way her scarred sockets followed him sometimes.

His parents' marriage had disintegrated gradually. Father always said she had been a laughing, vibrant young woman once, when he'd fallen in love with her, even though she was magi and he was just a soldier, captain of the squad assigned to protect her. Though the Crusade had been cruel to her, leaving her burned and broken, Father had stayed loyal to her, and soon after their marriage Alaron had been born. For a time they had been something like happy, then Tesla had turned back into herself, tormented by her disfigurement. Her screaming used to wake the whole house as she unconsciously set the bed linen alight, tortured by nightmares of dark faces closing in. During the daytime she was bleak and bitter, taking it all out on Vann. It had seemed to the young Alaron that she was trying to drive her husband away, despite all he'd done for her. He didn't understand her, and neither did Vann. Father had taken Alaron and moved into their current house in Norostein when he couldn't bear it any more, leaving Tesla behind in the Manor with servants to tend her. He paid, and Auntie Elena sent money whenever she could. Alaron sometimes suspected his father had never forgiven himself for not staying.

Alaron had only met his Aunt Elena a few times. She was a curt, hard-faced woman with a dancer's body. Last time she'd questioned him at length over his skills, listened blank-faced to his statements about what was and wasn't fair in the world and then lost interest. She was no friend of his father's either – he'd heard them arguing after he was sent to bed. He hadn't seen her for four years, but at least she kept the money coming.

The woods were tangled and dank, the trees choked with twisted vines and ivy. Crows were the only birds that thrived, and their harsh cawing grated on the boys. Then Anborn Manor suddenly loomed out of the trees, revealed in all its dilapidated glory. The lawns had degenerated into matted clumps thick with frost and the pond was covered in black ice. There were broken shutters and missing roof tiles, and dead moss blackened the walls. The whole edifice looked as if it were slowly tumbling down. A single wisp of smoke rose from one of the many chimneys, blue-grey against the stark sky.

'Look, there's Gretchen,' said Alaron, pointing to Mother's housekeeper, his old nurse, who was lifting an armload of firewood. She was wrapped in a faded red blanket that was stained with ash and dirt. Her hair was white as the frost.

'Master Alaron,' she wheezed, 'come in, come in – I'm about to open the oven.'

After they'd tethered the horses beside an old stone water trough and kicked a hole in the ice Alaron hugged Gretchen. Ramon offered to rub the animals down while Alaron helped her with the wood. *She has to be sixty by now*, he thought with a faint chill. She'd aged badly these past few years.

Alaron found his mother in her old rocker in the sitting room, wrapped in a blanket. She cringed at the sound of the door opening. He had once seen an oil painting of her, done before she left for Hebusalim: she'd been a vibrant, redheaded beauty, like a robin dancing in the sunlight. Her hair was grey now, and her eyeless face ghastly.

'It's me, Ma.' He went up to her and kissed her forehead. She smelled of confinement and old age. He backed away quickly and found a seat.

'So, you've finally remembered you have a mother, eh?' Her voice rasped like sandpaper.

'You know I had exams, Mother. They finished last week.'

'Did you?' she said, with little interest. 'All grown up now, eh? Off to fight the rag-heads, are you?'

'I don't know yet. Father wants me to work with him.'

'Better that than war, boy. I should know, shouldn't I?' She clenched and unclenched her ruined hands. The healers had tried to repair them, but they were near-useless.

'*Everyone* is going—'

'Let them go – they're all fools. Let 'em all burn. You stay whole and safe, boy, that's my advice, take it or leave it.' She scowled. 'Is Vann still trying to pawn you off on that self-important little Weber girl?'

'Uh, yes.'

'Huh. Don't waste yourself on her, boy. Do I hear your thieving Silacian friend outside?'

'Uh, yeah. Um, the governor was at the exams. For the first part, anyway.'

'Belonius *rukking* Vult?' She leaned forward. 'Silk-mouthed piece of dung sold us all down the river at Lukhazan. I wouldn't trust him to tend piglets.'

Alaron gave up trying to have a normal conversation and looked about. The windows were so dirty you couldn't see through them. Heat radiated from the overloaded fireplace. He wished he'd never come, just like always.

Finally Ramon came in, flushed from seeing to the horses. 'Good morning, Lady Tesla. There's a windship over the valley, flying in from the northeast. Is there a shipping lane through here now?'

'No, they all swing north of here and take the Kedron Valley into Bricia. They must have a blind navigator.' She sneered bitterly.

'Come and see, Al,' said Ramon. 'I reckon it's one of the Norostein fleet.' They excused themselves quickly. 'How is she?' Ramon whispered.

'Good,' Alaron replied. 'In one of her better moods.' It was true: she hadn't sworn at him yet, or called him an ungrateful wretch.

Outside, they shaded their eyes and squinted at the silhouette making its way towards the Manor. 'What are they doing?' Alaron wondered aloud. 'There's nothing out here. They're going to be dragging their keel through the woods if they don't get some lift.' He squinted. 'Look, that's a landing signal,' he added in surprise, pointing to a rigger waving a pennant.

'*Rukka mio*, it is too!' Ramon exclaimed.

The shadow of the windship fell over them and a huge anchor plummeted from the hull, its chain rattling. The anchor struck the turf, gouging the lawn until it bit and dragged the ship to a halt. Shouting men furled the sails, ladders were thrown down and a squad of soldiers descended, led by a sergeant. 'We're looking for Lady Tesla Anborn,' he said. 'Does she dwell here?'

'Yes sir,' said Alaron quickly, trying to make a good impression. 'She's inside. I'm her son.'

The sergeant was an older man with a bristly stubble and heavy jowls. He seemed friendly enough. 'Vann's boy, eh? My name's Harft – I know your Da.' He called up to the windship. 'This is the place, Grand-Magister, and she's in.'

'Excellent.' A mage leapt lightly from the side of the windship and floated some thirty yards to the ground, his control immaculate.

He was middle-aged, balding and sleekly plump, dressed in rich red and gold clothing, with an iron chain about his neck: a council mage. Alaron thought he recognised him from the city, though he couldn't recall the name. 'Who are these boys, Harft?'

'I'm Alaron Mercer, sir,' Alaron said. 'This is my friend Ramon Sensini. We're student magi, sir.'

The council mage took in Ramon's foreign name and looks with a narrowing of the eyes. He looked at Alaron. 'My business here is with your mother,' he said brusquely. 'It is council business.'

Alaron wondered what on Urte it could be. 'My mother is an invalid, sir. I'll take you to her.'

The council mage shrugged. 'Very well. Your friend can wait here. I am Grand-Magister Eli Besko. You'll have heard of me.' He strode towards the house. Alaron threw a worried glance at Ramon, then hurried after him. The sergeant grunted and followed.

Grand-Magister Besko paused to allow Alaron to open the door for him and then strode into the house, ignoring Gretchen. 'Show me to Lady Anborn,' he ordered, and Alaron felt a coil of anger at the man's manner, Grand-Magister or not. But he did as he was told.

The sergeant came in behind, throwing an apologetic look at Gretchen.

Tesla Anborn stiffened as Alaron opened the door to the sitting-room. 'Mother, there is a council mage here. He says that—'

Besko interrupted. 'My name is Grand-Magister Eli Besko. You will know of me.'

She wrinkled her nose. 'Besko? Found an office job during the Revolt, I recall. Yes, I remember *you*, Eli Besko. How is your *fourth* wife? Managed to find one you can quicken yet? It's a shame buggery doesn't work that way.'

'I will keep this brief,' Besko stated, his face colouring.

'Good. The less time you spend here the better.'

Besko scowled, then drew himself up. 'Your sister, Elena Anborn, has betrayed the emperor. She has been declared a traitor and a price placed upon her head. Her assets are subject to seizure. Consequently her majority share in Anborn Manor has become the property of the Crown. You are hereby evicted, with effect from month-end. If you have any contact with her, you are to report it to the council immediately. That is all.' He looked around the gloomy room. 'It will probably benefit your health to get out of this rat-infested pit anyway.'

Alaron stared at the man in horror, but his mother just laughed harshly. 'So, Elena finally became a liability to that shifty creep Gurvon Gyle, did she? I hope she sold him down the river for all he had.'

Besko ignored her. 'Madam, you have until 30 Noveleve to find some other filthy hovel in which to end your years.' He half-turned away, then paused, looking at her slyly. 'I understand you have a good library here.' He jingled a purse before her blind face. 'I have gold.'

'Go and stick it up your boyfriend's arse.'

Besko snorted, spat into her lap and turned.

He ran straight into Alaron's fist.

Alaron had been seething from the moment Besko addressed his mother, and his temper stoked higher at every word. Besko's message shocked him: that Elena could be a traitor was inconceivable, however little he knew her. That the council could strip away his family's property was surely wrong. And the man's manner was insufferable. He was swinging before he'd even thought the thing through, and his fist hammered into the man's nose with a satisfying crunch, sending the Grand-Magister reeling.

Before he could follow up, big arms enveloped him from behind and Sergeant Harft hissed in his ear, 'Stop it, you fool!'

Alaron struggled furiously until Magister Besko's bleeding furious face pushed into his and all of the air in his throat stopped moving. For an instant he didn't recognise what the Magister was doing, then he panicked, flailing desperately, unable to make a sound. He tried to counter the Air-gnosis, but without a periapt his efforts were pitiful. His vision swam as Besko laughed and pulled back his fist.

'Sir, stop – he's just a boy—' Sergeant Harft swung Alaron bodily away from the blow. 'Your career, sir!'

That made Besko pause. He wiped his bloody nose on his sleeve and glowered at the sergeant. 'What does it matter if I throttle the little turd?' He twisted his hand and the force tightened around Alaron's throat.

His mother snarled distantly as Alaron felt himself begin to pass out, and then all of a sudden the pressure was gone and he fell against the sergeant, gulping down air despite the pain.

Besko spat again. 'Ah, I suppose you're right, Sergeant. He's not worth it.' Besko's face loomed in front of Alaron. 'Hear that, boy? You're not worth it, and you never will be.' He turned back and repeated, 'Out by the thirtieth, you old hag,' then stormed out of the room.

Sergeant Harft gently set Alaron on his feet. 'Are you okay, lad?'

Alaron tried to speak, but his throat was agony. He nodded.

'I'm sorry, lad. I had no idea what this visit was about. I am sorry, ma'am.'

'Get out of here, Harft,' Alaron's mother snapped, then her voice mellowed. 'And tell your Maggie hello from me.'

Harft nodded as he backed out. 'Yes, ma'am.'

Alaron sat on the floor and massaged his throat.

'So, you've got the family temper, have you?' Tesla said. 'There might be hope for you yet. But you've got about as much sense as your aunt.'

'Wha—?' Alaron tried again, as the pain in his throat lessened. 'What did Auntie Elena do?'

'I've no idea,' Tesla snorted. 'Volsai business. They're all evil rukkers, those pricks. Your aunt fitted right in, I'm sure. She was a heartless little snot. But she knows how to sink a knife in. I hope she gave those bastards hell.'

The Great Hall of Norostein was packed with the well-to-do of Norostein, especially the magi, for this was a night for all of the descendants of the Blessed Three Hundred to show off their wealth and status as the newest graduates were welcomed into the fold. Marriage alliances would be made or confirmed, careers would be launched. Rich non-magi paraded their own children, hoping to catch

the eye of the young men and women who were the centre of attention: the day belonged to the graduates.

Normally the governor presided, but as matters of state required
his presence at the Winter Court in Bres, the Noros king was here.
His position had been emasculated since the Revolt, but the twenty-
two-year-old king was nonetheless an important figure. His father
had been executed after the Revolt and he himself had spent most
of his life confined in Lukhazan Palace. The slim, rather timid young
man looked out enviously at the real powerbrokers of his kingdom.

Alaron was in his best grey robes. His hair had been cut and glowed
reddish in the gnosis-lamps festooning the hall. His father was with
him. His mother was still at the manor, after his father lodged papers
with the council to forestall the eviction. The papers proved Elena's
funding was legally a gift and therefore could not be confiscated,
and thus Tesla Anborn could not be evicted – but without Elena's
payments they could not afford to keep the manor anyway. It made
Alaron's graduation all the more imperative.

Ramon, standing beside Alaron, was tricked out in his Sabbadai
best, but neither could match the opulence of the Pure as they
swanned about in gilded velvet hose and doublets, fingers adorned
with gold rings, their fine leather boots polished to a mirror-finish.
All the women sighed at Malevorn, Seth and Francis as they swaggered past, bowing to all of the graduation candidates from the girls'
Arcanum, kissing hands and making florid compliments that had
the girls simpering and blushing. Alaron watched the trail of adoration they left behind with disgust. Then he saw the Webers arrive
and ducked behind a pillar, but he hadn't been quick enough. Gina,
a serious-looking girl, detached herself from her father and walked
towards them. Her straight blonde hair was coiled into an old-
fashioned bun; she looked like she was intent on going straight from
schoolgirl to matron.

'Hello, Alaron.' She held out her hand. She was wearing a green
and gold velvet gown with a plunging neckline that drew his eye
despite himself.

'Uh, hi,' he answered weakly. He stared at her hand. *What—? Oh yeah!* He flushed red and bent over it, not quite making contact.

Gina struck a pose. 'How did your exams go? Are you confident? My best was in Clairvoyance and Divination.'

'Um, good. Yeah.'

Ramon leaned in. 'Buona sera, Donna Weber.'

She snatched her hand away. 'Oh, hello – are you still here? What was your name, sorry?'

'Shaitan. This is part of my realm.'

Gina curled her lip faintly. 'Mmm. Oh look, Father wants me.' She pointed to where her father was bending Vann's ear. 'Shall we join them, Alaron?' She offered her arm.

'Um, I – I'll just get a drink. Ramon?'

Gina sighed irritably and stalked away.

'Changed your mind again, amici?'

'She's an insipid cow.'

'Nice wide hips, though,' observed Ramon. 'Good for child-bearing.' Alaron blushed while Ramon cackled, discomforting the well-to-do families about them.

'You're disgusting,' declared Alaron. 'I'm going to miss you.'

'Of course you are. Being stuck alone with Donna Weber will be no fun for you at all. No sense of humour.' Ramon snickered. 'Fills a bodice nicely, though.'

Naturally, the Pure couldn't resist calling past. 'Ah, the two failures,' sneered Malevorn. 'I'm surprised you bothered to turn up at all. Neither of you will pass – especially you, you little Silacian slime,' he told Ramon.

Francis Dorobon looked down his nose at them. 'You know, my kingdom has thousands of Rimoni scum in it. You can't trust any of them. They're all thieves and liars.'

Ramon eyed Francis. 'Then why don't you go back and see how long it is before you get a stiletto in the back, O Beloved King?'

'My family's restoration to the throne of Javon is well in train,' Dorobon said loftily. 'The Crusade will ensure my rightful place is returned. I think my first act as king will be to round up all the Rimoni vagrants and have them crucified.'

Alaron took a step towards Francis, angry words forming, but Malevorn interposed himself and they stared into each other's eyes, noses nearly touching. 'You have something to say, Mercer?'

All of the beatings he had taken at Malevorn's hands flashed before his eyes, and every drop of resentment sang in his mind. 'Yeah, I've got something to say. You're a gutless coward who—'

Malevorn spat in his face and he spat back, his spittle striking a small shielding an inch from Malevorn's face. The pure-blood blew it back nonchalantly, spattering Alaron's own spit into his face. 'Got something in your eye, Mercer?' He smiled. 'Don't make an exhibition of yourself just yet. You wouldn't want to be thrown out and miss the big show.' He turned away.

Alaron grabbed his shoulder. 'Hands off, you little worm,' he snarled and grabbed Alaron's wrist, wrenching it painfully. 'Don't ever touch me again. *Ever.*' He shoved Alaron back and he and his friends swaggered away.

Alaron winced, but the worst thing was seeing other mage-born parents smirking behind their hands at his discomfort.

A bell rang and a herald proclaimed the beginning of the ceremony. They filed into the main hall where the governor heard plaintives and supplicants. His ornate throne remained empty in his absence; the king had to sit in a plainer seat below it. All about the room, the pillars and arches were carved into leaf-motifs gilded with gold paint. The painted ceiling depicted the ascension of Corineus. Crystal chandeliers captured and radiated the myriad gnosis lights, and the guests glittered no less. Ladies wearing necklaces with centre-stones of priceless sea-pearl walked gracefully on the arms of magi luminaries. The talk was boastful, while unseen currents of rivalry and influence pushed and pulled.

Alaron tried to restore his spirits by picturing himself as one of them. *I am a quarter-blood after all. That's not so bad. If I can distinguish myself on Crusade . . .* He pictured an audience with the Noros king, no longer a puppet but with full regal authority. *Rise, Lord Alaron, Emancipator of the Realm, approach the throne of your grateful king!*

Right now, the king looked more like a sulky youth as he called for the ceremony to begin. 'Lords and Ladies of Noros, I ask Grand-Magister Besko to begin proceedings,' he said without enthusiasm.

Besko! Alaron felt a tightening of his throat, as if his windpipe could remember the man.

The Grand-Magister began a speech written by Governor Vult, recalling the great traditions of the Noroman magi, speaking of the past glories of those who had graduated from these two premier colleges, Turm Zauberin and Saint Yvette's Arcanum. Names of the better-known past graduates were invoked, many of them present in this room and all of them pure-bloods. None of the generals of the Revolt were named except Vult himself, though many were graduates, and Auntie Elena didn't rate a mention either. The speech did recall Vult's own 'happy memories' of college life, commended the graduates for their efforts and wished them well for their glittering futures in service to the emperor. To Alaron it went on for ever.

Then Principal Lucien Gavius took the stage. He too rattled on for hours, and Alaron's impatience became feverish. He reassured himself by rating his own performance in the exams. By his reckoning his final mark should be in the seventies, well above the requisite fifty-nine and enough for a bronze star – lowest of the merit awards, but still respectable.

Then Gavius was joined on stage by the principal of Saint Yvette's, who called forward her graduates. Gina looked radiantly confident as she received a silver star, a very creditable graduation. *No wonder Da is so keen on her.* He bit his lip, feeling as if the walls were closing in, narrowing his future.

Then it was the turn of the boys of Turm Zauberin. Gavius beamed about the room. 'Lords and Ladies, some years stand out more than others, and this is of course due to the quality of the candidates. This year, we have been blessed with not one but three candidates of unsurpassed quality. I truly believe this year will one day be recalled with wonder, that three such blessed young men illuminated our ancient and revered towers.'

Ramon made a gagging gesture to Alaron.

'The first of these exceptional young men is Malevorn Andevarion.'

Malevorn stood and walked into the middle of the room to collect his results. Mothers' eyes brightened, ageing spinsters licked their lips and daughters clutched their breasts. With his black hair curled about his shoulders, his mature and regal face caught the myriad light and reflected it as if he were haloed, the embodiment of the legendary warrior-magi of the Rimoni Conquests. 'Malevorn is the son of Jaes Andevarion, the great general whose service to the emperor is well-remembered for valiant courage in the face of adversity,' Gavius went on. Alaron snorted softly; Malevorn's father had been a failure and a suicide, disgraced by his defeats at Robler's hands in the Revolt. 'Malevorn has been a revelation, not only for his superlative skill and impeccable breeding, but also his single-minded pursuit of excellence. He has been a model student, ever courteous, thoughtful and supportive of his fellows. He has even attained the status of trance-mage, the first in many years whilst still at college.' This revelation earned an appreciative gasp and rich applause. Alaron watched Malevorn soaking it up, visibly fighting to look humble. *If only they knew what kind of bullying creep you really are*, he thought dourly. Then he reflected, *It probably wouldn't make a jot of difference. They'd admire you even more.*

Gavius awarded Malevorn a gold star, the highest merit. 'Malevorn has accepted a commission in the Kirkegarde, the protectors of the faith. A career of unsurpassed glory awaits.' Gavius took up a periapt of pearl and placed it into his waiting hands. Malevorn could no longer contain himself. He raised his hands to the skies and roared, displaying the glittering gem. Everyone in the crowd applauded at this apparent display of youthful exuberance. Alaron saw it as sheer triumphal arrogance.

After a minute of milking the applause, Malevorn moved to stand to the left of the king's throne. The king looked envious, and oddly insignificant beside him. Gavius started again. 'The second of my "Golden Trio" is Francis Dorobon, the rightful king of Javon. Francis has been a model student who will be sorely missed. To know him is to understand the true nature of breeding, both in terms of gnosis and in terms of manners, dignity and carriage. I commend to you,

Lords and Ladies, Prince Francis Dorobon of Javon.' More applause, more swaggering. Another gold star.

Alaron watched all of this back-slapping with distaste. *When I get my periapt, I'll accept it quietly, not prance around like a show pony.*

Gavius said, 'Normally we give the graduation periapts in alphabetic order, but I am taking the liberty of slightly amending the order. I apologise to these young men for the slight change of protocol when they are clearly dying to know their results. But it is only proper to now welcome to the stage the third of my Golden Trio, Seth Korion, son of Kaltus Korion, Marshal of the South.'

More restrained applause rippled about the room. Alaron wondered whether it was because people remembered Korion from the Revolt, or whether they just knew that Seth was a little prig with no backbone. *It would be nice to think it was the latter, if unlikely,* he admitted to himself.

Gavius fussed over Seth for a while, but his words were more hollow than those bestowed upon Malevorn and Francis. He noted that General Korion couldn't make his own son's graduation, due to the same need that had summoned the governor away. 'It must be something big,' Alaron heard someone mutter. Seth looked stiff and pale as he bowed before the Grand-Magister, receiving his gold star.

You shouldn't have even passed, Korion, Alaron thought grimly, remembering the boy's breakdown at the weaponry test. *I wonder who the exalted Marshal bribed to ensure his son wasn't failed.*

The three graduates stood alongside the throne, not looking at each other. Alaron wondered how they really got on. Egos that size always bump, his father said whenever he saw powerful men together. But Gavius was graduating Boron Funt, who was of course joining the Church. Gron Koll was next, smirking all the while as if he had just played a tremendous joke on everyone there – but none of his 'friends' shook his hand now that they were parting ways. He gave no sign of caring.

Gavius then called for attention. 'Lords and Ladies, I call Alaron Mercer.'

Alaron's heart lurched. He walked forward, feeling as if the air were turning to treacle. He saw faces turn curiously to see the next candidate, politely clapping. He bowed to the king as if in a dream and stood expectantly before Gavius, just wanting to get this over with. *Keep your head down, play it cool.* He caught his father's eye, and he nodded encouragingly.

'Lords and Ladies, the candidate Alaron Mercer, Mage of the Third Rank, has earned a bronze star for his efforts in the examinations.' *Phew!* He allowed himself to smile, as Gavius continued, 'But there is another test our students must pass.' He had adopted a sombre tone. 'That is the test of *character*. In the case of Alaron Mercer, we have found a young man whose ill-temper, insolent bearing, atheist leanings and violent manner are ill-fitted to bear the periapt and serve the empire. We therefore withhold the periapt and declare Alaron Mercer a failed magi. He is forbidden to practise the gnosis or to bear a periapt henceforth, at the pleasure of the Crown.'

The whole crowd stared, utterly stunned. Alaron felt his knees wobble. Only the conviction that he was hallucinating kept him from falling to the floor. But Gavius looked solid and real as he drew himself up, pointed condemningly and thundered the renunciation: 'Alaron Mercer, the Kore and the empire reject you! Get you gone from this place!'

The room was utterly silent. Every eye was upon him. No one had been failed for years, and certainly never on these sort of grounds. He felt as if the ground was gone, that he was both floating and falling, for ever hanging before all the judging eyes. Malevorn's face was alight with pure pleasure. Francis Dorobon was beaming, his features twisted into gloating joy. Seth Korion stared at him wide-eyed, like someone who has just seen a dead man sit up.

Then his father was shouting, 'Gavius you fat shit – you can't do this! You show me your Charter! You show me what gives you the right! I challenge you, you bloated sot – *show me!*' Other voices were raised, but Alaron couldn't tell what they were saying. His ears were ringing, and the words meant nothing. He stared blankly at the fleshy face of the headmaster, and then at the confused and impotent face of the king. Besko was grinning gleefully, pointing a finger at the door. Hands clamped onto his shoulders as sudden fury made him lunge forward, but the guards had him firmly and dragged him out of the hall into the vast emptiness of the reception hall. He saw his father being pulled along behind him, not struggling but shouting, 'I'll see you fired, Gavius!'

I've been failed. This can't be real. This can't *be real.*

The guards released them at the top of the stairs. His father put his arm around Alaron's shoulders. 'We're going to fight this, son, I promise you. They can't do this – not on a *character assessment.* I'm going to take this all the way to the governor if I need to.' He squeezed Alaron tightly.

Alaron had a sinking feeling in his stomach. The faces of the Pure floated before him, Besko's face and Gavius' smirk. He thought about Governor Vult, as pure-blood as they come. What would he care of an injustice done to a quarter-blood merchant's boy? *They'll never let me pass.*

Vann Mercer fought hard for his son, but Lucien Gavius refused to see him and the council stalled him at every turn. His own work suffered while he wasted hours trying to see council members. The Weber family disappeared from his social circle, and so did all the other magi families he knew, to his pain and surprise. He had thought many genuine friends.

Ramon had gained the minimal pass allowable, conditional upon his joining a legion in time for the Crusades and serving for four years. He stayed with Alaron almost every minute. It didn't occur to Alaron until later that it was to ensure he didn't harm himself, as almost every failed mage tried to do. But even Ramon couldn't stay for ever; he needed to return to his village in Silacia, to see to his mother and arrange his affairs before his legion duties commenced.

'I will be married before my feet touch ground,' Ramon joked before he left, but that just reminded Alaron that the Webers had broken off negotiations. He could not even bring himself to wave goodbye.

The festival of the Birth of Corineus passed him by. His father bought presents on Alaron's behalf, because his son didn't have the courage to leave the house. There was no love for failed magi out there; they were easy targets for every bully in the neighbourhood, with no protection from the authorities.

When Vann Mercer finally cornered the Mayor, he was told to stop wasting council time and to desist from his harassment of city officials. He stalked out, vowing to see the governor himself when he returned from the Winter Court. But Alaron curled up into a ball beneath his rug beside the fireplace and closed his eyes. He lay there for hours and let the fire go out.

12

Council of War

The Gnosis

The gnosis is the power of God, granted unto the magi to uphold the Kore.

THE BOOK OF KORE

The powers of the magi come from Shaitan himself.

THE KALISTHAM, HOLY BOOK OF AMTEH

The gnosis is a tool. There is no evidence that Kore or any other deity was involved in its discovery, nor that any divinity has moral control over its wielders.

ANTONIN MEIROS, ORDO COSTRUO, 711

Forensa, Javon, on the continent of Antiopia
Octen/Noveleve 927
9–8 months until the Moontide

Elena saw Cera change day by day as responsibility was thrust upon her. She helped where she could, but there were so many new challenges, decisions and crises that Cera was forced to cope with. Borsa became a substitute mother, wiping away tears of grief and frustration and fury, and she kept Timori sheltered and happy and away from Cera when she needed to focus on the tasks at hand. She had a knack for knowing when seeing her little brother, hugging him close and reassuring him, was just what Cera needed too. That reassurance was becoming harder and harder as the silence out of Brochena stretched into weeks.

The succession laws meant Timori was legitimately king, with his elder sisters legally regents until he turned sixteen – but laws needed swords to enforce them, and a good portion of the Nesti Army had been left in Brochena with Olfuss. In the meantime, Paolo Castellini was charged with readying the Nesti for war. He threw himself with smouldering intensity into drilling the men. He had all the archery targets painted in Gorgio colours; the soldiers liked that.

Lorenzo recovered swiftly, thanks to Elena's healing-gnosis. She was pleased at his recovery, but worried that he saw the shared ordeal as something that bound them together. She did not let him kiss her again – though he didn't stop trying. She didn't quite know why she resisted, especially when she thought of Gurvon and Vedya together, but she resisted the temptation. It would be an ill use of Lorenzo's affections.

At his request, Harshal ali-Assam became their liaison with the Jhafi. When the Rimoni families quarrelled, the Jhafi were usually happy to watch the fracas and align themselves with the winners afterwards. 'This is different,' he told Cera, rubbing his smooth scalp anxiously, and outlined a proposal to bring the Jhafi properly into the Nesti fold. 'The Gorgio won't expect that.' The Gorgio detested the Jhafi, prizing their own 'racial purity' – even if that made them ineligible for the elected kingship. 'There will be a price,' Harshal warned. 'If I can get you Jhafi aid, it won't come free.' He vanished into the desert next day, with Cera's approval.

'Let us learn who our friends are, if Brochena is now hostile,' said Cera, and despatched messengers not just to Brochena but to Loctis and Baroz and even Krak di Condotiori. The couriers were hand-picked by Paolo, and Elena scryed them, following their progress gnostically until distance swallowed them. They were beaten home by a crowd of refugees, including high-ranking Nesti officials with tales of regicide and invasion. The Nesti soldiers had been surprised and overwhelmed in the small hours by a Gorgio army they'd never even suspected of being there. The survivors were chained and sent north to the Gorgio mines.

The refugees confirmed the fate of the king: Olfuss Nesti was dead, and Alfredo Gorgio was in Brochena, surrounded by his soldiers and supporters. He had told the court that Cera and Timori were also dead, and that news had paralysed the people. Fear kept the peace, for now, and the presence of Gurvon Gyle, Rutt Sordell and other magi he'd brought in reinforced that fear.

Solinde was alive, to their relief, though the traders told her the princessa was aligning herself publicly to the new regime. 'She is whoring herself to the Gorgio,' they muttered darkly, telling tales of Solinde dancing with Fernando Tolidi at court, and the handsome Gorgio knight emerging from her bedroom every morning.

Elena tried to reassure Cera. 'There are dozens of ways the gnosis can be used to seduce someone, Cera. You must believe in her.' She could see Cera's faith in her sister wavering. Solinde was legally a regent too; the Gorgio could use her to give their presence the semblance of legitimacy.

Cera created a new Regency Council. Elena was appointed to it, as were Paolo and Harshal ali-Assam, and Lorenzo, Cera's newly appointed chief of her personal guard. They met in the meeting room of Krak di Faradi, though the noise of reconstruction after Samir's rampage was audible through the walls. Elena and Cera let the men settle first before entering. Elena's cheeks were smeared with two bloody lip-prints, which drew first curious and then understanding eyes from those already present.

Several Nesti nobles who had escaped Brochena after the coup were also there: Pita Rosco, the balding and cheery Master of the Purse; sour-faced Luigi Ginovisi, the Master of Revenues, a counter-point to Rosco's optimism; Comte Piero Inveglio, a well-moneyed merchant-prince with wide experience and sound judgement, and Seir Luca Conti, a grizzled knight, representing the landed nobles. He'd brought many of the Nesti men-at-arms safe out of Brochena with him. Signor Ivan Prato, a young intellectual Sollan drui, sat opposite the suspicious and pricklish Godspeaker Acmed al-Istan. They were still hoping to hear from other Jhafi, from Riban and Lybis, but that would depend on Harshal, who had just returned, looking tired but satisfied.

The Amteh had a ceremony, used for public meetings when Jhafi women were present: the Mantra of Family. By naming all present as family before Ahm, the women were allowed to bare their faces. Cera gestured to Scriptualist Acmed, who spoke the words in Jhafi and Rimoni, then Elena and Cera lowered their cowls and Cera brought them to order.

'My lords, you have all heard the news: my father is dead and his head has been placed on a pike on the walls of Brochena Palace.' Her voice quivered with outrage. 'Alfredo Gorgio has come south with his soldiers and occupied the city. Half our soldiers were slain or made captive. There are hundreds of new widows, and I hear the wailing of the women day and night. My sister has become the play-thing of Fernando Tolidi. If he marries her, Tolidi could claim to be rightful regent.'

Comte Inveglio leaned forward. 'Permit me, Princessa: were you yourself to wed, even such a union as proposed by the Tolidi to Solinde becomes irrelevant.' Inveglio had a young and eligible son. 'Your husband would be Pater-Familia, and therefore regent, until Timori is of age. If she weds, then so too should you.' A graceful gesture encompassed those about the table. '*Simplicio!*'

'I assume you would propose one of your sons, Piero?' remarked Luigi Ginovisi, provoking a storm of comments from all sides.

Cera raised a hand and tried to get silence, but got none until she slapped the table.

'Gentlemen! You can disagree all you like, but I will have quiet, as my father would!' She glared, and the men mumbled sheepish apologies. '"Do not marry or war in haste",' she quoted. 'So said my father, and so say I. I do not need to wed: I am Solinde's elder, and she is not yet of age. Without my approval her marriage is illegal. And since Alfredo Gorgio is telling the people that the real Cera and Timori Nesti are dead, that we are imposters, even if I did marry, it wouldn't sway anyone.'

Everyone acknowledged the truth of her point.

'What we need to do is retake Brochena. There are Gorgio in the Royal Palace, and that is a gauntlet thrown in our faces. *That* is what concerns me: my father cut down the Dorobon banner six years ago! Do you want to see it raised again?'

The men growled and clenched their fists at the thought.

'Do not marry or war in haste, the princess says,' said the Godspeaker, 'words from *The Kalistham*. Your father must have read them there. I agree, you should not marry in haste – at least, not in such haste that you do not consider more options than Comte Inveglio's son. There are many strong princes among the Jhafi, and many more swords to be won than an Inveglio could bring you. You have been a virgin long enough, Princess. It is time for you to become a woman, for the sake of your kingdom.'

Cera frowned, uncomfortable at having her virginity discussed so frankly. 'I repeat, I will not marry in haste, to anyone, no matter race or creed. I am not a prize on a game-board! This meeting is about military solutions to a military problem. Am I understood?'

The hawk-faced Godspeaker looked ill-pleased, but Cera pushed onwards. 'Seir Luca, what are our numbers and dispositions?'

Luca tugged on his beard, and reported, 'Princessa, the Nesti maintain a standing force of some one thousand spears, but we can deploy seven times that number at need. The Brochena civic guardsmen stood aside when the Gorgio struck. Who knows where their loyalties lie? Their officers must've been bought off by Gyle before his magi struck.' The knight glowered up at Elena. 'Yet here we have one of his agents at our table.'

Elena glared at him in the sudden silence. 'What are you trying to say, Seir Luca?'

The old knight looked her in the eye. 'Your "colleagues" have killed our king. Rutt Sordell sits at the right hand of Alfredo Gorgio. But here you are amongst us, just as Sordell sat beside King Olfuss.' He stabbed a finger at her. 'Did you know what was planned, Donna Elena?'

Every eye turned to her. Elena took a deep breath, spread her hands placatingly and said, 'That is a fair question – I was, after all, in the pay of the enemy. But let me stress that word: I *was*. I had no more idea what was to happen than anyone here. I believed we were here to stay. And I swear to you all: I had no idea that he was about to do this.'

'He?' repeated Comte Inveglio. 'What "he" is this?' Although he knew the answer, of course.

'"He" is Gurvon Gyle, Comte.'

'Your former employer?' Comte Inveglio enquired, rhetorically.

'As you know.'

'And your lover,' he added, and a small hiss ran around the table.

She felt herself redden, though she'd expected the question. 'No, that was long over.'

'"Long over", is it? When did you last lie with him?'

'A year ago, or more – he has another, and frankly, she is welcome to the lying prick.'

'Was King Olfuss aware of your entanglement?'

'Probably – you were, obviously,' she said dryly. 'But I still didn't know of these attacks. Why did *you* not see it coming?'

'Maybe because no one was whispering it in my ear over a soft pillow,' said the Comte. 'Yes, I know you are still here, Donna Elena, and I know that you fought and killed Samir Taguine – but how do we know he wasn't an expendable pawn in your schemes? How do we know this is not a ruse to win our greater trust and fool us yet again? I believe Gurvon Gyle is the subtlest of men, and such a scheme would be typical of him – so what guarantee do we have that your continued presence here is not part of his master plan?' He looked around the table. Heads bobbed, some slowly, some quickly.

Cera's face was tight and drawn. 'Ella saved my life, and Lori's and Timi's – I saw what she did!' she cried, and Lorenzo nodded emphatically in agreement as she continued, 'This is a waste of time, Comte. I trust Ella, and so should you: she has given up all she owns to stand beside us now. She has lost her fortune, forsaken it to protect my brother and me. She deserves our trust. She *has* my trust.'

Inveglio frowned. 'Has she really forsaken her fortune? If it is held by the man she *says* is no longer her lover, then what has supposedly been "lost" can as easily be restored.'

Elena slapped the table and stood up. 'Fine. I will leave the wards intact. If you want my advice about your enemies and what they will do, send for me. If you don't trust me, work it all out for yourselves.

I am at the service of Cera and Timi. The rest of you can do what you like.'

'Stay!' snapped Cera. '*I* decide who comes and goes here: *I* am regent. You have pledged your service to me, so you come and go at my pleasure.' She glared about her, looking every inch her father's daughter. 'Understand this: Donna Elena is my trusted protector. Without a mage here this meeting cannot remain secret – remember why Father hired magi in the first place! Without Elena we might as well invite Alfredo Gorgio to join us here and now.' She looked up at Elena. 'Last night, before both Drui Prato and Godspeaker Acmed, she swore loyalty to the Nesti, under the highest and holiest blood-oaths, before Sol and Ahm. Her life is mine to command, her hand is mine to give in marriage, her wealth is mine to bestow. Is this understood? Ella is one of us now, until death.' She pointed to the bloody lip-prints on Elena's cheeks. 'Do you wish her to swear again, before you?'

The men mumbled into their laps and shook their heads. Cera motioned, and as Elena sat down she met Inveglio's eye and he gave a tiny nod. *Good, well done.* The conversation had gone as he and she had planned it earlier: if she were to be of use to them they needed to remove any doubts the men might have about her loyalty. Her mind went back to the chapel last night: the incense, the knife slicing open her palms. *I give my life to the Nesti.* It hadn't been a hard decision – in fact, she had taken it the moment she intervened against Samir. Yet she had still felt an almost religious joy as she spilt her blood into the Nesti family chalice cup and watched Cera sip it, then press bloodied lip-prints on both cheeks. Among Rimoni there was no higher binding. To doubt her now was to doubt Sol himself.

'Very well. I will hear no more on this matter. Onwards!' said Cera. She turned to her left. 'Harshal, you've been talking to the emirs. What is the Jhafi reaction to the death of my father?'

Harshal bobbed his head a little nervously. 'Naturally, they are concerned. They believe the Dorobon will return, and keep Javon neutral in the shihad. They are unhappy about this. The Harkun tribes are talking of an uprising against all Rimoni, a purging of the land. The nomads see no difference between Nesti, Kestrian, Gorgio or any other Rimoni House.'

The Nesti men exploded in disgust at this. 'This was a barren desert with a few nomads scuffing around the water-holes before we came,' Ginovisi snarled. 'There was no wealth here, nothing at all! We planted the olives groves and the vineyards; we found the mines and developed them! This land thrives through Rimoni sweat and toil!' Heads bobbed in agreement.

Harshal scowled. 'With respect, these are the words that exacerbate the anger of my people. You speak like there was nothing here before you came, but every city in Ja'afar stood for *centuries* before your arrival. You built none of the Dom-al'Ahm, none of the palaces of the emirs. The wealth you generate here seldom touches the Jhafi, though our men labour in your mines and vineyards and olive groves. We have a truce between us, and some intermarriage amongst nobles, but most Jhafi have few dealings with Rimoni. We are separate nations who happen to occupy the same land.'

Another eruption, this time more defensive, and again Cera had to slap the table to get silence. She motioned to the Godspeaker, who gave her a grudging nod of thanks. Stroking his long beard, he said, 'I too have spoken extensively with my people after services at the Dom-al'Ahm. Our people share your sorrow, Lady. Our grief and anger at the murder of your mother and aunt is real. They were Jhafi, and they were well-loved. We remember the unjust rule of the Dorobon. We are with you in spirit. But we wish to know these two things: what of the shihad? Your father had not given his pledge before he was murdered. And, more importantly, when will you Rimoni finally become one with we Jhafi?' He raised a hand to forestall interruptions. 'Yes, you have followed the Guru's stricture and intermarried, but always as the superior partner: you take a Jhafi noblewoman and make her into a Rimoni so that you can breed people eligible for the kingship. But you remain Sollan, and the young Jhafi girls taken to wife must convert. All of your customs are Rimoni. You attend our religious ceremonies if you must, and then run off to find a drui to *cleanse* you! You pay *lip service* to the Guru.'

He ignored the rumbling from around the table and said sternly, 'You sit on the wealth, you do not spread it: there are no Rimoni poor, but among the Jhafi, except for the ruling families, there are no rich! Your rules prevent all but a few Jhafi from voting when the kingship comes up for election! You look to the Jhafi for support when you are desperate, but do nothing to earn that support before-hand. So now we say: *Why should we support you?*'

A hubbub burst out, but Cera immediately slapped the table and shouted, 'Silencio! *Silencio!*' She glared about her. 'Gentlemen – stop and think before you speak. Stop jumping to defend us as your first reaction: I asked Godspeaker Acmed to join us because it is time we discussed the questions you don't like to hear.' She pointed to a bust of her father. 'One of my father's favourite sayings was "Truth is Perception". It means that what you *believe*, however right or wrong, that is your *truth*, and it will be shaped by who you are, what you've seen, your gender, your race, your religion, your history. So when Godspeaker Acmed tells you that the Jhafi don't love the Nesti, do *not* tell him that he is wrong and they do! Listen to him, and ask yourself: "Why is this their Truth?", and "What can I *learn* from this?"'

The room fell silent. Elena shivered; it was as if Olfuss Nesti were speaking through his daughter from beyond the grave. She watched them, reading their reactions. Pita Rosco, who hadn't said much yet, was nodding slowly. Luigi was scowling. Lorenzo and Harshal were exchanging harmonious glances.

Finally Rosco spoke up, rubbing his chubby chin thoughtfully. 'So, what is it that would align the Nesti and the Jhafi, Godspeaker? What is the price?'

Acmed narrowed his eyes. 'Spoken like a man of money, Master Rosco. I do not talk of coin, though: I talk of faith and brotherhood, and equality before law and before Ahm. We have been bought with gold before, but the money always finds its way back into Rimoni coffers. We have been gifted land that was ours anyway and never yours to give. Rimoni gifts always come with price tags! What will seal an agreement between Nesti and Jhafi must be more fundamental, and though it must start at the top, it must reach the common people.

'Let the Nesti embrace the Amteh Faith. Let the Princess marry a Jhafi prince and bear him Amteh children. Let the Rimoni share the secrets of the vines and olives and mines that make them so wealthy! Let the bread of the Rimoni feed the Jhafi poor. Let the iron of the Rimoni mines find its way into the armouries of the emirs. Let seized land be returned, or at least purchased at a fair price. And let the Rimoni and the Jhafi join our brethren in Kesh and purge the lands of the infidel. These are the things that will win the hearts of the Jhafi and finally make us one nation.'

Cera raised a hand, cutting off the opening mouths of her advisors. 'Wait, gentlemen, for one minute. Reflect on what the Godspeaker has said, then give me considered responses, not emotions.'

Elena watched her and wondered just where her gentle young princessa had gone. Cera was acting like some Senator of Rym, not a virginal young woman. But this part of her had always been there, in the way she bossed her siblings, and how she had gobbled up every word her father spoke. It was in the way she would argue the world's faults and injustices with Elena for hours on end in the blood-tower, surrounded by scrolls of the philosophers and Rimoni senatorial speeches, texts on the deeds of the emperors and religious tracts. She was always a thinker. *I just hadn't realised she could be a leader. And I bet she won't want to give it away when the time comes, either . . .*

As soon as the minute was up, Comte Inveglio raised his hand. 'There is no way we'll be giving weapons and armour to the Jhafi. The output of our mines is the basis of our power – we found 'em, we're mining 'em. Our soldiers must have superior equipment to compensate for our numerical disadvantage. Impossible! *Suicidal!*' He glowered at the Godspeaker.

The drui, Prato, said gently, 'A person's faith comes from the heart. All Nesti children are exposed to both religions. They have chosen to be Sollan – this is what is in their hearts.' He gave a faintly superior smile. 'I have no objection to their being educated in both faiths, of course, but they must be permitted their own choice.'

Pita Rosco was frowning. 'I can't see how we can do more to feed the people. We Nesti have always prided ourselves on our generosity to the poor. We distribute bread, we give water from our wells. If the Jhafi can't see that . . .' He shrugged helplessly.

Next Lorenzo spoke. 'We understand that before he was murdered, the king had elected to join the shihad. But until we can oust the Gorgio from Brochena, we are powerless to do so, even if we did wish to incur the wrath of the Rondian legions and battle-magi. Neutrality may not sit well with any of us, but prudence demands it.'

'And our princess refuses to marry,' remarked Comte Inveglio. 'It would seem that none of the Godspeaker's suggestions are practical.' He looked about him. 'Do we need the Jhafi to win?'

Alfredo Gorgio has you outnumbered about ten to one, thought Elena. *You bet you do.*

Godspeaker Acmed snapped, 'Typical Rimoni – all you offer are sops to buy our souls, and you don't even bother to conceal it.' He turned to Cera. 'If these terms are not suitable to you, perhaps Massimo di Kestria will find them more palatable? Or Stefan di Aranio in Riban?' He started to rise. 'I knew it was a waste of time talking to you.'

'Please, Godspeaker,' Cera said quickly, 'I have not said that I reject your ideas, nor that I agree with what my advisors have said. Ahm willing, we can find a path through this maze.'

'Ahm does not negotiate,' Acmed muttered.

'But men do,' replied Cera calmly, 'and so does this woman.' 'Personally, I find the Godspeaker's suggestions to have great merit. Obviously, these ideas challenge us, and your concerns are all valid. They are a step into the unknown, a leap of faith. We have always dealt with the Jhafi as we would an outsider, yet the Godspeaker is correct: we share a nation, and so their concerns must be heard and addressed. Here is what I propose: we take each one of these suggestions and examine it closely, but not from the perspective of what is wrong with it, but what is right about it. You will have until the end of the month, and your guiding mantra must be: *How can I make this happen?*. I want your most open minds, gentlemen. I want practical, positive plans. We need the Jhafi – and they need us.'

Gurvon Gyle had used this method with his team in the past, and Elena had suggested it to Cera. The men didn't like the idea, but grudgingly agreed to try it. They parted, arguing softly, but their steps were purposeful.

Cera sagged into her chair. Suddenly she looked seventeen again. 'They wouldn't have argued with Father,' she muttered.

'You'll just have to get used to it, Cera. Men argue – but arguments are good; they give you options to choose from.'

Cera exhaled. 'But they're so exhausting!'

'You did well.' She squeezed the girl's cold hand. 'They argue, but they gave respect too.'

Cera lifted her chin a little. 'They did, did they not?'

Promises of aid came in from the provincial lords who feared the return of the racist, oppressive Dorobon family. Massimo di Kestria, Lorenzo's older brother, was the first to respond to Cera's call for help, but the most important response came from Emir Ilan Tamadhi of Riban, a way-station town the Rimoni had never settled in great numbers. Lord Stefan di Aranio was the Rimoni ruler there, but the emir was far more influential. The hard-line Jhafi believed him a Rimoni servant, while most Rimoni saw him as a Jhafi troublemaker. He came east with a large contingent of Jhafi fighting men and built a great tent-city and camel-yard outside Forensa.

Ilan Tamadhi also brought the news they had been half-expecting. 'I have news of your sister, the Princess Solinde,' he told Cera apologetically as she greeted him on the palace steps. 'She is to marry Fernando Tolidi. This has been proclaimed in Brochena Cathedral.'

Cera hung her head. 'Does she seem at all unwilling?' she asked, so softly that Elena, standing close behind, barely heard the question.

'I am sorry, Princessa, but she seems willing. Alfredo claims Tolidi's marriage to Solinde gives Tolidi legitimate claim to Forensa. He says they will march after the wedding and take what is theirs.'

As soon as they were alone, Cera surprised Elena by throwing her arms about her and sobbing tearfully, 'They're going to try and kill us all, Ella – Timi, me, you, all of us! They're going to kill us all!' She clung to Elena like a child.

She's been holding all her fears inside her . . . I forget she's still just a girl. Elena stroked Cera's long hair uncomfortably, thinking, *Borsa is better than me at this*, and murmured, 'We'll be all right, Cera. Next week the Regency Council reconvenes. We will find a way to win.'

'What if there isn't a way?' Cera whispered.

Yes, Elena, what then?

Elena lay on her bed in her tiny chamber outside the nursery. There was no light but the tiny lamp beside the bed. She had lowered her wards, and now she held a little piece of wet clay, a conduit for Gurvon, an Earth-mage, to help him channel. It was slightly risky – he was the more powerful mage, and could do real damage if she wasn't careful. But she had never been one to shy away from risks.

An eye formed in the clay, then another and a mouth. 'Elena.' His voice was in her mind, not her head, despite the movement of the lips in the clay.

'Gurvon. Where are you?' There was a faint echo: he was distant, then.

'Not telling. You?'

'In Pallas, rukking the emperor.'

He didn't laugh. 'By the Kore, Elena, what are you doing?'

'Following my conscience. How could you imagine that I would just stand aside and let you murder the children I have been protecting for all these years?'

'A conscience?' he sneered. 'Whatever passed for your conscience you kept in your coin-purse.'

'I found something worth more to me than money, Gurvon. You wouldn't understand.'

Those clay lips pursed. 'Do you even know how rich we are? We're richer than kings, Ella! We're set for the life we always dreamed of.

Remember that manor by the lake where we were going to grow old together?'

'You and me, Gurvon – and Vedya makes three?'

'Just you, Ella. There's never been anything between Vedya and me.'

'I'm not a fool, Gurvon.'

'You love me, Ella – you told me so yourself.'

'And you laughed!'

'Elena Anborn in love? I thought you jested – but it was true, wasn't it?'

'What would you know of love?'

The clay face grimaced. 'Touché. Well, there is no doubt about who has come out of it better, is there? I have all the money, and you've nothing but a death sentence.'

'Do you have something pertinent to say, Gurvon? If not, I'll just break this link—'

'No, wait! I do have something for you: a final offer. Walk away, Ella. Go to Hebusalim, and I'll send you your money there, every fennick of it. You'll get an Imperial Pardon and you can walk away a free woman. You can go anywhere on Urte you want – except Javon. You'll be out of the game.'

'More lies.'

'No, Elena, I *swear* this is a genuine offer. They want you out of the way, Ella.'

'I'm not abandoning Cera and Timori to you, Gurvon, or *your* emperor, so you can tell his Majesty to go and screw himself. And I never want to see you again.'

The little clay face pursed into a regretful expression. 'But you will, Elena: mine will be the last face you ever see, right as the blade goes in. We're going to come after your little princessa and her kid brother. I've got the whole team here with me: Rutt, Arno, Vedya and the rest. Abandon them, Elena – leave now. It's your only chance.'

'You know I'd never accept such an offer.'

'No, I don't know that. The Elena I knew would.'

'Then you never really knew her, did you?'

'Damn it, Elena, *listen to me!* Surrender to me and I'll protect you – you're my link to the old days, to the Revolt. They were glorious times, Elena: the joy of living, the thrill of the hunt, the best days of our lives. I don't give a shit about Samir, or Vedya. It's you I want, Elena. It's always been you.'

She stared into the little ball of clay and her eyes misted over. Yes, there were good memories, hiding under bridges, screwing beneath the stars, that fox face inches from hers, taut with anxiety or laughing ironically, Gurvon kissing her; sliding into her, making her feel . . .

But there were other things she had tried hard to forget: plunging her blade between the ribs of unsuspecting watchmen; blood spurting from the throat of a farm boy who'd blundered into the middle of a raid; men burning like torches, or drowning as she flooded their lungs; a Rondian officer, screaming as Sordell burned out his eyes with a poker. Things she *needed* to forget.

'Go rukk yourself, Gurvon. I will be the last thing *you* see, not the other way around.'

Those clay lips pursed angrily. 'So, it's true then: you have gone safian. Have you fallen in love with your little princessa?'

'Oh, grow up, Gurvon.' She felt a ball of fury working its way up her throat. 'There is something here you wouldn't recognise: something worth preserving. These are good people, and now they're *my* people, and that's worth more to me than your money – or your so-called "love".'

'When did Elena Anborn ever give a rukk about "love" or "goodness"? What the Hel happened to you?' He sounded genuinely bemused.

Good question. Not sure I even know the answer myself, and yet here we are. 'I could never explain it to you, Gurvon. I'd need to use too many other words you don't know the meaning of.'

'Then you're dead, Elena. You've signed your own execution order.'

The clay ball suddenly became a fist-sized flea-shape that leapt at her face. It splattered against her shields, but as it fell back it was already reforming to spring again. She encased it in blue fire and burnt it dry, smiling grimly at his grunt of discomfort.

'Was that your best shot, Ella?' he taunted as the clay fell to dust, then he was gone.

She lay on the bed for a few minutes and reran the conversation in her mind: *Analyse and question.* What had he hoped to achieve? Did he really think he could turn her this late in the game? Where was he – and what was that faint echo? *That echo . . .*

She sat up, suddenly excited, wrapped a gown about her and went to find Cera.

The midmorning light was pouring into the council chamber from the high windows. They were all prepared for another long day, but there was a new energy about the Regency Council today. Elena and Cera had been awake a lot of the night, cocooned in blankets as they discussed Gurvon Gyle, and now there were plans to be laid.

'All right, gentlemen, Time for you to report.' Cera looked at Pita Rosco. 'Pita, you and Paolo were looking at the question of the poor relief for the Jhafi. You may go first.'

Pita Rosco outlined a scheme for wealth distribution that would gradually enrich the Jhafi without sending the marketplace into chaos or impoverishing Rimoni families. There was much about share-holdings and ownership rights and the renegotiation of land-based voting that made Elena's head hurt, but Cera followed with what looked like real interest, then commissioned a sub-committee to follow through. As the day passed in intense but largely civil debate, Elena and Cera began to believe they might just get through the day without serious conflict.

Naturally, that didn't happen.

Drui Prato started the last item of the day: religion. 'Princess, you asked Godspeaker Acmed and me to find the land some sort of religious accommodation. Clearly this is impossible. Our faiths are so divergent.' He looked disdainful, while the Scriptualist folded his arms and stared into space.

Cera leaned forward. 'So how have you spent the last three weeks, Signor?'

The drui blinked. 'I have prayed, Lady, for wisdom.'

Cera's eyes glittered dangerously. 'Did anything come to you? Any great insights, Signor Ivan? The wisdom of doing as your Regent demands, perhaps?' she asked acidly.

Prato's face went red; he was clearly unaccustomed to criticism from any but a more senior cleric.

She turned on the Godspeaker, who was smugly enjoying his rival's discomfort. 'And what of you, Godspeaker Acmed? How did your attempts to engage with the Sollan brothers go?'

'They would not have wished to talk with us,' the Godspeaker replied flatly.

'That is not what I asked.'

'I am not accustomed to being spoken to thus by a woman – or any man. My status—'

'Your status is beneath mine when you sit at this table. You should be grateful I listen to you at all. I have endorsed your right to speak here, and I have backed your proposals—'

'This is *not* endorsement! This is a sham!' the Godspeaker interrupted. 'Negotiating – swatting around fanciful ideas? This is nothing but a frivolity, a girl's game. A strong leader would not do this!'

Ah, thought Elena, *and here it is. It's a shame it's him. Inevitable, though* . . .

Cera's face went still and cold. 'Only a *strong* leader, Godspeaker? Is *that* what you respect –*strength*?' She almost spat out the word. 'So what exactly is *strength* to you? Is strength *tyranny*? Is strength screaming at servants, beating them? Is strength sending armed troops against the weakest to crush bread-riots? Or inciting violence and calling it God's will?'

The Godspeaker's face went white with anger. 'Princess—'

'*Silencio*,' she roared. '*I have not finished!*' She got up and began to circle the table. 'Is strength the ability to wield a sword?' She snatched a blade from one of the guardsmen and tossed it to Elena. 'Ella, deal with this toy.'

What are you doing, girl? Then she understood, and exerted the gnosis. Both Earth and Fire were needed and she was a poor Fire mage, but her power would suffice . . . She twisted the blade of the sword into uselessness, then handed it back to Cera, who dropped it onto the middle of the table. The men looked uneasily at Elena as she sought to conceal the effort the spell had cost.

'Maybe strength is in gold?' Cera plucked a diamond ring from her finger and threw it out of the window. A dozen pair of eyes watched it sail away. Their mouths hung open.

Elena grimaced inwardly. *I suppose she'll want me to go and find that for her afterwards.*

'Maybe strength is in holy books.' Cera picked up a Sollan Holy Book from the table. For an instant Elena thought she might throw that away too, but instead she dropped it next to *The Kalistham* and pushed them both away from her. 'All of you have been looking at me, thinking you can bully me into doing whatever you want. Well, I can do that that too: I have at my back the greatest warrior in this kingdom. Shall I ask *her* to show you how completely I can bully you if I so choose?'

Elena walked softly to her side, thinking, *Careful, Cera: you need their hearts, not their fear.*

Almost as if hearing Elena's thought, the princess let her voice soften. 'If this is about respecting force, then you may try me – but like my father, I believe leadership is not about bullying, but about consent and about vision. I am *legally* the regent of Javon. If I am not, then who rules? Alfredo Gorgio? Or maybe one of you?' She looked pointedly around the table. 'Would you like to fight with one another for supremacy and weaken us all? Or will you follow this woman, who has never turned away advice? Who is determined to find a solution that unifies us all?'

The men swallowed, then looked at each other. Finally Inveglio said, 'Princess Cera, though I am uncomfortable with your frankness, I recognise what you are trying to achieve. I give you my support.' He looked about the table. 'We of the Rimoni all do,' he added, a challenging note in his voice, daring his colleagues to disagree, but they all nodded.

Harshal ali-Assam raised a hand before the Godspeaker could draw breath and said clearly, 'I too also support you, Princess Cera.' His action forestalled whatever else the Jhafi lords might have said. Ilan Tamadhi gave his nodded approval with a faint frown, then all eyes turned to Godspeaker Acmed.

He sighed, then said grudgingly, 'We continue to talk, for now.'

Cera smiled. 'Excellent. Then here is what we will do. I will pledge to you that within a year, whether we have reclaimed Brochena or not, we will have implemented as far as possible all of Godspeaker Acmed's proposals. Will you accept that? My father said that a ruler must have legitimacy, will and vision. I have the legal right to rule, until my brother is ready to take the throne, and I intend to do so. Signori, I am a woman, but I have the heart of a man and strong men about me. I have a vision that I believe in our hearts we all share, of a united people. This is my quest, my lords: to regain and hold what belongs to Javon – to Ja'afar. Our sovereignty.' She glared at the Godspeaker, who was clutching his holy book protectively. 'Do you still think me weak, Godspeaker?'

He smiled a little. 'No, Lady. The princess is . . . *formidable.*'

'If it helps, don't think of me as female, signori; just think of me as Regent. For I tell you this: I will not wed until Timi comes of age. Get used to it. Everything else might be negotiable, but that isn't.' She half-smiled. 'I enjoy doing this and I'm not going to throw it away,' she said lightly, earning small grins from the men. 'Signori, look at yourselves. You are the best men I have. I look at Pita and Luigi and I see cleverness and knowledge of the forces of the market. Luca and Lorenzo and Elena, you are my weapons and my armour. Ivan and Acmed, you are my wise owls, who will show me a path that is right and seen to be right by the people. I look at Paolo and I see unquestioning, undying loyalty. When I look on Harshal I see my mother's people, unbroken generations wedded to this arid soil, and likewise I see my father's line when I look upon Comte Piero. And when I look upon Timori, I see my own heart, beating in my chest.' Hand to her breast, she went down on one knee. 'I ask you to serve, signori. I ask you to serve and I will serve you.'

Of course, no one could refuse her. Elena had seen officers win over unruly squads before. It took gumption and confidence and, more than anything, purpose. Cera had done that: she'd made them feel special and important, but she had left no doubt that she was in charge.

She looked around her Regency Council again and smiled. 'Signori, we have achieved much today. We have a commission to examine grain prices and how we can affect them. We will declare the Senate at Brochena invalid and illegal, and having resolved this, we are free to amend the Legalus Re as we will until normal rule is restored. And my religious guides will progress their investigation into religious accommodation.' She eyed Prato and Acmed meaningfully.

'But more importantly, I want you to reflect on this: *Your* voice is being heard, by *me*. You have the ear of the power who guides this land. Speak and I will hear you.

'In ancient Rimoni when war was declared we would go to the fields and throw a javelin into a piece of land that represented enemy territory. I will do that, before the people, tomorrow afternoon.' She clapped her hands together. 'Now we have one last item to discuss.' She turned to Elena. 'Ella?'

Elena raised her hand, 'Signori, I have had contact from Gurvon Gyle.' She heard their intake of breath. 'He offered an Imperial Pardon and to return my gold if I abandon you.' She made a disdainful gesture. 'I hope it goes without saying that I refused – I'm sure Gyle knew I would. But I learned one important thing: he contacted me via a relay-stave – we magi use them to boost our energy when talking to each other over *extreme* distances. They create a small echo during contact.' She learned forward and looked around her. 'Do you understand what that implies? *Gurvon Gyle is not in Javon* – he would not need a relay-stave if he were. He has gone home!' She grinned. 'Probably to explain to his employers why Cera Nesti still lives. We have an opportunity, signori, to take the fight to our enemy.' She lifted her head. 'This is not an opportunity I intend to pass up.'

On the last day of Noveleve, following the ancient tradition of her people, Cera threw a spear into a piece of ground festooned with Gorgio flags while thousands of Rimoni and Jhafi cheered. Drui and

Godspeakers hectored the crowds, though the people were already simmering with rage. They shouted angrily as they were reminded of the Dorobon's past outrages, the murder of King Olfuss and Queen Fadah Nesti, and the plight of poor Princess Solinde, being abused in captivity by the cowardly, Jhafi-hating Gorgio. Cera was proclaimed Queen-Regent before the people, and both Rimoni and Jhafi cheered enthusiastically, then she sat with Emir Ilan as food and wine were distributed. Traditional music began and the people danced as one. They were at war.

If anyone was looking for the Rondian mage-woman and wondering why she wasn't at Queen-Regent Cera's side, they would have looked in vain. For Elena Anborn was already hundreds of miles away, soaring towards Brochena on a windskiff.

13

Contact with the Enemy

The Noros Revolt

The Noros Revolt of 909–910 was the most romantic but least successful of the post-Crusade resistance to Pallas' exploitation of vassal states. As the Imperial debt burgeoned, lesser kingdoms were made to pay more. Noros gambled that a couple of quick victories would garner support from similarly afflicted neighbours, paving the way for a negotiated peace, but after initial setbacks caused by complacency, the Rondians overwhelmed the Noros legions. The scandalous surrender of the key city of Lukhazan merely hastened the inevitable.

The punishments were harsh: the king was imprisoned, authority was transferred to a Rondian-appointed governor and the land was occupied by Rondian legions. Noros has languished ever since.

ORDO COSTRUO COLLEGIATE, PONTUS

The Winter Court, Bres, Rondelmar, on the continent of Yuros
Noveleve 927
8 months until the Moontide

Trying to reason with Elena had been a stupid risk, Gurvon Gyle reflected resentfully. Did they think her such a fool as to surrender? It showed what limited intellects he was dealing with. But Lucia had been away – sainthood had its duties – and Emperor Constant had demanded he try. Without her, the emperor's stupid order had been impossible to refuse. He'd tried to give away as little as possible, but who knew what she'd picked up?

He walked alone into another secret chamber, the natural habitat of the imperial schemer. Belonius was already there. He had distanced himself from Gyle the moment the news of Elena's betrayal had reached them, but that was no great surprise. That was how Vult was.

All eyes watched him as he strode to the table. He'd flown nonstop for three weeks, most of the time in filthy weather. The crossing of the ocean had been particularly harrowing. The most frustrating thing was having to be here at all, but as soon as they'd heard of the thwarted assassination attempt the whole of Constant's Inner Council started demanding his head – as if he could have known that hard-hearted Elena Anborn would do something purely out of compassion. It was unthinkable! And how the Hel had she survived Samir? The man wasn't known as 'The Inferno' for nothing.

I gave them more than they could have achieved themselves, he thought sourly. *I brought down Olfuss Nesti and delivered Brochena to them. The Dorobon are preparing to return. I need to be on the ground in Javon, supporting Sordell, dealing with Elena – and instead these lackwits have dragged me five thousand miles around the globe so they can put me on trial. How dare they!*

He bit his tongue. *Careful, Gurvon. No anger. Confidence. Determination. Emphasise the gains. Reassure. Survive.*

The emperor sat illuminated on his throne. Everyone else sat in shadow, even Mater-Imperia Lucia. Gyle was careful to genuflect first to her, to acknowledge her supremacy – and buy her support. If that upset the emperor, too bad. 'May I sit?'

She moved a hand. 'Of course, Magister. You must be tired, having come such a long way.' Her voice was cool and composed; no apparent pre-judging from her, he noted with appreciation. He looked at the shadowy figures. Dubrayle was absent, no doubt counting money in Pallas. Tomas Betillon looked cross at having been dragged all the way from Pontus. *He probably feels he could have hanged me just as well there.* Kaltus Korion was screwing trophy-girls in his monstrosity of a palace near Bres, so he'd not had far to come. *He'll be pissed off to be dragged out on a cold day, though.* Grand Prelate Wurther looked back at him placidly. *He probably doesn't give a shit what's decided as long as there is mulled wine afterward.*

He glanced at Belonius Vult, who smiled serenely back at him and gave a small, encouraging wink. *Ah, a krone either way, Bel? You never change!*

Tomas Betillon started it off, 'What the rukking Hel is going on, Gyle? You said your people would exterminate the Nesti – not half of them! You said we could trust that bitch Anborn and instead she's killed your best man and gone native! So why haven't we strung you up by the balls already!'

Wurther chuckled as if the governor had made a particularly amusing jest. 'Tomas makes a good point,' he murmured. 'I thought you said you had people you could trust.' He tutted and glanced at Belonius, his eyes narrowing slightly. 'Of course, Gyle is *your* man, Vult.'

Belonius looked back mildly. 'Gurvon has never let me down . . . before.'

Gyle looked at Lucia. 'May I, Majesty?' She inclined her head neutrally, giving him leave to speak, and he turned back to the men. 'Gentlemen, no one was more surprised than I at Elena Anborn's treachery. The fault is mine, for I didn't see it coming. I didn't understand that her loyalties were shifting. If I had realised, I would not have left Samir alone with Elena, for he was strong but she is clever. My lord Korion always says no plan survives contact with the enemy, and thus it proved, but it is how you recover from setbacks that marks you out. We must have the fortitude to strike back. We must have the adaptability to learn from our mistakes and deal with the new circumstances.'

He looked at Lucia. '"Battles are not won by strategies but by how you adapt your tactics,"' he said, quoting Korion again. He noticed the general was actually *preening.*

'So what is your plan to retrieve the situation, Master Gyle?' Korion asked, far less hostile now.

Good, at least you're thinking I might have a future. 'I have new resources in the region already: six magi in place, more on the way. I have three major themes on the tabula-board, each independent of the others. One: Rutt Sordell will direct the Gorgio in crushing the Nesti.

Two, I will insert an agent into the Nesti. Three, I will accelerate the Dorobon restoration. Let us not forget what has already been achieved: we have eliminated Olfuss Nesti, seized his capital and hold his second daughter captive. I ask for your confidence, for I know how to adapt and evolve my tactics to finish the job.'

'So what you are saying really is, "Yes I screwed up, but you're stuck with me, so trust me to fix it", with some nice quotes to win over Kaltus,' Lucia remarked dryly.

He felt himself redden slightly at this precise appraisal. Betillon growled in agreement. Korion's eyes narrowed suspiciously, trying to work out if he had just been rebuked. Wurther looked watchful, trying to read Lucia's mood. Vult's face was smooth and unlined, serenity personified.

'As it happens, I believe you are right, Magus Gyle,' Lucia went on, to his immense relief. 'I am a forgiving woman, and I believe that sometimes things go wrong just because they can. Utterly unpredictable events do occur to upset the best of plans. Your confident presentation here tonight has reassured me.' Her eyes reminded him that he was utterly indebted to her. She whispered into his mind, <Well done, Magus. You didn't panic and run. You didn't try to hide or pass the blame. You have plans to turn the situation around. But if you fail again you are worse than dead.>

Betillon looked sour and the emperor disappointed, but everyone else was nodding appraisingly. He caught Vult's eye. Belonius was smiling as if relieved for his friend. *Sure, Bel. Thanks for everything.*

'So, what is your plan to ram that Anborn slut's head up her own shit-hole?' said Saint Lucia lightly. She tinkled with laughter at her own profanity. The men guffawed.

If she's a saint, I am too. 'Right,' Gyle said, leaning forward. 'Here's what we're going to do . . .'

14

The Road North

Hebusalim

. . . and likewise thee, Hebusalim, birth place of the Ahmed-Aluq. All worship-pers of the Faith must come to thee ere they die, to be assured of a place in Paradise.

THE KALISTHAM, HOLY BOOK OF AMTEH

Northern Lakh, on the continent of Antiopia
Shawwal (Octen) to Zulhijja (Decore) 927
9–7 months until the Moontide

'Have you and he done it yet? What was it like?' Huriya, her voice both pitying and curious.

'I've been with you all the time,' Ramita parried blandly. *It's none of your business – but no, it hasn't happened yet.*

'He came to your rooms last night while I was still in blood-purdah,' Huriya noted. She poked Ramita's arm. 'So did it happen?'

'He only came to check on my room. He didn't stay. Look, we're coming to another village.'

Huriya peered out the window. 'Another primitive dump, like all the others. Do you think he can even manage it?'

'Huriya!'

'All right! You're just being very dull, that's all.'

She counted back the days. She had married on the eleventh. They had left the ceremony early, and her last sight of her family home was of it all lit up, the whole neighbourhood there, everyone partying feverishly. She had been petrified of the consummation, but Meiros had retired to another room, leaving Ramita and Huriya in a bare room furnished with nothing but sleeping pallets. Huriya slept, but Ramita lay awake for hours, dreading his tap at the door. But he never came, and she was left feeling hollow and strangely unfulfilled, the test she had been preparing herself for still hanging over her. She slept at last, and woke up bleeding.

'You menstruate in the Full Moon,' Meiros observed when she told him next morning, 'so you will be fertile as the moon waxes, the second week of each month.' It was Shanivaar, Sabbadai in his tongue, the weekly holy day, and he let Klein take her and Huriya to a nearby temple. By the time they got back, the wagons were almost packed. Huriya was full of cheer. 'We are leaving soon, Jos says!' 'Jos' was Captain Klein, apparently. Huriya was fascinated by his bear-like frame and shaven skull. Ramita thought him repulsive.

Amidst the bustle of packing, her parents arrived with her clothes and possessions, and Huriya's things too. They didn't come to much, even with the gifts from the wedding. They exchanged gossip about the festivities, who had said what to whom, who had got rolling drunk. Father spoke of finding a new house, right beside the river. One with marble floors. It sounded unreal.

Father was obviously pleased that his dutiful daughter had achieved this new wealth for the family, but not all was well. He was worried about Jai. 'He went off after you left and has not come back,' he admitted.

'He spoke loudly about how the Amteh faith is more manly than the Omali. I don't like it,' her mother said. 'They are young and foolish boys, he and Kazim. Who knows what they will do?'

Ramita spent a few precious minutes more with her parents, chatting of inconsequential things that would be nothing to do with their future lives. 'I pray for you both, all the time,' Mother whispered to Ramita, her eyes wet. 'I will miss you every moment. Don't let that horrible man mistreat you, Mita.'

Horrible man or not, they bowed low to Meiros when he arrived back from some errand, and words of gratitude tumbled out of them in torrents. Ramita felt embarrassed, but she cried when they left.

'We leave now,' Meiros told them, and so they did. That had been five days ago, and their small caravan had been rocking and jolting and bouncing their way north ever since. They had two carriages, one for the girls and one for Meiros, and two wagons for supplies. The men clattered alongside on horseback. Carriages were a nightmare, Ramita decided, uncomfortable and nauseating. After a couple of days of throwing up the morning meal they had decided to forgo breakfast entirely; instead they stuck to fluids and fell on the evening meal ravenously.

They had been allowed to attend temple in a squalid village yesterday, where the local children had perched everywhere and stared, like a flock of crows waiting for something to die. Tonight Meiros had promised them better; they would stay at the haveli of an acquaintance of his.

Meiros' acquaintance turned out to be a raja, the sort of man an Ankesharan could never have aspired to meet. He lived in a palace with one hundred acres of gardens. Lean-tos were propped against the outside walls for the gardeners. Outside the walls there was no drainage and the stench was awful, yet inside the garden walls was a paradise of verdant lawns, marble fountains and statuary, birch trees swaying in the soft breezes. The raja was a portly man with huge waxed moustaches that curled in complete circles. 'Welcome, welcome, thrice welcome, Lord Meiros,' he cried, holding out his hands in welcome. 'My heart trembles to greet so august a personage.' He bowed and scraped as he walked backwards, leading them towards his palace, his eight wives openly gaping. Ramita wrapped her shawl tighter about her as she walked behind her husband. Meiros was wearing his cowled robes, and he tapped the ground with his heavy black staff at every step. Huriya was a step behind Ramita, peering about with no sense of decorum.

Introductions went on for ever, until at last the girls were taken by the wives into the women's palace. The walls were whitewashed, then painted with intricate floral patterns in red and green. Every arch was curved and fluted into pretty designs. But the paint was peeling and the corners were dirty. She glimpsed unused fountains with dirty ponds. 'Times are difficult,' the head wife, a plump, imperious woman, remarked as she took them to a suite of rooms overlooking a courtyard full of flowerbeds, filed with winter-blooms. A peacock strutted outside.

Huriya leaped for joy as soon as they were left unattended. 'Separate rooms,' she cried. 'A night without your snoring – this is the life!'

'A night without your farting,' Ramita countered. 'Bliss!'

They wagged tongues at each other and slammed the adjoining doors, laughing.

Servants showed them the baths and they pulled out their bathing salwars. It felt strange to change into the voluminous shifts in front of the servants, for neither of them had ever been attended upon before, but the water was warm and scented, and roses floated on the surface. The eight wives crowded into the waters around them, asking all about Baranasi and the road north. Huriya did most of the talking, spinning a concoction of fantasy about Ramita and her.

Eventually the chief wife spoke, 'Are all noblewomen of the south so dark-skinned?' she asked frankly. All the raja's wives were fair, and plump too, in stark contrast to the two girls, who had the sun-blackened skin of the marketplace, and who felt positively skeletal beside them.

'Oh yes,' Huriya answered them, to cover Ramita's confusion. 'We Baranasi are known for our dark skin – but everyone knows the fairest-skinned women are from the north,' she added, making the eight wives coo self-importantly. Huriya set about describing an elaborate palace where she and Ramita had lived until her marriage to the Rondian magus. She spoke of saree-length fashions in the Baranasi court as if she were an intimate of the emir. She gossiped airily about fictional court ladies, while Ramita just nodded and agreed that yes, it was just so. It was like a game.

'So,' the chief wife gave Ramita a conspiratorial wink, 'your husband, he is very old . . . Can he still stiffen his tool when required?'

Huriya giggled uncontrollably while Ramita's face burned and she contemplated sinking beneath the waters and drowning herself.

They spent several days at the raja's palace, enjoying the rich food and the entertainments: an endless variety of musicians and dancers and jugglers and fire-eaters. One man had a dancing bear – but it was scarred and timid, and Meiros clicked his tongue in disapproval and it was sent away. They viewed the menagerie, where brilliant birds sang overhead while jewel-coloured snakes slithered into the shadows. Tigers endlessly paced foetid cages and a painted, pampered elephant left droppings the size of a man's head in the dirt at their feet. They came away fascinated and appalled.

Meiros had a long, intent conversation with the raja, then summoned Ramita to be inspected. The raja praised her beauty, though his palpable fear of Meiros made his opinion meaningless. He said something in a low voice to Meiros, something full of assurances and promises, and the mage looked pleased as he ushered her away. 'Your name will be known to the mughal's vizier within days,' he whispered to her. 'Vizier Hanook has promised his friendship to you, Wife.'

Why would the mughal's chief advisor have any interest in me? Wives are just for breeding. They are unimportant – and I am the least of all wives . . .

Meiros read her thoughts in that unnerving way he had. 'Wife, you are Lady Meiros now, and Vizier Hanook will be grateful of your friendship.'

Grateful of my friendship? Parvasi save us! She spent dinner in a daze.

After dinner, dancers filed into the room: dervishes of Lokistan. Ululating madly, spinning like tops in a torrent of colour and sound, they were captivating, and the girls clapped and cheered and stomped their feet. The raja's wives, catching the girls' excitement, yelled and stamped their approval too. Afterward one of the younger ones whispered to Ramita, 'Normally we have to be quiet, but with you here, raja could not risk offending your husband by telling us to remain silent.' She smiled softly. 'That was such fun.' She looked fourteen and was four months pregnant.

'Good night, Huriya!' Ramita kissed her friend on both cheeks as they parted outside their rooms. 'This has been the best day so far.'

Huriya grinned back at her. 'You are smiling, Mita. That's good. It makes me smile too. We are going to be so happy in the north. You'll see.'

She woke to a cold hand on her shoulder and almost screamed as another hand came around her mouth, stifling her cry. The waning moon poured its light through the thin curtains, showing her the cowled figure that held her. 'Shhhh.' Her husband. She felt a clutch of dread pull at her guts.

'Quiet, girl. I won't hurt you,' he rasped. She could smell alcohol like a cloud about the cowl. He pulled the hood back, so that the moonlight illuminated his lined face. It made him appear older still, deepening the furrows, brightening the ridges.

'I thought . . .' She trailed off. *I thought I was safe until my fertile week.*

His voice was sympathetic, almost introspective, and she couldn't tell if he were talking to himself or her. 'It is wrong to leave these things undone. They grow to appear insurmountable obstacles if we do not confront them. They assume a greater importance than they warrant. It is not such a big matter.'

He handed her a small vial. 'Apply this oil. It will ease matters.' His hand shook, whether from age or uncertainty, she could not tell. Taking it mutely she turned away, knelt and hitched up her night-dress. Her skin felt clammy in the night air. She unstopped the vial and felt a soft, fragrant slickness on her fingers. Trying not to shudder, she reached between her legs and smeared the oil on the lips of her yoni. She felt him move fully onto the bed and turned in alarm.

'Do not look at me,' he whispered. 'Stay where you are.' She felt those cold hands on her thighs, pushing up her nightdress, baring her to him. His weight settled behind her and he manhandled her legs apart. She winced as his fingers touched her genitals, a bony digit prodding inside her, spreading the oil. She buried her head in the pillow to stifle herself: this was her duty. She heard him spit, and then a wet, rubbing sound. She waited and waited, trembling, her buttocks going cold, until at last she heard him grunt, then sigh. She nearly cried out as she felt the tip of his member against her yoni lips, pushing through her folds until she felt a tearing that made her grit her teeth. The penetration went deeper and his hips, cold as his hands on her flesh, clapped against her buttocks. She held her breath, tense and frightened, as his groin jerked in and out, once, twice, a dozen times, and then he gasped and she felt a hot wetness inside. He sagged against her slightly for a moment. When he pulled himself out, she fell forward onto her belly, fighting tears.

He sighed regretfully. 'I am sorry,' he whispered. 'I am not the man I was.' He retreated to the end of the bed as she curled into a foetal bundle, looking away from him. 'See, girl: it's not so bad.' He pulled down his robes and stood painfully: just a pale ghost of a man, drifting away. Gone.

A few seconds later Huriya bounded in and perched on the end of the bed. She watched Ramita piss semen and urine into the slop-bucket with unflinching eyes. 'So, how was it?'

The next stop was not a village at all, but a major city. Gradually the farmhouses were infiltrated by closer-packed, squalid lean-tos and poorly constructed hovels: the jhuggis that surrounded all the big towns. The stench of faeces and rotting food filled the air, smoke dirtied the sky and myriad voices assailed them as they fought their way through the dirty streets. 'This is Kankritipur,' a boy shouted in response to Huriya's call as he chased a chicken around their carriage. Then he jumped on the footpad and peered in the window hole. 'Pretty ladies, chapatti money,' he begged cheerily. Ramita pressed a few copper coins into his hand. He looked slightly hurt and put out his hand again.

'Imp, that's enough,' snapped Huriya, and he waggled his tongue rudely and jumped down, laughing. Another face replaced his, a filthy-faced girl with half her teeth missing, miming an eating gesture. 'No mamma, no papa. Please, beautiful ladies.'

Huriya rolled her eyes. '*Chod!* We're going to have every beggar in the city hanging off the footplate at this rate.'

They wound slowly through the squalor until they passed through the city gates, where soldiers beat the beggars until they dropped off the carriages like ticks from a dog. They moved from that desperate chaos into a richer, more frenzied pandemonium. Tiny shops lined the streets and men and women called their wares at the very tops of their voices, marketing through sheer volume. Woven shawls, supari leaves, sarees, scarves, knives, roots and leaves; cardamom from Teshwallabad, ginger from the south, even Imuna water from Baranasi, sold in tiny flasks for holy rites. The soldiers rode close by and Klein shouted angrily as faces constantly pressed into the windows, beggars with missing limbs or hideous diseases, young girls with babies at the teat.

Just when it felt like it would never end, they swung into the courtyard of the guest-house and relative quiet descended. They stumbled from the carriages, almost dazed. 'What a dreadful city!' exclaimed Huriya, not noticing or caring that the staff all stared at her with narrowing faces. 'What a stinking shit-hole!'

Meiros didn't come to her that night though, or the next, or the next, until it felt like it had been just a bad dream. Ramita finally regained the ability to sleep.

Huriya grew more and more animated the further north she went, flirting with the guards, giggling uncontrollably at her own daring, clutching her mouth to mute her own hilarity. She had eyes everywhere. Nothing passed her notice. Ramita envied her this never-ending voyage of discoveries, but she could not share in it, instead retreating further and further into herself.

Beyond Kankritipur was Latakwar. They struck the banks of the Sabanati River during the week of the waning moon. The river was wide but low, more than two-thirds mud. Crocodiles glided near the barges that ferried them across the dark, sluggish water. To the west and east were distant hills, with the hint of larger, grimmer promontories beyond, but to the north, the horizon was flat. The land was grey-brown, the sparse grass brittle and dry. Gold and green bee-eaters flitted amidst the bushes and kites circled high above. Once they even saw a cobra on the roadside, sidling backwards into a crevice, hooded and hissing. There were still people – always people – sun-blackened farmers labouring in the fields, bony children driving skinny cattle with sharp horns and quick tempers. They replenished their water barrels, bought an extra wagon full of feed and swapped their horses for a bevy of old camels. The town of Latakwar was wholly Amteh, the only places of worship Dom-al'Ahms, their domes crusted with windblown dust. The whole town was similarly glazed. The men were all dressed in white, the women wore black bekira-shrouds. They had a slow, distant manner, as if nothing were important enough to hurry about when exertion cost so much in sweat and energy in this dry, burning heat.

They slept in Latakwar for two nights and as the waxing moon rose, signalling her fertility, Ramita's husband finally returned to her bed for his brief, awkward fumblings. She felt like a piece of livestock as he pumped his seed into her while she knelt with her buttocks in the air. He wouldn't let her look at his body, though the few glimpses revealed nothing horrific, just a pale, somewhat bony frame that was surprisingly well-formed for such an old man. *He is vain*, she realised with a start.

'Do I please you?' she found the nerve to ask him this time as he rose to leave.

He frowned. 'You will please me when you quicken,' he answered tartly. 'My seed is thin, as is typical of magi. We must rely on persistence and good fortune.'

'And the blessing of the gods,' she replied.

He snorted. 'Aye and that.' He left her to lie alone, until Huriya came in, chuckling softly.

'I asked him how it went,' Huriya giggled. 'He just looked at me. I think he might actually have a sense of humour, if you seek it hard enough.'

Ramita looked aghast at her friend's effrontery. That night she prayed for the blessing of Sivraman. But she bled, as she always did, on the first night of the full moon, so they unfurled the blood-tent and she reacquainted herself with being alone. Her husband's disappointment hung over the caravan like a pall of smoke. Huriya joined her in the blood-tent a few days later, as usual, and they retreated again into their own tiny world.

When Ramita emerged from blood-purdah a few days ahead of Huriya, she found they were hundreds of miles further north. All week she had watched the featureless lands roll by. The last week of Zulqeda, or Noveleve, as her husband called it, the dark of the moon: the air was freezing-cold at night, so that she had to use two blankets. She was looking forward to spending a couple of nights away from Huriya. Her friend was losing all her girlish modesty and a new creature was emerging, one obsessed with wealth and men, who speculated ceaselessly about both. And her excitement at the journey was making Ramita irritable. It was tiresome, but she couldn't fight with her only friend, so she tolerated it. For now it was just a relief to be alone.

That night Meiros came and sat with her after dinner, beside the small fire Klein had built her. He pressed a book into her hands and she took it, trembling. She had never even touched one before. The lines and squiggles were odd, meaningless things that spidered across page after page. There were pictures though, of strange people with pale skin and oddly cut clothing. 'This is a child's atlas of Urte,' he said. 'It will help you learn Rondian.'

That night was a new type of awakening for her: more wondrous, more spiritual and awakening than any flesh-and-blood experience. These symbols contained *language*. They contained *knowledge*. Ramita dutifully intoned the sounds associated with each symbol and repeated them back to him until he was satisfied. Finally he put the book aside and mounted her, apparently for pleasure rather than duty. It wasn't too awful, and he left her the book when he departed. She clutched it to her as she slid beneath her blankets, her mind bursting with this new thing. She fell asleep when her eyes could no longer take in the pictures swimming before her eyes.

From then on, she rode with Meiros in his carriage so she could continue learning to read, leaving a disgusted Huriya alone. The landscape had turned entirely to sand, a sea that rose and fell in golden waves. There were no trees, just rocks where snakes and lizards basked, or jackals snoozed in the shade, awaiting dusk. The camels walked slowly onwards, phlegmatic, surprisingly gentle animals. The camels in Aruna Nagar had been bad-tempered creatures, whipped and beaten by their owners into obedience, but these were well-cared-for, and they rewarded that care. Beneath the awning, the heat was almost bearable.

Meiros rode with his hood lowered, allowing her to study him. His long, thin hair ill-suited him and his beard was a lank thing that she longed to trim. His eyes were haunted, but he smiled sometimes as he taught her his tongue. He apologised that he had not brought a windship to speed their passage, but he said it would have attracted too much attention. She wasn't sorry; she had never seen the legendary flying ships and the thought of going up in one petrified her.

She was slowly losing some of her fear of her husband. Behind the gauzy curtains of the carriage they were able to converse more freely, and she discovered he was a patient man for all his curtness. He seemed younger when he relaxed. 'It's the desert air,' he said when she was bold enough to remark on this. She thought it was more likely being away from all his cares for a while.

Not all his teaching was of language. He taught her a mantra, a little chant, to hinder magi seeking to learn things from her mind – only for a while, but long enough to seek help. The notion frightened her, that these people could read her private thoughts, so she practised hard at maintaining her concentration on the mantra, no matter what distractions there might be. Meiros told her she learned well, which pleased her. He also taught the mantra to Huriya, who picked it up quickly.

She also learned a little about the place they were going to. 'Hebusalim is a sacred city to the Amteh,' he told her, 'one of the three holiest. That is another reason why they resent the Rondian occupation. It was a major city even before the Bridge was built.' He told her about the sultans of Dhassa and old wars, but she was interested in more immediate things.

'Who is the Justina you sometimes mention?'

Meiros paused in midflow. 'Justina? She is my only daughter, the child of my second wife.'

'Does she live with you? How old is she? Is she married? Does she have children?'

He was amused at the sudden torrent of questions. 'Yes, she lives with me, but she has her own apartment and comes and goes as she pleases. No, she is not married; she has lovers, I suppose, but that is none of my business. She has no children – we magi do not breed easily or often, I'm afraid. As for her age . . .' He looked her in the eye. 'Justina is one hundred and sixty-three years old.'

Ramita went cold. It was so easy to forget that magi were not like other men. After a pause she asked, 'What does she look like?'

He thought for a moment, then said, 'She looks like a typical thirty-year-old woman, I suppose. She has long black hair and pale skin. She is accounted a beauty – she inherited her mother's looks, obviously,' he added self-deprecatingly.

Ramita pressed on. 'What happened to your wife?'

'She died of old age, forty years ago.' He gazed into space. 'She was the daughter of another acolyte of Corineus. We married when I settled in Pontus.'

'Who was Corineus? Is he not your god?'

Meiros shook his head. 'No, not back then, anyway. Baramitius and his ilk made him into a god afterwards, but to me he was just Johan – somewhat mad, incomprehensible, charismatic, compelling, but utterly human. He changed my life, several times over. I was a youngest son of a Brician baron, with no prospects beyond a career in the legions. Then Johan came to our village and lured me away. It was the time of the Rimoni Empire – we were all of the Sollan faith then, and the drui taught that salvation could be found through following personal vision, so travelling preachers abounded. I heard Johan Corin in the marketplace, talking about freedom and equality, and I was captivated. He painted a vision of a world governed by love, truth and understanding: a dream world. He had his woman, Selene, and a dozen other followers, and I walked away from the life my family had prepared for me and joined them that very day. I was just thirteen years old.

'For several years we wandered all over Rondelmar, teaching Johan's version of the Sollan faith. We slept in fields or under trees, on the outskirts of those towns where the authorities had turned us away, but others welcomed us, and Johan's following grew. Soon we were dozens, then a hundred, and by the following spring we were nearly two hundred-strong and growing daily. A new word was being whispered everywhere: "Messiah", which means "saviour". Corin became "Corineus" and people said that he'd come to lead us to a better life here on Urte. The legion commanders became frightened of our numbers, and when trouble flared and several of us were killed, Johan personally intervened and persuaded the legion commander to stop the violence. From then on we started to hear all these stories of miracles and great deeds – all nonsense, of course, but by midsummer we numbered more than a thousand. Johan – *Corineus* – began to speak more and more pompously, of visions sent to him from Sol and Luna. Selene announced that Sol and Luna had transformed Corineus and her, making them brother and sister, and she began calling herself "Corinea".' Meiros shook his head. 'It's almost funny now. Beware, Wife, of people who claim to speak the words of God. They will be lying. Most of the world's biggest liars claim to speak for God.'

'But priests—'

'Especially priests! Never trust a priest – and never, *ever* trust a magi who claims his gift comes from Kore or Ahm or Sol, or anyone else.' He waggled a finger at her. 'Never!'

'But you got magic from your god, that's what Guru Dev taught me.' In fact, Guru Dev had told her the magi got their powers from demons of Hel, but it felt unwise to repeat that, just in case.

Meiros laughed. 'Ha – yes, well . . . the Kore have done well out of that little myth.' He leaned forward. 'The secret of the gnosis is contained in a thing Baramitius made called the Scytale of Corineus. Baramitius was a great one for secrets, and for potions. He was Corin's oldest disciple, an alchemist – he was the true miracle worker. He discovered the liquid he called "ambrosia". Any who survived drinking it gained the gnosis-power to manipulate nature. I did not see any god that night.'

She looked up at him, confused, wondering. 'Did you see demons of Hel then?' she asked without thinking, then she almost swallowed her tongue in fright at what she had said.

To her vast relief, Meiros only laughed. 'No, nor angels either – I have never seen any demon nor angel, Wife, and nor do I expect to.' He chuckled heartily. 'The gnosis has nothing to do with any god, do you understand?' He jabbed a finger for emphasis and then paused and stared at it, as if amused by his own animation. Ramita felt a curious warming towards him. He reminded her of Guru Dev.

'No, the Scytale had nothing to do with religion,' he went on. 'Johan Corin intended the drink to open our minds to God – he got the idea after taking Sydian opiates, which ought to tell you much of his state of mind. Baramitius laboured to make Johan's vision a reality – he even tested his experimental brews upon fellow disciples – some died, but Johan concealed this to protect him. I only found out about his experiments years later, and I was appalled. Anyway, Baramitius eventually found what he sought, and got permission to administer it to the whole flock.

'On the chosen night Corin told us we were to imbibe the wine of the gods and ascend to greet them. A legion had surrounded our camp, sent by some alarmist townsfolk, but Corineus was adamant the ceremony would go ahead. We gathered in north Rondelmar, on a balmy day in late autumn. The wolves were beginning to howl in the wilds, but we all went about garlanded with flowers and dizzy from drink. Corineus made a slurred speech about sacrifice and love and salvation as the ambrosia was shared out. We each got just a drop, and at a sign from Corineus we raised our cups to our lips and drank. Outside the camp, the legionnaires were closing in.

'The fluid moved slowly from the belly to the heart. It was truly debilitating: we all collapsed. It left us conscious, but unable to function. To me, everything was frozen and magnified; I could even see the separate colours of the rays of light that showered down from the face of Luna. Deeper and deeper we all sank and as light ebbed away, a shimmering opalescence seeped through the air and clung to our bodies. I heard someone cry out in an incredibly slow, deep voice for their mother. *Mother?* I thought, and suddenly I saw her, my own mother, as clear as daylight, sitting at her table hundreds of miles to the south, and she looked up, seeing nothing, but calling my name. All around me, voices murmured, invoking parents, siblings, children, all the loved ones they abandoned when they joined Johan's flock, and perhaps they all saw them, as I saw her.

'But then everything changed again as our languor became infected with pain. As one, the whole thousand-strong flock cried out as agony took us and it grew in intensity, like talons ripping our innards apart, until we could bear no more. Some lost consciousness, some expired. I clung to the hand of a girl beside me, ripping at the turf with my free hand, but that girl's hand was my lifeline, keeping me grounded, keeping me sane. It felt like the earth was fraying and we were falling through it, into darkness – but we were not alone in that emptiness for long. Now the faces of the dead were surrounding us, people I knew: those who had died on the road with Johan, others from my childhood. They said nothing at first, then they howled at us, and came at us with their spectral hands clawed. I called upon Sol to protect me, and somehow armour appeared on my chest and a sword in my hand. I held the girl behind me and chopped at the ghosts, driving them away. All around me I saw others doing the same, or similar. Some burnt the spectres with fire, others blasted them away with pale light or gusts of wind. But many of us perished, helpless, unable to find the means to defend themselves like I and others had. I fought like a mad thing, hewing and slashing in desperation . . . and then suddenly the ghosts and the darkness were gone and we were cast up from that dreadful sea onto the cold shores of daylight, naked in a sea of corpses.'

Meiros shuddered at the memory. 'I came to myself lying with an arm around that girl, the woman who became my first wife. Beside me, a young man, a good friend, lay dead, his body twisted, his eyes wide open, his face frozen in a silent scream. Beyond him lay another, and another. Then I saw a living man, and other survivors gradually staggered upright: maybe half of us at most. The rest were dead or insane. Our eyes were drawn to the centre of the dell, where our leader had been. Johan and Selene lay immobile, and even from where I was I could see he was covered in blood. Someone began to wail, and Selene sat up. She lifted her hands, bathed in blood, and turned to the prone form beside her. I will never forget the sound of her scream. In the midst of her transformation, beset by some vision, she had slammed a dagger through her lover's heart.'

Ramita was beginning to feel nauseous, and she rather wished Meiros would cease his tale now, but he was caught up in the past, barely seeing her. He went on, 'I remember someone tried to grab her and she swung her hands at him and her fingers became knives, and she slashed his throat open. Then she ran, before any could think to stop her. Our Master was dead, his lover fled, and we thought we had lost our minds. I saw one man hold up his hands to implore Heaven and fire bloomed from his fingers. I saw another with tears streaming from his eyes which floated up to form rings about his head, a halo of salty water. A woman drifted upwards, panicking as she left the ground. For myself, my only concern was to keep the girl with me safe. What we'd shared had bonded us for life. I was surrounded by light and a barrier of stone was building up at my feet. Everywhere, every survivor was performing uncontrolled miracles, and in the mayhem some killed with accidental thoughts; others lost control and destroyed themselves, bursting into flame or petrifying themselves. It was chaos – Hel on Urte.

'And in the middle of all this, the legionaries, five thousand fighting men, charged out of the mist. Some six hundred of us had survived Baramitius' potion. Maybe a hundred of those had gone completely insane, and another hundred had not manifested any powers at all. The four hundred-odd who had attained power had almost no control; all we knew was that if we thought something, it seemed to happen.

But when the legionaries attacked we found the focus and will to resist.

'We destroyed them with pure elemental power: Fire and Earth and Water and Wind, and pure energy – that was all we had then; the refinements came later. That first battle was just slaughter, and I was not alone in being nauseated by the carnage; a number of us swore never again to use such powers to kill. But Baramitius and Sertain, who became the first Rondian emperor, they revelled in their victory: for them, this was the Purpose, the salvation Corineus had promised. They saw themselves as young gods, and they vowed to destroy the Rimoni and rule the world. And so they did, but by then I and many others had left them.'

Ramita remembered to breathe. 'What did you do?' she whispered.

'I walked away. I had never been a violent man, and I was truly sickened by what we had wrought, even though we had not attacked first. I took the hand of the girl beside me and when someone asked where I was going, I said, "Anywhere there is no blood", and some followed me. We stumbled through the carnage, the burned soldiers, dismembered limbs, headless torsos, and everywhere there was death. Johan Corin's peace-preaching flock had become a savage mob with horrendous power. So we left, and close on a hundred came with me. The hundred or so who had manifested no power were ostracised, and they also left, but not with me. The remainder went on to over-throw the Rimoni Empire and establish their own. The "Blessed Three Hundred".'

Meiros sighed deeply. 'For those with me, our only choice was flight. We marched through the Schlessen forests and over the Sydian plains. Of course we had to fight along the way – wherever we went the local tribes saw only helpless wanderers and tried to take us as slaves. Non-violence is a pretty ideal, but it's virtually impossible in this world. But at least we weren't part of the butchery that Sertain inflicted upon the Rimoni. At least we were better than that.'

He looked up at her and said, 'Wife, I do not wish to speak of this any more. Not for now.' He looked for a moment like a tired old man, whose spirit was long broken, kept moving only by the empty promise of continued existence. She had a momentary desire to hug him, to try to comfort him.

'I don't need your pity, girl,' he suddenly growled. 'Go back to your wagon. I would be alone.'

They reached the northern edge of the desert the next evening. After exchanging the camels for horses their pace increased dramatically and the days blurred as they rattled along endless hard, stony roads, often pressing on even through the night. Ramita made slow progress in her language lessons with Meiros. He did not visit her bed in the way-stations but locked the girls in their rooms with a tracery of light about the doors and windows: wards, he called them. They were supposedly to keep them safe, but other than making the doors give off sparks when opened, they had no other effect she could see.

For three weeks they travelled in this manner, circling the major cities, sleeping in the countryside. But one afternoon, Ramita was awakened from her slumber in the carriage by Huriya, who was shaking her excitedly and crying, 'Mita, Mita, look! Jos says it's Hebusalim!' She pulled aside the curtain and they gazed out over a wide valley, a fairytale sight: all lit up with house fires and lanterns and torches, with a massive Dom-al'Ahm rising amid the spires of palaces. They could see huge city walls, and wide roads lit with glittering white lamps, and everywhere, the tiny shapes of people, like ants scurrying about a disturbed nest. It was breathtaking.

'Hebusalim,' she breathed. Her new home.

Huriya wrapped her arms about her. 'We're here – we've arrived! By the gods, I thought we would never end this journey. I'm so happy!'

Ramita looked at her flushed and animated face and thought, *Yes, my sister you really are. I wish I was. I would happily just turn around and go home* . . . But she tried to look pleased.

The winding roads through the city were choked with people, and Jos and his men were watchful. The clamour of the markets was deafening. There were Rondian soldiers everywhere, dressed in red and white uniforms with golden sunbursts on their tabards: imperial legionaries from Rondelmar, Meiros said shortly. They looked grim-faced and hard, and Ramita saw a local man shoved aside brutally when he got in the way. Some of them recognised Captain Klein; when they called out to him she recognised Rondian words Meiros had taught her. The recognition sent a small thrill through her, a tenuous sense of connection to this alien place.

'Look! We're nearly at the gates to the city!' Huriya exclaimed. 'I wonder if this is the very street where my father fought the magi and Ispal saved him?'

Ramita tried to see it in her mind's eye, but it was too dark and the mounted soldiers were blocking most of the views. She could make out lean, bony Keshi and the rounder, paler visage of the local Dhassans, who called themselves 'Hebb' to differentiate themselves from their rural cousins. She particularly studied the white-faces of Rondian traders walking the souks with armed guards – mostly local men, she noted – at their backs. Everyone she could see was male. 'Are there no women here?' she asked Huriya.

'They'll all be at home, cooking,' the Keshi girl answered. 'But look, there's one!' She pointed to a black-shrouded shape scurrying into a doorway. 'Bekira – ugh!' Both girls groaned, already missing the light cloth and colourful hues of Lakh. In Baranasi Huriya had dressed as an Omali most of the time. Here, they would both have to be bekira-robed – the Amteh's cover-all public garment, named for the death shroud of the Prophet's wife, had originated in Hebusalim. It was a dismal prospect.

It was well after midnight when they rolled up a wide boulevard to the Eastern Gate, but they were waved through with no delay, into the closer-packed streets of the inner city. They began to see Hebb women more frequently, still shrouded, but with bared heads. Their faces were pale gold, their black hair luxuriant, curling. Many were clinging to tipsy Rondian soldiers. There were many taverns and the air stank of ale and rang with strange songs. Huriya called out to Klein, 'What is that racket?'

'Schlessen drinking songs – welcome to Hebusalim, the cesspit of Urte!' He laughed as they pushed through a crowd of bawdy soldiers and local women, one of whom had her caramel-coloured breasts bared. She was laughing uproariously as two lurching men held her upright.

Ramita was shocked. 'This place is a den of vice,' she remarked disgustedly. 'Did you see that woman? This is a holy city!' she shouted out the window. The men turned and the woman burst out laughing. To her alarm one of the soldiers took a few steps towards her, but Jos Klein yelled, 'Make way for Lord Meiros!' and everyone backed away.

They fought free of the crowds after that, rumbling into a side street. A tall white tower appeared ahead of them, illuminated by the waxing moon and filling the sky, gleaming like an ivory tooth. Chains rattled and they heard heavy gates swing open. Faces peered out from the windows of houses lining the street, then vanished again as the caravan rolled forward into a small courtyard. Marble walls glittered in the moonlight; gilt gleamed coldly in the torch-light. Their carriage stopped before steps ascending to imposing gates of wood and iron. Servants and stable-hands swarmed around them, darting between the irritable horses.

Someone opened the girls' carriage door and helped them out. Meiros was already out and was talking to a small bald man. Both turned to the girls as they stepped unsteadily onto the ground.

'Ah,' intoned the bald man obsequiously, 'this must be the new Lady Meiros.' He spoke Keshi with an oily accent. Ramita stared at him dazedly, wondering for an instant who Lady Meiros was before she remembered and thrust her hand towards him. He kissed the air above it, not quite touching her with either lips or hand. 'An Indran beauty, my lord,' he commented to Meiros, as if appraising a broodmare.

'Wife, this is my chamberlain, Olaf. He will show you to your rooms.'

Olaf simpered at her, then he looked at Huriya and licked his lips. 'My lord, did you purchase two? Do the Indrans marry in pairs?' He gave a small laugh.

'Her maid,' replied Meiros shortly. He turned as a tall shape in a dark blue robe detached itself from the shadows. 'Daughter.'

The blue-robed figure curtseyed. 'Father,' came a cool, deep voice. 'I see you have returned from your shopping expedition. Did you get any bargains?'

'Don't be rude, Justina,' sighed Meiros. He looked shockingly weary to Ramita, who hadn't seen his face for three days. It was as if returning to Hebusalim had erased the youthful vigour he had shown in the deserts. 'I have a new wife. Her name is—'

'I don't care what her name is!' snapped Justina. 'You old fool, have you finally gone senile? I've been half-crazy wondering what you were doing. Slipping away with no word, no contact, and now I find you've been *courting*? For Kore's sake, Father, an *Indran* – what on Urte are you doing? Have you gone mad? The Order has been in uproar.' Her face, glimpsed beneath the hood of the robes, was ivory, her mouth a vermilion slash, contorted in scorn.

'Peace, Daughter. I will not—'

'Ha – dotard!' Justina whirled and stamped away into the shadows.

Meiros let out a heavy sigh and turned back to the girls. 'I apologise for my daughter,' he told Ramita. 'She is highly-strung at times.'

Ramita stared at the floor.

'Come.' Meiros led them to a panel of carven wood set into the wall which contained what appeared to be a dozen intricately carved doorknobs. 'I know you are tired, but listen carefully: this palace has several security levels, wrought from the gnosis. I will explain it more fully when you are rested, but for now it suffices to know that I will grant Ramita the third security level, which gives access to all places but my tower. Huriya, you will have the fourth access, giving you the same as Ramita, but no access to my personal quarters. Wife, grasp the third doorknob from the left as if you were wishing to turn it. Grasp tightly and hold on. This will hurt a little, but Olaf will give you salve.' He held up his left hand, palm open, and Ramita saw for the first time a fine tracery of scarring. She shivered, but reluctantly grasped the handle with her left hand.

Meiros touched a gem set above the doorknobs, closed his eyes and whispered something. Suddenly a stinging heat surged through her hand and she shrieked, pulling it away. Olaf seized her hand before she could close it and pasted an oily goo that smelled of aloes onto her stinging palm. Through sudden tears she saw livid patterns etched into her skin.

Huriya looked ill-pleased, but she endured the marking stoically. Meiros then muttered something about Justina and left the girls alone with the chamberlain.

Olaf chortled under his breath as the old mage scurried after his daughter, then remembered himself. 'Come, ladies,' he said, 'let me show you to your rooms.'

Ramita was given a whole suite on the top floor of the building. Everything was white marble, which would stay cool in the hottest sun, Olaf told them. Servants brought their luggage while a dusky-skinned pregnant woman filled a copper bath with water that came steaming out of a pipe set into the wall. 'Running hot water,' Olaf commented as if this sort of miracle were commonplace. There were small sofas beneath each window, and below, a courtyard with a pond and fountain. Even the privy was alien: a chair with a padded rim instead of the usual squat-hole. Ramita wondered whether you were supposed to squat on the rim or sit on it – both looked possible, but she was too embarrassed to ask. The bedroom was vast, the canopied bed the size of her whole room in Baranasi.

The sudden remembrance of home brought tears to her eyes and she clung onto Huriya. Olaf looked puzzled at her distress. 'She is tired,' Huriya hissed. 'You may go now. I will look after her.'

Olaf looked momentarily flustered, then bowed his way out. Huriya led Ramita to the bath and helped her in. The Keshi girl's face was aglow with pleasure, but Ramita felt only an all-pervading inertia. 'I miss my mother,' was the closest she could come to expressing how she felt. 'And Kazim.'

'Silly,' Huriya whispered. 'We've arrived in heaven. I miss nothing at all.'

15

Mage's Gambit

The Studies

There are four major Studies of gnosis. These are the areas where the person-
ality of the mage comes to the fore, affecting the types of gnosis at which they
will be most competent. It has been said that a mage's affinities reflect what
manner of person they are. Indeed, one obvious example: a mage whose nature
is hot-tempered is often a Fire-mage. But it should be noted that sometimes that
affinity is more subtle: not all fire-magi are hot-tempered, for fire can be many
things. It is not enough to know your enemy's affinities – you must also know
their soul.

SOURCE: ARDO ACTIUM, SCHOLAR, BRES 518

Brochena, Javon, on the continent of Antiopia
Decore 927
7 months until the Moontide

Elena called her single-masted war-skiff *Greybird*. She had given it a
carved figurehead, and worked ash into the varnish to colour the
sleek hull. It had swivelling wings, giving it greater stability and
control, if you knew what you were doing. It was sixty feet in length,
small enough for one person to pilot, large enough to bear three
passengers. As she guided the craft westwards through the night
skies towards Brochena the waxing moon shone down on the faces
of her companions as they peered over the sides, any initial trepidation about flying long gone. Artaq Yusaini, a Jhafi warrior, sat in
the prow. Harshal had recommended him, saying, 'He can speak
both Jhafi and Rimoni, Donna Ella, he's loyal, and he's a killer.'

Artaq had a soft face and a gap-toothed grin. His facial hair was patchy and his skin blotchy, where some disease had caused pink patches. He didn't look like a killer – but he had more knives under those robes than Elena could credit. He was happy to work with a mage. 'If Ahm gave you whiteskins magic, then it cannot have been for virtue,' he told her, 'so therefore it is just a weapon, like my knives. So let us go and skewer some Gorgio.' He spat as he spoke the name.

Before the mast sat Luca Fustinios, a Nesti legionary. He was shorter than Elena by a head, but his compact, muscular form was well-feared in the wrestling ring; he was known to be the best in the ranks. He too was fluent in Jhafi after time in prison for strangling a rival over a woman. He had a cheery manner despite his reputation and crime, and he was Nesti through and through.

In front of Elena sat Lorenzo di Kestria. 'I'm going to Brochena to kill magi,' she'd argued. 'I want killers, not chivalrous knights. Lorenzo is too soft. He'll be a liability.'

'I cannot let you go alone with those two, Donna Elena,' he'd argued. 'Both are criminals. Even if I just watch your back and guard the skiff, I will go.' And Cera had overruled her.

Admittedly it had been nice to have someone familiar to talk to as they flew towards their destination, but she was apprehensive about what Lorenzo would see.

'That's Mount Tigrat,' called Lorenzo, pointing to a greater darkness to the north. 'Brochena is near, thirty miles maybe.'

She nodded her understanding. As the little craft creaked and tilted Luca Fustinios gripped the edge of the craft and looked back at her to ensure that this was a planned manoeuvre and not the beginning of a dive into messy death. She waved reassuringly at him. 'I'm going to land west of the city, away from the lake,' she told them. 'We'll have to move quickly then: I want to be within the city walls by dawn. Our first target – Arno Dolman – will be near there, working on the outer defences.'

Arno Dolman was primarily an Earth Thaumaturge. He was a big, strong man, and normally placid, though he had a temper if he was pushed. She had seen him scoop granite with his huge, muscular hands as if it were sand and mould it like clay. She liked Arno, regretted that he was now an enemy. He was the only other member of the team who'd been in the Revolt with her. She had disliked Gurvon's recent recruits: they were talented, but they were also bordering on psychotic.

Getting Arno out of the way first made sense as his affinities were all about the practical and the tangible. If she isolated him carefully he wouldn't be able to alert the others. After that, it would be harder to keep her attacks secret. *But first things first: let's deal with Arno . . .*

She began to feel like her old self, thinking of targets and weaknesses, the strategies of killing. Since she'd saved Cera and Timori from Samir she'd felt herself becoming a different person, one she liked more, but not the person to handle this mission. For this she needed the old Elena, who backstabbed enemies, sacrificed friends and enjoyed the vertiginous highs of life on the edge. Five targets, then she could put that Elena away, like a dress that no longer fitted, and never bring her out again.

It was something to hope for. She sent her mind questing outwards, concentrating on Arno. She recalled his thunderous brows and heavyset visage, that could smile or scowl with equal intensity. He had the shoulders of a bull, but surprisingly thin legs. He was a primal, basic man: simple, strong, blunt. And reliable. *Sorry, Arno – but if you didn't want to come up against me, you should have refused to come here.*

Arno Dolman found himself fighting a growing sense of anger all day. *Why was it always me doing the hard work while the others mince about the palace?* he thought. *And why did Gurvon leave Sordell in charge, when all he ever did was pick away at the future in his tower or fawn at Alfredo Gorgio's feet – lazy, arrogant, Argundian slime. Those two new recruits are snotty little pricks too, no use at all when it comes to practical matters, and neither is Vedya, the bitch. I'm the only one doing any work here. We've got to fortify this stupid sprawling mess of a city before the rukking Crusade begins.*

Brochena was the capital, and it'd been sucking people in like a sponge. It'd outgrown its defences years ago. The Dorobon had strengthened the walls and the Nesti had ripped them down again – allowing Alfredo Gorgio to march ten thousand men right into the capital unchallenged.

What's Elena doing? Why'd she screw Samir over? Is she angling for a bigger cut of the spoils – that'd be her style, the bitch. Gurvon had been furious; he'd grabbed everyone he had to hand and flown them to Javon – and ever since they'd arrived, Arno had been stuck here working on the walls. 'Someone must rebuild the fortifications around the inner city, Arno and you're the best there is,' Gurvon had told him. Manipulative bastard. But what about the others helping? Hel no! Gurvon had pissed off back to Bres on some fool's errand, leaving Sordell and his bum-boys prancing about with the Gorgios while Vedya was whoring as usual.

Perhaps he'd slept badly or something, but today all the things that irritated him were flaring up, and Arno could feel his fury rising. He used it to fuel his gnosis and plunged his hands into the rock again, drawing the stone up like toffee and shaping and strengthening it. Already a mile of new stonework enclosed most of the western side of the old city: two weeks' solid work. Today he was sick of it.

He lifted a block of stone that an Indranian elephant would have struggled to move and slammed it into place. All day long he'd been pushing himself to the limits, eager to have some real progress to show for all his rukking effort. Gurvon said the Nesti brats were still in Forensa, but what if they were marching? You couldn't ignore that possibility, not when that sneaky bint Elena Anborn was involved.

He spat, wishing he could trust someone else apart from Gurvon. Back in the old days he'd felt a sense of camaraderie, but not these days. When Vedya joined it all went downhill fast – that Sydian witch was pure poison.

He shook his head furiously. *Where is all this anger coming from?* He lifted another block and slammed it onto the first, almost staggering with the effort. If he could just finish this section by sundown . . . He threw everything into it, gnosis-power, muscle-power, all of his will. *We've got a deadline to meet, damnit!* He was conscious that the four soldiers guarding him were staring at him in awe. He felt a savage pride in his skills. *Yes, look at me: see what a* real *mage can do.*

He plunged his hands up to his elbows into the two massive blocks and shaped them like dough as he blended them into one, squared the edges and made ready for the next block. He felt almost dizzy with the exertion. He gasped and looked around. *Kore's Cods, it's evening already.* He looked out over the filthy hovels of the lowlife Jhafi. Unusually, there wasn't a single face in sight. *Scared of the big Rondian mage are you, you scum?*

He rubbed his face, groaned. *What's wrong with me? I'm not usually like this . . .*

But there's more to be done, a voice whispered inside him, and he thought, *Yes, there is more to be done.* He bent over another block, as big as the other two, almost reeling with the effort.

Just one more, that insidious whisper urged.

An *external* whisper!

Rukka! It all became clear: he'd been goaded like a bull in an Estellayne arena. He spun about him as the shadows closed in, but he didn't have time to shout more than, 'Ware!' before a small shape had appeared behind the backmost soldier, pulled him backwards and slashed his jugular. Blood sprayed across the stone, black in the twilight. The guards tried to draw weapons, but all about them others had darted in, stabbing at necks or beneath the left armpit, and they all fell, choking out their final breaths. The closest attacker glided towards him, her faded blonde hair caught in a pony-tail, cold eyes glittering.

'Elena.' *You bitch, I should have realised—* 'How long have you—?'

'All day, Arno.' Her voice was soft, almost sad. 'Egging you on. Got anything left to fight with?'

'You bet I have!' He hurled the great stone at her, though the effort made him stagger. The rock shattered against a square pillar, bringing down part of the wall he'd just erected. But she was already gone.

Behind! He swung the hammer in a complete circle that nearly took off the bitch's head as she reappeared, but as it whistled over her head he was pulled into a spin by its weight. He steadied himself and swung again. The blow skidded off her shields, visibly unsettling her.

Ha! 'I can take you, Elena—' He swung again, but she somersaulted off the walls and down to the hovels below. He glared down at her, then gestured, forming a gnostic stone-serpent thrice her size from the rocks at his feet. It erupted in a cloud of dirt, and he reeled with the effort. His vision blurred, and for a second he saw three Elenas below him. He blinked dazedly: there were still three. The snake ploughed into the middle one, encountering nothing but air and illusion, then smashed into a hovel below and its head shattered. Jhafi voices screamed.

But the real Elena was running up the stonework, barely touching it. He screamed a command and the headless stone-snake lunged after her, but the bitch was too fast and his construct crashed itself against the wall and expired in a cascade of rubble. He tried to follow her with his eyes and with his gnosis, but she was heading in three directions at once. *Damned illusions—*

'Stand still, you safian bitch!' he roared, and brandished the hammer.

<*Keep away from him,*> she snapped into the minds of Lorenzo, Artaq and Luca. <*Hold your fire.*> She slipped away to the right. *We have to finish this before he thinks to call for aid.* She left a spray of illusory glimpses to confuse matters as she landed, catlike, ten yards from him and let him see her.

'There you are,' he bellowed, stupid with exhaustion. His hammer fell, but she was already out of reach, showing him a fistful of gnosis-energy before sending it at his shields, even as she called, <*Fire,*> into the minds of her men. Three crossbows rattled as one.

It wouldn't have worked if Arno had been fresh: he was a half-blood Earth-mage of frightening strength. But she'd spent the whole day pricking at his mind like a gnat, enhancing his fears, driving him to exhaustion.

Her gnosis-bolt fused his shielding and centred all of his defences to the front, and the three crossbow bolts fired from the sides and behind encountered no resistance: one took him in the biceps, pinning his arm to his chest. Another took him in the neck, breaking his spine, while the third slammed into his belly. He collapsed and fell from the half-made wall to sprawl on the earth below. As Elena reached the lip of the wall he jerked and went still.

The three men walked to the edge and cautiously peered over. Elena leapt down lightly, wary of any movement, or the sudden expenditure of gnosis-energy. The others landed behind her, and as one they sucked in their breath.

Arno's eyes flickered open. A gurgle came out of his mouth, then a gout of blood. As clearly if he had spoken aloud, she heard, *<Elena – I should have . . . sensed you.>*

<Sorry, Arno.> She could almost feel the dreadful pain he was enduring.

<Why did you . . . do it, Elena? Wasn't your share . . . big enough?>

<It had nothing to do with money, Arno. It was about love, and right and wrong.>

His eye widened slightly, incredulous, then a sharp burst of agony nearly took him. Elena lifted her hand, gnosis-fires kindling. *<Do it, Elena. Kill me—>*

<Sorry, Arno. Not quite yet.> She raised her blade and cleaved his neck in two. His head rolled clear in a fount of blood. She bathed her ghastly trophy in healing-gnosis, sealing enough blood inside his head to keep his soul locked into his skull, steeling herself against Arno's horrified mental cries.

The men above her gasped as they saw his lips and eyes moving, and Lorenzo asked, 'What are you doing?' His expression was horrified.

'You'll see.' She took the head and rolled it into the waterproofed leather satchel she had brought for the purpose, then hefted it over her shoulder. Lorenzo looked at her and she saw his illusions about her begin to die. She felt a curious sense of loss. Faces peered out of the lean-tos, and a Jhafi warrior appeared, one of Harshal's contacts. He saluted her wordlessly with his scimitar and vanished again.

She looked at the men. 'Okay, one down. Four to go.'

Which one next, Lady?' Artaq asked her quietly.

'Sordell. Like Arno Dolman, his whereabouts is predictable. Rutt is like a man with a scab that itches him so badly that he cannot help scratching it. That scab is called paranoia, and the way he scratches it is to try and see into the future.'

'He can do that?' Artaq looked impressed. Luca made some primitive warding gesture.

'Many magi can, but it's not easy and it's very unreliable. I like to think of it as a way of clarifying planning and rounding out the data. I did some divining myself before we left to fine-tune my plans.'

'Did you see us as successful?' Lorenzo asked.

'Well, of course – but that could just be because I can't conceive of losing, so I wouldn't take it too seriously. But Sordell does: he's one of those nervous types, and he can't make a move without Gurvon holding his hand. He'll be terrified that something will go wrong on his watch, so he'll be up there in the Moon Tower, trying to see what it is.'

'Will he see us coming?' Luca asked perceptively. 'With his spells?'

'Perhaps. But one magi can usually hide from another, and from spirits set to observe them. A good diviner can play games with another too, feeding them wrong data.'

'Are you a good diviner, Donna Ella?'

Elena smiled down at the little Rimoni. 'Better than Sordell, actually, but I don't like to boast. He thinks I can't do it at all.'

Luca looked at her appraisingly, not the way men usually looked at women, but as if trying to strip away the flesh to the powers that lay beneath. 'Do you have any weaknesses at all, Donna?'

'A good cheese from the Knebb Valley gets me every time.'

The Rimoni chuckled and shook his head appreciatively. 'Do you have a weakness for shorter men?' he grinned.

She laughed and waved a dismissive hand. 'Not usually, but you'll be the first to know, Shorty.'

The starlight was sufficient to guide them as they wound their way through the pre-dawn. She wondered where Gurvon was – even the swiftest of windships wouldn't have got him to Pontus yet if he was travelling back from Rondelmar.

'What about we men, witch-lady?' asked Artaq. 'Do we survive this night, from your divining?'

She paused, losing her levity. 'Without a scratch,' she lied. 'Let's go.'

The outer limits of Brochena were alive with Gorgio patrols during the day, but at dusk they pulled back to the Inner City to provide tighter night-time patrols for the bureaucrats who made their homes there. But Elena was an illusionist and the men were used to moving stealthily. By the second hour after dusk they were in place. So far it looked like no one had noticed Arno Dolman was dead.

The palace of Brochena was a square with four great towers, each rising like a cathedral spire into the darkness. The Sol Tower was the dwelling of the Royal Family; Elena and the children had lived on the upper floors. Its golden roof caught the light like a beacon; it was the first thing people saw when they journeyed across the plains to the capital city. The Dorobon had built the towers, part of an ostentatious building programme which had nearly bankrupted the realm. There was already a pale luminescence coming from the ghostly Moon Tower, which was roofed with crushed quartz. The uppermost floor was open to the elements. Elena pointed: that's where Rutt Sordell would be, worrying at his fears. The chief knights of the Guard were in the Angel Tower, and the Jade Tower housed the guest-quarters for visiting dignitaries, as well as Elena's *Bastido*, in the top room.

Elena led them up the walls, creating footholds with Earth-gnosis as she went. She slipped behind the sentry at the foot of the Angel Tower. A single blade flashed, and as he fell, she muffled the sound with gnosis. He looked about seventeen, but Elena felt nothing but relief at having silenced him without giving themselves away. Lorenzo's eyes narrowed as he looked at the dead sentry, and his glance at Elena was troubled, but he stepped into his place without a word as Luca and Artaq dragged the body aside.

Sorry, Lori, but I was never the woman you thought I was, Elena thought regretfully. She took the leather bag from her back and took out Arno Dolman's head. The mage's eyes flickered open as she turned it in her hands. He was too far gone to speak, but that didn't really matter. Vedya had once told her that the Sydians used to be head-takers, believing they gained the strength and knowledge of those men whose brains they consumed; she had talked like she'd tried it herself. To a magi, the brain housed the gnosis, and that meant she held Arno Dolman's waning powers in her hands. His intellect was fading, but for a short while longer his powers were hers to command, if she had the stomach for it.

She glanced up at the tower and along the walls: there were sentries, but none were too close: the Gorgio had grown complacent, confident their enemies were far away and that Gyle's magi would keep them safe, a mistaken notion, and one she intended to correct. She looked at the Moon Tower, grey under the starlight without Mater-Luna to wash her opalescent walls white. It had been one of the first things she had noticed when she came here four years ago: that the towers of Brochena Palace stood over sixty yards tall, but only forty yards apart. She smiled and went to work with Dolman's head.

Rutt Sordell was nervous. It was a familiar feeling, this perpetual state of queasy unease, that somewhere, some unexpected factor was about to make itself known. Right now he was concerned about the Jhafi relations: the blithe contempt of the Gorgio lords for the race that outnumbered them eight to one irritated him. All through dinner Alfredo Gorgio had stroked his silver goatee with self-satisfaction as he voiced his ambitions for the return of the Dorobon and the restoration of his family's dominance beneath them. His smugness was sickening.

Some days Sordell wished their mission was to ruin the Gorgio instead, but then he remembered he despised the Nesti equally, albeit for different reasons.

Abruptly he decided all these Gorgio lordlings around him were unendurable. He stood and without a backwards glance stalked away. If that wasn't 'diplomatic', well bugger them and rukk Gurvon too, for going off to Bres at this crucial stage of the plan. He waved to Benet and Terraux and his acolytes fell into place behind him as he stomped out of the hall. They were recent graduates from an Argundian college, his own picks, neither yet twenty. The dining hall fell silent until he and his acolytes were out of sight, then redoubled in noise, but he didn't care. He was a weak-chinned man with lank hair. Worry was ageing him early, lining his pallid brow, plucking at his retreating hairline. He had shaping-gnosis, and when he exerted it he could make himself look younger, more handsome, but it took so much energy that he could rarely be bothered. And he could be charming if he felt like it, but he rarely did – what did the opinion of lesser men matter to someone like him? Let lesser beings like Vedya Smlarsk barter their powers for beauty; he had a higher purpose. Tonight he wanted the company of the stars, not mere humans. He needed to examine the future, see what the latest events portended.

He wondered what Elena Anborn was doing. He loathed her, for so many reasons. He hated that she was senior to him in Gyle's cabal despite being only a half-blood. That sickened him: that he, Rutt Sordell, a pure-blood mage of an old house, was forced to play second fiddle to a mere woman just because she spread her legs for Gyle, who had always been blind to her faults. He hated the way she was always undermining him, pouring contempt on him whenever he made even the smallest miscalculation. It had given him a real feeling of satisfaction to see her show her true colours in betraying them. Now, at last, he had been recognised as Gyle's number two. Arno Dolman had never been in the running, but he had worried that Vedya would use the same wiles as the Anborn bitch to win preeminence – but fortunately Gyle had seen sense.

Gyle's absence worried him – what if something had happened? He glanced back at Benet and Terraux. They were good enough at parlour seductions and blackmail or blasting helpless spearmen, but they'd be no use in a real fight, not against someone like Anborn.

He'd been divining furiously all week, but despite being almost certain she was penned in Forensa, the worry persisted.

Fuls was the guard at the door of the Moon Tower, a fellow Argundian, his flowing brown hair half-covered by his traditional conical helm. He let Fuls start reaching for his keys before unlocking the doors himself with a small gesture. He enjoyed these little demonstrations of power; they set him apart and made people nervous to be around him: they made up for so many things.

Benet was laughing at one of Terraux's quips. He glared at them, gesturing at them to hurry up, then, fuelled by nervous energy, bounded effortlessly up the stairs, leaving his acolytes behind.

The Moon Tower's top room had three great windows. Though they looked as if they were open to the skies, they were permanently warded, preventing birds, insects, even the wind, from intruding. Divination worked best under starlight – it was all to do with energy flows and disruptions; he'd written his thesis on it in college . . . ah, he missed the college where he had been regarded as heir-apparent to the headmaster until that unfortunate event when he'd been caught practising Necromancy – but they were *orphans*, not even real children . . . All those lost years, wasted years, until Gurvon Gyle had taken him in, restored his periapt, given him a new purpose. Gyle deserved his loyalty for such friendship, for valuing him properly. One day he would replace Gyle, when he retired, but he was prepared to wait, not like others, who'd made foolish plans to take over. They'd always resulted in bloody demises; Gyle always knew when someone was plotting against him.

He shut the door on Benet and Terraux. Tonight he needed to concentrate: there were rumours of Harkun movements in the north, where they were seldom seen. He lit the brazier in the centre of the tower room, added powders to the flames, then used the currents of smoke to channel his questions into visions. Time soared by unnoticed as he conjured visions and interpreted them carefully, determining the status and hostility of the natives. News flooded in from the spirit world: visions of campfires in the deserts, of Jhafi moving in larger than normal numbers – it was worse than he had thought.

He would advise Alfredo Gorgio to send some of his men back north, maybe even send one of the team. Arno perhaps? But the walls . . . He cursed. Vedya, then. It would be well to get her out of the capital before she damaged relations with the Gorgio further through her mindless promiscuity.

He registered in passing the tiny flare of Dolman's Earth-gnosis-powers, over to the west, beside the Angel Tower, but his mind was scanning the future, trying to determine where the Jhafi might be massing, where they might strike, who might lead them . . . suddenly some deep instinct made him look up, just before the Angel Tower lurched and he heard men screaming as the whole tower fell towards his own Moon Tower with irresistible, inevitable force. A more resolute mage than he might have had time to act, but he was frozen, both body and mind, unable to make the transition from the metaphysical to the material before all around him disintegrated as one tower struck the other.

Elena was already running above the courtyard, on a path formed from Air-gnosis, her three warriors following the trail of sparks she left, not daring to look down as they ran on nothing, held aloft by her powers alone. She had marked exactly the right spot on each of the towers, years ago, and now she had called up Dolman's fading gnosis and expended most of it on the Angel Tower, to set it toppling in just the right direction. The Angel Tower wobbled, and for a moment it looked like it could go either way, before falling exactly as planned. She caught her breath as horrified screams erupted from inside, echoed from without as the men patrolling the battlements became aware of the unfolding destruction.

The cupola of the Angel Tower struck the Moon Tower a third of the way up, shattering against it and sending debris flying outwards, over the moat and into the plaza beyond. She felt lives being extinguished as people were crushed and prayed they were the enemy, not innocents. A crossbow bolt glanced off her shields and spun away. 'Keep up,' she screamed over her shoulder, trying not to think, *One counter-spell and I'll lose all three of them.* She plunged into the clouds of dust billowing from the ruined edifices and out to the plaza before the keep, where the Moon Tower had fallen.

The plaza which had been so dark and silent a few seconds ago was in chaos. Lanterns were appearing in windows and faces peered wide-eyed at the debris strewn everywhere. The cobblestones of the plaza were shattered, and wooden beams jutted here and there from the piled rubble like the bones of some giant fallen beast. There were only a few bodies – the Moon Tower was not used for general accommodation. She could see the shattered body of a serving woman, and an Argundian, Rutt Sordell's personal guard, Fuls. She sprinted down the currents of air, sending gusts ahead to clear the dust and reveal her prey.

She found Terraux first. The nasty little snot was already dead, pulped beneath a shattered wall. She couldn't find Benet at all, but she'd felt him die; no loss there either. But where was Sordell? *There!* She landed lightly and fired a gnosis-bolt into the broken body. It jolted the prone, twisted form, but Sordell didn't stir. She still approached cautiously, though his body was a pulped mess of torn flesh and shattered bone. He'd been trapped inside the falling tower and unable to use Air-gnosis to fly free. With no affinity to Earth-gnosis, all he'd been able to do was wrap himself in shields and hope. Such protection might work for instantaneous impacts, like weapons or missiles, but shields couldn't withstand tons of rock raining down, and the result was the broken shape before her.

But Sordell had other resources: he was a Necromancer, and they were tougher to kill than cockroaches. She had seen him rise from apparent death before and she was taking no chances now. She fired another bolt into him, and this time she heard a tiny sigh even as Artaq closed in on him.

'Artaq, stay back!'

'He's dead, lady. I'll take his—'

Black light flashed from a twitching finger and caught the Jhafi warrior in the face. He screamed, his back arched and he fell. Even as Elena ran towards him she fired more bolts of energy at Sordell. His flesh was quivering in some unseen wind, rising up with jerking, unsteady movements. *A soul-drain! Rukka!* There was no help for Artaq; she could see that already.

As Sordell's eyes opened she flung herself at him, her sword gripped in both hands. She punched through his shields in a flare of coruscating sparks and buried her sword in his gut. Blood sprayed and his flesh writhed frantically, trying to close itself. Sordell hurled a soul-drain at her too, but she met it with healing-wards, which weakened his attack. But she could not escape his ferocity unscathed: she felt the skin on her face dry, felt her hair wither like desiccated grass. Her lips split as she screamed in defiance and her fingers twisted, even as she threw her weight onto the pommel of her blade and drove it into his chest, through his heart. He flailed beneath her, and the skin on his face peeled away to reveal the muscles and tendons and sinews beneath, pulsing red and purulent yellow, as he howled.

'Take his head!' she screamed. *'Cut it off!'*

Sordell tried to climb up her blade, his heart spitted but his body, fuelled by Necromancy, fighting on. One purple-lit hand reached for her and gripped her throat, and as it tightened it seemed to be drawing the blood from her veins. Energy throbbed down into his arms, healing them, reviving him even as she struggled to counter his attack. 'Kill him!' she croaked as the fangs of his spell sucked her vitality away. He grinned madly up at her, his body reforming about him despite her efforts.

A blade swung, a sweep of silver that cleaved Sordell's neck in two, wielded by a man screaming in fury. As the steel severed the neck it struck the stone beneath and the blade shattered. Sordell's dreadful visage emptied and his fleshless skull rolled sideways. Elena fell to her knees over his body, propped up on the blade that still skewered his heart. Her hands were twisted with age, like knotted firewood. She felt hollow, broken, and it took all her strength just to look up at Lorenzo, who stood beside her, his broken sword in his hand.

'Lori—' Her voice was a withered croak. He backed away, raising a hand. *Gods, how bad is it?* Beyond him, Luca was backing away from the fallen Artaq. There was a hole in the Jhafi's head where his face had been. That would have happened to her without her shields and healing-gnosis. All around them bells were ringing and voices shouting.

Luca gasped, 'Donna Elena!' and he pointed to Sordell's head.

She half-glimpsed an eight-inch-wide multi-legged insectoid thing sliding from his mouth. She raised her twisted right hand and sent a weak bolt, but she was too slow; the hideous thing scuttled into the rubble and was lost from sight. *Damn!*

'What was that?' Luca gasped.

'What's left of Sordell,' she rasped. She tried to find Vedya mentally, but she had no strength left. 'We must go – Vedya will come, and if she catches us, we're done.'

Luca bent over Artaq, said a few words, then left him where he lay. Lorenzo was still staring at her. 'Elena, can you—? What happened?'

'This is . . . nothing. I'll be fine . . . just took all I had.'

'Your hair,' he said. He looked almost nauseous.

'What?' She tugged a strand from her ponytail and sucked in her breath. It had gone silver-grey. 'It's nothing, Lori . . . could have been much worse.' She climbed to her feet, feeling desperately frail. Sordell's attacks had pushed her to the very limit.

Lorenzo came over and reluctantly put an arm about her and helped her up. He looked like he could scarcely bear to be touching her. 'Sorry, Lorenzo,' she cackled mirthlessly. 'I guess you won't be wanting my kiss any more.' She grimaced inside at how hysterical and hideous her voice sounded – and at the self-pity of her words. As she clung to the young knight, he looked at her, his face unreadable, but he didn't let go of her. 'I'll claim one later,' he said in a low voice.

'Get us out of here and I'll freely give it,' she croaked, her sword shaking in her clawed hand.

Luca Fustinios suddenly took to his heels, leapt a pile of broken masonry and started rummaging around amidst the strewn rubble. 'Lady Elena – *look!*'

'What? Luca, we have to get out of here, now—'

But the little Javonesi was ignoring her. He bent over something, then straightened carefully, holding something in his arms. He turned towards them with a beaming grin. He was holding Solinde Nesti. The princess was unconscious and battered, but she was undeniably alive.

Lorenzo squeezed Elena's arm and whispered, 'Sol et Lune, the princessa!'

Elena stared, stunned. *She must have been in a lower room of the Moon Tower*, she thought, *but how could she possibly have survived? Was she shielded, or imprisoned in a warded cell?* But all her questions could wait; right now they had to get out of there. 'Let's get her away from here,' she rasped.

<*Elena – is that you?*> Vedya's mind teased hers.

Damn. 'We've got to go, now – Luca, can you carry the princessa? Come on—' She tottered free of Lorenzo's arms and poured what last scrap of energy she could summon into her legs, trying to counter Sordell's spell. She felt utterly stricken – an unwanted preview of old age. Her limbs felt like frail twigs, and it hurt her tortured throat to breathe.

But fear whipped them all along and they broke into a slow trot. At first they ran through empty streets, then hooves clattered behind them and they swerved into an alley. After another block Luca handed Solinde to Lorenzo and loaded his crossbow. He ran back a few steps, dropped to one knee and fired down the alley they had just left.

A horse shrieked, and they heard it crash to the cobblestones, its rider screaming.

Elena? Ah, there you are. Vedya's tinkling giggle filled her mind.

'Faster,' she croaked, screaming inside in frustration and terror. *We can't survive Vedya, not when I'm so far gone . . .*

Booted feet echoed behind them. Luca had already reloaded; now he fired again, and as they heard another death-cry, someone yelled, 'It's a dead-end! They're trapped!' from somewhere nearby.

It better not be a rukking dead-end, Elena thought as her mind filled with images of what Vedya would do to her if she caught her. 'Run!' she whispered.

<*I'm coming, Elena,*> that insidious whisper cooed in her mind again, and she sensed the Sydian witch's approach, three hundred yards above and behind them and closing by the second. 'Get through the walls, Lori, and then run,' she croaked calmly. 'Take the princessa to safety.'

Luca ran past them, guiding them to the gap in the walls where they had slipped through, one of the many points Dolman hadn't had time to fix. He pushed Elena through, then helped Lorenzo carry Solinde through. An arrow flew out of the darkness, struck the wall and pinged away, followed by another that flew through the gap. Luca grasped a support strut in the half-completed structure and pulled with all his strength until a section of the wall fell inwards, sealing the gap. They turned away from the blockage and found themselves at the top of a slope that led down to the close-packed shacks of the Jhafi.

Lorenzo led the way, Solinde in his arms, mercifully still unconscious. Luca helped Elena down. Though his eyes betrayed his horror at what Elena had become, he didn't falter. Barely had they reached the Jhafi shanties when an incandescent shape appeared above the walls. Vedya wore a silk dress, red as blood, and her waist-length black hair flew about her like the wings of a raven.

'Do you have a plan, Ella?' Lorenzo whispered, pulling her into the lee of a half-built wall. Luca knelt and reloaded his crossbow, as his eyes tracked the witch.

Not really. 'Get under cover, damnit, before—'

Vedya swooped over them and a vivid blast of blue fire erupted from her finger and struck Luca even as he fired. His bolt was snatched away by the torrent of energy that picked him up and flung him against a mud-brick wall. His mouth was open in voiceless agony and he started twitching, as if being moved by the invisible strings of some puppet-master.

Vedya vanished behind a roof, no doubt wary of a counter-strike, but Elena didn't have the energy.

Lorenzo put Solinde down and stood over her, his broken sword in hand, scanning the skies. 'What is the plan, Elena?' he demanded.

I had a plan, but in that plan I was fresh and undamaged. 'We have to draw her in, Lori, and take her down with weapons. She isn't a fighter.'

'But all she has to do is stay up there and the Gorgio will be on top of us!'

'I never said it was a good plan.' She struggled to put one foot beneath her. On the ground Solinde moaned. *I do this for you, Princessa.* She grimaced in pain as she stood, then tottered out into the narrow alleyway. A bright shape swooped towards her like one of Kore's angels.

Vedya Smlarsk first met Gurvon Gyle at Northpoint, the tower placed by the Ordo Costruo where the Leviathan Bridge was anchored, south of Pontus. She had come with her man, Hygor, to look upon the great tower – the Tower of the Eye, the Sydians called it, *Ureche Turla,* where the hated magi gazed out eternally over the Bridge. The Bridge itself was deep beneath the waves, midway through its tide-cycle. Ureche Turla was a mighty sight: as delicate as an ivory carving, yet a mile high, festooned with massive cables and platforms where windships could dock. The blue light in its uppermost tower room shone like a star.

Vedya's mother had seduced a Bridge Builder mage nineteen years previously, though she was already married. There was no shame in the seduction – all knew that to bear a mage-child was to bring wealth and status to the clan. Her mother had been nubile and skilled in the arts of the flesh. She was often called upon to conse-crate the sacred union with the priests on feast days, when they would mate before the tribe to bring blessings upon the harvest – though they were nomads, horse herders, they would settle in spring to grow a single harvest of barley, oats and wheat to sustain them through winter.

Vedya grew up a privileged child, one whom men fought over. The few magi the tribe had managed to breed lived together in the Sfera, or Circle, sharing an intense rivalry and kinship, teaching each other what snippets of mage-craft they learned. All the Sfera were part-Rondian, of course, mostly quarter-bloods and eighth-bloods, but Vedya was a full half-blood, with affinities to water and animals. When she bled, she was married off to a powerful man, Hygor of the Armasar Rasa clan, as his fourth wife. He took her virginity before the whole clan at the height of the wedding celebrations while his three other wives watched her with dark unreadable eyes. He was twice her age. She was thirteen.

That night in Pontus she became aware of another man watching Ureche Turla. Hygor had already noted him, wary hunter that he was. At first she thought the stranger, clad in Sydian leathers, one of the clan, but as he approached, the wind pushed back his hood, and the moonlight revealed that he wasn't Sydian at all; he was Rondian. And he wasn't watching the tower. He was watching *her*.

Hygor growled: an outsider looking openly upon a Sydian woman was an unacceptable challenge to her husband's manhood. This man didn't look like a fighter, but neither did he cringe when Hygor strode angrily towards him. He was smallish for a Rondian, with a ferret-like face and a compact body. Hygor no doubt intended to kill him – until he saw the crystal pulsing at his throat. The man was a vrajitoare, a mage.

Vedya had feared for Hygor. He was a good mate: he was virile and protective and he favoured her above his other wives. But the vrajitoare had raised a hand in peace, and he and Hygor had talked. The vrajitoare knew the Sydian tongue. When Hygor returned, it was with a stunned look upon his face. In his hands were three woven leather bracelets, each set with twelve diamonds, each stone alone worth one hundred horses. She remembered the tremor she felt when she saw them. Hygor reached out and broke her bridal neck-lace, spilling the pottery beads onto the rocky hillside. 'Wife, you are no longer my wife. You belong to this man.' His eyes were like plates, luminous in the moonlight.

She had fallen to her knees and wailed – it was expected. But her mind was already moving forward, even as Hygor walked away.

'My name is Gurvon Gyle,' the vrajitoare told her as he silenced her grief-cries with a gesture. 'You belong to me. Come.'

She missed Hygor and the simplicity of tribal life sometimes, but her first child to Hygor had left her barren, so she could no longer strengthen the clan. Her daughter would enrich the Sfera, but she brought Hygor nothing more now. She was worth considerably less than three thousand six hundred horses. Hygor had got a very good price for her.

At first she had been confused: this man Gyle would not consummate their marriage, instead spending his nights with a tired older woman who was also not his wife. But gradually things became clearer to Vedya: she was merely Gyle's servant; the other woman, a hostile, cynical creature called Elena Anborn, was his lover. Gyle had purchased Vedya not for his bed, but to teach her, to *realise her potential*, he said, to make her useful to him. So she learned how to shield, and how to blast enemies with energy, and other skills even those of the Sfera didn't know: wonderful things; how to fly, how to read minds, how to deceive people. They opened up her horizons, clever Gyle and his cold Elena.

Gradually the thought grew in her mind that were she to supplant Elena in Gyle's bed, she would enjoy greater status and privilege among the other vrajitoare he employed. She noticed that their relationship was based on habit, old memories, remembered passions. When she spied on them, she saw the dull, uninspired way they coupled briefly, then rolled apart, and how they talked, sharing ideas but never dreams. It was easy to drive a wedge between them: she was young and beautiful, exotic, comfortable with her body and her desires. She had performed before the entire clan with Hygor many times, and witnessed others, learning new tricks to please a man – and herself. It was easy to drop hints, to expose a little flesh for his eyes only. She could be patient, for him – and there was much more for her to learn, once she understood their purpose: to kill enemies for money. That came easily to her too.

It wasn't hard to find ways to be alone with Gurvon Gyle. The first time, in Verelon, he had fallen upon her without finesse, taken her quickly, guiltily, but the next time she had slowed him down and taught him how to enjoy her fully. And though she had no pretensions of intellect, she was a good listener; it took no great mind to know Gyle wanted to be thought wise, not to be contradicted, as Elena always did. And he believed himself to be a masterly lover – all men did. She knew better than most how to make a man feel good. With his body enslaved and his mind engaged, he was hers.

She had enjoyed watching the realisation come upon Elena Anborn that her lover was being stolen. It was amusing to witness the way she pretended it wasn't happening, how she humiliated herself trying to look more beautiful, while Gyle found reasons to send her from him. He might have pretended to Elena that she was still important to him, but they were empty words: Vedya ruled Gurvon Gyle.

Vedya swooped above the forest of crude buildings that fringed the inner walls of Brochena, seeing with night-sighted eyes. Elena Anborn hobbled out of cover, her face hooded, her movements awkward. *Is she wounded?* Vedya licked her lips. Now was the time for the pupil to become the master. The little crossbowman lay twitching in the open and she blasted him again, enjoying his death-spasm. There was still no counter-strike from Elena, to her surprise.

Has she nothing left? She fought a sense of exultation and focused on the second man below: a Rimoni knight, cowering under cover . . . And Jhafi, hundreds of them, huddling like beetles in a rotting log. Vedya knew many ways to destroy an enemy. *This will be amusing,* she thought as she started building a fresh attack based upon mesmerism-gnosis.

With a harsh cry she sent a wave of despair through the minds of all in the vicinity. She felt old men and women of the Jhafi imagine their own deaths, and their hearts gave up beating. Children dreamed the deaths of their mothers and wailed in utter despair. Men suddenly thinking themselves castrated howled in agony, hands clutched to their groins as they grovelled in the dirt. Women clenched their wombs, imagining them shrivelling and cancerous. All the while she expected the bent figure of Elena Anborn to counter her, but nothing came.

She has nothing left! She concentrated next on the Rimoni knight, slid inside his mind, knew him in a heartbeat: a young man, infatuated with Elena Anborn. *What is it with this shrivelled old woman?* His sexual awakening had come at the hands of an older woman and in his mind he had interwoven Elena with that now-dead lover. But this night he had seen the ruthless killer behind Elena's fair mask. Vedya crowed as she saw him relive the way Elena's youth had been destroyed by Sordell; his mind showed her just how horrifically disfigured Elena was now, like a shattered egg, the yolk spilled, the shell broken. His confusion was a tangible thing, an easy weapon to grasp.

<She's an abomination> she whispered into his mind. <She cares nothing for you. How she looks now: that is her true appearance! See the hag within exposed, her vileness laid bare! Strike her down, rid this world of her—>

Vedya exulted as she saw him step from the shadows behind Elena's back. This was truly her hour. She glided down, parrying a feeble mage-bolt. Elena's hood fell back, exposing aged skin and coarse grey hair. She was bent like an old woman, her hands clawed. The knight was four easy strides behind her, his sword raised – it was broken, but still a foot long, still lethal.

Vedya spoke to distract her. 'Elena. You're looking your age.'

Elena straightened slightly, her prematurely old face grimacing with effort. Behind her the knight swung, but somehow Elena twisted, did something that made the knight collapse as if deflated. Vedya recoiled in alarm, but Elena's leg buckled and she fell to her knees, gasping for breath. The light within her periapt dimmed. She looked like some toothless granny, begging for gruel in the markets.

Ha! Vedya landed, stepped in and slapped her, her hand cracking across Elena's face. No shields softened the attack, and the satisfaction of that physical blow was *magnificent*. Elena tried to raise her own sword, but Vedya stamped on her wrist. Bones snapped. Elena whimpered in agony and Vedya slammed a bolt of gnosis-fire into her. As she convulsed her mouth opened in a wordless scream as her skin seared and blistered. The energy crackled, frying her. One more would kill her.

No – too merciful. She knelt above her, the woman who'd taught her more about the gnosis than any other: her mentor in magic, her rival in love, now utterly helpless beneath her. 'Elena, *darling*, do you remember teaching me the *Soul-Devourer*,' she whispered, 'how to consume the mind and powers of another? That is what I shall do to you, and your soul will dwell eternally in mine, shrieking in despair and rage as I take everything that was once yours: your powers, your memories. You will be at my disposal, helpless within me for the rest of my life.' She slid her mind through Elena's remaining shields. The woman's resistance was pitiful. *See, I remember the spell well* . . . She let the snake of her gnosis coil about the tiny, fragile core that was all that remained of Elena Anborn's power and opened her jaws to swallow.

A dry voice whispered inside her mind, <*You didn't think I'd taught you properly, did you?*>

The darkness changed. The lights went out and she screamed. And kept on screaming as a billion claws pulled her into oblivion.

Elena came to herself slowly. It had been such a gamble! She had been totally emptied out, her stamina gone, her powers all but spent. Countering Vedya's manipulation of Lorenzo had used up her last reserves – all but the one sliver she forced herself to hold back, the only slim chance she had left. If the Sydian had used mage-bolts or stabbed her, or simply sat and waited for the Gorgio soldiers, Elena would have been helpless – and now dead. But Elena had taught Vedya that the Soul-Devourer technique was always the best way to destroy a helpless mage, for it would give the devouring mage greater power. That was true, but it was also something of a trap, for it opened a path for a counter-blow, one that could only be blocked if you knew the technique. Elena had never even mentioned that to Vedya, let alone taught her that technique. *Always have a plan* . . .

Now her rival's empty carcase was lying in the filth of the alley, her glassy eyes lifeless. She was as dead as it was possible to be: her soul was gone for ever. The spirit world would never receive her, no Necromancer or Healer could ever restore life. That tiny spark of awareness that had flowed into Elena had dissolved and gone.

Beautiful, manipulative, obsessive Vedya had simply ceased to exist.

What a monster I have become. But I live and I have her life-energy, until it dissipates . . .

She pulled herself up. Ignoring her bloodied knees, she dragged herself through the stony dirt of the alley to Lorenzo. She rested her head on his chest. It rose and fell shallowly. *Thanks be . . .*

She used some of what she had taken from Vedya to send calmness to the surviving Jhafi, huddled unseen in the surrounding hovels. There were dozens dead, and many more who would be mentally scarred for life. She closed Luca's staring eyes, berating herself for being unable to protect him, then turned to the Rimoni knight.

She sent a little wakefulness into him and cushioned his mind as consciousness returned. When he woke and his eyes found her face, she heard him stiffen and gasp. He threw her off him and cringed in the dirt. 'Diablo,' he hissed, '*don't touch me.*'

How much was the remnants of Vedya's spell she couldn't tell. *Oh Lori. I warned you not to come.*

The hue and cry died down; the Gorgio had seen Vedya's demise and now feared to follow. Jhafi men came out of the rabbit-warren of buildings and found Elena, huddled protectively over the prone body of Solinde, with Lorenzo in a daze nearby, his face turned away. These men were loyal to one Mustaq al'Madhi, ostensibly a trader, known as, amongst other less salubrious nicknames, 'the Sultan of the Souks'. But Mustaq al'Madhi had a complicated personal code which currently favoured the Nesti among the Rimoni noble families. Elena and Solinde were wrapped in bekira-shrouds, then the three survivors were borne through the tangle of alleyways ripe with the smells of rotting food, human and animal waste and the sweat of unwashed bodies. The smoke of a myriad cooking fires set Elena coughing helplessly, like the oldest crone in the market.

Behind them, more Jhafi men were carrying the bodies of Sordell and Vedya and shouting in triumph, waving weapons produced from hidden caches. Drums started beating and torches lit up the night, gleaming scarlet and orange off bared scimitars and knives. They wound their way to Dom-al'Ahm Plaza, where Mustaq al'Madhi awaited them, surrounded by his fighting men. Some had brought meat-hooks for the corpses of the hated magi. His brutish face was beaming as he clapped Elena on her shoulders, nearly sending her sprawling.

'This is a night of glory, Lady Elena!' he shouted exultantly. 'Five of the devils! It is a shame that Shaitan Gyle was not here too, to taste the same bitter defeat.'

If Gurvon had been here this would not have happened, she thought numbly, but what she said was, 'Bring me scrolls, to pin on their bodies.'

Her voice was so cracked that even al'Madhi, who barely knew her, noticed. 'Lady, you are afflicted?'

'Just temporarily, Mustaq. You need not worry. I will be fine again soon.'

He backed away a little at this reminder of the dreaded gnosis, but he remained friendly. 'You have given much for us, lady,' he said. 'We will tend you. Everything we have is yours. May Ahm bless you eternally.'

I don't know that Ahm cares much for Rondian magi. She bowed in thanks, nevertheless. 'I will keep the princessa with me,' she told him. 'She must be restored to the Queen-Regent.'

'And put on trial, Lady,' he added grimly. 'She has been with them.' He spat eloquently.

'And put on trial,' Elena agreed, sadly.

The Gorgio soldiers did not leave the Inner City, but ranks of legionaries manned the walls, peering out over the Jhafi dwellings as rejoicing spread like wildfire. The drums beat all night and whooping cries echoed around the shanties. Threats were called up to the Gorgio, goading them:

'Come, come and join our celebration.'

'All your magi-devils are dead.'

'Would you like to mourn the fallen? Come to the Dom-al'Ahm tomorrow.'

'Death to the Gorgio; long live the Nesti!'

Some of the Gorgio solders were visibly champing at the bit to attack, but discipline and the shouted orders of their officers held them in place.

Dawn found the Outer City wreathed in smoke. Alfredo Gorgio himself came and peered out across the city. He looked shaken. The soldiers locked down the Inner City. Paralysis gripped Brochena.

For the next few days Elena closeted herself in a room of Mustaq al'Madhi's house. She mostly slept, and when awake concentrated on healing herself, especially the broken wrist, to make sure the bones were not permanently weakened. In the mirror she was confronted with a vision of what old age would look like. She told herself it wasn't so bad: a gaunt face, but fine-boned, not unpleasant, but still it made her weep. Her hair was grey, but she could see blonde at the roots, so she took some shears and cut it all back to the regrowth. It made her look alien, but it was better than looking seventy. *Let them think it's a fashion decision.*

After that, she set about restoring herself to the woman she had been. As the days passed, her vigour gradually returned. Full recovery would take months; for now, her face had more lines and the hair growing back with gnosis-assisted speed was a paler blonde with silver strands. She looked frightful for a couple of days as her skin flaked and peeled off, but the skin beneath was smooth and glowing – though being half-killed by Necromancy was never going to be popular as a beauty treatment.

Lorenzo did not come near her. She wanted to help him, but she was the last person he wanted to see, so she made Solinde her main concern. The princessa regained consciousness the day after her rescue, but she was sullen and refused to talk to anyone. Elena had taught Cera and Solinde mind-blanking to prevent magi from prying in their minds. Now Solinde used Elena's own teaching against her, refusing to let her into her mind. She could not say how she had survived the Moon Tower's fall. Perhaps she had just been extraordinarily lucky.

Mustaq and the other headmen managed to restrain the Jhafi population from assaulting the citadel, though some of the younger men fired arrows at men on the walls. The word went round: 'Wait. The Nesti are coming.' But it was the Gorgio who moved first, a few days after Elena's attack. Trumpets blared and a legion marched from the Inner City, down the Kingsway to Dom-al'Ahm Plaza. As row upon row of soldiers filled the square, the Jhafi silently encircled them. A cohort secured each flank, while the fifth cohort marched in the centre. The legion commander rode amidst a plethora of shields raised about him in a tortoise formation to the meat-hooks that had been hung in the centre of the plaza. Every Gorgio legionary looked at them once, reading the signs writ large and bold, and winced.

The headless corpse of Arno Dolman hung upside down, his intestines entwined about the hook. A huge nail tacked a sign to his flesh that read *The Man of Stone*. Beside him hung the grisly but unrecognisable remains of Benet and Terraux, with the legend *The Blasphemous Twins* pinned above them, referring to a well-known cautionary Amteh parable about homosexuality. Rutt Sordell's head was on the top of a spike, the rest of his body impaled lower down. His sign read: *Slayer of the King*. Beside him, Vedya's perfect body was similarly defiled, and her scroll read: *The Whore of Shaitan*.

The next day, the Gorgio fled the city.

The news of the enemy's flight spread swiftly. Mustaq al'Madhi led his men cautiously into the Inner City the next day, surrounding Elena, who was shrouded in black and carried on a palanquin. The Jhafi warriors treated her with deference and fear. The drums and cymbals beat out the rhythm of vengeance and children danced in triumph as their elders sacked any Rimoni house not flying a Nesti pennant and butchered families who had publicly aligned themselves with the Gorgio usurpers. There were few of those, luckily, but they came across some grisly sights as they wound through the streets.

When they arrived at the palace, they stepped carefully through the wreckage of the fallen Moon Tower and circled towards the main gates, which stood invitingly open. 'My men have scouted,

Lady Elena,' Mustaq told her as he helped her down, 'but we have found something strange. We need your assistance, if it pleases you.'

Her hands shook, but she could straighten herself again, and her sword hand and wrist had regained some of their old strength. She hobbled along using a rough staff to balance her while her mind searched ahead. There was refuse everywhere. One deserted court-yard was littered with discarded tack and harness; another held dozens of broached casks – whatever wine the Gorgio could not take with them, left to run into the drains in an act of spite. Cats crawled through the wreckage, mewling and hissing, and in one place squab-bling violently over something: the right arm and leg of a man protruding from a shallow grave. His flesh was rotting in the midday sun.

At their approach, the cats backed away, yowling. Mustaq signalled and a couple of men wrapped cloth about their noses and mouths and began digging. It didn't take them long to uncover a naked man, tall with long golden hair: Fernando Tolidi, Solinde's Gorgio sweet-heart.

Why would they kill Fernando? Elena wondered, but she was distracted by more men running into the courtyard, shouting in agitation: there were more graves in the gardens. Elena put a hand to her mouth and hurried along with the crowd.

Hundreds of crows rose like a black cloud from a square in the shadow of the Royal Tower. The Jhafi stiffened, some fell to their knees, wailing, and Elena herself reeled at the dreadful smell. The last act of the fleeing Gorgio had been to butcher the palace's Jhafi staff. Elena felt a terrible weight of guilt fall upon her as they walked across the bloodstained square. *None of this would have happened if I had not come.*

She looked down on the bodies of the women and men of the servants' quarters, their eyes sightless, their faces locked in their final expressions of terror or resignation. There were forty-eight of them. She felt tears running down her cheeks, and closed her eyes. She let grief wash through her. It wasn't cleansing at all.

After a time she sent her mind questing ahead, seeking life. *There – up, to the left!*

She led the Jhafi men cautiously, but there were no hidden archers or ambushes. Each room looked partially ransacked, as if the Gorgio had seized anything they could carry of value as plunder in a hurried escape. But in one room, hidden amidst a pile of debris and fallen tapestries, she found a large locked chest. Mustaq sidled forward and gingerly prised it open with a crowbar. When the lock snapped with a crack, they all jumped.

Inside was a Jhafi girl, her dirty face tear-streaked. She shrank into the chest, whimpering pitifully.

'Hush child,' Mustaq murmured. 'This is Lady Elena of the Nesti. She will not harm you.'

The girl looked unconvinced. She had a dark face, with a child's upturned nose, and was skinny as a broom. Elena remembered her now: *Tarita*, one of the younger maids, fourteen or fifteen years old, and tiny, well short of five feet tall. She had been a sparkling, cheeky girl, prone to forgetfulness – once she had absentmindedly carried a pitcher of cold water up to Elena's chambers for bathing, forgetting it was supposed to be heated. She had feared a tongue-lashing, or worse, but Elena had gently jested with her, and she had been quick to join the joke, telling Elena she could no doubt warm it with magic. She was in shock now. Elena wondered how she had escaped.

'Tarita,' she said softly, 'will you heat some water for my bath?'

The girl almost smiled, then hid her face. It took time to coax the girl into her arms. As a Jhafi woman led the girl away to care for her, Elena told herself, *I must not forget her. We need to know what she saw.*

There were no other survivors, just rooms strewn with broken furniture and discarded non-essentials. The tower room where *Bastido* lay waiting hadn't been touched. She'd primed *Bastido* to attack on *cinque* if anyone else came in, which might've had something to do with that. Her own room had been destroyed, of course. Someone, Vedya, she presumed, had taken the time and trouble to go through her wardrobe and rip up every piece of clothing she owned, then she'd pissed on everything. It stank and it hurt a little, but she'd expected it.

At least I was wearing my gems.

The Nesti retook Brochena in an atmosphere of carnival two weeks later. The hated Gorgio had come, and they had shown their true nature in murder and regicide, but they had fled without battle. Cera Nesti's courage following the death of her family was already legendary, and the celebrations were spontaneous and genuine. Elena waited with Mustaq al'Madhi and his Jhafi on the main steps of the palace as Cera's party wound through the streets. The cheering and singing grew closer while Elena sweated beneath her hooded robes.

The Queen-Regent didn't keep them waiting too long. Elena dreaded assassins in the crowd, but Cera negotiated the throng safely, touching the hands of well-wishers, a heroine to the masses crowding the plaza. She was composed, her gestures controlled. The girl had gone; she was a woman. *She is born to this.* The thought made Elena both proud and apprehensive.

As Cera climbed the stairs, her eyes found Elena. She frowned at her shroud. Elena had written, but reading was not the same as witnessing. Elena's healing-gnosis had softened most of the effects of Sordell's necromancy, but she was not yet her old self. Her silver-blonde hair was half an inch long, her face was lined. She looked ten years older, by normal human standards.

Cera worked her way down the line, greeting the waiting nobles and heads of bureaucracy, until she reached Elena. At her first close sight of her protector, the Queen-Regent gasped and swallowed. Then she masked her features and embraced her. 'Ella – *Deo!* What have they done to you?' She ran her hand over Elena's scalp. 'I hardly recognise you.'

'I heard short hair would be the look this winter.' Elena winked.

Cera seized Elena's hand and kissed it, then pulled her into a tight embrace. 'You have won us back the kingdom, Ella.' Her whisper was fervent. 'You are a miracle-worker!'

'Oh, it's just my job,' Elena replied drily.

'I love you, Ella. You are Sol et Lune to me.'

'Shhh! That's blasphemy, Cera – it'll annoy the drui.' She patted her cheek and gave her a serious look. 'Solinde refused to attend. I can't get through to her – she's shielding from me, and if I use gnostic force to break through, I'll hurt her. The Jhafi want her executed for treason.'

Cera's face clouded. 'Later, Ella. Today I have to look happy.' She leaned forward and whispered in her ear, 'Mustaq's people have slaughtered a thousand Gorgio sympathisers and he's given me a list of three thousand more.' Her eyes met Elena's. 'What do I do?'

Elena swallowed. 'Say nothing. Talk to me later.' She squeezed her hand, then stepped back and curtseyed. 'Later.'

Cera looked at her for an instant longer, then she regained her composure and swept on to the next person, a smile once more on her lips.

Elena slipped backwards through the crowd, troubled, whilst all around her people rejoiced. She noticed Lorenzo following her with his eyes, but he looked away when he realised she had noticed.

Four of them made the decision: Cera, Elena, Comte Piero Inveglio and Mustaq al'Madhi, who had become indispensable with terrifying efficiency. After a measured beginning, the meeting became increasingly acrimonious. Finally Mustaq was on his feet, jabbing a finger at Inveglio. 'When the Gorgio came, all manner of people in the Merchant and Crafts Guilds flocked about them, grubbing for money, shamelessly rolling over like dogs for their new masters – there must be a reckoning!'

Inveglio protested, 'But most of those on this list – I know them! – had no choice but to comply. When a usurper places a knife to your throat, only a fool denies him!'

'You are protecting your friends, your "business associates",' Mustaq spat. 'These people got rich on Gorgio money; they suckled at the enemy teat, and now my people demand retribution.' He redirected his demands to Cera. 'The Gorgio slaughtered the palace servants like *animals*! These people abetted that by their fawning upon the Gorgio. There must be a purge, sanctioned and run by the Nesti, or blood will flow without sanction, this I promise you!'

Cera turned to Elena, her tones a little pleading. 'Ella, what should I do?'

Elena looked at her appraisingly, thinking, *This is what kingship is, Cera: not all parades and pretty speeches, but wielding the knife judiciously.* 'There was a Rimoni poet, Nikos Mandelli, who advised the emperors of Rym before the coming of the magi. He wrote extensively about how to rule an empire. The Church banned his writings, but they have been recovered and distributed among the magi. In his book *Imperator* Mandelli said that a ruler must be both loved and feared. Sometimes this can be achieved with kindness and mercy, but sometimes harsher means must be utilised. Your goal is to secure the Nesti in power. You cannot permit those who supported the Gorgio coup to continue without sanction; that would weaken your standing with the majority of the people. Your path is clear.'

Mustaq stabbed his finger at Elena. 'As the jadugara says!' he exclaimed triumphantly while Comte Inveglio buried his head in his hands and Cera swallowed, her face white.

'Prison and trials, not killings!' she demanded as Mustaq bowed and strode from the room.

For a week Cera gave Mustaq his head, and Nesti soldiery carried out what was required. The streets were filled with squads of men making raids on the accused merchants and the dungeons beneath the Castel Regium filled up. Inevitably it got out of hand as the lists got longer and longer. Elena suspected the bureaucrats administering the lists were taking bribes from people to settle scores. There would be months of trials before anything could be done, and in the meantime the gaol was bursting at the seams. Worst of all, possible collaborators' names were being leaked to the public and then targeted by lynch-mobs. Those scenes took Elena back to places like Knebb during the Revolt. They were not memories she wanted to revisit ever again.

It all took a toll on Cera. The waves of guilt and sickness at what she had unleashed gave way to a new coldness and remorselessness that was frightening to see in the eyes of one so young.

Elena was scared for her. *She reminds me of me, during the Revolt . . .*

After seven days Cera lifted martial law and the Nesti soldiers returned to keeping the peace. She ordered a city-wide clean-up to wash away all traces of that week, and it went ahead alongside the funerals. She ordered the reconstruction of buildings, which took time, while the dungeons beneath the palace overflowed. The people no longer cheered her unquestioningly, and she began to dread public appearances. 'Half of them hate me now,' she wept into Elena's arms.

Despite this, she presided over the endless trials of the alleged collaborators, fining all but the most genuinely extreme cases. Some saw it as leniency and weakness, others as mercy and strength. She came to terms with one of life's truths: you can't please everyone.

By the last day of the year, Timori had recovered enough to sleep in his own room, as long as Borsa slept outside his door. Cera had moved into the royal suite, though she was visibly uncomfortable to be sleeping where her dead parents had once slept, and Elena had Rutt Sordell's old chambers outside Cera's doors, which she hated. The rescued Jhafi girl Tarita became Elena's maid, revealing a gift of laughter that Elena badly needed, especially on mornings when she came back from her work-outs bent double with pain. The girl turned fifteen shortly after they'd found her, and she appeared to have put whatever horrors she had seen behind her quickly. She knew how to play tabula and to Elena's embarrassment she usually won. *Some master strategist, whipped at the Game of Kings by a maid.*

Lorenzo remained wary, whether horrified by what he'd seen Elena do, or as a result of Vedya's mind-manipulation, though he was always polite. And Solinde continued to behave like a stranger.

Cera enlarged the Regency Council with selected Jhafi leaders, including Mustaq al'Madhi. She reaffirmed their commitment to the shihad, and envoys were sent to Salim, Sultan of Kesh. Alfredo Gorgio was declared outlaw, and they prepared for war against the Gorgio, though they were in no condition for such a conflict.

The matter of Fernando Tolidi's death nagged at the back of Elena's mind, but she was too busy to deal with it. Solinde refused to be reconciled, and it was beginning to look like she must either go on trial or be quietly removed from the arena. The prison beneath Krak di Condotiori in the southern mountains was the traditional place for high-ranking political prisoners. They prepared for her transfer.

It was six months until the Moontide and Brochena rang with activity. Spies told them that Gurvon Gyle had been spotted in the Gorgio stronghold of Hytel. The Gorgio were severely weakened, having been harried by Jhafi all the way home, but if the mage was still with them, that was reason for caution.

It was from Hebusalim that the most puzzling news came: the head of the Bridge Builders, old Antonin Meiros, had remarried – even more shocking, his new bride was a Lakh girl from a family no one had ever heard of. Had the old mage gone senile? It was disgusting, the old goat purchasing some poor girl. The Hebb called for his head in the streets of the villages and the Kesh burned him in effigy while singing of shihad. The few windships that flew from Pontus spoke of mustering legions. The world was arming for war, and Javon had no choice but to follow suit.

16

A Piece of Amber

Periapt

A mage's powers can be amplified by attuning himself to certain tools which take the gnosis energy and focus it. For example, a periapt made of wood can double the efficiency of a 'spell', and a piece of amber or a crystal can amplify it further. Many will have a variety of periapts for different workings. A pendant is best deployed for protective work; a rod or wand for delicate and narrow-focus work; and a large staff for offensive or large-scale workings. But do not make the mistake of believing that the periapt itself is more important than he who wields it. The gnosis comes from within.

ARDO ACTIUM, SCHOLAR, BRES 518

Norostein, Noros, on the continent of Yuros
Decore 927 to Febreux 928
7–5 months until the Moontide

Alaron sat and stared at the ashes in the fireplace. He had barely left his bedroom for three weeks. Daylight glimmered through the ill-fitting shutters and he could hear the muffled sounds of the street: outside life carried on, but his life couldn't. When Headmaster Gavius had given his verdict, he had effectively killed him. He felt as grey and cold as the ashes.

His father had tried talking to him, but he had retreated to his bedroom and locked the door. His piss-bucket was almost full, the rank odour filling the air. He'd not washed in days, his hair was greasy, his scalp itched, and he couldn't eat, but he barely noticed. Those final moments kept replaying in his mind and he repeated the same questions, over and over: was it the thesis, or the scene at his mother's house, or was he truly unworthy? Why wouldn't they let his father appeal the decision? Why had Muhren ripped into his thesis like that – and who had stolen his notes?

He tried occasionally to rally himself, but the impossibility of his predicament was too much: there was no going forward. They had stripped away his future and left him a figure of ridicule and derision. He couldn't even show his face in public now. He considered fleeing, maybe to Silacia, to live with Ramon, but he could muster no energy to do anything but sleep.

He shivered. The fire had gone out again. He fell to his knees and started scooping handfuls of embers into the bucket until a still-glowing coal seared his fingers. He hissed in pain as a cloud of ash billowed across the room. *Fire was my element*, he thought bitterly. *I was going to be a Fire-mage. Now I can't even put out the embers without burning myself.*

'Alaron? Are you going to wallow in self-pity in there for ever, or do I have to come in and get you?' It took him several seconds to recognise the voice, then he floundered to his feet. *Cym? Shit!* There he was, clad only in a filthy nightshirt, in an ash-covered room that stank worse than a privy.

'Alaron?' Cym hammered on the door again.

'Go away!'

'No – open up, you gutless fool.'

He picked up the piss-bucket, lurched to the window and flung open the shutters. His right hand still hurt. Panting, he tipped the bucket into the filthy alley behind the house, ignoring whoever snarled a heartfelt curse up at him as he slammed the shutters again.

'Alaron: open up!'

'Wait, I'm— Um, can you wait downstairs? *Please?*'

'Why?'

'I need to wash!'

'You've got ten minutes or I'm walking out of here and you'll never see me again.'

'Hel and damnation,' he swore as he heard her walking away. 'Don't go – I'll be down, I promise!' All the stable hands were away with Vann at the fur markets in Geidenheim, so he had to draw his own water from the well. Cym was nowhere to be seen, thankfully. He felt weak as a child, standing barefoot in the freezing courtyard and trembling like a leaf as he tipped buckets of clear water over his head until he felt clean again. But it brought back some clarity. *Cym is here* – but she'd gone back down south, hadn't she? He scurried into the kitchen, wrapped in a wet robe, to find the fire had been banked up and a pail of water was simmering above it. Cym was sitting on the cook's bench, clad in her familiar gypsy skirts, her tangle of black hair caught in a ponytail and hidden beneath a bright patterned scarf, her golden earrings glinting in the firelight. He nearly wept to see her.

'You look bloody awful,' she told him flatly. She gestured towards the fire. 'I've heated some water for you. Use soap. And shave.' She got up. 'I'll wait outside. I have no desire to see your malnourished body, even accidentally.' She looked him in the eye. 'You're a complete idiot, Alaron Mercer.'

He hurried to pull off his robe, then used a cup to scoop the warm water over his gelid skin. He managed a rudimentary shave, though he was shaking so badly he nicked his face several times, then he ran upstairs to find clean clothes, terrified she would be gone before he was even half-presentable. He threw on the first things he could find, ran fingers through his wet hair and ran back downstairs.

Cym was in the kitchen. She looked him up and down, then held out a hand to him. 'You may approach,' she said regally, and he moved tentatively to bend to kiss her hand – but she suddenly snatched it away and quick as light slapped his cheek, a stinging blow that made him reel.

'What on Urte were you thinking, you fool? Ramon told me everything! Punching a city official? Blathering about the Scytale of Corineus to a room full of Rondian magi – are you rukking suicidal? Are you a moron?' Her eyes were blazing.

'You've seen Ramon?' he managed weakly, rubbing his cheek.

'My family's caravan went through Silacia and we stopped at his village. He was very worried about his friend Alaron Numbskull, who buggered up his own future. And now I get here to find you're determined to mope yourself to death.'

'I'm not moping, I'm just . . .' His voice trailed off weakly.

'I thought you might have a bit more *spine* than this, Alaron: after seven years of sneaking out to teach me mage-craft, risking expulsion *every day*, I thought you had a little more *cojones* than this.'

'But you don't understand—'

She folded her arms and glared at him 'Don't I?'

He leaned against the bench and folded his own arms. He felt feeble in the face of her fire. 'When they fail you, that's it: you're screwed for ever. You can't use a periapt, so your gnosis is impaired, and if they catch you using it, they imprison you – or worse. To the people, you're one of God's rejects, you're fair game for – well, everything. And all the time you're faced with what you should have been. I was going to be a Fire-mage and go on Crusade; now I daren't even join the legions as a ranker, because the men will tear me apart. I can't help Da's business as he hoped, or build that windship keel he wanted. I'll never be able to repay him the cost of the college – and now Mother's going to have to leave the manor. The whole family – we're going to be ruined. And it's all my fault.' He buried his face in his hands, then whispered, 'I think I should just kill myself.'

Cym snorted. 'Just like a boy: no guts. First thing that goes wrong and they're snivelling about ending it all.' She stood in front of Alaron, prised his hands from his face and cupped it. 'Alaron Mercer, you and Ramon gave me something incredible: you taught me, when no one else in Yuros would. Even if you were both shit-useless teachers who spent most of your time trying to peer down my front. But I owe you. I want to help you – I *can* help you, if you've got the guts to help yourself. So are you going to go back into that filth-hole you call a bedroom and whimper about suicide, or are you going to reclaim your life?'

'That's not fair,' he protested.

'Poor boy, life isn't fair.' She pulled a leather cord at her throat and drew a honey-coloured gem from beneath her blouse. It was crudely cut, but it glimmered in the dim room. He sucked in his breath.

'This is an amber periapt my people stole from a mage in Knebb,' Cym told him, letting it spin tantalisingly in her grasp. 'If you want it, it's yours.'

He reached halfway, then pulled it back. 'But . . . that would be illegal. If I got caught—'

She pulled it over her head and dangled it before him. He wavered, unable to think clearly, reaching, then stopping. She sighed, exasperated, and hung the gem on a kitchen hook. '*Rukka mio*, Alaron.' She gripped his shoulders. 'You've been cheated – doesn't that make you want to fight back? Get angry!'

'It's not that easy – I can't just—'

'You *can just:* take up that periapt and become the person you want to be.' She turned and walked out of the kitchen, snapping, 'Use it!' over her shoulder.

'Wait, Cym!' He rushed over. 'How was Ramon?'

'The little twerp was fine. He worries about you. He'd just done over some thugs the local familioso sent, and now he's considering offers from said pater familioso to join his gang. That's how things go in Silacia.'

Alaron tried to grin. 'That's good.'

'Huh – if you say so. The little prick asked me to marry him. As if!' She turned to go.

'Cym,' he said frantically, 'the periapt – the law—'

'*Law,*' she sneered derisively, 'that's just the current opinion of whoever's in power – it's got *nothing* to do with what's right.' She tossed her head. 'The periapt is yours to keep, if you've got the guts. See you, Alaron.' Then she was gone, slamming the door in his face. He flinched and went back to the fire. Finally he reached for the amber periapt and stared into its murky heart. He was lost in its depths for hours.

When Tula the cook came home, he barely noticed. But he did eat the bowl of stew she gave him.

*

'So, how are you, Alaron?' Vann Mercer asked.

Alaron looked up from staring into the fire, the amber gem clutched in his fist. He'd not heard his father come in. 'I don't know, Da.'

Vann pursed his lips. 'Your grandpa, Kore hold his soul, always said you need to think of the destination you want, and then work out the road. So what do you want from life?' Vann settled into his armchair beside the fire and waited for a response.

'I don't know – I'm only eighteen.'

'Most lads your age are married with children by now, Alaron.'

'Yeah, well, that won't happen now, will it?' He swallowed and fell silent while his father puffed his pipe, waiting patiently until his son finally found his voice. 'All my life I thought I would be a mage – I can't *be* anything else. But the authorities – the college – they say I'm not *allowed*, that I'm not *suitable*. But I did fine in those tests, Da, I earned a Bronze Star, they said it out loud – but they didn't graduate me! And my thesis was sound, whatever they said – it was certainly good enough for them to steal my notes—'

'What?' Vann leaned forward, suddenly intent.

'I meant to tell you – someone stole my thesis notes, right after I presented it—'

'From here? Why didn't you tell me?'

'Um . . . I didn't think it mattered, not after they'd failed me—'

'You didn't think it mattered that someone robbed you of your thesis notes *during* the exam? Alaron, that's wrong – utterly wrong. We have to tell Captain Muhren—'

Alaron broke in, saying hurriedly, 'No, not him!'

'What do you mean, "not him"? Jeris Muhren is my friend, and he's Captain of the Watch. If anyone can find your notes, he can. Maybe we can get you reassessed. I'll see him—'

'No, Da, please—' And he started to tell his father how Muhren had belittled his thesis, how he'd punched Eli Besko – somehow he'd forgotten to tell Da that too – and once opened, his mouth just kept pouring out words: 'I just wanted to be a battle-mage and join the Crusade, Da. I wanted to be famous – I wanted *respect*. I've endured

seven years of constant scorn from those highborn shits at school –
Malevorn Andevarion is the most spiteful creep on Urte and he got
a rukking gold star, Francis Dorobon isn't fit to rule a fishbowl, let
alone a kingdom, and Seth Korion, he's just a joke. Why should they
have *everything* when they don't deserve *anything*—?' And then he was
crying, acid tears that stung his eyes. He felt his father gather him
into his arms, like he had when he was a child, and as dusk became
night he clung to his father, oblivious to the passing of time.

Finally he drew back, wiped his eyes and whispered, 'What should
I do, Da?' He stared at the amber gem, still clenched in his hand.

Vann Mercer looked at his pipe, which had gone out, and laid it on
the mantelpiece. 'You must do what you need to, Alaron; I've no special
wisdom to share. I was just a soldier who fell in love with a mage;
nothing in my life could have prepared me for that marriage, or raising
a mage-child. I love you, but I have absolutely no idea how you should
live your life. What I do think is that a great injustice has been perpe-
trated against you. I knew about Besko; Harft told me. But this theft,
on top of everything – that stuns me, and that's why I want to talk to
Jeris Muhren about it. He's a good man, whatever happened during
your thesis presentation. Son, you've been cheated of your birthright,
and I don't have the power to overturn that, but I'll fight it, any way
I can. But in the meantime, your friend has given you a gift – and
Alaron, whatever else happens, I'm prouder of you than you can begin
to imagine for what you've done for that girl. And what kind of person
spurns a gift from a friend? If you want to take up that gem, and if it
means you need to run, you'll always be my beloved son.'

That was too much. Alaron started crying again, and he cried for
ever.

When he awoke in the middle of the night, lying beside the kitchen
fire, he pulled out the gem and began to tune it. It felt curiously
exciting to be an outlaw. When Cym returned a few days later, she
squeezed his hand and promised to call again soon, and Alaron dared
to dream once more.

*

Plane. Smooth. Rub. Cut. Sand. He was bundled in layers of clothes and his hands were wrapped in wool mittens, but his breath billowed from his mouth, the cold biting deep. New Year had gone, barely marked in their silent household. The river was frozen solid, and the heavy clouds dropped fresh white drifts nightly. Winter's grip might be unrelenting, but it was 928: the year of the Moontide, and that gave the passing days an extra shiver of excitement.

A kind of spring had come to the Mercer household. Alaron was running weapon-drills every day as dawn rose over the glittering frost. He had a new gem, hidden beneath his shirt, and a zest in his step; everyone noticed that energy was most apparent when the Rimoni gypsy girl called by, but it was none of their business, so the cook and stablehands took care not to be caught noticing.

Alaron had a new project. It didn't matter suddenly that he had no wood-shaping, and only the most mediocre Air-gnosis. He was going to make a windskiff. It wasn't an especially rational decision, but he had made up his mind, so every morning he went through the drills to limber up, then he dug out his father's tools and started work.

While Alaron worked the wood, his father was off accumulating stock. Vann was determined to travel to Pontus and cross the Moontide Bridge, along with thousands of other traders who had decided to risk the war, in the hope of trade with the Hebb and Keshi. The Crusade did not preclude all commerce; there were fortunes to be made.

His mother was now ensconced in an apartment on Eastside, together with her books and a new cook. Anborn Manor was up for sale, and old Gretchen was going to stay and serve the new owners. Alaron had visited his mother on Eastside, though it was painful: she appeared to have no understanding of why she'd had to leave the manor – but she did remember him punching Besko, and she laughed about it every time he visited, until he began to feel that maybe it had been the right thing to do after all, regardless of the consequences.

He was hammering in a nail when he heard a voice he'd hoped

to never hear again. 'Mercer,' it drawled. 'What are you doing?'

He put down his hammer before it began to feel like a weapon, very aware of the illegal periapt hanging out of sight about his neck as he faced the newcomer. 'Koll.'

Gron Koll hadn't changed much in the last few months. His face still looked like an acne farm, and his hair was just as oily. But his clothes were richer now. He stroked his fashionable sable robe as he sauntered into the snow-covered yard, sniffing faintly. 'What a come-down, eh, from dreaming of the Crusade to bashing in nails? Too scared to step outside his house – just as well, though: there's a bunch of lads just aching to see what a failed mage can do in a fight. Bugger all, apparently.' He spat on the snow. 'So, how are you filling your time, Mercer?'

'Just pottering,' Alaron replied, fighting to stay calm.

'Not been tempted, Mercer? You know—' He waggled his fingers. 'Must hurt, to be barred for ever, after seven years' training . . .' He walked around Alaron, peering maliciously. 'You're a rukking waste of space, Mercer: you should just fall on your sword so you don't waste air that real people could be breathing.'

Alaron clenched his fists, but stayed where he was.

'I thought I'd just pop in, see how you were doing, before I go to watch the muster. That's what real men are doing: mustering for the march – real men, not faggots like you, Mercer, you cock-sucking piece of degenerate merchant-trash.'

Something went red behind Alaron's eyes and he took a step forward. Koll's hand went to his periapt, his eyes lighting up—

Both of them jumped as another man entered the yard and called, 'Hello?'

'Rukk off and wait your turn,' Koll said, smirking – and suddenly the young mage jerked as if pulled by puppet-strings and started convulsively smashing his head against the stable doors. Blood splattered as his lip split, over his beautiful clothes, before he slumped to the ground, dazed.

'I'm sorry, Master Koll, I missed what you said,' said Captain Muhren. 'What was that again?'

Alaron smiled grimly as Gron Koll dragged himself to his feet, gasping, then staggered out of the yard. 'I'm telling the governor about this,' he mumbled through his swelling lips once he had reached the safety of the gateway, then he was gone. 'I'm telling on you' had been Koll's mantra at college.

Alaron let out his breath slowly, then caught it again as Muhren turned back to him and asked drily, 'A friend of yours?'

He shook his head, then stopped, terrified the captain would spot the periapt he was wearing.

'So, young Mercer: how are you keeping?'

Alaron took a deep breath and tamped down a sudden surge of anger. 'I'm well, sir, for a *failure*. Though maybe I might have passed if the proof of my thesis hadn't been ridiculed so completely.'

Muhren sighed and pointed to a bench just inside the stable. 'Mind if I sit?'

Alaron nodded, not trusting himself to speak, but his temper burst forth and he cried, 'How *could* you, sir? I researched that thesis – I checked my facts, more than you did – and you *lied*, in front of everyone, and ruined my life—'

Muhren let out his breath slowly in an icy cloud. 'I'm sorry you feel that way, lad,' he said calmly.

Alaron stared. 'You're *sorry* I *feel* that way? For *rukk's* sake, you're *sorry*?'

Muhren raised a hand, a pained expression on his face. 'Hush, lad! Hush.' He took another breath and said, 'Yes, I'm sorry, but it was an impossible situation.'

'An *impossible* situation? I can hardly have been the first student to present questionable evidence and speculation for the thesis,' he started, then, 'Hel, *rukking* Seth Korion had just spent an hour trying to defend Vult's surrender at Lukhazan, in front of the governor himself, the goddamned crawler! Did you rip into him, tell everyone that his evidence was second-hand shit? You're just as gutless as everyone else.' He jabbed a finger. 'My father welcomed you to his hearth, and you *destroyed* me.'

Muhren let out his breath heavily. 'Alaron, listen, you left me no choice. I couldn't let you go on like that, not in front of that audience – as it was, I think I did enough, but—'

'Did *enough*? You did more than enough: they *failed* me! They won't even let me appeal—'

Muhren raised a hand. 'Alaron, let me finish: yes, you are angry and you have every right, but just stop for a second, will you? Your father asked me here; he says you've been robbed. Can you tell me about that? Without ranting?'

Alaron stared at him. *I'm not sure I can*, he thought, then he took a deep breath. 'Okay. Sure. When I got home that day, someone had been through my things. My thesis notes were gone. Nothing else.'

'Why didn't you report this?'

'Who to?' he said bitterly. 'If it wasn't Gron Koll and his mates, then it was the governor, or even you – so who the Hel could I report it to?'

Muhren said quietly, 'Ah, I see. I have indeed let you down, and I am doubly sorry for that.'

'According to you my thesis was a load of shit anyway,' he muttered as a wave of self-pity washed over him. 'So who would even care?'

Muhren shook his head. 'No, Alaron, that's just the point. It wasn't a load of shit; in truth, it was too plausible for comfort. I was convinced, and others were too. No one knew about Langstrit's arrest in the old town except Vult himself, probably, and maybe two or three others who are still alive. I just wish you could have been a little less accurate, or come to the wrong conclusion. But you said right out loud what a few people with very powerful connections have been whispering for more than a decade, and that's why I was trying to talk you down. I think you may well be right: the Scytale of Corineus really is lost, here in Norostein.'

His words hung in the air and Alaron felt his skin go slick. He bowed his head and tried to breath.

'Do you know what that piece of knowledge is worth?' Muhren asked, then shook his head, answering his own question. 'No, and neither do I. It's priceless. If Argundy had the Scytale Pallas would fall. If the Rimoni got it – by Kore, if the Dhassans or the Keshi got it we'd be fighting the heathen right here in Yuros, and we'd be losing. There isn't enough gold in the whole empire to buy that Scytale. The power to make Ascendants is the Imperial Throne's greatest treasure, given only to their most trusted servants because they can't risk making just anyone an Ascendant. And now you've voiced what only a few have dared whisper: that the Scytale's lost . . . The emperor himself must be trembling every waking minute as he awaits news of some new Ascendant cabal come to destroy him. Can you imagine that?'

Alaron couldn't. He whispered, 'I just thought it was an interesting thesis topic . . . I thought I was being clever. I never really thought I might be right . . .'

They both fell silent for a minute, then Muhren questioned him about the theft: when had he noticed it, had he tried to work out who did it? He hadn't. He'd been too broken to do anything that afternoon.

'If you remember anything, if you think of anyone who might be connected, come to me,' Muhren told him. He offered his hand, and Alaron slowly took it. Some part of him had begun to forgive the captain. 'Good lad. You call me if you remember anything else. Or if Gron Koll comes back.'

After Muhren left Alaron just sat and watched the snow falling, wondering. He wished Ramon or Cym were here to talk to, but they were far away, and he was alone.

Vann Mercer drove and Alaron bounced around painfully in the back of the wagon. But Cym was sitting opposite him, and that was worth any amount of discomfort. They were on the road to Anborn Manor on a silver-sky day, their breath fogging in the still air. *We're off to break a few laws*, Alaron reflected wonderingly as he stroked the hull of the skiff he and Cym had made.

Cym's caravan had returned in mid-Febreux as spring woke the countryside, and now they were waiting on the unkempt lawn in front of the manor, under poor Gretchen's worried gaze. She'd been alone here at the manor for some months, and she shared all the common fears the citizenry had of gypsies. Six gaudy wagons ringed the lawns and their owners spread out across the grass. There were more children in one spot than Alaron had seen since college, clad in a rainbow of colours and swirling about like butterflies. Their clamour was deafening. The Rimoni men were clad in white shirts and black leggings; their hands rested on their knife-hilts. The women, wrapped in shawls, were scowling in suspicion. Cym'd warned them that the Rimoni didn't like magi, but they were here to cut a deal.

Willing hands helped Vann to empty the back of the wagon and lower the hull onto the ground, then Alaron directed the men as they bolted the mast and rudder together, and dealt with hanging the sail and untangling and fixing the rigging while his father sat with the head of the gypsies, Mercellus di Regia, Cym's father, a tall, lithe man with flowing hair and an impressive moustache – a man who had made love to some unknown mage-woman and come away with the child – obviously a man to be reckoned with. He and Vann sipped coffee together and laughed over the confusion playing out before them, like lords enjoying a comedy troupe.

Alaron had hoped it would all be a bit more serious, but he wouldn't even have got this far if Cym hadn't appeared in the yard the previous week and offered to help. She was better than him at whatever they did, in this instance, enchanting the keel of the skiff so that it would absorb and utilise air-thaumaturgy. He looked across at her where she sat perched among the gypsy women, ignoring the young men hovering about her, muscular-looking youths with long hair and faces that didn't look capable of smiling. They all looked at Alaron with superior hostility. *But you lads can't make things fly*, Alaron thought. *Of course, I'm not sure I can either yet*. There'd been no chance of any test flight in the city, so they'd had no chance to practise – but if it worked, Cym's father would buy it for a lot of money. *So it had better work*, he thought.

At last the skiff was ready. It was just a small two-person craft, single-masted, with a deep keel and six retractable landing forks. The woodwork was a little rough, he had to concede, though Cym had helped, and she was a half-decent Nature-mage, which he certainly wasn't. She was a better Air-mage than him, too, but he knew the theory and had better training, which helped him feel like it was still mostly his project. Working alongside her had been wonderful; better yet was taking her hand and helping her board the skiff in front of all those glowering gypsy boys. All the children went 'Oooo' as they settled in readiness for the maiden flight.

'Ready?' he asked confidently.

Cym frowned. 'Are you sure you know how to steer this thing?'

Alaron shrugged. 'Nothing to it.' Actually there probably was, but he could remember a few things from college – and anyway, what was the worst that could happen?

His father was holding a cup of thick black coffee. He gave an approving nod and Alaron waved back, then he turned his mind to the flight. Air-gnosis had always been hard for him, for he was an Earth-mage, the diametric opposite. But as he'd worked he had found a small affinity – and he'd also found that he'd enjoyed building the skiff, when he wasn't picking splinters out of his fingernails.

I'd never have finished it without Cym, but she would never have known how to start without me. He closed his eyes and let the gnosis throb into the keel. The craft gave a small shudder and lifted slightly. He locked eyes with Cym in growing excitement as she poured in her own energy, slowly saturating the keel until the whole craft was straining against the moorings.

'Cast off!' he called, Cym translated into Rimoni and the young men jerked the slipknots mooring the skiff. It rose into the air, two feet, three feet, six, a dozen. Everyone gasped in excitement – and then a sudden gust swirled through the glade and filled the sails. Cym gave a small squeal and he grabbed at the tiller.

'Turn!' she shouted, pointing at the trees before them, and he laughed at her discomfort and pulled the tiller about so that they glided lazily about the glade. Below them, the Rimoni cheered and the children ran after them, waving wildly. He felt a swelling pride as he waved back. Even their fathers were on their feet.

All sorts of hopes bloomed inside him, but as they turned, they lost the breeze and the heavier aft end of the skiff dragged about so they were facing into the wind. *That's bad, isn't it?* he thought, trying not to worry. The sail flapped against the mast, then caught the wind again, but on the wrong side, and they began to drift slowly backwards, the tiller now useless.

That's definitely bad, he admitted, while Cym screamed, 'Alaron – do something!' and gesticulated frantically behind him to where the giant window of his mother's drawing room loomed.

'Shit – take her down,' he cried, trying to release the gnosis in the keel, but it was circulating inside the wood and he couldn't draw it out quickly enough. Cym scrambled under the sail, but that just shifted most of the weight to the rear and the craft tipped backwards. Cym fell into his lap with a squeal, and below them the gypsies howled in dismay as the tip of the mast struck an upstairs window.

'*Rukk!* Stop—' Cym's full weight fell onto him and her forehead caught him a dizzying blow. The craft lurched again, levelling out, then the drag from the mast made it pendulum forward and the rudder smashed through the drawing room window, right where his mother normally sat. The mast sheared off, dragging against the window frame, and the canvas ripped on the shards of glass falling all about them. He clutched Cym and tried to shield them both from the glass and timbers as the hull propelled itself into the room, smashing through an oil-painting of Lord Gracyn Anborn before wedging itself in the hole and settling amidst the ruined furniture.

Gretchen opened the door beside them, shrieked and vanished. Outside, all was silent. Alaron buried his face in Cym's hair and prayed this wasn't happening. She smelled of cloves and patchouli, and her body was firm and warm. Perhaps this was all a dream?

'Alaron, let me go, you idiot,' she hissed at him. She shoved herself backwards and staggered to her feet. '*Rukka mio!*'

He lifted his head and gazed about him. The room was a sea of debris. The broken mast was still fastened to the hull by tangled rigging, and its tip jutted out through the shattered window. There was broken glass everywhere.

Cym sank to her knees, her shoulders shaking. It took him a few seconds to realise that she was laughing hysterically.

But all that work . . . He felt more like crying than laughing, but when a sound finally gurgled up out of his throat, it was somewhere between the two. He rolled clear and lay panting in the midst of the destruction.

A few seconds later, a multitude of children peered through the window, chorusing, '*Ooh!*'

'Cym?' he finally managed, 'do you think your father will still want to buy?'

There had been no deal, of course, but they had parted on good terms. 'My daughter will help your son again,' Mercellus told Vann. 'This is better than the circus.'

Alaron didn't feel too bad, all things considered. Yes, it had been a disaster, and yes, the Rimoni had laughed uproariously . . . but Cym had put her arm around his shoulder and kissed his cheek. 'We'll make it work properly next time,' she had whispered in his ear. That was worth more than gold.

Alaron sat alone in the stables of Anborn Manor, watching the rain plummeting down. It was the end of Febreux and Vann was away again. Cym was gone too, off with her kin, travelling somewhere in the lowlands to the north. The wind was moaning about the eaves like a man in pain, and the trees bent and branches whipped about. He hadn't seen another soul apart from Gretchen for weeks, but that suited him, as he poured all of his concentration into the skiff. They had decided to repair it here, where he didn't have to be so cautious of anyone sensing his gnosis. He worked on the house too, repairing the damage his skiff had caused as well as the depredations of winter.

He read up on piloting too. There was more to it than he'd thought.

'Perhaps if you'd read all that first, we wouldn't have crashed,' Cym remarked before she left.

'But that isn't the way men learn things,' he'd tried to explain.

Somehow his crippling depression had been jettisoned like ballast in a storm. Being active and having a purpose had helped, but mostly it was the company, he realised: people to share things with, to work alongside, to laugh with, to commiserate with. Even just a friendly cup of tea and honey cakes with Gretchen was enough to get him by.

He used the amber periapt sparingly and discreetly. Elsewhere, the legions were drilling and men and munitions were pouring into the capital, readying for the great march to Pontus. He would be one of the few young men left behind when six Noros legions marched off – but he was oddly content rebuilding the skiff and gently fanning the small fire he had built from the ashes of his life.

The spring rains had set in, so there would be no chance to test his repairs that afternoon. He settled his hand on the keel and closed his eyes, feeding it, gently exhaling his energies into the timber. If he had had his eyes open, he would have seen the wood take on a soft lustre in the dim light of the shadowy workroom.

He suddenly stiffened as a small surge of Air-gnosis flooded up the keel to greet him. He opened his eyes and groped about, feeling for the hammer. Someone moved in the gloom and he froze, his heart hammering.

An old man was standing at the opposite side of the workbench, staring down at his hands, which were touching the other end of the keel. Though tall, he was stooped, and his white hair was wild. His unkempt beard had twigs sticking out, and his eyes were unfocused. He looked like he'd been dragged through the undergrowth. Mud and grass stains smeared his ragged clothing – which, when Alaron looked closer, turned out to be just a nightshirt. He was soaking wet, as if he had just walked in out of the downpour.

'Kore's Cods – who the Hel are you?' Alaron gasped, more startled than afraid.

The old man cowered. '*Mmngh!*' he choked, then flinched at the sound of his own voice. '*Mmngh!*' He clapped a hand over his own mouth and fell to his knees.

'Sir – sir?' Alaron grabbed a horse-blanket and ran to him. 'Here, let me help.'

The old man looked up at him, his eyes wide with dread. '*Gggnhh!*' His eyeballs rolled back in his sockets and he toppled over, senseless.

Alaron yelled to Gretchen for help.

17

Desert Storms

Ingashir

While farmers till the arid soils, other men sit in the hills, watching them. And at the most propitious time, those watching will sweep down, massacre the farmers and make themselves rulers of the farmlands. They then slowly forget whence they came, while in the hills more watchers gather . . .

QUINTUS GARDIEN, OBSERVATIONS OF ANTIOPIA, 872

Northern Lakh to Kesh and Hebusalim,
on the continent of Antiopia
Shawwal (Octen) 927 to Safar (Febreux) 928
9–5 months until the Moontide

A wagon rumbled into the encampment and within seconds it was surrounded by young men all fighting like jackals for the tiny sacks the soldiers threw down. Someone tried to climb up, took the butt of a spear in the face and toppled backwards into the uncaring press. Kazim fought no less viciously than the others. The last time he'd eaten, two days ago, it'd been a tiny morsel of mashed chickpeas. He clubbed a boy in the back of the head and snatched up his portion, then fought forward to grab another three of the little sacks from the wagon, ducking as a spear-butt whistled over his head. Then he was staggering out, smashing a foot into the belly of one of those who preferred to lurk on the fringes and ambush the dazed victors of the fray as they emerged.

Whatever he had expected of the shihad, it had not been this. They had been part of the march for three weeks now. For four days

296

they had walked north through the dry heat of winter, begging food and places to sleep along the way. At first people were generous, as the Amteh faith was prevalent here in northern Lakh. 'Blessings of Ahm' were generously handed out: dry breads and leaf-plates filled with daal and fresh well-water. But when they arrived three days later at their first staging camp, their tiny group was swallowed into the chaos. Haroun went to find the Godspeakers to ask what was going on while Jai and Kazim sought food and water. But the only supplies here were secreted in wagons guarded by a contingent of soldiers. A thin man who'd been there a week told Kazim not to approach them. 'They don't care if we starve,' the man growled.

'But this is the shihad,' Kazim exclaimed.

'Tell that to the soldiers and see where it gets you.' The other man laughed grimly. 'All I want to do is kill Rondians, but at this rate we'll never live long enough to get there.'

Kazim went to talk to the soldiers anyway. They all had chainmail and domed helms with spikes, and curved swords. Their beards were braided and their eyes were little pieces of coal. They were Keshi mercenaries in the service of the mughal – and they were roasting chickens on their fires and swilling fenni.

One, a captain, strolled to meet him. He had a scarred face and a world-weary air. 'Piss off, you little shithead,' he snapped, to a chorus of laughter.

'But we have no food,' protested Kazim, 'and you have plenty.'

The captain bit off a haunch of chicken and swallowed. 'Yes, we do,' he agreed. 'And you don't. Get lost, *mata-chod*.'

Kazim stood his ground. He was the same height as the soldier and was bigger-built. Still, the soldier had a sword. His eyes flickered to the men behind. They were all armed and would take this man's side in any fight. *This isn't a good idea.* He backed away a little, but tried one last time. 'Please sir – a chicken – I have rupals.'

The captain snickered. '*I have rupals*,' he mimicked mockingly. 'One chicken? Okay, let's call it one hundred rupals, shall we?'

'One hundred rupals – I could buy ten chickens for that at home!'

'Then go home!' The captain turned away.

'Okay, one hundred rupals.'

The soldier smiled nastily. 'Price has gone up. It's two hundred now.'

Kazim glared angrily, while his stomach wept at the smell of the roasting birds. 'Okay. Two hundred.'

The captain pulled a spitted chicken out of a fire and held it out. 'Money first,' he said, waving the chicken as if teasing a pet dog. Kazim fought to keep his temper in check. He held out the money, all he had, the captain snatched it, then dropped the chicken to the dirt. As Kazim instinctively dived for it, Jai yelled, 'Kaz—'

The captain's boot crunched into his jaw and light burst inside his skull. He felt himself fly head-over-heels, backwards into an empty nothingness.

When Kazim came to, his jaw was throbbing, but it didn't feel like it was broken. He opened his and looked around dazedly. Jai was hunched over him. It can only have been a few seconds, because the captain was still standing over him, laughing. Kazim glared back, memorising his face.

'Come on,' hissed Jai. He was holding the dirty chicken. The scuffle had brought onlookers, ragged men who were staring at the chicken.

Kazim spotted a broken stick lying in an open fire and grabbed it, then got unsteadily to his feet. 'Stay behind me,' he hissed at Jai, and walked forward determinedly. *The first person to try me gets this stick in the face.* But no one did; they just parted and let them through, gazing hungrily after them. They split the chicken with Haroun, but Kazim was careful to take the biggest portion. *I'm the warrior here,* he told himself. *I have to stay strong.*

For the next six days all they had to eat was a little bread they'd begged from nearby farms. The soldiers drew their swords when approached. Someone created a Dom-al'Ahm from old bricks, only a waist-high thing, with pots for domes, where Haroun and other scholars led prayers. They prayed for victory over the infidel, but it was the prayers for food that became louder and louder.

Then the wagons began to arrive. Initially there were just three wagons a day to feed eight thousand men, and eighty per cent of them failed to get anything to eat that first day, but gradually more supplies arrived and at last they could at least feel they were not weakening further. Desertions racked up as the winter sun baked them, and there was wild talk of storming the soldiers' camps – but they all knew that was suicide. There was nothing to do but pray and make do, or go home.

Finally, after another week of desperately fighting for food, the captain who'd kicked Kazim rode a horse into the midst of the camp. There were no latrine pits, and with barely enough water to drink no one could wash. Many were ill. The air stank of urine and faeces. The captain wrinkled his nose and announced that they were to march north. 'Glory awaits!' he shouted, his face mocking as he ran his eyes over the ragged marchers.

'These are trials to test us,' Haroun told them as they staggered to their feet. 'Paradise was never earned without suffering.' He had been ill for most of the past three days. His eyes were yellow.

Moving was better than sitting. The soldiers ransacked the farms they passed, forcing the farmers to cook for the passing column, while the younger farm-women were kidnapped and raped. Any men who resisted were spitted on lances and left on the roadside. The fury that Kazim, Jai and Haroun felt mounted with each passing step. *This is the shihad*, they shouted inside, but words failed whenever the hard-eyed soldiers came near, seeking amusement. A thousand times Kazim thought of turning back, but Ramita was somewhere ahead, and he could not abandon her.

Instead he focused his hatred on the soldiers, and most especially on Jamil, the one who had kicked and humiliated him. Whenever he saw Kazim he smirked and mimed eating a drumstick. The soldiers of his company revered him, but to Kazim he was Shaitan incarnate.

He barely noticed the miles and miles of road and dust on this endless march. Diarrhoea beset them, and they squatted in rows beside the path and shat liquid. The grim humour of the other marchers sustained him, joking about bleeding feet, runny bowels and rank water. But Kazim and his friends stayed aloof from the rapes. 'We are not animals,' Haroun said. 'Others might forget who they are and why we are here, but we will not.'

Haroun talked to those around them as they walked, finding out their stories. A surprising number were converted Omali, men bereft of home and family, seeking companionship or wealth or just food. None had ever seen a Rondian, or had a personal quarrel with them – but the Infidel had stolen the Holy City, they were quick to add, so they must die. They listened dutifully to Haroun's pious admonitions to duty, but still they stole and raped their way north remorselessly. Only big towns with active garrisons were spared, and even then there was violence.

Everywhere they went, Kazim would ask whether an old ferang with two Lakh women had passed through, and several villages and towns remembered such a caravan, coming through more than a month before – they were probably on the other side of the Kesh desert now, an old man told him as he smoked beside a well. The oldster offered him a puff of ganja as he watched the resting marchers lying about like casualties. 'You're losing ground by the day, travelling with this lot,' the old man remarked.

'We're going to fight the Rondians for you, old man,' Kazim told him harshly

'Good luck, boy. I doubt they are trembling at the prospect.'

Kazim surveyed the prone marchers, searching for a retort, then gave up. *The old bastard is probably right.*

Over the following weeks the column crawled forward, barely managing more than a few miles a day. They bypassed the northernmost cities of Kankritipur and Latakwar and instead camped beside the Sabanati River, where they bathed in the muddy water and drank their fill – only for many to come down with dysentery afterwards. Crocodiles took a few more.

Kazim, Jai and Haroun escaped pretty much unscathed, having latched onto the supply-wagon that followed Jamil's men, the best-fed soldiers they'd seen, and made it to the verge of the great desert in better condition than most. They were listening in as Jamil lectured his men about the desert, telling them their worst enemy would not be the raiders, but the heat, which would make their armour hot enough to boil eggs on. There was no water, so they must carry it.

Haroun calculated that there were only one thousand water-flasks, and there were more than three thousand marchers preparing to cross, so they prepared: Kazim mugged a weak-looking fellow after dark and stole his flask, and Jai did likewise, while a dying man gave his to Haroun in return for prayers. That put them in better stead than most, but there was barely enough food for a third of their number, and the soldiers kept the weapons locked in the wagons – they would be armed in Kesh, they were told. *They are wise,* Kazim reflected, *because if we could get blades, they would all be dead.* The marchers were given no tents, uniforms or boots; only the soldiers had these.

We'll be lucky to ever get to Hebusalim, Kazim thought grimly, staring out over the desert, watching crows and vultures and kites circling high above. They themselves had been reduced to frying lizards and small snakes; they would have to move if they were not going to be forced to eat the rations set aside for the crossing – but still they weren't moving, and the reason was in plain sight: an Ingashir scout on a camel, watching them from a high rock to the northwest. The soldiers were nervous about setting off while the raiders were watching their every move.

'I can't see we have much choice,' said Kazim. 'The Ingashir will find us whatever we do. Can't they at least give us spears?'

'God's will be done.' Haroun intoned flatly. As usual.

His piety was beginning to grate, but it was about all that could be said about their situation. Kazim looked at Jai, who had been very quiet for the past two weeks. Kazim was beginning to suspect why: his friend always managed to get them water . . . and he was a good-looking boy. There were rumours about certain of the captains – but water was life here . . . *It wasn't supposed to be like this.*

They set out the next evening under cover of darkness, and of course it was a fiasco. Without torches to see what they were doing, half the gear got left behind, and none of the units were where they were supposed to be in the order of march. The trail of animal and human faeces marking their passage meant a blind man could track them, let alone an Ingashir scout.

'Maybe all this fertiliser will cause the desert to bloom,' Haroun joked wearily.

By dawn the column was being watched by a dozen Ingashir, who trotted away disdainfully whenever the soldiers tried to whip their horses towards them. Birds of prey swarmed above, calling incessantly. Sand got into every fold of clothing, into mouths, nostrils, ears, hair. Kazim felt like he was shitting grit, his nethers were so raw.

The marchers quickly began to weaken. The first day, those who fainted were given room on the wagons, but by the second day they were just left behind. Kazim hated them for giving up; he hated the watching Ingashir, arrogant and untouchable – but most of all he hated the soldiers, who cared nothing for them. He longed for an Ingashir archer to fell Jamil and all his smirking men, but the nomads kept their distance, and after two weeks they disappeared altogether, which encouraged everyone. As the oppression of being watched lifted, the men sauntered along in a more relaxed fashion, boasting of what they would have done if the nomads had dared come closer.

Haroun pulled Kazim to one side. 'The Ingashir are still out there, even if we cannot see them. Be on guard, brother.' He slipped something hard and cold into Kazim's hand. It was a curved dagger. 'Given to me by a soldier. I can think of no more worthy recipient than you, my lionheart.'

Kazim embraced Haroun quickly. 'Thank you brother. Thank you from all of my heart.' But his eyes sought Jamil, not the Ingashir.

The Ingashir attack came three days later, on the seventeenth of the desert crossing, after another night marching under the waxing moon, at the point where turning back was beyond them and the next oasis far in the distance. They came at dawn, as the marchers were about to make day-camp. The guards were tired and lax; the men were exhausted, thirsty and hungry. The Ingashir came from out of the rising sun so that they were difficult to see, and any defending archers would have the sun in their eyes. It was so perfect it could have come from a military textbook.

For the hour before the attack, Kazim had been trailing the third supply wagon with a crowd of others who'd broken ranks to try and ensure they would not go hungry. The faces around him were dulled with weariness. The dry wind that had risen out of the north sent stinging gusts of sand into their faces, so every man had wrapped a scarf around his head, impairing visibility. As the eastern sky lightened and the moon sank in the west the soldiers began calling the halt, and Kazim shoved his way towards the supply-wagons. Around him men jostled, but no one pushed him, not even those who fought in packs: they were all wary of his speed and ferocity.

A beady-eyed youth from Kankritipur was pointing towards the rising sun. 'What's that?' he asked.

'What's what?' someone replied as a shaft of red light stabbed the gloom and hands rose to shield eyes.

'I thought I saw something moving over there,' the boy maintained. 'See?'

Kazim peered: a flock of birds had taken to the air, a great black cloud of them. He blinked as the birds arched upward and dived towards them. *Not birds – arrows!*

'Watch out!' someone called, but the men were transfixed, their mouths open in curious wonder.

Kazim dived behind the line of men, but no one else moved.

A shaft struck the Kankritipur boy in the chest and exploded from his back, pinning him to the ground as he fell, his feet kicking and arms jerking like a dropped puppet. Then the rest of the flight of arrows decimated the column, taking men in the chest, the belly, the limbs, through eyes and mouths. Three men in front of Kazim went down; one silently, dead immediately from a shaft straight to the heart; the other two screaming and clutching limbs. There was a momentary respite, then a second flight of arrows flew and the desert floor trembled with the rhythm of hooves. The column disintegrated, the marchers running westwards, or seeking shelter. Kazim ran to the nearest wagon, stuffed small bags of lentils into his belt-pouch and snatched a flask from the driver, who was slumped sideways in his seat, an arrow jutting from his chest. Two of the horses were down.

More arrows flew as an ululating cry erupted from the east: the Ingashir were ready to charge.

Kazim estimated the nomads would reach him in about sixty heartbeats. He grabbed some cured meat, then ran back to where he had last seen Jai and Haroun, keeping low to the ground. 'Jai!' he called, as the rumbling of hooves from the east grew louder. The soldiers were forming a line, facing east. A cloud of arrows struck them and they wavered. 'Haroun!'

Someone crouching behind one of the wagons waved: Jai. Kazim ran towards him, shoving aside men racing in the opposite direction. The arrows were sporadic here as the raiders concentrated their fire on the soldiers. The ground was already littered with the dead and wounded, and most of the marchers were now pelting westwards willy-nilly.

Kazim leapt onto the wagon Jai was hiding behind; the driver was gone, but the horses were whole and holding firm. He snatched up the reins, shouting to Jai and Haroun, 'Get on, brothers!'

The eerie wailing cry of the Ingashir grew louder. Kazim cracked the whip and the wagon jerked into motion as the first of the Ingashir, all in white and riding pale horses, topped the ridge and surged down the slope, waving curved swords and screaming to Ahm. A thin line of soldiers stood between them and Kazim's wagon. He hoped they were as good at fighting Ingashir as they were at bullying their own. 'Fill a pack each with rations,' he yelled over his shoulder. 'Be prepared to jump if we have to!' He whipped the horses into a trot and guided them towards the west.

Somewhere behind him a girl screamed, and Kazim glanced back incredulously. Haroun had lifted a blanket and there she was, curled in a ball. There was no time to dwell on it. Kazim flogged the horses while the Ingashir tore towards the waiting soldiers, but the defenders were too few and too thinly spread. The nomads blasted through them like arrows through cloth. The few survivors tried to gather in spiky clusters. Nomad archers fired into them from point-blank range, but most rode on, seeking easier prey. Several saw the wagon moving and spurred towards it.

Kazim expected an arrow at any moment; he hunched over involuntarily. The horses had poor traction in the soft sands and the wheels were slewing wildly. He heard the girl shriek again, and Jai shouting, Haroun praying as they careered into a running man and went over him in a wet crunch. Kazim lashed the horses and they began to catch up with the fleeing marchers – then a chorus of dismay came from ahead and first one man and then others spun and ran back, flinging aside their meagre burdens. 'We're trapped!' someone howled.

'There are raiders to the west as well,' Haroun shouted in Kazim's ear. 'Go south!' He clambered up alongside and seized the reins. 'I will drive, Kazim; you must fight!'

Kazim rolled back into the wagon as a complete stranger tried to leap aboard. He was another marcher, but Kazim smashed him in the face with his boot and he was gone. The girl clung mutely to Jai, her face terrified. Then she seemed to focus on something behind Kazim, who turned as an Ingashir raider galloped in, his raised blade angling towards Haroun. Without pausing to think, Kazim lunged forward and thrust his dagger into the path of the blow. Steel rang and his arm was jarred numb, nearly knocking the small blade from his grip. Narrow eyes focused on him and he felt a small thrill of dread: this was it, the real thing, live or die. An overarm blow lashed down on him, but he jerked aside and let it pass, then lunged as far as he could and plunged his dagger into the rider's arm, right up to the hilt. There was a gasp of pain, and the scimitar dropped from the raider's splayed hand onto the wagon seat. He grabbed the man's sleeve and pulled, and the rider screamed as he came off his horse and went under the wheels of the wagon. Haroun and Jai threw themselves about to prevent it from rolling, righting it only as a second rider galloped up behind them.

Kazim grasped the fallen scimitar. He tossed the dagger to Jai, then leapt to the back of the wagon. He landed on one knee, scimitar raised to parry, as Haroun brought the wagon about to face south. The second rider reared before him and attacked. Kazim blocked two heavy blows, then slashed and missed, almost overbalancing. More blows rang on his blade, then the wagon bounced and knocked him off his feet. For an instant he was helpless. but the girl startled them all by throwing a pack, which struck the nomad, knocking him half out of the saddle. Jai whooped as a mounted soldier came up behind the dazed rider and swung at his back. The nomad yowled and plummeted to the ground.

The soldier galloped alongside the wagon. It was Jamil, and the captain took them all in with one glance and to their shock yelled, 'Kazim Makani, stay close!' Then another nomad attacked, forcing Jamil to spin away and parry. The captain fought deftly, blue sparks coruscating weirdly along his blade as the metal belled.

A youth from Lakh running behind them took a flying leap at the running-board. 'Help, help!' he called, pulling himself aboard, slowing them further, then a nomad drove a lance into the boy's back, blood erupted as the boy screamed, and then he was gone, just another dead shape on the desert floor. The nomad ululated savagely and spurred his horse alongside, just out of reach. With an evil smile he drew his bow.

'Haroun!' Kazim shrieked, but before the archer could fire, Jai's arm went back and with a throw that bettered anything he had ever shown on the kalikiti pitch at home, he skewered the man's shoulder with the dagger. The man howled and pulled away. They burst through a crowd of their own men and found open sand before them. They were at the rear of the column, and behind them was a confused string of unarmed men running hither and thither, panicking – and doomed.

Kazim slapped Haroun on the shoulder. 'Let's go! This lot are dead already!' Haroun cracked his whip and they accelerated again – then a lone horseman galloped out of the press towards them.

'Go! Haroun, go!' Kazim shouted as he stared back at the pursuing rider. Haroun lashed the horses up a short rise and into a dell, and the battle dropped out of sight behind them, though the cries of the trapped and wounded rang clear enough. The lone rider topped the rise and plunged after them. It was Jamil. Kazim spat and prepared to fight anyway.

They were a good two hundred yards south of the fighting when the captain caught up. He had a slash down his right arm and his scimitar was limp in his hand. His eyes focused on the girl. 'The girl's mine, Chicken Boy,' he shouted.

'Come and get her then,' Kazim snarled back.

The soldier closed in, wincing as he hefted his blade. 'Don't be a fool, Kazim Makani,' he gritted.

'You're not having her, you piece of dung.'

Haroun slowed the wagon. 'Stop it, stop it – we are all brothers here,' he cried. 'The enemy is back there!' He pulled the horse to a standstill. 'We are brothers here – please, put up your blades!' For the first time, Kazim realised his friend was weeping for the shihad.

He looked down at the girl, who whimpered as she clung to Jai. She was plump and soft-looking, utterly out of place here. 'Who is she to you?' he snarled at Jamil.

'Mine, is who she is. Release her.'

Kazim stood his ground, his scimitar raised, unwavering. He *knew* he could take the man, and he was longing to do so. 'Get lost, Jamil. We don't want or need you. Go, before the Ingashir come.'

'If any of you touch her, you're all dead.'

'Piss off, you ugly prick,' Kazim shot back.

He thought the man would attack, but he didn't. With a fierce scowl, he wheeled his horse and galloped away towards the west. He watched him until he was out of sight. Then he leapt into action himself. He and Jai unharnessed the horses and loaded them with provender: food, precious water, blankets, then mounted the girl on one and led the rest. They chose to go southwest, where the shadows still clung to the dells and the sand was harder. Behind them, distant screams could still be heard as the Ingashir hunted down the remnants of the column. After a few hours they found rocky ground to cover their hoof-prints, and then a low-lying dell

where they hid for the rest of the day, wondering how on Urte they
had survived.

No one came near in the daylight hours and at dusk they roused
themselves. Jai had spent the entire day with his arm about the girl,
who had not said a word but was fully able to cry at great volume
if not comforted. Haroun had been praying all day, asking Ahm why
he had seen fit to have his own warriors destroyed. His constant
mutterings were driving Kazim slowly insane, but he restrained his
temper. They were all afraid, and who could guide them to safety if
not Ahm Himself?

'Are we not your children, Great One?' Haroun wailed bitterly. 'Do
not the Ingashir worship you, even as we do?' But by evening his
face had hardened. 'An example has been made,' he told Kazim. 'This
has been an object lesson in failure. There must be an accounting.'

Kazim thought this the understatement of a lifetime, but he had
more practical concerns: where now? North, into the unknown, or
south, though that would be the end of his dreams? How could they
avoid the Ingashir? Was there enough food and water? Was it better
to travel during the day or the night? The answer to each question
was: 'I don't know.'

At least there was food, and they ate a cold meal of dried meat
and breads, washed down with a small flask of arak and some water,
all from the wagon's spoils. Tanuva Ankesharan's best cooking could
not match so wondrous a feast as this scavenged meal. 'What shall
we do now?' he asked Haroun afterwards.

The young scriptualist was rocking back and forth on his haunches,
hugging his knees. 'Brother, I know not. My head tells me we should
return south and demand retribution for these dreadful losses –
more than three thousand men, underfed, under-provisioned and
unarmed, thrust across the hostile desert, only to be ravaged by
nomads? It is intolerable – where was the protection? Where was
the leadership? Why were we not armed and trained in Lakh before
setting out? Why did so many of our brothers have to die so needlessly?' He was distraught and angry, stabbing the ground with his

knife, as if pouring his grief and anger into the sand. 'The Ingashir will be watching the back-trail. We do not have the provender to go back. It is six days northwards to the next oasis, I heard a soldier say last night. Perhaps we can find it? All I know is this: Ahm has spared us three.' His eyes flicked to the girl. 'Maybe even us four, alone of all those men. If ever you have doubted, cast that doubt aside. Ahm is with us and He will guide us.'

Kazim looked at Jai, sitting with his arm awkwardly about the soft Lakh girl with big moist eyes, not made for deserts and danger. She clung to Jai as if he were her personal messiah.

'I want to go home,' Jai said miserably.

Kazim took a deep breath. 'So do I, brother. But I came to rescue Ramita from the ferang demon. If Ahm is with me, I shall not fail.'

A dry chuckle echoed about the stony dell and Kazim leapt to his feet, spinning here and there, brandishing his new scimitar.

A shadowy rock on the edge of the dell rose and became Jamil. 'What "demon" do you speak of, Kazim Makani?' His blade was sheathed and he was moving freely, no sign of the wounds inflicted that morning.

How did he get there? How long ago? Kazim thrust his scimitar towards him. 'Stay away from us!'

'Hush boy – do you want the Ingashir to hear you?' Jamil stalked closer, his hands open. 'See, I come in peace. I am here to help you.'

Kazim took a step forward. 'Liar! You're just here to take our water and this girl. She can't even speak now, you piece of dung!'

Jamil halted. 'You wrong me, boy: I have not harmed the girl. I found her like that on the second day into the desert. Some fools had smuggled her into the march and misused her. I've been protecting her ever since. And I'm not here to steal anything. You may not believe me, but I have been looking out for you. Who do you think gave Jai water during the march? Who warned the worst of the marchers to leave you alone? Who ensured you were always fed during camp? I've been watching out for you since before we met.'

'You kicked me in the head!'

Jamil shrugged. 'My orders were to ensure my watch over you was not obvious. But I don't really care whether you believe me or not. If you want to survive, you'll travel with me.' He looked at Jai. 'And if your friend abuses the girl, I'll disembowel him.'

'Jai wouldn't hurt a girl,' Kazim shot back. He made a gesture of dismissal. 'We don't need you.'

Jamil gave an arid laugh. 'Do you not? You've no idea where to go, how even to ride your horses. I would say that you desperately need me. Come now, maybe your pious little friend here can give us a sermon about Ahm having sent me to guide you. There is none better He could have sent: I've lived among the Ingashir, and I know the desert. I can get you across, and all the way to Hebusalim too.'

'But why are you looking out for us?' Kazim asked.

He shrugged. 'Those are my orders. And because of your father.'

Kazim stared. 'My *father*?'

'Yes, Kazim, son of Razir Makani. My *benefactor* commanded that I seek you among the march after you left Baranasi.' He put one hand on his scimitar hilt. 'I know why you march – I even know the name of the "demon" who stole your woman.'

Kazim felt a frisson of fear and excitement. *Who is this Jamil?* 'I must rescue Ramita!' he cried.

'Indeed. I can help you – if you let me.'

Kazim looked at Jai. 'Is it true about the water?'

Jai nodded, looking embarrassed. 'He told me not to tell you.'

Kazim turned back to Jamil. 'How can we trust you?'

Jamil shrugged, pulled out his sword and sent it spinning into the sand to Kazim's right. He followed it with his dagger. 'Will that do? Keep them until you are ready to trust me.'

'Don't expect them back soon.' Kazim took a deep breath. 'You say you know the name of the Rondian who stole Ramita?'

'I do, and I shall tell you when we reach Hebusalim.'

Kazim bristled. 'Tell me now!'

'In Hebusalim,' Jamil repeated inflexibly, 'and not before. I will not argue this point. That is my last word on the subject.' He stood waiting, his face expressionless.

Kazim hissed in frustration, glancing at Haroun, who gave a warning shake of the head. 'Very well,' he sighed, 'for now, you can guide us.'

Jamil gave a low, mocking bow. They all stared at him, waiting for direction. Eventually Haroun asked him, 'Well, Captain, where should we go?'

Jamil half-smiled. 'Nowhere, yet. You must learn much before you are fit to travel this desert.'

Jamil kept them in the dell for two days, until he deemed them ready and the Ingashir gone. During the daytime he showed them how to halter the horses with ropes and trot them about the dell, always on muffled hooves. He never missed a detail, a badly set blanket on a horse or a poorly muffled hoof. Jai and Haroun were clearly terrified of him, but Kazim felt more unease than fear. The question of the identity of Ramita's abductor gnawed at him.

The girl mostly slept, flinching when anyone but Jai approached her. Only Jai could coax her to eat or drink, and at night she huddled against him, causing him embarrassed discomfort.

'How could this have been allowed to happen?' Haroun asked Jamil on the second night, his face disillusioned. 'All my life I have been told of the great shihads: huge armies of men drawn together by their love of God, marching as one to purge our lands of the infidel. But what we have seen was dreadful. How the Rondians must laugh at us.'

Jamil had no words of comfort. 'Blame the Mughal of Lakh, if you want, or Salim, the Sultan of Kesh. Or the zealots, who couldn't organise a fuck in a whorehouse.' He spat. 'Shihad has been declared by the Convocation, but Salim refuses to allow the mughal to move armies into Kesh – of course the mughal's armies pillaged southern Kesh during the Second Crusade, so you can't entirely blame him. Kesh and Lakh have fought many more wars against each other than against the whiteskins and the hatreds run deep. I myself have slain more Lakh than Rondians in the two previous Crusades.' Kazim wondered how old the man was; he had to be at least forty to have fought in two Crusades, yet he looked younger than that.

Jamil went on, 'The official routes are closed by Salim's armies and the mughal is sulking, but the Godspeakers of the Lakh Dom-al'Ahms wanted to feel important, so they issued the call to arms regardless, and it was answered by people like you: untrained, ill-equipped, with no provision made for food or supplies. And because they cannot cross the deserts to the east where Salim is guarding the best roads, some fool decides they must march across the western deserts, right under the noses of the Ingashir! Pure genius! None of the marchers are armed, in case they mutiny. Each column divides into a few thousand so that they can be provisioned, therefore making them small enough that the Ingashir can wipe them out piecemeal. Did you know you're the third column to march out this winter? To the best of my knowledge none have arrived. The Ingashir are laughing like jackals.'

Haroun looked up from where he was sitting, his head buried between his knees. 'You make it sound so hopeless.'

'It is hopeless.' Jamil shrugged. 'Until Mughal Tariq stops pouting and comes to an agreement with Salim, nothing can be done. Men arrive, the local area can't sustain them, so essentially they are thrust out into the desert to fend for themselves. And Mughal Tariq is four-teen, so don't expect mature decisions from him any time soon.' He leaned forward. 'In truth, Vizier Hanook rules Lakh, and that shifty bastard won't be losing sleep over a bunch of poor Amteh-Lakh perishing in the sands. He's Omali, you see; he wants Lakh purged of the Amteh.' He spread his hands. 'So you see, my young friends, if we're going to make it, it's up to us.' He looked at Haroun. 'Keep faith, young scriptualist. Ahm protects best those who protect them-selves. We're going to make it, if you do as I tell you.'

Kazim stared at his feet. What he told them was nothing like the world he had imagined, with rulers with high purposes and noble aspirations, but it fitted well with the world he had seen on the march: sordid, squalid and brutal, and meaningless. 'Who are you, Jamil? How do you know all these things?'

'I'm just a man of the Amteh, Chicken Boy. I have lived in many places, by my sword and my wits. The mughal's army was a convenient place to be, not for the first time. Just know that my masters mean you well.' He looked up at the stars. 'Get some sleep. We rise before dawn and we ride all day.'

'We're travelling in the daytime?' Kazim was surprised.

'Indeed. It is in fact the safest time for us to travel, while the Ingashir rest.'

They rose at dawn. The sun lit the eastern sky red and gold, glorious, remote. There was no wind, no clouds, and the air was dry, but it was clean. They kept to the low places, Jamil occasionally scouting ahead, but they saw no sign of the nomads, even at the site of the massacre, where hundreds of jackals and vultures fought over the unburied corpses. As noon approached they walked the horses on muffled hooves. They saw no Ingashir that day, nor the next, and on the afternoon of the third day Jamil removed the muffling from the horses' hooves and allowed them to trot. The mute girl wrapped her arms about Jai's chest and pressed herself against his back, but apart from a small squeal the first time they broke into a trot she uttered no sound.

Kazim began to see signs of life he'd not noticed when marching amidst the thousands of the shihad: the marks that snakes left on the sand, little spider-webs woven between boulders. Tiny birds followed them, swooping about them chasing flies. There were lots of flies.

They prayed five times a day. Jamil joined them as Haroun recited texts from memory to guide them. The girl watched silently, her eyes following Jai wherever he went. One day, as they prepared for their midday nap, Jamil spoke quietly in Jai's ear and the two of them built a small blood-tent for her, complete with red ribbons. She was reluctant to leave Jai's side, and only settled when Jai laid his blanket across the flap so that she could see him. Jai had been planning to marry one of the bevy of mindless chatterers who frequented Aruna Nagar Market, yet he was caring for this clinging camp-girl like she was a younger sister. *I guess your life isn't working out as planned either*, Kazim thought.

He put an arm around Jai's shoulder at breakfast. 'How are you, brother?'

'I'm scared witless,' Jai admitted, 'but I have to look after Keita.'

'That's her name?'

'She talks a bit to me. I've promised to look after her.' He set his shoulders. 'So I guess I have to.' His voice held a faint tinge of regret, of dreams quietly disposed of, but not quite forgotten.

Kazim hugged him. 'I'll look after her too, brother. She will be as a sister to me.' He looked Jai up and down. He was leaner, his beard and moustache fuller. He looked more adult. He was improving with the scimitar too. They drilled each night before sleep, and Jamil seemed faintly pleased – not that he ever said so. 'You're looking like a real Lakh warrior now. Let the Rondians beware.'

Jai's mouth twitched distantly. 'I don't care about the Rondians. I just want to find Mita and Huriya and bring them home. And take care of Keita, of course. She's from a village near Teshwallabad. We can take her back to her family on the way south.'

'I hope it's that simple, brother.'

The only men they met were three Ingashir who appeared before them like ghosts one morning. Jamil went ahead and spoke to them in their own tongue, and the raiders let them pass. Kazim watched their back-trail for the rest of the day, but there was no sign of pursuit. Jamil caught him looking back and praised his caution, but added, 'You're better to watch forward, boy. The Ingashir prefer to lie in wait rather than pursue. Come, ride with me and I'll show you some survival skills.'

So he went ahead with the warrior and learned something of scouting: reading the terrain and using it to approach high places unseen. How to watch where the birds did and didn't go. Things to look for in the sand and the stones. How to tell how old a campfire was, or when water might be near.

To the west, the hills of Ingash rose stark and brown. On the clearest days, they could see above and beyond them to the remote snow-capped mountains. To the east, the horizon was dead flat, empty.

The Prophet had walked this wilderness, speaking with Ahm and Shaitan for one hundred days. Kazim knew the story, the Great Temptation, and it made him tremble to think they might be walking in the Prophet's very footsteps, but Jamil just grunted when he said as much. He was scanning the northern horizon, where a faint darkness, brownish-purple, was stirring. There was a faint, acrid wind and the skies had become utterly empty.

'Let's go back to that last wadi and await the others,' he said. 'We'll go no further today – or tomorrow, if I'm not mistaken. There's a sandstorm coming.'

They retraced their journey to the dried-up watercourse set between high banks of rock. Moving hastily, they unburdened the horses and tethered them, then Jamil set Kazim to hammering staves diagonally into the ground so they buttressed the bank before lashing the leather tent to them. By the time the others arrived the wind was beginning to keen. Jamil was everywhere, urging the horses down on their knees and covering them, creating lean-tos of blankets and packs against the riverbanks.

'But it might rain and fill the riverbed,' shouted Haroun, worriedly.

Jamil laughed bitterly. 'It won't rain here for another seven months, Scriptualist. Save your breath and work!' He lashed together another tent and shoved the girl inside. He thrust some food into Jai's hands and pushed him inside after her, crying, 'Seal it off!'

The wind began to scream, frightening the horses as much as them.

'Won't the horses run off?' shouted Kazim.

'Where to?' the warrior shouted back. 'They'll stay put, don't worry. Distribute the packs and water. You're with the scriptualist. Pray hard!'

The sand began to lash them, stinging blasts that made them stagger, but they were almost done now. Haroun was sealing the last few gaps with rags. Kazim crawled in beside him. Jai waved from the mouth of his tent, then pulled it shut and fastened the ties. Jamil stalked towards them. He put something into Kazim's hands: a shovel. 'Stay inside and you'll be fine, Ahm willing,' he shouted, then he was gone. Kazim tied the flap shut.

The tent quivered in the wind, which let loose a menacing wail. Kazim was pressed up against Haroun. The young scriptualist looked at him and brandished a flask. He took a sip, then held it under Kazim's nose and the sweet smell of arak filled his nostrils. 'It won't be all bad in here, brother,' Haroun shouted as he leaned back against the wadi wall. 'One day Ahm will have perfected me so that I do not need such earthly pleasures. But thankfully, that day is not yet at hand.'

Kazim settled in beside him and accepted a sip. The bitter liquid burned its way down his throat. Jamil had said it could last for days. It was almost too loud to talk, so as long as the tents held, there was nothing to do but pray or sleep. Or drink.

'Haroun, did I do right, back at the ambush?' he asked much later, when the noise outside dipped momentarily.

Haroun blinked. 'You saved our lives, Kazim. You were magnificent.'

'It doesn't feel that way. I killed a raider – I pulled him under the wagon wheels – but I also rode down one of ours, and I threw another fellow off the wagon so he wouldn't slow us down. So I killed one enemy and two friends – in fact, I have killed three Amteh so far on this shihad, and if you count the men whose food I stole, I may have killed more. Will Ahm forgive me?'

'You know better than that, brother,' Haroun said. 'A dead man cannot redeem your woman. Ahm loves you, Kazim Makani; that I know. But let us pray, and it will ease your spirit.'

So they prayed, and he gained a kind of peace from it, but as usual, his mind couldn't dwell on higher things for long. He was alive and others weren't. *You have to go on*, he told himself. *Don't dwell on it.* He settled down to wait out the storm, wishing he could trade places with Jai and have a soft female to press against. *Lucky bastard!* Though Keita probably wasn't interested, so perhaps it was worse for Jai, locked up with a girl who wouldn't screw, knowing Jamil would gut him if he forced himself on her – not that Jai would ever force a girl. So he was probably just lying there with a rock-hard cock and nothing to do with it. Kazim grinned at the thought.

Outside the noise rose to deafening. The sand slashed at their tents, making them shudder, but so far they were holding. When they had to pee or shit, they used the lee-ward corner, and buried it; Jamil had left a small hole unlaced there, so the smell never became unbearable. Though it was midday, the dirty brown darkness was more like twilight. There was nothing else they could do, so they shared the arak until it was gone, and finally, feeling lightheaded and bored, they were tired enough to sleep.

Some indeterminable time later, Kazim woke to a narrow shaft of sunlight pouring in through the little air-hole. Outside he heard the keening call of a kite, and a horse nickered softly. The air inside was sour, and Haroun was muttering in his sleep. He looked at the spiritualist: his beard was fuller than when they'd first met, and curly, falling to his collarbone. His white robes were frayed and stained under the armpits. It was strange to think they had met just a couple of months ago. It felt like for ever.

Kazim rubbed his own burgeoning beard. He wondered if Ramita would like the look, or if she'd nag him to shave. He tried to picture her face, wondered where she was. Did she still think of him as he did of her, or was she with child already, and caught up in her own cares?

He shook away these depressing thoughts and examined the tent flap. He could feel sand banked halfway up it, so he unlaced the top and crawled out over the mound. His legs were aching from being bent for so long; straightening them was agonising. Outside, he light was dazzling, but the air was still. Sand had piled everywhere; the wadi was full almost to the lip on the other side, but Jamil had sited them in the lee, which had got off far more lightly. Jamil himself was saddling one of the horses. He smiled with genuine warmth and called, 'Sal'Ahm.'

Kazim looked about. The sun was low to his left, which must be east if this was morning. 'Is all well?'

'All is well. Rouse the others; we should eat.' He indicated a small camp-fire, where a tin pot was steaming, and Kazim's stomach growled in hunger.

Buoyed by the thought of food, Kazim woke Haroun, and then tramped up to Jai's still- closed tent. He peered through the air-hole. Jai's eyes were closed. The girl's head lay on his chest, her hair loose over her bare shoulder. She was also asleep. He sniffed, and at the smell of sweat and bodily fluids thought, *My friend's a lucky bastard*, then shouted, 'Jai, wake up!'

His friend opened his eyes and peered up at the air-hole. 'I am awake,' he whispered, with a smile of puzzled contentment.

'Then get your arse out here and do some work,' Kazim told him. 'Unless you are so weakened from screwing you can't walk?'

'I'll be five minutes,' Jai said, running his fingers through Keita's hair. She stirred and murmured something throaty. Jai grinned up at Kazim. 'Or maybe ten.'

They wound their way north as the moon waned and vacated the night sky. Weeks flew by, each day like the other. Though supplies ran low, Jamil kept strict rationing and they did not go short. The captain was no longer scouting ahead; he said there was no need. The ground was rocky now, and the sand coarser, and small spiny bushes grew in the lee of the rocks. Fat blue-black flies hummed about them ceaselessly, but avoided Jamil. That wasn't the only unusual thing Kazim had observed: sometimes he saw a faint blue light within his tent, and sometimes he appeared to be talking to himself in one-sided conversations. But he'd been true to his promise to guide them safely, and he treated them all with more respect now; When he called Kazim 'Chicken Boy' now, he was teasing.

Kazim felt a kinship with them all unlike any he'd felt before. They had survived the massacre and the sandstorm and crossed the desert. They prayed together and ate together, and if Jai was the only one allowed to screw Keita, no one complained. The girl cooked for them now, and she was losing some of her baby fat, turning into a woman. Of course, her belly would be swelling soon enough if Jai wasn't careful. Kazim mentioned this as they walked the horses to a tiny muddy pool Jamil had found.

'She's a dark moon bleeder,' Jai replied, 'so we were careful last week. She'll need the blood-tent again any day. Jamil says we're only a couple of days from Gujati, the most southern settlement in Kesh.' He glanced back the way they had come. 'I'm going to miss the desert, sort of.'

'Me too. There's something about it . . . but I'll be glad of a bath.' He cast his mind forward to Hebusalim, to Ramita, imprisoned somewhere: the caged bird he would free. *We're coming, my love.*

Two days later as the setting sun cast long shadows into the darkening east, they topped a rise to find a cluster of thirty-odd mudbrick huts before them, gathered about a well. They were too tired to enjoy this moment of triumph – they had been on the march for three months and the new year was already two months old. But they were finally in Kesh.

18

Lady Meiros

The Ordo Costruo

Some of those given immortality by Corineus lacked the zeal and fire to join the overthrow of the Rimoni Empire. These ingrates fell under the leadership of Antonin Meiros and wandered for many centuries before washing up in Pontus around 700. They took the name Ordo Costruo (from the Rimoni word for 'builder') and among many engineering feats constructed the Leviathan Bridge, in the early 800s. Chapters of the Ordo Costruo dwell in both Pontus and Hebusalim. They claim to prize knowledge above faith, and place themselves above God in many heresies large and small. For this reason they are widely abhorred, except by the greedy and grasping merchant-princes.

ANNALS OF PALLAS

Some enemies come bearing weapons and uttering blasphemies and so you know them. But worse are enemies who come with gifts and gracious deeds. You know them not as foes, until too late.

SALIM KABARAKHI II, SULTAN OF KESH, 922

Hebusalim, on the continent of Antiopia
Moharram (Janune) to Awwal (Martrois) 928
6–4 months until the Moontide

Ramita and Huriya paced the gardens of Meiros' palace in Hebusalim, wishing they had wings and could fly over the walls. It felt like a prison, when there was so much to see outside. The central court-yard was sixty paces square. The crushed marble underfoot glowed in the sunlight, and the carved reliefs of the marble buildings shone so brightly that the girls covered their faces with gauze headscarves. The sky was clear, the air was scented with the fragrance of the flowerbeds. Somehow the smells of the city never reached this place. Water tinkled musically in the fountain of carved fish exploding from stone shaped as spume – more water wasted in a minute than Ramita's family used in a day. She had thought it was drinking water, until a condescending servant had told her, 'If madam wanted a drink, she had only to ask.' The fountain water was not drinkable, the servant said, though it looked fine to Ramita, a lot cleaner than the water she used to lug home from the Imuna. People here were clearly over-delicate. There were plants blooming here that she did not recognise; she couldn't work out how they would be used, but Huriya giggled and told her they were decorative.

Decorative?

They had arrived four days since, and something like a routine was being formed. The girls wanted to go out and explore the city, but her husband forbade it. There was constant shouting outside, but the soldiers would not let her walk on the battlements of the red walls that surrounded the house, so she had no idea what it was about. The palace covered four acres in the heart of the city, she had been told, but she was allowed only in her own rooms, her husband's study and the central garden, and it was suffocating. Only the tower rooms had a view of the city, but she was forbidden entry. The tower stood like a pale fang, rising three storeys above the walls. It was accessible only from her husband's rooms.

By the time she presented herself in her husband's study for Rondian lessons the deep furrows on his brow had returned. He was surrounded by letters and missives and looked beaten down again. His thin hair was tangled by worried fingers. She glimpsed a hall where supplicants waited, a mixture of Rondian merchants and Hebb traders in their check-patterned headdresses, including some women in the black bekira-shrouds that even Rondian women wore in public. Meiros acknowledged her distractedly, then told her his daughter Justina would see to her language tutelage from now on. That had been three nights ago. In the evenings she could see light limning the shutters of his tower-rooms. He did not come to her chamber, and she suspected that he had not slept since returning.

Justina Meiros ignored her requests for language lessons. Olaf was apologetic, but no help. 'Once the trouble on the street dies down we will summon cloth and jewellery traders for you, Lady Ramita,' he offered, as if this would satisfy her. *What trouble?* she wondered.

'But Rondian speak I desire me!' she burst out in mangled Rondian. 'Book need I nigh! Nigh! *Nekat chottiya!*' It was very frustrating. Olaf didn't seem to understand.

When Huriya asked Olaf about the troubles in the street he said, 'Because of Madam.' Huriya passed this on, and Ramita laughed nervously: trouble because of her, in the streets of this foreign city? Huriya must have got the words wrong.

On holy day her husband spoke to her briefly before he left under heavy guard to attend a Kore service at the Governor's Palace. This governor, Tomas Betillon, was rumoured to eat children, the servants told Huriya. 'Betillon is a pig,' Meiros remarked with distaste, 'yet I must dine with him.' He looked like he wished to spit.

'Olaf said that there was trouble in the streets because of me,' Ramita remarked curiously, staring at the intricate mosaic on the floor.

Meiros had grimaced. 'Someone has put it about that I have kidnapped a Lakh princess, and have her imprisoned in my tower. Some of the Hebb are burning my effigy and calling for my stoning.' He chuckled dryly. 'This is normal here, Wife. Don't let it concern you. It flares up, it dies down.'

'Justina will not teach me,' Ramita complained, feeling curiously neglected.

Meiros grunted and dashed off a note. 'Take this to Olaf. Justina has obligations to this family, whether she likes it or not. It will give her something constructive to do instead of painting her face and nails.' He stood. 'I am sorry I have been busy, Wife, but next week you must attend a banquet with my colleagues, and you must be ready.'

After breakfast Olaf took Ramita to Justina's quarters. Ramita waited impatiently while Olaf haggled with Justina's housemaid. She wished Huriya was with her, but her friend had been allowed to go with the servants to Amteh worship in the city. Huriya had been full of excitement about seeing Hebusalim. Ramita had asked Olaf to give Huriya some money for the markets, and he had casually handed over enough coins to make even Huriya's eyes bulge.

Finally a servant came out and led her through to Justina's private courtyard. Two women were sitting cross-legged on Keshi-style low leather seats with no backs, beside a tiny fountain. Incense perfumed the cool air. Both women wore blue mantles. They looked at her distantly as she entered. Justina waved Ramita to one of the seats, then continued conversing with the other woman.

At least it gave Ramita the chance to study Meiros' daughter for the first time. She had a long narrow head, and her complexion was pale as porcelain. Her full lips were stained red. Her face was mature, but her complexion was clear and smooth. Meiros had claimed his daughter was more than one hundred years old, but she could not tell if this was true. She was a mage; who knew what was possible? Her lustrous black hair had no trace of grey. She wore simple jewellery, but it was all gold. A ruby as red as her lips hung from a gold chain and pulsed at her neck like a heartbeat: a periapt, one of the magical gems of the magi. Justina had a forbidding beauty, as if she had been sculpted, not born.

The other woman was far less fearsome. Her soft, round freckled face was framed by a tumble of golden curls. She too wore a pulsing jewel at her throat, a large sapphire. She smiled reassuringly. 'Hello,' she said slowly in Rondian, 'you must be Ramita.' Her voice was warm and sultry. 'I am Alyssa Dulayne. Welcome to Hebusalim.' She spoke as if trying to coax a cat to be petted.

Ramita ducked her head, licked her lips. 'Hello.'

'So she does have a tongue,' observed Justina tartly.

Ramita caught the gist of Justina's remark. 'Some little Rondian, I have. More Keshi. You Lakh have?' she added, sticking her chin up a little.

Alyssa chuckled. 'A good point, Justina. Do you speak her tongue?'

Justina Meiros wrinkled her nose. 'I don't, and neither do you, Alyssa. Apparently Father expects me to have this girl ready to face the vultures at the next Ordo Costruo banquet. How ridiculous.'

'What is "rikuless"?' Ramita asked, trying to quell her dislike.

Justina faced her, looking down her nose. 'Ri-dic-u-lous. It means "silly". Do you know silly?'

'I am not silly,' Ramita said levelly.

Justina sighed. 'I never said you were. Kore's sake, Alyssa, what am I going to do?'

The fair woman laughed gently. 'Well, why don't you leave it to me for a while? I'm better at this sort of thing than you are.' She smiled at Ramita, who felt a sudden fear of what this nice-seeming woman might mean.

Justina drained her tiny cup and rose. 'Yes, why don't you, Alyssa? I have no patience at all.' She bent over, kissed Alyssa's cheeks and vanished into her suite. Ramita rose, thinking herself dismissed.

'No, no, sit.' Alyssa patted the chair Justina had vacated. 'Come, sit with me.' She poured green tea, serving Ramita before herself, then she leaned forward and cupped Ramita's face in soft hands that smelled of rose-water. 'I'm not going to hurt you. I'll be very gentle, I promise.'

Ramita looked at her, puzzled, then the mage-woman's gold-flecked brown eyes caught hers, like a hook catches a fish. Her words meant little, but they trilled like a lullaby. Ramita felt strange, caught somewhere between sleep and alertness. Tiny details seemed huge, but she couldn't have said whether there was anyone else in the little courtyard. Alyssa's voice brought echoes of Meiros' lessons to the surface of her thoughts, like bubbles rising in a fountain, and other words were added, a stream of them, as if Alyssa were chanting them into her mind. She felt them sink slowly inside her and slide into orderly formations, schools of words swimming in an ocean of thought. Associations formed, with colours, with numbers, with actions . . . She felt her eyes fall closed with an almost audible click . . .

Perfumed hands caught her face and gently shook and she blinked, startled. 'It's all right, Ramita,' said Alyssa, smiling with satisfaction. 'That went well, though it was hard work getting you to open up.' The Rondian woman had a sheen of perspiration on her brow, Ramita noticed in surprise. Surely they had just been sitting for a few moments?

Then it suddenly dawned on her: Alyssa was speaking in Rondian, and she'd *understood* her! Ramita gasped and threw a hand across her mouth. For a second she felt a panicked sense of loss, until she realised her Lakh words were waiting for her, ready whenever she wanted. 'You Rondian me teach?' she asked out loud.

Alyssa giggled. 'Have you taught me Rondian?' she corrected. 'Yes, a little – but we're going to do this for most of the rest of the month so that you can understand Rondian perfectly. All I've done is imprint some more advanced grammar and some vocabulary.' She pointed up at the small square of sky above them. The sun was gone, away to the west. Ramita felt a dizzying wave of tiredness as Alyssa said, 'We've got a long way to go, Ramita Ankesharan-Meiros. A long, long way.'

'Why not Husband do this?' Ramita whispered.

'Oh, I imagine Antonin would not risk it while travelling. Mind-to-mind work like this can be all-consuming, and if you'd been attacked, he would have been almost helpless. And maybe he thought it would scare you; I'm much less intimidating than him. Now he's returned, he's very busy. But I find I rather enjoy it.' The jadugara rose a little unsteadily to her feet. 'It will take weeks for you to be fluent, but by the time of the banquet I hope you'll be able to converse comfortably with the other magi.' She surprised Ramita with a quick hug. 'You have a nice mind, my dear, wholesome and good.'

Ramita flushed at the strange compliment. She stammered something and tried to rise, but Alyssa sat her back down gently. 'Wait a little – you'll be dizzy if you try to move too soon.' She left, with a friendly waggle of her fingers.

Ramita felt exhausted, but the sound of the fountain was soothing. She wondered if Huriya was home yet and started to rise again, but Justina, reappearing with a steaming pot, said firmly, 'Sit down, girl.'

She poured out spicy chai and pushed the porcelain mug into Ramita's hands. 'Drink some of this before you try to do anything.' She sat opposite, half in the shadows, and pulled up her hood. She could have been carved in marble. 'That sort of working is more draining than you realise.'

Ramita took a sip. The chai was sweet and strong, just as she liked it. 'Thank you,' she said, then mischievously added, '*Daughter*.'

'Don't call me that,' snapped Justina, 'I'm not your "daughter", you backwater pagan.'

'Baranasi *nehin* "backwater"!' she snapped, 'and Lakh *nehin* "pagan". You are.' How dare this arrogant woman criticise her home town or her people!

'*Nehin*? Don't you mean "not"?' Justina asked scornfully. 'Find a dictionary!'

'What is "dictionary"?'

'A book of words. Alyssa didn't do a very good job, did she? Or maybe you're just not a good pupil.' She leaned forward. 'I don't care who you are or where you're from. I don't agree with what my senile father has done to you, and if I had my way we'd send you right back. If any further proof were needed that he has lost his mind, his wedding a Lakh peasant is it.'

'I *nehin* peasant, jadugara. My father is a trader in Aruna Nagar.'

'I don't give a *neffing rukk* whether your peasant father owned one piss-pot or two,' Justina snarled. 'You're in Hebusalim now, at the front line of a war, and no matter what price my idiot father paid yours for the right to bed you, you are worth nothing if you can't get pregnant damned fast. My advice to you is to shut your cheeky gob and spread yourself like a good little whore, and just maybe you'll get out of this alive.'

Ramita's temper flared and she raised her fist, thinking *I'll show you* – and instantly her whole body was frozen, and Justina's red ruby was glowing rich as blood.

Her icy eyes transfixed Ramita where she sat. 'Never *ever* raise your hand against a mage,' Justina Meiros whispered. 'Never, unless you have the power to kill them.' She stood up and walked around Ramita, whose body remained locked in place. 'You must learn to control your temper, mudskin, or the first person who goads you is going to have every excuse to burn your face off.'

Ramita's heart drummed helplessly and her whole body was slick with fear.

'Alyssa will teach you to speak like us, and I will give you a few pointers on who to talk to and who to avoid, but do not ever make the mistake of thinking that you are one of us. Until you are with child, you are nothing but a particularly expensive whore. Now get out.'

As Ramita fled on wobbling her legs, Justina's cold voice followed her. 'By the way, what is a "jadugara", bint?'

Ramita clutched a pillar by the door and let her legs regain a little strength. She turned her head. 'Look it up in a dictionary, *Daughter*,' she said clearly. Then she ran.

To her surprise, she heard a sudden burst of harsh laughter.

Ramita tottered back to her room. She needed Huriya, to tell her what had happened, but as she went to pull the door-curtain aside she heard a rhythmic thumping sound and a quiet *uh uh uh*, a girl's voice. She peered carefully inside, at the hairy bulk of Jos Klein jolting into Huriya's open body, tiny beneath him. Huriya's head turned faintly towards the door as if she knew Ramita was there. Then she arched her back and tossed her head with fervent abandon.

Ramita slipped away to her huge, lonely bed. Kazim's face haunted her dreams.

'Husband, Huriya has told me of a shrine to Sivraman, here in Hebusalim.' Ramita proudly said the whole sentence in Rondian. It was the week of the waxing moon and she was sharing coffee with her husband. Though Ramita was not allowed to leave the palace grounds, Huriya was, under guard and during the day, and a Lakh trader from the spice markets had told her of the little Omali temple.

'What of it?' Meiros asked distractedly, reading a letter. 'Hebusalim has shrines to the Kore, the Sollan, the Ja'arathi and the Amteh faiths – every religion in Antiopia can be found here.'

'But this is my religion, Husband, and I wish to pray there.' This was her fertile period, until the end of the full moon. Meiros had come to her chambers for the first time the previous night, but his manhood had failed him and he had shuffled away, leaving her untouched and humiliated. She knew there were things women did to excite men, but she had no idea what, so if he couldn't manage, then it was in the hands of the gods – which was why going to the shrine was vital. 'Sivraman rides the great bull, he lends us the animal spirits of fertility,' she explained.

He looked utterly discomforted, and she smiled to herself. *I can make this jadugara blush!*

Finally he relented enough to agree that the pandit of the shrine could visit to bless them. Huriya brought the holy man, whose name was Omprasad, to Casa Meiros the next evening. He was so thin he was practically a walking skeleton. His beard fell to his midriff in a dirty grey tangle, and he hobbled like a man who had walked the length of Antiopia – and he had. His tattered white loincloth barely covered his privates, and his only other clothing was a dirty orange blanket. He had no fingers on his left hand, just scarred, seared knobs, and he stank ferociously.

Ramita looked at Huriya. 'My husband will not allow this if he is not clean.'

Huriya's eyes lit up. 'Olaf,' she called loudly, mischief in her eyes.

Pandit Omprasad's face was so transported when he sank into the warm water of the marble bath that Ramita feared he would expire then and there. The menservants cast sullen looks at the girls as they washed him, which they ignored. *Do they think themselves better than a Lakh holy man?* Ramita thought. *Well, they can just do as they're told.*

Eventually Omprasad was washed and clothed in second-hand servants' attire, then fed while they waited for Lord Meiros to return home. When the old mage joined them in the little courtyard Meiros looked at the old holy man and gave a nod of resignation. 'You'll have to tell me what to do.'

Ramita beamed with relief and pleasure. She squeezed Huriya's hand. 'He will bless us,' she announced, excited to have persuaded her husband to do this for her.

Omprasad spoke lengthily, wheezing and coughing a lot, and none of it made much sense, but that wasn't relevant; what was *important* was the blessing of the gods; what was *relevant* was clasping her husband's hand and watching *him* do something for *her*. As the pandit traced a pooja mark on her forehead she could feel Sivraman's third eye on her. She would conceive soon, she knew it. She felt renewed determination to see this nightmare through.

While Huriya saw the old man out, giving him a bundle of food and some coins, Ramita took her husband's wrinkled hand and walked him solemnly towards her private chambers. But as soon as they were out of sight of the servants Meiros pulled her to a halt. His eyes were amused, but also sad. 'Wife, stop: I appreciate what you are doing. I appreciate your optimism and your willingness to do your duty, but I am tired and I am old. Last night I failed, and tonight I have even less energy: I am worn out.'

She refused to be put off. 'Then allow me to help you relax, Husband,' she said meekly.

He seemed about to refuse, but instead he shrugged his assent, and she led him down the small passage that connected their rooms to the small courtyard where the waxing moon shone down. She called for hot water, soap, a razor, bathing oils and incense sticks, and sat him on the cushioned seat, then knelt at his feet. She had done this for her father when her mother was in the blood-room or the temple, and now she sang softly as she worked, pouring hot water and oil, massaging with hard fingers, paring ill-kept nails, making his joints crack. Occasionally she glanced up, and she watched his gaze go from puzzled wariness to relaxed resignation.

Finally she was done and he sighed, 'Thank you Wife. That was pleasant.'

She stood up and worked up the courage to touch his head. 'I haven't finished, my lord.' She had a plan. She started by pushing her thumbs into his temples and gently worked them, to ease his headache, then she wrapped his head in a warm wet towel and plucked up her courage. 'Will you permit me to trim your hair and beard, Husband?'

She felt a strange tickling sensation in her mind that made her shiver, then it vanished and he said gruffly, 'You may.'

She wet his beard and lathered with the sweet-smelling soap, then, swallowing a sudden attack of nerves, picked up the blade. His eyes were closed, his face unreadable. She used the razor tentatively at first until she was sure she had got the hang of it, then she shaved clean his cheeks and throat with careful sweeps, and used scissors to shorten the beard to just an inch long. It took years off him, and for the first time she could see the younger man he'd been: a dogged, patient face, strong-jawed, with a firm mouth.

She turned her attention to his hair, lathered his scalp well, took a deep breath and lifted the razor. The long, uneven, tangled tresses clung to his scalp like dried-out weeds: they had to go. She worked patiently and carefully, taking her time, removing every hair from his scalp and ensuring there was no trace of stubble. Then she rinsed his head, and finished by massaging in a musky oil.

When she was done, a new man sat before her. His scalp was already tanned from the years of encroaching hair-loss, but this new baldness brought out the strong lines of his skull. He no longer looked like some neglected ancient, but regal, timeless. And the smooth scalp felt velvety to touch.

She suddenly became aware that she was bent over him, stroking his scalp. He raised a hand to her face and pushed away a loose tress that had fallen from her hair combs. She looked down and then froze as he pulled her face down to his and pressed his lips to hers.

His mouth tasted of bitter tobacco – almost unpleasant . . . but not. He had not kissed her before, ever. He pulled her onto his lap, sitting astride him, and contemplated her face. His right hand caressed her shoulder and he examined her salwar. 'Is this dress of yours a favourite?' he asked softly.

Huh? 'No,' she whispered.

'Good,' he muttered. He waved his hands, his eyes flared pale blue and every stitch fell apart. She suppressed the desire to claw herself free – sometimes, she forgot that he wasn't an ordinary man, but never for long, not when he could do things like that. It took all her courage to hold still as he pushed aside the cloth and kissed her left breast, above her heart. She wondered if he could hear it thumping. His hands slid down her back and pulled away the remnants of her clothing entirely. In a dreamy daze – *don't think, do* – she unlaced him and wriggled herself onto his erect manhood. She was already moist, with no need for the oils, and she received him easily and rode him gently, the restricted movement keeping him hard inside her, but slowing release, while her own juices flowed sweeter and hotter. Involuntary noises began to escape her throat and she could feel something heavy and sluggish stirring deep inside and rising to the surface of some hidden lake. Almost, *almost* – she was near that climax she occasionally experienced with her own fingers, but never with him, not yet . . .

He stifled a cry and his whole body jerked up and into her, making her cry out and almost triggering that blissful release . . . *almost*. She arched her back, half-disappointed, half-exultant, and she offered up a prayer to Sivraman and Parvasi, for a child to bless this night.

His hand, warm now, stroked her cheek. 'Thank you, Wife.'

'Thank the Gods, Husband,' she whispered piously.

'The only divine thing here is you,' he told her, kissing her forehead.

He held her for a long while, before wrapping her in a shawl and giving her leave to go to her rooms. She prayed for conception, staring out at the moon, until she fell asleep. All the next week he treated her with tenderness, and twice more the mood came upon him to take her onto his lap and let her move until he expended inside her, but she still bled when the full moon waned.

There was no condemnation in his eyes when she told him, only a resigned disappointment and a pledge that they would try again, next month.

'And Wife, if and when it pleases you, you are welcome to attend me in my chambers.' He had more energy somehow, as if what they shared had reignited his zest for life. He attended his work with more vigour, and in the evenings his voice carried a certain feistiness that hadn't been there before. But that invitation, well-meaning and gently made, made her feel guilty: yes, her husband's company was amiable, and their coupling had become – well, almost pleasurable. But surely it was but a shadow of the rapture that could and should have been? In her dreams Kazim would come for her, sweep her up onto a white horse and they would ride and ride, for ever . . .

Casa Meiros, like most of the Ordo Costruo houses, lay on the west side of Hebusalim. The city's vast population, some six million when the Leviathan Bridge opened, had dwindled to perhaps half that since the Crusades began twenty-four years ago. Dhassans had paler, softer features than Keshi, and their language and traditional dress predated the Keshi, they claimed. They subscribed to a milder version of the Amteh, called 'Ja'arathi', based more upon the teachings of the Prophet's disciples, with gentler, more liberal interpretations of the Amteh strictures. The city's special place in the Amteh and Ja'arathi cosmos was sealed not only because it was the Prophet's birthplace, but it was also the resting place of Bekira, his chief wife. The huge Dom-al'Ahm was named *Bekira Masheed* in her honour.

Fewer than sixty thousand Rondians dwelt in the city, living in an enclave around the emir's palace. Half of them were non-combatant support to the six legions stationed in the area: four on the Gotan Heights to the east, the other two in the city itself. Each legion had its full complement of five thousand men, including a dozen battle-magi.

Meiros took Ramita by carriage through the city, driving westwards to the rise upon which sat Domus Costruo, the Palace of the Builders. He was to preside at the quarterly banquet.

Domus Costruo was a cross-shaped building of glittering gold-flecked black granite. The central hall was positioned beneath a massive gold-plated dome, on the interior of which was a massive painting telling the story of the building of the Leviathan Bridge.

The banquet hall was in the west wing, to catch the last of the sun. The marble floors remained cool, even under the hottest summer sun. The Arcanum Guard, the legion recruited in Pontus to guard the Ordo Costruo, filled the grounds.

Ramita checked out her husband from the corner of her eye. She'd been confined to her blood-room for days, her only company Alyssa and her gentle, subtly-tiring language teaching. 'You look tired, husband,' she said in Rondian, pleased with her progress. This magic of the Rondians did have some good points.

Meiros yawned. 'Yes, I am tired. The Kore Inquisition sent a delegation, and their presence has sparked some vicious debate. Those bastards seized Northpoint – the tower at the Pontus end of the Bridge – which permitted the First Crusade. Like it or not, the Ordo Costruo's primary function is now the maintenance of the Bridge, for the emperor's use. Old wounds.' He stroked his shaven skull, as if still unused to it. 'I'm getting too old for this – though I'm told I look younger since you came, Wife.'

She smiled dutifully, fighting her apprehension about the coming evening. 'Lady Justina has warned me to be careful tonight, Husband.'

'Justina likes to be dramatic. Stay near me and I will look after you.'

'I won't let you down.'

'My dear, you will be the talk of the banquet.' He smiled.

The carriage rolled up a long boulevard lined with palm trees. Trumpets blared as they halted and doormen in red jackets helped them out. Arcanum Guards lined the entrance as Meiros led Ramita up the stairs; she supposed it a credit to their discipline that only half of them stopped and stared, open-mouthed. She presumed none of them had seen a saree before. Or a woman's bare midriff in public, possibly.

Justina had threatened to burn all of her sarees rather than allow her to wear one in public, but Ramita had sought and obtained Meiros' blessing, as much to get one over Justina as any other reason. She wore the most ornate of the new collection Vikash Nooridan's wife had purchased with such great pleasure in Baranasi. The close-fitting gold bodice was embroidered with blue glass beads, which matched the elaborate blue patterns stitched by hand across the saree and bearing the auspicious marks of Gann-Elephant, so skilfully devised that every fold revealed a new pattern, each subordinate to the whole. The final fold she had pulled over her head to shroud her face. Her flat stomach was adorned with a belly-ring of gold. She had her bridal bangles on, and a nose-ring chained to her left ear. Huriya had pasted a bindu gem to her forehead, a scarlet ruby, and her fingernails had been painted by one of Justina's servants in one of her own polishes. Her lips were coloured dusky red. Huriya had painted henna patterns on her hands and feet that morning. 'You will turn every head,' she had whispered while Justina ranted. 'Don't listen to what that jealous old hag says.'

Meiros smiled softly at her. 'You look radiant, Wife. Magnificently alien. And very beautiful.' She was surprised at the grateful affection she felt at his words.

He guided her to the top of the steps, where a timeless-looking man with grey hair met them, gawping openly at her. She came up to his chest – were all of these whiteskin men giants? He was Lord Rene Cardien, he told her, eyeing the henna uncertainly as he bent over her hand and letting go nervously. His eyes kept crawling from her bodice to her waist and back.

'If all of the men are going to spend the evening ogling you, I'll get no sense out of them,' Meiros remarked quietly as they passed inside the massive doors.

'Is that not the plan?' she asked pertly. Everyone in Aruna Nagar knew there were men whose bargaining skills collapsed when confronted with a pretty face. She wasn't the prettiest girl in the market, but she'd certainly learned how to flash a smile at the right moment.

Meiros glanced at her curiously. 'I may have underestimated you, Wife,' he whispered. He sounded pleased. 'But be careful: not everyone here is an old lecher like Rene Cardien. No cheek, remember!'

She bowed her head humbly as they entered a massive hall. Motes of dust danced in the columns of dusky pink light shining through high windows. Their footsteps echoed as they walked between statues of commanding-looking men and women in flowing robes, rendered with astonishing realism in white marble shot with seams of emerald and vermillion. Meiros paused briefly next to one, a slim, lissom woman with big eyes. 'Lynesse, my first wife.' He pointed to the statue opposite, an imperious woman with her arm pointing skywards. She looked grim and haughty. 'Edda, my second wife.'

'Justina's mother?' Ramita whispered.

'Indeed. Alike in all things,' he said ruefully.

Ramita repressed a giggle as he led her onwards to where the magi were gathered. Silence fell and every head turned as they were announced.

They had discussed the question of curtseying, not easy in a saree, so he told her not to curtsey at all. 'It's a Rondian gesture, Wife; your clothing is making a statement about *not* being Rondian. Remain standing, and let them all get a good look at you; let them fully realise that you are a foreigner here. Dare them to bend towards you – remember, you are my wife, and they will not want to offend you, for that would be to offend me.'

With 'Lord and Lady Meiros' still ringing in the air they paused to let the gathering absorb them. Meiros wore a simple cream mantle; Ramita was a glittering doll, brighter than every woman in the room. Then he led her into the crowd and faces and names quickly became a blur: male magi married to female magi; single magi of both genders; non-magi spouses of magi. Everyone was deferential, and with an unexpected touch of pride she thought, *My husband is the mightiest man here.*

They were offered glasses of some kind of bubbling wine that was obviously a luxury, but she accepted only a fruit sherbet, as a good Lakh wife should. It looked like she was the only non-drinker there; her father had once told her that all Rondians were sots.

What surprised her most was that almost half the magi were clearly of mixed Antiopian descent, Hebb mostly, she guessed, looking at the dark hair set against pale olive complexions, but there were some striking combinations. One voluptuous woman, introduced as Odessa d'Ark, had dark olive skin and nearly blonde hair: she looked almost offended by Ramita's saree, but stared at it avidly, as if already planning her next ball-gown. 'The fashion stakes have been raised,' Meiros whispered as they passed on.

Thus far she hadn't even been called upon to open her mouth. She was just beginning to feel a little confident when Justina arrived. She was wearing a silver brooch of a snake coiled about a staff, the symbol of the order of healer-magi she'd founded. Ramita noticed most of the women present were also wearing it. Justina was on the arm of a man whose clothing almost out-glittered Ramita's.

She left her partner to come and acknowledge Meiros. 'Father,' she said, and curtseyed elegantly.

Meiros eyed the man with her doubtfully. 'Him, Daughter?' he said in a low voice.

'Oh, Father, don't be a grump. Emir Rashid happened to arrive in the next carriage to mine and offer his arm. Be nice, Father, this is a party.'

The emir, who would have shamed peacocks with his glittering brilliance, glided towards them. Justina waved her hand airily, as if displaying an exhibit. 'Rashid, this is my father's new wife, Ramita.'

She stared up at the man and caught her breath.

It wasn't just the costume of opal, mother-of-pearl and even real pearls, woven into a piece of finery that shimmered like a glittering snake. It wasn't just his perfect, haughty, beautiful face, framed by braided hair and an elegant goatee; it was all of those things, but it was also the confident poise and the grace of a dancer or a swordsman. His eyes, the most piercing of emeralds, glittered beneath his manicured brows. But mostly, she saw Kazim in his natural athleticism and utter belief in the power of his own charm, and for a small second he *was* Kazim, striding towards her across the floors of this dream palace. She almost said his name.

She swallowed as a cool hand gripped hers and his lips caressed her hand. '*Namaste*, Lady Meiros. Rumour does you no justice,' he said in Lakh, his voice rich and his accent perfect. 'I am Emir Rashid Mubarak al Halli'kut and I am your servant.'

'Uh, *Namaskar*,' she started. 'It is wonderful to hear my own tongue again, Emir.'

'It is a pleasure to practise it, Lady Meiros.' He straightened, preening a little.

He loves himself passionately, she noted.

Meiros' rasping voice was a contrast to the emir's rich timbre. 'Emir Rashid, I did not know you have spent time in Lakh?'

'Oh, I get everywhere, milord, sooner or later.' He looked at Ramita. 'Good evening, Antonin. Lady.' He swirled away to greet Lady Odessa with a florid bow. Ramita had to tear her eyes from him.

After a time the novelty of being looked at but not talked to became frustrating. She was Lakh, and Lakh people were gregarious by nature. There were so many fascinating people here – the legendary Bridge Builders themselves – and yet all she was permitted was to listen to small talk, to simper and smile. She felt restless, and her nerves dissipated, worn away by boredom.

'Um – where's the privy here?' she whispered at last.

Alyssa, hovering nearby, volunteered to guide her. 'How are you enjoying the party, Ramita?' she asked, as she led the way through endless corridors.

'It's not like a real celebration,' Ramita sighed. 'There is no music, no dancing – it's not really fun.'

'A party for fun – what a novel idea,' Alyssa mused drily. 'We don't really do those here.'

'None of you seem to actually like each other,' Ramita commented. 'I can tell: everyone is so formal! At home, if you don't like someone, you don't invite them to your parties – well, except everyone just shows up anyway. But you don't have to let them inside and if they make trouble, you just tell one of Chandra-bhai's boys and they sort it out.'

'It sounds like you have more fun than we do. Everything here is politics: who you talk to, what you say, who you dance with, some-times even what you wear.' She giggled. 'I think all the women will be trying to be more colourful next time. But the older ones are shocked at seeing your belly, of course.'

'At home it is normal. Do you think I made the right choice of what to wear?'

'You did; you've caught everyone's eye. Especially the most handsome of the men.' She winked at her. 'I think you've made all the right impressions.'

Ramita felt a sudden flush of confusion. 'I only wanted to establish that I am Lakh and have a right to be myself. I have no desire to attract any other sort of attention.' She stuck her chin out. 'A Lakh woman is faithful to her husband.'

Alyssa smiled knowingly. 'My dear, what lovely sentiments. But when you've been married to the same bore for half a century, you may feel a little different. And your husband is so old – some of us wonder if he can still . . . ?' She gave a sympathetic sigh. 'We're all dreadfully sorry for you, my dear. All we want to do is make your time here as painless as possible, before you are sent home.'

Ramita felt a strange sensation inside her. 'Sent home? But I will conceive soon.' *Is this what they all think, that I'm just a momentary distraction, even this woman I thought my friend?* 'You'll see.'

'Of course, dear.' Alyssa leaned against the wall, her face suddenly calculating. 'But to whom, I wonder? So many of the younger men are crying out for fresh meat.'

Ramita flushed red. 'To my husband,' she said, gritting her teeth. *Do I really have no friends here at all?* She fled to the privy, locking the door behind her. For a time she sat there, trying to regain her composure. When she emerged, Emir Rashid Mubarak was leaning against the wall where Alyssa had been waiting. The woman was nowhere in sight.

'Lady Meiros. Or may I call you Ramita?' Rashid asked smoothly in Lakh.

She had to swallow twice before she could speak. 'My lord.' She moved to step past him and he put a hand on her arm: soft, but steely.

'Allow me to guide you, my dear,' he said. 'It's not easy to find the way in this maze.' His hand was huge upon her forearm, and she felt herself trembling as he walked her through corridors she didn't recognise into a small courtyard filled with the rich smell of frangipani. Leafy branches filled the space, enclosing them.

The emir turned to face her, though he was so tall that she came only up to his chest. He still gripped her arm, and she found his proximity intimate and subtly threatening. 'So, Ramita, it must be hard for you, to be taken away from those you love.' His mellifluous voice caressed her senses. 'Family, friends, lovers . . .'

'I don't recognise this courtyard, Emir.' She tried to keep the fear out of her voice.

'Did you have any young men in your life, back in Baranasi? Any handsome young men?' For a second his face caught the light strangely and again she was staring up into Kazim's face and he was whispering to her on the rooftops, one of those many nights lost in the past, so few months and so many lifetimes ago. She tried to pull herself from the emir's grip, but he held her firmly. 'Wait, Ramita – don't be afraid. I'm here to help you. I'm a romantic, you see. I want to see you live happily ever after. I have a soft spot for young lovers. Like you and Kazim.'

Her heart nearly stopped. *He knows about Kazim – and what else does he know?*

Footsteps scraped behind them. 'Rashid.' Antonin Meiros' words were harsh and ugly after the beauty of Rashid's voice, but to her, in that moment, they rang like bells.

The emir's mouth twitched. 'Ah, Antonin. I found your young wife wandering, clearly lost.' He held out Ramita's hand as if she were a prize. 'I return her to you. I trust you will be more diligent in future.'

'Oh, I shall, Rashid, I shall.' Meiros took Ramita's hand gently in his. 'Come, Wife. They are ready to serve the meal.' He walked her slowly back to the hall, but she barely heard him. Her mind was racing. How could the emir have known—? She had not even thought about Kazim tonight . . .

Then she had a sickening thought: someone had been allowed freely inside her mind. Alyssa could have picked her mind over at leisure. She felt a chill, like the coils of serpents writhing in the darkness.

*

'You did well, Wife,' Meiros said as they were driven home. 'You were silent, courteous and composed.' He looked sideways at her. 'What passed between you and Rashid Mubarak?'

She carefully blanked her mind. 'It was as he said – but only because Alyssa left me on my own.'

'Alyssa? That is not like her. Something must have called her away.'

Or someone? She almost voiced her suspicions, but stopped. Meiros had known Alyssa Dulayne far longer than she had, and both he and Justina evidently liked her. *Very well*, she told herself, *but I will end my lessons with her.*

'Was the banquet a success?' she asked. There had been no dancing and little laughter. It had been a tense and joyless occasion, in her eyes.

Meiros grunted. 'It was just a continuation of the whole week. Nothing you need concern yourself with.' He sounded drained once more.

'Whatever concerns my husband concerns me,' she replied determinedly.

He looked at her. 'Very well: I founded our Order to promote peaceful use of the gnosis. But when the Inquisitors seized Northpoint, they forced me to choose between the Bridge, or war. Rightly or wrongly I chose the Bridge, and since that time, the Imperial Inquisitors have effectively controlled the Order. We were allowed to continue functioning solely to preserve and maintain the Bridge, and this has split our Order. Some members have been bought out by the Inquisitors and now give them their loyalty. Others just keep their heads down and do as contracted. Many of the Order now wish to fight, but we have been pacifist for *centuries*. We have neglected the arts of war, and we are too few. To fight would be to risk complete destruction.'

'Which side do you take, Husband?'

'I take the side of peace, as I always have, but it is not easy, though as founder I have right of veto. The militants outnumber the pacifists, but they are divided between Crusade and shihad. Rashid Mubarak favours the shihad. Rene Cardien leads the Crusader faction.

I stand between them, trying to hold the Builders together in adherence to our founding principles of education, commerce and peace.

'Wife, I am losing. My son is dead. My daughter squanders herself. Only my divination holds out hope, that if you and I have children, they will somehow save the Order – that is why you and I must be fruitful, though it will be twenty years before our children are ready to play their part. We must survive this Moontide, and the next, and it feels like a forlorn hope. But I have lived this long, and I can endure longer.' He squeezed her hand. 'I'm sorry to lay such burdens upon you, my lovely wife.'

He looked almost lost, like a small boy. She had understood only a fraction of what he said – politics was hard, and she had more pressing worries. *What else did Alyssa learn of me?* The thought made her feel ill, but for now she pushed aside her fear. She put a hand over his and squeezed.

Captain Klein let them into the house and she followed Meiros up the stairs. He walked her to her door, but she shook her head. '"A good wife should stay with her husband when he is troubled and sooth his brow",' she said, quoting Omali scripture.

He gave a small smile. 'I fear I will not be good company, Wife. I am so very, very tired.' He kissed her goodnight gently and hobbled away.

Her dreams that night were disturbing, images of Kazim and Rashid overlapping, confusing her, leading her in circles, while Alyssa watched, laughing callously. She woke more than once, wishing she was not alone.

The banquet marked the end of Janune, the first month. Febreux and Martrois drifted by and still she did not conceive. She refused further language lessons, and had Huriya shut Alyssa out the one time she visited. She was still too frightened to make her suspicions known to her husband, as Justina's friendship with Alyssa clearly ran deep. Suddenly nothing felt safe. She felt isolated despite the growing warmth of her relationship with her husband and Huriya's constant friendship. When she had travelled north, she had feared all manner of real and imaginary perils, but she had never thought to make offerings against loneliness: no one visited her, and even Huriya and the other servants had more freedom than she did.

But her bubble of safe solitude burst at the end of Martrois, when Huriya came bursting in one morning, threw herself at Ramita, crying, 'Mita, Mita – you will not believe this, but I've seen him – in the souks! I spoke to him!'

'Spoke to whom?' Ramita asked, shaking off her sister. 'Who have you seen?'

'Jai – I've seen Jai, right here in Hebusalim—'

'Jai? My brother Jai?'

'Yes, idiot, your brother Jai – he's here in Hebusalim.'

'*Here?*'

'Yes, here!' Huriya's vivid face was inches from hers. 'It's so wonderful – Kazim is here too!'

The whole world lurched.

19

Offered Hands

Kesh

The Keshi call their land the forge of civilisation, where impurities are burned away. Life is surely ancient there. The plains are littered with old tombs; the caves are decorated with primitive drawings. The Amteh Faith began here, where the Prophet Aluq-Ahmed had his revelations. Though much of the land is barren, around all water there are throngs of people living on top of each other like ants. There are arguably twice as many people in Kesh alone as in all of Yuros.

ORDO COSTRUO COLLEGIATE, PONTUS

Kesh and Hebusalim, on the continent of Antiopia
Awwal (Martrois) 928
4 months until the Moontide

Kazim had thought that they would travel northwest from Gujati, but instead Jamil sold the horses and took them east at a leisurely pace through a maze of low broken hills where snakes basked on the rocks and jackals yowled. The new moon, a vast crescent, covered a third of the sky for most of the night and part of the morning. Jamil seemed to know all the small waterholes in unexpected places, and Kazim became progressively more nervous over just who the captain was; there was no escaping the fact that they were entirely in his hands now. Haroun had no qualms at putting his life in Jamil's hands, but Kazim and Jai still exchanged wary glances.

On the third day, with hours still to go until sunset, Jamil made a pleased noise in his throat and pointed to a distinctive pillar of

343

rock, a massive shaft the size of a house, with another as big lying athwart it. 'Ha! We have arrived,' he announced, and led them to a sandy space beneath the pillar. To their surprise it was heavily carved and shaped, and a door was set in the stone. As Jamil went in they glimpsed a sizable room within the rock. He emerged with a small gourd in his hands. He unstoppered it, took a deep swallow and winced. 'Fenni!' he said, and handed the gourd to Kazim. 'Sit down, relax. We've reached our destination.'

Kazim took the gourd and sipped – *chod, the fenni was strong!* – and stared truculently at the man. 'Our destination? Here? I want to go to Hebusalim, not the middle of the Kesh desert. This is not our destination – if it's yours, you can stay here, but I'm going.'

Jamil grinned infuriatingly, and Kazim bridled, longing to smash that smile off his face. 'What are we doing here?' he shouted. 'Why aren't we going north? Just who the Hel are you?'

'Me? I'm the one who pulled your fat out of the fire and babied you across the desert, that's who.' He lounged against the stone. 'I'm the man who can get you to Hebusalim faster than any other, and right now that's all you need to know.'

Jai put a hand on one shoulder, Haroun grabbed his arm and they pulled Kazim away. They hunched together in the lee of a great rock. At last he growled, 'Brothers, what are we going to do?'

Haroun patted his shoulder. 'Trust him, my friend. He has done all he said he would, and if he says he will take us to Hebusalim, he will. He is what he says, I promise you.'

Kazim rounded on the spiritualist, asking angrily, 'How do you know that?'

'He is our guide, sent by Ahm Himself,' Haroun answered emphatically.

Kazim rolled his eyes and looked at Jai, who shook his head and glanced at Keita. 'We don't have much choice, Kaz. Let's just keep our eyes open and see what happens. We've got nothing he couldn't just take, have we? So maybe he's genuine.'

Kazim slowly unclenched his fists. 'I'm sick of being led around by the nose.'

Haroun patted his shoulder again. 'Trust, my friend. Trust in Ahm and in Jamil.'

The Keshi captain produced real weapons from the stone room, and all afternoon he drilled Kazim and Jai, working them hard. Kazim imagined each blow was at Jamil's face – or Ramita's husband, whoever he was.

In the evening after the meal, he bolstered his nerves with the fenni, and whilst the others bedded down for the night he went and sat near Jamil. Jai and Keita were out of sight behind some rocks, but they were still in earshot. Kazim fought to stay civil as he asked, 'Jamil, how do you know my father? You do not seem old enough.'

The warrior was cleaning his helm with sand. He grunted. 'Raz Makani was older than me, but I knew him. We are distantly related, in a manner of speaking.'

'In a manner of speaking? What does that mean?'

'Just that.' He shrugged, uninterested. 'I'm a distant cousin.' He leaned back. 'Boy, I like you. You've got courage, and you think fast in a fight – if you didn't I'd have lost you when the Ingashir struck. I will get you to Hebusalim, and when we arrive, I will introduce you to some people who can help you recover your woman.'

'Then why have we come here? Why aren't we going northwest?'

Jamil put his hands behind his head and leaned back. 'You'll see tomorrow – and before you ask me why I'm being mysterious about it, I will tell you: you'll understand tomorrow. So stop being so spiky, lad, and get some sleep.'

Jamil shook them awake before dawn. 'Stand with me,' he told them. 'Don't do anything foolish.'

'I wasn't doing anything foolish in my sleep, so why wake me?' Jai grumbled. He put an arm around Keita. Kazim and Haroun blinked and looked around. The sun was still a distant gleam in the east; Luna's crescent hung to the west, and the stars were a sea of twinkling light.

Jamil raised a hand and pointed northwest into the sky. 'There.' His voice was low, and full of anticipation as a shape, darker than the night sky, flitted through the stars low to the ground.

At first Kazim first thought it might be some kind of bird, but the shape was wrong and the size too. 'Is that—?' He looked at Jamil and took a step back. 'Is that a *windship*?'

Jamil grinned wolfishly. 'It is what they call a "skiff", boy.' He bent over a lantern at his feet, lit it and swung it about his head.

'But aren't they Rondian?'

'No. It's one of ours.'

'*Ours*? But . . .'

'Don't tell anyone.' Jamil winked ironically. 'It's a secret.'

Kazim gaped, struggling to find his voice. 'But the Amteh preach that the magi are *evil*! Their powers are devil-bought – they are allies of Shaitan! You cannot just tell us, "it's one of ours": Rondian magic is evil, the magi are Shaitan-spawn, and we the Amteh are unstained. *This is known.*' He looked up at Haroun. 'Did you know about this?'

Haroun nodded slowly. 'Jamil told me a few days ago. Have faith, Kazim: if Ahm saw fit to give the enemy magic, would he not also give it to those of the true path?' He reached out to Kazim, who brushed the scriptualist's hand away.

'Don't touch me. You aren't my friend – you never have been. You're just like Jamil: you're in the pay of someone, trying to make me do what *you* want. You've never been my friend.' He stood up and walked away.

Behind him he heard footsteps, which stopped, then some muttered conversation. Despite himself, his eyes were drawn to the approaching windskiff. *A Rondian has married my love. I am going north to find her. And suddenly people are stepping forward to help me. Which means – what? This is insane.*

But it also looks like the only way to get to Hebusalim. Would they even let me go alone?

He walked back to Jamil. The skiff was much closer, bearing down on their sandy clearing. 'Who am I indebting myself to in accepting your aid?' he demanded.

'No one.'

'What, no honour debts? No "I owe you" understandings?'

Jamil shook his head, his expression unreadable in the pre-dawn shadow. 'No obligations.'

'I don't believe you. Who do you work for?'

'Come to Hebusalim and find out.'

'Then you are working for someone!'

Jamil looked mildly exasperated. 'Of course I'm working for someone – *everyone* works for someone, whether they know it or not. But I'm on your side, Kazim Makani. I want what you want.'

'And if I don't come with you?'

'Then you've got a long walk ahead of you.' Jamil half-turned away. 'And true love may not conquer all. That would be a shame. But, it's your choice.'

Kazim closed his eyes and groaned. 'My choice, my arse! You bastard.' He turned to Jai, ignoring Haroun, indeed fighting the urge to punch him, scriptualist or not. 'What do you think, Jai?'

Jai hung his head and murmured, 'I'm tired, Kaz, and so is Keita. Let's just go with them and think again when we get there, okay?'

Kazim threw up his hands in resignation. 'All right, all right: we go.' He stalked to his pile of belongings and shouldered them, jammed his new scimitar in his belt and bowed to Jamil. 'You win.'

'We all win,' Jamil replied evenly.

The skiff landed with a flurry of activity from the one man aboard, tugging on ropes to lower the sail while holding the tiller steady between his thighs. It was larger than it had looked from the distance, and yet it was disappointingly small. In tales the windships of the Rondians were huge things, castles of the air. This was barely sixty feet long, and it had been crudely hacked from a hollowed-out log.

The man was wrapped in a headscarf and flowing dun robes. As the hull crunched into the sand he leaped to the ground and came striding towards them, crying, 'Praise be to Ahm, Jamil, praise be.' He threw his arms around the captain and kissed his cheeks in greeting.

'We give praise, Molmar.' Jamil hugged the man back intently, then buffeted his shoulder. 'I trust you were not seen, my friend.'

'No, no, the Rondians are shut up in the Hebb Valley. We could put a fleet in the air in broad daylight out here and go unremarked . . . not that we will be that indiscreet.'

'No, we will not. Molmar, these are my travel companions: Haroun, Jai, Keita . . . and the sulking one is Kazim Makani. He'll get over it, once he's adjusted to the realities of the world.' Jamil clapped Molmar on the shoulders. 'If you can convince him that you haven't sold yourself to Shaitan for the power to fly that windship, he will come with us.'

Molmar raised an eyebrow. 'Ah, that. Lad, forget what you've been told. The gnosis – that's what this power is called – has nothing to do with Shaitan and devils. That's just priest-talk. It's—'

Jamil raised a hand to stop him. 'That's all they need to know for now, Molmar. How far can we fly in daylight unseen by the enemy?'

'There are no Rondian patrols this side of Saghostabad, trust me.'

'Good, then let's get under way.' He looked at his companions and gestured at the skiff. 'Throw any gear you want to take into the nets and if you need to shit or piss, do it now, before we take off.' He clapped his hands. 'I want to be gone from here in ten minutes.'

Just like this, my whole world changes . . .

Kazim sat in the prow, as far from the two Keshi warriors as possible. Jai and Keita huddled beside him; she was whimpering, her head hidden beneath a blanket. Haroun sat beside the mast. Jai and Keita had both vomited over the side within seconds of take-off, but Kazim had always stronger guts than his Lakh brother. Haroun appeared completely unmoved. Still, it was a frightening sensation, watching the ground fall away and the craft rise as Jamil hauled on the ropes and raised the single sail.

I am flying aboard a vessel powered by the arts of Shaitan – or not, apparently. What am I to think?

They swung stiffly in the barely moving air, then Molmar spoke softly and with a sudden rush a gust of wind came from nowhere and filled the sails. The nose dipped and straightened and as they picked up speed Kazim realised he had been holding his breath. He exhaled. For the first minute or so he fully expected them to plummet to the ground and die, then everything changed – not in the landscape, though that was astonishing, but inside his head: a sense of complete freedom filled him, which was entirely at odds with the way he appeared to have been manipulated by Jamil and whoever he worked for. It suddenly didn't matter: he was moving towards his love, and he was experiencing *this*. Whether it was enabled by Ahm or Shaitan, he could not deny that flying was *glorious*.

From above, the shapes of the land were revealed, details that had escaped them from ground-level. The sun rose and stretched its bright hand across the landscape, and in the southwest he could see the distant mountains on the horizon. The villages were like toys beneath him, herds were like beetle swarms. He saw a desert lynx, yawning on a rock below. Hawks shrieked indignantly at them and swooped away. The miles disappeared beneath them, but he never tired of the ever-changing views.

No wonder the Rondians are said to be arrogant: if this was how they travel they must think themselves gods.

They made stops twice-daily to relieve full bladders and bowels, rest and eat, always in the wilderness, and they flew well clear of the few towns they came across. Molmar knew the land well, leading them unerringly to waterholes at each stop. When they stopped at night for Molmar to sleep he occasionally got a glimpse of his unmuffled face. He looked uncannily similar to Jamil, and a deeper unease took Kazim. Again he contemplated walking away, but when he woke he could not resist the lure of flight.

They travelled like this for a week, covering more than two hundred miles a day. Molmar unrolled a map and taught him what the lines on the leather meant, and he stared at it for hours over dinner, memorising it, trying to picture places from the descriptions Molmar and Jamil gave him. He hadn't meant to talk to either of them, but after a while he felt like a fool and slunk into the circle about the campfire. *They are useful*, he reasoned, *but it doesn't mean I've forgiven them*. Nor had he forgiven Haroun, though his anger towards the scriptualist was harder to sustain. *Maybe I've misread him*, he thought; *perhaps his friendship is genuine*. But he'd never been very good at backing down.

For the first week they flew west, then swung northwest towards Dhassa. The waxing moon grew, dimming the stars, and as the plains became more populated, they changed to travelling only at night. Kazim found just as much joy soaring beneath the moon and stars, seeing the dim lights of campfires below and the way the waterways reflected the night sky. Eventually he asked Molmar to teach him how to use the rudder and set the sail. The first time he caught the wind and they began to skim across the sky like an eagle a burning exhilaration filled him.

Molmar chatted amiably, though he refused to tell Kazim how it was that Amteh warriors had the devil-magic of the Rondians. 'That's for others to relate, not me, lad.' If it hadn't been for his resemblance to Jamil, Kazim could almost have liked him.

Eventually, though, their airborne odyssey came to an end. 'We are coming to the areas where the Rondian warships are known to patrol,' Molmar told them, 'so we must part company, my young friends.' He set them down in a field just after midnight. He embraced Jamil and offered Kazim his callused hand. Kazim stared at the man for a long moment, then took it, and Molmar's face broke into a smile. 'My helmsman,' he chuckled, then looked more serious. 'Ahm be with you, Kazim Makani. May he guide your blade true.' And within minutes the windskiff had disappeared into the night sky.

Thereafter they travelled on foot from village to village, safe-house to safe-house. These were tended by the servants of Amteh scriptualists. Everywhere it seemed they were expected. Haroun spent most of his evenings with the holy men, but returned with snippets of news. Most of the talk was of the shihad, of course: Salim was supposedly negotiating with the mughal; Javon would soon join the shihad; the Rondians were reinforcing and refugees were already fleeing Dhassa in anticipation of disaster. They saw many such people on the road, weighed down by their belongings, stoically trudging through the dust.

At the end of the month, under a full moon almost as bright as day, they entered Hebusalim in the back of a curtained camel-cart. The Godspeakers in Baranasi had claimed that Hebusalim was besieged, under constant attack, but though Kazim saw no sign of armies or fighting, the inner city walls were strongly manned and there were many ferang guards on the gates.

'The sultan musters his armies east of the Gotan Heights,' Jamil told him. 'No one but insane Rondians makes war in midsummer. The Convocation did not reach agreement in time to mount a winter campaign – after ten years of wrangling we should be grateful they reached agreement at all.' The Keshi captain's voice was bleak and cynical.

They did not enter the inner city, but turned into the tangle of streets in the outer city. There were people and noise everywhere, feverish commerce and raucous religion, traders and Godspeakers vying for customers, verbally bludgeoning passers-by with their promises of paradise.

'They are desperate to squeeze as much from their businesses as they can before they flee the Crusaders,' Jamil remarked. 'The markets will be open past midnight – the traders have starving families and opium habits to feed. This city has become a cesspit.' His voice was only mildly condemnatory.

They passed whiteskin soldiers clad in chainmail and red tabards, drunkenly cursing and shoving their way through the alleys. They looked big and stupid. Jai had his arms around the shivering Keita and Haroun's head was buried in a scroll, leaving Kazim with only Jamil to talk to.

'There are rooms awaiting you near the Dom-al'Ahm,' Jamil said. 'There is someone you need to meet.'

Kazim looked at him. '"No obligations", remember?'

'Of course. But if you wish to see your woman, we can help you.'

'"We"?'

Jamil just smiled.

Bastard. 'Stop toying with me,' he growled.

Jamil leaned towards him. 'Look around you, Kazim: this is a Hebb city, under the thumb of drunken whiteskins with less wit than the camel pulling this cart. How did this happen? Because Antonin Meiros and his Ordo Costruo allowed it to happen. Because he refused to do what decency and righteousness demanded and drown the emperor's legions. He continues to compound this treachery by not reversing that decision, not aiding the shihad. This evil, lecherous creature is rolling in the mountain of gold the emperor paid him for that betrayal.'

Kazim listened with little interest. 'I'm here for Ramita, nothing else.'

Jamil jabbed a hand finger into Kazim's arm. 'It affects you, Kazim Makani, because Antonin Meiros has recently revealed to the world that he has a new wife.'

Kazim felt his whole skin tingle. He met Jamil's eyes, barely comprehending.

'He has a new Lakh wife,' Jamil continued remorselessly, 'named Ramita Ankesharan.'

Kazim stared. 'But Meiros – he died years ago – he is just a legend, not a real person—'

'He is a jadugara who has stolen your woman,' Jamil replied in a low voice.

Kazim felt his throat constricting: Meiros: the bogeyman of every tale of the Crusades, Shaitan Incarnate himself. 'My God, Ramita!' He put his head in his hands. 'How long have you known?' he whispered. 'Why didn't you tell me sooner?'

'Would you have believed me? And if you did, would you have come, or would you have given up and gone home?' Jamil asked, studying him intently. 'Now you are here, and know the truth. What will you do about it?'

'You thought it would scare me.'

'Does it not? Antonin Meiros is the most powerful mage in all Ahmedhassa.'

He remembered the tale of Ispal and Raz, told to him so many times: flying magi and firestorms, and Meiros betraying the Hebb after all he'd done for them. Was it even possible to steal Ramita back from such a man? 'Why do you help me?' he muttered.

'Because your enemy is our enemy, Kazim. You have come to win back your woman and we applaud your courage. We stand with you. We will aid you. Accept our help.'

Kazim looked at him levelly. '"We"? Who is "we", Jamil?'

'*We* are the Amteh – the true Amteh, not the mainstream of the faith, but a select brotherhood, dedicated to ridding this land of the whiteskins. We have acquired Rondian gnosis, though I cannot yet reveal how. *We* have the ear of the Sultan of Kesh. *We* move the Convocation; *we* are the power that guides the shihad. And we want to help you rescue your woman.' He held out his hand. 'Only we can aid your quest. Will you accept our aid?'

What choice do I have? I know no one here; I don't know where she is, or how to get to her. Without help I'm lost. And Antonin Meiros *has my Ramita . . .* Slowly, reluctantly, he took the offered hand.

Kazim sat on the dirt of the arena, panting slightly, his back propped against the wall, slurping from a water jug. His clothes were filthy, his face ran with perspiration. A blunted scimitar lay on the ground beside him. Ten yards away, the burly Hebb youth he had been sparring with lay writhing in the dust, clutching the welt across his face and moaning. *Well deserved too, you smart-mouthed little shit.*

Jamil was sitting on the wall, accepting coins from the other warriors with him. He waggled a heavy purse at Kazim, grinning: third bout today, third win – and that was after spending the morning drilling. Jamil told him he was good. He longed to try himself against the Keshi himself, just to see.

Haroun was somewhere with the scriptualists, and Jai was with Keita, of course – he was virtually married to her. He wished Jai joy, but he really thought he should forget her – after all, he could hardly take her back south when all this was over. Ispal Ankesharan would have a fit if his eldest son arrived with some homeless chit.

The arena was well away from the areas where the Rondians were.

White-skins who entered the Southside ended up with knives in their backs, Jamil said, unless they had gold for opium, and then they might just be allowed to live – provided they intended to keep returning.

A newcomer leapt down into the little arena. He was clean, and his kurta and pants were silk, embroidered at the neck and seams. He picked up the fallen youth's blunted blade and tested its weight. He had well-oiled shoulder-length hair, a beautifully trimmed beard and piercing green eyes. His boots were soft leather, expensive: surely some nobleman's son – a Hebb, by the look of him, but paler than most. He probably never went out in direct sunlight, to preserve his pretty skin. But he was muscular, lithe and well-balanced. Kazim had seen his sort in Baranasi. Lakh noble families bred them by the score: perfumed pretty-boys, skilled at weaponry and poetry, with the morals of a snake.

The newcomer glanced down at Kazim. 'You fight well, for a Lakh.' His voice was odiously melodic.

Kazim stood up. He wasn't that tired; the three bouts he had already won had been easy. 'I'm not Lakh, I'm from Kesh. And my opponents were only Hebb, and everyone knows they're gutless cock-suckers.' He lifted his blunted blade. 'You are clearly typical of the breed.'

The young noble smiled mildly. 'I've killed for less than that, boy.' He prodded the squirming Hebb boy at his feet with his boot. 'Get up, worm.' He pulled the boy to his feet, as if to see him off, but instead whirled suddenly and shoved the boy straight at Kazim.

Kazim had been half-expecting something, but not that; he caught the winded youth with his left arm and ducked low as the newcomer stepped in and rained a flurry of blows at Kazim's head.

Kazim responded by using the semi-conscious youth as a shield, and the wooden blades cracked together time and again until Kazim straightened and flung the Hebb boy back at his opponent. The nobleman caught him, then thrust the hapless youth into the path of Kazim's next blow. His blade smashed into the Hebb boy's temple, knocking him unconscious, and the nobleman threw him aside. His lips parted into a fierce grin and his blade flickered, but Kazim had already darted away. He came back at the man, and the wooden blades clattered together and locked. Kazim moved in and hammered his forehead at the noble's nose, but somehow it didn't connect, and again he was pushed away. He circled, a little more wary now. The man was still smiling.

Arrogant prick. I'll show you! Kazim leapt into his favourite attack, launching himself forward to land in a one-legged crouch, his blade at high-guard, his left leg lashing out, but his foe danced out of reach and retaliated with a series of powerful blows. Kazim rolled away and came up in time to catch a high thrust and turn it aside. The nobleman laughed joyously and circled to his right. Kazim followed him, turning in a circle.

'Good, Kazim,' the nobleman purred. 'You are a fast learner.'

'Shut up, cocksucker.' Damn but the prick was good, leaning away that extra inch necessary to let the key blow of Kazim's next combination pass by his nose, then almost slamming the tip of his weapon into Kazim's belly with a counterblow. They whirled apart again, both panting now.

'Well done, Kazim Makani,' the nobleman said, circling out of reach and flicking up his blade, ending the duel. 'I think with more intensive training you'll be one of our best. We'll put you into more qualified hands, try you against Rondian straight-swords, too. Jamil will teach you, and I myself, at times.'

'You,' Kazim sneered back, 'what do you think you can teach me?'

The man's face went still. 'What indeed,' he said thoughtfully. 'Well, let's see—' His left hand jabbed and suddenly Kazim felt as if he had been caught and tossed by an unseen bull, sending him sprawling into the dirt ten yards back, right against one of the walls. The air slammed out of his lungs in a whoosh, but he regained his feet and somehow managed to parry the nobleman's blade. Then a boot smashed into his shin and he dropped to the ground again. An unseen fist grasped him, and then he was flying through the air and scraping his face in the gravel.

The nobleman was laughing now, and an emerald gem fell into

view about his neck. A greenish bolt flew at Kazim from the man's left hand, and as he dropped and rolled he saw it flash over him and burst against the stone wall. Another bolt stabbed towards him, forcing him to dart the other way, but as he came to his feet another unseen blow to the belly slammed him backwards and he struck the wall, slid down it and doubled over in the dirt.

The nobleman pushed the tip of his blade into Kazim's mouth. 'Who are you calling "cocksucker" now? Here, suck on this.'

Kazim jerked his mouth away and retched, no longer caring what the man might do to him. He felt terrified, but not so far gone that he would unman himself before this perfumed Shaitan.

To his intense surprise the man chuckled approvingly, then bent down and laid a hand on his shoulder. 'You still have much to learn, boy. The first lesson is this: do not antagonise a mage. My name is Rashid. I am the man Jamil brought you to meet. I can deliver you to your beloved Ramita.' He smiled as Kazim's jaw dropped. 'We should be friends, Kazim, son of Razir Makani. There is much we can do for each other.' Again he found a hand extended towards him, offering everything and asking nothing. *Yet.*

He took it, and allowed himself to be pulled to his feet. Rashid clapped his shoulder again. 'Come, eat with me and I will tell you about your Indran beauty and what she wore to the Ordo Costruo banquet last month.'

Kazim stared, his heart banging inside his suddenly flimsy chest.

Kazim spent the next week training with Jamil. As he had come to suspect, Jamil was also a mage, and he had no compunction about using his powers to win. Kazim finished every session battered and bleeding, and though Jamil would run his fingers over the cuts and welts and ease the pain, Kazim was left totally drained, with barely enough energy to eat. He had no time to see his friends, until Jai sought him out one evening as he was lying on the roof watching the myriad stars. It was colder here at night than in Baranasi, and the skies were clearer. It was Moon-dark, the last week of the month.

'What is it, brother?' Kazim asked, seeing Jai was badly unnerved.

'I saw Huriya today, in the souks,' Jai started, and Kazim shot up, almost shaking with excitement.

'Huriya – truly? You saw her?' He seized Jai's arm as questions poured out: 'How was she? Was Ramita with her—?'

'Slow down, brother! Huriya is well – she was alone, except for two Rondian guards. She took me to an Omali shrine, and we were able to talk for a while. Ramita is well – they both are, at least they are fed and have comfortable places to sleep. But Huriya says the jadugara keeps Ramita chained to her bed and has her every night. She can hear her screams, but no one intervenes.' Jai was trembling.

Kazim felt fury choke him. He stood up and started pacing the roof, clenching and unclenching his fists as visions of his beautiful love, her divine face creased in agony, overwhelmed his mind. He found tears streaking his face and wiped them away. He was desperate for some way to save her. 'We must free her, brother,' he cried, 'we must destroy that *animal* – it is our *duty*.'

Kazim clasped Jai's hand and embraced him. 'You are my true brother, Jai. We will crucify that madman and take back Ramita and you shall marry Huriya and we will be heroes – princes among men.' He gripped his shoulder. 'You and I, brother! We will kill Meiros and save our women.'

'But Keita—'

'Ha, forget that one. Huriya is far prettier – I always intended you would marry her.'

Jai looked uncertain. 'I don't think she'd have me, Kaz – she wants much more. She scares me, sometimes, you know.'

'Ha! Man, don't worry: I know my sister and she's perfect for you. But first, we need to think about how to kill that bastard Meiros.' He patted his sword hilt. 'These Keshi jadugara think they are using me, but I am using them. We will free Ramita and live as princes.'

20

This Betrayal

The Trimurthi

The Holy Trinity of the Omali faith are the three principal deities, known collectively as the 'Trimurthi'. Baraman is the creator, but his great task has been accomplished and he receives little direct worship. By contrast, Vishnarayan, who protects and sustains creation, and Sivraman, who presides over death and rebirth, are widely worshipped among the Omali.

ORDO COSTRUO, HEBUSALIM CHAPTER

Hebusalim, on the continent of Antiopia
Thani (Aprafor) 928
3 months until the Moontide

Kazim is here. She had dreamed of hearing those three words, had prayed to hear them – and now she had, they had destroyed her fragile peace. Over these four short months she had gradually let go of her old life and found some balance in her new one; she could go whole days without thinking of home. Her husband, at first so repellent, felt like a haven of safety.

But now it all came crashing back in on her: Baranasi's tangled alleys, the hurly-burly of her people, the warmth of her mother's arms, the laughter in her father's voice, the clamour of her siblings. And Kazim, on the rooftops, kissing her. Kazim, gazing up at the moon, daydreaming of travel and adventure, recounting his street battles with the other boys, or some last-ball victory at kalikiti. The warmth of his arm around her shoulders, the musky scent of his body; the feel of his whiskers on her cheek. She had been in love with Kazim all her life, but the thought of seeing him terrified her.

Her husband was gentle and considerate, but he was a mage: he could pluck stray thoughts from her mind at will. Just one idle thought of Kazim could doom him. She began to picture her husband's rage if he found her with another man, a mere human. What might he do to Kazim, or Huriya and Jai? She was almost paralysed with fear for them all.

She and Huriya spent hours together, their conversation swirling about wildly as they made and discarded a thousand plans: flight into the wilds; begging her husband on her knees to dissolve their marriage and let her go; imploring Kazim to leave . . . she even spoke wildly of killing herself, so that Kazim would give her up once and for all.

Huriya's ideas vacillated just as madly: one moment she was indignant that their brothers had come to spoil their rich exile from the drudgery of Aruna Nagar Market; the next she was voicing murderous thoughts of slitting throats and escaping into the night.

Worst of all was when Ramita was alone with her husband. She was terrified of him catching her frantic thoughts, so she pleaded illness, then had to endure his concern. He came to her chamber, clearly wishing to lie with her, but she pleaded tiredness and he left, puzzled and disappointed.

Finally Huriya hatched a plan, and next morning, Ramita begged Meiros for the right to go herself to the old Pandit Omprasad's mandir to pray. 'Please, lord,' she whispered, 'I wish to make an offering each day for a child. I dreamed this would be the only way.'

Meiros looked sceptical. 'You take your superstitions too seriously, Wife. What will aid your quickening is persistence. And eating well,' he added, eyeing her half-touched bowl.

'Please, Husband. Huriya goes there often. It is quite safe.'

'It might be safe for her, but she is not Lady Meiros.' He looked doubtful, and as he stared at her she felt her mouth go dry, her heart hammering. 'You are working yourself into a state over this. Cannot that priest-fellow come here as before?'

'The mandir – it is very sacred . . .'

'Is it? Oh, very well – but just once!' He thought for a moment, then said gently, 'Wife, if it would please you, I will have a small shrine built here, for you to pray to your gods.'

She felt a horribly guilty twinge inside. A few weeks ago she would have been overjoyed that he acknowledged her beliefs, but now it was just an impediment to her seeing Kazim. She tried to look pleased. 'Thank you, Husband,' she said, her voice low.

He frowned. 'Perhaps this visit will calm you down. You have been temperamental these past two weeks, Wife.' He stroked her hair. 'Don't be anxious. All will be well.'

She bowed her head, swallowing her fear.

Jos Klein stomped into the mandir, followed by five soldiers, and glared about the tiny enclosure. The stones were fouled by pigeon droppings and rotting berries from the cherry tree in the corner of the tiny courtyard. The shrine was a six-by-six-foot pillared square, roofed, open on three sides. Inside sat a rough-hewn statue of the god, just the shape of a sitting man smeared in dyed paste, identified only by a Siv-lingam and engraved trident. Before it was a sandbox filled with burnt-out incense sticks and marigolds. Smoke rose from a small cooking-fire Omprasad was tending in the corner. There were two other men in priestly orange sitting with him, with the same tangled, ashy hair and beards, but they were younger and fitter-looking.

Klein glared at them. 'Who are these?'

Huriya answered quickly, 'They are "chela", Captain, initiates of the Omali. They have been here a few weeks now. Morden has met them.' The soldier nodded nervously when Klein looked at him.

'Get them out of here,' Klein said, pointing to a middle-aged Lakh man and his family praying before the central shrine. They looked too frightened to protest, but stared curiously at the girls as Morden ushered them away.

Ramita was so afraid she could barely move. She kept her vision focused on the Sivraman idol and a stream of prayers poured from her lips as she fell to her knees before it. Huriya wriggled in beside her and they prayed fervently for several minutes. She felt ill with tension and lack of food.

'The soldiers will get bored in a minute and go and sit by the gates,' Huriya whispered. She pulled back her hood and called loudly, 'Chela, pray with us!' As the two young priests shuffled towards them, Huriya whispered, 'I've been doing this every day so that Jos' soldiers are used to it.' She sounded excited, as if this were some marvellous adventure.

The initiates knelt between the side pillars. Ramita's gaze flickered to the man who knelt beside her and her throat almost seized up as Kazim stared back at her, a world of longing in his eyes.

'Ramita,' Jai whispered from the other side, but she had eyes only for Kazim.

How changed he looked! His beard was fuller, his skin more weathered. His hair – well, clearly that was disguised by the ash, but it was longer, a real mess. She yearned to reach out and comb it with her fingers. And his eyes – *oh, his eyes*, so clear, pure, so full of light.

'Mita,' Kazim whispered and the timbre of his voice, full of longing, of the anguish of hope, vibrated through her. 'Mita, are you well?'

She nodded mutely, not trusting herself to speak. She glanced at Jai; his face was altered too. They both looked more mature, more manly. They had clearly been through much.

'Ahem,' coughed Huriya. 'Let us pray.' She spoke in Lakh. 'You can talk, but look like you're praying! We've only got a few minutes, so get on with it!'

Ramita wished she could reach out and touch him. 'My love,' she whispered, 'are you well?'

'Now that I have seen you. Huriya has told Jai of how you suffer, and it tears my heart.'

'Oh, it isn't so bad. I endure.' *What had Huriya been telling them?*

'You have such courage – I don't know how you manage to be so brave. But we will rescue you! I promise with all my heart – I promise on my Immortal Soul, I will take you away from this.'

She didn't know what to say. She stared at him while tears rolled down her cheeks and Jai loudly chanted ridiculous things, snatches of prayers, folk songs, even lists of market goods. She wished she could hug them both to her for ever.

Kazim told her he was living behind a Dom-al'Ahm, and learning to fight – and he promised there were men dedicated to stealing her away from Meiros when the time was right. 'If that swine Klein weren't here we'd do it now, but with a battle-mage to confront we can't take the risk.'

She blinked. 'Klein is a mage?'

Huriya whispered, 'He is – third-ranked, he tells me. That is quite powerful.'

Ramita felt even more nervous, but Kazim sounded confident as he planned out loud. 'If you can come back tomorrow, we might be able—'

'Lord Meiros forbids it. Next time, and all times in the future, I am to bring the pandit to Ramita at Casa Meiros,' Huriya answered.

Kazim groaned. 'Does he suspect?'

'No, he is just paranoid. I am amazed he allowed this visit, but Ramita was the perfect actress. Next time, one or both of you must come with Omprasad. You will be allowed into the public area, but we will find a way to get you into our quarters.' Her voice took on a lascivious tone. 'We'll find a way to get you two lovers alone.'

Ramita stared into Kazim's eyes, the thought of all that could yet be overwhelming her. She bowed her head and prayed through a rain of tears.

To see her, to see her weep, was almost too much. Seconds felt like hours; every word was heavy with meaning. But too soon their time was up. Jos Klein's massive frame cast a shadow over them as he bade them come, and Ramita furiously wiped her tear-streaked face. Kazim carefully averted his eyes from the battle-mage. He wished fervently he had his blade, but he also remembered the contemptuous ease with which Klein had pummelled him in Baranasi without even resorting to magic. If he was recognised, it would go very badly, so instead, he hunched over pathetically, not even watching as the girls left. Jai, who'd danced before the man at the wedding, was just as frightened, but neither was recognised, and in seconds, Ramita and Huriya had vanished through the gates to the mandir.

Once certain they were gone, Jai collapsed. 'By all the gods! I was sure he would recognise me!'

Kazim felt the same dizzying relief. 'Me too – he'd have remembered you for certain without the beard. And I just had to pray the dirt and turban were enough!' He glared at the gate, where the family banished earlier were peering in curiously. 'Why won't Rashid kidnap her from here?'

Jai put a hand on his shoulder. 'Patience, Kazim: we will manage. You heard Huriya: she can get us inside Casa Meiros.'

'Yes, I heard her.' His heart was burning in his breast. 'I bet Rashid didn't help today because he would have had no opportunity to kill Meiros.'

Jai glanced at him. 'They can't be serious about that,' he whispered.

'They better be, for I am!' Kazim said fervently. He looked up and swore, 'Ahm, hear me: I *curse* Antonin Meiros. He will die at my hand: I swear it.'

Huriya briefed Kazim and Jai the day before they were to visit Casa Meiros for the first time. She showed them the palm of her left hand, which was etched with strange patterns. 'See these lines? They allow me to open the doors that separate each part of the House. I can get us into most places, but not into Meiros' rooms; only Ramita can go there. But I have a plan. Meiros says we can use a place in the private courtyard as a shrine. We've taken Omprasad to Ramita's room to wash him, so I'm sure we can get you in too – as long as you look harmless. So make sure you do – and you must be *careful*.'

Kazim knew how well Huriya loved her material comforts, so for her to so actively aid them spoke volumes of her love for him and Ramita. 'Ahm will reward you, sister,' he said appreciatively.

It was with bent backs and ashen hair that they tottered beside the oblivious Omprasad the next morning. Emir Rashid had spoken to the old pandit, and now he truly believed Jai and Kazim were his pupils. His vacant face occasionally became confused when he looked at them, but he gave no trouble; ganja and a flask of fenni were enough to reconcile him.

At the gates to Casa Meiros, Jos Klein himself looked them over, but not too closely, and with no sign of recognition. A stony-faced guard searched them for weapons, but they'd not been so foolish as to bring any. Then they were through, and his thoughts rebounded, as they had all that sleepless night, to Ramita, and he felt his manhood stiffen.

A good job the soldier hadn't patted down that weapon, he thought, then told himself, *Be calm, you probably won't get to do more than look at her, for Ahm's sake!*

But when he saw her, clad in a shimmering silk salwar, with jewellery kissed by sunlight, it was all he could do not to prostrate himself. She and Huriya wore identical white salwars, but Huriya's dupatta scarf was orange, while Ramita's was green. He followed in a daze as Huriya led them all into the inner courtyard, touching the handles of the doors, then pausing until they slid open silently. She showed them a brand-new shrine, which had been purchased intact and concreted against the north wall. A newly carved figure sat within, of Sivraman and his consort Parvasi, with baby Gann-Elephant upon her knee. The detail was rough but not unattractive. Before it, a new Siv-lingam sat, gleaming in the shade. Staring at the phallic idol did nothing to calm his need.

There were a couple of Hebb maidservants watching, but apart from these onlookers, they were alone. As they knelt before the idol, the women in front, Huriya whispered in Lakh, 'The Master is at the Domus Costruo, miles away.' Kazim felt a thrill run through him.

Omprasad led them in prayer, chanting on and on in a droning voice, until the servants lost interest and went back to their tasks. The pandit's wavering voice filled the courtyard as he invoked all the gods, one by one. By the time he was finally done, Kazim thought he might die of longing. When Ramita rose and he met her eyes, all he could feel was his own need, echoed in her soft eyes.

Huriya led them to another courtyard, where food was laid upon a small trestle. She invited the three 'holy men' to sit and eat. Kazim felt a crushing disappointment as she and Ramita departed: was this to be just a cruel tease? But they returned, and his heart pounded when he saw they had swapped dupattas. Huriya, mimicking Ramita perfectly, said, 'Omprasad, perhaps one of the chela could bless our rooms?' She pointed at Kazim. 'It will take only *five minutes* – I can see you are hungry.'

Ramita stood, pretending to be Huriya, bowed slightly to Kazim and indicated that he follow her. She touched a doorknob, which flickered with light as the wooden panel slid aside and they entered a corridor of cool and shade. He stepped quickly to her as she turned and pulled her to him, his mouth finding hers as she crushed herself against him. He lifted her, pressing her against the wall, drinking in her taste, the feel of her mouth, her tongue, her body.

She jerked her mouth away. 'This way, next room,' she panted, and then she was kissing him again as they slid along the wall and fell through the curtained doorway onto a low bed, into soft sheets and a mattress that swallowed them up.

He pulled up her salwar as they wrestled and grasped her waist. She moaned into his ear as he lifted the skirting above her waist. Her face was frantic as he tugged off her leggings. She looked as if she might say something, but there was no time. He fell upon her, pulling up his kurta and freeing his rigid member, and kissed her mouth as he pushed himself inside her. She stiffened in pain until he reached the wetness within, then sobbed into his mouth as he filled her, spreading herself wide, gripping his waist with her legs. He plunged frantically: flesh slapping flesh, frantic gasps, an eruption boiling through his body, fighting to keep it inside for just a split-second longer, but it was all too much, *too much*, and he groaned in agony as his seed gushed and he was gasping, weeping, into her face, 'I love you I love you *I love you* . . .'

They gazed into each other's eyes, panting, skin slick, souls bared. It felt like for ever, but it could only have been minutes before they heard Huriya's voice, still mimicking Ramita: 'They are just finishing, I'm sure.'

He cursed, *so little time* . . . He stood up unsteadily and dressed quickly, watched her do the same. The wet stain filling the crotch of her leggings was hidden when she pulled her salwar back down. She looked bereft already.

'I will come again soon, and we will get you out of here, I swear it,' he whispered.

She gave a hesitant smile and pushed him out of the door. 'Go.' She grasped his hand quickly. 'I love you.' Then she followed him out again.

Huriya rose, a secret smile on her face, and raised her voice so anyone listening would hear her. 'Offerings must be made here daily for a week so that the shrine is properly sanctified. One or both chela must come here tomorrow at this hour. That will be all.'

Kazim struggled to regain his breath as he met Ramita's eyes. All his feelings for her were still boiling inside him, unsated by their brief encounter. *Tomorrow*, he mouthed and she nodded, looking nervous now. Omprasad led them, bowing their way out, until they were blinking in the dusty streets and fighting their way through crowds, buffeted by noise and odour.

Jai caught Kazim's shoulder. 'Did you—?'

Kazim nodded.

'I hope you can make good on all your promises to my sister, Kaz,' Jai said in a low voice, the protective brother.

His tone rankled Kazim. 'I have said so, haven't I? I will slit that old goat's throat and then I will marry her and be with her for ever. You will see.' He felt exhilarated. It had been so brief a taste of the ecstasies they would share, but it meant so much, to have claimed her, to have made her his – *his*, no matter how often Meiros misused her. 'You will see, brother!' He cast off his temper, put an arm around Jai's shoulder. 'Sweet as honey, she was – sweeter, an apsara, a nymph of heaven.'

Ramita knelt in the privy, slopping water over her loins, trying to clean herself. She almost screamed when Huriya slid the door open. '*Chod!* Can't I have some privacy?' She felt on the verge of hysteria.

'Shhh!' Huriya frowned. 'I've seen you pee and shit and vomit, and you've seen me do the same, and more – there is no such thing as privacy between us. So shut up and listen: I've asked for the bath to be filled. No one suspects a thing, I swear.'

'My husband will be home soon! I've got to—'

'Ramita, he won't be home for *hours* – relax, it's not even lunchtime. The only danger is you panicking. Calm down, I'll be right back.' She returned with a small drinking flask, the sort men carried. 'Here, sip this. It'll help.'

Ramita sat on the floor, trying not to cry, overwhelmed by the emotions she was feeling, part joy, part terror, part – something else she couldn't name. She sniffed the flask. 'What is it?'

'Arak – sip it, just a little.' Huriya knelt behind her and wrapped her arms around. 'Are you okay?'

Ramita nodded. 'I think so – I only meant to talk, maybe to kiss him, but he was all over me. It was . . . wonderful. Stupid, but wonderful.' She swigged on the arak and reeled, blinking.

Huriya purred, 'That's my girl. Better than that horrible husband of yours.'

Ramita tried not to think about that. Finally she managed, 'What if he senses—?'

'Don't worry, Mita: he's taught you how to hide your thoughts, you know that. You'll be fine – just think of other things.' She giggled. 'Even if he takes you himself.'

'Huriya, this isn't a game – the Amteh *stone* adulteresses – and I dare not even think what magi would do . . . I'm so scared . . .'

'Oh, there!' Huriya comforted her, stayed with her as she bathed, led her wrapped in towels to bed and sung her asleep. 'I'll tell your husband not to disturb you,' she whispered as she dozed off. 'Dream sweet dreams of your lover, whom you will see again tomorrow.'

It was the single most terrifying moment of Kazim's life, to enter Casa Meiros the next morning and hear a rasping voice behind him, speaking Rondian. His throat locked up.

'Who is this, Wife? Where is the old priest?' The discordant voice was almost enough to make him bolt: it was Antonin Meiros himself!

'These are his pupils, lord.' Ramita sounded meek and uncertain as she watched Kazim and Jai sinking involuntarily to their knees. *He'll know – he'll somehow know, and then . . .*

They heard the old man sigh. 'My reputation precedes me again. Get up, you two,' he said, walking past them with barely a glance. 'You say these fools have to come here every day this week?' The old jadugara sounded sceptical. 'More likely they just want free food.'

Huriya spoke up boldly. 'Only this week, lord, until the full moon, when Sivraman is in the ascendancy. Your wife blooms at that time. It is auspicious.'

'I am continually amazed at how many things are *auspicious*,' he growled. 'Oh, very well, if this makes you happy, my dear.' He patted Ramita on the head as if she were a pet dog. 'I must away. Get some repose, my dear: for someone who slept all afternoon and evening, you don't look at all rested. Don't worry so much. All will be well.' And he strode away, his pale pate gleaming in the morning sun.

Huriya pulled up her scarf and led the way. Kazim let out his breath.

This time they had longer. The servants lost interest not long into the meaningless distraction of the prayers, so there was no need for scarf-swapping. Ramita opened the door and he walked in boldly, whispering his love for her even as he grasped her hair, stroked her face, the curves of her body. There was time to disrobe, to suckle her breasts and glide his fingers through her pubic hair into her soaked yoni. There was time to go slowly, to feel her climax against him, her body jerking spasmodically as the rapture on her face sent him over the edge. There was time to semi-swoon, in blissful oneness, to share their adoration. There was time to whisper of love and eternity before they had to part once more.

But there would be only four more meetings before the full moon rose. He didn't know why Huriya had set this timeframe, but it must be necessary; she was cleverer than he. He comforted himself that they would strike soon, then he and Ramita could at last share their love openly, free from this nightmare.

Ramita lay in the warm bath alone, lost in reverie. She could still taste the ash from Kazim's hair on her tongue. She could remember how her silent shuddering orgasms had felt, first as he slowly worked her with his fingers, and again as he thrust inside her. He was the Love-God incarnate. His magnificent body, his astounding face, the way he could melt her with a smile, everything about him was perfect.

But now came the waiting as they tried to find a new way to be together. This week was over, and next week her husband would return to her chambers, seeking to finally get her with child. New excuses and plans were needed. It would be best if she didn't see him next week – she was a Full Moon woman, fertile when Luna was biggest in the sky, though women seldom matched the lunar cycle exactly. Yes, it would be sensible to not see Kazim next week – but how would she endure it?

'Ramita!' Huriya poked her head in the door. 'Lord Meiros is home early – get up, get dressed – wear a saree, that'll give you more time. I've told him you were bathing to refresh yourself.' Then she was gone and she heard her below a few moments later, greeting the master with a string of babble.

Ramita picked out a saree, a yellow and orange one, and let the patience required in getting it folded *just so* calm her. She pinned her hair and was about to emerge when Meiros hobbled in. He stopped short and a smile creased his face. 'Wife, what a lovely vision you are.'

She curtseyed, tried to look pleased. 'My lord.'

'Have those priest-fellows gone? Thank goodness; I'm getting sick of seeing them here.' He limped to her and cupped her cheek. 'Perhaps you can show me what they have done?'

She smiled uncertainly, took a breath and tried to pretend she was Huriya of the glib tongue. She led him to the private courtyard and showed him the shrine. Sweet frangipani and rose-incense filled the air – Huriya and Jai had finished it while she and Kazim were in bed. She explained to him what the triple-idol represented: the Death and Rebirth of Sivraman, the dutiful woman of Parvasi and the luck of Gann. She found herself enjoying it, displaying knowledge for one instead of always being the pupil, and Meiros showed every sign of being an interested listener.

'And what is this again?' he asked of the Siv-lingam.

She blushed. 'The phallus represents the – um – the manhood of Siv. The lips about it are the yoni of Parvasi. It is auspicious, ah, for fertility.'

He chuckled drily. 'What offerings are required?'

'A paste with egg and cardamom and vermilion – the husband tips it over the phallus and then the wife, kneeling here, drinks it as it pours down this channel.'

He raised an astonished eyebrow, then summoned Olaf. 'An egg, please, also cardamom and vermilion. And hurry – the hour may be *auspicious.*'

Ramita felt embarrassed to say the pooja words to her mildly amused and habitually sceptical husband, but he didn't mock, and he mixed the paste with his own hands and tipped it over the phallus. She knelt and drank the yolk, praying intently to cover her fear that he would somehow know what she had done that morning. But he just pulled her to his feet, smeared her hands with the paste in his and kissed her forehead. 'I take it the Omali do not consider it auspicious to copulate in their temples, like the early Sollans did?'

She looked shocked. 'No!'

'Good, because my old bones aren't up to these hard marble floors.' He led her upstairs to his room, and all the way she was terrified that somehow he would *know,* but he sat on the edge of the bed and watched her undress, as he liked to do, before pulling her onto him. She was startled to find herself responding more to his penetration, almost as if Kazim had loosened something inside her. It felt like betrayal, to climax with Meiros after the beauty of Kazim and yet, when the moment came, she could not stop it, and he swung her onto her back and rode her until he too came, and lay there afterwards, her body pinned beneath his. He gave her a foolish grin. 'You take years off me, Wife. I have not enjoyed coupling this much for longer than I dare think.'

It was all she could do to blank her mind, to try to hide the guilt and fear and a confused sense of betrayal.

Kazim's training had changed: now they also taught him how to disable or kill an unsuspecting victim. He had not imagined so many ways to take down an enemy: a stab to the kidneys or under the left armpit; a slash to the throat from behind; a knife driven up under the jaw into the brain; places where a single blow with a blunt instrument could stun. They showed him how to throw a variety of blades, and set him tests for silent movement.

They even gave him tips for fighting magi, which came down to a few simple principles: kill or knock them out with the first blow, and failing that, keep landing blows, causing pain, so they can't focus their powers. Never strike the same place twice, for their instinctive shielding will block the second blow, then they will counter and you'll be done for. Strike from behind when you can, silently.

It was simultaneously chilling and exhilarating, and Kazim lapped it up.

Most of the training was with Jamil, and he quizzed him ceaselessly about this secret order of Amteh magi. 'Who are you, really?' Kazim asked. 'You're a mage, but you're not in the Ordo Costruo, though Rashid is. You and Molmar look alike – are you all cousins? Was my father one of you? Is this magic handed down father to son?'

Jamil didn't shrug his questions away like usual. 'Rashid has given me permission to answer some of these questions, but I must first swear you to secrecy: *total* secrecy, brother. You cannot even whisper this to your woman.'

When Kazim nodded cautiously, Jamil told him, 'We are Hadishah.' He whispered it, as men always whispered when they said that word.

Hadishah – the Jackals of Ahm: even the name was one of terror. The most extreme movement of the Amteh, and outlawed by the sultans, even in Kesh and Dhassa. But everyone knew the stories: it had began as the creed of the nomads of Mirobaz, and gradually evolved into a kind of religious secret police, answerable to no ruler. The Hadishah were the cloaked figures who burned down the houses of blasphemers and stoned adulterous women, punishing them on the word of rumour alone; they stole children to bring them up in their order; they were a million things, truth and fable entwined. For centuries the sultans of Kesh and Hebb had tried to stamp them out, but now, with Rondians in Dhassa and the Convocation disunited, they had a new legitimacy. They were the new heroes of the shihad.

Kazim found he wasn't surprised, not deep down, but he was afraid. You didn't walk away from the Hadishah. They had revealed themselves to him, so like it or not, he was now theirs to use until death.

And they have this magic, this 'gnosis', too!

Jamil cocked his head. 'Guessed already, had you?'

'I had wondered. What does it mean, you telling me this?' he asked, watching Jamil carefully.

'It means we want to help you do something we would also like to see done. When Meiros leaves his house, he is on guard, and the wards he has built into Casa Meiros make it impregnable. Once a street mob tried to assault it, but no one could climb the walls, though they look low, or break the doors, which look so flimsy – and Meiros wasn't even there at the time. But your woman is the weak point. Your sister can get us inside, but not into Meiros' tower. Only Ramita can get us in there.'

'But how can you be magi?'

'How indeed!' Jamil laughed wryly. 'In truth, the usual way. When the Ordo Costruo settled in Hebusalim, they took lovers – naturally their Sollan church condemned it, and so did the Amteh, but that wasn't much good to the babies that resulted. Some were adopted by the Ordo Costruo, but we gathered many. Likewise, from time to time an isolated mage might vanish. We took them as breeding stock; to create our own magi. Like me.' His voice was hard and flat. 'I was born in one of these breeding houses.'

Kazim stared at him. 'That's disgusting!'

'It's perfectly logical. Magi are weapons, and we need such weapons to defeat the Rondians. But we have few bloodlines: hence the "family resemblance" you noticed.'

Kazim stared. 'But you're suggesting that my father– But that is impossible. He never – I–' *Chod! Is he really saying I am one of them?*

Jamil went on implacably, 'We ensure the brothels frequented by Rondian magi have fertile women. We kidnap, we set honey-traps, but male magi have thin seed, and female magi seldom conceive, so we have few bloodlines. So much inbreeding leads to many stillborns and deformities – my mother was born with no arms, and she died birthing me, at the age of forty-three, having given birth seventeen times.' He spat. 'This is what fighting such an enemy reduces us to. Every so often we capture another one, add some fresh flesh to the mix.' He pursed his mouth in distaste. 'I agree with you, Kazim: it's vile, and sometimes it makes me sick. It's as much a crime as anything our enemies perpetrate. But what are the alternatives? We must have the gnosis, and if we sin in the service of Ahm, that sin is forgiven: Victory justifies all.'

Kazim was horrified. 'But my father . . . Was he one of you? Am I?' he asked hoarsely.

Jamil met his eye. 'No, Kazim, you are not one of us,' he said.

Something in the way he said it gave Kazim pause, but still he exhaled in relief. The gnosis was too frightening to comprehend.

The Hadishah smiled grimly. 'Just because you do not have the gnosis does not mean you need not defend yourself from it, Kazim. Next week Rashid will commence that part of your training.'

Ramita knelt before the shrine in her courtyard and tried not to scream. She had a mad urge to take a knife, bare her loins and carve in until her blood poured onto the stone. The urge had been growing daily since she had woken and found her sheets unstained. She had always been regular, always on time, and now, when she least wanted to have conceived, she was late.

I must bleed, she told herself, *I must . . .*

She wanted to keep this secret until she had worked out what to do, but it was impossible: Meiros was exhilarated when he learned her blood-towels were unstained, that she might be with child. He had been diligent in his ploughing of her the previous week, as powerful as if her prayers to Sivraman had somehow infused him with long-lost youth. He could scarce contain his excitement, and she tried to feign the same emotions, but she was certain she bore Kazim's child – he had taken her when she was most fertile, and his seed was both youthful and non-magi. If she was pregnant, the child (or *children*) must certainly be his.

She tried to tell herself that it didn't matter, soon she would be stolen away and the parentage of any children would be irrelevant, but she could not dismiss her fears so easily. Her husband was Antonin Meiros: he was invincible. No attempt to steal her could ever succeed, so barring a miracle, in nine months a dark-skinned, non-mage child would tumble from her loins and all of the wrath of a centuries-old jadugara would come crashing down on her and all she loved.

Please, Sivraman, please, Parvasi, please Gann-Elephant . . . make me bleed!

But she did not, not all week, nor into the next.

21

Missing and Hunted

Thaumaturgic Magic

Thaumaturgy manipulates the base elements of the world and was the first and most obvious branch of magic. It is stunning to think that the entire Rimoni Empire was conquered by fewer than Three Hundred men and women wielding only Thaumaturgic powers. These days several thousand magi can scarcely control their empire and they have all sixteen of Ardo Actium's Studies to bring to bear. Of course, military tactics have evolved a long way since the time of the Liberation and whilst still princes of the battlefield, the magi are no longer so invulnerable. Nor are they all Ascendants.

ORDO COSTRUO COLLEGIATE, PONTUS

Anborn Manor, Noros, on the continent of Yuros
Martrois to Aprafor 928
4–3 months until the Moontide

Vann Mercer had managed to have the confiscation of Anborn Manor annulled, but without Elena's regular payments they were going to have to sell the dynastic home anyway. At least they would have the profits from the sale. Alaron worked on the manor, and the skiff when he had time, and he found he was enjoying seeing the old house beginning to regain some of its former grace. It was sad to think the home he'd grown up in would not be in the family much longer.

His days took on a timeless quality. It was easy to imagine that there was only this house in the whole of the world. Spring was blossoming in slow, subtle ways. Flowers bloomed in the long grass that had once been manicured lawns. The wind was sometimes gusty and cold, sometimes light and playful, but never silent. The snows cleared at last and the streams brimmed with icy melt-waters, though the Alps remained white. Gretchen polished, cooked and cleaned and her husband Ferdy did whatever it was that Ferdy did, which involved a lot of planning, but not a lot of finished product.

The isolation also allowed Alaron to practise with his illegal periapt as he slowly repaired the windskiff. He'd never excel at sylvan-gnosis, the manipulation of wood and plants, but with practise he was definitely improving. But he had another major concern now: the mysterious old man. After their initial panic, Gretchen had put him to bed and kept him there for several days, feeding him chicken broth and country remedies. He recovered quickly enough physically, but he appeared unable to speak. He could use the privy unaided, but he could not communicate, either by sound or in writing – and he had an almost uncanny knack of vanishing when occasional visitors called by.

Alaron had started talking to him while he worked on the skiff, one-sided conversations about what was wrong with the world. He was certain the old man was a mage; he hadn't imagined that tingle of alien gnosis that first day, though it never happened again. The old man was *someone*. But he had no idea who.

He hadn't seen Cym for more than a month, but she breezed into his stables-workshop one afternoon in Martroix, with the summer breezes wafting behind her, as he was singing loudly to himself, '— and the lady kissed the ro-o-o-o-o-sssse—'

'Ugh, Alaron, are you deaf? That's horrible—'

'Cym!' He was halfway to her before it occurred that she might not want to hug him at all and was left floundering awkwardly. 'Come in, come in.'

'I am in, you idiot.' She walked up and hugged him perfunctorily, then looked at the windskiff. 'Do you need some help? Huh, stupid question. You always need help.' Before he could reply she was smoothing the keel with sandpaper, enchanting it as she went, working three times faster than he could. She looked older, more grown-up: her hair was pinned up, her white blouse looked more filled-out, and her multi-layered patched skirt swayed enticingly as she walked. 'How are you, Alaron? Are you getting by?'

'Sure!' He smiled earnestly. 'I like it out here. Well, for now.'

'I'm glad you're putting my gift to good use. Have you learned how to pilot the skiff yet?'

'Um, I've read a lot about it, but I can't practise until we can get it airborne again.' He felt overjoyed to see her, but her arrival made him realise how lonely he was. 'Have you seen Ramon?'

'Nope. I imagine the Silacian sneak-thief is probably running his village familioso by now. I heard the Weber girl just got engaged – someone from Bricia. Life goes on, you know. Except here.'

'Life goes on here too,' he said defensively.

'No, you misunderstand me: it's good, to come back here where nothing happens. The rest of the world is turning to shit, men getting ready for war, people starving from hard winters and bad harvests, the usual. There are plenty of worse places you could be. You're even getting to use your gnosis a little.' She looked around the workshop. 'I called in on your father, by the way. He's moved your mother into your house; she needs constant care now. He told me to tell you he'll have to sell this place soon to pay for the care she needs.'

He winced. 'I should be there for him.'

'No, he knew you'd say that. He says, stay here, he'll let you know if things change. I think he actually quite likes having her there again. She's less cranky than she used to be, or so he says.' She suddenly stiffened, staring past Alaron's shoulder. 'Who's *that*?'

Alaron turned to see the old man had stepped out of the shadows. He had no idea how long he had been standing there. 'Uh, I don't know.'

'What do you mean, you don't know?' Cym stared at the old man.

Alaron shrugged. 'He just walked in, about a month ago. He can't talk and I don't even know if he can understand what I'm saying.'

'A month ago?' Cym walked around the old man, who followed her progress with a blank expression. 'The Norostein Watch have been going door to door for the last three weeks, looking for an old man, around six feet tall, with white hair and a beard.' She looked the old man up and down as if measuring him. 'They said he was suffering from memory loss. There's a reward posted.'

'Are you suggesting I should take him in and get the reward?' Alaron wondered.

Cym looked at him as if he had just farted. 'Sol et Lune, no! If those pricks want him, then it's probably better for him that they don't get him. And if they're offering a reward, then doubly so, 'cos it means the fool who lost him is in big trouble. You're looking after him well, yes?'

'Of course, but—'

'Then he's fine. Let the poor bastard enjoy some freedom. He's probably just escaped from paupers' gaol after years of maltreatment.' She waved her hand in front of the old man to get his attention, then greeted him in Rimoni and Schlessen, but the old fellow made no response. But when she went back to the keel and called up her sylvan-gnosis, the old man stared at the glowing lights emanating from her hands. 'Look, that's got his attention.'

'He's fascinated by gnosis,' Alaron said, having noticed it before. 'Did the Watch say what the missing man's name was?'

'No, that was one of the other odd things about it: no names were mentioned at all.' She looked at Alaron. 'Promise you'll hide him if the Watch comes looking.'

'Sure – but they never come out here.'

That evening Cym tried in vain to coax some words out of the old man. Afterwards they pored over the book on windskiff piloting before putting chairs together and having a hilarious time simulating the movements of rudder and sail to pilot their skiff. Cym announced eventually that she needed to sleep and skipped out of Alaron's reach before he'd summoned the nerve to try and kiss her goodnight.

He barely slept that night, thunderingly conscious of Cym in the next room, and it felt like he'd no sooner closed his eyes than he was woken by the thumping of mailed fists on the front door. He felt a clutch of fear and grabbed the sword leaning beside the door before running down the hall. It was sunrise, and Gretchen was standing in the kitchen doorway in her nightdress, wringing her hands.

'Who's there?' he called, trying to sound commanding.

'Norostein Watch. Open up!'

His mouth went dry, and he wondered where the old man was. 'Just a minute!' He made sure his periapt was hidden beneath his collar, then pulled the door open, his sword in his hand but not raised.

A square-jawed sergeant looked down at the blade, then up at him. There were three more watchmen standing behind him, looking bored. 'Expecting trouble, lad?' the sergeant drawled.

Alaron felt himself flush. 'We're a long way from town, sir. Anyone can pretend to be a watchman.'

The man grunted. 'True enough. But we are watchmen, worse luck, and we're looking for a missing person – an oldster who ran away from an asylum. Might be dangerous.'

Alaron's heart thudded, but he kept his face expressionless. 'No, sir. I've not seen him.'

'I didn't say it was a "him",' the sergeant observed. 'Crebb, take a look around the stables. Taultier, round the back. Mind if I come in, lad?'

'Uh, sure.' Alaron stepped back, his mind racing. The old man usually slept in the stables – and the skiff was there – the *illegal* skiff . . . He couldn't think of a single thing to say.

The sergeant stepped inside the door. 'You can put the sword away, lad. We're not bandits. Morning, ma'am,' he nodded to Gretchen, who looked outraged by armed men in *her* house. Then he looked down the hall and stiffened. 'Who's this?' He glanced sideways at Alaron as Cym came down the passage, wearing a dress of his mother's she must have hastily thrown over her head. Her hair was a tangled mess.

'Staria di Biacchio,' she answered smoothly. 'Alaron, darling, who are these men?'

'You're Vann's boy?' the sergeant asked. 'What are you doing out

379

here?' He ran an appreciative eye over Cym and grinned. 'Second thought, don't answer that. I can see why you were nervous: if you ain't married to her, you better pray her folks don't find out.' He addressed Cym. 'Your people haven't seen some old geezer mooching about, have they, Princessa? There's a reward.'

Cym shook her head slowly. 'I'll ask about, if the money is good.'

'Sergeant,' someone called from the stables, 'come and look at this.'

Alaron groaned inside as he and Cym followed the sergeant to the stables. They glanced at each other anxiously as the watchman he'd called Crebb flung open the stable door. The old man stood beside the upturned keel of the windskiff.

The sergeant walked straight past the old man as if he wasn't there and stroked the keel. 'What's this, then – a windskiff? But I heard you—' He stopped, and looked at Alaron meaningfully.

'Oh, that thing!' Cym strode through, smiling warmly. 'Alaron just cuts the wood. One of his friends in town does the actual – *thingy* – you know . . .' She waved her hands in a magical sort of way.

The sergeant nodded as if nothing were more reasonable. He continued to act as if the old man just wasn't there. 'Well, nothing here; and I can see we don't need to check the house.' He smirked and winked at Alaron. 'Wouldn't want to know how many other little cuties you've got tucked away, eh.'

He pushed the door of the stable shut behind him, then suddenly stopped and looked up at Alaron. 'Ah, have I looked in here yet?'

'Uh, yes. Just now.'

'Oh good. Well, that's that wrapped up then.' He was in some sort of daze – all of the watchmen were; it was weird – and within two minutes they had all disappeared back up the road.

All the strength in Alaron's legs evaporated and he sagged against the doors. 'Did you do that?'

Cym shook her head slowly. 'I never did a thing.'

'They walked past the old man like he wasn't there – they swallowed that bullshit story about the skiff without a question, then he couldn't even remember where he'd searched. Someone messed

with their minds in a big way.' Cym was already shaking her head
as he said, 'It was you, right?'

They both turned and looked at the old man. He returned their
stare, smiling vaguely.

Alaron looked at Cym. *'Who is he?'*

Cym stayed another week and they finished off the skiff. Alaron had
got used to having her around, but he still couldn't sleep for longing,
wishing for the courage to knock on her door at midnight. A hero
from one of the old folk tales would have just gone straight on in
and swept her off her feet, but she'd probably kill him if he tried
anything like that.

Then the Rimoni arrived, Vann Mercer riding alongside their
wagons, puffing a pipe and chatting to Mercellus di Regia. Cym's
father ran an appraising eye over the two of them when they appeared
together from the stables and Alaron had the uncomfortable feeling
that if he had laid so much as a finger on her during those past two
weeks he would now be extremely sorry, mage or no. The gypsy chief
pulled his moustache thoughtfully and finally nodded, after which
Cym hugged him affectionately while the gypsy boys went back to
staring at Alaron with postured menace.

This time the test-flight went much better: they managed to miss
both the house and the trees in the yard, and if they weren't always
in complete control, they managed well enough to ensure they didn't
crash, and landed safely. Money changed hands and Cym kissed his
cheeks and hugged him before slipping away to rejoin her people.
The black-eyed Rimoni youths eyed Alaron with a deal more respect
as they left.

'Well done, son,' his father said, 'On all counts.' And at Alaron's
quizzical look, he explained, 'Not making a fool of yourself with the
girl. And finishing the skiff and flying it without crashing.' He slapped
his shoulder. 'In that order. Now, how're the repairs going?'

Alaron grinned. 'Good. I'll show you the drawing room. I had to
put in new glass and everything—'

He talked with his father into the night, but somehow he failed to think about the old man at all. He had glimpsed him, standing beside the stable as they flew around the manor, but the Rimoni had not appeared to notice him and he had vanished again by the time they landed, and didn't reappear all evening. Alaron meant to broach the subject with his father, but it kept slipping from his mind.

The next day they unlocked his mother's library. Her books were gone, but there were other things left behind: old coins and medals, a rolled-up map from the Revolt with handwritten notes showing troop positions, and an old Keshi scimitar that had fallen behind a desk. Cleaning it all up took most of the day. They enjoyed one last meal with Gretchen and Ferdy and turned in. The Manor was sold; the new owner, Jostyn Weber – Gina's father – would take possession tomorrow.

'Ironically, Weber can only afford it because he married young Gina off to some vintners in Bricia.' Vann chuckled, then peered at Alaron. 'You're not upset about that, are you?' Alaron shrugged. 'I didn't think so – though we ought to be trying to get you married at some point. Just because you can't legally use your powers doesn't mean you can't breed magi; you're still a catch, lad.'

Alaron decided to ignore that.

Jostyn Weber arrived next morning to collect the keys. He had promised to keep Gretchen and Ferdy on, which pleased everyone. Alaron was relieved Gina wasn't with him.

After Weber had left, Alaron poked into the stables one last time, checking to make sure he'd packed all the woodworking tools. *I'm going to miss this place, Cym, the skiff. Everything, really . . .*

A hand fell on his shoulder and he nearly hit the roof.

The old man was standing beside him, his face expressionless, his eyes full of mystery. *How did I forget him?* Alaron's heart raced. 'Da,' he called, 'Da!' He didn't take his eyes off the old man, in case he vanished the moment he blinked.

When Vann arrived and saw the old man, his mouth dropped open, his pipe falling unnoticed to the ground. Alaron had never seen his father so shocked. He watched dumbfounded as he reached out to the old man as if trying to touch a phantom, but when he felt the old man's hand, Vann fell to his knees and kissed the old man's hand, crying, 'My Lord – my Lord—'

The old man stared down at Vann, and then across at Alaron, his eyes unfocused.

'Da?' His father was *crying*.

Vann wiped his eyes, staring up at the old man in awe. 'Alaron,' he whispered, 'it's Big Jari – it's *General Jarius Langstrit*.'

The anniversary of the Ascension, otherwise known as the Sacrifice of Corineus, was the most important religious event of the Kore, but in 928, as the Third Crusade loomed nearer, it took on even greater significance. Most legions were already marching to the staging camps in Pontus, soldiers, suppliers, messengers and myriad others choking the arteries of the continent in a massive eastward flow. Manipulation of the weather kept the main roads east dry, but resulted in tempests and flash-floods everywhere else. Vital crops were ruined by torrential rain, unnatural hail and unseasonal snowstorms, and farmers cursed and wept as young battle-magi flitted overhead on skiffs, oblivious and uncaring. There were scores of casualties in the camps too, as parochial pride demanded violent settling of scores. The whole continent of Yuros was in turmoil.

Despite this, at dawn on 18 Martrois, Sacrifice Day, silent congregations gathered in every city, town and village, cramming into churches and cathedrals to pray and give thanks for the Ascension of Corineus and the Blessed Three Hundred. White-clad magi kept vigil from dusk the previous day, emerging for the six-hour ceremony as the sun rose. Each of the Three Hundred was named aloud, to the tolling of a great bell, and descendants of that Ascendant would rise and lead the prayers. None of the Blessed Three Hundred were ever forgotten; magi would 'adopt' any now-extinct lines, so they would always have someone to stand for them. Only one was unclaimed: dread Selene or 'Corinea', the treacherous sister whose blade had martyred Corineus.

The last named was Corineus himself, of course. Prayers were led by the most senior mage present – in Pallas, that was Emperor Constant himself – and afterwards Mater-Imperia Lucia received the twenty-one genuflections the theologians had decided were due a Living Saint.

The ceremonies ended at midday and gave way to the biggest street party of the year, at which the local rulers distributed alms to the poor; men like Governor Belonius Vult were not the sort of people to neglect their reputations, despite other calls on the public purse, and the Sacrifice Day celebrations were always magnificent.

Alaron had grown up expecting to keep the vigil, to stand beside his mother and Aunt Elena before the people as the name of Berial, his progenitor among the Blessed Three Hundred, was read out. Another dream lost . . .

'Are you sure you won't come, son?' His father paused at the door. His mother, wearing a red-hooded cloak and gauze over her face, clung to his arm. Alaron liked seeing them together, even though all they ever did was argue.

'And see all those self-satisfied creeps being lauded by the ignorant? I don't think so, Da.' He waved them off cheerily, then filled the kettle, brewed some tea and took it upstairs to the lounge, which was now full of Ma's old books. Jarius Langstrit spent his days there, reading poetry. They had tried the histories of the Revolt on him, hoping they might trigger something, but he'd shown no interest. Alaron had managed to dissuade his parents from getting a healer-mage to look at him. 'If the Watch meant him well, they wouldn't be looking for him in secret,' he'd pointed out. 'They'd have announced that a national hero was missing and asked for his return, but instead they're sneaking around as if he's a dirty secret.' His mother took his side, and no healer-mage was called.

Tesla spent hours talking to the general. She had no more success in getting him to speak, but at least it was giving her an interest; she was more engaged than Alaron could ever recall her being before.

He found Langstrit in his usual seat and poured them both tea, then picked a poetry book at random and started reading aloud. The general tapped his finger in time to the rhythm and made displeased noises if he disliked the verse. He didn't care for war-poems like 'Retton's Charge', but he enjoyed old rural favourites like 'Gardens of Sol, Gardens of Lune' and 'Love like water runs through my hand'. Alaron had just about given up on him remembering anything.

The bells started pealing: the ceremonies were obviously done. Alaron got up and peered through the grimy windows in time to see huge flocks of doves exploding into the air from Cathedral Plaza, quarter of a mile away across the roofs. He wished for a second he was there; he had always loved Sacrifice Day whilst growing up. There would be money in his pocket, the smell of cooking sweets on the air, the best in performers and entertainments, his friends at his side – but now the thought of being there, a rejected outsider at the fringe of the crowd, hiding his face lest someone recognise him, had turned those fond memories to poison. A wave of misery swept over him and he fell silent.

A hand touched his and he saw that Langstrit was looking at him. The old man pointed to the open pages and the poem he had stopped reading.

'I'm sorry, old man – General, if that's who you really are. I just wish . . .'

The old man tapped the page querulously, the line where he'd stopped reading.

'Okay, okay—'

Mid-afternoon, Alaron was woken from his dozing by a sharp knock on the door. The old man didn't stir, so he shouted, 'Coming,' went down and opened the front door – and froze.

Cymbellea di Regia leaned against the doorframe. 'Happy Corineus Day, Alaron.' She kissed his cheek and breezed past. She was in her normal Rimoni attire, white blouse and colourful swirling skirts, but today she wore even more bangles and her gold earrings were bigger. Her loose ebony hair hung to her waist in a silken cascade. Bells on her ankles jingled as she walked. She was stunning. 'You look stressed,' she observed lightly. 'Oh and leave the door open,' she added.

'Why?'

385

'So I can get in too.' Ramon peered around the door, grinning merrily. He was clad in a black and silver doublet of velvet and leather cuffs. His thin black moustache made him look almost grown-up.

'Ramon!' Alaron gaped. 'What are you doing here?'

'Yeah, nice to see you too. We're looking for somewhere to stay; have you got a spare room?' Ramon grinned and hugged him. They had brought food and drink, lots of it, and they dragged Alaron into the sitting room, everyone talking at once.

'Ramon, you look like you're – well, rich,' said Alaron, puzzled. He was struggling to cope with his friend dressed in anything but worn-out hand-me-downs.

Ramon smirked. 'Of course I'm rich! I'm the only Rimoni mage for fifty miles in any direction from my town, so I can charge what I like. The local familioso are eating out of my hand. Life is good, if you don't mind a little paranoia.' He looked a bit fuller about the face and had a rakish confidence he'd never had at college. He remembered Cym telling him Ramon had asked her to marry him; at the time he'd not credited it, but now he understood how Ramon'd got up the nerve.

'I've got to join a damned legion for the Crusade, of course,' Ramon noted with resigned annoyance, 'but apart from that, all is well. So what about you, Al? Cym says you've been keeping a low profile after what those pricks did.'

Alaron sighed. His own life was so dull compared with his friends. 'Well, I can't use the gnosis in public, so I stayed at the manor for a while – Cym and I built a skiff together,' he added, emphasising the 'Cym and I' part.

Ramon laughed. 'I heard you flew it through a window and half-flattened the house.'

'Only the first time,' Alaron said quickly.

'And what's this about an old man?' he asked. 'I heard there's a thousand-krone reward.'

That much? Good grief! Alaron looked at him seriously. 'It's a secret – he just showed up at the manor.' He told Ramon the details, and ended, 'And he's upstairs.'

'Do you know who he is yet?' Cym asked.

'Come upstairs and I'll tell you,' he said.

As the three of them stood around the old man, he woke abruptly and peered at them all. His lips moved a little, and then he fell back asleep again.

Ramon looked at the others. 'Did you feel that?' He rubbed his temples. 'He rummaged through my mind – he used Mysticism or Mesmerism – and then left me alone again, but he could have done *anything* he wanted; it's like my shields weren't even there.' He stared at Alaron. 'Who is he?'

Alaron closed the door and whispered, 'Da says he's General Jarius Langstrit.'

'Isn't Langstrit supposed to be dead,' Ramon said with a frown, 'or mad or senile or something?'

'Da says it's him – and he would know; he fought with the general in the Revolt. He doesn't speak, and he uses gnosis without even knowing he's doing it. Da wants to go to the Watch, but I've talked him out of that, for now at least.'

'Why?' Ramon asked.

Alaron motioned for them both all to sit. 'I've been thinking about that. Remember my thesis? I said I thought Langstrit might have something to do with the missing Scytale—'

'The dreaded thesis again!' Ramon rolled his eyes.

'But if I'm right—'

'That's a big if, Al!'

'Yes, but let's say I'm right – Captain Muhren said – did I tell you about that? Well, later; anyway, if my thesis was right, it would explain everything: Langstrit is the only one of the rebel generals still alive. But he's got amnesia or something. So if you thought he was hiding the Scytale, wouldn't you hide him away until he becomes lucid enough to tell you where to find it?'

'But why would they keep him here? Why wouldn't they pick his brain apart in Pallas?'

'Maybe they tried that and failed? Maybe they brought him back here hoping the local sights would bring his memories back? Or maybe the locals kept him here and Pallas doesn't even know?'

'But – and this is all assuming your far-fetched explanation is correct – how did he get away if his memory is gone? And why would he come to you?'

'I don't know – perhaps someone rescued him, then lost him? Or his powers came back and he simply walked out without realising he was hiding himself? Maybe it's an experiment, to see what he does under his own volition, and they're tracking him . . .' His voice trailed off. *That* was an ugly thought.

'If they were tracking on him, there'd be a general identifier rune on him.' Ramon brandished a glittering ebony gem on a silver chain. 'Do you like my periapt? The previous owner lost it, can you believe that?' He winked, then turned back to the old man. He held up the periapt and concentrated. 'Nope, I think he's clean, unless it's been hidden by someone better at illusion than I am.'

'So most of the population then,' put in Cym, but she checked the old man too and shook her head. 'I agree with the Sneak; he's clean.'

The door opened and they all whirled into combat positions. Vann Mercer chuckled at the circle of determined faces and cried, 'I surrender – have mercy.' He looked at Alaron. 'Been discussing our guest, have you? I hope everyone is staying for dinner?'

'Actually Da, they're staying for a while, if that's okay?'

Vann Mercer smiled tolerantly. 'Of course.'

The company of his friends was balm to Alaron's lonely soul. Even his mother was happy as they sang seasonal songs and drank far too much mulled wine. He was envious of his friends' freedom, but he obtained promises of more frequent visits, and even made tentative plans to visit Ramon in Silacia.

'Alaron, you mustn't,' Cym laughed. 'They'll rob you blind.'

'Hey, I'm a mage,' Alaron protested. 'I can look after myself—'

'You're the most naïve greenbud on Urte,' Cym scoffed. 'Silacians eat fools like you.'

'Not all Silacians are thieves,' replied Ramon defensively, 'unlike all Rimoni!'

'Ha! 'pon my honour, that's it: a duel it is,' Cym announced, her eyes flashing.

Alaron called encouragement as Ramon and Cym defended their respective pieces of cake from the other's fork, manipulating them by gnosis. The cutlery clashed and darted and feinted, until Cym won and danced, crowing, around the room. In the corner beside the window, Vann and Tesla recited from memory rhymes by the poet Colliani to the dozing general, while the three young magi showed off gnosis balancing tricks, getting more ambitious and less accomplished with each glass of wine. It was the happiest evening Alaron could remember for years.

Finally they all helped get Langstrit and Tesla to bed, then found their own rooms. The boys took the stable at the back, leaving Alaron's room for Cym. They talked until they couldn't keep their eyes open, about everything – college, the Crusade, Langstrit – and about nothing at all. Ramon admitted to having a maid who warmed his bed back at home, which made Alaron feel like the last virgin on Urte. They wondered about Cym, and speculated whether she was about to be married off. 'I'd have thought she'd be wedded by now, not free to wander around doing what she likes,' observed Ramon. 'Usually Rimoni are worse than Silacians for marrying off girls as soon as they bleed.' He poked Alaron in the ribs. 'She's probably told her father she's waiting for you to propose, amici.'

It was a cheery thought to finish a wonderful night upon. But not one he could quite believe.

Everything changed on Freyadai evening, two weeks after Sacrifice Day. Ramon was making noises about returning home before he had to reconquer his own village. No one had heard anything about the hunt for the general for ages, and Alaron had begun to hope it was over. His parents were arguing downstairs about the arrangements for when Vann left on his trading run to Pontus, and the three young people were upstairs, reading to Langstrit, even after the old man fell asleep. Cym found a book of Rimoni poetry and read aloud, performing in her native tongue – only she and Ramon spoke Rimoni, but they all enjoyed her passionate rendition of the lyrical words. She was in the middle of Mecronius' 'Et il Lune Sequire' – 'And the Moon Follows', a lament for a lost love – when a throaty voice suddenly joined in the chorus.

They all turned and stared.

Jarius Langstrit was looking at them, his mouth repeating the phrase, over and over again.

'Get Da!' hissed Alaron, not taking his eyes off the old man, but before anyone could react the general fell forward to his knees and stared at his hands as they began to glow with gnosis-light. Fire scorched the air before him, coiling in patterns that etched themselves on the air. They gasped and took a step back, then Cym seized a quill from the desk, jabbed it in an inkwell and started scrawling, her eyes never leaving the burning pattern.

Every breath the General took was pained, as if he were labouring towards some profound utterance, and his eyes jerked from face to face as if he almost recognised them, then swung back to the blazing pattern hanging before him – then, just as suddenly, the energy inside him faded and his eyes rolled back in his head. He was unconscious before he hit the floor. They leapt to his side as the luminous pattern faded from sight.

Alaron put his ear to his chest. 'He's still breathing – get Da—' but Ramon was already gone, shouting for Vann as he ran.

It was an anxious hour before the old man woke again. They put him to bed and crowded around as Cym fed him spoonfuls of water. Suddenly he spluttered and his eyes flew upon. He looked like a trapped animal.

Vann stepped forward and held his hand. 'Sir, are you well? Are you in pain? Who did this to you?'

The general groaned and buried his head. No more words could be coaxed from him, no matter what they tried, but Ramon promptly cancelled his trip home. 'I'm not going anywhere with all this going on,' he told Alaron.

When they were finally alone, Cym showed them the shapes that had appeared during Langstrit's fit. They made a complex pattern, far more intricate than the runes they had learned at college. Runes were symbols from the primitive Yothic alphabet. The magi had assigned them to specific gnosis-effects as a form of shorthand, but they were just memory triggers, not intrinsically magical themselves. As Ramon said, 'Only babies and Seth Korion use runes while casting – but I've never seen one that complex.'

Alaron peered at the shape. 'Ma has a book on runes somewhere – it's got a lot more in it than they taught us at college. I'll see if I can find it.' He returned a few minutes later with a small volume. They couldn't find the pattern Langstrit had burned into the air, but they were filled with a new resolve and purpose. Something was happening, and it was happening to them.

Outside, the bell tolled midnight, ushering in the last day of Aprafor. It was two months until the Moontide.

22

Circling Vultures

Sainthood

It has been revealed unto us that the humble woman Lucia Fasterius, through service to Kore and the grace of His hand, has attained through her purity that state by which it is beholden to acknowledge her the divinity. Let her name and deeds be proclaimed!

ROYAL EDICT OF EMPEROR CONSTANT SACRECOUR
ELEVATING HIS MOTHER TO SAINTHOOD, PALLAS 927

Javon, on the continent of Antiopia
Martrois 928
4 months to the Moontide

Vultures circled high above, ever hopeful: the desert was no place for the ill-prepared at any time of the year and the scavengers knew it. But Gurvon Gyle never went anywhere unprepared. He sat cross-legged on a low rise in the foothills east of Lybis, watching the sun go down. His wards were blocking a bombardment of attempted communication, most from Tomas Betillon demanding explanations: why had the Gorgio taken fright and fled north? What of the tales coming out of Javon that Cera Nesti had returned in triumph to Brochena? *What was going on?*

These were damn good questions, and there would have been others had he not been able to control some of the information going to Hebusalim. Not all of it, though: Betillon would know soon enough about the corpses of Gyle's agents hanging in Brochena Plaza. *Damn you, Elena!*

The late sunlight glinted off the carapace of a black scarab crawling up his sleeve. How appropriate that the remnants of Rutt Sordell should have manifested as a dung beetle. He needed to find the necromancer a new body, but it needed to be a mage's body, otherwise Sordell would be incapable of using the gnosis. A living mage body wasn't easy to find. He was half-tempted to stamp on the filthy thing and have done with him: *I left you in charge, Rutt, and now look . . .*

He gritted his teeth in frustration and tried to think through his next step. Twice now Elena had destroyed his plans. He had talked his way down from the gallows after the first, but this latest setback would mean his head if he didn't set it right before the Crusaders arrived.

Damn you, Constant Sacrecour, for dragging me away, opening the door to Elena – you forced me to contact her, effectively telling her I'd left the continent . . . damned idiot.

But even he, who knew her better than anyone, hadn't really believed Elena would take them all on. To slay his whole team, each and every one of them of higher Blood-Rank than her: that was almost miraculous . . . but it was very much the Elena Anborn he knew. He would have had nothing but admiration for her astonishing feat, had it not endangered him.

Most galling was that he couldn't decipher her motives. Was this a personal vendetta because he'd taken Vedya to his bed? Or was she in love with one of the Nesti? Was it politics, religion, altruism or just opportunism?

I know you, Elena: love, honour – these things are nothing to you. Or they never used be. Her motivations had always been material or intellectual: head and coin, that was Elena, not heart and body. She was an old dog, like him – she *couldn't* have changed. He didn't *want* her to have changed. He missed her, strangely. Though Vedya had been far more beautiful, and *glorious* in bed, there'd been something about the relaxed informality of him and Elena that he needed. Vedya was nothing but ash now and already he could barely remember her face. That said everything.

Elena must have had aid. One against five wasn't possible – so had the Ordo Costruo helped her? Or some rogue Ordo Costruo from the half-Keshi faction? Now there was a thought – were some of the Builders abandoning their neutrality, taking sides at last? It opened up myriad lines of enquiry.

Even if it wasn't true, it might provide the story he needed: a plausible and acceptable reason for failure. It was so frustrating, to be reduced to this, but he needed *damned* good excuses because he was running out of friends. Belonius Vult had joined Tomas Betillon and Kaltus Korion in condemning this latest setback, so he probably couldn't count on Vult's backing any more. So the question was: had he run out of second chances? Was it time to cut and run?

He rejected that thought instantly. He still had Coin, the most talented shapeshifter he had ever come across, and he still had Mara Secordin, and his other mage-agents were even now riding the winds towards Javon. Elena couldn't hide, not with a queen to protect. She'd be on the defensive now, and that was fatal in this type of war. He was Gurvon Gyle, the Grey Fox. He had never lost a duel between spies before, and he never would.

Another questing mind touched his, one he dare not block. His mouth went dry. <*Mater-Imperia*> he greeted her respectfully.

The touch of Lucia's mind was viscerally cold as it echoed through the relay-staves. <*Magus Gyle. My son and the Grand Prelate have just burst into my chambers in an unseemly panic. They tell me Alfredo Gorgio has fled Brochena, that all of your magi are dead and that no one can contact you. They are demanding your recall to explain yourself to the Chief Inquisitor. What have you to say?*>

He swallowed and tried to keep his mind's voice calm and reasonable. <*Majesty, the news is correct: whilst I was in Bres meeting with your council, Elena Anborn led an attack augmented by Ordo Costruo magi, and slew my agents in Brochena. The Gorgio lost their nerve and fled the city. Cera Nesti now holds the palace.*>

<*You have proof of this Builder involvement?*>

A lie, or the truth? An easy choice. <*Yes, milady. Elena was able to attack all of my magi simultaneously and overcome them. I have certain knowledge that rogue Ordo Costruo were involved.>* He plucked a plausible name from memory. *<They were sent by Emir Rashid of Halli'kut.>*

<Certain knowledge?>

<There is no doubt, Mater-Imperia.> If you're going to lie, do it with conviction.

<How did she know you were in Bres, Magus Gyle? I understood you had taken some pains to ensure that she would not be aware of your absence.>

Emperor Constant was nothing compared to Lucia. Gyle knew whose protection he would rather enjoy. *<Whilst in Bres, I was persuaded by the emperor, Wurther, Betillon and Korion to contact Elena, to try and buy her off. Use of relay-staves is distinctive. Realising that I was contacting her from afar, she obviously decided to attack in my absence.>*

Gyle sensed anger on the part of the Empress-Mother, but when she responded her mental voice was still calm. *<I will speak with my son.>* She paused for a few seconds, clearly struggling with her temper. *<I am beginning to feel some admiration for the audacity of this Anborn woman. Her initial treachery was merely capricious. This latest act shows verve and cunning. Magus Gyle, we have a difficult situation now: the Crusades begin in two months, and we have lost our grip on Javon. We do not have time to bring anyone else in. We are dependent on you delivering what you have promised. Needless to say, your life depends upon it too.>*

<I fully understand that, Mater-Imperia.>

<Lord Betillon is demanding I send the Dorobon legion via windship ahead of schedule to Hytel and commence war.>

<With respect, he is wrong, Imperia-Mater. The Gorgio are broken. The Jhafi harassed them all the way north. Even if General Korion could spare the windships, the Dorabon arriving would precipitate the Shihad too soon. Please give me time.>

<So what is your new plan? What other resource do you have, and how will you proceed? If the Anborn woman has Ordo Costruo help, we must support you.>

<Mater-Imperia, the Javon situation is now very delicate. The Nesti have aligned with the Jhafi, and the death of Cera Nesti could throw the entire country into the hands of the shihad. We cannot let Cera forge an alliance with the sultan, so I plan to replace her. As you know, Coin is already in

place within the Nesti circle.> He paused, allowing the emperor's mother to comment, but she said nothing, to his relief. Coin was a touchy subject with her. And the shapeshifter was not yet where he needed her to be. *<Mater-Imperia, Coin is the only living shapeshifter capable not only of becoming either gender, but of completely hiding all gnosis traces. She will replace the real Cera and move the Nesti away from the shihad. Civil war will ensue, and the surviving Rimoni will have no choice but to turn to the Dorobon legions to preserve them.>*

He took a mental breath and went on, *<I have other agents gathering to infiltrate the Nesti and place Coin, as Cera, on the throne. I will be operating inside Brochena myself. You could best aid me by keeping Betillon and Korion off my back. I will deliver you Javon, I swear.>*

The Mater-Imperia was silent for some time, considering. *<Magister Gyle, I have said that I will back your plans and so I shall>* she said finally. *<I remain greatly angered, but if you can eliminate Anborn and replace Cera Nesti, I will consider our contract still valid. If you fail, however, there is nowhere you will be able to hide from me.>*

<I understand, Majesty. I will not fail.>

<Good. Betillon has burnt out most of his communication-rods ranting about your failures, so we will barely be able to communicate with you again until the Crusade has begun and we are re-established on Dhassan soil. We will await your notification of success eagerly.>

He sent his gratitude wordlessly.

<Also, Magister Gyle, I have this demand: take the woman Elena Anborn alive and send her to me. She will regret her treachery.> Mater-Imperia's mental voice would have corroded steel.

<As you command, Mater-Imperia.>

<There is one last thing: I must bow somewhat to the wishes of my son. He is anxious. He is sending a man of his own. You will have heard of Inquisition Grandmaster Fraxis Targon?>

Damn. *<Yes, Mater-Imperia, I have.>*

<He will be with you in a few weeks. Fail, and the Church's Executioner will ensure you do not slip away. My son thinks you should die immediately. I am protecting you, Magister. Do not let me down.>

<My eternal gratitude is yours, Mater-Imperia.>

The contact was broken and he was left to stare out at the darkening sky and contemplate the arrival of the Church's most feared Ascendant Inquisitor. He exhaled, noticing the faint quiver in his left hand and realising that he had not lost the capacity to feel fear.

23

Relearning the Heart

Corinea

At times, my wife the Empress Lucia says to me, 'Are not the fairer sex as well equipped both intellectually and morally to participate in the discourse of the high table?' To which there is one easy response that banishes all argument: Corinea.

EMPEROR HILTIUS, 870

Who was the real Corinea? Selene, the murderess who slew Corineus? A whorish harpy who benighted Corineus' flock, ensuring that so many of the Thousand were found unworthy of Ascension? Or is she just the excuse the Kore uses to oppress women everywhere?

SARA DE BOINEUX, GRADUATION THESIS, BRES ARCANUM 878

Brochena, Javon, on the continent of Antiopia
Martrois and Aprafor 928
4-3 months until the Moontide

Elena's Necromancy-wracked body was in turmoil. She failed to bleed at the start of Martrois, and for the first time in years did not accompany Cera to the blood-tower in the week of the new moon. Instead she went into her own tower and exercised to the point of exhaustion. *Bastido* could now defeat her on even the most basic setting, so she added bruises and welts from the fighting machine to her catalogue of pain – on top of the all-consuming task of re-establishing security inside the palace. Everyone, guard or servant, had to be mentally scanned prior to hire – though it was probably a waste of energy, for it would not uncover anyone trained in thought-conceal-ment. Those permitted access to Cera and Timori were cut to the bare minimum, and the family areas of the palace were segregated from the rest of the building. Fear of failure and desperation to regain her former athleticism drove her on. Every night as she collapsed into bed Tarita and Borsa nagged her to get more rest. She ignored them.

She had not thought herself vain, but she was more than upset at her inability to regain her youthful looks and lithe body. Her hair was slowly regrowing, a blonde-silver hue that was not too unflat-tering, but she had black circles beneath her eyes. Her joints creaked painfully; her tendons burned at every movement. She had no energy to spare for rebuilding herself: Gurvon Gyle was out there and she could not afford to relax.

The re-establishment of the Nesti proceeded apace. Cera had summoned her nobles to council, but before that there were hundreds of crises to deal with. The treasury, stables and granaries had been ransacked, and the Gorgio had been weakened, not destroyed: should the Nesti pursue when they themselves had been so denuded of men by Gurvon's initial strike?

Brochena buzzed like a hive, filled with frenetic energy. The Jhafi returned cautiously to the palace, first seeking news of missing rela-tives, and then seeking work. Cera herself attended the mass funeral for the murdered on the first Sabbadai of Martrois. She was visibly moved by the occasion, and Emir Tamadhi left her in no doubt about the feelings of the people: shihad was demanded, against both the Gorgio and the Rondians. Cera understood; she gave repeated assur-ances on both counts.

There was a lot of goodwill flowing from the liberation of the city, but one issue was still tearing Cera in two: what to do with Solinde. The people, especial the Jhafi, wanted her put on trial, for Solinde had fraternised with the Gorgio and publicly proclaimed her love for Fernando Tolidi. To protect her sister would be wrong; to not protect her would be weak and a betrayal of family.

It did not help that Solinde remained antagonistically unrepent-ant. The Jhafi claimed she had egged on the Gorgio, and she denied nothing, until at last Cera had no choice but to condemn her own sister to the dungeons in Krak di Conditiori, far to the south, where political prisoners were housed, guarded by Javonesi knights and Ordo Costruo magi under an ancient treaty with Antonin Meiros' magi. It was a delaying tactic and it pleased no one.

Mystery still shrouded the death of Fernando Tolidi. Elena could not work out how he had died, or why his body had not been taken north. There were no witnesses, and Solinde denied any knowledge. She showed no sorrow at all, which Elena found disturbing.

Before Solinde was sent south, Elena went to her cell. The princessa sat alone, staring into space, moving only to eat or to use the privy. She looked and acted traumatised, yet when she spoke, she was viciously sarcastic, and simmered with more hostility than fear, even alone with a mage. Elena contemplated her in puzzlement, unable to understand where the vivacious Solinde they all had loved had gone. Had Sordell done something to her, or was this a reaction to Fernando's death? It would take weeks of patient work to probe her mind and heal her of her terrors, but she would have one last try.

'Solinde, what did they do to you?' she whispered.

Slowly the princessa turned her head. Her eyes were flat, empty. 'What do you want, you old hag?'

Elena winced. 'I hoped to find some way we could restore you to the girl you were.'

Solinde lifted her chin and laughed bitterly. 'Why would I want to go back to being that gormless empty-headed bint and let Cera have everything? Don't think I haven't seen this, you and Cera, safian bitches plotting together. You disgust me.'

She had to stop herself slapping the girl – but someone, or some-*thing*, had got to her. *Gurvon, what have you done?* She almost went back to Cera to ask for permission to attempt some kind of mind-healing, but she was exhausted. *Maybe I can do something in a few months.* 'This won't be pleasant, Solinde,' she said calmly, 'but I have to place a binding upon you to prevent any mage from contacting you. If you are still linked to Gurvon, I must sever that link.' She reached out a hand.

Quick as a cat, Solinde leapt backwards, pressing herself against the walls of the cell as she cried, 'Don't touch me, witch, there is nothing wrong with me – keep away!'

Elena sighed and pinned the girl against the wall with Air-gnosis, feeling queasily like a torturer. 'This is a Chain-rune,' she told Solinde. 'It will hurt.' She placed a hand on the girl's brow, gnostic light flared and Solinde shrieked and writhed in pain for twenty long seconds before going limp. Elena checked her pulse, then lowered her to the bed. She hated doing this, but the Chain-rune, normally used to turn off a captive mage's abilities so they had no access to the gnosis, also cut off the mind from any gnosis-contact. If a mage was communicating with Solinde, the Chain-rune would break that link. *What she really needs is psychic healing, but she resists so violently. Damn this: why is there never enough time to do things properly?*

Elena left the cell with deep misgivings and watched the prison-wagon depart half an hour later with a sense of missed opportunity – but there was no time to dwell on it. Cera was in open court, hearing grievances from the commoners, and she needed to be warded.

After that day's session Elena accompanied Cera back to their private quarters. All day Cera had listened to complaints, giving well-considered answers. Elena was proud of her young charge, but she was distracted by hot flushes and attacks of the shakes. She wore a deep hooded mantle, under which she was dripping.

'Ella, you look terrible,' Cera said with concern, reaching out and flicking back her hood.

Do I? Elena looked at her dazedly as the whole world wobbled, fell sideways and went blank.

She came to in her bed, clad in a nightdress, with Tarita and Borsa fussing over her while Cera pressed a cold cloth to her face. Borsa placed a bowl of chicken broth into her hands.

'Do you think you're any use to me if you're dead?' Cera demanded.

'I'm sorry – I thought was recovering.'

Cera snorted. 'Recovering? You're killing yourself!' Elena hung her head as Cera began pacing the tiny room. 'It's my fault. I've demanded too much of you. My knights can guard me – nothing major is happening until the provincial lords arrive: that's in three weeks, so you've got eighteen days, during which you are *commanded* to recover properly.' She took Elena's hands. 'I need you to stop scaring me, amica. *Please?*'

Elena had no choice but to agree, and for the next week she found herself sleeping not just at night but for part of each afternoon. She was forbidden exercise, and the fainting episode had scared her enough not to protest. She even let Tarita and Bursa pamper her with moisturising oils and creams. Some nights Cera read her poetry, and Tarita played tabula, but other than that, she had plenty of time to think. It wasn't a pleasurable pastime.

With new eyes she examined her life. It was obvious to her now that what she'd believed was love had been nothing more than intense loyalty to Gurvon, as she'd tried so desperately to find a person or cause to tie her colours to; she'd needed to *belong* to something. Religion and greed had let her down: there was no creed or philosophy that she felt anything but amused scorn for. Wealth meant little, especially now she knew there was nowhere she would ever be safe again. She and Gurvon had been too successful. The Imperial Court would not want people like them around once they had outlived their usefulness. She had no loyalty to that Court, or its goals, and all those missions she'd told herself were necessary now felt like acts of evil. She'd abdicated her own moral responsibility by blindly doing whatever Gurvon told her. She had been an empty vessel which he had filled with poison. There was nothing she could think back on with pride since the Revolt, until she had thrown in her lot with the Nesti and foiled Samir Taguine.

She was so used to dealing with her own problems – or having Gurvon deal with them – that it never occurred to her to talk to anyone else. But Borsa came in one morning and after the usual pleasantries sat down beside her bed, began knitting and surprised her by asking, 'Who are you, Ella?'

Not how; *who*. Elena looked at the old woman in surprise and almost corrected her before she realised the question had been deliberately worded. She suppressed the impulse to tell Borsa to mind her own business, but she had never confided in anyone before, not even Gurvon – especially not Gurvon, in fact, for she dreaded appearing weak. She was tempted not to answer at all, but to her shock words came pouring out almost of their own accord. So she just let them come. Giving voice to her subconscious was strangely liberating.

So who am I now? she wondered. *I have a cause: Cera and the Nesti, because I believe in the conciliation and compromise that lies at the heart of their worldview. Because I respect and love Cera for her courage and convictions. I am proud of the way she confronts the daily challenges of leadership. I am proud that Cera is showing these men just how strong and capable a woman can be. I would be happy to die in the knowledge that I had died saving her.*

'But surely you must want more than just death, my dear?' Borsa answered when she fell silent, her needles clicking.

'Everything ends in death,' she replied. The assassin's answer.

'But don't you also want to live?'

'Of course – and I will stay alive as long as I can, for Cera.' She sat up a little, hugged her knees. 'She's building something good here. If I can keep her alive and in power, it might just take root. That would be enough. My legacy.'

'You speak like a man: death and duty and legacies.' She patted her arm. 'You're a woman, Ella.'

Elena looked down. 'I am what my role demands, Borsa. Cera relies on me for her security. If Gurvon kills her, Javon will be torn apart. Keeping her safe must be enough, for now.'

Borsa looked at her sadly. 'There is always more, my dear. You cannot go on as you have been. You drive yourself impossibly hard, and you let no one reach you. You let no one touch you, here inside.' She touched her heart. 'All the stress and fear build up inside you like pus, and you have to lance it with joy, or you will just keep on collapsing, more and more frequently, and then you will be no protection whatever to Cera or anyone else.'

She opened her mouth to do the usual Elena-thing and argue, but she stopped and considered what she was being told. *She's right*, she found herself admitting: *I'm destroying myself faster than Gurvon could. I'm exhausted all the time. Sleep doesn't refresh me any more, for even in sleep my mind worries and festers. I have to acknowledge it: I've about as much humanity as Bastido at the moment.*

She met Borsa's eyes. 'The most precious thing about Javon is that I feel I belong – I've not felt that since the Noros Revolt. After years of working with people I wouldn't trust as far as I could spit, it's wonderful to live with people I care for. I do understand what you're saying, that I could function better if I had some way to let the fear and anxiety go. But I can't see a future beyond this situation, Borsa. There are wolves all round us, and right now I can't see how we can survive, I really can't. I'm just one person – no other mage would be crazy enough to join us, not when they know what we're up against. Gurvon can just keep on hiring new people until he takes me down.' *By the Kore, it is hard not to cry right now . . .* 'I could deal with it when I cared only about myself. But now I'm afraid for everyone! I'm scared for Cera, for you, for Tarita, for Solinde, for Timi, for all of you. I'm frightened of failing and losing you all.'

'This is why you've been driving yourself so hard,' Borsa observed.

'Yes – yes, exactly. After what Sordell did to me—'

Borsa frowned. 'Sordell? What did he do?'

'He used a necromancy spell that drains life-energy: it debilitates and then disintegrates the victim, while proving energy for the caster. It was like being aged decades in the space of seconds. If my shielding hadn't been so effective, I would have died, like poor Artaq. Regaining what is lost is very hard. It would take months of inactivity and healing-gnosis to recover fully, but I must focus most of my energies on Cera.'

Borsa studied her thoughtfully. 'How can we help you?'

'I need a healer-mage, and I'm the only one in this kingdom!' She bit her lip, galled at admitting weakness.

'There is us, my dear: Tarita and Cera and me, all those who love you.'

'You're not magi – you can't help me!' She found she was shrieking like a harridan and clapped her hand over her mouth. 'I'm sorry, I didn't mean to shout—'

Borsa said patiently, 'I am glad to hear you shout. Perhaps we're not magicians like you, but of course we can help you, my dear: we can ensure you rest; we can make you eat and drink properly, even pamper you. I have no magic, but I've been a mother and a grand-mother and I've helped people recover from illness for sixty years. You need to heal your body *and* your spirit. You're afraid this weak-ness is terminal. My old husband got the same way as he got older: he lost all confidence.'

'I'm trying, Borsa—'

'Yes, you are trying – *too hard*. You need to be gentler on yourself.'

Maybe she really is right. She nodded slowly.

'And you need a lover,' Borsa added with a smirk.

Elena sat up. 'No, absolutely not – that would make things worse—'

'Ha! What would you know? Four years here and always alone in your bed? You need some love, girl. Love is a great healer. People who love want to heal; they have energy and ambition. And I don't mean chaste poetry-reciting love, I mean sweaty animal love.' She cackled warmly. 'You need to get your juices going, girl.'

Elena squirmed. Part of her agreed: healer-magi knew those in love gained something in gnostic strength and resilience, but quite apart from the lack of candidates, the thought of letting her guard down, now of all times, made her afraid on more levels than she could name. She glanced at her hands, still wrinkled from Sordell's spell months ago. *And who could love me when I'm like this?* She took shelter behind duty. 'I am here to protect the queen, Borsa; every-thing else is secondary.'

Borsa saw through her in a second. She reached out and lifted her chin. 'You are capable of love and being loved. Don't forget that, child.'

Elena looked down. 'I am not very lovable. Especially at the moment. And I can't afford entanglements.'

'We are all entangled, Ella, whether we want it or not. And if you open your eyes, you'll see that others wish to be entangled with you,' she added archly.

'If you're talking about Lori, forget it – after what he went through he wants nothing to do with me.'

'I rather think he is softening on that stance,' Borsa replied with a knowing look.

'What have you said to him?' she demanded hotly.

'I just pointed out a few things,' Borsa replied loftily. 'And what would be so wrong about it, after all? He admires you. He is courageous and handsome and well-liked. Just what is it you don't want?'

Elena closed her eyes and recalled Lorenzo's face, caught in the aftermath of Vedya's spells, filled with gnosis-induced hatred, and then she thought how emancipating it had felt to kiss him, to be wanted by another – to shake free of the shackles Gurvon had placed about her soul.

Whatever her face betrayed, Borsa saw. 'I think he is intending to come and see you, and in the meantime, rest. You might need your strength!' she added with a wink.

Elena's face burned. 'Get out, you dreadful woman! You are incorrigible!' she exclaimed, though she heard something she hadn't heard in her own voice in weeks, perhaps months: laughter.

Tarita frowned and moved a pawn forward, trapping Elena's last knight. 'You're not very good at tabula, are you?'

Elena scowled at her. 'Strategy games were always Gurvon's thing, not mine.' It was hard to focus; she was still so tired – but improving. Despite the humiliation of needing aid, Borsa and Tarita's babying was definitely helping. The only exercise they permitted her was gentle Indranian yoga, which was restoring her suppleness. She even treated herself to a glass or two of red wine a day, and it felt good. She had regained some of her colour, and thanks to the unguents Borsa and Tarita lavished on her, her skin was softening. Her hair, though still mannishly short, was returning to her natural honey-blonde. She was regaining a sense of well-being.

'Do you want another game?' Tarita asked, in that way she had of subtly crowing.

Elena shook her head irritably. 'I can't get interested today,' she conceded.

Tarita smirked, put the game-board aside and was ostentatiously scratching the wall with her fingernail – she was now winning, four-teen-two – when there was a knock at the door. She lifted her eyebrows and went to open it.

She didn't reappear, but Lorenzo di Kestria entered. He looked very subdued.

Elena clutched at the front of her nightdress. 'Lori – this is my bedchamber!'

'So it is,' he said softly. 'May I sit?'

'Modesty forbids—'

He looked about the room with a trace of his normal humour. 'Where is this Modesty person? I can't see her anywhere.' Then the levity vanished. 'Please. I need to talk to you.'

Elena swallowed and nodded.

The Rimoni knight sat in the chair Tarita had vacated, studied his hands, then met her eyes. He looked as she felt: tired and trou-bled. 'You told me not to come with you on that mission.'

'I shouldn't have let you.'

'No, you needed me – but you should have talked to me more first. If I'd known more about what a mage can do, I would not have been so shocked, and perhaps Vedya would not have been able to use me so against you.'

Elena sighed heavily. *True. Maybe.* 'Foreknowledge might have made you hate me from the outset.'

'I cannot hate you – I don't hate you now. It was only the sudden-ness of realising what you could do. Using fire is frightening enough, but the things you and Dolman and Sordell did – I was not prepared, and I should have been. You should have readied us, told us what to expect.'

Elena looked away.

'You don't trust easily,' Lorenzo went on, 'but I understand you better now.'

Elena glowered at him. 'You know *nothing*. I've blackmailed and murdered and betrayed good people and bad, all for gold; I've committed every sin you can imagine and nothing will absolve me.'

'But you told Borsa that life is behind you. It is who you *used* to be, Ella, not who you are now. The only absolution you need is your own.'

The sanctimony made her temper flare. 'Oh yes? Tell that to the widows and mothers I've left behind. These were not *victimless* crimes – I did not just kill other killers!'

He gnawed his lower lip. 'Maybe when this is done you can find a way to make amends – but you never will if you don't make it through this. Cera needs you. We *all* need you.'

'And I'm doing my best for you all!' she shouted back. Her words echoed about the tiny chamber.

Lorenzo flinched and filled his lungs as if about to shout back, but whatever he would have said, he swallowed the words unspoken and instead stood and strode away.

She stared after him with trembling belly and a bitter taste in her mouth. *Brilliant, Elena. Maybe if Cera comes in you can scream at her too.*

Elena recovered her strength in time for the council during the week of the Dark-moon. The court was packed with the retinues of the provincial lords. Massimo di Kestria, Lorenzo's elder brother, arrived with a swarm of golden-skinned Rimoni knights kitted out in Jhafi robes – the di Kestria family were one of the better-integrated of the Rimoni noble houses. The di Aranio family also arrived, with their many womenfolk. Lord Stefan di Aranio was a big, smooth-faced man with the manner of a merchant on a horse-trading mission; advantageous marriages were his stock-in-trade. His sons paid court assiduously to Cera, while clashing in private with their chief rivals, the local Brochena noblemen and the Gordini family of Lybis. Elena watched with amusement as the pieces on this particular tabula board moved, but Cera gave no signs of favour. There were rumours that Lorenzo had been ordered to renew his courtship too, and Elena discovered she had mixed feelings about that: though Lorenzo had not spoken to her since she had driven him from her bedroom, there was an unresolved tension between them that was fraught with complexity.

It was the full moon of Martrois and the skies were brilliant blue. Early summer heat was rolling across the plazas and festering in the alleys; mosquitoes were proliferating in the open sewers and down by the lake, though the Jhafi servants had an ancient recipe for candles that drove the insects away, so the palace was largely unaffected by them. Brochena was filling up with people, trade tentatively returning as the merchants felt out the new lay of the land. Many goods were still scarce and the people remained wary, the purges first by Alfredo Gorgio then by Cera still fresh in their mind.

It was odd to watch Lorenzo courting Cera. The queen-regent's young mind was too full of law and politics to care about small talk and dance-steps. At least she enjoyed his company, as they perambulated about the gardens while the court looked on and rival suitors simmered. Elena, always close by, found herself admiring his face and manner more and more, and witnessed Cera's polite indifference with puzzlement. *Hel, I've never been forward with men, but I'd take him on if I were in her shoes.*

'So, what do you think?' she asked one evening as she set the wards.

Cera, her skin gleaming bronze in the candlelight, pulled a nightdress on and shook out her hair. 'About Lori? I can't take it seriously.'

Elena snorted. 'I think he senses that.'

'Is he offended?' Cera asked, looking concerned. 'I can't afford to lose the friendship of the Kestrians.' She scowled. 'Though they're neutral on the shihad – they're supposed to be my allies.'

'They think that after the bloodshed, neutrality is best for our people. But they remain loyal.'

Cera sniffed and observed, 'If Timori was dead, they'd hold enough votes to gain the throne.'

Elena was shocked. 'Cera, these are the Kestrians – they are the truest of the true.' She was a little worried; her protégée was increasingly seeing plots everywhere.

Cera harrumphed irritably. 'Anyway, I don't wish to marry him, but his courtship prevents me from dealing with all the others sniffing around.' Her voice was tinged with disgust.

Elena sighed. 'Lorenzo understands that.'

Cera frowned. 'Am I that obvious?'

Elena laughed. 'To me, perhaps.'

Cera giggled. 'Poor Lori. I do like him – I had a crush on him once.'

'Once – but not now?'

Cera lifted her head a trifle pompously. 'No, I think I'm well past that part of my life.'

'Listen to you!' Elena laughed. 'Just like an eighteen-year-old, to think you're all grown up.'

'I have to be grown up,' Cera insisted. 'I meant what I said: I won't marry until Timi is king.'

Elena frowned. 'But some kind of alliance with the Kestrians—?'

'Ella, I've had all that from Pita and Piero and the others, I don't expect it from you. The Kestrians are with us anyway, so why make concessions when we already have what we want from them?'

Elena looked at her, a little surprised at her maturity and dispassion. 'Someone should warn poor Lorenzo so you don't break his heart.'

'Oh, I doubt he'll be so affected as all that,' Cera said dismissively. She looked at Elena with amusement. 'I see you're wearing make-up tonight, Ella. Maybe you hope to catch someone's eye?'

Elena threw up a hand. 'Just making sure no rumours reach Gurvon that I look unwell. I'm already worried enough that my absence from your side these past weeks will have been noted.'

Once she had set the wards, Elena retired. She slid between the sheets and closed her eyes as she conjured a handsome face before her, one that smiled intently as it looked into her eyes. The small illusion wasn't taxing and it gave her something to focus upon as her hands slid down her body. She took her time as her sighs became gasps and it felt like a small dam burst inside her as she climaxed.

She woke next morning feeling better than she had for weeks.

Lorenzo's courtship continued to fascinate and puzzle the court, which had thought to witness a blossoming romance and instead saw distant politeness and a young queen-regent whose eyes remained firmly on the issues of the day. 'What's wrong with the girl?' they wondered. 'Has she no juices?'

'Some people blame you,' Tarita told Elena boldly one morning.

Elena smiled at the young maid's frankness. 'Why?'

'Well, some say you are overly protective, and using spells to shield Cera's heart.'

Elena grunted. 'Is that all they say?'

'Oh, others think you have seduced her yourself!' Tarita giggled.

Elena snorted in disgust. *Have these people no originality in their filthy minds?*

Tarita grinned. 'Everyone is scandalised by you! They think your short hair is barbaric, and proves you're safian. Others say you want Lorenzo for yourself.'

Elena raised her eyebrows and fought to keep the blush from her cheeks. 'They do?'

'I started that one myself.' Tarita snickered proudly. 'I tell them you're randy as a goat for him.'

'*Tarita!*'

'You are – your sheets sweaty as a brothel. I have to change them every day. And people see you watching him. They think it's funny.'

She felt a flash of anger. 'Why funny?'

'Oh, only that you've shown so little interest in men until now.'

'Men have hardly shown any interest in me either.'

'That's not true – everyone says half the knights tried to bed you when you arrived. There was a barracks wager among them, who'd be first to seduce you.' She laughed aloud. 'The men boast a lot amongst themselves, mistress. They don't mean all that they say; it's just expected, that's all. It's normal for them to compete with each other.'

Elena flexed her fists. 'Well, if that's all they think of me, they can all go to Hel.'

'It was just men's talk, mistress – you should take Lorenzo as you find him, not on hearsay.'

'I'm not planning to "take him" at all,' Elena replied crossly, and stomped off to the queen's morning session with the Regency Council.

Being in the same room as Lorenzo and seeing the way that he too was growing into his role didn't help her much. He spoke well, displayed awareness of the strategic situation, displayed wit and gravity as appropriate. At times his eyes would meet hers, and she could tell that he'd forgiven her. He jested about claiming the kiss she'd promised him that deadly night, and teenage insecurities and flutters of the heart plagued her, she who had thought herself beyond such emotions.

You are ridiculous, Elena. Don't make a fool of yourself. He's two decades younger than you and you're hardly the prettiest woman at court. But she couldn't help herself.

Massimo di Kestria was still in his brother's ear though, and he was determined Lorenzo would uphold family honour – so Elena found herself walking through the ornamental gardens on Massimo's arm yet again, their eyes on Lorenzo and Cera while the baron bored on about his many children and the sun slowly fell toward the horizon, turning into a discus of pinky-orange light as it descended.

Massimo was about to launch into another diatribe when he froze, his mouth hanging open. Elena followed his gaze to see Lorenzo suddenly down on one knee before Cera in a pretty little rose bower.

His voice carried clearly: 'Queen-Regent, Cera, will you do me the honour of becoming my wife?'

Cera's face remained composed. 'Alas, Lorenzo, I cannot accept,' she replied in a measured voice. 'Though your company pleases me and your family are very dear friends to the Nesti, I have vowed to remain an unwed virgin until my brother attains his majority. Please respect this promise, and know that you have my utmost respect.'

Good Kore, she sounds closer to forty than twenty, Cera thought, her heart pounding with some kind of relief that she daren't examine.

Massimo's face had turned purple and he looked flummoxed. Elena whispered in his ear, 'Massimo, please give us some privacy,' and the baron backed off uncertainly.

Cera turned to Elena. 'Elena, I must rejoin our guests. Could you please ensure that Milord di Kestria is comforted and vouch for the veracity of my oath and of my feelings?' She bowed lightly, looked down steadily at Lorenzo for a second and then turned and walked away.

Elena stepped into the bower, conscious suddenly that she was alone with Lorenzo. 'Er . . . are you all right, Lori?'

Lorenzo climbed apologetically to his feet. 'I am sorry, Elena, that you have witnessed my discomfort.' He gave a cautious smile. 'I have never suffered rejection before.'

'Have you proposed marriage often then?' Elena asked drily.

Lorenzo gave her a crooked grin. 'In truth, my previous proposals have not been of marriage.'

Elena plucked a rose from the bower and pinned it to a buttonhole on his doublet. 'From what I have observed, there are many women about court who will not provide you much of a challenge when you get over your disappointment.'

'But it could be that I prefer a challenge,' he returned, looking her full in the face. 'When I get over my disappointment, of course.'

'You don't look *that* disappointed to me,' she remarked severely.

He suddenly looked uncertain again. 'Donna Ella, are we friends again?' He cocked his head as music started up. 'Shall we dance?' he asked, bowing in invitation. 'That is, if Rondian magi dance?'

She felt a dangerous heat in her breast. 'Not today – but we do apologise occasionally. I'm sorry for yelling at you. I know you meant well.'

He bowed again. 'Apology accepted. May we talk then?' He indicated a seat among the roses.

Elena smiled. 'All right, but not here. It's too public, and if one of Gurvon's agents is out there and notes us talking, you will be a target.'

'I'm Captain of Cera's guard, so I'm a target anyway, but I take your point.' He looked about the bower and she did too, suddenly enjoying the delicate scents and vivid colours. The city was blossoming, with frangipani and marigolds coating the green spaces in white and orange splashes of colour, filling the air with lovely scents.

'So,' he said, 'my courtship is over.' He smiled and admitted, 'I am relieved. She had no interest and if my brother wasn't being such an ass over it we could have spared everyone the fuss.'

'You should probably grieve publicly for a while,' Elena suggested awkwardly.

Lorenzo laughed. 'Truly there is no one like you, Elena Anborn. In this whole world I've heard of no one like you. Even your fellow magi women do not fight like you, with weapons as well as gnosis.'

'I know this – I've heard it from many men. What point do you wish to make?'

'Just that it does not repel me – and neither do your past sins, or your strange skills. Nor the scars on your body or your soul. I believe I see past them to the woman beneath.'

'I am twice your age, and I am a foreigner.'

'Yet you risk your life to remain here.' He looked back at her, the setting sun catching his face, painting it bronze, like the statue of some hero. 'My family despair of my ever settling down, but I have several brothers, and my brothers have many sons. I'm not needed at home.'

There was a restlessness in his voice she could empathise with. 'Is "settling down" what you want?'

'No: when this danger has passed, I wish to travel again,' he told her. 'I love to see new places.'

'I thought what I wanted was a manor beside a lake in Bricia.' *With Gurvon beside me.* 'But now I'm a traitor to my people and outlawed throughout the continent of my homeland. I have no home at all.'

'Then perhaps you too will find solace in the open road, Donna Elena?'

Her mind's eye showed her an image of herself, dressed in strange robes, standing in an exotic temple, with Lorenzo at her side. It wasn't an unpleasant thought. She swallowed slightly. 'Lori, if we live through this, who knows?'

He smiled softly at that. He had a nice mouth and she could remember the way it tasted. *But . . .*

She clenched her jaw. 'Lori, I need to tell you something.'

His face tightened. 'I sense it is something I won't like.'

'You won't. After the Noros Revolt, the Church commissioned Gurvon to destroy an enclave of magi who'd gone into hiding and were fighting on. It was a test – the Inquisitors could have done it themselves, but they wanted to see if Gurvon could be trusted to go after his former allies. They'd fled to a castle town in Schlessen. The population was sympathetic, they sealed off part of the keep and held it secure – with gnosis, defence is often stronger than attack, so they couldn't easily be taken.

'They thought themselves safe, but first Gurvon struck those he could reach, human outsiders, and used them to lure the magi out of the keep, singly or in small groups. Any we took were broken and sent back, barely alive, needing the gnosis to keep them living. The city folk began to fear interacting with the rebels. The magi had to pour increasing energies into keeping the injured alive and it quickly broke them down. They split up and we picked them off one by one.'

'And you think he will do the same here?'

'I know he will. Those closest to Cera and me will be the first targets.'

There was no fear on his face, only quiet determination. 'Where did you launch your attacks from?'

'We were hidden within the town. No one knew we were there.'

'And your role?' he asked bleakly.

'Gurvon likes to have someone inside. My role was to subtly sow discord and misinformation.' She sighed. 'These were old comrades; it wasn't hard. They believed I was one of them right till the end.'

He looked thoughtful. 'So you think he will attack this way: isolate us and pick us off.' He exhaled heavily, and she could see the fear now, the disquiet of a commander afraid for those in his charge. 'Is there an insider already among us?'

'There will be people at court he has already got his claws into. Wherever he goes, Gurvon finds out people's dirty secrets; he will be blackmailing courtiers and servants over their thefts, their adulteries and indiscretions.'

Lorenzo's eyes met hers. 'How may we best counter this, Donna Elena?'

'By sealing off part of the keep for our own protection. By restricting access to the safe area and constantly rotating who may enter. By being vigilant. We can make it hard for him, but that won't be enough. We must also counterattack where and when we can. We must use the eyes of the community. We will need Mustaq al'Madhi.'

'Mustaq is not to be trusted. He is the head of the largest Jhafi crime syndicate in Javon.'

'Then he is ideal. He will have eyes in places we cannot reach. Gurvon is probably already here, with the rest of his gang. Most of those I worked with are dead. I won't know most of the new ones. He may have found a new body for Sordell too.' All at once the shadows, even in the sunlit bower, were stirring like waking panthers. 'Let us go in.'

Lorenzo gripped her shoulder as she went to pass him. His hands were big and strong: a swordsman's hands, and they were warm through the cloth. 'Ella – what about us?'

They were the same height. She met his eyes, trying to read him. 'Is there an "us"?'

He didn't answer, at least, not with words. His other hand cupped the back of her head and he pressed his lips to hers. Her gasp of surprise became an open mouth that tasted his. Heat and wine and sweetness and a tongue that invaded her mouth, tasted hers then withdrew. She stiffened against him, and found she had no will to move away.

'So,' he breathed, 'you tell me, Ella-amora.'

Amora: lover . . . Her heart thudded. She felt horribly exposed before his soft brown eyes. She wanted to flee, to hide, to not deal with this. 'Didn't you just propose marriage to *someone else*, Lori?'

He sighed. 'It was pretence and you know it. What I feel for you is not.'

She swallowed awkwardly. 'Lori, for you to court me so soon after Cera would invite scandal, and it would invite Gurvon like a corpse invites the jackal. We cannot be seen together.'

He stroked her cheek. 'Then we will not be *seen*.'

The thought made her blood thunder.

'Must I woo you like a knight-errant?' he breathed in her ear. His arms stroked her shoulders, firmly, invitingly.

'I don't do poetry and dances,' she replied, trying and failing to make her voice light.

'What do you do?'

She made herself meet his eyes, summoned all her will and hardened her heart. 'I don't do anything at all.'

He sighed softly, not in the least put off. 'You still owe me a kiss, Elena.'

'You just had one.' *And it was delicious*, she admitted to herself.

'But I didn't need to ask for it,' he replied. He flashed a smile, bowed and walked away.

Cera had retired to her rooms after rejecting Lorenzo's proposal. Elena joined her there. Cera was looking wan. 'Ella, where have you been?' she asked. 'I don't like it when you're not with me.'

'Are you all right?'

'I'm fine. It's Massimo who's put out, not me.' Cera shrugged. 'He'll get over it.' Her face was shadowed with suspicion. 'They have always been honourable,' she whispered as if to reassure herself. She looked up at Elena with a sour expression. 'So tomorrow all the young men will be vying for my attention again. How tiresome!'

Elena studied her. 'What's wrong, Cera?'

Cera slumped onto her bed, plucking absently at her gown. 'Me – I'm what's wrong!'

Elena sat beside her and put an arm about her. 'My darling, what could you possibly imagine is wrong with you?'

417

Cera rubbed furiously at her eyes, pulled herself from Elena's grip and sat facing her. 'It was what Massimo said to me after I'd rejected Lorenzo – he took it back immediately, but I knew he meant it!'

Elena pursed her lips. 'What did he say?'

She hung her head. 'He asked if my father knew the kind of safian bitch he'd bred.'

Elena stared, speechless. *Why the arrogant, hidebound prick – I'll rukking geld him—*

'I don't dance, or make silly conversation with their young knights like the other women do, so they make crude jokes about me.' Cera's face tightened. 'They think any woman who is not some vacuous broodmare is *unnatural*. Why can't they see I'm just trying to protect the kingdom?'

Oh Cera, welcome to my life, darling girl. Men are never slow to scorn women who insist on wearing swords. 'I have heard such things all my adult life, Cera,' she said softly. 'People – men particularly – feel threatened by those who do not conform to the norms.'

'Politics and trade interest me, fashion and poetry and dance-steps do not,' Cera said.

'I know – but Cera, we've both heard that sort of rubbish before. What's really the matter?'

Cera hung her head. 'I need the people to love me, Ella. If they turn against me, we Nesti are lost. I won't give up my independence so the Aranios or Kestrians can stage a bloodless coup-by-marriage. The barons don't want a woman as regent. They want Timi as their puppet, and I won't have it.'

Elena squirmed uncomfortably. Being the kindly confessor was not a role she excelled at, but she was pretty sure Cera still hadn't revealed what had really upset her. 'You know what they're like; they won't change. But their aims are aligned with yours: they want Javon strong and united, so they will support you. And there are other concerns, Cera.'

She explained Gurvon's likely tactics, and they took supper together in Cera's parlour while planning how to seal off the royal towers and minimise the security threat. It wasn't until the bells tolled six times that Elena realised that it was midnight already. They both yawned.

Cera gripped Elena's arm as she rose to leave. 'Grazie, Ella-amica.' She pulled her close and hugged her. 'Being with you always makes me calmer.'

'My pleasure, Cera. Do you need help getting out of that gown?'

Cera stood and stretched, yawning again. 'Please. Poor Tarita will be fast asleep.'

As Elena helped her into her nightclothes, she stroked the dark curtain of hair. 'You are very beautiful, Cera,' she said softly. 'When you find the right man, he will be a lucky fellow indeed.'

Her words upset Cera again and she seized Elena's hand. 'I'm frightened, Ella – what if they're right about me?' she whispered. 'What if I do have that sickness in me?'

Elena frowned. 'It's not a sickness, Cera, it's something people are born with. The Rimoni Empress Claudia was one of their greatest rulers, and she kept a whole harem of girls for herself.' She braced herself to ask the question. 'Do you believe yourself to be safian?'

Cera hung her head. 'I don't know,' she said in a small voice. 'Why don't I want the boys they throw at me? They're all handsome and well-built and charming. What's wrong with me?'

'Cera, you're tasting authority and power, and you're enjoying it. You're seeing these suitors as a threat to that, that's all. I doubt you even see them as men; they're just pawns in the tabula of politics.'

'But I don't find them even a little bit attractive.'

'Cera, you're – what, eighteen? You're not yet grown-up. Many people don't develop any interest in the opposite sex until they're in their twenties. You're going through more than any young girl should, and you're holding up magnificently. You've got far more important things to worry about than whether your heart goes thump when a boy smiles at you. Frankly, I'm glad it doesn't.'

Cera ducked her head and nodded apologetically. 'I'm sorry. I'll sleep now. Thank you.'

'Goodnight, Cera,' Elena told her, feeling emotionally drained as she sought her own bed. The memory of Lorenzo's face swam before her as she slid between the sheets. In her dreams she watched him on his knees again, proposing alternately to Cera and herself, before turning into a knife-wielding Gurvon Gyle. He slashed and whirled and in a trice Cera was dead and Elena was staring in disbelieving horror at the dagger in her own breast. She woke unsure if it were nightmare or omen.

Gurvon Gyle sat entirely still, like a lizard on a wall afraid to move in case it is seen by a predator. And the man in the chair opposite was assuredly a predator. The decrepit room they shared had no other furnishings. The stone was crumbling, bugs crawled in the corners and it stank of rot and decay.

The man was weaving strands of light with his fingers. He didn't look like a torturer, but his reputation hung heavily about him. Inquisition Grandmaster Fraxis Targon was neat and clean, so fastidious that he shaved twice daily. He wore hair cream despite the crippling midday heat, slicking his thin blond hair and thin moustache. He looked like a shopkeeper. Only his eyes, so pale as to be almost white, betrayed the cold distance that he maintained from life. His stare was utterly dispassionate, utterly uncaring. He might rip a man's heart out with the gnosis as blandly as he crushed a cockroach. Rutt Sordell clearly thought so – the scarab housing Sordell's soul was hiding in Gyle's pocket, and had not stirred for hours.

The pattern of light frayed as the Inquisitor lowered his hands and scowled. Another blocked scrying. Targon could blast through Elena's wards, but that would alert her instantly, so for now they had to probe, and to rely on information from Gyle's small network of spies within the palace. None were highly placed, nor capable of taking aggressive action, but at least they were inside.

'Have a care you aren't detected,' Gurvon told the Inquisitor sourly. His agents had reported that Elena had formed a friendship with the commander of Cera Nesti's guard, Lorenzo di Kestria. They insisted it was just friendship, but the thought made his stomach tighten.

It is not jealousy. It is just a matter of honour that I castrate and disembowel the man.

'Her skill is insufficient to detect my probing,' the Inquisitor rumbled. 'I grow impatient at your caution, Gyle.'

'We need to get Coin into position first,' he argued.

'With the Anborn woman dead, no one could stop us.'

'No, but the whole of Javon would erupt into war against all things Rondian. It is only the continued reign of the Nesti Regency that is keeping that in check.' *Surely Mater-Imperia told you this*, he thought angrily.

'Mater-Imperia did tell me that,' Targon said, answering what Gyle had believed a private thought. He felt himself go cold. 'You play your little games of king-making and think yourself subtle and perceptive, Gurvon Gyle, but I was raised to the Ascendancy by Magnus Sacrecour and I will act as I see fit. When I choose to strike, I will strike, and you had best pray that you are well out of my way.' The Inquisitor leaned back in his chair. 'In the meantime, spymaster, I believe it is time to go on the offensive. The local criminals are hunting for you house-to-house. It is time to give them pause.'

Gyle redoubled the shields about his mind as he bowed his head. 'You will begin it?'

Targon nodded. 'And then you will start upon the princessa.' The man's smile never reached his eyes. 'Leave me and send in the serving girl.' His eyes were hooded. 'I must continue her instruction.'

Cera Nesti sat on the window seat, the perfumed night wafting through the open casement. Elena had set the wards – she had seen the grille of light as her protector lit them – and nothing else could get inside. She looked up as something landed on the sill just beyond the unseen wards. A crow?

'Shoo,' she called, 'get away—'

But the bird turned a beady eye towards her, and then *changed*.

There was nothing gradual about it: one moment it was a big black bird and the next a grey-clad man. She opened her mouth to scream, but he put his fingers to his lips and whispered, 'Shhh – wait.' He put a hand up as if reaching for her and the wards lit up, a mesh of blue-skeined light. 'See, I cannot reach you. This illusory form cannot penetrate Elena's wards. You are quite safe.'

She knew him. 'You are Gurvon Gyle.'

The man inclined his head. 'I am.'

Cera stared at the man, trembling slightly. *I should get Ella . . .*

Gyle raised a placating hand. 'I am only here to talk.'

She swallowed. Her enemy, so close – *what do I do?* 'Why should I talk to you?'

'Why shouldn't you? I cannot hurt you, so please, hear me out. I will be brief.' His face radiated sincerity. 'I do not wish to see you harmed, Cera, nor do I wish to harm your little brother.'

Elena was probably doing her evening exercises, Cera remembered. *Sol et Lune, this is my* enemy, *talking to me. Maybe I can learn something from this . . .*

She looked around, checking that she was alone, feeling guilty, as if she were betraying herself, then said, 'You killed my family. How could I trust you?'

Gyle looked sad, almost apologetic. 'I was commanded to remove Javon from the shihad. I had no choice. If you soften your policy towards the shihad, I will guarantee the safety of you and Timori.'

She felt her temper flare. 'My people would never let me – nor will my conscience.'

'When all of your house are ash and all those who have pinned their futures on you are dead, how will your conscience feel then?'

She sucked in her breath. In one sentence he had cut to the bones of her greatest fear. 'Ella?' she called, her voice quavering.

'Elena is in the Jade Tower exercising – unless she's *busy* somewhere with Lorenzo di Kestria,' he added archly.

He's testing me and I will not respond. But the queasy sense of fear his words aroused became a flash of temper. 'Ella slew your Sydian whore!' she fired back.

Gyle smiled blandly. 'Elena Anborn leaves a trail of destruction wherever she goes, girl. She has neither pity nor remorse. Do you think she's on your side? She's on her own side and none other.' His voice sounded pained, even regretful. 'I could tell you all about her, girl.'

His words awakened all her fears and she batted them away. 'Liar!'

'Calm yourself, girl.'

'Rukka-tu, Neferi!'

'Such language, Princessa!' His voice was condescending. He stood, effortlessly floating on the air. 'Cera, you have a choice: align Javon with the Crusade and you and your family will live and prosper. Choose the shihad and you will lose everything.'

She opened her mouth, but he was already gone.

She stumbled backwards to her chair and huddled in it like a child.

When Elena came soon after, freshly washed and glowing, she just *knew* that Gyle had spoken truly about her and Lorenzo. She couldn't articulate why the thought of her protector and her first knight together made her ill, but it did. So she didn't mention Gyle's visitation at all.

24

Manifestation

Magic

The term 'magic' is incorrectly applied by laymen to all gnosis-workings. To a mage, the term means the channelling of raw energy into bursts of fire, protective shielding and moving objects. A 'mage-bolt' can be a useful and often lethal weapon; a shield is vital to any mage in a dangerous situation and the 'telekinesis' applications of 'magic' are innumerable. Mastering magic is the first task of any student.

ARDO ACTIUM, SCHOLAR, BRES 518

Hebusalim, Dhassa, Antiopia
Thani (Aprafor) 928
3 months until the Moontide

Casa Meiros was in a state of semi-celebration since a healer-mage had confirmed Ramita's pregnancy. Antonin Meiros openly wept for joy, and treated her like an apsara sent from on high. He had told her a dozen times a day that she was the bravest and most wonderful bride in all of history, and his kindness had further softened her heart towards him.

It also doubled her guilt and shame, and she felt like the worry was driving her insane. The city was suddenly fearful as rumours of Keshi armies on the move intensified, and increased security meant no visitors. But Huriya was endlessly inventive, and persuaded Ramita to ask Meiros for the chela from Omprasad's temple to come and light candles for their peace and safety. So Jai and Kazim duly visited Casa Meiros, improvised some prayers to the Omali gods and then took tea in the outer quarters. Ramita was so desperate to talk to Kazim she could barely contain herself, but Kazim was clearly full of a different need. He kept glancing over her shoulder at the doorway, but the servants were hovering.

'Settle down, Kazim,' Huriya hissed in Lakh. 'You're like a bull in the mating season.'

'I *am* a bull!' he retorted. He looked at Ramita and groaned. 'How are you, my love?'

'How do you think I am? Pregnant to the wrong man, in daily danger of discovery and stoning, in a city where war could break out any moment!' Hysteria was threatening to break through any moment. 'We need to talk, Kaz, not go to bed.'

'But Mita—'

Ramita felt a sudden and alarming urge to slap him. 'Listen to me: I'm going to have a child, probably more than one, if my mother's line holds true, and when he realises they aren't his, my husband will have no choice but to hand me over for stoning. And don't think he won't come after you too. He may be old but he is Antonin Meiros, and he will pull you apart.' She dropped her voice to a hiss. 'You have to run, Kaz: go home, go anywhere, but go.'

'I'm not going anywhere without you, Mita. I love you—' His voice was almost loud enough to reach the ears of the housemaids. Huriya shushed him.

Ramita found herself wishing he had never come. 'Kaz, please listen to me: your only chance is to be so far away that he can't find you. Please go – you don't know what it's like here now. He's so happy, and I feel sick, having to lie and pretend. I could betray us with a stray thought at any second. I can hardly bear it. The only way I can endure this is if I know that you're safe. When Huriya next visits you at the temple, all three of you run. *Please*, if you truly love me.' She felt close to tears.

Kazim was unmoved. 'No, Mita, there is another way. I have friends who can help us. We don't have to leave you behind.'

'I can't come with you, Kaz. They might not pursue you, but they will come after me, whether they believe the children are his or not. No man can tolerate an adulterous wife and maintain face.'

'You're not thinking clearly, any of you,' Jai put in quietly. 'I have found a woman who can remove unwanted children from a woman's womb. If we can bring her here, pretending she's a midwife—'

Huriya looked at him scornfully. 'Antonin Meiros is never going to let some backstreet hag from the eastside near Ramita and his precious babies, you idiot. He's got magi-healers watching over her.'

'What if we bring the woman to the Sivraman temple and then have Ramita visit?'

'Oh and the soldiers are just going to stand by as this woman sticks a poker up Ramita's passage, are they? That's even assuming Meiros lets her leave the palace grounds now she's pregnant.' Huriya glared at Jai. 'What did you need to find such a woman for, anyway? Is your Keita knocked up too?'

Jai nodded miserably, and Ramita felt like someone had punched her in the throat. 'Jai? You've got Keita pregnant? Oh, sweet Parvasi, what are you boys thinking with?' She stood. 'Just get out! You're children, not men.'

Kazim grabbed her arm, then looked round. The servants were fortunately chatting amongst themselves, not paying them any attention. 'No, Mita, please: hear this. I have a plan.'

'You have a plan? Two thoughts that follow one another in logical sequence? I wouldn't have thought it possible – what on Urte did I ever see in you, you fool?' she hissed harshly.

Kazim flushed. 'Mita, we're doing this for you – I love you, you know that. I have a plan, and good people who will help.' He leaned forward. 'Don't give up hope. Just hold on a few more weeks, then everything will be resolved.'

'In what way? What is your plan?'

Kazim leaned forward, his face intent. 'We're going to kill him.'

She felt the colour drain from her face and her bones weakened. *No – that is wrong. It is* impossible. *It would be evil.* No— 'You can't,' she whispered. 'You cannot.'

Kazim shook his head, misunderstanding her. 'Don't worry, it will be well planned. We can do it.' His voice brimmed with suppressed excitement. 'We will kill him and become heroes of the shihad.'

Her husband lay behind her in the gathering dusk, his body pressed against her back, his arm around her. The air was warm, even though the sun had gone and the silver of the waning Mater-Luna lit the room. Three weeks had passed since she'd last seen Kazim and Jai. She would have bled this week, had she not been truly pregnant, but she hadn't, of course. Her belly was swelling, even this early. Her breasts were tender and she woke queasy most mornings. *I will have twins, even triplets, like Mother.*

That night, to celebrate, Meiros had produced a dusty bottle of wine and prevailed upon her to enjoy a glass of heady pale amber fluid that had tasted divine: a chard from Bres, he'd told her. 'This is to celebrate the conception of our children, Wife.' He was so clearly relieved and happy that she found herself feeling genuine affection for him. And then he had done patient things with his fingers that had brought her as much pleasure as she had ever derived from her body before entering her gently. Despite the guilt and the fear, there had been long moments of bliss in their coupling.

'It will not harm the babies?' she had asked anxiously, but he had just laughed and reassured her.

Now he sat up abruptly, a decisive look on his face. 'Wife, there is something I need to tell you.'

She sat up also. 'What is it?' she asked anxiously.

He stroked her arm. 'Do not fret; this is good news, not bad. I had hesitated until your condition was better-established, but it can be delayed no longer. I apologise that I have not spoken sooner, but this is something you must know, about when a male mage mates with a female non-mage. The act of carrying the child to term necessitates a sharing of body tissue between mother and child, and this results in a manifestation of the gnosis in the mother. Normally it is temporary, and minor – too minor to have any real effect. But I am Ascendant, and you are carrying twins, and I believe the manifestation will be potent and permanent.'

Ramita sat up and hugged her knees. 'What do you mean, lord?' she whispered. It sounded like nonsense, but it was clearly important to him.

Meiros put a hand on hers as if to comfort her. 'What it means, my good and brave wife, is that in a few weeks those first manifestations will become apparent.'

'"Manifestations"? What does that mean?'

'Manifestation of the gnosis, my dearest wife. You will gain the gnosis and become a mage.'

25

The Jackals of Ahm

The Second Crusade

The First Crusade in 904 was a journey into the unknown, but in 916 we knew what we were getting ourselves into. The Ordo Costruo had lost all authority and the Inquisition controlled the Bridge. By now we had tens of thousands of soldiers, civilians and Kore-convertees already in Hebusalim, besieged but holding out. The Hebb were a beaten people. The enemy now was the Keshi. After we defeated them in open battle, they resorted to insurgency. We had to respond in kind. The First Crusade could aspire to glory, but the Second Crusade represented a loss of innocence. It was kill or be killed.

GENERAL GREN PAKARION, BRICIA IX, MEMOIRS, 920

Was once not enough? No, for the hunger of Shaitan is insatiable.

GODSPEAKER GHIZEK OF BASSAZ, 916

Hebusalim, on the continent of Antiopia
Thani (Aprafor) 928
3 months until the Moontide

The Hadishah had many safe houses and hideaways dotted about the city, and it was to one such house Jamil brought Kazim and Jai on a market day in the third week of Thani. The streets were growing tense and the legionaries were patrolling in larger numbers. The mighty Rondians were nervous, and the whole city sensed it.

They were afraid of the Hadishah more than anyone else, Jamil told them. The cruelty of the Jackals of Ahm was legendary: they stole Rondian children, then sent back the mutilated corpse once they'd secured the ransom money. They torched captured legionaries alive. Many Hebb thought them too extreme, un-Amteh – but the Hadishah were fighting when so many weren't, and though people deplored their methods, all of northern Antiopia cheered their successes. While the sultans prevaricated, the Hadishah were making war.

Jamil and Kazim were sparring when Huriya, clad in a bekira-shroud, burst in. She was shadowed by the doorman of the safe house. She was bursting with news she insisted Kazim's superiors needed to know, and ten minutes later Jamil was leading them along an alleyway and beneath the street into a long cold room lit only by guttering torches. Rashid sat cross-legged at the head of a low trestle table set about with squat cushions. He looked tense. Jamil bowed low to Rashid. 'Master, this is Huriya Makani, the maid of Ramita Meiros.'

She prostrated herself, but Kazim could see his sister's eyes calculating.

Rashid eyed her with interest. 'Jamil tells me you have news of some development, girl?'

Huriya spoke quickly, her voice frightened. 'Lord, the Magister told my mistress that in bearing his child, she will become a mage herself. She told me that it is like an infection. Is this possible?'

Kazim heard himself gasp, 'No!'

Rashid stroked his chin. 'I know women bearing mage-children gain a weak and temporary form of the gnosis. This is known.'

'But Meiros has told Ramita it will be strong and permanent,' Huriya insisted.

Rashid and Jamil exchanged dubious looks 'I've never heard . . . I will need to make enquiries.' He looked at Huriya with more interest. 'You have shown a quick wit in coming straight to us, girl. What is your mistress' state of mind?'

'She is distraught, lord. She does not know who the father of her children is. If it is the Master, signs will soon appear of this "gnosis".' She looked imploringly at Jamil. 'All our lives we have been told that the devilry of the magi is derived by communing with demons, but

Ramita is a good person, lord! It is not her fault that she was picked out by the Master!' Huriya's eyes looked moist with tears, but Kazim knew his sister; she seldom cried needlessly.

Kazim's own mind was reeling. How could his sweet Ramita be *poisoned* in this way? But . . . 'Surely this is irrelevant, sister – I am the father of the child, not Meiros.'

Huriya flashed him a pitying look. 'And what if you are, brother? Lord Meiros says she will begin to display signs within the next month. *What will happen if she does not?*'

Kazim finally understood and he felt his stomach lurch. 'We must strike—'

Rashid chopped his hand down and said impatiently, 'Be silent, Kazim Makani. Let me think!' He stood and began to pace. 'Antonin Meiros will be at Domus Costruo all next week, then he will be with his inner circle at Southpoint the following week. To strike at the old man openly would be suicidal; the only chance is when he is in repose, and the only person who can do that is his wife.' He looked at Huriya. 'You are closest to Ramita Ankesharan. You have reported that she has been severely abused. She is sympathetic to our cause?'

Kazim opened his mouth. 'Ramita hates him—'

Rashid raised his hand again. 'Quiet, Kazim! I asked your sister. Do not speak unless addressed.' He looked at Huriya intently. 'Tell me truly.'

Huriya glanced at Kazim, then ducked her head. 'Ramita has not been abused. Her husband treats her well and is gentle with her. She has some fondness for him. I don't believe she would betray us, but she has . . . grown accustomed to him.' She looked at Kazim. 'Sorry, brother. I didn't want to hurt your feelings by having you know that she cares a little for him.'

For a burning instant Kazim wanted to slap her, hard. 'I don't believe you. She— When she and I— *She was eager* – she hates him, I know it.' His eyes felt as if they had been bathed in acid.

Rashid didn't look at him. 'So you do not believe she can be relied upon?' he asked Huriya intently.

Huriya answered warily, 'Ramita loves Kazim, but she does not hate Meiros. She wants to escape and live with Kazim, but if this could happen without her husband's death, she would be happier. She is not someone who could ever kill another person.'

'Would she open the door to Kazim, knowing he held a dagger?'

'Possibly, lord, but not certainly. It would be safer were I to open that door instead.' Huriya looked Rashid in the eyes, and for all his pain, Kazim marvelled at her daring.

'Ah: so you would become our gatekeeper, would you?' Rashid's voice took on a calculating air.

Huriya didn't flinch. 'I believe I could serve you, lord.' Kazim recognised her manner, all the way from Aruna Nagar: bargaining with bluff, cheek and some knowledge of the true price of the goods.

Rashid half-smiled. He leaned forward and did something that made his eyes flash pale-blue, and Huriya looked momentarily startled. Something had passed between them. She looked genuinely scared, and bit her lip. Rashid laughed aloud. 'What an *interesting* mind you have, girl. And yes, *obviously* the gnosis has nothing to do with the demons of Hel if I can do it.'

She coloured, still afraid, but she also looked pleased, as if she had made a wager and won.

Rashid turned to Kazim. 'Your sister has the same blood as you, Kazim, and great aptitude mentally. She will receive the same training as you.'

Kazim stared at Huriya. She would receive Hadishah mind-training – why would she need that? Huriya smiled coyly and said, 'Meiros himself has taught me some mind-shielding techniques already, so that enemies cannot learn of his doings through me.'

Rashid looked at her appraisingly, then clapped his hands. 'Very well, we will proceed. Kazim, final preparation and initiation will begin immediately. By the time Meiros is back from the Southpoint, you will be ready. Huriya, you will liaise with Jamil and me to create the opportunity to enter Casa Meiros. In the meantime you must keep your mistress calm and oblivious. I deem she cannot be trusted to remain silent on this matter.' He glanced at Kazim, challengingly, but Kazim bit his tongue. 'It is important that Ramita does not panic or show concern if no signs of mage-blood appear. We will research this phenomenon ourselves to better understand it.'

Huriya said confidently, 'I can do that, my lord.' She was more composed than Kazim felt.

'Why did Meiros choose Ramita?' Rashid asked Huriya suddenly.

'Ramita's mother's line produces many children. She says he believes his children will bring peace to the world.'

Rashid snorted. 'Then he is deluded – there is no such thing as peace!' He shook his head dismissively. 'Well girl, you have become important to us. What reward do you desire?'

Kazim watched her consider. She'd always been too clever by half, but to make bargains with Hadishah lords was another matter. He marvelled at her nerve. 'The safety of my mistress and myself will be reward enough, great lord,' she answered eventually, but her eyes were sly.

Rashid looked amused. Kazim sensed something else pass between them mind to mind. Rashid looked skywards, as if considering, then looked at Jamil as if inviting his thoughts before he nodded to Huriya, who looked pleased. He wondered what bargain had been sealed. *Do I really want to know?*

<You hear me, Kazim? Answer with a thought, not words.> Jamil's mental voice was impatient.

<Ye— yes.>

<Good, well done. Now, think of darkness and silence whilst I chant. You will know you have shut me out when my chanting fades from your mind.> Jamil started to chant the Holy Book in his skull while Kazim frantically tried to shut it out. It seemed to take for ever, but finally, there was nothing.

<Well done.>

He could not tell if hours or minutes had passed, but Jamil didn't stop. He took him through more and more such exercises, and each time it got easier. Finally he said, 'Enough, Kazim. Stay away from Casa Meiros from now on. Meiros could pick your brain too easily, if he had any suspicions.'

Kazim sighed. He'd not seen Ramita for so long now, and the last time had not gone well. He missed her, longed to know what she was doing, but he had other worries too. He looked at Jamil intently. 'What did Rashid promise my sister?'

Jamil considered him for a moment, then said, 'She asked for the gnosis.'

Kazim was aghast. 'Huriya – but— Even I can't use the devil-magic, and I'm a *man*—'

Jamil laughed. 'I'm not sure your masculinity is the key determinant.'

'We are not like you. My father was not a Shaitan-spawned jadugara!'

'I never said he was, Kazim.' Jamil's face was patient.

Kazim's jaw dropped. 'My mother – was she—?'

'No, her neither.'

'Then why does Rashid think my sister can gain the gnosis?'

Jamil shrugged. 'I don't know, but he is my commander and it is not my place to question.'

Kazim's training had redoubled: silent movement, picking locks, climbing wall and trees, using ropes or bare hands; he took to them all with ease. Jamil told him a normal trainee would have started training from a young age, but he'd never had a better pupil. 'You are a natural athlete and fighter, Kazim: you are born to this.' The praise was both cheering and chilling.

It was not just physical work; Jamil fed his mind: Rondian words and grammar, knowledge of the Hadishah network; codes and passwords that relied on complex grids of symbols; safe houses and key contacts. The Hadishah operated in small cells, and they had few dealings with each other. Though the pouring of information was one-way, Kazim felt like he knew Jamil better than anyone – Jai, Huriya, even Ramita – even better than he knew himself. He trained physically for eight hours a day, absorbed knowledge mind-to-mind for another eight, and slept the remainder. It was punishing, but he felt a new self emerging: he could kill with his bare hands or a well-

434

placed kick; he could throw with power and accuracy; he could kill with a dozen everyday things. He could run tirelessly.

Days ran together, and they so lost track of the moon and stars that it came as a shock when he was told this phase of his training was over. It was dark-moon; three weeks had passed, eighteen days in which he had not thought for an instant of Ramita. He sent his apologies to her in fervent prayer.

It was time for his initiation as Hadishah. Haroun was being initiated alongside him, as a scriptualist. Kazim had never decided if Haroun had latched onto him in genuine friendship, or whether it had been more calculated; he'd not forgotten that Jamil had been watching out for them on the march, and that Haroun had known. Nevertheless, side by side, hours on end, they learned together *The Kalistham*'s passages on shihad. A Hadishah must understand shihad, and why there could be no pity for the heathen, however innocent or weak or fair-seeming. Even a child brought up as a heathen was a threat, for what they would become, so all infidel must die. It was a simple truth, and unyielding.

Ramita must convert when we marry. For her soul, she must cleave to the Amteh.

This training was less physically demanding, but it was mentally draining. Eight hours of learning at the feet of a Godspeaker, eight of sleep, eight to spend as he willed – which meant more training with his blade, often just himself alone, flowing through the rhythmic dance of the sword with increasing surety and confidence. He thrashed all who sparred with him, even older men of the Hadishah. Only magi like Jamil could stand up to him now. He took grim pride in his prowess.

On the final day he fasted all night alongside Haroun. The only words they had exchanged in the whole five days had been the call and response of prayer, but the last task the Godspeaker set them was to make peace with each other. Kazim spoke aloud his anger and fury at Haroun's manipulations. Haroun refuted this, claiming Jamil had sworn him to secrecy. The Godspeaker called upon Kazim to forgive, and somehow, in the midst of this emotional intensity, he clasped Haroun to him, purged of his anger, and genuinely forgave.

He had been compelled to several acts of forgiveness. *All things are God's will*, the Godspeaker told him. He had to forgive others their weakness: Ispal Ankesharan, for his desire to elevate his family; Jai for his softness; even forgive Ramita her compassion for her husband. *These things are not evil*, the Godspeaker said; *reserve hatred for those whose evil is wilful, born of selfish desires and blasphemy. Even forgive Antonin Meiros his need to create new life, forgive the Rondians their barbarity, for none of these can help who they are. Only the pure in faith can transcend themselves above their instincts. Forgive – but do not forget, and when you strike, let not pity nor forgiveness stay your hand. Become the blade of God.*

When he sliced his palm and swore his loyalty to the Hadishah and his bashir, Rashid, he did so with a remorseless sense of purpose. His will was as hard as his edged steel.

Afterward, Rashid shared iced arak with Kazim and Haroun. The sweet aniseed liquor was heady after their privations. It was the last week of the month. In sixty days, the Leviathan Bridge would rise from the sea, the sky would fill with windships and the Rondians would begin their long march across the ocean, bringing fire and war. The nightmare would begin again.

Rashid tapped the table. 'Before that, Antonin Meiros must die, then the Ordo Costruo will split, freed from his craven neutrality. Many of the order are Amteh. Freed of their strictures, they will join the shihad. This Crusade will be different, I swear: this time, victory will be ours and the Rondians will be purged from Antiopia for ever.'

It was an intoxicating thought. Rashid touched Kazim's shoulder. 'You are the best swordsman I have seen, Kazim Makani: the match of your father, whose prowess you never saw. To you, God willing, will fall the most critical blow of this holy shihad: the blow that ends the long and evil life of Antonin Meiros. Haroun, you will be Kazim's contact and sponsor. You will supply his needs, give him prayer and encouragement. You will keep him strong. I myself will deal direct with you.

'Now, this is the situation. The Rondians have sent an Imperial Ambassador, supposedly to negotiate a peace, but all know this is a pretence, to lure the Dhassans and Keshi into a false sense of security. This ambassador is named Belonius Vult. Meiros will be with him constantly next week, then he will return home: this is when we will make our move. I cannot give you the exact date for your strike, so be ever alert: when it comes it will arrive at short notice. Patience is your prime virtue for now, Kazim Makani: you need to be focused, calm and patient. But the time to strike is coming.'

26

Patterns Burnt into Air

Runes

There are certain aspects of the gnosis that are common to all magi. These are the 'tools of the trade', so to speak: the erecting of protective wards, the ability to send and block gnosis-contact, the sealing of barriers and portals, and many other applications. Each has been assigned a Rune – a symbol from the language of the old Yothic peoples of Schlessen – to identify it. Hence the phrase casting a rune has passed into magi speech along with terms like spells and wards and the like.

ARDO ACTIUM, SCHOLAR, BRES 518

Norostein, Noros, on the continent of Yuros
Maicin 928
2 months until the Moontide

'Master Mercer,' the quiet voice hailed Alaron as he scurried through the twilight streets of Norostein, his hood up to avoid recognition. He had left his illegal periapt at home in case some over-diligent guardsman searched him before he entered the council library. With so many gone eastwards, as legionaries or in the vast supply trains, the streets felt oddly empty. The wind was rising and high clouds were scudding across the face of the crescent moon. The summer was in full bloom, its humid heat sapping strength and alertness.

Alaron stiffened as Jeris Muhren detached himself from a wall a few feet away. The rough-hewn watchman looked dangerous in the half-light. Alaron knew he should salute the captain, but he hadn't fully forgiven him. Under his arm was a notebook filled with hundreds of the more arcane runes he'd found in the library, but he still hadn't found the one Jarius Langstrit had burned in the air last week.

'How are you faring, lad?' Muhren asked.

Alaron found his forced softness irritating, but answered, 'Well enough. We've been forced to sell our country house and my mother is so ill that my father has had to take her in again even though they separated years ago. Father is so in debt thanks to my failure at college that he must go east to try and trade his way out of impending bankruptcy. Meanwhile I cannot practise the art I trained in, or show my face in most of the city for fear of been assaulted. So life is just *wonderful*. Thank you for asking.'

Muhren winced at the sarcasm. 'I have said I am sorry, young man, but you left me no choice—'

'*No choice?* Who was going to believe me? You could have just laughed it off – they'd have forgotten anything I said within ten minutes.'

Muhren shook his head. 'Lad, the councilmen listening had their ears flapping madly. And it wasn't that which condemned you – I spoke to Gavius afterwards and he assured me that my disagreement with your theories wouldn't fail you. He gave me his word.'

'His word,' spat Alaron. 'Lucien Gavius' word?' He threw up his hands. 'You must be—' He stopped. *Keep your mouth shut for once, Alaron: it's already done. You've got a periapt, you're alive and you have other secrets to protect.*

'Lad, they were set to pass you; Gavius promised me that. But a week later you threw a punch at Eli Besko. Did you not think that might have consequences?'

'But that fat creep—'

Muhren stopped him with a peremptory gesture. 'That "fat creep" is now acting-governor. The council approves all graduation, you know that. Even if he richly deserved your blow, which he probably did, you should have had more sense. I'm not your enemy, boy and I've given my support to having the decision overturned.'

'Much good that's done so far,' Alaron observed bitterly. He shuffled uncomfortably. 'Anyway, have you got something to say or can I go?'

Muhren looked to be wishing he could bawl Alaron out like one of his guards. 'You're a difficult little sod, aren't you? All spikes and prickles, just like your Aunt Elena. Yes, I have something to say. You may have heard that there is a search on for a missing old man?'

Alaron stiffened. 'I have heard, sir.'

'Do you know anything about it?'

'No. Why, should I?' he added truculently.

Muhren looked skywards as if searching for patience. 'If a watchman gave me even half as much lip he'd be in the stocks. No, there is no particular reason that you should know, except that old man has some connection to your thesis. He played a prominent role in your thinking, and I have been wondering why he should go missing at more or less the same time. I'm just exploring connections.'

Alaron licked his lips. 'I don't know anything, sir. Who is he?'

Muhren shook his head. 'Best you don't know – but if you do find something, please, come to me. Don't go to the council.'

So you know his name: that's interesting. 'I thought you were the council.'

Muhren glared angrily. 'On your way, boy – and don't think you can talk like that to everyone. I'm being soft on you for Vann's sake. Yes, perhaps I could have handled things better – but you would do yourself more good if you kept a respectful tongue in your head.'

Alaron glowered at him. As he stomped away he heard the captain sigh and head off in the opposite direction.

Back home, Alaron joined Ramon and Cym in the living room. Mother was in bed, fighting off a cold, and Langstrit was dozing in an armchair. The general's condition was unchanged. Alaron and his friends tended to each, feeding them, cleaning up afterward and settling them for the night. Vann Mercer was out finalising a shipment. He had already sent three wagon-loads east, and was trying to confirm the final load that he himself would drive to Pontus. He would be leaving soon, and he was visibly worried for Alaron and Tesla. The presence of the general was no doubt gnawing at him too.

'Did you find anything?' Ramon asked Alaron as he sipped the Silacian wine he had bought in town. The red liquid made Cym's lips fuller, more enticing – but she looked like she would slap anyone who said so. Alaron drifted off into a reverie, wishing he and Cym were alone.

'Hello, Urte to Alaron – did you find anything today?' Ramon asked loudly.

Alaron blinked and swallowed a mouthful of beer to cover his confusion. 'Huh?' The small table in front of him was covered with books from his mother's library, and were full of rune-variants they had never heard of. 'Oh, yeah – um, the last book I went through was by Rohinius of Pallas. I'm not sure it's helpful. Many magi don't use runes, or make up their own to obfuscate how they operate. The symbol Cym copied could be unique to whoever cast it.' He sucked on his bottom lip. 'It's hopeless.'

Ramon steepled his fingers. 'It's certainly not simple. Cym could have traced the thing wrong, or it could just be a rare rune we've not yet found – or it could even be a common rune that everyone knows, but disguised by the caster. I agree, it's not simple, but it's still the only clue we've got.'

They fell silent. The moments dragged on until Cym looked thoughtful. 'I know I've not had your formal training, but here's a suggestion. Instead of focusing on the rune, why not look at what it seems to have done to the general?'

Alaron looked at her admiringly. 'That's actually a good idea.'

'What do you mean "actually", ginger-mop?' Cym enquired with a mix of whimsy and danger.

'What he meant to say was "that's not a bad idea, *for a girl*",' Ramon threw in cheekily.

'No, that's not what I meant at all—' Alaron threw a malevolent look at Ramon. 'You're washing up tonight, familioso boy.'

'Guests don't have to wash up,' Ramon replied quickly.

Cym arched an eyebrow. 'So what about my suggestion, rat-face?'

'Uh, yeah, good idea, as I was just saying.'

Alaron leaned forward. 'Yeah, it's *brilliant*.'

Cym preened. 'Si, I'm brilliant.'

Ramon laughed. 'All right, okay, so let's think: the general has no memory of who he was. Is there a rune for that? We weren't taught any.'

Alaron leaned and picked up a slim volume. 'Yes, here, in Rohinius: Rune of Erasure – but it's on the forbidden list, which is why we didn't learn it. You've got to apprentice to a Church mage to be taught this stuff. Blanking someone's mind is Mysticism: it takes a lot of training. And it's illegal.'

Ramon whistled softly. 'Whoever did it meant business, then,' he murmured.

'But he's also got his unconscious use of the gnosis,' Alaron pointed out. 'What would cause that?'

'Maybe it's the amnesia?' Ramon wondered. 'Maybe he's forgotten he can do gnosis, but does it anyway by instinct.' They all glanced at Langstrit, who stirred and looked up at them, and for a second Alaron thought he was about to say or do something . . . but his face remained blank.

'I sometimes think he's just on the verge, and then it goes again,' Cym whispered, putting all their thoughts into words. 'It gives me the willies.'

'But why can't we detect any gnosis-traces? We've all tried.' Alaron folded his arms, trying to think, then said suddenly, 'Hang on; what if it's a Rune of the Chain, but too weak to entirely suppress his gnosis – wouldn't that leave him able to do some workings?'

'Perhaps, yes,' Ramon agreed. 'I'll tell you something else, too. We've tried to scry him and got nothing. What if there's a Rune of Hiding cloaking him?'

'Can one rune do all of that?' Cym asked.

'If a trance-mage cast it, I imagine so,' Ramon replied. 'A trance-mage can do several workings at once. If there's a Hiding-rune over him, that would explain why the council can't find him. If he's under both Chain and Hiding runes, he would be invisible to scrying, or any sign of the gnosis.'

Alaron tapped the table. 'Okay, so we're guessing runes of Memory-

Erasure, Hiding and the Chain.' He pulled out his notebook. 'Everyone knows the Hiding-Rune, it's basic stuff.' He sketched it out.

'And the Chain is well-known,' Ramon added. 'We got taught it in Year Six – remember when you got asked to demonstrate it and Malevorn blew out of it in twenty seconds?'

Alaron scowled. 'I've been trying to blank that name from my memory. Thanks for ruining three months of hard work.'

'Try a Rune of Erasure,' Cym offered. 'Apparently they're very effective.' She peered at Alaron's notes. 'Does your Rohinius tell us how to cast it?'

'No, he just says what it does.' Alaron tapped his empty glass. 'The actual rune-shape means nothing, it's just a symbol used to represent a gnosis-working, in the same way that a letter of the alphabet represents a sound. It's the act of will and the mental training that makes the gnosis work. So the pattern is essentially meaningless.'

'Then why did it appear at all?' Cym asked.

Alaron leaned back, looking up at the ceiling. 'Now *that's* a thought. Why not think about "why?"'

'I suppose we can,' Ramon said tiredly. 'We've tried "what symbol" and "what effect", so why not "why" for a bit? According to the official stories, the general suffered a breakdown after Robler's final surrender in Knebb Valley, but Alaron's thesis has him wandering aimlessly in Lower Town, arrested and vanished. If his memory was erased, it presumably happened prior to his arrest – but why?'

Alaron put up a hand. 'Because he knew about the Scytale of Corineus.'

Ramon rolled his eyes. 'You and your damned thesis—'

Cym leaned forward. 'No, Ramon, we should at least consider it: let's say he knew where the Scytale was, and so when he surrendered someone wiped his mind to remove that knowledge.'

'Why would they do that? Surely they would have wanted to learn where it was?'

'Perhaps they did, then they erased his knowledge so they were the only ones left who knew.'

'You have a devious mind,' Ramon said approvingly.

'Why thank you, sir.'

Alaron considered. 'It's possible: Langstrit goes to meet someone, who turns on him and erases his memory. That way only the other man knows what happened.'

Cym stroked her chin. 'Wouldn't it have been easier and safer for the mystery man to just kill him?'

Ramon nodded. 'Yes, I'd have just killed him.'

'Spoken like a true Silacian,' Cym snickered, 'but I do think we're onto something. Someone wanted to silence the general. It might not even be to do with the Scytale – we don't know for certain it's missing. But it could be what's behind it all. If we could return his memory, perhaps we could find it – imagine that—'

Alaron couldn't pretend it hadn't crossed his mind: to find the Scytale and become an Ascendant; what wouldn't he be able to do then? He'd have real, world-changing power . . . He found himself looking at Cym and Ramon with different eyes. They were of Rimoni stock; what would they do with the Scytale if they found it? Restore the lost empire, throw off the yoke of Rondian rule? If he had the power to change the world, wouldn't he want to free Noros from the empire?

If it truly was the Scytale they were hunting, it could be the beginning of a war like no other.

They were all silent, lost in their thoughts.

Finally Alaron said, 'We don't know for sure it is the Scytale. I could've been wrong about so many things. But we can't hide the general for ever, and we can't just leave him as he is. He's almost helpless – he even needs to be reminded to eat and drink. If we can do something to help him, we should. We owe it to him.'

'No one's suggesting we give him up, Alaron. Let's not get ahead of ourselves,' said Ramon, 'but you're right to have raised this. What do we do if the most powerful artefact in the history of the world falls into our laps? Of course I'd love to see the Rondians thrown out of Silacia and the Rimoni Empire reborn, but I can't think of a single Silacian I'd trust with that much power, much less a Rimoni.' He glanced at Cym and coloured slightly. 'No offence meant.'

'Some taken nevertheless,' glowered Cym.

Alaron put up his hand placatingly. 'We should make an oath. If we find the Scytale, we will keep it a secret and only tell people each one of us agrees to tell. What do you think?'

Ramon stared at Alaron and Cym. 'All right.'

The two boys looked at Cym. 'Of course,' she said lightly. 'Let us swear.'

They clasped hands solemnly. Ramon elected himself spokesman. 'We three hereby undertake that should we gain the Scytale of Corineus, we will limit its use to those whose admittance we all three agree. We will act only in ways agreed by us all. The friends of one are the friends of all. The enemies of one are the enemies of all. Our fellowship will never be broken, unto death. This I swear.'

'I so swear,' said Alaron, feeling a surprise welling of emotion that thickened his voice. *These are my dearest friends, and we are bound unto death.* He blinked back tears.

'I so swear,' Cym chimed in a second later, with a small note of hesitancy that caught Alaron's attention. He looked at her, but her face was the same as always: lovely, unreadable, mysterious. She winked at him and his mind eased.

They toasted themselves awkwardly and sat. 'Of course, we're putting the cart well before the horse, but at least we're prepared,' Ramon said. He looked down at the three runes they'd drawn, then pulled out the paper with the fiery lines Langstrit had projected and said excitedly, 'What if this is a whole *series* of Runes, all displaying at once? Look, the Hiding-rune could go here – no, hang on, yes: *if it was backwards* – look!' He sketched quickly, then held up what he'd drawn. 'See, Cym had it round the wrong way round—'

'I did not copy it wrongly,' Cym grumbled as they all leaned forward. Ramon traced his finger through the tangle of lines and yes, there was a Rune of Hiding. They all began making suggestions as they realised that this way round, the pattern could also accommodate a version of the Chain-rune.

'But there's no Erasure-rune in what's left,' groaned Cym.

'Then maybe it isn't the Erasure-rune,' Alaron suggested hesitantly.

'Look, see the lines through here and here, those are part of the Chain-rune and the Hiding-rune; imagine they aren't there. That leaves this line and that squiggle and a curve there . . . All we need to do is find a rune that includes that shape—'

'Or more than one rune,' added Cym. 'We might still be looking for more than just one.' She looked out the window. 'It's midnight – I heard six bells a few minutes ago.' She yawned. 'We should finish this in the morning—'

'No, not when we're on a roll,' Alaron said briskly. 'I'll make some coffee.'

'All right. I'll get the coffee, Alaron, you two get the general to bed.' Cym got up, stretched and sashayed downstairs, watched wistfully by the two young men.

'Mind on the job, Alaron,' whispered Ramon, handing him a book. 'Her father would gut you.'

After an hour of working through the piles of notes and roughly copied runes they had to admit they'd got no further. Cym groaned, and yawned again. 'Now what do we do? Can we sleep yet?'

'Not yet,' Ramon answered, his ferret-like face alert and his voice still lively. 'Just because the poor general has been struck by two common runes, it doesn't mean the other one or two aren't from a Study. It'd have to be something Theurgic or Sorcerous – it wouldn't be Elemental, although I suppose it could be Hermetic.' He reached down to another pile of books and started flipping through them. 'Every spell is represented by a rune, so let's go – should only take us an hour or so.'

In fact it was less than half an hour when Alaron blinked, looked back and forth a couple of times to make sure, then whispered, 'Look, I've got it: the line from this symbol fits that line, and the other lines overlay these two. It's a Spiritualism spell called "Transfer Recall" – listen to this. It takes the consciousness of the person and sends it into something else, usually a crystal.' He looked at them. 'So what do you think?'

'It fits,' Ramon agreed. 'I've never heard of it before, but it could be the one.'

'The Church hoards all the most powerful knowledge,' Alaron said. His mother always said that. 'So it looks like whatever was cast upon the general was a multiple-casting: this Transfer Recall spell, plus a weak or flawed Chain-rune and a Hiding-rune. That must be it.' He clenched his fist in victory.

'Why would anyone do that to him?' Cym asked.

Ramon looked thoughtful. 'Let's think . . . Perhaps he and a friend know about the Scytale. The army has surrendered, the Rondians are closing in, so they make a run for it, but his friend needs to cover his own tracks: no one knows of his involvement, but the general is very well-known. He can't bear to kill his friend, so instead he steals his memories, leaves him on the streets to be taken care of by the people and makes a run for it.'

Cym frowned. 'Okay, so that's a possibility – but if so, where is this mysterious friend now?'

'Who knows?' Ramon said, stretching. 'Maybe he sold it back to the Rondians?'

Aaron was struggling with a new thought. 'Why did we see the runes at all?'

'Not this again,' grumped Ramon impatiently. 'We've been over that—'

'No, listen: he *made* those symbols appear – but why display the spells someone's cast upon you?'

Ramon put a finger up. 'Maybe it's the last thing he remembers?'

Alaron nodded emphatically. 'Exactly what I'm thinking: when someone uses a rune, they trace it in the air and it leaves a trail of light, right? So that rune-pattern – or patterns, in fact – were the last thing Langstrit saw as his memory got fried, right?'

His friends nodded in unison.

Alaron felt inspired, and the words poured from him. 'A multi-layered rune like that would take a trance-mage, right? But since when does a trance-mage even *need* to trace a rune? Those guys can do it all with a thought; no words, no gestures, it's just will and execution. You saw Malevorn – the bastard had outgrown using visible runes and audible words by Year Four. Yet whoever cast that multi-rune had to be a trance-mage, and he used the standard symbols that are universally taught, writ large in fire – *as if he wanted them to be seen.* And think about this: why is it the wrong way round?'

Cym and Ramon were nodding thoughtfully. 'Okay, why was it the wrong way round?' Cym said.

Alaron thumped the table triumphantly. 'You were standing in front of the general, but what you copied turned out to be the wrong way around. So if the caster was the person who left those rune-marks . . . *then the caster was General Langstrit himself!*'

Ramon reached out and shook Alaron's hand. 'You're right, amici – you must be. The poor bastard did it to himself – and you know what? That means if he left those rune-marks to be found, then they are meant as clues and he wants someone to undo it.' He puffed up importantly. 'And that means us.'

27

A Trail Gone Cold

Lukhazan

It is impossible to write about the Noros Revolt without considering the Surrender of Lukhazan in 910. At the time Robler's armies had been forced to quit the Knebb Valley. Before Robler could retreat to Lukhazan, Vult surrendered the city, which almost trapped Robler and gave the Rondians a direct line of march on Norostein. The fall of Lukhazan, supposedly impregnable, made Rondian victory certain. Robler never spoke to Vult again, nor did any of his subordinates.

ORDO COSTRUO COLLEGIATE, PONTUS

Magi and windships care nothing for fortifications, and castles in modern warfare are more death-trap than refuge. Holding Lukhazan was impossible. My critics are simpletons who refuse to acknowledge the strategic and tactical realities.

BELONIUS VULT, SPEAKING TO THE
ROYAL WAR CONDUCT ENQUIRY, NOROSTEIN 911

Norostein, Noros, on the continent of Yuros
Maicin 928
2 months until the Moontide

Alaron didn't tell his parents of their discoveries. They didn't want to distract Vann Mercer, not when he needed to go to Pontus to save the family from bankruptcy. They were also scared Vann would put their information into the hands of Jeris Muhren, and Alaron still didn't trust the watch captain. So the unravelling of the clues remained a secret.

'When do you go, Da?' Alaron asked his father, who was dealing with piles of paperwork.

'Next week.' He looked tired. 'How are you, son? Are you going to be able to look after things here when your friends go home?'

'Sure. Ramon'll be here until the end of Maicin, and Cym says she'll stay longer if I need. Mum is – well, you know—' He flinched slightly. 'She's not too bad really. I think she likes being back here.'

'What are we going to do about the general?' His father ran his fingers through his thinning hair. 'We can't keep him here for ever, even leaving aside the risk we're taking. At some point we'll have to put him in the hands of someone who can look after him properly. I should speak to Jeris Muhren.'

'No! I can look after him. The council doesn't mean him well. And he's making progress.'

For a moment Vann looked as if he might argue, then he relented. 'Just until the end of Junesse, Alaron. If he's no better by then, you must go to Jeris Muhren. Promise?'

Alaron considered. Surely they would have solved the mystery by then. *And if not, well, Da will be in Pontus.* 'Okay,' he said, then something occurred to him. 'Do you know who found the general, back on the day after the Surrender? The actual person, I mean?'

Vann frowned. 'No – but the Watch should have a record. I'll ask Jeris, if you like . . .'

'Uh, no, it's all right, thanks. It's nothing really; I was just curious,' he said quickly, excusing himself. He hurried back to his friends. 'I just asked Da about who might have found the general and he said the Watch should have records. That would mean asking Muhren, but I don't trust him.'

Ramon waved an airy hand. 'We should be able to find an eye-witness and take it from there. As long as we're discreet.' He grinned. 'That means me. No one trusts gypsies and Alaron couldn't do discreet if his life depended upon it. Just give me a day or two.'

Ramon had been using his status as a legion battle-mage to use the Arcanum library, returning each day with diligently copied notes for the others to pore over. If they were right about the rune then the general's memories had to be captured in a crystal and hidden somewhere.

'So if we discover the crystal, we can put his soul and body back together,' Ramon told them. 'And I found out who arrested General Langstrit.' He smirked like a well-satisfied cat.

The following day Alaron met Hans Lehmann, the watchman Ramon had identified, in a run-down tavern inappropriately named the Summer Dream. The dark little room reeked of pipe-smoke and the stink of the sewer that ran past the one open window. The beer was watery and the landlord had sausage-breath.

Lehmann had been a sergeant of the Watch during the Revolt. With all the young men away fighting, the Watch had been reduced to those men too old or infirm to fight; he'd been over fifty then, just a few years off retirement. He was more than seventy now, and though his once-muscular frame had run to fat, his eyes were clear and he was happy to talk about the old times. His eyes lit up at Vann Mercer's name, which filled Alaron with pride.

Alaron asked about the general, and Lehmann sighed. 'If I close my eyes I can still see Old Jari that morning. He looked totally lost. The surrender, I guess, it must have hit him hard.'

'Wasn't the general supposed to be in camp?' Alaron prompted.

'I wouldn't know, lad. Trudi, the chapel's cleaner, found him first—'

'What chapel?' Alaron interrupted eagerly.

'The one by the oak on the north side of Pordavin Square. Jari was wandering around inside when Trudi found him. He was crying his eyes out, but he wouldn't speak, didn't seem to know his own name. Trudi sent a boy to find me and my mate Rodde. We sat him down, closed up the chapel and were just wondering what to do next, but word must've spread because some Palace men came and took him away.'

'King's men, you mean, or Rondians?'

'Our own king's men, lad, but they was under the thumb of the Rondians – you see, the Rondians, they was occupying us, but they was stretched so they let us oldsters police Lower Town. Some o' them who cry-babied at Lukhazan was paroled; one of 'em was put in charge of the Watch: a sharp young fella, name of Fyrell.'

Alaron felt his eyes pop out. 'Darius Fyrell?' he whispered.

'Aye, that was his name, he was one of them the Rondians set up to transition power. The fella what sold us down the creek, he was involved too.'

'Belonius Vult?'

Sergeant Lehmann spat on the floor. 'Aye, him.'

'But wasn't he imprisoned after Lukhazan?'

'The Rondians paroled him. He was up at the Governor's Palace even then, filling the Rondians' ears with our secrets and his own pockets with gold, I don't doubt. He allus was a shifty beggar.'

'So, Fyrell, he was working for Belonius Vult, who was working for the Rondians—'

'Aye, that were the way of it. Didn't make them palace lads too popular with the folks. Anyway, there was a fair few skulls cracked before Fyrell got his hands on the general, but in the end they cleaned out the chapel and took the general away. No one's ever seen him since. They had Old Jari killed, I reckon. Poor bastard.' He finished his beer and looked meaningfully at Alaron, who took the hint and waved for another pint. 'You're a gent, lad, just like yer dad.'

'Why don't people know this?' Alaron asked. 'All the books say Langstrit surrendered with Robler.'

'Well, that's books for you, full o' lies. The generals was rivals, lad, feuding like Silacians. Vult and Langstrit hated each other, and Robler favoured Langstrit. Old Jari, he were a tough bugger, and Vult were a strutting peacock. I allus figured Fyrell saw a chance for Vult to get Langstrit to himself.'

'What happened to the others who saw this?' Alaron asked. 'Rodde and Trudi?'

'Both in the grave, lad. Trudi was old even then, and Rodde, he were knifed in a tavern brawl a few months later. Nasty, that were: took him a week to die.' He tutted morosely. 'All the young men was away fighting and the young women, they kept off the streets to protect themselves from those dirty Rondian bastards. I doubt anyone under fifty saw the whole thing play out. They'll be mostly in the ground now – it were a long time ago, after all. I may be the last person as saw it all.' His face clouded over.

Alaron pushed his own beer across the table to him and rose, his words of thanks most probably unheard, for Sergeant Lehmann was staring out the window, his eyes glazed and moist.

Alaron and Cym found the chapel on Pordavin Square, right where the old watchman had said. It was more than six hundred years old, and originally Sollan: there were still traces of the dedications to Sol and Luna. But the door was broken and the whole place stank of rot and urine. It had escaped demolition only because it housed some historic gravestones, the last remains of some of the first magi to settle in Norostein – it was illegal to destroy anything pertaining to the magi.

They looked around, but there was nothing to see; the floors had been scoured long ago, there were no furnishings and the walls were peeling and covered in mildew. It was a sad, neglected place.

'Is this where he did it, do you think? Where he cast all those runes on himself,' Alaron asked.

'Who knows?' The gypsy girl fixed Alaron with a look. 'If we do find the Scytale of Corineus, I believe we should take it to the Ordo Costruo. They're sworn to peace. What do you think?'

Alaron swallowed. He hadn't expected her to spring that question without warning. 'I don't know,' he replied. 'No one trusts Antonin Meiros any more, do they? He lost the Bridge, so who could trust him with the Scytale? Maybe he'd just give it back to the emperor.'

'The Rondians have been lording it over everyone else for too long. If the Ordo Costruo have it, they can regain control of the Bridge and stop the wars.'

Alaron looked at Cym's lovely face framed by a cascade of black hair. He just wanted to make her happy. 'You're probably right,' he said, hopefully.

'I'll hold you to that,' she told him, her face solemn, and tantalisingly close.

'Don't forget Ramon has to agree too,' he warned her nervously. *If I leaned closer I could kiss her—*

She turned away. 'He'll come round,' she said. Her shape was outlined by the light streaming through the door. She looked angelic, and out of reach. 'There's nothing here,' she added. 'Let's go.'

'So where does that leave us?' Alaron wondered aloud. 'The chapel's empty. Unless we can find out what Fyrell took away with him, we're at a dead end.' He ran fingers through his hair. 'Twenty years – that's such a long time. The governor's men probably destroyed everything. The trail has gone cold.'

Ramon grinned. 'If this was Silacia, I'd take a few lads and have a quiet word with Fyrell – except we're in Norostein and Fyrell's a Magister who could blow us all to Lune.'

'Fyrell's probably nothing to do with it any more,' Cym muttered. 'It's Vult we need.'

'He's in Hebusalim,' Ramon said, 'it's all over the Arcanum.' Ramon had confirmed his own enlistment that week, and was due to fly to Pontus on a windship in early Junesse, in less than a month's time. 'He's acting as ambassador for the emperor.'

Alaron rubbed his face. 'The chapel's empty, we've got nothing to go on. We're at an impasse.'

Cym looked at Ramon. 'He really doesn't understand how things work in Rimoni, does he?'

Alaron eyed them both uneasily. 'What do you mean?'

'Well, it's pretty obvious what we need to do,' Ramon said, licking his lips. 'I bet Vult guessed the other generals had the Scytale, and he was angry at being left out. When Fyrell brought in Langstrit with his brain fried, Vult thought that it had something to do with the Scytale so he made Langstrit vanish. He's probably spent the last twenty years trying to solve the very same problem we're working on now. But I bet Langstrit hasn't ever manifested that Rune-puzzle for Vult, so all Vult has is a man with amnesia, so does he kill him, or hold on to him and hope he recovers? Clearly he chose to wait.'

Ramon's explanation seemed to fit the facts. He went on, 'Vult has been governor for years now. The report on Langstrit is too important to leave lying around, but too secret to entrust to his staff, so it'll be amongst his personal effects. So obviously we have to break into Vult's house and find it.'

'You're both mad!' Alaron said incredulously. 'This is *Belonius Vult* you're talking about: the Governor of Noros, a *pure-blood* – he'll have wards and probably traps, and he might even have spirit guardians, constructs – and we don't even know for sure the information's there – this is *ridiculous!*'

'Oh, it'll be there,' Ramon replied confidently. 'Think about it: personal and sensitive information like this will be in the Residence, which is quite separate to the administration area. He's not married, so there'll be no one there but guards after sunset. A determined and clever mage could gain access easily. After that it's just a case of finding the safe-box and we're in.'

Alaron thumped the table. 'This is *insane* – the slightest error will bring the Palace Guard down on our heads. The moment his wards are triggered he'll be instantly aware of what we're doing.'

'Vult's in Hebusalim,' Ramon insisted. 'Aware or not, he won't be able to do anything.'

'Maybe not personally, but he'll contact someone pretty damn quick. Probably Fyrell himself.'

'No, he won't: Alaron, these are his personal effects we're talking about. He wouldn't trust Fyrell with it any more than us—'

Alaron threw up his hands. 'Talk sense, won't you? We don't have a snowflake in Hel's chance of succeeding, and when we fail we'll end up dead or arrested or both. Talk sense—'

Ramon stood up. 'I am talking sense! Are you chickening out, Alaron?'

'I'm not chicken!' Alaron stood too, and poked Ramon in the chest. 'There's a difference between courage and suicide, short-arse. Trying to break into Vult's place is idiocy.' He appealed to Cym. 'You agree with me, surely!'

'It is a suicidal idea,' she started, 'but I agree with Ramon. It's the only way forward. We're at a dead end, otherwise.'

Ramon gesticulated expressively. 'Look at it logically: of course there will be guards, but the palace can't be that well-protected because Vult wouldn't trust anyone else's wards but his own, and he certainly wouldn't want anyone but him in his private study. He'll be thousands of miles away – he may not even sense it, but even if he does, he'll not be able to do anything about it. The palace should be easy pickings. What sort of magi can't get past a few watchmen?'

'But what about his wards?' Alaron said doubtfully. 'Even a simple locking spell set by a pure-blood is beyond any of us – so how will we ever get past wards set by someone as powerful as Vult?'

Cym struck a pose and pointed at Jarius Langstrit, slumbering in his armchair. 'Ta-da! I give you one Ascendant Mage. He's got enough power to blow through Vult's wards like they weren't there.'

Ramon's mouth twitched. 'Cymbellea, bella amora mio! You are a genius.'

'But he can't even tie his own boot-laces,' Alaron objected. 'How will you get him to help?'

'I know how,' she insisted, and Alaron looked at her, then sat down resignedly.

'Okay, okay. But what do we even know about breaking into buildings?'

Ramon laughed aloud. 'I'm a Silacian. It's in my blood.'

28

Divinations

The Javon Settlement

The Javon Settlement of 836 remains possibly the most remarkable piece of diplomacy ever. The Lakh philosopher Kishan Dev convinced the factions of Javon who were destroying themselves in civil war to adopt a mixed-race elective monarchy. That this remarkable compromise was even agreed speaks volumes about the desperation of the times, but does not diminish its unique achievements.

ORDO COSTRUO, HEBUSALIM CHAPTER, 927

Sister, there has come amongst us a guru from Indrania! His ideas beggar belief: he would have us pollute ourselves in the name of a craven peace that benefits no one. The Nesti give him credence, unbelievably, and his influence spreads. It is the beginning of the end.

LETTER FROM LETO GORGIO TO HIS SISTER UNA, JAVON 836

Brochena, Javon, on the continent of Antiopia
1–12 Maicin 928
60 days until the Moontide

The remains of a young Jhafi woman lay on the steps to the canal. Elena knelt and stared down at the wide-open eyes, the shocked visage and the torn and bloodied nakedness that ended at the girl's belly. Her hips and legs were gone, bitten clean away. More blood than could be believed covered the steps.

The girl was Mustaq al'Madhi's niece, his brother's daughter. The women of the family were screaming and tearing at their hair while the men beat their chests and howled threats. Beside her, Lorenzo started vomiting again. She sympathised, but she'd seen worse.

Mustaq's face was a mask of controlled fury. He stalked to her side. 'This was done by Gyle?'

Elena nodded. 'Mara did it – Mara Secordin, one of his assassins.'

'Ahm protect us!' The Jhafi headman glanced at his wailing relatives and lowered his voice. 'The women were bathing. They say something huge reared out of the water and bit the poor girl in half—' His voice was both awed and scared. He used these bathing ghats himself. 'How is this possible?'

Elena dropped her voice to match his. 'Mara is an Animagus, a beast-mistress. She has made a particular study of water-beasts.'

'The women said it was a fish, five times the length of a man, with a mouth full of teeth!'

'It's called a *shark*. I have seen such beasts: they dwell in the oceans. Mara found a living one once, trapped in the tidelands. She dissected it and learned its shape, but its nature affected her. That can happen to an Animagus who spends too much time in beast form. She's lost most of her humanity.'

Mustaq looked sick and murderous. 'Gyle targets my family.'

Elena nodded. 'He does: he has learned that you are hunting him and he thinks to warn you off.' She ran her eye over the headman. 'He thinks to frighten you into standing aside from the conflict.'

Mustaq scowled. 'We of the Amteh know no fear,' he boasted, though his voice was hollow. 'We do not abandon our allies.' He put his hand on Elena's shoulder. 'Tell Cera not to fear. We will remain true.' He nodded emphatically, then said, 'I must comfort my brother.' He turned and hurried away.

Lorenzo groaned and stood. He rinsed his mouth with water and spat.

'Come on,' she whispered, 'we can't do anything more here.'

They made their way back into the haveli of the al'Madhi family, passing shocked children and womenfolk. There was no comfort they could give, so Elena led Lorenzo to the nearest Sollan church, a tiny shrine near the palace walls. The drui was away, and the shrine was empty. She pulled back her hood. Lorenzo's face was pale beneath his tan and he swayed slightly as he clutched at her. Gradually he steadied, but she could still feel him shaking.

'Now you see what we're up against,' she whispered.

He squeezed her almost painfully tight, then fell to his knees before the altar, and started praying silently, fervently.

Elena remained standing. *I'm going to kill you, Mara. Somehow I will find a way . . .*

After a time, Lorenzo climbed to his feet, trembling still, but with a different heat; the aftermath of horror was turning into a need for consolation. It was a familiar reaction – she'd felt it herself during the Revolt – but she stepped away. 'Lori, come: we must report this to Cera.'

His face was full of grief and need. 'Ella,' he whispered, 'please: I just want to hold you.'

'Not here,' she replied, 'not now. This is a holy place.'

He reached for her, but instinct took over and with a whoosh of gnostic force she hurled him away and sent him sprawling among the pews. The weight of his armour smashed through the wooden bench and he sprawled crookedly in the broken timbers.

'Oh shit! Lorenzo, I'm so sorry—' She hurried to him.

Lorenzo sat up, his face both alarmed and angered. '*Rukka mio*, Ella!'

'I'm really am sorry!' She offered a hand.

His Rimoni pride and temper were roused, but he clenched his teeth and accepted her hand to get to his feet. Then he let go and raised both his hands carefully. 'See, I'm not touching you.' He circled away from her as if she were a dangerous animal.

'I'm sorry, Lori, but I don't let people grab me like that, not by surprise—'

'I only wanted to hold you, Ella,' he whispered. 'I mean you no harm.'

She hung her head. 'I know, Lori. I do know that. I'm just not used to being that close to anyone.'

He put his hands on his hips, his eyes shining with frustrated passion. 'Why do you still push me away, Ella? Are we not adults;

may we not speak frankly?'

'All right, let's do that.' She glared back at him. 'You said you understand me – but you do not.' She began counting off fingers. 'First: I'm a mage: you don't grab us and expect to keep your hands! Two, I respect the Sollan faith enough to not desecrate the chapel. Three, I'm fertile this week and I cannot risk pregnancy. Four, I might travel with you after the shihad, but that is two years hence.'

She thought he might storm off, but he didn't. 'All right, my turn.' He too raised his fingers. 'One, I apologise for startling you. Two, the drui make love to priestesses during certain ceremonies so I don't think they'd mind too much. Three, I'm not familiar with your courses so how would I know when you're fertile? And four: I'm a man, not some swooning poetic hero who can be fobbed off with some decade-long errand for the Questing Beast! I'm not asking for undying, eternal love. I'm asking for you to acknowledge your desires. If you want me, stop flirting and be mine!'

Her temper flashed. 'Flirting? I do not *flirt—*'

'No? Who made eyes at me the whole time I was humiliating myself with Cera? Whose gaze follows me every time I enter the room. As mine follows her!' He looked about to seize her again and she had to quell the urge to lash out. She stayed stock-still as he slowly reached out and gripped her forearms. 'See, Ella? No harm is done when I touch you.'

Her heart thudded painfully against her ribcage as he stepped in and swept an arm about her and pressed his mouth to hers. The rough scrap of his chin chafed and his strength was alarming. But her legs turned liquid. The kiss went on for eras, and when he lifted his lips from hers she heard herself protest as she gulped in air, trembling.

'Was that so bad, Ella?'

Her senses were spinning, her strength gone. 'But Gurvon . . .'

'Ella, I am already in the sights of the enemy. We both know that. What is it you truly fear?'

Good question. Intimacy? Something I can't control? Falling in love? Her lips quivered, but words wouldn't come out.

He released her. 'Elena, speak plainly: will you accept my love or not?'

She was barely able to remain standing. 'Lori, do you know the jest about porcupines? "How do porcupines make love? Very carefully." We magi are like porcupines. I'm twice your age, but I've only made love with two men in my life. One was a boy, we were both seventeen. The other was Gurvon.' She hung her head. 'I do not count the times I have allowed myself to be had while on a mission, for those are not acts of love.'

His eyes explored her face, his expression twisting as he sought to understand. 'Ella—'

She interrupted, desperate for him to understand. 'Even with Gurvon, we were both fiercely protective of our minds. Being naked with another scares me – naked of defences, I mean. I have killed male magi by letting them take me just so I could get inside their defences. I dread another doing the same to me, so do not think I am just playing with you: my fears are real.'

He understood, which made her affection for him billow like sails catching the wind. 'Elena, I hear you, but I am no mage, and I am no danger to you – quite the opposite.' He stroked her hair. 'My heart is in your hands. I will understand if you return it to me unused.'

The selflessness made her eyes blur. 'Thank you, Lori.' She gnawed her lip, utterly torn between duty and desire. 'Please, let us speak again, in a few weeks. There is so much happening right now and I need to keep my head clear to think. Please?'

He bowed. 'You give me hope, Ella. Thank you.'

They returned to the palace in silence. They needed to report to Cera and Paolo Castellini. And to make some kind of plan. *I must find Mara*, Elena kept repeating, *I must find Gurvon . . .*

Elena re-ignited her wards on the blood-rooms while Cera watched, then filled a copper basin with water and readied herself for the work she had to do. She still felt tired; the fear and stress remained, and the possible healing power of love was untested.

Because I'm too gutless to try . . .

Cera pursed her lips. 'Remind me how Divination works.'

Elena turned her attention to the matter at hand. 'Divination is a way of asking a question of the so-called "spirit-realm". When a person dies, their spirit leaves their body and floats free. This spirit is essentially energy and identity. Some claim they pass on to a another place, a Heaven or Hel, if you like, but we don't know. What we do know is that many spirits remain present but unseen here on Urte for a long, long time, observing the world. They're like a giant cobweb covering the world, travelling as fast as thought on dry land – though the seas block their movement – and communing with each other constantly, sharing visions and information. They watch all we do. Does this make sense?'

Cera nodded. 'The drui says the same: there are spirits, the ghosts of the dead and they can observe us. My mother believed they speak to us, and if we know how to listen, we can hear them.'

Elena prodded a finger into the water in the basin and stilled it. 'Sorcery is a Study based upon communing with the spirit-realm. Sorcery comprises Necromancy, Wizardry, Clairvoyance and Divination. Necromancy concerns the recently dead. Wizardry is the command of spirits to perform gnosis for you. Clairvoyance is seeing and communicating through the spirits, and Divination is the art of trying to see the future; that relies on asking the spirit-world a question, based upon what the spirits have observed, and then extrapolating that information into a prediction. Remember: we are not actually *seeing* the future – that's impossible. What we're seeing is a wider view of *now*.' She looked at Cera. 'Do you understand? The best I can give you is a likely prediction, not a certain outcome.'

When Cera nodded, she said, 'Then what question do you have?'

'Ask this: who are the agents of Gurvon Gyle in Brochena and where are they?'

Elena grunted impatiently. 'Cera, magi can hide themselves from the spirits. Questions about other magi are seldom usefully answered.'

'Not all agents are magi – ask, please.'

'Very well.' Elena called energy to her hands and flung it into the water with an abrupt gesture, making the water steam. She didn't need to speak aloud, but she did so anyway. 'Spirits, does Gurvon Gyle have agents in Brochena? Reveal them!' She spoke in Rym and repeated in the Jhafi tongue.

The steam cloud went murky, a pool of night hanging in the air, and Cera, her face pale, leaned as far from the dark cloud as possible. Shapes flickered in the darkness, almost too faint to be seen, then faded, half-formed.

Elena peered intently, focusing on the shapes that formed and following the tingling strands of the gnostic web out into the city. The responses came slowly: the Past, a web of small lights and a spider, crawling . . . The Present: a thinner web with gaping holes, a dark shape flowing through the gaps, the spider hidden . . . The Future: a busy spider, feeding, repairing and the murky outline of a red glove and a spinning coin.

All fairly clear and predictable, apart from the red glove, whatever that means. I'll need to research it. 'You see what I mean?' she asked Cera. 'It is pretty obvious: his network was damaged by the death of his magi. Undoubtedly some of those slain by Mustaq in the purges were his men. But it tells us nothing; magi can hide from the spirit-watchers, so what he is really doing cannot be divined.'

'What were the two last shapes?'

'A red glove and a coin. Usually a coin means bribery and a glove manipulation, but I don't know why the glove should be red. It is the colour of passion or anger, usually. Or it may refer to the colours of one of the noble houses, perhaps. I need to think on that.'

'The Kestrian colour is red,' Cera noted.

'In Yuros we associate red with the Church,' Elena replied, irritated at her recurring paranoia.

Cera scowled and produced a sheet of paper. 'Here are some more questions to ask.' She leaned back. 'We have to do this.'

Elena sighed and acquiesced, fighting the oncoming migraine that Divination always brought. Some of the questions were easy, others harder. The red glove, the coin, the spider, all recurred, along with a lizard slithering among the shadows. The gloved hand sometimes held a dagger . . . She felt her mouth go dry. *He's going to strike, and it's going to be soon.*

Elena took a sip of cold tea and tried to clear her pounding head. She suddenly realised it was dark outside; she'd been divining all day. Her hands shook, spilling the tea, and she placed the cup down clumsily. 'Enough, please – I'm exhausted, Cera.'

The queen-regent scowled. Her face was also weary. 'What have we learned, Ella?'

'Gyle's agent, this Red Glove, seeks to bring another factor into play. A glove often symbolises disguise or hidden control. The rolling coin will be about corruption. And lizards often symbolise shapechangers or turncoats.'

Cera took this in with visible dread. 'What can we do, Elena?' she asked at last. 'It could be *anyone*, striking from anywhere.' She huddled into her chair. 'It's all so hopeless – I have to find a way to preserve the family, but our enemies hold all the cards. It is *so* unfair.'

'Life is seldom fair,' Elena pointed out, and Cera glared at her.

'I *know* that. You've told me a million times. We're all sacrificing so much and trying so hard. Why is destroying things so much easier than building them? Why does God let this happen?'

Elena wrinkled her nose. 'Which god? Ahm? Kore? Sol?'

'Any of them! Why should men like Gyle have so much power?'

Elena flopped back against the back of her chair. The divinations had left her dispirited and fighting a losing battle against a migraine. 'The prizes go to the winners, Cera, and there are no rules. Those who play fair and honourably invariably lose: that is the true lesson of life. There are no gods, no justice, only winning.'

Cera hung her head. 'That's so *empty*,' she whispered. 'That's an awful philosophy – you can't actually believe that? You must believe in more, Ella.'

Must I? She rubbed her temples, groaning. *Oh Kore, just let me rest, girl!* 'Of course I do, Cera – we all do. We try to find meaning in whatever we do. I want what we all want: love, happiness, dignity, respect. Security, a good wine and some Brician cheese. And sleep.'

She half-smiled, looking wan. 'I am sorry. I was very poor at Ethics and Philosophy at college.'

Cera rubbed at her temples. 'It's all too much, Ella.' She looked up. 'So all I can do is preserve my family as best I can, however I can.'

Elena nodded sadly. 'That sounds as good a reason as any other.' She clutched her temple. 'Rukking Sordell never got headaches from doing this,' she muttered bitterly.

Cera hugged her and helped her to bed. 'Grazie, Ella. Thank you for everything. ' She kissed Elena's cheek. 'Sleep well,' she added sadly.

'See you in the morning,' Elena moaned, though it was only early evening and she hadn't even eaten. She was unconscious before Cera left the room.

The queen-regent locked the door to her blood-room and went to the window to watch for crows.

'Do you remember the last time I visited Brochena openly, Cera? About two years ago, now – doesn't time fly? Do you remember that little talk we had?' The queen-regent's face coloured as Gyle gave her a conspiratal grin. 'I kept my side of the bargain, didn't I? I've told no one our little secret.'

Cera Nesti's lower lip quivered. She looked like she wanted to flee.

'Your secret is safe with me, Cera,' he put in hastily. 'There is an old Rimoni saying: "Those who share a virtue are bound; but those who share a vice are bound tighter". We share the same vice, Cera. We like to spy on people.'

'I'm not like you at all,' Cera retorted, but her voice was uncertain.

'I rather think you are. Remember when I caught you in the spy-passages in Brochena Palace? You knew them all, didn't you? You used to slither into them late at night to watch your courtiers in their bedchambers.'

Cera hung her head guiltily. 'You said you had something to say that was to my benefit,' she muttered, shifting uncomfortably. 'So speak, or I'll go and tell Elena.'

It was an idle threat, and he ignored it. 'But you shouldn't have spied on me, should you?' He waved an admonishing finger. You just had to know what Elena and I got up to, didn't you? What did Rondian magi do in bed – did they shapechange and rut like demons?'

Cera hid her face in her hands. 'Go away,' she whispered.

'I knew you were there, of course. No one ever sneaks up on me. It must have been disappointing, to see nothing but the curtains.' He leaned towards her, right to the edge of the wards. 'We made a bargain, didn't we: that I'd not tell anyone what you did, if you told me all the secrets you learned.'

Cera nodded mutely as he grinned at her. 'Don't be ashamed: it's natural to want to know secrets. We both share that need. We are bound by our vice, closer than virtue.' He gave an intimate smile. 'Did I not improve the concealment of your secret hideaways, and create wards to muffle sound better? Did I not keep them secret from Elena?' He smiled. 'We are very alike indeed, Queen-Regent.'

The girl was curled into the window-box like a foetus in the womb, but she was listening to every word as he went on reeling her in. 'Cera, you still creep through those passages, don't you? You know all their vices, don't you: Pita Rosco's affairs; Comte Inveglio's money problems; young Prato's penchant for self-flagellation, even Lorenzo di Kestria's ambition. How it must burn you, to know that the people you rely on are so unworthy of trust!'

'Elena says that I can trust them,' Cera whimpered.

'Ah, but can you trust Elena?'

'I have to,' she whispered hoarsely.

'No, Cera – no, you don't have to trust her at all.'

'I won't hear this,' she hissed, but still she made no move to leave.

'Watch her with Lorenzo di Kestria. If Timori died, there would be no Nesti with the right lineage to stand for the kingship. Which way would your faction vote? Why, to your trusted allies, the Kestrians – yet you allow this same man to guard your very life . . .'

'Elena has read his thoughts – she says he is true—'

'Which is why I say: watch him and Elena. Be warned, Cera: he conspires against you. With Elena as his consort, he could seize the kingdom.'

'She's loyal to me – she has sworn—'

'But he can give her things you can't, Cera, a strong lusty young man like that.'

Her face twisted as if she'd swallowed a beetle. He watched his words take root, watched them burn through her mind and distort her feelings. *I have you, my little queen-regent. Now to reel you in.*

'Cera, I know you struggle to trust me. I am a mercenary, we both know that, and my loyalty can be bought. But I tell you this for free: only I can preserve your rule. Elena believes you will fail, so she seeks to tie herself to the Kestrians. But I believe in *you*, Cera. We are so alike, and our interests are so aligned that it must be destiny: I want this realm stable and disconnected from the shihad, and this will preserve your rule. Elena and the Kestrians want to drag Javon into disaster while selling you into marriage slavery to the Jhafi. Only I can save you, Cera.'

A door rattled and the queen-regent started guiltily. He felt a thrill of fear as he heard Elena calling. Cera glared at him, rubbing her eyes furiously. 'How can I believe a word you say?'

'Watch Lorenzo and Elena,' he told her, 'then you will know.'

Elena called again, 'Cera?'

He gave the girl his most reassuring smile, while wishing he could just slide his gnosis through the wards and seize her soul. 'Farewell, for now,' he whispered and broke the connection.

29

Envoy

The Leviathan Bridge

*For all the destruction its making has enabled, I still am in awe of the Bridge
itself, and I say this without reservation or cynicism (no, really). What a thing
it is, this wonder Antonin Meiros wrought! To stand upon that span, hundreds
of miles from land, is the stuff of dreams. If I close my eyes, I can still hear the
waters roar and feel the thrumming of the stone beneath my feet. I have seen
wonders, palaces and Dom-al'Ahms and holy places . . . but it is that Bridge that
I will remember until my last breath.*

MYRON JEMSON, ARGUNDIAN, IN JOURNEYS EASTWARDS,

901

*Hebusalim, on the continent of Antiopia
Jumada (Maicin) 928
2 months until the Moontide*

Ramita sat upon a stool watching the bustle in the main courtyard
of Casa Meiros. Huriya sat at her feet, watching just as avidly as men
scurried like monkeys on bamboo scaffolding, lashing the thick poles
together to create a temporary pavilion. Tradesmen were filling the
kitchens with meat, spices, lentils, olives and flour. The air was rich
with baking breads and slowly simmering spiced meats. It had been
like this for the past week, but this finally was the day. Her husband
was coming home, and he was bringing his important guests, ferang
envoys. She was clad in a new sky-blue salwar, the colour Meiros
favoured most. Though she was enduring morning sickness, her condition was not obvious yet.

468

But soon my belly will grow and grow, like Mother's does, and I will turn into an elephant . . .

Someone below shouted and silk curtains of soft yellow and white to block the sun unfurled down the sides of the pavilion. Musicians were setting up and tuning in a corner. Olaf was shrilling orders, wringing his hands, the stress almost too much for him.

It was weeks since Ramita had seen Kazim, and she could scarcely remember that madness of desire. Her husband was kindness and gentleness embodied; why had she ever wanted another man? What had she risked everything for: a few frantic couplings? Ridiculous – *suicidal . . .*

There was still no sign of any manifesting of the gnosis, and it gnawed at her. How long would it be before her husband or his daughter suspected the truth about her pregnancy? Though Meiros' visits home had been sporadic these last few weeks, Justina was increasingly present, personally inspecting every tradesman and servant who entered, frightening them all with her cold manner and visible use of the gnosis as she rummaged through their minds. Even Huriya dared not bring Kazim or Jai here now.

To her surprise she missed Meiros' company. Though she could not say she truly loved him, he made her feel safe. And she increasingly craved the animal heat of mating; perhaps the pregnancy was turning her into an earthier being. Though he was not the lover she'd dreamed of, her husband pleased her – and at least lying with him wouldn't have her stoned to death.

'You should run,' she told Huriya daily, but her adopted sister refused, promising to stay with her no matter what. So she hung on, in hope and desperation that somehow the babies had been fathered by Meiros. Or perhaps she was just paralysed by fear.

She feared Justina's eyes upon her too. She had shown no interest before, but now she was watching her all the time. Perhaps she envied her state? Not that she was any more pleasant; she never included Ramita in her afternoon teas or gaily-lit parties in her private garden, where she and a stream of magi women could be heard singing and dancing to music from both continents. Instead Ramita and Huriya were left to rot in their chambers, excluded, but always watched.

Her only consolation was in her faith: daily she offered long, intense prayers to Sivraman and Parvasi: for her family back home in Baranasi; for Jai and Kazim, who she hoped had seen sense and fled; for the manifestation that would prove the children were Meiros'. Mostly she prayed for her death, should her perfidy be revealed, to be swift and painless. She could not say if the gods heard her.

'Ramita, there you are.' Justina Meiros stepped from the archway behind them, her flawless face cowled. 'You should already be inside; come,' she ordered peremptorily, and led the way. The girls trailed in her wake as they made their way down to the pavilion. They were seated beneath the cool drapes just in time. Ramita's place was at the front, to the right of the main seat where her husband would sit. On his left would be the guest of honour, this Rondian man Belonius Vult. The chairs were massive, carved and cushioned, draped with yellow and blue silks. She had a moment of fright, that she, a market-girl of Baranasi, was to eat with these lofty people. It was not twelve months since she had been taken from her home. It was frightening, how quickly life could change.

Jos Klein led an honour guard into the pavilion, and Ramita felt a small flutter of comfort when her husband appeared behind the guards. His eyes sought hers. He looked tired but energised. His shaven skull gleamed in the soft light within the tent, and his short beard jutted in exactly the style she had cut it. She forced a fond smile to her lips. *This is my husband, whom my secret lover wants to kill.* The thought made her hand quiver and she buried it deep.

Behind Meiros glided a silver-maned man with a trim beard and cheeks smooth as a child. He carried himself with the utmost elegance. His imperial purple robes were rich and lined with gold. Presumably he was the Imperial Legate, Belonius Vult. Behind him was a man she assumed must be Governor Tomas Betillon, a wary, sullen-looking man with wobbling jowls wearing half-armour. Huriya said there'd been several attempts on his life; she'd picked up tales in the markets about this man stealing children from the streets. But everyone here was according him careful deference.

Following them were a dozen more men, eight Ordo Costruo magi and four Rondian magi, aides to the governor or the Imperial Legate. She rose to her feet as Meiros approached and he kissed Ramita's cheek in greeting. 'Wife, you look radiant,' he whispered. He kissed Justina and turned to present the Rondians. 'Lord Belonius Vult, let me present my wife, Ramita.'

She took a breath, curtsied, and proffered a hand, keeping her eyes lowered. She felt a cool grip and lips pressed against her hand. 'Honoured, lady, my congratulations on your impending mother-hood.' Vult's voice was pleasant and smooth. When she looked up, his eyes measured her distantly.

'And my daughter, Justina Meiros,' Meiros continued.

Vult turned to take Justina's hand, but she withheld it, to Ramita's surprise. Vult acted as if nothing had happened. 'Lady Justina, a pleasure to see you again. Has it truly been twelve years?'

'During the last Crusade, Lord Vult: I believe I was trying to prevent your men from sacking a healers' refuge.' Justina's voice was chilly.

'I recall it well. War is a terrible thing, lady. A shocking waste.'

'Yes, it is always far easier to plunder uncontested.' Justina turned to Betillon. 'I have met Governor Betillon before. Introductions are not necessary.' Her look was as icy as her voice. Betillon grunted dismissively and ignored her. He peered curiously at Ramita, but made no move to greet her.

Antonin Meiros ignored the awkwardness and gestured for them all to sit. Drinks were served; Ramita had sherbet, but Justina had no compunction about drinking alcohol with the men. The conver-sation revolved about the loquacious Belonius Vult, who was full of anecdotes: Rondian aversion to spices; the quality of Dhassan jewellery; the forthcoming wine harvests; the difficulty with head-winds this month flying over the ocean, and other trivialities, which he directed at Meiros, Justina and Betillon. Antonin clearly found his company genial, and even Justina seemed to thaw somewhat.

By contrast, Betillon was a disgusting eater and drank heavily. He barely followed the conversation. His eyes trailed lingeringly over Justina's breasts and occasionally Ramita's, but he was not openly rude. The rest of the table interacted congenially, but pinned between Antonin and Justina, Ramita said little and ate less. Finally Belonius Vult addressed a question to her, asking with a smile, 'And when are we to expect your happy event, Lady Ramita?'

'Early next year, lord,' she replied, flustered at being noticed.

'Ah, so you are, what, two months along?' Vult remarked. He turned to Meiros. 'Tell me, Antonin, is it true what they say about the wives of Ascendants and gestational manifestation?'

Antonin smiled proudly. 'We are awaiting the first signs. It could happen any day.'

Vult inclined his head and looked at Ramita. 'And are you prepared for the manifestation, Lady Ramita? Are you ready to become a mage?'

'I don't know how any woman could call herself ready for such a thing, milord,' she answered carefully, and Meiros nodded approvingly at this answer. Beyond him, she saw Betillon glowering in silent contempt, no doubt at the thought of another non-Rondian gaining the gnosis in this manner.

Meiros caught and deflected other questions cast her way, then she was packed off to allow the men to discuss their business. Justina left too, gracing Vult and her father with a curt inclination of the head.

Huriya met Ramita outside. 'How was it?' she whispered.

Ramita glanced at Justina. 'It went well, I think.'

Justina looked back at her coldly. 'Well enough.' She looked like she wanted to spit. 'I loathe breathing the same air as that bastard Betillon.' She stomped away without a backwards glance.

Huriya whispered in Ramita's ear, 'She's grumpier every day.'

'I think she's sad,' Ramita commented.

'I think she's a bitch,' sniffed Huriya. 'Perhaps her lover has dumped her.'

'What lover?' Ramita wondered. 'No one ever comes here.'

Huriya wrinkled her nose. 'Who knows? She has her own apartment in the Domus Costruo. There's someone, I'm sure – or there was.'

Ramita remembered Justina arriving with Rashid Mubarak at the Domus Costruo banquet and swallowed a nasty taste in her mouth.

'Madam does not wish to be disturbed at the moment,' Olaf said.

'I don't care, I need to see her,' Ramita snapped. She shoved past the chamberlain and into Justina's courtyard. Seeing the fountain where Alyssa had taught her Rondian while plundering her memories brought on a sweat. She rang the bell that hung in the garden, then sought shade. The air was dry, a desiccating southeasterly raking the city. Nothing moved between midday and sunset now; people slept, or lay in the shade and tried not to move. Even the plump purple flies grew dozy and slow.

Justina emerged looking as if she had just risen from her bed, though it was early afternoon. Her shapeless mantle looked like it had been thrown on and her feet were bare. She ran fingers through her tangled midnight tresses, yawned and asked, 'Well, what is it?'

Ramita made a supplicating gesture. 'Justina, I need your advice, please. It's been two months and I have no sign of your "gnosis manifestations". My husband is busy; he hasn't had time to tell me what they are, what they look like. I need to know – it's making me anxious.'

Justina Meiros rolled her eyes, but she sat on a stone bench and gestured for Ramita to join her. This close, her hair gave off a redolent scent, one Ramita recognised at once from the backstreets of Aruna Nagar. *Opium.* Her pupils were dilated and her movements languid.

Ramita wrinkled her nose and made to stand. 'I'm sorry, mistress, you are engaged. I will go.'

Justina caught her arm and pulled her back down. Ramita realised she was naked beneath her mantle, and smelled of sweat and arousal. She edged away, wishing she had never come.

'No, you've already interrupted me,' Justina said in a slurred voice. 'The manifestations can happen any time in the first trimester, according to the scrolls. At first you'll think you're ill, or hearing voices, then something'll happen, a little accident, usually related to the element that you'll be most closely bound to – you might set fire to something, or push your fingers into a wall. It's like what happens to teenagers when they first attain their gnosis. I torched a prayer-book in a fit of temper when I was twelve. Something similar will happen to you.' She slumped back against the wall.

Ramita rose, wanting only to get away. 'Thank you. I'm sorry to have disturbed you.'

Justina looked her with glazed, suspicious eyes. 'That's assuming your pregnancy is due to my father, of course,' she said with slow hostility, 'because the other reason nothing has happened yet could simply be that nothing *will* happen, because like your little maid you've been rukking some guardsman or servant while everyone's back is turned.' She stared at Ramita with the insolent appraisal of the drunk.

Ramita's heart skipped a beat and it took all her strength to turn back and glare at Justina as if the suggestion were beneath her contempt.

Antonin Meiros came home properly two weeks later, late in Maicin. Ramita bathed his feet. Her belly felt tighter, and she could see it beginning to swell. Her mother had always got big early and she expected she would too.

'Twins, or triplets?' Meiros smiled, touching her belly fondly.

Ramita's mind was full of anxieties: about Justina, about the babies and whose they were, about Kazim and Jai, about Huriya's refusal to abandon her. But she kept her thoughts still and quiet. She smiled and asked him of his day.

Meiros was morose after the negotiations: 'Betillon is a pig. His very presence undermines everything. Vult says the emperor wants to re-establish peace and trade, with new borders and a market between, in the no-man's-land. It would sound reasonable were it not that Hebusalim is not theirs, that the Rondian Imperial Treasury is drowning in debt and there are already forty legions massed in Pontus. They will not keep their word.'

'What will we do?' Ramita asked anxiously.

'We will move to Domus Costruo. No force on Urte can storm our Citadel without magi-support. Our priority is the safety of our families and the Bridge.'

'Can you not stop the Rondians from crossing this time?'

Meiros sighed heavily. 'The Inquisitors control Southpoint and Northpoint, my dear. The time for that is lost.' He stroked his shaven scalp regretfully. 'There are so many Rondians here permanently now; half of the Hebb have direct commercial links to them. They are all threatened by the shihad. Even if I could shut the Bridge, Salim's armies would still run amok: he will slaughter anyone who has ever dealt with them. It would be a bloodbath. That cannot be allowed to happen. We must ride this out, protect who we can and pray for a return to peaceful trade when this period is over.

'People forget all the Ordo Costruo have done for them: buildings, aqueducts, healing orders, and trade. The Bridge was the greatest agency for good this place had ever seen, and through it money has also flowed into Yuros. Emperor Constant must eventually realise that his crusades are cutting the throat of the goose that lays golden eggs. Vult himself acknowledges that these invasions have almost bankrupted the empire. I am sure he will come to reason and seek peace – I know it.' He stroked her tight belly. 'And our children will preside over that peace, my dear wife.'

She forced a smile. Her husband's hopes sounded blind to her, but what did she know of statecraft? For a second, his shaven head looked like a skull. Then he yawned cavernously and his head fell forward onto his chest. He started, and looked down at her. 'I'm sorry, my dear, I'm falling asleep. Will you help me to my room?'

She helped him to his bed but when he rolled on his side and offered her a space, she feigned illness and bid him goodnight – not because she had not wanted to stay: the idea of curling under his protective wing and pretending all was well was very attractive. But to stay felt like an act of betrayal, both to him and to herself.

This is the man my lover wants to kill.

30

Dressed to Steal

'Magic Spells'

Prior to the Ascendancy of Corineus, all cultures had in their folklore tales of magic – the ability to do the inexplicable and miraculous. Many of the words used now in the practice of the Gnostic Arts are derived from such sources – wizard, sorcerer, spell; the list goes on. We magi know that the ability to wield the gnosis does not depend on saying special magic words, but the myth persists among the common people.

ORDO COSTRUO COLLEGIATE, PONTUS

Norostein, Noros, on the continent of Yuros
Maicin 928
2 months until the Moontide

As soon as his father left for Pontus, Alaron and his friends started a systematic surveillance of the Governor's Palace, and discovered Belonius Vult was to be absent for two more weeks at least. The three felt a little like the infamous Kaden Rats, a group of magi who'd turned to crime half a century before and subsequently led the authorities a merry dance through Bricia and Argundy. 'Of course, the Kaden Rats were pure-blood nobles, not a ragtag group of rejects like us,' Ramon noted. He'd put himself in charge of the plan to break in: 'I'm a Silacian,' he told them. 'It has to be me.'

The top floor of the Merry Magpie Inn commanded a fine view of the palace's back entrance. The window seats were perfectly placed for them to reconnoître the movement of guards. Alaron made soft comments that Ramon surreptitiously noted down or sketched. The table was littered with goblets; the boys had been there all after-noon. They were the only customers in the upstairs room so busi-ness was nonexistent for Prissy, the bored-looking prostitute in the corner.

A barmaid came up and scooped up the empties. 'Another round, young sirs?'

'Mmm,' murmured Ramon, not looking up from his notepad.

Alaron jerked around. 'Huh? Yeah, sure.'

The barmaid looked at the empties, then at the bored whore. 'You lads ain't paid for nothing yet, nor spent any coin with Prissy. I'm thinking it's time I saw the colour of your money.'

Ramon absently flashed a gold Silacian auros and she nodded her approval.

'You've got an auros?' said Alaron when she'd gone.

'It's a *Silacian* auros – it's mostly lead. I wouldn't swap a Rondian silver for it, but these morons don't know that.' He glanced at Prissy, who had caught the glint of gold and was now heading for their table. Her breasts were almost hanging out of her dress. 'Alaron, could you help that poor girl – her laces have come undone.' He went back to his writing.

Prissy waggled herself helpfully at Alaron, who did his best to look the other way. 'Well?' she said in something approximating a seductive purr, 'wanna bury your face in these?'

'He doesn't,' Ramon said without looking up, 'he's saving himself for the woman of his dreams. Which is rather sad as she's not inter-ested.' He rummaged in his pouch and produced a silver Silacian foli, which he pressed into her hands. 'Look, take this and go away. I'll treble it if you never talk to us again.'

'Quadruple it and you've got a deal.'

Ramon frowned. 'You want me to pay you four foli *not* to bed you?'

She shrugged. 'It was your idea.'

'What's your normal rate?'

'Three silver.'

'So you're saying you want *three* to sleep with you and *four* if we don't?'

'Um, yeah.'

'Okay, here's another two. Start without me and I'll catch you up later.' She pouted and stomped away, but not before she'd pocketed the coins. Alaron tried to work out who had won that exchange, but gave up and went back to thinking about Cym.

The next round arrived. Ramon took a slurp of sour red wine, winced slightly and let a cheery smile play across his face. He was clearly enjoying playing at criminals.

'By the way, Cym *is* interested in me,' Alaron told him. 'I'm just waiting for the right moment.'

'Uh-huh. In your dreams, lanky. Is there still a man in the watch-tower?'

Alaron peered back to the palace. 'Yes, but he'll come down at dusk. Anyway, Cym came back and helped me when I was at my lowest point. She gave me a periapt, free of charge.'

'Nothing is free, Alaron: she *owns* you, as if she didn't already. I bet she's tried to talk you into giving the *you-know-what* to her Rimoni pals if we get it.'

'No, she hasn't.' He decided not to mention Cym's suggestion of the Ordo Costruo.

'We don't want to start a war with it, Al. We should just keep it secret and live quiet lives of luxury and crime,' said Ramon with relish.

'I'm not a thief and neither is Cym—'

'Oh please, she's *Rimoni*: to be a gypsy is to lead a life of crime.'

'They used to have an empire,' Alaron retorted.

'And they lost it and were nearly wiped out. Now they're forbidden the ownership or even the rent of land so of course they're all thieves now. I'm just being realistic. If we take the view that we're totally in it for ourselves, then we can quietly set about accumulating money without having to make awkward choices that will all lead to war and misery anyway. It makes perfect sense.'

'But it's not *right*.'

'According to who? Alaron, you need to dry behind your ears. The Rondians run the world because they're the biggest pack of bullies, not because they're nice people – they've got nine-tenths of the magi, including all the most powerful ones. They tax us and demand tribute from us and generally roger us up the arse, and why? Because they can! If they realise someone has found their precious Scytale, they're going to smash the pillars of heaven to get it back.'

'But by then we'll be Ascendants too.'

'Al, it took the first Ascendants *years* to master the gnosis. You and I aren't in the same field as them in terms of knowledge and skill, regardless of our blood-strength. Even as Ascendants we wouldn't last ten minutes against the Pallas Kirkegarde. If we find this thing, we'll need to keep it utterly secret.'

Alaron scowled, trying to think of a rational counter-argument, but he couldn't. 'It's just not *right*.'

Ramon rolled his eyes and went back to his mapping.

'Why are we so rubbish at the gnosis?' Alaron asked miserably.

Ramon frowned. 'Speak for yourself. I'm competent enough; it's just that I'm only a sixteenth-blood. That's the lowest you can be without having no power at all. But I get by.'

'Yeah, but I'm a quarter-blood. There are lots of quarter-bloods who are accounted powerful, so what's wrong with me?'

Ramon fixed him in the eye. 'You really want to know?'

Alaron blinked. 'Of course!'

Ramon reached out and tweaked his nose. 'It's because you have no self-confidence. You don't believe in yourself and you're afraid of the gnosis.'

Alaron had been preparing himself for something complicated and beyond his control, not *this*. He was silent for a moment, then said vehemently, 'I do have confidence! I know a spell will work when I cast it – I'm only afraid when doing the sorcery stuff, you know that. Hel, if I can fight Malevorn knowing right from the start I'm going to lose, then I'm hardly going to be afraid of a little spell not working, am I?'

Ramon shrugged. 'Suit yourself. It's pretty clear to everyone else. You fight Malevorn because you can't control your temper, but you've never once believed you'd beat him.'

'He's a pure-blood – I never stood a chance—'

'Of course you didn't – because you were mentally already beaten. You were just feeding his ego. If you'd really wanted to take him down you'd have knifed him in his sleep. You never tried to win, you were just fighting to get a badge of honour that said "I tried".' Ramon tapped the table. 'Your first experience of the gnosis was to see your mother's face and all her nightmares. It's no wonder you're petrified by what the gnosis can do.'

Alaron felt like he'd been slapped. 'I thought you were my friend!'

'I *am* your friend, idiot. That's why I'm telling you this. Look, once you accept the gnosis and learn to fight to win, you'll master all your fears and become a half-decent mage. So harden up, stop doubting and believe in yourself. It really is that simple.'

Alaron hung his head. 'So why didn't *you* do something about Malevorn?'

'Because it was an Arcanum tiff. It wasn't important. You might think college is the beginning and end of the universe, but the truth is that all that shit is just trivia. You'll have forgotten it all in a few years – or you should have. Alaron, just *toughen up*. We're in the middle of something that could be truly huge and if you're going to play your part, you need to put your best foot forward.' Ramon leaned forward. 'I've learned more in six months in a Silacian village than I ever did in college. The familioso stuff, it isn't pretty.' His voice took on a haunted quality. 'At home I'm the familioso problem-solver: someone has a problem, they go to the Pater, and he sends for me. I fix it. You're still sheltered from that side of life, but you won't be for long. Harden up, amici.'

'How?'

Ramon rolled his eyes, then put a hand over Alaron's. 'Mostly you need to stop thinking negatively about yourself. Never say "I can't"; say "I can". Be positive.' He took a sip of beer. 'Alaron, inside your shell of insecurity and incompetence is a tenacious mage and a natural leader – I see flashes of it when you lose your temper. But you need to draw that out of yourself while you're calm.'

Alaron wrinkled his nose. 'I can't— Uh, okay, I'll try.'

'Don't *try* – *do*.'

'And you can do all this?'

Ramon grinned. 'Of course. I'm a genius.'

Ramon's access to the legion barracks and battle-mage records room gave him the opportunity to copy the plans of the palace. 'It was so damned easy it was embarrassing: one look at my legion badge and that overrode any concern of me being Silacian. Complacency, that is what it is.'

He built them a three-dimensional map of the palace using Earthgnosis and sat back, grinning smugly as the others examined it. Alaron contributed some tiny illusory guards and had them walk the routes he had observed so they could work out the blind spots. They really did feel like the Kaden Rats reborn.

The five-storey Governor's Palace was in the shape of a massive H, with a massive sloping roof and a turret at each point and at every intersection. The ground floor of the governor's wing was dedicated to entertaining, and linked to the huge kitchens. The second floor was given over to more intimate entertaining and decorated with statues, art, rare artefacts and treasures of the state. The third floor was for staff facilities – the great central staircase bypassed it completely. The fourth floor, guest suites, was almost always empty. The top floor, which enjoyed fine sunset views, was for the use of the family of the governor, though Vult had been widowed some years previously and his only child was grown up and lived in Pallas.

'The study and his bedroom are on the top level,' Cym noted, 'but which one will have his personal stuff?'

'Study, I'd think,' Ramon replied.

'No, bedroom,' Cym replied. 'This is stuff he only thinks about occasionally. He'll have secretaries and servants coming and going in the study.'

'We shouldn't restrict ourselves to those two rooms,' Alaron said. 'Remember Fyrell lecturing us on protecting valuables? There are two ways you can do it: one, you load up wardings and hope no one comes who is too strong for you; or you go for stealth and cunning and hide them under veiling spells, relying on outwitting any enemies who might come looking. The problem with wardings is that they're detectable to other magi; they basically say "here are my valuables – are you good enough to take them?" That doesn't sound like Vult to me.'

They mulled that over. 'What will we be facing?' Ramon asked. 'What studies does Vult use?'

Alaron put his hand up. 'I can tell you that,' he announced. 'Like all good Noros babies, I was raised on stories of the Revolt. I found this one in Ma's library.' He brandished a battered copy of *Generals of the Glorious Revolt*. 'It say here that Belonius Vult is "a noble and urbane general beloved of the people. He is at his most deadly to the craven foe in the arts of Sorcery and the elements of Air and Water. His mastery of Divination allows him to foresee all turns of the game." He grinned at them. 'It was written prior to Lukhazan, obviously. But it does give us an idea what we'll be facing.'

'If he's mostly a diviner and clairvoyant, he'll be of limited use when it comes to protecting his stuff,' Ramon commented. 'Most sorcery is fairly limited unless you're there in person. And Air-magery is not great for traps, and nor is Water. This is good – I was worried he'd be a Fire-mage, and have all sorts of nastiness waiting for us.'

'What if he used a friend, like this teacher Fyrell, to enhance his defences?' Cym wondered aloud.

'It's not impossible,' Ramon acknowledged, 'but it would take a lot of trust for him to leave his defences in the hands of someone who could deactivate them, rob him and then reactivate, all the time playing the innocent. I don't think Belonius Vult is the sort of person who gives out trust like alms on Beggars Day.'

'What does your book say about General Langstrit, Alaron?' Cym asked.

Alaron found the page. 'Here it is: Ha! You'll like this: "Though from Argundy's far vales, Jarius Langstrit heard the resounding call for freedom and came prepared to expend his blood upon the slopes of this mountain kingdom for the cause of justice. A master of the elements, the fell-handed Argundian loves nothing better than to bring the wrath of fire and lightning upon the foe, whilst his illusions cloak the presence of our boys from the cowering cheese-munchers". "Cowering cheese-munchers" – I love it!'

Ramon pulled a face. 'So the general is an Elementalist – handy, but Sorcery is the weakness of Elementalists. Ordinary runic magic should be fine, provided I can get him to do anything. What about any spirit-guardians Vult might have left?'

'No problem,' Alaron answered. 'Vult's not a Wizard, or a Necromancer.'

'But how are we going to get inside?' Cym wondered.

Ramon put his hands behind his head and leaned back. 'We'll get in. We just need to investigate a bit more and a way will open to us. Trust me.'

Alaron looked at Cym. 'Did the Silacian familioso just say "trust me"?'

'Alaron?' a vaguely familiar voice called as he walked up to the Governor's Palace; he'd planned on going inside this time, to see what kind of reception area there was, how it was manned and guarded. He wore a cloth cap and a light scarf despite the heat, but it obviously hadn't been disguise enough. So much for getting in without attracting any notice. 'Alaron Mercer?'

He cursed under his breath and looked up into a freckled face framed by braided blonde hair. He groaned internally: his almost-fiancée Gina Weber. 'Uh, hello Gina,' he responded as he sought an excuse to move on.

Gina was wearing a grey dress and a modest headscarf covered the braids which showed she was still unmarried, but there was an engagement ring on her left hand. She was smiling like he was an old friend. 'It is you – I thought it was! What have you been up to?'

'Oh, looking after Ma, mostly. Dad's gone east on business. Not much, you know.'

Some of the desolation of his reply must have triggered her memory, for she suddenly coloured and apologised. 'I'm so sorry about the graduation thing. It seemed very unfair.'

'Tell the governor that,' Alaron snapped, regretting it when she flinched. 'Sorry, Gina, it's not your fault. Anyway, we're still trying to petition the governor – better get on, eh?' He tried to walk away, but she came with him.

'I hope your petition is successful, I really do. I thought you were – well, you know, a decent person.'

He swallowed, suddenly a little choked up. It had never occurred to him to worry about what she thought of him. 'Yeah, well, thanks for that, Gina. No hard feelings. You seemed like a decent person too.' He met her eyes, possibly for the first time ever. 'Good luck with your marriage to that Brician fellow.'

Her face clouded. 'We won't actually marry until he gets back from the Crusade,' she said quietly.

'Well, I hope he makes it. What was his name again?'

'Blayne de Noellen. His father has a big estate and lots of horses near Fellanton. He's from an old half-blood line, like our family. Father was quite pleased—'

'Good, good— Excuse me, Gina, but I have to go.' He fought an unexpected sense of regret – not that he had really wanted to marry her, but that future had been safe, normal. Now here he was, contemplating a crime that could get him executed. 'Goodbye, Gina.'

'Watch out at the governor's office,' she said suddenly. 'There's a young mage there who's an absolute creep. He's their security man now that the legions have marched. He keeps propositioning me, the slime.'

'Any useful battle-magi has gone east, so I'm told,' Alaron remarked. 'Just the arseholes and losers left, huh?' he couldn't help adding morosely.

'I don't think you're either of those things, Alaron,' Gina told him. 'Good luck – let me know how it goes. I'm around here a lot. Unmarried mage-women like me who aren't good at fighting or healing do most of the communication tasks. I'm working as personal secretary to the watch captain.'

'Jeris Muhren?'

'Yes,' she sighed. 'He's wonderful. If you'd like to meet him one day I could arrange it – he already knows about you. I've heard him dictating letters to the governor on your behalf.'

Alaron felt a flicker of surprise: so Muhren hadn't been lying when he claimed to be trying to help him. 'I've met him already. Look, thanks, Gina, but I've got to go. I might see you around.'

She gave him an encouraging smile. 'Good luck, Alaron.'

He set off, then turned back. 'Do you know Malevorn Andevarion?' he asked her, trying to sound indifferent. Her resultant blush told him all he needed to know. He stomped away.

He climbed the stairs to the west wing, passing assorted guards and statuary. Inside was a cavernous foyer, filled with more statues, including a huge one of Vult, and ceiling murals of the Alps. A bored-looking man sat at a large desk confronting rows of men and women of all ages. The room had an oppressive air of stillness, as if the supplicants had been there so long that invisible spiders had woven unseen webs about them.

Alaron sat as if he were another petitioner and began to take mental note of what he could see of the lay-out.

'Alaron Mercer,' purred a voice behind his shoulder that made him shudder.

Alaron stood warily, confronting Gron Koll. The last time he had seen Koll's sallow face, Muhren had just pounded it into a pillar. Sadly, Koll had healed, but the cure for acne still eluded him. He was wearing the red and blue uniform of the governor's staff. 'Koll. I'd heard only the dregs were still in town. I guess seeing you here proves it.'

Gron Koll allowed a faint sneer to curl his lips, as though baiting by inferiors were beneath his contempt now. 'The best men get the best positions, Mercer. Only the knuckleheads went east. The clever ones don't need to go grubbing around deserts to make their fortunes. I'm Personal Aide to Acting-Governor Besko. He's got his eye on you. And so have I, you and your little group of foreign scum that hang around your father's house day and night. Does your gypsy slut give good sport?'

Alaron fought the urge to hit the smirking youth whilst quelling alarm at the news that their house was being watched. 'You and Besko are a lovely couple. Let me know when you decide to make it official.' He turned his back to go.

Unseen fists gripped his throat, squeezing the air from his windpipe whilst lifting him kicking and choking into the air. He was peripherally aware of shocked supplicants staring as he fought to breathe through Koll's gnosis-choke. He was horribly afraid that Koll would probe his mind, but instead Koll just giggled as he spun Alaron slowly in the air. His vision started turning ragged, coming in and out of focus, and he felt himself beginning to black out when he was dumped on the floor, cracking his skull as he fell. He gasped for air like a beached fish as heavy hands picked him up and he was half-dragged, half-carried out the door and down the steps. The two watchmen left him sprawled on the ground in front of a small group of onlookers. He lay there, trying to inhale through tortured throat muscles.

Koll's voice slithered into his mind from the top of the stairs. <*Come here again and it'll be worse, you lowbred scum.*>

'Alaron?' Gina Weber bent over him and soothing, balm-like gnosis suffused his throat muscles until blessed air flowed in without pain once more. He coughed and retched.

'Gina, darling, don't waste your time on that failure. Tomorrow night after work, perhaps?' Gron Koll called, his voice oily and mocking. 'Wear that lovely green dress.'

Gina ignored him as she helped Alaron to his feet. 'You know him? Oh, that's right – he was one of Mal's friends. What a creep,' she murmured. 'Come on, I'll help you home.'

It's 'Mal' still, is it? Alaron let her steady him until his legs regained their full strength and he was able to stand under his own steam. 'Thanks Gina,' he croaked. 'I can make it from here.'

She looked at him with a pitying face. 'Is there anything I can do?'

He shook his head, feeling nothing but helpless rage at Koll, Gavius, Muhren and everyone else who had ruined his future. *When we've solved this Langstrit mystery, I'm going to leave here and never look back.* He glared at her, then remembered his manners and softened his look. 'Sorry. Thanks again, Gina.'

'That's okay,' she said quietly, looking at him oddly, almost as if he were a child. 'Well, then. Nice to see you,' she said, slightly awkwardly, and backed away.

She actually *wanted* to marry me, it dawned on him. It wasn't a peripheral thing, not to her. *What on Urte did she see in me?* 'See you around then,' he muttered and fled.

They set the evening of Torsdai, 22 Maicin as the night for their raid on the Governor's Residence. Ramon reacted with vindictive delight at the thought that Gron Koll would be guarding the building. 'We knew some mage or other would be there – good to know it's that bastard.'

Alaron frowned. 'I'm not so sure. Koll is no pushover.'

'It's ideal! For one, he's a known quantity. We know what he's good at – Illusion, obviously, and Air-gnosis – so we know how to beat him. Two, I've been wanting the chance to beat the shit out of him for seven years.'

'He's not easy,' Alaron warned. 'We've both duelled him at college. He's tough to beat.'

'It won't be a square fight,' Ramon said. 'We can't afford the time and noise. He has to go down with one hit.'

'No killing,' Cym warned them. 'It doesn't matter how much you hate him, we can't afford that.'

The boys muttered their reluctant agreement.

'Good,' she pronounced, 'because I've thought of the best way to do this . . .'

So it was that Alaron found himself wearing a large green dress and a pale blue half-cloak, and thus cowled, with Ramon on his arm, he tried to walk like a woman through the twilight streets. 'This is the worst plan ever,' he muttered sourly.

'Hush, gorgeous,' Ramon hissed.

'Arsehole! You should be the one in the dress. You might even like it.'

Ramon stifled laughter. 'You look lovely, Alaron. Good enough to kiss.'

Alaron scowled. 'Don't you dare!'

'Shhh! And don't pull faces, you'll spoil the effect.'

Gina was a moderately tall girl, bigger than Cym or Ramon, and only a fraction smaller than Alaron. Her hair was a problem, but Cym had somehow came up with a blonde wig. After that, it didn't really take much work at all to make the transformation, especially with some judicious use of normal disguising techniques: a little padding here, a little make-up there. They even pierced his ears so he could wear earrings. He felt mortified, a complete fool, and his ears stung, but Cym was right: it did have to be him.

'One moment you're telling me to toughen up, next moment you're putting me in a frock,' he complained.

Ramon chuckled. 'Part of being tough is taking a hit for your friends, Al. Doesn't have to be a physical blow – being tough enough to put on a dress is part of being in a team.'

'Really?'

'Absolutely.' Then Ramon spoiled the pep talk by bursting into uncontrollable laughter.

The sun was gone and the waning moon hung in the eastern sky. There weren't many abroad in the streets, and the Watchmen weren't about to harass a girl on the arm of a battle-mage, so they were left alone as they headed for the private entrance to the Governor's Palace. It hadn't taken much research to find out that the governor's new aide was using the guest rooms of the Residence; Koll was ill-liked among the staff, to no one's surprise.

Ramon left Alaron at the corner of the square and went to join the others in a nearby alley. Alaron crossed the plaza, his head bowed, trying to walk like a woman and praying he didn't meet anyone.

He wasn't that lucky.

'Hello, young Gina,' came a rough warm voice, and Alaron stole a glance, pursing his lips. Damn! Some young bureaucrat, he couldn't think of the name. He hoped Gina wasn't too friendly towards him normally.

'Hello.' He used Shaping to soften his tones and Mesmerism to encourage the other to find him as expected, just as he'd practised for the last two days. It must have worked, because the young man appeared to be taken in.

'Visiting someone?' he asked curiously.

'Just a friend,' Alaron said softly, flicking his head at the Residence.

The young official screwed his face up. 'Gron Koll?' he said disgustedly. 'Well, there's no accounting for taste, but I'd have thought better of an *engaged* woman like you.' He tipped his cap tersely and marched away.

Sorry about your reputation, Gina. Once he was sure the young man was out of sight he hurried on: the third night-bell had already sounded. He would only get one chance if Koll was there. Failure would be fatal. He came to the servants' door and knocked, his hand trembling.

He had to wait for a several seconds before a middle-aged woman's voice called, 'Who's there?'

Alaron summoned all his courage and spoke in Gina's voice. 'I'm here to visit Master Koll.'

He heard a disgusted sigh, then, 'What name shall I give?'

When he said 'Gina,' he heard a small curse.

The viewing slot opened. 'Let's look at you.'

He met the servant's eyes through the slot and reaching out with the gnosis. *You see Gina Weber, no doubt about it. Let me in.*

Mesmerism wasn't one of his best affinities, but the maid was busy and not expecting anyone else. 'Very well,' she grunted tiredly. She worked the locks open and let him in. Light shone from the kitchen and cooking smells filled the hall. The woman looked about forty, with flour on her hands. 'I'd have thought better of you, lass,' she said resignedly. 'Come on. I'll show you to the parlour.'

She led him down a hall; outside, Ramon and Cym should be leading Langstrit across the square, ready to follow him through, if he was able to see off the guard and Koll.

The cook called to one of the guards who were casting dice in the foyer. 'Kurt, take Miss Weber to the parlour . . . Charles, go and fetch Slimetongue.' She sounded disgruntled.

To know you is clearly not to love you, Gron Koll, Alaron thought. *Slimetongue – ha!*

The guard, Kurt, led him to a small armless chair in a tiny round room overlooking the square. He reeked of rusty mail and sweat. He peered at Alaron curiously.

Guards of magi houses were often taught shielding techniques, so Alaron put extra effort into his mesmerism. *You see an attractive woman, but she is not for you. Leave.*

There was little resistance. Kurt sniffed and turned away. 'What do you want to see Koll for?'

'None of your business, guardsman – but I'll be sure to mention that you asked.'

Kurt flinched. 'Uh, sorry, miss. Didn't mean nothing by it.' He hurried away.

Alaron, finally alone, looked around curiously. The ill-lit room was cluttered with books and tables and desks and the smell of lamp-oil. He heard footsteps and tugged his hood into place.

'Gina,' purred Gron Koll as he entered the room. 'What a pleasant surprise! I hoped you would see sense after all.' He stopped beside a decanter and splashed brandy into a glass. 'No sense in pining for your fiancé for two years, is there?'

Alaron watched out of the corner of his eye. *Come closer, Gron you prick.*

Koll ambled towards him. 'You know, Gina, I really was a little disappointed at your concern for that cretin Mercer, the other day. He got what he deserved. He's beneath the likes of you and me.'

'He's nothing to me,' Alaron risked saying, patting the seat again, conscious of Koll's eyes studying him. He hoped the mimicking was effective as he couldn't risk mental contact.

Koll slurped noisily and replaced the glass. 'He's nothing at all,' he agreed, 'but *I'm* someone; the Acting-Governor's Personal Aide. While those fools are off soldiering, I'm filling my purse here. I could fill your purse too,' he added with a guffaw. 'Both your purses!' He loomed over Alaron, who forced himself to keep his head down. He felt Koll reach out and grasp the corner of the hood. 'Malevorn's told me you were quite the little wettie.' He snickered throatily.

Kore give me strength . . .

Something thumped in the hall and Koll swivelled, pouting. 'Damnit, I told them—'

Alaron slammed a bunched fist into Koll's belly, his illusory disguise vanishing as he struck, but Koll didn't notice; he'd doubled over in time to meet Alaron's other fist, straight to the jaw. His head snapped back with a crack as he fell. Alaron leapt onto him, ready to strike again, while he sent a mental jab into his opponent's brain. Koll's eyes rolled back and he went limp.

Gotcha!

The door opened and Ramon slipped inside. 'How'd you do, Al?'

'Done.' *Damn, that felt good.*

Ramon grinned. 'Well done. I got the guard, and the kitchen staff don't know what's going on. Anyone else we need to deal with?'

'No, I think we're clear,' Alaron said as Cym pulled General Langstrit inside. She bent over Gron Koll. 'This is him? Ugh; he looks the molester sort, doesn't he? Now, let's see . . .' She closed her eyes and blue light seeped from her fingers into Koll's temples. Then she leaned back, panting slightly. 'He'll be out for hours,' she told them.

Alaron grinned at Ramon. 'I nailed the bastard,' he whispered. He mimicked a one-two combination.

'I'm absolutely green with envy, amici.'

Cym smiled. 'Sorry, but he's not going to remember you thumping him, Alaron. He'll think he's spent the evening asleep after too much drink.' She straightened. 'Let's go.'

They left Koll and crept silently to the main foyer, then up the stairs. A serving girl passed them on the servants' level, oblivious to their presence. They reached the top level undetected.

Cym turned to the boys. 'So, bedroom or study?'

Ramon pursed his lips. 'My money's still on the study.' He peered down the shadowy halls. 'First scan for wards: and don't trigger them. Slow and cautious, remember. Cym, that's the study; Al, check the bedroom door.'

Alaron touched it gingerly; almost instantly the door was limned in pale light. 'Warded,' he whispered.

'So is the study,' Ramon reported.

Alaron met the Silacian's eyes. Now that they were inside Vult's quarters, the potential for disaster was unlimited. *And I still don't think either study or bedroom is correct . . .*

He walked off down the hall.

'Where are you going?' Ramon whispered irritably.

Alaron pointed to the door he was making for: the room marked as spare on the plans. There were no wards on the door, so he slowly pushed it open.

His first thought was that it was a chapel, until he saw the medals and war honours. The wall was decorated with legion banners and captured standards. The plinth itself bore a life-size bust of Vult. The room was indeed a shrine: to Belonius Vult himself.

Cym slipped in behind him, her gnosis-lit eyes pale and translucent in the gloom. 'Look at all these,' she said, taking in the bust and the medals. 'Vult must have the ego of a Sollan demi-god.'

Ramon peered in. 'What are you both doing?'

'Alaron wanted to look in here,' Cym whispered to him.

'Stay focused, damn it,' Ramon fretted. 'Bedroom or study?'

'Hold on a second—' Alaron's mind began to race. *Let's just say that the files are here. It's not impossible – it's not the obvious place, but it's convenient to both bedroom and study . . . If I were him, I'd want my secret files at hand. I'd want them to just appear, but only to me. I'd use . . .*

He smiled. *I would use a Rune of Summoning.*

He walked over to the bust and examined it closely until he found the small mark etched into the base. He pointed it out to the others. 'Look, a Rune of Summoning.'

'Is it?' Ramon peered at Alaron intently. 'So?'

'Remember how they work?'

Ramon scowled. 'Of course: you touch the rune, think of the object

and call it to you. We did it at college. But not very well,' he added
pointedly.

Alaron pulled a face. 'The caster is the only one who can use it.
But you can override someone else's summoning by planting your
identity into the spell. We did it in class.' *Once.*

'You think you can override a pure-blood mage's spell?' Ramon
asked. 'No chance. It's probably warded, too.'

Alaron stared at the little mark. *It probably is warded – a touch-ward,
one you can't even see until you trigger it. That's what I'd do.* 'We knew
we'd be breaking a warding or two sometime,' he whispered. Before
the others could react – and before he could think about it too much
– he plunged a gnosis-lit hand onto the symbol while casting a Binding-
Rune into it.

If it is here, then this will – oh shit!

The eyes on the bust opened and focused on him. A stab of gnosis
drilled into his skull and latched on. He felt his body stiffen, his
heart beginning to race.

<*Speak the password*> snarled Belonius Vult's voice, emanating from
the stone bust.

He was dimly aware of Ramon and Cym reaching out to him, but
all he could feel was flowers of pain blooming in his breast. His body
went rigid as knives of acid pierced him through. A bubble of sound
swelled up inside his throat as his chest constricted. His lungs began
to fail, leaving him airless, his sight and sound going dim.

A dazzling burst of light exploded around him and he screamed
silently, his back arching, his legs giving way. But it was not death;
it was life. Something snapped inside his skull and he could hear
again. Awareness followed. He was lying on the floor, clutching his
face, moaning, with Ramon's hand over his mouth. Cym was holding
him, trying to confine his limbs – he must have gone into convul-
sions. But neither of them was looking at him; they were staring at
Jarius Langstrit, whose hand was gripping the bust of Belonius Vult.

It had cracked all the way down the middle.

Ramon knelt over him. 'Al, are you okay?'

Alaron clutched at his head. 'I think so – what happened?'

'It was a Mesmerism trap,' Ramon replied. 'I thought you were a goner, but then the general grabbed the bust and it broke.'

'Hel, Alaron,' Cym snarled, 'that was unbelievably stupid, even by your standards.' She peered at the bust. 'Did it work?'

Alaron looked up at Langstrit, who was staring at the bust with a look of vague interest. 'I dunno. Hey, maybe me being endangered moved the general to act?'

'Obviously,' answered Cym crossly.

'Did you know that would happen?' he asked her.

She rolled her eyes. 'No – my idea was to have him touch any wardings we found and hope his instincts took over.'

'Oh. Isn't that rather heartless?'

She met his eye and shrugged slightly.

He swallowed. 'Okay.' He pulled himself to his feet and reached for the broken bust, but Cym pushed him to one side.

'Wait, let me check it first. You look half-dead.' She placed her hand on the rune-mark and closed her eyes. 'Okay, interesting,' she said after half a minute. 'The ward is gone, but the Rune of Summoning is intact, and it's got some kind of imprint on it. You did it, Alaron. Unbelievable.'

Alaron exhaled and tentatively placed a forefinger on the symbol, triggering the Rune of Summoning. 'General Jarius Langstrit,' he tried, and there was a hissing sound as one of the wooden wall panels peeled back and a scroll-case floated through the air towards him. The panel closed silently. Cym caught the scroll-case, beaming excitedly. She peered at the label and her grin widened. 'You were right, Alaron: this is it, I'm sure—' She thrust it into her belt and looked at Alaron. 'You're still an idiot, though. That could have killed you.'

Ramon, examining the wall panel, quickly drew his hand back. 'It's still warded. They're poised to explode if anyone tries to break in. If we'd taken a crowbar to the walls, the files would have been immolated.' He had a faintly admiring look on his face, as though rethinking his security arrangements at home.

'Vult must be paranoid,' Cym remarked. 'Perhaps he's secretly

Silacian.' Suddenly she stiffened and her eyes widened, round as saucers. Alaron and Ramon felt it too: a sudden oppressive hammering, as if a thousand smiths were pummelling the air itself, trying to smash into the bubble of space they were in. In his mind's eye, Alaron thought he could see the ghostly outline of an outraged face forming, pounding against his Rune of Hiding. All three threw renewed energy into their wardings, but the attack was worse than anything they had ever come across in training. Alaron felt his protections begin to slip as pain knifed through his skull, and then—

—the attack broke apart, gone between one breath and the next. Jarius Langstrit was standing like a statue with one hand raised defensively over them.

'The general blocked it!' Alaron whispered wonderingly. 'That must have been Vult, trying to see who triggered his wards.'

'Then we have to go,' Cym hissed. 'Vult's next step will be to contact his underlings.' She pulled the general towards the door. He came blankly, as if everything that had just occurred meant nothing, already forgotten.

Ramon hurried after her.

Alaron looked about the room. There could be another attack any second. But he couldn't help himself. He touched the Rune-mark on the bust again. 'Alaron Mercer,' he said aloud. Another panel peeled back and another sealed scroll-case emerged. He snatched it out of the air, tucked it inside his cape and hurried after the others.

They made it out without incident, leaving the staff and guards mired in their gnosis-induced slumbers. The square was empty, as were the alleys they fled into.

They had done it. They beamed at each other exultantly.

Ramon took Alaron's arm with a mischievous grin. 'So, can I walk you home, my lovely? I quite like tall girls,' he added with a grin.

'If you don't get me home in five minutes my mother will gut you,' Alaron replied.

'Why do they all say that?' the little Silacian sighed.

The walk home seemed to take an eternity, but they made it unchallenged, and with no sign of the alarm being raised behind them. Whoever Vult might have contacted locally to investigate the break-in was acting discreetly. It wasn't until they got inside and locked the door behind them that they finally felt safe. They threw themselves into a group hug, pulling Langstrit into their huddle, whooping joyously.

Alaron felt someone pinch his behind and yelped, jerking out of the clinch. 'Who did that!' he demanded, while the others roared with laughter.

Ramon winked at him. 'So, honey, can I help you out of that dress?'

Once they were all changed and settled into the armchairs of the lounge Cym opened the Langstrit scroll-case. Tesla was already abed, and Langstrit dozed in his favourite armchair.

'So: let's see what's in the general's file,' Cym said, pulling out a handful of tightly wrapped pages headed with the seal of the Watch. 'Look: "Arrest Report for Prisoner L" – this is it. And here it is, the contents of the chapel—' She set the papers down, beaming excitedly. Alaron thought she'd never looked so beautiful.

Ramon poured drinks and they toasted their success. 'Amici, much though I want to read it all tonight, I think we should get some sleep first. *But well done, us.* We got in, Alaron got to biff Koll, we got what we wanted and we got out undetected. Perfect.'

'Well, not exactly undetected,' Cym reminded them. 'Vult knows he's had a break-in.'

'He's in Antiopia,' Ramon replied smugly. 'He won't be back here for weeks, and there's nothing to tie us to the break-in. We are geniuses; step aside, Kaden Rats, there's a new gang in town.'

They finished their drinks and went reluctantly to bed. Alaron didn't mention the second scroll-case. In retrospect it was an utterly stupid thing to have done – but it was too late now. He waited until he could go to the privy alone so that he could examine the papers privately.

Inside were his thesis notes. He began to tremble with rage. Vult really had stolen them, or more likely, had got someone else to do it. Then his eyes fell on the only other item in the file, a one-page letter folded up amidst the notes.

> To: Lucien Gavius, Principal of Turm Zauberin, Norostein
> From: Belonius Vult, Governor of Noros.
> You are instructed to fail the student Alaron Mercer. On what grounds
> is up to you, but I suggest misconduct. However, you are not to cast
> the normal Chain-rune upon him, nor monitor him for ongoing posses-
> sion of a periapt. The Watch have also been so instructed. Refer any
> queries to me, or in my absence, to Captain Muhren.
> BV

He stared and stared, and then he wrapped his arms about his
sides and began to tremble. Vult had secretly sanctioned his use of
a periapt? Why? And if a Chain-rune was supposed to be cast upon
a failed mage, why hadn't one been cast on him?

Vult wanted me to still have access to the gnosis – why?

There could be only one reason why: Vult must have divined something about him after seeing his thesis. *So Vult wants me to search for
the Scytale . . .*

He recalled the words about Vult in *Generals of the Glorious Rebellion*:
'His mastery of Divination foresees all turns of the game.'

31

Lovers

Sorcery

Sorcery strikes to the very heart of the most perplexing and unsolved mysteries – that of the after-life and the soul. Whilst the gnosis appears to prove the existence of some form of life after death, it does not prove – or even hint at – whether that after-life has a purpose, is a reward, or is in fact little more than a protracted fading-away, the tail-end of dying. The existence of God is neither proven nor disproven. Nevertheless, with Sorcery, one can commune with spirits and enlist their aid (Wizardry); speculate upon the future (Divination); communicate over distance (Clairvoyance); or manipulate the dead (Necromancy). Whether any of these uses should be legal is a matter for the moralists.

ORDO COSTRUO COLLEGIATE, PONTUS

Brochena, Javon, on the continent of Antiopia
Maicin 928
2 months until the Moontide

In the aftermath of the Revolt, the Rondian legions went from town to town throughout Noros, seeking out the more famous rebels and – despite many having been pardoned – executing them, as a warning to the populace. Elena recalled one in particular: the headsman had paused, nonchalantly, the axe poised above the victim's head. The boy on the block – and he was only a boy, barely nineteen – had sobbed as he waited to die. There had been for no reason for that pause; it had been deliberate and cruel, the executioner enjoying his moment in the sun as he played to the crowd.

She knew now how that boy had felt. *Gurvon's axe is above us all. I can feel it.*

Everyone was affected. Cera was distant, always busy; she never spoke of personal things any more, reminding Elena of a bad phase she had gone through a few years back, spying on people. She'd turned secretive and mean-spirited for a while, until Elena had managed to snap her out of it.

Timori was often tearful, and gave Borsa a horrid time. Elena wished she could spend more time with the boy, playing like they used to, but she was so busy and so tired. Even Lorenzo was awkward with her, his eyes full of longing and his usual smooth manner rumpled by uncertainty.

I wish I could just ride away – but where would I go? she wondered.

After another fruitless day searching the slums – Mara had struck again, this time at one of Mustaq's kinsmen – she stumbled back to her chambers. Tarita ordered a pair of hefty servants to bring buckets of water to fill the old half-wine-barrel she used as a bath. She heated the water herself with the remains of her gnosis and sighed with relief as she immersed herself.

'Are you hungry, mistress?' Tarita asked her.

'Not really,' Elena admitted. She tipped more water over her head, enjoying the enveloping warm wetness. 'I should be, but I'm too tired to eat. I'll have a big breakfast tomorrow.' She stood up and accepted a towel.

'You have a fine body, mistress,' Tarita told her. 'Very strong and athletic.'

'But not very feminine,' Elena replied, rubbing herself down.

'I think your form would please any man.' Tarita said with her usual disconcerting frankness. 'Does Lorenzo di Kestria like your body?'

'*Tarita!*' Elena rolled her eyes as she wrapped the towel about her and sat on the bed, wondering what to wear that evening. 'You have no sense of propriety, do you? How old are you now?'

'Ah, I don't know precisely – fifteen, I think. I bleed.' She sniffed. 'Why?'

'Just curious.' A nagging thought surfaced in her mind. 'Tarita, how did you come to be in that chest when the Gorgio began killing the Jhafi staff?'

'You've asked me this before, mistress: I saw what was happening and I hid.'

'Where? Surely not in that trunk for a whole day?'

'Why not? The soldiers only came in once, and they were in a hurry. I was frightened they would find me, but an officer came and took them away with him. After that, everything went quiet.'

Elena finally remembered what it was that had been nagging her. 'Who locked you in the chest, Tarita?'

The girl froze, and Elena instinctively walled herself with shields, in case Tarita did something aggressive. Her fears were misplaced; instead, Tarita whimpered and backed away.

'I won't hurt you, girl, but I must know,' Elena said firmly.

Tarita slumped to her knees on the floor. 'Please, mistress – I was going to tell you, once I knew it was safe, I promise.' She took a deep breath and looked at Elena. Her face was pallid beneath the deep tan of her race. 'It was Portia, mistress.'

'Portia? *Portia Tolidi?* Fernando's sister? Why would she do that?'

'Because Fernando was my lover,' she whispered.

'What?' Elena stood up, towering over the girl, who cowered on the floor. 'He was *what?* But Solinde—?' Whole new vistas of questions burst into being around her.

Tarita cowered on the floor, her eyes bruised with fear. 'Fernando made Portia promise to keep me safe, mistress. Please – I was going to tell you, but if my people found out I'd lain with a Gorgio they would kill me.'

Elena sat down in the water again, thinking furiously. 'Why didn't Portia take you north?'

Tarita gave her the look she usually reserved for when Elena made a stupid tabula move. 'Because the Gorgio were killing all the staff – if I'd been found in the north, I'd have ended up just as dead. Portia was kind to me, for her brother's sake.'

Elena reached down, lifted the girl's chin and looked deep into her eyes. 'Your secret is safe with me, Tarita. I swear that.' She was still thinking furiously. 'So what happened to Fernando Tolidi?'

'He was killed, about a week before you came and drove off the Gorgio.'

'He was killed? By whom?'

'Princessa Solinde killed him,' Tarita replied unflinchingly.

'Great Kore! *Solinde?* You're serious?'

The girl lifted her head defiantly and repeated, 'Princess Solinde killed him.'

Elena stared at her. 'Surely you're mistaken—'

Tarita looked back up at her, her dark eyes flashing. 'You can disbelieve if you wish, mistress.'

'I don't understand.' She pictured the bitter, vicious creature who had confronted her after they had pulled her from the wreckage of the Moon Tower and tried to match it to the happy, vivacious girl she had spent four years with. *Great Kore!*

She patted the mattress beside her. 'Sit here, Tarita. Please, tell me what happened.'

Tarita rose gracefully to her feet and sat shyly next to Elena, careful not to touch her. 'Mistress, Seir Fernando was aide to the Gorgio ambassador. He was courting Solinde, but the princessa was off-limits for — well, you know what.' She preened slightly. 'I was not a virgin and he took a liking to me, so when he came back to his rooms after dancing, with his passions aroused, he wanted a woman. He wanted me.'

Elena stared at the girl. She'd have been what, fourteen? *Gracious, the lives we live.*

'Then you went to Forensa with the queen and Princessa Cera and Prince Timi. The palace was preparing for the arrival of the sultan's emissaries. Then Magister Sordell killed good King Olfuss and the Gorgio entered the city. There were thousands of soldiers and they were forcing many of the women, but Fernando protected me.' The girl stared at the floor. 'He said he loved me.'

And maybe he did, Elena thought. He was only eighteen himself. He wouldn't be the first to fall in love with a servant – or the first to pretend love if it enabled him to enjoy a naïve young girl's body either. 'Did you love him?'

Tarita squirmed uncomfortably. 'I *liked* him. We really didn't spend time together, mistress. We just rukked, then I would go back to my duties. Maybe we would have come to love each other.'

'What happened between him and Solinde?'

'The princessa was very distraught – her father was dead and she was a prisoner. I saw her after, and she was crying. Fernando was trying to console her, but she hit him – I saw the handprint.'

'Was he angry?'

'No, he was sad. He was a good man, mistress. He felt sorry for her – he said she was really just angry with his clan, not him. The princessa was kept locked up for a long time. Lady Vedya arrived, and she wouldn't even allow any servants into Solinde's rooms. Then after a few weeks, Alfredo Gorgio announced that Solinde and Fernando would marry, and they began courting again as if nothing had ever been wrong between them. We all saw them walking together, and she looked happy.'

Alone with Vedya, and then a change in behaviour. 'Go on,' Elena said grimly, thinking, *I have to get Solinde recalled back here so I can question her.*

'The whisper went round that Solinde and Fernando would marry in secret on the next holy day, and Fernando told me that evening. He said I couldn't be his maid any more and he made Portia promise to look after me.' She scowled. 'At least I wasn't with child. But I was not pleased at all.'

Elena put a hand on the girl's shoulder. 'I'm sorry.'

Tarita pouted, then shrugged. 'I suppose it had to happen some-time.' She leaned towards Elena. 'Then it all went horribly wrong. There were these awful noises, in the middle of the night – they woke the whole palace! The two of them were shouting really dreadful things at each other, horrible obscenities, then someone screamed and one of the knights broke the door down. Fernando's chest was covered in blood and there was a knife in his heart!'

'And Solinde?'

502

'She had pulled a sheet over her face. They told us she was shouting in a strange voice—'

'Strange? In what way strange?'

Tarita shrugged. 'Just strange. She sounded – well, *different*, not like Princessa Solinde . . . she wasn't speaking *words*, just wailing, like at a funeral.' She shuddered. 'She had stabbed Fernando many, many times. Then Magister Sordell arrived and threw everyone out.'

'Not Gurvon?'

'Magister Gyle was away – this was just before you came back and killed the evil ones,' Tarita reminded her. 'Magister Sordell put it about that Fernando had attacked the princessa and she had defended herself. Then he locked her in the Moon Tower – for her own protection, he said.'

Elena raised her eyebrows. 'He *protected* Solinde? After she'd murdered a Gorgio?'

Tarita looked like she wanted to spit. 'I suppose she had more value than Fernando,' she said bitterly. 'Anyway, a few days later you came and killed them all. But Lady Cera should bring back her sister and make her pay,' she added in a low voice.

Elena took a deep breath. 'I wish you had told me this before I sent Solinde south.'

Tarita hunched over a little. 'I couldn't tell anyone.' She reached out and clutched Elena's hand in hers. 'The men – they wouldn't understand. I slept with a Gorgio!' she whispered hoarsely. 'I don't want them to hurt me.'

'I'll keep your secret, Tarita, I promise you. Thank you for trusting me with it.'

'You are a good mistress,' the maid said in a small voice, and then, after a moment, 'Will you ask Lady Cera to give Fernando justice?'

'Yes, I will,' Elena replied, squeezing Tarita's hand.

First though, I'll need to exhume his body and ask it a few questions, and hope to Hel I can make sense of all this.

Many aspects of Necromancy were illegal throughout the Rondian Empire, for good reasons. To create an *undead* by imprisoning a soul

503

in their own or another body violated all human sensibilities, and not only was every instant a torment for those souls, but they were a danger to the living: their bodies were oblivious to pain and their need to feed on other spirits to continue their half-lives made them murderous.

Javon, having not previously been home to magi, had no specific laws against Necromancy, but, regardless, Elena had no intention of getting caught.

Fernando Tolidi had been hastily buried in one of the palace crypts beneath the now-ruined Moon Tower. As a nobleman, Fernando was owed a proper burial, but the expectation was that his body would be sent north at some point, once relations with the Gorgio normalised. So in the meantime, he'd been nailed into a coffin and interred without ceremony in the crypt of some long-extinct dynasty, where he'd been left to rot away unregarded.

The gnosis was Elena's key and illumination. She checked Cera was asleep, Tarita silent and Borsa snoring in the next room before slipping down to Fernando's current resting place. The padlock came open in her hand with little effort; the gnosis muffled the noise of the grating hinges as she opened and closed the door, then lit a torch. Alone in the cold chamber, Elena went grave-robbing. The graves of almost five hundred years of sheiks, emirs and Godspeakers lay beneath the palace, a maze of Jhafi dead that would take hours to fully explore. But Elena needed only the Rimoni crypts, easily recognisable by the angel-encrusted, Sol et Lune engravings on the rows of stone sarcophagi. She muttered a quick prayer for the dead as she navigated her way through them. It was easy to imagine ghosts peering after her, or shades stalking the shadows in her wake. At times the dead did sleep unquiet, when some poor soul's transition did not go as it should, instead leaving it haunting its own remains. Sometimes they could be deadly dangerous. But here there was only the cold, rotting damp of the grave: unpleasant enough, but not perilous.

Fernando had been laid in a stone sarcophagus, his name etched hastily on the top. She placed her torch in a holder on the wall to free her hands and lifted the lid, wincing at the stench of death within. She paused to wrap a scarf over her nose and mouth, took a deep breath and prised open the coffin.

No effort had been made to prepare the body for burial. The corpse of Fernando Tolidi was in advanced decay, horribly swollen to twice its normal bulk by the gases trapped as the internal organs decayed. The fingernails, toenails and hair had continued to grow, but the face had fallen, the rotting flesh clinging to the shape of the skull beneath. His eyes were open, bulging white orbs staring sightlessly upward. His swollen tongue had forced the mouth apart and lines of dried blood ran from his eyes and mouth as if he had been weeping ichor. But all this was normal decomposition.

It's no wonder there were legends of the living dead well before the gnosis made it possible, Elena thought. She quelled her nausea; what she was about to do was difficult and more than a little dangerous. She was going to use Fernando's body as a link to his soul – a Necromantic summoning to bring the spirit back to its corpse. There was every chance it would be futile – Necromancy was not her forte, and his spirit might have already dissipated or passed on. Or worse, she might attract the attention of something more dangerous.

Purple light, the colour of Necromancy, oozed from her fingers onto Fernando's gelid skin. There was nothing left of him here but a cadaver, but a residue of his essence remained for a time in the body. Using it, she began her call, soundless in the human world, but felt like a pulse by the spirits, like vibrations on a web, attracting the spiders. She tried not to think of it that way, though.

Fernando Tolidi . . . Fernando Tolidi . . .

She lost track of time while she called, feeling only the sheen on her brow, the beads of sweat, the light touches on her mind, until at last she felt stirrings, as if something large had swum near her in deep waters, a thing of shadow and distant hissing voices, and then . . .

I . . . am . . . was . . . Fernando . . . Tolidi . . .

She caught an image, a self-image of a well-made young man with an equine face. His semi-opaque form drifted towards her, a look of fear on his face. He reached the other side of the coffin.

Don't look down, Fernando, look at me, she told him, but he looked down anyway, saw his own rotting body and cried out in sorrow and horror. His spectral form began to disintegrate.

She walked around the coffin as he backed away. *Fernando, look only at me*, she commanded.

His face turned back towards her, unwilling, terrified. *What have you done to me?*

I need to know who killed you.

He looked at her in confusion, his eyes haunted. He clutched at his breast, as if touching an embedded blade. *I can't remember – why can't I remember my own death?*

Elena sought to soothe him. *It's normal. The mind erases pain and trauma.* She felt a sudden prickling of her senses as other spirits crowded about them now, watching intently. She needed to get this over with. *Be still*, she told Fernando's ghost, and she held out a hand, aglow with purple gnosis, and reached inside his spectral skull. A shudder ran through him and images flicked into her mind:

A young woman, Solinde, naked on top of him, his hands gripping her as she rode him, his pleasure mounting, ascending towards release . . . He looks up at her as she looks down . . .

It's not her!

Shock, disbelief; he's shouting, inchoate words of denial and horror, shoving her off him . . . a thin, white body sprawls, and then that face is shouting back at him and a dagger flashes . . .

There's numbness as blow after blow hammers into his chest, and it's so strange because he can't feel a thing and yet there is blood everywhere. He can still see a bony face, blood all over the white skin, the acrid tang of blood. Darkness is rushing in like water, pulling him under . . .

Elena disengaged from the vision as it faded. 'Thank you, Fernando,' she said, aloud and into the spirit world. 'Go in peace.'

The big face looked down at her and he tried to reach for her, whether in threat or gratitude she couldn't tell, because some unseen wind shredded him and blew his soul into the void.

Elena held onto that indistinct image: a thin, boyish face with short red hair. No one she knew . . .

The mausoleum felt watchful now, sentient. Summoning one spirit invariably attracted others. She backed out, waving the torch about her, knowing her fears were not groundless: she knew of beings that could be lurking, and she whispered words of banishing. The echoing silence mocked her, but though there was nothing else here, she did not feel safe until she had regained her rooms.

She lay wakeful long into the night, wishing she could talk to someone – *all right, with Lorenzo* – but it was late, and she had too much to think about.

When eventually she slept, she dreamed the bloated body under the slab was her own.

'Lady Elena, how are you faring?' Pita Rosco sat himself beside her as the rest of the Regency Council filed in. The group was somewhat changed these days, with Seir Luigi Conti gone north, where he was penning in the Gorgio. Comte Piero Inveglio was still there, urbane, suave as ever, and still peddling his sons to Cera at every opportunity. It had become a good-natured joke, though with a serious undertone. Don Francesco Perdonello sat with the council now, the prime bureaucrat of the Grey Crows, to advise on Civil Service matters. He always brought a retinue of experts, and had become a major player. He and Pita Rosco were at constant loggerheads over finances.

'Pita, I've never been better,' Elena lied brightly.

Pita raised a dubious eyebrow, but didn't challenge her words. Lorenzo came in and Elena found something important to do in the corner while the young knight joked with Pita about a wager.

Cera led in the remainder of the council: Luigi Ginovisi, still Master of Revenues, and still grumbling. Godspeaker Acmed al-Istan, trying to persuade the council to make positive steps towards the Amteh demands. The Sollan Faith was now represented by Josip Yannos, more senior than Ivan Prato. Yannos was a stern, grey presence who would argue the smallest point as if it were life and death. The Regency Council was thirty-strong now, and each councillor had his own retinue. It was too big, Elena kept telling Cera. She was working on getting Cera to adopt a smaller Upper Council instead; one more boring, divisive meeting should persuade her.

Cera sat, and everyone took their places. Elena slid into her customary position beside her, but the queen-regent didn't even spare her a glance as she opened the meeting. 'All of our time is precious, gentlemen, and I am sick of fixing gate tolls and salt quotas, then finding we're out of time to debate the shihad. This is a decision, not an invitation to argue. Understood?'

They all knew her well enough by now to just bow and agree. Elena had heard a few of them hankering back to the old days, 'when Olfuss at least let us talk'. But she had also heard them agree that Cera ran the council well, and by and large they were fiercely loyal to her. She felt a familiar surge of pride in *her* princessa. All those nights tutoring her on politics and leadership were bearing fruit, far beyond what she could ever have envisaged.

Though I miss the girl she used to be . . .

Cera recapped their position: their agents in Kesh reported massive columns of men winding their way west towards the Hebb Valley. A trader reported that Tomas Betillon had instituted a brutally enforced curfew in Hebusalim. The Rondians had sent Belonius Vult on some kind of diplomatic mission to the Ordo Costruo. In the north the Gorgio were quiescent, but they were building tall wooden gantries, the type used to dock windships. The Dorobon were coming, it was rumoured. Even if Javon ignored the Crusade, war would still come. But this was all days or weeks old; without Gurvon Gyle's web of informants fresh news was precious.

They debated the shihad extensively, but no one could agree on anything. Sending their soldiers south if the Gorgio were about to be reinforced by the Dorobon would be madness – but rebuffing Sultan Salim's demands would also be suicidal. In the end they voted narrowly in favour of the shihad, and only on Cera's casting vote. Lorenzo had voted against, Elena noted, which had not pleased Cera.

It was a long meeting, and even the most argumentative councillor was ready to leave when Cera announced one last matter. 'Elena has asked me to bring Solinde back from Krak di Conditiori,' she said baldly.

This made everyone stop their end-of-meeting banter and stare. 'For what purpose?' Comte Inveglio asked at last. 'She still faces charges of treason and has not yet been tried. Can we risk a public trial at so delicate a time?'

Pita Rosco raised a finger. 'We should make an example of her – it will show the people that we are determined to confront this matter head-on—'

Cera raised a hand. 'Elena wishes only to question her concerning events surrounding the death of Fernando Tolidi. The transfer will be low-key. Whether she is sent south again will depend on the answers we get.'

'Then why does Donna Elena not go south herself and save us the trouble of a difficult and dangerous prisoner-transfer?' Pita grumbled.

'Because I cannot spare her,' Cera responded flatly. 'This is for your information; it is not a debate.' Then she softened a little. 'Solinde is still my sister, and I too want to see her again. I want to know whether she put the Gorgio ahead of us. If she did, I will have no pity.' Cera's voice had a hollow, haunted tone. 'But that is for another time.' She stood abruptly. 'That is all, gentlemen.'

As the men dispersed, Cera plucked at Elena's sleeve and bade her walk with her, a rarity of late. 'Elena, part of me would be happy for Solinde to stay in the dungeons of the Krak for ever,' she admitted. 'I'm not sure how to deal with her any more.'

Elena said sympathetically, 'I will question her as quickly as I can, then we will send her back. You don't even have to see her.'

'But I do, Ella – of course I have to see her.' Cera straightened her back, her mind already moving on. 'Next week the sultan's emissaries are arriving. What do we tell them?'

'That we'd love to dance, but we've got a full card?'

Cera suppressed a smile. 'That might be about all we can say. I doubt Salim will be amused, though. Nor the Jhafi. If the Dorobon return, I can't afford to have my armies in the Hebb Valley.' She yawned bleakly. 'Lorenzo di Kestria voted against us supporting the shihad,' she noted. 'I was surprised.'

'I think Lorenzo believes we can only deal with one problem at a time. He believes the Gorgio–Dorobon alliance is the issue we must confront.'

Cera scowled. 'Usually the Kestrians vote with me,' she growled. She glanced at Elena. 'I thought you had him better trained than that.'

'If that was a jest, it wasn't funny, Cera.' *She thinks I'm sleeping with him. Who else does?*

Cera said coldly, 'I merely meant that you and he usually agree on most matters. There was no need to take offence.'

Elena flinched. 'I apologise, your Majesty. I'm tired.' *Deathly tired. Tired enough to make mistakes.* She bowed, conscious that the exchange had been overheard by several of the council. 'Please excuse me.' She hurried away, thinking, *What's got into my princessa? Where's the girl I used to know?*

She climbed the stairs wearily, considered another bath, but chose meditation instead. She went to her tower-room and bowed apologetically to Bastido, whom she'd been neglecting of late, before casting off her cloak and weapons. She pulled open the shutters and bathed in the crimson light of the falling sun for a while before pulling off her breeches and outer tunic, unrolling the thin mat she kept in the corner and beginning her routine. The art of yoga had come originally from Lakh, but after the Leviathan Bridge had opened it had been learned by many magi of Yuros, deemed useful as both physical and mental training.

She had been working for half an hour and was beginning to sweat when the sound of her door opening pulled her mind back to the present. Her eyes went to her sword. She relaxed slightly when she saw that the intruder was Lorenzo di Kestria, though her skin prickled at being alone with him.

'Donna Ella, may I interrupt?'

She looked down at herself, clad only in perspiration-soaked undergarments, then up at him. 'Lori, if you walked in on another woman like this she would have every right to scream.'

He glided past her to the window. 'I know, I'm sorry. I presume upon your goodwill.' He turned, his face gilded by the sunset, and extended a hand. 'We said we would talk again after you had returned from the blood-tower. You have returned, and I wish to have that conversation.'

Oh my . . .

She allowed him to draw her up. Her knees had lost all strength, and all of the wet heat in her body began to flow to her belly. And below. 'I should dress,' she muttered distractedly.

He prevented her by simply enclosing his arms about her from behind. They were firm and warm; they felt as strong as castle walls. She sank into his grasp almost involuntarily.

'I enjoy watching you. You move with such grace,' he murmured in her ear. 'Like water.' He gently turned her so that they faced out the window. 'Here in these dry lands, water is precious.'

Together they stared out over the sea of mud-brick houses to the desert horizon and the stark shapes of the mountains to the west. She tried to remember what forests looked like, and couldn't. She couldn't rightly think of anything, except how good his arms felt wrapped about her.

'Tell me of Indrania,' she said hastily, trying to give herself time to think.

He smiled fondly. 'Ah. The people there say Lakh, not Indrania. It's the strangest land in the world, perhaps. The red dirt, the dusty green of the trees, the minarets rising white above the red roofs. The vibrancy of the people and the colour. You have never seen colour until you have been in a Lakh market. The women wear such dazzling, beautiful fabrics, the richest reds and greens, the brightest yellows and oranges, all glinting with gold embroidery and studded with gems. The patterns are intricate, the detail incredible.' He stroked her arms. 'One day I will take you there, if you wish it.'

A vision of freedom and movement: a hope to pin her colours to. 'I do wish it, Lori. It sounds wonderful.'

'There is freedom in movement. The road calls and you leave all cares behind and allow it to take you away, to where dreams await.'

She sighed and sank into his enfolding arms. He kissed her left ear, then her right, and she squirmed pleasantly. He nuzzled her neck. 'May I claim that kiss now, Ella?'

She turned in his arms and faced him, his eyes inches from hers. She exhaled gently, hopelessly. 'You may.' She pressed her mouth to his and drank in his kiss. His mouth tasted of coffee. She felt her defences crumble as she let him guide her to the yoga mat, gently lowering her onto her back, kissing her throat, feeling his stubble rough on her neck and cheeks. His hand slid inside her sweaty tunic and stroked her left nipple, then unbuttoned the shirt. The decision taken, she was filled with urgency to get it over with, but he was in no mood to hurry and his movements became slower, more languid, his kisses gentler, less urgent, his touch more playful and teasing.

He bared her carefully, praising her with whispered murmurs as he slid down her body. 'There is a Lakh text, a guide on the art of love. The first book describes the non-penetrative pleasuring of a woman,' he told her and then he kissed her mound and ran his tongue down her cleft, his touch so exquisite it froze her. She clutched his curling hair and held him there as he tormented her with his mouth for what felt like hours, licking, sucking, until she came apart in a flurry of explosive climaxes, her whimpered cries hanging damp in the air.

Only when she had recovered did he slowly climb her body. 'The second book concerns the penetration of the woman,' he told her as he filled her. She squirmed beneath him, tried to rock her hips, but he stilled her. 'Slower, *amora*, always slower.' He felt huge inside her, and when at last he began to move, it took all the breath from her body. They wrapped about each other, every movement building on the last, her senses filling with him: the way he sounded, felt, smelled, moved, all-pervasive and glorious. Her native reserve vanished and she found herself crying out, panting for breath as at last he pounded into her, bellowing like a bull as he came inside her convulsing body. It felt like aeons before she could think again. Her loins were slick with fluids, her skin with sweat.

'That was wonderful,' she whispered.

'Thank you.' He gave a slow smile, strangely serious, almost appraising.

'What are you thinking?' she wondered suddenly.

'That you are a wondrous being. A magi, capable of all manner of miracles.' He eased himself out of her and lay half-astride, his face pressed to hers. 'But you are a woman, before all else.'

'No, I'm not. I'm the queen-regent's Champion – that, above all.'

He looked into her eyes. 'You are a woman first to me.' And he kissed her reply away before wrapping her in his arms possessively.

She kissed his cheek, suddenly shy now that the urgency of her need had been sated. For now. She felt a confused mess of hopes and fears churning inside her. Though her instincts were to draw away and gauge what this meant, it had been wonderful – better than she had dreamed.

'So?' she asked him playfully, 'what did you wish to talk about?'

He grunted. 'Women! Always in bed they talk talk talk.' He laughed, but it was he who filled the silence, speaking of places he'd seen. The room filled with shadows as the night came on, but Elena barely noticed, her mind following his words, envisaging what he described.

'The road sounds good,' she murmured when Lorenzo paused at last.

'It is a good life,' he agreed. 'But it can be lonely too. You're never certain of your welcome, wherever you go. A misunderstanding, a loose word and you find yourself on your own and having to move on. Some towns can be very unwelcoming. Others open their arms to you.'

I bet they do, she thought, eyeing his handsome face. 'I'm sure you were able to charm your way out of anything dangerous, sirrah.'

He gave a lopsided smile. 'Of course – exotic strangers always hold a certain charm, don't you think? Like yourself, Donna: all the men here are fascinated by you.'

She looked sceptical. 'Appalled, horrified, maybe. When I first arrived the knights were outraged that a foreigner – and a woman at that! – could be considered more capable of protecting the royal children than they. They have taken every opportunity to criticise me, to disparage me and outdo me – and some of them still had the cheek to try and woo me as well!'

'It must be difficult for you here, unable to give anyone a hold over you by showing them favour and affection.'

'Exactly: when a man takes a woman, he has *conquered*. He is victorious, he has *triumphed*, while the woman is *ruined*, *sullied* by that same act. A man beds a little court-bint and everyone thinks the better of him; his prowess is established. But those young girls are left tainted by their succumbing.'

'So other men here have also tried to seduce you?' he asked, deflecting that line of conversation.

She decided to let it go. 'Some of them – the cocky ones. But most think I'm a freak: a female warrior-mage. I could not be more alien to them. If they could beat me in a duel or bed me, they could place me somewhere in their little pecking orders. I spent my first year here under siege.'

'It sounds exhausting, being you,' Lorenzo observed after a few moments.

Elena looked back at him, trying to sort through her feelings. He was charming and he was honest. That he was not a mage meant he could never know her fully, but she could relax with him as she never could with another mage. And the sex had been truly magical. It felt as if he were some kind of lodestone, pulling her flesh towards him. His voice was low and throaty, just the sort she liked. Carnal images were filling her mind again.

'So, do you have a copy of this Indranian sex-manual?' she asked slyly.

He grinned, leaning back. 'Of course! It can be good inspiration to liven things up on a slow night. It is based upon the four principles of pleasure.' He raised a finger. 'One: That all bodies can give and receive pleasure. Second, that until we understand our own desires, we are closed to full enjoyment of pleasure. Third, that pleasure may be transitory, but it is a glimpse of the eternal bliss of God's house. Fourth, that the key to pleasure lies not in the body, but in the mind. The book is fond of the number four; it groups the myriad couplings it depicts into four primal acts. It devises four phases of love-making and associates them with the cycles of the moon. It's also rather picturesque. The Amteh have banned the book, but it is easily available, even in supposed Amteh towns. I know of one scriptualist who adapted it to Amteh customs. Here in Ahmedhassa, the people enjoy their pleasures, whereas Rondians are reserved and prissy about them, in my experience.' He raised a teasing eyebrow.

She ducked her head, recalling the brief couplings that she and Gurvon had used to indulge in, more a purging of need than a celebration of it. 'So I become yet another of your conquests,' she observed.

'I have, well, much experience of women,' he replied, not quite apologetically.

The idea didn't repel her as she thought it might. 'Then I'm in good hands.' She smiled.

'You are,' he replied confidently. 'And speaking of hands—' He slid his hand down her belly, cupped her mound and began to tease her again.

She moaned softly and surrendered once more.

Stealth was something Cera Nesti had learned from an early age, in hide-and-seek games with her siblings. She knew how to move soundlessly, to know when to pause and when to go, or to stop, utterly still, and remain so for minutes on end. By now it was second nature. And she'd seen enough.

There was a tiny viewing space high on the wall overlooking Lorenzo di Kestria's bed. She had taken to watching it when he courted her to see if he was faithful. After she'd rejected him, he'd become promiscuous for a few weeks. It had been queasily entertaining to watch him coupling with a different girl each night.

But this time it was Elena she saw slip into the knight's chamber, and some part of her soul turned to ash. It was evident that this was not their first time from their easy familiarity. As the grunting, gasping frenzy of their coupling burned her ears, she crawled away, tears stinging her eyes.

Gyle will say this proves they plot against me . . .

Her bedroom adjoined her father's old reading room, the nexus from which the spider-web of passages and tunnels over Brochena Palace radiated. She stumbled into the room, collapsed on the divan and sobbed soundlessly, her shoulder heaving violently with the effort of keeping her grief silent. She twisted in a paroxysm that began as sorrow and finished as rage.

There was a shadow perched outside her window. She staggered to it and threw it open. 'You were right!' she gasped hoarsely. 'You were right about them!'

The projected form of Gurvon Gyle bowed its head. 'I grieve for you, Cera,' he said simply. 'Elena has no loyalty but to herself. Her support for you was only ever a ploy, to gain independence from me and a new pension plan for herself.'

She wanted to smash something. She wanted to scream. A dark future opened before her: of awakening to find Elena crushing a pillow over her face while Lorenzo knifed Timori and seized the throne; the massacre of all the Nesti as the Kestrians swept into power. Of Elena and Lorenzo, coupling in her own bed, King and Queen of Javon.

'How can I save myself?' she heard herself ask.

Gurvon met her eyes. 'You must proceed with caution, Cera. Try to arrest them and you will bring everything to a head. Your position is precarious, but not hopeless.'

She swallowed. *I'm doing this for my family.*

'The issue will be forced when Solinde is brought back. You will note that Elena has invented some pretext to have her returned? This is so she can be slain at the same time as Timi and you. If they left her in the Krak, where the Ordo Costruo have sovereignty, she'd be a rallying point. By bringing her back, they make ready their coup.'

She shuddered. 'I never thought of that. I'll countermand the order—'

'No, let it happen. It will be the catalyst to freeing you.' He raised a hand to her, palm out. 'Cera, I have a plan – but you must trust me.'

She sucked in her breath. *He is Gurvon Gyle. He killed my father and mother. How did it ever come to this?* Then the image of Elena's enraptured face as she rutted with Lorenzo di Kestria obliterated her doubts. *Rukka Hel, I hate these magi!* She met Gyle's eyes. *But it seems I must trust one of them . . .*

'What must I do?'

'Firstly, send Lorenzo di Kestria to retrieve Solinde from the Krak – it must be him. And then summon Harshal ali-Assam in secret and—'

'Harshal! You mean—'

'No, I don't mean he is my agent – he is not. But he has contacts among the Jhafi, including a man called Ghujad iz'Kho, who—'

'That's a Harkun name!'

Gyle sighed slightly. 'Yes, Princessa, it is. Are you going to interrupt everything I say?'

Cera clasped her arms about herself and shook her head.

'Excellent. Now, here is what you must tell Harshal . . .'

Everyone knew the participation of Javon in the shihad would be decided today, so it was with sinking heart that Elena watched the way they arrayed themselves about the council table. Emir Ilan Tamadhi, Harshal ali Assam and Scriptualist Acmed al-Istan sat on one side, with Comte Piero Inveglio, Seir Luca Conti and Pita Rosco lined up opposite. Conti was standing in for Lorenzo, who was travelling to retrieve Solinde. Josip Yannos was sitting at the foot of the table.

I wish you were here, Lori. At least you know how to find compromise. But Lorenzo was riding south to fetch back Solinde. She missed him with both body and soul.

Cera arrived, looking red-eyed and nervous. She had become even less communicative in recent weeks, colder and harder and more distant; there was obviously some internal dialogue going on inside her that she would not share with Elena.

No one else appeared to have noticed the change; they no longer treated Cera as if she was either young or female; instead, they argued with her, joked with her and deferred to her as readily as they ever had with Olfuss.

But that did not mean they always agreed with her, and the shihad was the most divisive topic of all. They had run out of time: the ambassadors for Salim, Sultan of Kesh, were due in Brochena within the week, at which point either they agreed to join the shihad, or they became its target.

Scriptualist Acmed made the case for the shihad. 'You must understand that only one body can speak for the whole of the Amteh, and that is the Convocation. The shihad is a sacred obligation to make war. It has not been decreed against the Kore before. The First Crusade took us by surprise, and the feuding of Kesh and Lakh meant no Convocation could be possible for the Second Crusade. Once it is confirmed that the Third Crusade has begun, every able-bodied man in Kesh and Dhassa and Gatioch and beyond will take up arms and march to join Salim's armies. This includes my people, the Jhafi. The obedience they owe to the throne is one thing, Queen-Regent, but this is an obligation to Ahm Himself!'

Ilan Tamadhi nodded quickly in agreement. 'The fact that you Rimoni are Sollan is recognised, your Majesty. The Jhafi will not take up arms against you and your people, but you cannot stand in the way of this call to arms. Already many young men have gone south of their own volition.'

It was so: reports from the Krak di Conditiori, the gateway out of Javon, spoke of young Jhafi streaming out of the country to join the armies mustering in the Zhassi Valley.

'But the true danger is here,' Piero Inveglio replied with a measure of exasperation. 'It is almost certain that the Dorobon will arrive in Hytel with at least one legion. Are we to let them ravage Javon unchecked?'

Acmed spread his hands. 'My people believe the Gorgio to be finished. They do not think the Dorobon will return. The queen-regent has defeated them.'

'But is that what you believe?' Luca Conti growled. 'What are you telling your people in the Dom-al'Ahms?'

'That the Convocation has spoken and we have no choice but to respond,' Acmed replied sharply, with a hint of challenge to his voice.

Elena frowned. *What he was really saying was, 'I control the people, not you.'*

'In 904 the Dorobon conquered Javon with a single legion,' Comte Inveglio reminded the room. 'We overthrew them only when they grew complacent and we managed to poison Louis Dorobon and half the magi. They will not be so lax again. Do you want to see your homeland destroyed while your people are off being slaughtered in Hebusalim, Godspeaker?'

'It is God's will that we march to Hebusalim,' Acmed replied obstinately.

The four Rimoni slapped the table in frustration. 'What is it you want?' Pita Rosco demanded. 'What concession? Lay your cards on the table, damn it!'

'There is no bargaining with Ahm!'

'Ha! There is no bargaining with you,' Luca Conti drawled disgustedly.

'Do not impugn a holy man,' Ilan Tamadhi snapped. He eyed the Rimoni lords firmly. 'Listen, you know me: I have supported the guru's strictures, and I love this land. We are not fools: we know that answering the shihad will cost Javon dearly. We know the risks – but to speak against the Convocation will rouse the common people against us, and that will destroy us even sooner.'

'And still you put your precious faith ahead of the wellbeing of your people,' Pita Rosco complained.

'Yes, my faith is "precious" to me,' Acmed thundered back. 'It is the centre of every man's life, or should be—'

'I agree on that point, if no other,' growled Josip Yannos.

'Gentlemen,' Cera snapped, slapping the table, 'this is unseemly. I want a solution.'

'Apparently there is no solution,' Comte Inveglio rasped. 'They would march off to death or glory, leaving the Rimoni to face the Dorobon alone.' He looked at Ilan Tamadhi. 'Or is there a solution?'

'Those who speak against the Convocation are inviting death,' Ilan replied, his expression neutral.

'Are you threatening our queen-regent?' Luca Conti snarled, and Elena wished once again that Lorenzo were here.

'No,' Acmed put in, 'no, we are not. The queen-regent is beloved by us all. You Rimoni are not threatened by the shihad, not unless you align against it. But the Gorgio must be your problem.'

The argument went round for hours, a storm-tossed sea of words that crashed against the will of the Convocation and broke apart. Elena feared a breakdown, but Cera kept stepping in. At last she asked Elena to speak about the capabilities of a Rondian legion.

'The Dorobon are Rondians from the north,' Elena told the council. 'They are wealthy beyond your reckoning, with all the arrogance that brings. They are closely aligned to the emperor, and highly favoured – the Dowager, the wife of Louis, who you poisoned, has the ear of the Empress-Mother Lucia Fasterius herself. They will invade by windship before the year is out. That is not a guess.

'The Dorobon legion is extremely well-equipped. Though five thousand men does not sound like a lot, these will be mostly mounted, many on gnosis-creatures designed for the battlefield. They will bring winged steeds, and at least a dozen battle-magi. They will be of many levels of blood-purity, but many will be stronger than me. A force like that could destroy an army ten times its size.'

While they were still taking this in, Cera asked, 'What of an army *twenty* times their size?'

Elena blinked. They all did. 'Well,' she started, 'if they held together, if they were not panicked by the awful losses they would incur – even pure-bloods tire; even a construct-beast can be brought down . . . but there is no such army, not here in Javon.'

Cera stabbed a finger in the air. 'Yes there is.'

Everyone looked at her blankly.

'The Harkun,' she answered their silent enquiry.

Every man in the room except Harshal ali Assam rose to their feet, the expressions on their faces ranging from shock to scorn to outrage, but Cera did not flinch.

Finally they fell silent to allow Comte Inveglio to lead the protests. 'Queen-Regent, the Harkun and the Jhafi have been at war for centuries. Their atrocities are legendary – even in my time we've had to fight them on our southern borders. Those memories still haunt me. They torture captives to death and enslave our women. Even the Keshi will not deal with them – they are *animals*, Queen-Regent!'

Cera turned to Harshal ali-Assam, and Elena watched with interest. Harshal had obviously known Cera's suggestion was coming; she wondered what had already been negotiated. *And why was I not included in this discussion?*

'Harshal, I believe you have contacts among the Harkun?' Cera asked. 'Tell us of them.'

Harshal stroked his shaven skull. 'I have made contact with the Harkun through a man of mixed blood. His name is Ghujad iz'Kho and he is known in all the major nomad camps. The Harkun enter our southern marches through mountain passes hundreds of miles east of the Krak. They are impassable in winter so they summer here, in the cooler north, then winter in Kesh. They are devoutly Amteh, but do not acknowledge the Convocation, nor do they swear allegiance to Kesh or Gatioch. They are fiercely independent, and very warlike.'

'Precisely,' exclaimed Pita Rosco. 'Warlike and lawless and owing no allegiance to anyone – let them into our lands and they will run amok!'

'It's only the height of the Pedrani Rift and the forts atop it that keep them out of Javon proper,' Inveglio added. 'Without that natural border we would be overrun.'

'Yes, yes,' replied Harshal quickly, 'we all know this. But the Harkun are not mindless barbarians. They are Amteh, and they adhere to the codes of the Prophet. They also live in the real world. Our commerce with them remains valuable. I have met one of their chieftains, and he can read and write and speak articulately.'

Comte Inveglio grunted, unimpressed. 'Regardless of that, why should they fight alongside us? Would they restrain themselves from plundering whilst in our lands? And how would we make them leave afterwards?'

'By giving them what they want,' Cera responded levelly.

'Which is what? Our lands to graze and our children as slaves?'

'We can promise them all of that, for all that it will matter,' Cera replied. 'They will cease to be a problem after we send them in first against the Dorobon.'

Her words hung in the suddenly silent air. Elena stole a stunned glance at the girl, her heart a lump of ice in her breast. *Great Kore, did my little girl just say that?*

Even Acmed was lost for words, though he recovered quickly. 'You would send the men of an entire people to their deaths just to soften up the Dorobon for the kill?' He blinked thrice, his eyes glazed.

'These are desperate times, my lords,' Cera replied, her voice devoid of emotion.

'They would never agree,' Pita Rosco said in a shaken voice. 'If they are as intelligent as Harshal says, they will know that a pitched battle against a Rondian legion is tantamount to suicide.'

Harshal shook his head. 'They have heard tales of the Rondians, but they do not credit them. They think they are stories made up by the Keshi to explain their defeats.'

'Then all the more will they panic when they confront the reality,' Elena put in. 'When winged gnosis-beasts soar upon them and the battle-magi bring fire and lightning they'll run like devils.'

'Not so: the Harkun are raised to the blade from childhood. They are utterly fearless in battle,' Cera replied, stubbornly backing Harshal.

'But they've not faced magi!' Elena retorted. 'Remember your own men, when the Dorobon came last time? Believe me, in the Noros Revolt we took on the Rondians head-to-head, with our own magi. The battlefields were wastelands, for years after! This will be beyond the ken of the nomads; they'll think themselves facing all of Heaven and Hel, and they will flee and not even be shamed in doing so. They will believe themselves caught in the end of all times.'

'They will fight,' Harshal responded. He looked at Cera. 'Ghujad iz'Kho claims they have more than one hundred thousand warriors.'

'And we Javonesi can almost equal that number,' Cera added. 'That's enough men to finish the job when the Dorobon battle-magi have expended their powers against the Harkun.' She looked about the table. 'It does not matter what we promise the Harkun; we will never have to deliver. And we will be freed of two problems with one blow.'

So cold and calculating – it's a plan such as Gurvon might concoct. Elena hung her head. *Yet these were the lessons I taught her myself.*

'Even if we can do this, what do we tell the sultan's ambassadors?' Ilan Tamadhi asked, frowning. 'Will the shihad be appeased?'

Cera shrugged. 'I believe so. I have a plan for that too . . .'

Two days before the end of Maicin, Queen-Regent Cera Nesti sat upon her throne with her Regency Council and court gathered about her to receive the emissaries of Salim, Sultan of Kesh. The portly Faroukh of Maal, an uncle of the sultan, was here, and with him was the renowned Amteh scholar, Godspeaker Barra Xuok. They took turns at beseeching her to aid the shihad.

'Join us in this righteous quest to rid the world of the invaders, Majesty – surely all the blood in your veins cries vengeance, for you are of the Rimoni, alone of the folk of Yuros you do not bow the knee to the Rondian emperor. You are also Jhafi: you have felt the heel of their oppression, right here in Javon. You have felt the scourge of their magi – your spirit is with us already, Queen-Regent, so let your body join it, united in one purpose.'

Faroukh unfurled the white banner of the shihad, the crescent and star foremost, framed by the four scimitars representing the four corners of the world. At the centre of it was embroidered a castle and a word: *Hebusalim,* the goal of this shihad. 'The Lakh are with us; all of Antiopia rises as one. Let not the Jhafi be denied their place in this holy brotherhood.'

Elena watched from a hidden alcove, as her open presence would be inflammatory. She did not wish to be present, in any case; she felt shut out of this matter. After the last meeting she had told Cera her plan was manipulative, deceitful and destructive, but Cera now believed herself above being criticised by her bodyguard. 'You're an outsider, and you offered no solutions of your own,' she had said, her voice harsh, dismissive. 'You gave me no support, just scary stories about the might of your own people. Perhaps you'd be happier back among them.' She had stormed out, and had not spoken a word since to Elena that was not a direct order.

To be estranged from Cera's affection was horrid, and with Lorenzo away, Elena felt isolated and afraid. Borsa was busy with Timori, preparing him for his ceremonial role greeting the ambassadors. There was only Tarita's company to console her.

If only it didn't all feel so suicidal. She remembered the devastation battle-magi could wreak: the ruined bodies, burnt beyond recognition; the bulging faces of men drowned on dry land; the corpses of men torn apart by construct-creatures with hideous powers. What hope did Javon have, even if Cera sold her soul to gain Harkun aid?

Finally, the Keshi finished their appeal, a beautifully choreographed finale that found Faroukh on one knee, holding the banner of the shihad, while the Godspeaker clutched the Amteh Book with his right hand pointing up to the heavens. Elena, like the whole court, held her breath, their eyes on the eighteen-year old-girl who held the fate of their land in her youthful grasp.

When Cera spoke, her voice rang out clearly. 'Lord Faroukh, Godspeaker Barra, I have heard your words. I have heard also the words of the people of Javon, from northern Hytel, where the Gorgio hold out against the just rulers of Ja'afar, to the fortresses on the Rift, warding us from the Harkun; from Lybis, whose farmers just want peace, to Baroz, which hungers for war.

'All men speak of the justice of the shihad – none would have their lands sullied by the ferang. I hear this, and I echo it, but just as in battle, you cannot take your eye from the man before you to face the distant threat. Nor can we Javonesi turn our backs upon the Gorgio. We must crush them, to be one people once more.

'Nor can we allow our borders to be violated. We know that our southern fortresses have stood between independence and slavery to the Keshi in the past. I cannot blindly say to Sultan Salim, "Send me your warriors that we may crush the Gorgio." Even in the days of the shihad, that much trust is not permissible, though it aches my heart. But I ask you this: allow me to raise the banner of the shihad, here in Javon: a special banner, blessed by the Godspeaker, bearing the legend "Hytel". Let us raise shihad upon the Gorgio and Dorobon and then, once purged, we will take up the banner of the Hebusalim shihad.'

Elena observed the murmuring of the court, listening to Cera's plan, an attempt to convince the Keshi that Javon resisting the Gorgio and the Dorobon was sufficient call to arms to appease the Convocation. The secret negotiations prior to this reception had been inconclusive.

She held her breath as they all did, waiting to hear the ambassador's response.

Faroukh conferred with his Godspeaker, then he turned back to Cera. 'Queen-Regent, we have heard your request. We acknowledge its wisdom and the love it shows for both of your peoples, and for peace, and for Ahm in Paradise. Sultan Salim has given me some discretion to reach accommodation with you. Your proposal has many points in its favour.'

The court went utterly silent, hanging on the ambassador's words.

'Lady, Salim the Great will look upon your request with favour. But he would urge me to note that it runs counter to the will of the Convocation, which summons all warriors of the shihad to the conflict in Hebusalim.' He paused significantly, as the court took this in. 'However, Mighty Salim also notes that the Convocation gave the leadership of the shihad to him alone. It does not remove the right for him to protect what is his.'

What is his? Elena leaned forward from her vantage. *What does that mean?*

Faroukh bowed to Cera. 'Salim is a great admirer of your courage and intellect, lady. He has heard of your valiant and victorious struggles against the treacherous Gorgio and evil Dorobon. He has heard the reports of your gentleness and beauty. He humbly asks for your hand in marriage.'

Cera's mouth fell open.

'Were you his bride, dear lady, he would acquire the right to protect you, even as he protects his own household. Then he could grant your request without impugning the shihad.'

Cera's hand went to her heart. 'Emir Faroukh, I am overcome. So lowly a person as I, a mere regent with no right to the throne once my brother comes of age, is unworthy of Salim the Great's notice.'

Oh, well said! Elena almost clapped her hands, aching to be beside the girl. *You remind him that he cannot have Javon just by marrying you.*

The emir bowed, his composure unruffled. 'Lady, Salim does not wish to claim the throne of Ja'afar. He wishes only to secure his northern frontier. He would expect nothing more than the right to have an observer at your council table until your brother attains his majority. He would not even require your presence in his court until after this war is fought.'

'My lord Sultan Salim is generous,' Cera whispered, her voice husky.

'Then you accept his proposal?' Faroukh asked warmly.

Cera looked around.

<Take a break, confer!> Elena urged her silently.

Cera heard; she turned her head and met Elena's eyes. Then she turned away. 'I accept the sultan's magnanimous proposal,' she murmured.

The Jhafi at court burst into raptures, while the Rimoni looked stunned.

When finally there was silence, Faroukh bowed again. 'We are overjoyed, dear lady. Let me be first to give you obeisance as my future queen.' He fell to his knees, placing his forehead on the floor. His fellow ambassador, a holy man, bowed. The Jhafi all prostrated themselves, while the Rimoni looked increasingly discomforted.

When Faroukh rose, he cried, 'I show you the wisdom of great Salim,' and made a resplendent gesture. One of his aides unfurled another banner and a murmur ran through the court.

It was a shihad banner, like the first, but bearing the name of Hytel, the stronghold of the Gorgio, in its centre. The sultan had anticipated Cera's acceptance. 'Let this banner go before you as you conquer the north, and thereafter may you ride to war in Hebusalim. And after the victory: a wedding!'

Cera stood. 'Thank you, my lords. But I must hear the will of my people before I commit to this path. My acceptance is not enough; I must have the agreement of those I rule.'

Their self-congratulatory smiles froze on their faces as Cera addressed the court. 'My people, if there is any person present who wishes to speak against the Hytel shihad, or my acceptance of this marriage proposal, I invite you forward now, without fear of censure.'

There was a pause which stretched uneasily as Elena wrung her hands, unable to work out whether this had been a victory or a great defeat. *Gurvon would know . . . Damn this!* She could not read all the nuances; she could only watch as the silence stretched and people shuffled awkwardly.

At last Comte Inveglio stepped forth. 'I have only this to say,' he shouted. 'Long live the Queen-Regent and death to the Gorgio!' He went on his knees before Cera, and suddenly the whole court was doing the same. Cera stood in the middle of all of this, apparently lost for words.

'Long live the Nesti! Long live Javon! Death to the Gorgio!'

Elena picked at her food, watching Cera from her alcove on the balcony above the feast-hall, where the queen-regent was hosting a celebratory banquet. She looked ill-at-ease seated beside Godspeaker Barra Xuok, who seldom smiled. Elena was also uncomfortable; she had not lost her fear that this evening would end in blood. She wanted nothing more than to pack Cera back into her warded tower again, away from potential assassins.

A tall robed figure stepped into her alcove. 'Sal'Ahm.'

Elena rose quickly. 'Sal'Ahm, Lord Faroukh. Are you permitted to address one of Shaitan's spawn?' she added wryly.

'My faith is strong. I'm sure I can resist your wiles,' the sultan's uncle answered with a faintly ironic smile. 'How may I address you?'

'"Donna Elena" is fine. I expect you think I have some evil influence over the queen-regent and are wondering therefore how I have let the events of this afternoon happen,' she observed, gesturing to the chair beside her.

Faroukh sat and held out his goblet to a servant for refilling. The Godspeaker might not drink alcohol, but evidently Faroukh did. 'I admit it has crossed my mind, Donna Elena.'

'A plan never looks so good when your enemy approves of it, eh?' She met his eye. 'You're very casual about talking to the likes of me.'

'Donna Elena, I have met several magi of the Ordo Costruo. They are men and women who laboured for the people, turning Hebusalim into a garden. I have also met men like Tomas Betillon, who have betrayed agreements and done evil. Thinking men like me wonder how the magi can be servants of Shaitan and yet act in so many different ways.'

Elena gave a tight smile. 'Your thinking does you credit, at least in my eyes.'

'Were you expecting Salim's offer? Do you approve of your queen-regent's acceptance?' he asked.

'I think you would have given us that banner anyway,' Elena replied carefully.

Faroukh shook his head. 'Having made the offer publicly, a refusal would have ended all negotiations, and all hope of friendship. A sultan cannot be publicly refused, Donna Elena.'

Oh, Cera. You knew that, didn't you? And they trapped you. She held her tongue prudently.

'Will you go to war under the shihad banner, Donna Elena?' he enquired.

Elena met his eye. 'If the queen-regent goes to war, I will be there, under the *Nesti* banner.'

'Why is that, Donna Elena? You are ferang. You do not belong here.'

Elena suspected her reply would be reported all the way up to Salim himself. 'Because I love this people, this land and my princessa. I have made holy vows to serve the Nesti, and I will fulfil them. This is my home now, and anyone who wants to get to Queen-Regent Cera must come through me.'

Faroukh inclined his head. 'Heard and understood, Donna Elena.' He raised his goblet to her, then finished it in one swallow. 'Thank you for your time. It has been a pleasure. Sal'Ahm on high.'

'Sal'Ahm,' Elena replied, and the sultan's uncle rose, bowed and was gone.

Tomorrow there would be public announcements, displays of the banners of shihad, celebrations. But tonight stretched cold and lonely before her. Cera would doubtless continue to ignore her, and Lorenzo was far away.

32

The Ghost of a Dog

Necromancy

You speak as if Necromancers are inherently evil. But do you not want the knowledge the dead hold? Would you have murderers go free when I can ask their victim who killed them? Would you allow spirits to linger in torment for want of a mage who can bring them peace? Not all that Necromancy can do is moral, but fire burns, does it not? Like all Crafts, Necromancy is a tool; it is the use it is put to that may be questioned by this committee, but not the tool itself.

DARIUS FYRELL, WAR CRIMES HEARING, NOROSTEIN 911

Pontus and Norostein, on the continent of Yuros
Maicin 928
2 months until the Moontide

Mordai, 25 Maicin 928
There was no fanfare for the arrival of Belonius Vult back into Pontus after two nights on a windship above the ocean. He used Clairvoyance to send ahead his instructions: *Tell no one I am here, not even Korion. I need a skiff and crew, ready to leave for Norostein within an hour of my arrival.*

He'd been forced to leave the diplomatic mission in Hebusalim early – not that it mattered; the most important meetings had already taken place, with Meiros and Betillon, and the secret one with Emir Rashid. He had more pressing matters to attend to now: finding whoever had broken into his personal quarters. *Who dared?*

It was incredible, that someone would have the nerve to take *him* on. And how had they known where to look? Had that guttersnipe

Gron Koll thought to rob his master – no, it surely wasn't Koll. Someone tremendously powerful had blocked his counter-strike. He'd been on the verge of breaking through and at least learning the identity of the robbers, even from across the ocean, when his scrying-assault has been shattered. The strength of that blow still unnerved him. He had only ever felt that level of power wielded by Church Inquisitors.

The windskiff he'd requested was waiting for him when he landed and he was in the air again inside an hour. The skiff was lightweight and full-sailed, built for speed, and the two young magi piloting it were on extra money to get him to Norostein by Freyadai night. The wind whipped his hair as he sat beside the mast, staring ahead as the night turned slowly to day, his mind racing. He would be able to contact Fyrell tomorrow or the next day. How much he could tell him was debatable, but he needed someone there to get the investigation started discreetly. He wondered which files had been taken – all of them? Many were personally incriminating, but most were more damaging to people he currently wanted to protect. Whichever had been taken, it was imperative they were recovered.

Who the Hel has robbed me?

'You did what?' Ramon leapt to his feet and stared at him, his eyes bulging.

Alaron hung his head. 'I needed to know,' he said defensively. Once he'd realised that he'd probably signed all of their death warrants he knew he had to confess.

Ramon swore and cursed, but Cym just looked away, perhaps calculating how much time they had until someone worked out the Alaron Mercer file was missing and came looking for him. Either that, or she was deciding precisely how she would kill him.

'For Kore's sake, Alaron,' Ramon shouted, 'we all knew your graduation failing was a fix – anyone with half a brain could work that out! And *obviously* it had to be ratified by the governor! You didn't need to steal the rukking file to know that!'

Alaron hung his head. There was no point arguing. Ramon was right.

'So, when Vult gets back he'll find two files missing: one, the Langstrit file, and two, the Alaron Mercer file. So it should take him, oh – about *two seconds* – to send a squad here. Kore's cods – are you a complete rukking idiot?' Ramon balled his fists furiously.

'I'm sorry,' he muttered. 'I'm really, *really* sorry. I didn't think—'

'No, you *never* think! You just *do* things, and then stare at the broken pieces with a gormless look on your face.' Ramon was shaking with rage. 'We'd just pulled off one of the thefts of the century, and for once – for *once* – you'd actually been really smart. And now you tell us you followed that up by doing the equivalent of painting our names and addresses on the walls as you left.' Ramon threw his hands up in fury and stomped out, as if afraid of what violence he would commit if he stayed.

Alaron buried his face in his hands, wondering almost in passing what his mother was making of all the shouting. Cym came and knelt beside his chair and put her hands over his. 'Kore's Blood, Alaron, but you're such a fool,' she murmured, a pitying look on her face. 'What are we going to do now?'

He'd been thinking about that himself, all night long. And he was grateful she wasn't screaming at him too. 'Well, I think we have two choices,' he started. 'We could run far enough away that he can't follow us, but I don't think we're capable of that. The other option is to solve this in the next few days. The maps say it's five thousand miles from here to Hebusalim. Even Vult can't make that sort of journey in less than a week. I reckon we've got until the first of Junesse, and then he'll be here and I'll be dead.'

'That sounds right,' she said, touching his cheek. 'You really are an idiot, you know. But you're interesting to be around. We need to make plans. I'll go and pacify Ramon.'

He tried to thank her, but she just waved a hand and left him alone, his eyes full and his throat so tight he struggled to breathe, thinking, *I'm not too clever, but I'm lucky in my friends.*

They returned a few minutes later, Ramon still clench-fisted and simmering, Cym with a matronly look on her face. Alaron looked at her gratefully. 'Ramon, Cym, I'm really, *really* sorry. The only one he can pin the break-in to is me – it's my fault, and I deserve the consequences. If I were you I would run and leave me to it.'

'No, you wouldn't,' Cym said. 'You'd stay and help, just like we're going to. You're an idiot, but you're loyal to a fault.'

'One of many faults,' Ramon growled. He still looked ready to spit, but Cym put a warning hand on the Silacian's shoulder. 'Vult can't get here for days,' she said, 'so we'll solve it by then. Then we'll hide you somehow until we work out what to do next. We're not going to leave you in the lurch.'

'However richly you deserve it,' Ramon muttered. He glared at Alaron, and then forced a grim smile. 'Well, instead of having the leisure to solve this in our own time, we've got about four days before a legendary pure-blood mage descends upon our sorry arses. So let's get on with it.'

'I mean it,' Alaron insisted. 'If you go, I'll not—'

'Yes, we got that,' Ramon said sarcastically, 'now shut up and concentrate. Realistically, we probably only had about a week to solve it anyway, before we all had to get on with our lives, so apart from having attracted the attention of the most powerful man in Noros, what's changed, eh?' He held out a hand. 'Where's that bloody arrest report?'

They spent some time poring over the Watch Report, penned in the flowing hand of Special Constable Darius Fyrell, bane of their college lives. Fyrell had left a detailed written report of the arrest, the skirmish that followed and the condition of the general, which was just as he was now: disoriented, with memories and self-identity gone. He did note marks on Langstrit's hands and forearms, recently inflicted, as if he had been either tortured, engaged in combat or caught in a gnosis energy blast.

Fyrell had also listed what he found in the chapel:

General Langstrit, wearing commoner's clothing and his periapt (emerald set on neck-chain).

A flask of gnosis-brewed truth serum, partially consumed and detectable upon the general's breath.

A bowl of milk, mostly consumed, containing a fast-acting and lethal poison.

A dead wolf-hound, identified as JL's favourite, recently deceased from ingestion of said poison.

A sheath of papers containing writings from the Scriptures, with possible encryption markings.

A scratching in the paint of the floor, reading 'JL 824: Argundun my wife'.

The rest of the scroll-case contained the Scripture pages mentioned under item 5: sheets pulled from a Kore Scriptorium, with red markings under various letters. There were also several pages of notes in a different hand, probably Belonius Vult's, which looked to be attempts to solve the encryption. Judging by the crossings-outs and increasingly ragged writing, it hadn't been going well. The final page looked like it had been screwed up several times before Vult decided to keep it. It contained a complex chart of numbers and letters and lines drawing conclusions. The final line appeared to be his conclusion, a series of dotted lines, each containing a letter. Vult had got most of the way through, then stopped. What he had 'solved' read:

W R O N G | A G A I N | B E L O _ _ _ _

Ramon laughed aloud when he saw that. 'So the old general outsmarted Vult – good on him.'

'But if Vult couldn't solve it, what hope have we got?' Alaron asked worriedly.

Ramon shrugged. 'I can solve anything.' He'd recovered his normal good humour somewhat, though he still shook his head disbelievingly whenever he looked at Alaron.

'It's all the murder investigations they have in Silacia,' Cym observed tartly. 'It sharpens their minds.'

'My mind was already a razor, Cym-amora.' Ramon frowned. 'Let's assume that Belonius has worked them over thoroughly. So does this mean there is a real clue here, or was it just a puzzle Langstrit left to annoy Vult?'

'Or both,' Cym added.

'Or both,' Ramon agreed. 'So, Fyrell gets the word that Langstrit is in Lower Town. He arrives with his men, cracks a few skulls and grabs him. Langstrit has a few burns and his mind is gone. Inside the chapel there is a poisoned dog and traces of a truth serum. What are his conclusions?'

Alaron tried first. 'How's this: someone was trying to get information out of Langstrit. They threatened him with the death of his dog and when threatening didn't work, they killed it. They hurt him with mage-fire – so they're a mage. They fed him the serum, he told them what they want, so they destroyed his mind and left the other stuff to taunt Belonius.'

Ramon shook his head. 'No, no, we know that is exactly what *didn't* happen because we know something that Fyrell and Vult haven't worked out yet: *Langstrit did this to himself.* I'm sure Vult hasn't seen the rune we deciphered, so they were working under the assumption that there's another party involved, someone who erased Langstrit's mind. That puts a whole new slant on it, doesn't it?'

Cym agreed. 'It means that Langstrit did all of this himself: he swallowed the serum, he burnt himself. *Sol et Lune*, he even poisoned his own dog – so why would he do that?'

'It knew too much,' Ramon sniggered, before waving a placating hand. 'Sorry, bad joke.'

'What it might mean,' said Alaron carefully, 'is that Langstrit hid the Scytale and wanted to leave a trail for friendly eyes. If we hadn't seen the rune, we would believe someone else was involved too.'

'Vult must be terrified that whoever that person is will show up one day and demand some answers – for Lukhazan, and a few other things. How does he sleep?' Cym wondered.

'Badly, I hope,' Ramon said. 'So: why would Langstrit take truth serum if he's about to erase his own mind?'

Alaron pulled a long face. 'I can't think of one good reason – unless it's just a distraction to hide the real clues.'

'I agree,' Cym said. 'The truth serum only makes sense if he were being tortured, not if he did it to himself. It's a false trail.'

Ramon rubbed his nose thoughtfully. 'Okay, that's possible.'

'But why would he kill his own dog?' Alaron wondered. 'That makes no sense at all.'

They were quiet for a long time.

'What about this, "JL 824: Argundun my wife"?' Ramon asked eventually. 'Is that year significant to the general somehow?'

Alaron consulted *Generals of the Glorious Rebellion*, but there was nothing there. He found what he needed in another of his mother's books. 'Langstrit was born in 824,' he reported excitedly, 'and he was married for a long time ago, to a mage-woman called Beatta. Hey, don't Argundians call themselves "Argundun"?'

'Yes,' Ramon said, 'but why scratch it on the floor of the chapel?'

There was another long silence.

Cym leaned forward. 'Who or what burnt him if he was there alone? Maybe it was just another attempt to throw everyone off the scent?'

Ramon jabbed a finger at her. 'Probably – but it would also have messed up all the psychic residue in the chapel.' He snatched up the sheet containing the runes-pattern they'd been studying for so long. 'Look – remember that squiggle in the rune that we couldn't explain? It could be a "wild energy" sigil.' He looked pleased with himself. 'That means the burn-marks were deliberate and self-inflicted. Langstrit knew that other magi would try and investigate, so he covered his traces.'

Alaron sat up, feeling like they were making progress. 'So what next?'

'Let me think about that.' Ramon looked hard at Alaron. 'Don't think I didn't notice what Vult said in that memorandum: he told Gavius and Muhren not to intervene if they saw you using a periapt. That is absolutely non-procedural. Vult wanted you to have a periapt.'

'He's a Diviner. I think he's Divined something.'

'Agreed. After he heard your thesis, he must have asked: "Who is this boy? Is he right?" He must have been crawling out of his skin trying to figure out what he'd missed. And then Langstrit escaped from wherever he was being held—'

'I did wonder if perhaps he pushed Langstrit my way,' Alaron mused. 'If he'd been getting nowhere with him, maybe he thought we might unlock the problem for him?'

Ramon whistled softly. 'Possible, amici – but no, unlikely. No, I think he just Divined that you might be onto something and decided to give you some rope.'

'You mean we're leading him to the Scytale?' Cym looked aghast.

'He will believe so.' Ramon pulled a face. 'But what choice do we have now?'

'I wish there was someone we could trust who would help us,' Cym said. 'There must be *someone* in this city who wouldn't just turn us over to Vult or rob us and use the information for themselves.'

'You would think so,' Alaron agreed, 'but there's no one I can think of. I don't trust the Church – and don't even mention the Watch. That memo suggests that so-called hero Jeris Muhren is in this up to his eyeballs.'

'Not necessarily,' Cym disagreed. 'He could be totally unaware and just following orders.'

'You just fancy him,' Ramon grinned, and when Cym blushed girlishly, 'Ha! Knew it!'

'He is a friend of my father,' Cym said, a little sheepishly. 'He's always been decent to my family.'

'We can't risk telling him anything,' Alaron repeated, piqued by Cym's reaction to Ramon's jibe, and Cym nodded grudgingly. They all winced a little as they heard Tesla start another coughing fit in the next room.

'I don't like your mother's cough,' she added quietly to Alaron. 'She's not as healthy as she pretends.'

It was another thing to worry about – not what Alaron needed.

Tydai, 26 Maicin 928

The valleys of East Verelon had been transformed into a floodplain, Belonius Vult noted grimly as his windskiff roared above. Repeated weather-working by Air-magi as the legions traversed the Great Road had left a trail of devastation; storms, flash floods and furious gales battered the farms and villagers, ruining crops and houses. Half the trees had been ripped up by tornados and hurricanes, and dead cattle floated in the miles of trapped floodwaters. The air stank of rotting bodies and muddy water, heated by the summer sun until the land was nothing but a series of tepid lakes of cesswater. All along the Imperial Road, miles-long caravans were bogged down in the sludge.

What a rukking waste of time and money, he thought.

They had flown all night, only putting down near dawn for his pilot-magi to get some rest. He himself had barely slept, consumed with anxiety over what awaited him in Norostein. Still, tomorrow Norostein would come within his clairvoyance range and he would be able to set things in motion. In the meantime, there were many other issues to consider. He let his mind run free . . .

What was Gurvon doing? Had he struck against Elena Anborn yet, or was this some elaborate game Gurvon and Elena were playing to hold the emperor to ransom? *Perhaps I need to distance myself further? A year ago we outlined a programme of conquest to the emperor: does it still hold? Will the events in Javon ruin it all? Can we trust this Rashid Mubarak, on whom much rests? Is Antonin Meiros a senile fool or cunning snake? Why did he marry a Lakh – who is she, really?*

A worst-case scenario haunted him: that someone else had gained the Scytale of Corineus . . . Where in Hel was Jarius Langstrit? How had a helpless, mind-erased old man managed to escape custody? And why did his divinations constantly tell him that Tesla Anborn's son was a factor? Tesla, Elena's sister – was that connection significant? Who was the hidden hand here; the mage who had destroyed Langstrit's mind, then vanished?

What am I flying back into?

Wotendai, 27 Maicin 928

Tydai had passed without any breakthrough and the search for clues was becoming desperate. On Wotendai Alaron visited General Langstrit's last remaining relative: the widow of his son, Ardan. She lived in Quatremille Parish, a poor area near the lake. Ardan Langstrit had been a mage, but he had married for love: a milkmaid named Kyra from the Knebb. Ardan had served in the Revolt, but he had been captured at Lukhazan and his health had been destroyed by the prison's dreadful conditions. By the end of the war he had looked older than his father.

'So you're Vann and Tesla's son,' Kyra Langstrit said, staring at Alaron across her kitchen table. 'I can see a little of both of them in you. Everyone thought well of your father,' she added. Kyra had grey-streaked hair and a sad face. Ardan Langstrit had been the Principal when Alaron and his friends started at Turm Zauberin, but once Vult became governor he'd been displaced by Lucius Gavius. Ardan had hanged himself soon after, leaving Kyra with no income, no looks to attract, no sophistication and a country woman's caution of charlatans. She'd been gradually selling off her husband's estates to survive and now rented a room in her own house, clinging on like a limpet, with no hope of a better life. She was forty-four, and already dead.

'What do you remember of the general?' Alaron asked, wondering if this was a waste of time. *Yes, she has a sad life, but still . . .*

'Old Jari? I don't even know if he's alive or dead – no one can tell me. He would have been one hundred, four years ago. Of course, he is a mage, and they live longer lives than we unblessed folk. I do wish I could have had children, but my Ardan was taken from me too soon . . .' She trailed off, and blinked the tears from her eyes.

'And the general?' Alaron prompted gently.

'Oh, he was always kind to me. You know he had a dog? Lovely old thing. I wonder what became of it – Nye, he called it. He was a funny dog, that one: dead loyal. He loved old Jari, he did, and Jari loved him back. He used to walk him every day, even during the siege, down from Old Town, across the Mint Bridge and all the way to Pordavin Square. He reckoned the old boy could do it blindfold.'

Alaron rolled his eyes. 'Did the general ever speak of Belonius Vult?'

'Who?'

'The governor – the general at Lukhazan?'

She shook her head. 'I never concerned myself with men's talk; left that to Ardan. Would you like another biscuit?'

*

Alaron went home to report failure. 'It was purgatory,' he groaned to the others. 'She went on and on about absolutely nothing – she knows nothing about the general, or even her husband. She didn't even know he'd been fired from the college! She must have been living in cuckoo-land even then.'

It hadn't been a good day. They'd eliminated a few possibilities, but it didn't feel like progress. Alaron went to bed shaking with worry. He was on the verge of begging his friends to run for it. It wasn't fair to leave themselves in the firing line when Vult returned or when Muhren came knocking.

One more day, and then we'll all have to run . . .

Belonius Vult pulled the ball of light in his hands into a wider sphere, cloaking it in illusion so that his mage-pilots could not eavesdrop, and reached out with his mind. *<Darius, answer!>*

Fyrell's face appeared immediately within the ball of light: black-bearded, with beak-like nose above a thin-lipped mouth. *<Magister Vult! How may I serve, master?>*

<There has been a break-in at my residence, Darius. Question Gron Koll. Be as hard as necessary. But do not enter my residence, understood?>

<A break-in? Who would dare, master?>

<Who indeed, Darius? At this stage, you need only ask questions; do not act on the answers you gain. I will be there on Freyadai.>

<In two days – are you not in Hebusalim?>

<Do you hear any relay-stave echoes, Darius? I'm over Verelon. Meet me at the docking platform on Freyadai. I will warn you of my imminent landing. I expect a full report on arrival.>

He broke the contact and let the ball of light dissipate. Fyrell was usually reliable, but he was not to be trusted, of course – too much pent-up ambition. Already he was chafing at his rank in the college, wanting more, too soon. But for now, he was the best tool at hand.

Though Koll was hired on Fyrell's recommendation . . . Are you involved in this, Darius?

Torsdai, 28 Maicin 928

Alaron took a turn bathing his mother's forehead that afternoon; her fever had risen and he had sent for a healer. They were running out of time to sold the puzzle, so Ramon and Cym had turned their attention to hiding Alaron from Belonius Vult.

Tesla slept poorly and her ruined face looked corpselike. His father had kept a painting of his mother done before Tesla flew off to Pontus and the carnage of the First Crusade. She had been lovely, with a determined face and a mane of red hair. Her sister Elena had been in the portrait too, angular and moody-looking. The painting was in storage; he wondered aloud where his Aunt Elena was.

'Causing trouble, I don't doubt,' Tesla rasped. She grimaced and groped for a glass of water. 'Elena will be at the heart of things, she always was. And giving the bastards Hel. Don't be fooled by what Besko said, boy. If he says "betrayal", you can bet it means something more like "plot thwarted". Perhaps she's even grown a conscience. Stranger things have happened.'

'No one screws with Aunt Elena, right?'

His mother chuckled, a rasping sound that turned into a cough. 'Mind your language, boy,' she warned as an afterthought. 'So, what are you and your friends doing that's such a big drama?'

'Just trying to help the general, Ma,' Alaron replied cautiously.

'Seems to necessitate a lot of arguing and shouting and running around,' Tesla remarked dryly. 'Making any progress? Still all friends?'

'Not sure.'

'On which point?'

'The progress. Yes, we're still friends.'

His mother turned and focused her eyeless gaze on him. 'You're in trouble, aren't you, son?'

'No, no – not at all–'

'That bad, is it?'

Alaron hung his head. 'I had to steal something. It might be pinned back to me.'

She stiffened slightly. 'Idiot boy. Didn't your aunt teach you anything, or that jackanapes Silacian? You never, *ever*, leave a trail. Who did you rob?'

He couldn't lie to her. 'The governor.'

She went dead still and he saw the beginning flicker of flames about her fingers. He hurriedly reached out and clutched her hands closed. They were painfully hot to touch.

'The governor? *You robbed Belonius Vult?*' She clutched his arm and wrenched him close. 'You need to go to Jeris Muhren – he'll shield you. Vann and he fought together. Go to Muhren—'

'I can't, Ma. Muhren is in it with Vult.'

'Impossible.' Her voice was flat and absolute. 'They *despise* each other.'

'It's true. They're partners in something shady. But Cym's family know a cellar in an old warehouse down by the docks in Old Town that's deep enough to block scrying. We can hide there, wait it out. Ramon has been preparing it, laying down food and water. Cym's people will keep an eye out for me and I'll take care of the general. They remember what he did for them in the Revolt. It'll all be fine. And Cym will look after you for a while, until I can come out again.'

'You'd be better off running to Silacia, though you should have left by now.' She bared her yellowed teeth. 'Why hasn't Vult been here already?'

'He's away, Ma, but he'll be back any day now.'

She wrapped her claw-like hands about him and held him against her bony frame. 'Oh, you foolish boy.'

Alaron didn't move until his mother fell asleep. He disentangled himself and went back to the lounge, poured himself cold lemon tea and sat staring at the sheaf of notes. Ramon had started working on the phrase 'JL 824: Argundun my wife', but he'd not got further than writing 'anagram?'; 'code?'; 'Scripture?' and a series of doodles.

I hate puzzles. Why kill your favourite dog, then wipe your own brain? And what on Urte does this stupid phrase have to do with anything?

He was still sitting there when the others returned. He'd forgotten to drink his tea, but he was trembling with excitement. The room was almost pitch-black and Alaron could scarcely make out the papers any more. The general snored in an armchair.

Cym pulled the curtains open. 'You'll go blind working in the dark.'

Ramon trailed in behind her, carrying bags of vegetables. 'What's up, Al?' he asked. 'You look like Corineus just touched you.'

'I just had a thought, that's all.'

'I guess that'd be pretty stunning for you.'

Alaron made a rude sign. He'd been sitting there turning the thought over in his mind for an hour or more. 'I think I've solved part of the mystery of the dog,' he said, trying to sound nonchalant.

They looked at him expectantly. 'Well?'

'I was looking at that phrase – 'JL 824: Argundun my wife'. This might sound dumb, and unless you know the name of the dog it wouldn't work, and even then you have to know that Langstrit killed the dog himself, which Vult and his lot don't know, but—'

'Alaron, you're babbling,' Ramon said tersely. 'Spit it out, amici, spit it out.'

'Uh, sorry! You know that number: 824? I noticed it matches the number of letters in the phrase with it: "Argundun my wife". See? An eight-letter word, a two-letter word, then a four-letter word. And if you take the last letter of each – the eighth, the second and the fourth, you get three letters: N, Y and E: Nye: the name of his dog.'

Cym cocked her head. 'That's a clue?'

Ramon was more enthusiastic. 'You know, you might be right. It isn't all that sophisticated, but it might mean something. Any further thoughts, Al?'

'Well,' Alaron replied, 'the poison he used on the dog reminded me of something from Necromancy lessons. It was made from mottle-hood, which is known to enhance the likelihood of the spirit lingering close to the body. We did a whole class on them, remember? They're called shadow-poisons.'

'Wouldn't Vult know that?' Cym enquired doubtfully.

'Only if he's a necromancer,' Ramon responded. 'His profile in the *Generals of the Inglorious Rhubarb* doesn't suggest that. Necromancy is part of Sorcery, which he doesn't seem to do, and it's associated with Earth and he's an Air-mage, the diametric opposite.'

'So you think *Alaron* might know something *Belonius Vult* doesn't?' Cym pulled a face.

'Put like that, it does seem far-fetched,' Ramon agreed, winking at Alaron.

'I'm going to ignore you both and carry on,' Alaron said. 'Mottlehood is common enough: people use it to kill weeds, mostly, not animals. But if you wanted to create a ghost, that's what you'd use.'

'The ghost of a dog?' scoffed Cym.

'The ghost of *Nye*,' Alaron corrected, 'a dog whose master walked him every day from Old Town across Mint Bridge, all the way to Pordavin Square and the chapel where Langstrit was found.'

Ramon blinked. 'You think that the ghost of his dog could lead us to the next step of the puzzle?'

Alaron shrugged. 'Why not?'

'But was Langstrit a necromancer?'

'He was an Earth-mage, and necromancy is Earth-related, so that suggests some affinity. We need to take another look at that chapel, by night. Necromancy is an affinity of mine, even though I'm rubbish at it. It works better at night-time, but I need to prepare.'

Ramon shook his hand. 'Good work, Agent Mercer. We may yet save your butt.'

Ramon led them through the winding alleys of Pordavin, effortlessly avoiding the Watch patrols. It was moon-dark and the pre-dawn glow in the east was still faint, so the silent streets were lightless. They were all clad in dark clothes, and grateful for the scarves muffling their faces; Noros was high above sea-level and the nights were always cold. Dawn was still two bells away. Alaron had scarcely slept, but he felt invigorated by this possible break-through.

They slipped into the chapel on Pordavin Square unseen, and were relieved to find no beggars inside. The flooded floor had only partially drained, which had probably kept the homeless out. The stagnant water stank abominably. Ramon made a florid gesture at it. 'Alaron, the floor is yours. Well, the puddle is yours, anyway.'

Cym closed the main door to prevent their lights reaching the street. Alaron steeled himself as he splashed through the main chapel to the side chapel, where the dog's body had been found all those years ago. He glanced back at Ramon, seeking reassurance.

'You can do this, Al,' his friend whispered. 'Confidence.'

Confidence . . . Alaron nodded and closed his eyes. He called to mind the small things he'd got right in college and blanked the failures. Ever since Ramon's lecture at the tavern, he'd been trying to convince himself that he was capable of leaping the hurdles he'd always fallen at before. *But necromantic-gnosis – ugh!* Fyrell had taught Necromancy, and he'd hated all of Fyrell's classes, so he'd always done badly. Mostly he hated the way it felt: necromantic-gnosis was horrible, manifesting as a gelid purple energy that oozed through his fingers like slime. And he hated being around corpses; the horrible cold-jelly feel of dead flesh and the stare of lifeless eyes terrified him.

Toughen up, he told himself. *You've no choice now. Do this, or Vult will slaughter you.*

The gnosis came painfully, leeching the heat from his body. As he sent out his call, it felt like a million rats with dead flesh clinging to their teeth turned and hissed at him. There was a murmur of half-heard voices in his ears, the voices of those who had died here. He blanked them out, focused only on his call.

<Nye, Nye . . . here boy!>

His normal sight faded and instead he could see dark shadows creeping from corners, sliding along the walls: half-seen faces, lost souls, drawn like moths to flames. <Nye, *faithful hound*, Nye.> He imagined the dog he had seen in the picture-book and sent that image out. <Nye . . . >

'Alaron?' Cym's voice was ragged. She suddenly snatched her hand back as a new crack silently appeared in the wall she was standing against.

A chill voice seeped through from some deeper place beyond. *<Who calls? Who dares?>*

Cym backed away as a human shape imprinted itself like a wet stain on the stonework. Without thinking, Alaron raised a hand and muttered a spell to banish the dead. Something shrieked, an inhuman sound, and the shape was gone.

Wow, I did that!

'What happened?' Ramon gasped.

Cym backed towards the door. 'Alaron, I'm not sure this is a good idea—'

'I'm not liking it either,' Ramon admitted. 'Get it over with, will you?'

Alaron called again, focusing on the dog. He wished he'd actually met Nye, but of course he'd not been born then. He knew the breed, though – perhaps that would help? *<Nye, come here, boy!>*

A damp furry body rubbed itself against his leg and he shrieked and almost hit the roof. He stumbled and landed on his backside as a wolfhound padded out of the shadows, with lolling tongue and matted fur, faintly limned in purple light. Alaron almost forgot to breathe.

The others sucked in their breath as they saw the hound too.

Alaron reached out a tentative hand. 'Nye? Nye, here boy, here—' The ghost dog came and nuzzled him, his spectral nose as cold as ice. Alaron felt weary relief, and an awed sense of accomplishment. *I did it!* After being the class joke in Necromancy, he had solved a riddle that had defeated Fyrell and Vult, thank you very much. *Take that, you pricks.*

He looked across at Ramon and as he smiled, faintly dizzy from the effort, the little Silacian grinned back encouragingly and whispered, 'Well done, amici.'

The dog snuffled at him as though learning his scent. He stroked it tentatively and then laughed as it responded with a happy wag of the tail and a nudge that knocked him off his feet. He cautiously bound the hound's essence to his, and then released his call. The dog remained, ghostlike, but solid enough to touch. 'Hey, Nye, nice to meet you, boy.'

'He likes you, Alaron,' laughed Cym, kneeling down and cuddling the wolfhound.

'Huh. The *ghost* dog likes *Necromancers*,' Ramon sniffed. 'I find his taste suspect in the extreme. So what now?'

'I don't know,' Alaron replied. Nye's fur had a slightly insubstantial feel, as if it were made of smoke. He had the creepy feeling he could pass his hands through him if he wanted to. He kept his touch light. 'Any ideas?'

'Let's ask him,' Cym suggested, as Nye bounded towards the door, wagging his tail. He neither disturbed the water on the floor nor made any sound.

'Do you speak dog-language, Cym?' Ramon laughed. 'In Silacia we say that dogs and Rimoni share the same family tree,' he added teasingly.

'As do rats and Silacians,' replied Cym, quick as a flash. 'Just look at him, stupid: he wants to go outside. You don't have to be a mage to see that. He wants to show us something. Come on boy, shall we go walkies? Shall we go?'

The ghost-dog waited at the closed door, whimpering softly. Ramon opened the door and peered outside. 'It's still dark,' he said. 'What should we do?'

'I'm not sure I can hold him in this world once the sun comes up,' Alaron replied. 'I think we have to chance it and let him out. If someone sees us, I'll follow the dog and you guys try and draw them off, yeah?'

'Ha! Classic Robler – so that expensive education wasn't for nothing after all.' Ramon bowed. 'Lead on, General Mercer.'

Cym pulled the door fully open. Nye gave a sharp bark and dashed across the square, turning every few yards to check he was being followed. Alaron wrapped an illusion of shadow about himself and ran after him, the others in his wake. They crossed the square, trailing the hound's faintly luminous form. Fortunately, Nye's route led through less populous ways, where the soldiers seldom patrolled. On the one occasion a patrol came near, he melted into the darkness so thoroughly that Alaron feared he'd lost him, but when the clanking and the lanterns had subsided, there was Nye, wuffling softly, urging them on.

They took the Mint Bridge over the Leille River, and Alaron began to feel his time listening to Kyra Langstrit hadn't been wasted after all. 'He's retracing the path his master walked him each day. Langstrit was teaching him the route,' he said excitedly. They had to dodge another patrol near the Royal Mint before they started descending towards Old Town and the lake. Nye bounded happily under the aqueduct, ignoring the water thundering above their heads, then took a side-street through the Silver Market, spooking a pack of wild dogs who backed down an alley, snarling timidly, before fleeing.

They entered a small square in Old Town and as they approached, Nye cocked his leg and sent a ghostly stream of piss against the door, all the while wagging his tail.

Ramon choked back laughter. 'He's marking it for us,' he laughed. 'Brilliant!'

They examined the door, which fronted an old stone crypt, the type noble families favoured on their city estates. They stared at the crests and Kore Angels above the entrance. The grey stone was weathered, but the locked door was freshly painted, in the green hue traditionally used for crypt doors. The family name on the crypt, *De Savioc*, was an extinct dynasty, the last descendants of one of the Blessed Three Hundred. There were several such sites about the city, still sacrosanct, though the mage-families themselves had fallen into ruin.

'"De Savioc".' Alaron turned to the others. 'I've never heard of them.'

'You're the only local among us, Al,' Ramon observed.

Nye trotted back to Alaron, looking up expectantly. The first shaft of sunlight broken over the mountains in the east and the sky went from grey to pale blue. Nye whimpered; suddenly he looked translucent. 'We'll come back tonight,' Alaron said, then, quickly, 'We're going to lose him—' and he slapped his thigh and called, 'Come on, boy!' He whirled and ran for home.

He ran all the way, Nye bounding eagerly beside him. He fumbled open the door, the dog sniffed once, then barked and tore into the house, Alaron on his heels.

Jarius Langstrit was sleeping in the armchair by the cold fireplace, but he awoke as Nye ran towards him, barking happily, and recognition seemed to run through him. The hound put his paws in the general's lap and nuzzled him happily, and the old man stared down at him, then began to ruffle his fur, his face blank but tears rolling down his cheeks.

'Nye,' he whispered. '*Nye.*' They were the first words he had spoken since he had appeared.

Alaron felt his heart trip. The others pounded in behind him, panting; they clapped him on the shoulder as they peered into the room, then he heard them gasp too as they heard the general repeat the dog's name, over and over, as he hugged the wolfhound. The dog's tail pounded the floor delightedly.

Perhaps this will cure him, Alaron thought, but as the sun rose outside, the dog started to fade away. With a regretful snuffle he turned and was gone, bounding away into some dark place that acknowledged no walls, his final bark slowly echoing into silence. The general stared after him, his cheeks wet, a wondering smile on his face.

They couldn't coax any other words from Langstrit, so they were left whiling away the day in feverish impatience. Ramon went to Bekontor Hill to check whether Vult had arrived, using the pretext of booking his passage to Pontus – he was due to rejoin his legion in a few weeks. A small flotilla of windships was already assembling, getting ready to take the magi to join the Crusade.

Meanwhile Alaron read up on the de Savioc family in one of Tesla's books. They seemed remarkable only for their dullness. 'In a world where nobodies like us end up on quests for the greatest treasure of the empire, this lot have managed a footnote in a horse-breeding manual,' he told Cym. 'The only interesting one was the last of them. He got killed in a duel over gambling debts. His last words were: "What were my odds?"' He chuckled morosely.

They spent the rest of the day packing all the clues from their quest in a chest, ready to transfer to the cellar they'd prepared as Alaron's hideaway. Ramon got back from the landing towers. There was no word yet of Vult.

Cym agreed to stay with Tesla and the general while Ramon and Alaron returned to the de Savioc crypt. They set off at dusk. In Old Town the wealthy lived behind high walls and locked and guarded doors. The streets were always quiet and they reached the crypt unchallenged. Ramon worked the lock open with studious application of gnosis and within a few seconds they were both inside and the door closed behind them. Alaron lit a torch.

The difference between this and the previous chapel was pronounced. All but one of the sarcophagi were marble, and expensive shades of marble too: reds and greens and blacks. The one plain stone sarcophagus belonged to the unfortunate gambler, Roben de Savioc, the last of his line.

'So, what are we looking for?' Alaron wondered aloud.

Ramon was staring at the headstone of one Alvo de Savioc, Roben's father. 'That,' he replied after a few seconds. The marble was worn and cracked, and the moss growing in the cracks had all but obliterated the family crest, a set of keys and the words JEUNE ETERNAL: for ever young.

'What?'

Ramon poked a finger at the script. 'Look: the first and last letters are discoloured: J and L.'

Alaron sucked in his breath. 'J L. Jarius Langstrit.'

Ramon nodded. He had his periapt out and was scanning the tomb. 'Ha – see this?' He wiped the moss away just below the letters J and L. 'There—'

Alaron peered. A phrase was scratched into the stone: *Voco Arbendesai*. His mind clicked over. 'It's wizardry – "Voco" means "Summon".'

'And "Arbendesai"?'

'It's a name – all spirits have names by which they are summoned.' He gripped Ramon's shoulder excitedly. 'We're almost there, Ramon.'

*

It was dawn over the Alps. Vult felt the updrafts, breathed in the clear, cold air. He had slept, finally, until woken by a tentative touch on his mind. *<Magister Vult – answer!>*

<Mater-Imperia?> He licked his lips.

<Where are you, Magister?>

<I am flying back to Noros, Imperia-Mater. I can explain . . . >

<Good. Because I am not accustomed to finding that one of my envoys has abandoned his post without explanation. There is a rumour that you panicked because assault is imminent and fled the field. The name of Lukhazan has been raised repeatedly here in Pallas. Explain yourself, Magister Vult.>

The grip she took of his mind tightened as she spoke and he felt a cold dread that she might be able to reach down from her tower in Pallas and tear out the inside of his head. He marshalled his defences, establishing a new barrier within himself, not challenging the grip she had, but prepared to contest any further intrusion. Only then could he think rationally.

Something close to the truth was required – but not the real truth, of course: never that. The stakes were too high. *<There has been a security breach at the Norostein Governor's Palace, Mater-Imperia. Information may have been stolen that is critical to the empire.>*

When she replied it was in an even, concerned voice. *<What information is that, Magister?>*

<That is yet to be ascertained. I felt the breach and followed it back. I almost scryed the intruders, until someone broke the link.>

<Then your thieves have talent, Magister. You must be anxious.>

<It is unnerving, Majesty. There are few I would rate capable of such a deed.>

<Do you have any suspects?>

<Until I land and can be briefed, no.>

He awaited her displeasure, but when she responded again, she remained sternly cordial. *<I must have a soft spot for Noromen, Magister Vult. I have had to forgive your compatriot Gyle twice, and now I do the same for you. I shall expect a full report. Keep me appraised of developments. The list of those capable of such an outrage would be small, Magister, but the names on it are alarming, I deem.>*

<I am suitably alarmed, Mater-Imperia.>

She laughed. <Yes, I am sure you are. May that alarm fuel your hunger to solve this matter. But Magister, I am not amused at you abandoning your post. It frightened the garrison at Hebusalim, and scared men make poor decisions. I will not forget this. Find your thieves and deal with them. Keep me informed.>

<Yes Majesty,> he replied, but she was already gone.

Next morning Alaron was breakfasting early, on his own. Cym was still sleeping and Ramon had gone to the land-towers – but Alaron had barely finished his porridge when the door burst open and Ramon hurtled in. 'You've got to move, Alaron – they're expecting the governor tonight. We need to get you and the general to that cellar now—'

The enormity of it all hit Alaron like a punch to the belly, but Ramon didn't let him hesitate. Evidently going into hiding at a moment's notice was normal for Silacians. 'Come on, Al, let's move!'

Dusk found Alaron fifteen feet below ground in a hidden cellar beneath an abandoned wreck of a cottage. He was perched on a pile of sacks, wondering how on Urte he was going to be able to endure the coming night, here beneath the ground with no one but the general and a pile of books for company. At least a dose of gnosis-fire had dealt with the fleas. But life looked like it was going to be pretty miserable henceforth.

The hatch above was wrenched open and Ramon clattered down the stairs, clad in dark clothes. The general stared at him with a passive face and disinterested eyes. Ramon sniffed and wrinkled his nose. 'What a sewer.'

'Thanks,' Alaron scowled, from his lumpy mattress of flour-sacks. 'What were you expecting, the Royal Suite?'

'No, just less filth and decay.'

'Thanks for raising the point. I'll have the maid clear up – oh, hang on, no maid—'

'Stop sulking, Alaron. Your father dealt with worse during the Revolt.'

'Yeah, but that was patriotic,' Alaron muttered sourly. 'I suppose your *tavern room* is comfortable?'

'Not bad,' Ramon said, 'thanks for asking.'

'Huh. So, are you here to help, or what?'

'To help, as always.' Ramon held up a clay pot. 'Silver compound, for the summoning circle.' They both knew the theory, but Ramon had no affinity for Wizardry himself, so it was left to Alaron to once again take up a Study he had always been more than a little frightened of. Wizardry involved calling and binding the spirits of the dead who haunted the earth as servants. They were mentally linked to each other, a web of dead souls, constantly being renewed as some passed on and others died – but there were others, still superstitiously called 'daemons'. These beings had been around for millennia, and the eldest daemons were very strong – and much prized by wizards; once named, they could be summoned and controlled.

Though a wizard could summon a daemon without a circle, only a madman would summon an unknown daemon without one. A summoning circle would confine the daemon until it could be subdued; the circles could be attuned to the specific powers of known spirits, tailored to hide identities and detection or filled with illusions and traps: this was all part of the varied arts of Wizardry. A full wizard's summoning circle could take hours to inscribe.

Like Necromancy, Alaron had always found Wizardry terrifying. Never mind that the entrance exams had suggested that he had an analytic and logical mind well suited for such Studies; the truth was he was gut-clenchingly scared of all these dead souls and daemons – and just the threat of having his mind destroyed if he failed to subdue the summoned being was the stuff of nightmares. He had hoped to never again use Wizardry in his life, but it didn't seem to be working out that way.

I did Necromancy the other day . . . I can do this, he told himself firmly.

The painstaking inscription and the preparation of the inner circle took all night, though the boys worked well together. Just before dawn, Alaron experimentally activated the summoning circle with a light touch of gnosis and gave a grunt of satisfaction when a scintillating column of semi-opaque light arose inside. The silver liquefied and fused. He walked around it, looking for gaps, then deactivated it, so that he didn't burn off the valuable ingredients. 'It's done!' he announced, and immediately felt immeasurably tired, wanting only to sleep for ever – but he was excited too.

A few months ago I'd have fallen apart at what we're going through. But I can do this, he thought. He showed Ramon the circle. 'The inner circle is for the daemon and the outer one is for me, so that if I screw up, the daemon can't get at the rest of you. It looks good. I think we're ready.'

'Then we'll do it tonight.' Ramon peered at Alaron. 'You'll need to sleep, amici. You need a fresh mind to take on a daemon, si?'

Alaron felt surprisingly confident. 'We can do this,' he insisted. 'Hey, what do you reckon the general will say if we can restore him?'

Ramon chuckled. 'Something along the lines of: "Who the Hel are you clowns?", I imagine.'

Alaron tried to hold onto the light moment, but couldn't. 'Imagine being so desperate you'd destroy your own mind and just take it on trust that someone would find you and repair it for you.'

Ramon said soberly, 'Si – maybe he's crazier than we are.' He glanced at the sleeping Langstrit. 'I should go. We both need to rest for the summoning tonight.'

'And maybe battle an uncontrolled daemon, if I screw up,' Alaron worried.

'Or fight off Vult, Fyrell, Muhren and half the Watch,' Ramon added lightly.

Alaron looked at him miserably. 'I'm sorry, Ramon. I should never have taken that file, I know—'

'Done is done, Al. We'll just have to be cleverer now.' Ramon stood up and clapped him on the shoulder. 'Don't panic, amici. We're nearly there. *Tonight!*'

Alaron pulled him into a rough hug. 'Thank you, my friend – thank you for everything. Without you here, I'd already be dead.'

Ramon cocked his head impatiently. 'Don't make me cry, Al.'

Alaron hugged him again. 'I mean it, Ramon. You're my best friend.'

'And you are mine, Al. But you're still an absolute moron.' Ramon pushed him away. 'What does that say about me, eh?'

Alaron tried not to succumb to claustrophobia as the hatch shut above him. He settled into the darkness, alone with the silent general. He thought of Cym, watching over his mother, and sent his love. It would have been hypocritical to pray when he despised the Church, but he came close to breaking ranks on that score, for sheer terror at what might happen to the people he loved.

Be safe, all of you. Please, be safe . . .

Freyadai, 29 Maicin 928

A bitter north wind blew Vult into Norostein before dawn. He stood dizzily and stretched as the windship settled on the paved terrace above the city. The Air-magi who had piloted Vult nonstop since Pontus simply rolled onto their backs on the deck and groaned, their relief needing no words. They had met his wishes, and exceeded them. The stars glittered off the snow-covered slopes of the Alps thousands of feet above them, the barrier to the south, the throne that gazed down upon them, as implacable as Mater-Imperia Lucia herself.

He threw a pouch of gold onto the deck as he left. Let them fight over it; that was the way he had always run his underlings. Let the wolves rip and tear at each other, then he would adopt the winner. It was how he'd found Gurvon Gyle, and Darius Fyrell. And here was Fyrell, waiting loyally.

'Master!' Fyrell bowed.

'Darius.' He placed a hand on his shoulder, then reasserted his distance. 'Brief me, my friend. What did Gron Koll have to say about this outrage?'

'Little, my lord. He claimed to have drunk too much and slept through it all,' Fyrell sneered.

'Had he?'

Fyrell grimaced. 'His memories had been altered, so we may never know what he really did. The overwritten mind is difficult to restore.'

Vult felt his eyes narrow. 'Who did it?'

'Someone skilled enough to remove their own traces. The trail is cold, I'm afraid.'

Vult harrumphed irritably. *Predictable, but annoying.* 'Take me to the Residence. I must determine what has been taken.'

Alaron felt the scrying attempt in the timeless darkness of his cellar. It touched him faintly before the weight of stone obscured it. The art of the Clairvoyant was related to Air-gnosis, so Earth could thwart it; the simplest way for non-magi to escape the seeing eyes of a mage was to go underground. The Rimoni had not realised that in time to save themselves, but the Silacians in their mountain fortresses had learned quickly, and others had followed. If you cannot shield, you dig.

He's back – Belonius Vult's here . . . Alaron felt a surge of fear, but quelled it. They had come so far – they were ahead in this game, so long as they held their nerve. He breathed out the fear and lay back on his flour-sack bed. All he could do was wait and rest now, and hope the others were safe.

Cym was in the kitchen when someone hammered on the door. Tesla was asleep upstairs and Tula was at the market. She pulled open the door, holding her periapt behind her back, ready to flee or fight.

There was a crowd of Watchmen below on the steps. A tall, grim-faced man with flowing locks and a dashing countenance stepped to the fore. She knew his face well; Jeris Muhren and her father had been friends for many years.

'Norostein Watch,' Muhren announced. 'We have a warrant for the arrest of Ala—' He paused, belatedly registering Cym's presence. 'Cymbellea di Regia? What are you doing here? Where is young Mercer?'

'He's not here – he went with his father to Pontus. I've been hired to be his mother's maid,' Cym lied smoothly, surreptitiously pocketing her periapt.

'Does your father know you're here?'

'Of course.' She feigned regret. 'I'm sorry but no one's home but Madam, and she is asleep. You can come back at midday, once I've washed and fed Mistress Tesla. She gets awfully tetchy this early in the morning – she's apt to fire-blast people.' She looked down at the soldiers meaningfully. 'You know how these insane battle-magi get.' She watched them flinch at the thought.

Jeris Muhren laughed abruptly. 'Indeed I do!' He turned back to his men. 'All right, lads: Jensen, you will remain outside the front door. No one comes or goes.' He turned and bowed up the stairs to Cym, a wry look on his face. 'For your protection, Mistress di Regia. I'm sure you understand.'

Cym scowled, seeking a way out of this fix.

Muhren glanced at his men. 'The rest of you, get out and start canvassing door-to-door.' He waited until the men had tramped away and then closed the door behind him. Cym felt herself colour. 'Well, young Cymbellea, perhaps we need to have a long talk,' he said in a voice that brooked no refusal.

Belonius Vult stared at the figure on the other side of the desk. 'What do you mean, you can't find him?' He leaned forward. 'I know who broke into my offices, Captain Muhren: it was Alaron Mercer, and I want his goddamned head for it!'

It had been something of a relief when Vult had put two and two together: the Langstrit file was missing, which was alarming, but the Mercer file was the only other one taken, and that was intriguing.

I have cast Divinations concerning you, boy. You and the Scytale of Corineus . . .

After hearing the boy's thesis, which mirrored the truth alarmingly, his Divining had revealed greater opportunity to gain the Scytale himself if he arranged for the boy to work on it as a failed but free mage – it was a low probability, but better than none. He'd divined again after finding which files were missing. The boy was active. Something was happening here, a web of conspiracy concerning the missing Scytale, and an opportunity like no other beckoned.

I can take nothing for granted, he thought, eyeing the man opposite him. Muhren was a former Revolt battle-mage, a Langstrit man, one of the hard core of soldiers who had fought to the bitter end. He'd been there on the alpine slopes when Robler had finally surrendered. He knew Vannaton Mercer, no doubt. He also knew Mercellus di Regia, the notorious Rimoni bandit who'd aided the Revolt. It could be no coincidence that di Regia's daughter had been found at Mercer's house. *I can't trust Muhren, I never could* . . . Vult had been trying to have Muhren removed for years, but the position of watch captain was appointed by the king, not the governor.

No one is untouchable, not even you, Jeris Muhren, he told himself, before saying smoothly, 'Very well, Captain. I want the search for the boy intensified. And I will question this gypsy girl myself. And the mother.'

Muhren's reply was crisp and neutral. 'I'm sorry, Governor. The questioning of suspects is a Watch duty.'

Vult glared at Muhren. 'Then I will attend the questioning,' he rasped.

'I'm sorry, Governor,' Muhren repeated, in an infuriating textbook-reciting manner, 'The questioning of suspects may not be observed except by arrangement with the watch captain.'

'Then arrange it, Watch Captain.'

'I'm sorry, Governor, but I see no grounds to permit you.' He stood and saluted, then strode out while Vult fumed.

Who the Hel do you think you are, Jeris Muhren? I'm the rukking governor! With a frustrated snarl, he returned to the so-far fruitless and aggravating work of trying to scry Alaron Mercer. If only he could remember the boy more clearly. He paused. Wasn't Gron Koll a contemporary of Mercer? It was time to see if that oily young man could redeem himself after his failure on the night of the theft.

That's if Fyrell left Koll alive and with his sanity intact.

33

Southpoint

Shaitan

The King of Evil in the folklore of Antiopia, Shaitan and his hordes of afreet (pale-skinned demons with magical powers) plague the virtuous, but are constantly defeated as they are powerless against men of faith. Though the myth of Shaitan and the afreet predates the advent of the Rondian magi into Antiopia by millennia, the parallels that the people of Kesh and Dhassa draw are obvious.

ORDO COSTRUO, HEBUSALIM CHAPTER

Hebusalim, on the continent of Antiopia
Jumada (Maicin) 928
2 months until the Moontide

The Rondian Imperial Envoy, Belonius Vult, had flown home in high dudgeon. Negotiations between the Rondians and Salim continued, but without Ordo Costruo input, which was frustrating Antonin Meiros. Meanwhile Governor Betillon was losing control of the streets. Casa Meiros could not keep out the sounds of marching soldiers and distant shouting; sometimes stones struck the walls. The air was smokier and the carrion birds more plentiful.

As Jumada ended, Meiros told Ramita that he had a surprise for her. 'There is something I wish to show you, Wife, whilst you can still travel. Prepare yourself first thing in the morning for a day and a night away. You need pack only clothing; I will take care of all else.'

Ramita was puzzled and intrigued, but the prospect of getting out of Casa Meiros was wonderful. The whole household was preparing for evacuation to Domus Costruo, which meant their home would probably be looted, but even her husband could not guarantee their safety if they remained here once war began. Eventually, a concerted assault would break through.

Despite this, Meiros was almost light-hearted when he came to her courtyard the following morning. There was a gentle breeze blowing, and Luna was sinking in the west, kissed pink by the rising of Sol. Ramita wore a red and yellow salwar, a silver nose-ring and ruby-studded rings and bangles. Her hair was plaited down her back. Her belly was subtly rounder, but she felt well.

'Are you ready, Wife?' Meiros enquired kindly. 'Then come to the lower courtyard.'

Huriya took Ramita's arm, not because she needed the help, but because Huriya was nervous at letting her go. 'Ramita, what if this is some trick to lock you away somewhere he thinks is safe?'

'I'm sure he wouldn't do that, and anyway, I would insist you were with me.' She kissed Huriya's forehead. 'We'll be back tomorrow, he says.'

In the central courtyard a strange sight awaited: an old carpet, fully twenty feet long and eight wide, had been laid out on the stone. Its deep maroon, black and white patterning was faded but still beautiful. At one end was a small pile of blankets and baskets. Olaf had just finished placing a wine bottle inside a bag. Jos Klein was leaning against the wall, his bullish face unhappy.

'My dear, please take a seat,' Meiros said to Ramita, indicating a pile of cushions in the middle of the carpet.

Puzzled, Ramita settled herself on the cushions, wondering what was happening. Were they going to picnic here in the courtyard? It seemed very odd. Meiros sat beside her, patting her knee, his lined face boyish with anticipation. She caught a small glimpse of the child he must once have been and a foretaste of the children in her belly . . . if they were his.

'Well, Wife, are you ready?'

She nodded, still not understanding, and he raised a hand, which held a gemstone she had never seen before. She felt a tremor and a rippling, and then suddenly the carpet rose into the air, bearing them both and all of their luggage. She gasped and clutched her belly in terror. 'Husband!' she heard herself shriek, and her stomach lurched as the ground fell away. Huriya was yards below already, staring upwards with round eyes and open mouth. Meiros gave a laugh of sheer delight, made a twisting gesture with the gemstone and suddenly they were soaring, up and away.

'Don't worry, we are perfectly safe,' he shouted.

Ramita clung to him, her eyes screwed tightly shut, until, eventually, she found the courage to open them. They were impossibly high, though she scarcely felt the air rushing by, as if it were being deflected by some unseen shield. The carpet barely rippled; their stack of baskets and blankets lay unmoving, and only the tassels whipping furiously indicated that they were moving at all. But below them, the city unfolded in incredible detail, receding further with every second.

They appeared to be making for the hills to the north, which were many times higher than they were flying. Ramita finally had the courage to pull away from her husband's protective grip and look around properly. It was wonderful and terrifying, and when she looked back at Meiros' face, intent but merry, she lost her fear and began to enjoy the sensation. They went rocketing past flocks of birds that swooped away, startled. An eagle soared past and called out, and when Meiros mimicked it, the great bird turned aside disgustedly, making them both laugh.

'My second wife made this for me,' Meiros told her. 'Edda was an Air-Mage and I am not. She made this linking-gem: it channels raw energy and converts it to Air-gnosis. Such things are very inefficient, but they work. Occasionally I take it out and fly on my own.'

'She must have loved you,' Ramita said, wonderingly.

'On a good day.' He laughed. 'She was like a tempest: she had a terrifying temper and a restless nature. She could sulk for months, then suddenly all would be forgiven and there was nothing she would not do for me. But it could be wearying.' He smiled at her. 'She was as unlike you as I can envisage.'

How could he ever have wanted to marry me after someone like that? She was surprised to feel a twinge of jealousy. *I would never be able to give anyone so wondrous a gift.*

Meiros stroked her shoulder. 'She died a long time ago. You bear an even greater gift inside your womb, my dear wife.'

Ramita smiled dutifully, but thinking of the children inside her led to other thoughts too frightening to ponder. She closed her mind down and concentrated on the journey.

They were flying northwest, faster than galloping horses, and Meiros made the carpet swoop on the updrafts and dart through the narrow valleys. Shepherds tending flocks in the rocky dry lands peered up at them in disbelief; camel-drovers gaped while their herds chewed phlegmatically. They followed a pass through the hills to a huge sloping plain and she heard a thunderous sound ahead that rose like a distant storm. A pale blue star twinkled ahead, and at last she understood: Meiros was taking her to see the legendary ocean – and the Leviathan Bridge!

She clutched his hand, afraid again, as Meiros piloted the flying carpet above a wide road where tiny shapes travelled: camel-carts, wagons, galloping messengers, all heading towards the white tower that rose before them. He talked to her as he flew, instructing as always: 'The Bridge needs concentrated energy to withstand the seas, drawn from two sources. One is the land itself. The closer we get, you'll see less vegetation and no birds at all. But most of the power comes from the sun. There are huge clusters of crystal inside each tower that trap solar energy – in fact, they draw energy from any living thing, so no one can remain there long. The Ordo Costruo magi who look after the Leviathan Bridge work in shifts, making sure all is well. The Imperial Inquisitors oversee us,' he added bitterly.

The shimmering white tower was so tall – a mile high – that it could not be real. It terrified her. But she also felt grateful to see it, this wonder of the age. She squeezed her husband's hand, thankful for the gift of this flight and for his reassuring presence.

Meiros was perspiring freely. 'Edda's gem burns energy like nothing else – but we're nearly there.' He guided them about the tower in a spiralling descent. She saw robed magi on a balcony two-thirds of the way up, waving to him, and he called out greetings, then they were off again, swooping down the ramp on the north side of the tower and into a wall of wet mist. She clung to him, crying out in alarm as the roar she'd heard before amplified tenfold. Then they broke through the mist and she almost screamed. They were over the ocean.

She stared at the tortured seas of Oceanus pounding the walls of the land. The sight left her full of mute dread and awe: towering cliffs formed a rampart against the seething waters, a sheer black wall that had stood for eternity. But the ocean hammered ceaselessly at the defences, and everywhere there was evidence of its gains: rock falls, carved gullies, undermined ledges.

Meiros pointed, his eyes alive with pleasure. 'The ocean gains only a few yards each year, and we have ways of repairing the cliffs. As long as we are vigilant, the tower will never be swallowed by the sea.' He took them in another swooping arc, almost skimming the giant waves, and then up, up and over the ocean. He pointed downwards to her right and she saw the dark line beneath the waves, hundreds of feet below the water level and yet, when the waves troughed, clearly visible. 'There she is,' shouted Meiros. The pride in his voice was unmistakable. 'The Leviathan Bridge, rising from the deep. The pressures it withstands beneath the waves would level mountains. But the power of the gnosis and the skill of the engineering keep it strong.'

Ramita gazed, open-mouthed. *I am just a market-girl from Baranasi. How is it I am here?*

'The Bridge rises from the sea for two years in twelve,' Meiros shouted. 'The moon has an irregular orbit, and this, together with other influences we still don't understand, exerts greater and lesser pressure on the globe and its pull upon the oceans. Every twelfth year, that pull creates extreme low tides in this region, allowing the Bridge to be revealed.'

'What is a "globe"?' Ramita asked.

'A globe is a sphere. That is the shape of the Urte.'

She raised her eyebrows. 'No; the world is flat, like a disk. Guru Dev told me. It is known.'

'Your guru needs to come to the Ordo Costruo for some higher education,' laughed Meiros. 'The Urte is round, and is circled by the Moon.'

'And the Sun?' Ramita frowned, perplexed.

'Oh no, we circle the Sun.'

That made no sense at all.

'Trust me, Wife: these cycles are well-established. The Bridge may be traversed during a two-year period, one year either side of absolute low tide,' Meiros continued as he swung the carpet back towards the shore.

'Why ?' Ramita asked curiously, hoping it wasn't a silly thing to ask.

'That is a very good question.' He stroked her shoulder affectionately. 'Back in the 700s, the demand for windships outstripped supply – they take years to build, and they have a very small capacity, which limits supply and causes runaway prices. The merchants monopolised trade and gouged everyone. They behaved like despots.

'I had been studying the possibility of a bridge, but I ran into many problems – the engineering was hard enough, but the politics were worse. The windship merchants didn't want the competition, and neither side wanted a land-link at all. But I convinced the Pontic High Council and the Sultan of Hebb that both would benefit from it.

'Of course, I wanted to build a bridge higher than the highest tide, one that would be constantly open, but when we did the calculations, we found we couldn't. The bridge could not stand without Earth-gnosis, which meant it had to be anchored to the earth. To keep the bridge open all the time would require underwater pillars a mile high in places, but we could not build them so tall, not with enough strength and suppleness to bear the stresses. To draw enough power from the earth they had to be shorter. This meant we were limited to working with the twelve-yearly absolute low tide. We utilise five of the giant crystal-clusters to absorb energy, and this sustains the Bridge against the waters. There is an undersea ridge that runs from Pontus to Dhassa – without that, it would have been impossible. We built three more towers on a small archipelago roughly halfway across. The High Council and the sultan were all happy enough with a temporary bridge, and the land-based traders were delighted. The windship merchants weren't too pleased, but they get by well enough regardless. So really, the Leviathan Bridge was a compromise of engineering and politics.'

Ramita didn't really understand it all, but she was content to let him talk. It was enough to have seen Southpoint Tower and the dark shape beneath the waters; it was enough to hear him so proud and paternal. Inside, she tried to suppress the turmoil she felt, caught between her love for Kazim and his passionate wildness and her growing fondness for her young-old husband and the wonders he showed her. Who was she, Ramita Ankesharan, to have walked the halls of Domus Costruo and seen the Leviathan Bridge from a flying carpet? Who was she, to have conversed with Rondian emissaries and shared the life of a living legend? She struggled with the growing feeling that she could never go back and be a simple wife in Baranasi.

Abruptly she was angry with herself. *You are being seduced by riches and wonders, you fool! This old man only wanted you as a broodmare – it is Kazim you love . . . Oh please, oh Gods, please, let him be miles away, travelling home with Jai.* She huddled in the crook of her husband's arm and tried to quell her fears. 'Husband, may we return to land now?' she asked in a small voice.

'Is flying not to your taste, dear wife?'

'I think I could come to like it,' she admitted, 'but I have had enough for now.'

He chuckled sympathetically and sent the carpet whooshing back towards the cliffs.

Meiros took them a mile inland, some two miles from Southpoint Tower and landed gently. He staked blankets over the flying carpet in a small steeple-walled tent shape, open at one end, looking out at the sands. Gulls circled, their hard black eyes glinting in the sun, calling constantly, until their voices and the pounding of the waves lulled her to sleep.

When she woke, it was to him kneeling beside her, gently shaking her shoulder. It might have frightened her, not long ago, to have him leaning over her, but now it did not alarm her at all. It was dusk, and the light was slowly melting away.

'Wife, come: there is something we must do.'

She sat up and stretched, and he pulled her to her feet. 'What is it, husband?'

He grinned, almost boyish, and winked conspiratorially. 'I need to show you something.' He nodded at the mighty pinnacle of Southpoint. 'Something to do with the tower.'

He led her a little way off, then after looking around somewhat furtively, he waved a hand and she gasped as the sand and rocks were suddenly scoured away by a tiny swirl of wind. Then she almost swore as she saw a trapdoor set into the desert floor, about a foot below the surface. She looked at him as he stilled the winds. 'What is this?'

'A secret.' He blew away the last of the sand. The door was wood, carved with filigree silver lines. There was an intricately carved knob on the left-hand side which reminded her of the security knobs at Casa Meiros. 'This is the beginning of a tunnel that runs all the way to Southpoint. As yet, the Inquisitors do not know of it.' He took her right hand, the hand not scarred already by the Casa Meiros security. 'This will hurt – I am sorry, but you have felt the sensation before.'

She nodded, bracing herself, and voluntarily placed her hand on the knob.

It stung, but she held firm until Meiros gently withdrew her hand. He didn't give her salve this time but instead exerted his powers, leaving the palm numbed and the scars already looking weeks old. 'Look about you, Wife,' he said quietly. 'Mark this place in your mind. There may come a time when you need to come here on your own.'

On my own? 'Why, lord?'

'I do not know, precisely, but I believe it important that you know this. Beneath Southpoint is a chamber from whence the flow of energies supporting the Bridge is controlled. Within it is a silver globe that channels the solar energies of the tower and turns it into the Earth-gnosis required to power this Bridge. Only an Ascendant can withstand the energies of that chamber. Only one of my blood can alter the energy flows.' He smiled grimly. 'Even the Inquisitors cannot unmake that connection.'

Is he telling me this for our children to know? Does he think he will not tell them himself? The thought gave her an uneasy chill, but she dared not voice it. 'Is this related to your prophecy?' she asked meekly.

He looked at her measuringly. 'I have told you that I have foreseen our union resulting in children whose lives are integral to the restoration of peace and justice. In those divinations – they are not prophecies, just predictions – knowledge of the chamber beneath Southpoint Tower is vital. I don't know why.'

Ramita nodded dutifully, not understanding at all.

He stroked her head affectionately. 'Do you think you can remember this place?'

She looked about her and waggled her head confidently. 'Achaa.'

He smiled and waved his hand, strewing the deep pile of dust and rocks back over the trapdoor and covering it. 'Then that is all we can do for now. There are Inquisitors inside the tower and I would not reveal either this tunnel or you to them.' He took her hand. 'Let us go and eat – all this plotting and intriguing has made me hungry.'

Back at their camp, he fussed over the food while letting her doze again. Hours later she woke to the smell of slowly roasting lamb, turning of its own volition above an open fire. It smelled wonderful. Meiros sipped wine, gazing away towards the tower. It was the last week of the month; the darkmoon, and the stars glittered above in the moonless sky, diamonds on sable.

'How may I help, Husband?' she asked, sitting up.

He turned towards her, looking more relaxed than she had ever seen him. 'All is done, I believe.' Plates and cups were laid out beside the fire, where little wicker baskets of fruit and salad and cheese waited, covered with cloth. 'Come and sit with me.'

She wrapped a shawl around her shoulders and joined him. They talked of small things, like favourite foods of childhood, and watched the stars. 'See how bright they are with Luna on the far side of the globe,' he told her.

'No, the moon is dark because Parvasi drinks its light to give her hair lustre.'

'Does she just? Who is this Parvasi again?'

'I have told you this before,' she scolded good-naturedly. 'She is the goddess of fertility and devotion, and it is to her and Sivraman that I prayed for children.'

Meiros touched his cup to hers. 'And your prayers were answered.'

'Of course. Parvasi hears the prayers of the dutiful wife,' she answered automatically before inwardly cringing. Perhaps these children were Parvasi's punishment upon her for her infidelity – but how could new life be a punishment? *Please, Parvasi, permit me to raise these children, whoever their father.*

'Parvasi is a very gentle goddess, like my good wife?' Meiros enquired kindly.

'Parvasi is kind, but when there is peril, she has other aspects far more terrifying. When the lands are troubled by evil, she takes the form of the warrioress Darikha, who rides a tiger and has many arms filled with weapons. She is very fierce.' She lifted her chin slightly. 'Lakh women are dutiful, but we are courageous, like Darikha-ji.'

He studied her face. 'Yes, there is fierceness too, not easy to spot, but sometimes you unmask it. Determination. Courage. You have many qualities that will serve you well as a mage.'

She shuddered at the thought, but Meiros perceived her fear. 'You must not be afraid. The gnosis is an extension of who we are, and you will learn to embrace it, I promise you.' He stroked her arm. 'When you assume the mantle of mage, I will teach you how to be both Parvasi and Darikha.'

She swallowed and looked away. Too many emotions pounded her. *Why is it that I respect you so much, even care for you, when I love Kazim and yearn so much for him? How am I going to bear this, whatever happens?*

'You look sad, Ramita.'

She looked up at him. He had called her Ramita, not simply Wife as he normally did. *Ramita.* She swallowed a small knot of emotion. 'I'm not sad, just . . . overwhelmed. There is so much happening – children, a strange land. Some days I don't know where I begin and end.'

He drew her against him and kissed her forehead. 'Ramita, I have grown very fond of you. I am proud of how well you have adapted to so much. I know you must chafe, to be left alone so often and unable to go out. I promise you, when this Moontide is over, you and I will take the children to Baranasi to meet your family. We will go to places where there is safety and you can walk around freely. I know that you have given up much for this marriage. Everyone else gained from it but you – you lost, yet you have given me so much. I know that it is too much for an old man to expect the love of a young woman like you, but please believe me when I say that I will protect you and care for you until the day I die. I am more than fond of you, my dear.'

Her eyes were heavy with tears. She blinked them away. 'The meat is ready,' she said huskily.

They ate, and afterwards lay in the tent, she cradled against his body, his arm around her, his body the warmest thing in the cool of the night, his hand upon her belly, his breath on her neck. He slept, his breathing soft and regular. She wondered what he had been like when he was young, or even middle-aged: wise and strong, feared by kings.

I like him. I never thought I would, but I do. And he cares for me. Would he forgive me if he knew I had been unfaithful to him? Because I swear, if he did, it would never happen again, even for Kazim, who gave me nothing but brief madness and a full womb. I wish you had never come, Kazim, my love.

They breakfasted late on eggs with bread and onions. The coastal desert was at peace, empty of all but a few birds, the constant rumble and crash of the water softened by distance. He pulled her down beside him under the open sky and made love to her, cradled in the same position they had slept, lying behind her and inside her, a slow and lingering pleasure. 'The healers say it makes the birth easier if conjugal relations continue throughout the pregnancy,' he assured her. 'Or at least, that's what I paid them to say,' he added with a chuckle. He could have been thirty in that moment. She wished that they could stay here longer.

But they had to return, flying all afternoon in the blazing sunlight, battling a headwind, though they still raced along faster than horses, and soon the Hebb Valley sprawled beneath them. Meiros grimly pointed out six windships in a row outside the city walls. 'Six Rondian Warbirds. Betillon has reinforcements.' He increased the speed of the flying carpet, swooping south towards his gleaming, needle-like tower. The air of the city had a rank smell from above, like a smoke-filled latrine, and Ramita wrinkled her nose in distaste. The desert air had been so clean.

They alighted in the courtyard just before sunset, and she realised she felt profound regret at being back. Just for one day and night, her life had been almost perfect, the world of the magi filled with more wonders than terrors. She let him kiss her lips and hugged him tightly in return.

He stroked her brow, his voice apologetic. 'I am sorry, Ramita, but I must go to the Domus Costruo and find what the advent of these warships means. Dine judiciously, and sleep well. I will see you in the morning.'

Huriya was full of questions, but she did not want company that night and eventually Huriya took the hint and left sulkily. Soon after Ramita heard Huriya's door click as she admitted someone, probably Klein. But Ramita could not sleep, torn between guilt for a young lover and yearning for the safe arms of an old man of whom she was more than fond.

34

Revealed

Sorcery: Wizardry

The greatest of all Studies. Once you master Wizardry, you have mastered every aspect of the gnosis, for there is nothing you cannot do. Nothing!

GILDEROY VARDIUS, WIZARD, PALLAS 846

Norostein, Noros, on the continent of Yuros
Junesse 928
1 month until the Moontide

Torsdai, 4 Junesse 928
A dull rapping roused Alaron from his reverie and a few second later, the hatch opened and Ramon flew down the stairs, looking anxious in the pale blue glow of Alaron's gnosis-light. 'Dim that, you idiot,' the Silacian snapped.

Alaron released his gnosis-light, only for Cym to call out irritably, 'Hey, who put out the light?' He rolled his eyes and lit the candles with a flourish of his hand.

Ramon wrinkled his nose. '*Sol et Lune*, it stinks in here.'

Alaron scowled. 'You try living in it,' he grumbled. He watched Cym clamber down and look around warily. 'How long has it been? How many weeks?'

'Don't be silly, Alaron, it's only been a couple of days – and it's not like you're in a prison cell.' She grabbed Ramon's sleeve and they both shuffled guiltily. 'Uh, we need to tell you something.'

'What?' he demanded suspiciously as his friends looked at each other sheepishly. '*What?*'

Cym stepped forward. 'Well, it's like this. We've had to tell someone about our little problem.'

'*What?*'

'Stop saying that and calm down. It's for the best. We didn't have any choice anyway.'

'What have you done? This is *our* secret, for Kore's sake—'

'Well that's rich, coming from the fool who left his identity all over the theft of Vult's files,' snapped Ramon. 'Do you want to live down here for the rest of your life, or do you want some help in getting out?'

Alaron stared at them, feeling like the ground had been cut away from his feet. 'Who have you told?' he asked weakly.

His friends looked at each other apprehensively. 'It's for the best,' Cym repeated. She glanced up at the hatch, and Alaron realised it was still open. 'It's okay,' she called hoarsely, and two booted feet descended, bearing a cloaked man who lowered his cowl to reveal blond locks tumbling over a chiselled face.

'Muhren?' Alaron spat. 'You told Jeris Muhren – what the Hel are you thinking? He works for Vult, you idiots—'

The watch captain waved a hand, closing the hatch, and said calmly, 'Actually, I don't. I serve the law and the city of Norostein.'

'Ha! Everyone knows the Watch is in the governor's pocket.' Alaron glared at his friends. 'I can't believe you've done this.'

Cym tried to put a hand on his arm, but he shook it off angrily. 'Alaron, he came to the house when I was there with your mother. He has Tesla in his protection and he's hidden us from Vult. Vult is furious with him—'

'How do you know that?'

She frowned. 'Alaron—'

'You don't know, do you? You've only got his word – they're probably working together, and now he knows exactly where we all are. I suppose you've told him everything—'

Muhren wasn't listening; a cone of gnosis-light had bloomed in his hand and was washing over a blinking Jarius Langstrit. 'By the Kore, it's true! You've found him . . .' He fell to his knees, seizing the general's hand. Langstrit watched him, his face blank. 'General Langstrit, command me, sir – how may I serve?' They were startled to see a tear in the captain's eye, but Langstrit stared back at Muhren incuriously, his expression utterly blank. 'Do you not remember me, sir? Muhren, Battlemaster, third cohort of the Ninth—'

The old man didn't react at all and finally Muhren looked at Alaron. 'Is he—?'

'I told you, he doesn't remember anything,' Cym said, slightly impatiently. 'Men never listen.'

Muhren bowed his head, then stood, his eyes on Langstrit. 'You won't understand what this means to me, but during the Revolt General Langstrit saved us so many times. He and Robler were our banners; they were miracle-workers. For most of the Revolt we were outnumbered ten to one or worse, but we always came through. They knew the name of the least soldier, especially Old Jari. We loved him – we *still* love him. It's eighteen years, but it seems like yesterday . . .' He blinked hard. 'We thought he was dead, and now you've found him.' He looked at Cym. 'I confess, I did not really believe what you told me.'

Ramon walked to one side. 'Jarius,' he called softly, and the general turned and looked at him. 'He hears when people say his name,' Ramon told Muhren. 'It's built in to what he did to himself.'

Muhren stared. 'How do you mean, "What he did to himself"?'

While Ramon quietly explained their guesses about Langstrit, Cym put a hand on Alaron's arm. 'Look, I know you don't like it, but in the end it was Vult or Muhren. I asked your mother and she said we could trust him. Without him, we're going to get caught. Vult is back – he's already raided Father's caravan. Only the captain can protect us.'

Alaron sat down and put his head in his hands. 'This was *our* quest – *ours*. *We* found the general. He needed help and *we* gave it. Even assuming you're right and Muhren isn't really in Vult's pocket, you've given away control of the whole thing.' He jabbed a finger at Muhren. 'What's he going to do if we do find you-know-what? Let us walk away? I don't think so—'

'Would Langstrit?' Ramon replied. He exhaled heavily. 'Face it, Al, someone's going to come after it. At least the captain has a testified history of human decency.'

'He believed my thesis, and he's been watching me ever since,' Alaron snarled. He looked at Muhren. 'You've been spying on me, thinking I'll lead you to the damned Scytale so you can restart the Revolt.'

Muhren raised a placatory hand. 'Enough! Let me explain myself before you unleash that famous Anborn temper, Master Mercer.' He looked about the circle of faces. 'Yes, I know what you hunt. And I presume you all know something of me: I'm a half-blood and I fought in the Crusades – and in the Revolt. I am loyal to my king and country. We did well, for a time, but then the emperor put Kaltus Korion in charge, and Korion targeted the people, knowing we couldn't protect everyone. The outlying farms went first, then the villages and towns: there were massacres, looting, kidnappings and all the rest – poisoned wells, torture, forced starvation. The promised aid never came. Whenever we fought the enemy we were still winning, but there were many more of them and the odds kept lengthening. In the end, we lost, but we also formed a bond. We who fought that Revolt are bound by suffering.

'Maybe you are old enough to remember the years that followed? The bread queues and shortages; bartering for food because we had no coin, and the parades of the defeated, wrapped in chains, headed by our own king. I was one of those paraded: I could show you the lash-scars on my back. Emperor Constant made an example of us. So it's fair to ask: do I just want to start another war?

'The answer is complex: do I want Noros to stand free and independent? Of course I do. Do I hate the Rondian throne and wish to see the power of Pallas broken? Of course. But would I plunge my own land, only eighteen years on, with our manpower weak and our farms and commerce barely beginning to recover, back into conflict? No. Absolutely not.'

He looked at the general. 'If someone handed me the Scytale of Corineus, what would I do? Ever since I heard Alaron's thesis I have been wondering that. I would like to think that I would hide it again, for a time, until our land was stronger, and then I would gather trustworthy men, men of honour and virtue, and we would make it our Crusade to rid ourselves of Rondian occupation, to force Pallas to give us our independence. But not by open war. We would do it like Meiros and his Bridge-Builders. They stood apart, gathered power and gave the people their time and energy – just as I try to do in my own small way by keeping the peace.

'But Pallas brooks no rivals. When Pallas sees a power that might challenge it, it stamps it out, whether it's foreign or their own people. Pallas is the enemy of freedom. And I am the enemy of Pallas. To bring down Pallas cannot happen without blood. Pallas will never surrender. So in the end, there must be blood spilt.

'You are acting for the good of the general, of course you are, but try telling me you have not dreamed of what you might do with the powers of an Ascendant? And try telling me you think Pallas would sanction it.

'If I worked for Vult he would be here now, and he would rip the knowledge you have gained from your minds and continue the search himself. If I were such a man, I could do the same – but I am not. Vult and I are not allies; we have never been allies. He resents any man he cannot suborn or destroy, and he particularly hates those who remember his conduct in the Revolt and what he did at Lukhazan.'

They all looked at the watchman, and then at each other. 'So what do you propose?' Ramon asked.

Muhren considered before speaking. 'Here is my offer. I will shield you from Vult. I will help you restore the general, and if we can do that and the Scytale is not found, we will leave it at that. My beloved general being restored would be enough. Perhaps he will even return to the public arena and cast down Vult and all he stands for, and if so, I am his man.

'If the Scytale does come to light, then I swear that I will not attempt to claim it. In return, I would ask you to give it to the general and accept whatever reward he gives. I know him to be an honest and considerate man. If we can agree this, I will swear on whatever you wish – my honour, my periapt, or a holy book: whatever you wish. But please, let me help you.'

They fell silent for a time. Langstrit watched Muhren as if he were vaguely interesting, but there was no recognition in his eyes. Ramon scratched his ears thoughtfully, his expression neutral. Cym met his gaze placidly, apparently in agreement with the watch captain.

'And if we don't?' Alaron asked.

Muhren looked up at him. 'If you don't want my help and you're prepared to risk Vult on your own, what can I do? It's not in my nature to force you. But I beg you, do not do that. Belonius Vult is like no one you have ever encountered. He was an indifferent and self-serving general, but he is a serpent when it comes to intrigues, and he is a deadly duellist. He has friends at the very top, even in Pallas – that is what this governor is: Pallas' hand in Noros. He never forgives a slight, and his enemies do not survive long – and that includes me. As soon as my term in office is over, I will fall hard and fast. If he is aware of your search, he will find you. This will be more important to him than anything else. He has curtailed a mission in Hebusalim to be here. He knows what is at stake.'

He paused to let them absorb the warning before continuing, 'Your father and your mother know me, Alaron; so does Cymbellea's father. I knew your Aunt Elena – I even carried a torch for her, for a while. I beg you, please, trust me.'

Alaron felt the weight of all of their eyes upon him, even Langstrit's. *Why does it come down to me?* he thought sulkily. He rubbed his face, feeling the unwashed skin, the itchy stubble. *What choice do we have? We're in over our heads already. We're playing at treasure hunters, but the treasure will destroy us. And I can't hide here for the rest of my life.*

He thought of the humiliation of his thesis presentation. *I was putting my head in the noose, and he tried to warn me off. And Gina told me he was writing letters in my support* . . . He hung his head, then stood and offered the watch captain his hand. 'I'm prepared to give it a chance,' he managed to say.

Muhren stood and took his hand in his powerful grip. 'I won't let you down, Alaron Mercer.' He looked at the others. 'I hold myself bound to keep you safe and to restore the general: I swear this on my gnosis.'

Alaron, Ramon and Cym looked at each other, then Ramon gave a decisive nod and turned to Muhren. 'Well, we'd better fill you in . . .'

They brought him up to date, taking him through the trail of clues they had followed, though Alaron stopped short of telling him what they'd found in the de Savioc tomb. When they reached that point in the narration, he paused and reached out tentatively for Ramon's mind. *<So, do we tell him? If he's honest, we'll learn pretty fast whether we're fools or not>*

<You've always been a fool, Al.> Ramon winked. *<I don't think we have any choice. Either we trust him or we don't. There are no half-measures.>*

Alaron spoke aloud: 'The final clue was in a tomb the ghost-dog led us to. We think it's the name of a daemon – we think if we summon it, it will bring the memory-crystal Langstrit constructed and hid. But before I tell you the clue, we have to agree to use it here, with everyone present.'

Muhren half-smiled. 'Still not convinced, are you? I suppose that's fair enough.' He pointed to the summoning circle on the floor. 'I'd assumed that wasn't just decoration.' He walked around it, peering carefully. 'This circle has been well-drawn.'

'Are you versed in Wizardry, Captain?' Ramon enquired warily.

'It is one of my strengths,' Muhren replied.

'I'm doing the summoning,' Alaron blurted.

Muhren frowned. 'Are you sure, lad?' He raised a quizzical eye, then glanced at Cym. 'I gather you have a periapt, but this summoning may not be an easy one. You don't know what manner of being Jari chose.'

Alaron stood up. *Have confidence. Toughen up.* 'I'm doing it.' He glared about him.

Muhren inclined his head. 'Very well. But you will need a further outer circle, to prevent Vult or any other mage from detecting the surge in energies created by the summoning. I can draw one of those for you, but I'm due on night watch inside the hour. Let us return here tomorrow evening, after I have completed my shift and slept. I will create the dampening circle and then Master Mercer may assay the summoning. Agreed?'

That sounded reasonable – and Alaron wasn't ready to go ahead with the summoning, not after this new shock. 'If you can bring some hot food, that would be even better,' he told the captain boldly. 'I've not had a hot meal for days, and neither has the general. And we need more blankets – and can you take out the slop-bucket?'

Muhren raised an eyebrow. 'Gods, you test my patience, boy.'

Cym stepped lightly between them. 'He annoys us all, Captain. It's part of his charm.'

Freyadai, 5 Junesse 928

It was late afternoon when Alaron was awakened first by Cym and then Ramon arriving. They cooked the food they'd brought using Fire-gnosis and fed the general, then they sat about waiting apprehensively for the arrival of Jeris Muhren. Or Belonius Vult.

'You trust Muhren?' Ramon asked, munching a honey-cake.

'I'm getting there.' Alaron mopped his brow, sweating despite the cold air of the cellar. 'I think he'd do anything for the general. I'm not so sure he'd do as much for us if push comes to shove.'

'In Silacia, we say, "Have your friends to dinner, but your enemies to breakfast". It means you should keep a close eye on them. So let's do that, si?'

Muhren himself arrived soon afterwards, cloaked in dark wool. He went first to the general and examined him anxiously. 'You have taken good care of him,' he admitted, before joining the others beside the summoning circle. 'Vult has informers in my Watch, of course, but I know who they are. It was easy enough to shake them.' He looked at Alaron. 'So, you are still resolved?'

'Of course,' Alaron said irritably.

'Then shall we begin? I will inscribe the dampening circle.'

The young magi watched with interest as the watch captain went about his task. They'd been taught the working, but Ramon had never mastered it and Alaron had forgotten it – he'd never thought to need such secrecy. After a painstaking hour, Muhren fused the silver dust with a flash of energy and declared himself satisfied. 'Master Mercer, the floor is yours.'

Alaron took a deep breath, glanced at Ramon for reassurance and began, 'Okay, here's what we learned. There is a tomb with "JL" marked on it, and then we found the words "Voco Arbendesai" inscribed underneath. We believe that is a summoning phrase for a daemon.'

'What does Arbendesai mean?' Cym asked.

'It doesn't have to *mean* anything,' Alaron replied. 'We think it's a name – wizards give names to daemons and bind them to that name so they can be summoned over and over again. Fyrell taught us how to do it. I had one I called "Rabbit Hat".' He blushed slightly at the juvenile name.

'Mine was called "Cymbellea",' Ramon smirked. 'Hel, was it ugly!'

Cym flicked an insolent finger at him.

Muhren grunted. '"Voco" followed by a name is the standard invocation for a daemon. I agree with your interpretation. But remember, this "Arbendesai" is likely to be far stronger than the weak daemons you bound at college.' He frowned at Alaron. 'I do wish you would allow me to do this.'

Alaron knew the request was reasonable, but he still shook his head. 'I'll do it.' He fought to calm himself: *cleanse your thoughts; release all distractions, fears, anger. Be certain. Be single-minded. Be focused.* The words could be applied to all of the gnosis, but most especially to wizardry, where uncertainty could be deadly.

He stepped over Muhren's dampening circle and activated it, then stepped over the protective circle and activated it too. Though he could still pass it, a spirit could not. He was locked inside with whatever he summoned. He faced the inner circle and spoke one word: *Angay*, the Rune of Beginning. The lettering and lines before him ignited in a silver glow. A shaft of light rose before him, coming to a point a few yards above his head. The air suddenly smelled of burning and heat. *I can do this.*

Outside the summoning circles his friends were arrayed about, ready to intervene if required. Even the general was watching. His craggy face was serene, but the light caught his eyes disturbingly.

Alaron turned back to the centre. Within the central circle where the summoned spirit was to appear Alaron had placed a bowl containing water laced with his own blood, to provide a connection for his gnosis. In it lay the body of a dead crow, something for the daemon to inhabit. He held a wooden rod in his left hand to direct his energies. In his right hand was the amber periapt that Cym had given him. He exhaled thickly. *Okay, let's go.*

He raised the tip of the wooden rod into the paste bowl and let gnosis energy flow. When he pulled it out, the residue smouldered on the tip of the thin piece of wood. '*Arbendesai,*' he called softly, suffusing his voice with the gnosis to make it heard in the spirit-realm. He repeated the word, again and again, in a gentle whisper: '*Arbendesai . . . Arbendesai . . .*'

For minutes, nothing happened. He felt the others shuffling anxiously. *Damn, I was so sure . . .*

Something hissed inside the circle.

Alaron had to stop himself jumping backwards as steam began to rise from the bloody water and flowed into the body of the crow, fleshing it out. It stood suddenly, flapping its wings and flexing its legs and spine experimentally. Then it focused on him.

By Kore . . . He felt all the others lean in. 'Arbendesai!'

A disembodied voice chuckled inside his head. <*Who are you, fool? You're not Langstrit.*>

Alaron braced for the inevitable assault. Unseen claws latched into his brain and the world seemed to lurch, like the heaving of a boat on the ocean. A toothy face with leathery skin hissed at him and he almost fell. *It's an illusion,* he reminded himself, *you're still in the circle, standing.* But the tiny cellar vanished and suddenly he was in a vast ballroom at the palace. It was the graduation ceremony. The king was staring down at him, drooling. Lucien Gavius, bloated and hostile, thundered his verdict: *FAILURE!*

Behind Gavius were row upon row of Malevorn Andevarion, Francis

Dorobon, Seth Korion, Gron Koll and Boron Funt, hundreds of each of them, all chanting, a rising crescendo: '*Failure, failure, failure, failure . . .*' They marched towards him, pointing in condemnation.

He tried to blank it out, but the sound pierced his skull like knives, louder and louder. '*Failure failure failure failure failure!*' More people joined in – his father; his mother, her blasted eyes weeping. Ramon was chanting mindlessly. Even Cym, nuzzling up to one of the Malevorns, letting him put his hands inside her blouse, kissing him as he groped her . . .

Failurefailurefailure . . .

But I didn't fail the tests – I was rejected because of Vult. You'll have to do better than that. He lashed the daemon with blue fire and heard it screech obscenely. '*Submit, Arbendesai!*' he cried.

The daemon wasn't cowed; it sent images of the batterings he had taken from Malevorn on the training ground; pictures of Cym, lewdly coupling with Malevorn; Ramon, impaled upon meat-hooks, screaming for death – anything it could think of to shatter Alaron's concentration. He fought back, lashing it with pain, with fire, with ice. It shrieked and whined and cursed and howled, feeding him images of Tesla's eyeballs exploding in flames, and of Vann, dead in a ditch in Verelon, until he lost his temper fully and thrashed it with a whip of gnosis-fire.

Suddenly he felt a hand on his shoulder and he almost leapt in fright. It was Muhren. His hand was shimmering and his voice strained by the pain of reaching into the protective circle. 'Easy, lad. You've won. Don't kill it.'

He looked down to see the crow was thrashing weakly in the muck of the summoning paste, its feathers singed and smoking. 'Uh – oops—' He let the gnosis-whip fade. 'Uh – Arbendesai, do you submit?'

'Yesh,' the crow squawked thinly. 'I've already *rukking* said so three times! How may I serve you, you over-enthusiastic moron?'

Ramon laughed aloud.

Alaron threw his friend a withering look. 'You must . . .' He trailed off and looked around. He hadn't really expected to get this far. 'Um, guys, what exactly do we want it to do?'

Ramon guffawed again. 'Sol et Lune, you're an amateur! We want it to bring the Memory Crystal, or give us the next clue.'

'Yeah, we want you to—'

'I'm not deaf,' the crow said irritably. 'Are those your commands?'

'Er, yes.'

The crow gave a little bow and hopped onto the edge of the bowl. 'I am yours to command, master,' it said with extreme irony.

Alaron looked questioningly at Muhren, who nodded. He cautiously removed power from the protective circles, stepping back. Sometimes spirits got it into their heads to attempt to kill the summoner, even at this juncture. But the crow merely took to the air and flapped experimentally about the room, yelping as it banged into the walls. 'What are you doing?' he asked it at last.

'Learning how to fly, obviously. Did you think I was a crow in the hereafter? Or before then?'

'What were you?' Alaron asked curiously.

'Buggered if I can remember.' It landed on a chair near General Langstrit. 'This old bastard called me up eighteen years ago and gave me a name. Once I retrieve his hidden treasure I can finally get free of this damned binding and move on. So if you don't mind, I'd like to get on with it.'

Alaron watched it warily. 'I'll be scrying you,' he warned.

'Yes, yes,' the bird replied tiredly. 'It's in both our interests for me to do what I'm told. Just let me get on with it, eh?' Springing into the air, it flew straight at the hatch, throwing it open with its own gnosis, and soared up and out into the night.

Alaron found he was swaying and tried to fight off sudden dizziness.

Muhren clapped him on the shoulder. 'Well done, lad. You need to follow him mentally now, to make sure nothing interferes, and feed him energy if needed. We'll stand guard.'

Ramon shook his hand as he sat and readied himself. 'Well done, Al.' He grinned. 'That's an interesting subconscious you've got. Vividly imagined.'

'Huh?'

'Didn't you notice, Al? Everything that daemon hit you with was visible to us.'

Alaron replayed the mental duel in his mind. *The graduation – Cym and Malevorn –* 'Oh Kore—'

Ramon sniggered. 'An interesting insight, that's all I can say.'

Alaron glanced at Cym, who raised an eyebrow and stared back. 'I can explain – those aren't things I think about . . . it was just trying to get under my skin—'

Cym regarded him frostily. 'So, who was the pretty boy at the graduation? Perhaps you could arrange a meeting, if that's the sort of thing you think I'd enjoy him doing to me?' Her voice could have corroded metal.

'Give him some space,' Muhren growled. 'A daemon uses whatever lever it can find. I've seen things that would turn your hair white when I've had to summon a daemon, and I'd like to think my conscience is largely clear. Give Alaron credit: he stood up to it. We saw less than half the battle, and he won it.'

Alaron looked at the watch captain gratefully. Then he closed his eyes and sent his awareness off after the daemon-crow as it flew through the twilight sky above the city.

Arbendesai returned within two hours, preening and puffed up. In its claws was a small pouch of damp-stained leather, encrusted with old dirt. 'Ha – got it, no problems.' It placed the pouch in Alaron's hands and hopped about as if expecting a reward. 'I would dearly love some cheese,' it announced meaningfully. 'I haven't had cheese since the last time I saw the old gent in the corner. Love cheese, I do.'

Muhren checked the large quartz crystal inside the pouch and verified that it contained gnosis-energy of the correct type before Alaron fed the crow a wedge of hard cheese from his rations. When it had finished, with much smacking of its beak, he dismissed the spirit, leaving a newly fresh crow corpse lying inside the summoning circle. The others watched Muhren with equal measures of anticipation and apprehension. He was the only one of them who had seen a memory crystal before.

'To release a memory crystal requires a linkage to be formed,' he told them. 'It's going to take time and effort.'

They made sure the general was sitting comfortably, then Muhren sliced open the old man's palm. Langstrit didn't flinch but watched the crystal with a curious expression, as though some part of him knew what it was. Muhren folded his bloody fingers about the crystal and light flashed as he triggered a gnosis-link between the blood and the crystal, then sat back to quietly feed that link. The old man gave a sudden sigh and folded back into a prone position.

Cym stifled a cry. 'Is he all right?' she whispered.

Muhren checked Langstrit's breathing and pulse. 'He's fine,' he confirmed. 'This will take hours,' he told them, 'and I had better return to my duties before I am missed. You'll need to take turns to gently feed the crystal with a small but steady stream of gnosis. The light it exudes should not exceed a candle-light. Can you do that? Mistress Cymbellea, perhaps you can go first?'

Cym learned swiftly, as always. Muhren was surprised at her aptitude and strength. 'Who was your mother, Cymbellea?' he asked.

Cym didn't look at him. 'Family secret,' she replied, the same words she always used.

Muhren grunted. He turned to Alaron. 'This trust you demand runs both ways, Master Mercer. I expect you all to still be here when I return at dawn.'

'We'll be here,' Alaron said tiredly. 'And so will the general.'

'Then I will go and check on what is happening in the city. Vult will not have been idle.' Muhren left without another word. The general lifted his head to watch him go. The glow of the crystal in his hand lit his eyes and seemed to be trickling through his veins.

They took turns as Freyadai night wore on, sleeping in shifts, focused on their task. They had no idea what was happening above, whether Vult was closing in or oblivious, but the exhausting task and the need to rest afterwards kept their minds occupied and their fears suppressed. Time became irrelevant, something measured only by the heartbeat of the old man in their care.

When Muhren returned, well before dawn, Ramon was taking his turn with Langstrit while Alaron and Cym rested. The Rimoni girl was asleep, her face unguarded. She looked like a divinity to Alaron, the hardness normally present in her eyes absent.

She woke when the hatch opened, saw Alaron watching her and scowled. <*What?*> Her mental touch was like her hand, deft and hard.

<*I was just thinking how beautiful you are when you sleep,* > Alaron replied with uncharacteristic boldness.

<*Idiot.*> She looked away, her cheeks colouring faintly.

I complimented her and she didn't throttle me. His heart soared.

Ramon, feeding the general some water, eyed his withered body. 'Look at him – he's lost nearly twenty years. It's going to be a Hel of a shock for him when he wakes.'

'It will,' Muhren agreed. 'I'll take over now. Get some rest, lad.'

The moment came soon after: the general gave a small cry and they all crowded around him. The old man was muttering, his face jerking about, then he cried out again, as if in pain, and his eyes flew open.

'Great Kore!' he shouted, and looked about him wildly, his eyes desperately frightened.

Muhren reached out and grabbed his shoulders. 'General Langstrit, sir – it's all right – you're with friends.'

The general stared at him, then visibly reeled. 'Jeris Muhren, is that you? Where am I?'

'My dear general, you are back. You're really here – I can't believe it.' He pulled the old man into his arms, and Langstrit hesitantly returned the embrace before looking about him at the dimly lit faces surrounding him.

'Muhren, who are these children?'

Alaron bowed, feeling a surge of pride. 'Mercer, sir, Alaron Mercer. My father is Vannaton Mercer and my mother is Tesla Anborn.'

'Tesla had a boy? Of course, you were born in the second year of the war. Great Kore, how long has it been?' He clutched his chest suddenly and looked down at his half-naked body. A visible shock ran through him. *'How long has it been?'*

'It is 928, sir,' Muhren replied carefully. 'About eighteen years.'

Langstrit's legs gave way; only Muhren's strength kept him upright. '*Eighteen years*,' he whispered. 'I never thought it would be so long. I thought three years, maybe . . . *Eighteen* – my Lord Kore–' He looked at Alaron. 'I know your father, boy. And your aunt.'

'I know, sir,' Alaron replied proudly. 'My father speaks of you often.'

'I'm Ramon Sensini,' Ramon put in. 'This is Cymbellea di Regia. It was we who followed the clues and brought you back – with the captain's help, of course,' he added.

Langstrit stared at them all, clearly still shaken. 'Then I thank you, all of you – thank you, with all my heart, thank you.' He looked down at his own body again, and a shudder ran through him. Cym draped a blanket around him and he huddled into it. He accepted food and drink, and calmed himself with visible effort. At last he said, 'I had better hear the tale, Jeris. Best I know the worst. Tell me everything.'

It was near dawn by the time Langstrit had heard the answers to his most burning questions. Though Muhren did most of the talking, filling him in on recent history and current events, the young people spoke most about the quest to restore him to himself. He grew calmer as he listened, and even chuckled once or twice as they explained how they'd found and unravelled the clues. 'I had in mind it might be someone like your Aunt Elena following the trail, young Alaron. The multi-rune I left was primed to appear before certain people only. I only included descendants of the specific people I named as an afterthought – a fortunate afterthought, as it turns out.' He grinned at Alaron, who ducked his head, smiling.

They all liked the general, now that his personality had emerged; his vibrant energy and gruff humour was endearing. Muhren was clearly devoted to him, and now they could see why: General Langstrit exuded leadership, and gave respect as readily as he expected it.

Finally, he declared himself satisfied, although he had grown more and more worried as they told him about Vult's presence. Alaron tried to apologise for exposing them by stealing his file, but Langstrit waved it away. 'Mistakes are made, lad; that's life. We learn, we make amends.' He turned back to Muhren. 'Vult clearly suspects your involvement, Jeris.' He looked about the group. 'So, the Scytale, and what to do about it.'

He took a swig of the dark beer Muhren had bought with him, his favourite. 'The Scytale first. Young Alaron was right: Fulchius – the Noros canon – stole it and brought it to Noros the year the Revolt broke out. Fulchius had fallen out with Mater-Imperia Lucia over the Crusade, so he stole the Scytale and fled to Noros, intending to create a rival to Pallas. Robler brought me in, along with a few others, all Noros veterans of the Crusade. When we drank the ambrosia Fulchius created, Robler, Modin and I ascended; the others failed and died. Fulchius had hoped that the act of creating ambrosia and showing we were in earnest would be enough to force the Rondians to nego- tiate – he didn't think Lucia would risk open war. He underestimated her.

'By the final defeat, Fulchius and his fellow canons were dead and only Robler and I were left of our inner circle. When surrender became inevitable, we decided we had to hide the Scytale and I took it on myself, so that Robler would be genuinely ignorant of what happened to it. We had already begun to think we would have to conceal the Scytale when we were besieged here in Norostein, so I had laid the groundwork. I did my best to cover my tracks, and to set a puzzle that only a friendly party could solve. I knew I would fall into hostile hands when the eventual surrender took place – I'd anticipated that I would be taken to Pallas, but obviously Vult managed to gain control of me and hid me from Lucia. By then I had erased my own memory.'

They all reflected on this. Alaron wondered if he could have ever had the courage to do the same.

Langstrit spoke again. 'All of this leads to an important question: what to do with the Scytale when we recover it? There are only two courses: to destroy it, or to use it. To destroy it would be wrong, I believe – for all the evil that has been wrought, the gnosis has also done much good. It's the key to righting the wrongs of this world.

Pallas will never fall of its own accord, so a stronger force must arise to eclipse it. To destroy the Scytale is to condemn us to Pallas' domination for ever.

'Great things can grow from small beginnings. Just as the magi sprang from a few fortunate individuals, so together we can grow something special, something vital. We must use the Scytale, carefully and seeking only the sort of mage who shares our aims. I have tried open war, and war failed. We must try something else. It will take years, but with patience, we can create a network of allies and break Pallas' power.'

'Give it to the Ordo Costruo,' Cym urged, as she had once suggested to Alaron.

Langstrit shook his head. 'They may prove to be allies in the end, but they were compromised by the Crusade and now Pallas controls them. How could we be certain that Antonin Meiros would aid us? For now we must look to ourselves and those we can trust.'

Cym frowned, looking like she wanted to argue.

'How will we retain control of the Scytale if we go about adding others?' Ramon asked.

'You told me of your own pact, and I agree with it. Let we five become the new Keepers of the Scytale. Please believe me, I do not seek to cheat you, or to plunge this land into war again. I do not seek to open old wounds. I only want the opportunity presented by the Scytale to rebalance the wrongs that Pallas inflicts daily.'

Muhren was nodding as Langstrit spoke, but Alaron needed to look at Ramon for reassurance before agreeing. Cym gave her assent last of all, clearly fighting her doubts.

Langstrit gathered their hands together in the middle of the circle. 'Let us be the Ordo Pacifica: the Order of Peace. We five shall be the Inner Circle, to stand as equals dedicated to bringing peace to Yuros. Peace shall be our banner. War will be our enemy. Are we agreed?'

Alaron felt a sense of unreality – these were the sort of things that legendary magi swore, not a motley collection of people like them. It felt pretentious. *I am a failed mage*, he thought. *Cym is Rimoni and Ramon is Silacian*. It was surreal. *But here we are – and it feels right.*

He looked around the circle. Everyone looked so determined, and it made him feel braver.

They released each other's hands and sat down again. It was a few moments before Langstrit spoke up once more. 'Now we must recover the Scytale, lest we be accused of putting our cart before the horse. We have a few problems to overcome: I buried it deep, and I still have some issues to resolve regarding gnosis-workings.' He raised a hand and, grimacing, strained to produce a very modest gnosis-fire. 'One, I'm out of practice. Two, I'm currently bound in a Rune of the Chain, put upon me by Vult himself. Fortunately, my power after Ascending surpasses his – that enabled the instinctive use of the gnosis you tell me I occasionally displayed. And as you can see, I can still produce a little force when I try. But I must be fully unbound to be of use: I can do it myself, but in doing it, Vult will be aware of exactly where I am.'

'Do we need to remove the Chain-rune at all?' Ramon asked. 'Can't we regain the Scytale without you?'

Langstrit thought for a moment. 'Probably, yes – recovery of the Scytale will require only moderate Earth-gnosis and Water-gnosis – and knowing where to look. As I didn't know who would come looking, I didn't protect it so strongly that only an Ascendant could regain it. The clues had to be enough to lead the right people to it, while keeping the wrong people away.'

'We can remove the Chain-rune anytime,' Muhren said. 'What we can't afford is to be found.' He pursed his lips, considering. 'Does the Scytale itself have powers that will aid us once we have it?'

The general shook his head. 'Sadly, no. Fulchius told me the Scytale is not an artefact of intrinsic might; it's a repository of knowledge: how to make the ambrosia in such a way that precisely suits the recipient. It is of no use in battle.'

'So where is it?' Alaron finally asked the question burning in his mind.

Langstrit looked up. 'Ha! Of course, I haven't said, have I? It's beneath the waters of the lake in the flooded area of the Old Town. Inside the plinth of a broken statue of the king, actually. It's inside a metal cylinder about eight inches round and two feet long, lined with lead to keep out the damp.' He looked at them. 'We need to get to Lower Town undetected, and one or more of us will need to go down under the waters to find it – preferably me, as I know exactly what I'm looking for.'

Lower Town was around a mile north of where they were, spread around the shores of the lake. It was a good twenty minutes' walk through curfewed streets. Langstrit described the route carefully, and the whereabouts of the statue, in case they had to split up.

'What are our chances of being detected along the way?' Alaron asked.

'Small, if you stay here,' Ramon replied.

'Huh?'

'Think about it Alaron: you're the name and face Vult knows. He can't detect the general, Muhren can block him and he doesn't know Cym or me – so it's safer if you aren't with us.'

'But—' Alaron stared at him in frustration.

'I know, amici, but it makes sense. You are the rod that could bring the lightning down on us.' He waved his hands apologetically. 'I'm sorry.'

'He's right, Alaron,' Muhren said. 'Look, it doesn't matter which of us gets it: we're all going to share in it. We'll only be gone an hour – and then we can work out how we're going to get the Scytale out of Norostein.'

Alaron slumped and hugged his knees. *It makes sense . . . but it's not fair.* He felt numb as he listened to the others getting ready, gathering their weapons, putting their cloaks back on. Langstrit, dressed in some of Vann's old clothes Cym had found, looked much more confident now, reconciled to what had happened to him and ready to make the most of his rescue. He buckled on a sword, his face clouded by memories.

Ramon patted Alaron's shoulder. 'We won't be long, amici. I promise.'

Alaron watched as Ramon led the way up the ladder, Muhren behind him.

Cym gave him a small wave and a wink. <*Back in a jiffy, Alaron.*>

Ramon pushed open the hatch at the top of the stairs, something *twanged* and the Silacian gasped and folded in half, clutching his belly as he fell backwards on top of Muhren. Alaron cried out in horror as he saw the feathered tip of a bolt protruding from Ramon's stomach. Muhren caught Ramon, then twisted and hunched over, shielding him with his body as flames washed down the ladder.

Souldrinker and Assassin

Heathen

*To all religions, those outside the faith are heathen, an enemy whose very exist-
ence endangers the soul, for if the heathen can exist without God, their example
undermines the faithful. Therefore all religions are at war with those who deny
them. At least the Amteh are frank about their wish to put all heathens to the
sword. The Kore mouths platitudes of tolerance, but murders just the same.*

ANTONIN MEIROS, ORDO COSTRUO, 643

*Hebusalim, on the continent of Antiopia
Jumada (Maicin) to Akhira (Junesse) 928
1–2 months until the Moontide*

Kazim knelt in prayer, alone in the largest Dome-al'Ahm in Hebusalim,
prostrating himself to heaven, asking Ahm's forgiveness and blessing.
The enormity of his mission was beginning to fully dawn upon him.
It had never been just a game, not really, but training was not reality.
To perfectly execute a killing stroke with a blunted wooden knife
was not to drive a steel blade into a man's heart.

Footsteps echoed in the vast space and he turned to see Rashid,
Jamil and Haroun, striding across the stone floor. They were booted,
despite the prohibition on footwear in an Amteh holy place, and
part of him was offended by this subtle expression of Hadishah arrogance, but the thrill of trepidation was greater. Was this the moment?

It felt like he had been preparing for ever, that this daily cycle of
exercise, eating, prayer and sleep was some kind of nightmare wheel
that would never stop turning. The only person he saw every day

was Haroun, who quietly read him the words of the texts, of self-sacrifice, of striking the necessary blow, of the evil of the unbeliever. He could have quoted them backwards now: *the Only God is the One God who is Ahm. There is no salvation for the Unbeliever.* But they were just words; only the act of killing Antonin Meiros could release him. Only through death could he live again, somewhere far away, just Ramita and him, with their children.

'Kazim,' said Rashid. 'Come.'

He led them to a Hadishah safe house, deep below the house of a merchant near the gold souk. They were admitted silently, unquestioned and unchallenged. There was an underworld here, dealers in opium and gambling and money, all in the service of Ahm. The Hadishah ruled that world, and Rashid led the Hadishah. Kazim saw fear mixed with reverence in all who recognised him. He wondered what role the man lived openly; he had seen or heard virtually nothing since he came here, and Hadishah did not ask more than they were told.

They descended, the deepest into the earth he had ever been, to a dimly lit pillared cavern some hundred paces long. An old woman stood hunched over before a plinth with an open book on a stand. To Kazim's amazement, Rashid fell to both knees and prostrated himself before her, and the others did the same. Kazim hastily followed suit. *Who is she, that Rashid kneels to her?*

'At last,' the old woman said. Her harsh, dry voice was oddly familiar. Despite himself, he lifted his head, and he realised that he did know her after all: the ancient crone in Aruna Nagar Market who had first told him that his fate was tied to Ramita Ankesharan. A thousand questions boiled up, but he swallowed them fearfully as her eyes pierced the gloom and fixed on him.

'Sal'Ahm, Kazim Makani,' she rasped. She rose and offered him her arm. The others, even Rashid, remained behind as she guided him to an alcove that she had obviously prepared. There was a brazier and a few artefacts – a knife, some small crystals that looked like large chunks of salt, and a pair of beaten copper goblets.

She motioned for him to sit on the richly patterned carpet that covered the floor, then, moving stiffly, sat cross-legged herself. 'My name is Sabele,' she told him. Her irises were yellowish, he noticed with a shudder – amber-coloured, like a jackal. 'You may call me Grandmother, though that is not precisely correct.'

Grandmother? He studied her fearfully. *She is another Hadishah mage. This is a test.*

'Rashid argued against my seeing you until after the deed is done,' the crone told him. 'He felt the risks were too great.'

'What risks?' he found the nerve to ask.

'The risk that you fail and my presence is torn from your mind under questioning.' Her voice was cool and emotionless. 'I recognise the risk, but I overruled him.'

She overruled Rashid. He nodded nervously.

'Rashid does not know all that is at stake. He knows what you are, but he does not know *all* that you are.' Sabele leaned forward. 'He does not know what we can gain if we play our hand correctly. He has chosen you for this mission because he deems you capable, because your sister or this Ramita will open the door for you, because you are Raz Makani's son. But he does not know all that Raz Makani was.' Her eyes met his intently. 'Nor do you. It is time you learned.'

He was suddenly afraid of what he was about to be told.

'Raz Makani was a descendant of mine,' Sabele said, 'as was Falima, his wife.' Then she suddenly changed the subject. 'Do you know the tale of the Rondian magi, of Corineus and his followers?'

Kazim nodded; Rashid had told him. 'They gained their Shaitan-powers, destroyed the Rimoni and conquered Yuros,' he replied.

The woman sniffed diffidently. 'I was there,' she told him, and he felt his skin go cold.

The woman's eyes challenged him to disbelieve. 'I was born in Yuros almost six hundred years ago. I was one of Corin's followers; we drank ambrosia together. But only one third of the thousand people gathered there gained the gnosis and became magi. Fully one third died in their sleep. But that left another group: those who did not gain the gnosis that night, but who did not die. I was such a one.'

'But—?'

'Hear me out, boy.' She put a finger to his lips. 'Listen. Those of us who failed to gain the gnosis that night were left in a strange position: witness to the miracle, but not party to it. Those who had gained the power declared that we had been proven unworthy, and once they destroyed the Rimoni legions and established their rule, they turned their attention to us. Sertain and his cronies wrote a holy book for their new religion, the Kore, and in it they named us "Kore's Rejects". First they hounded us, then they went so far as declaring us heretics and condemned us to death.' Her voice was harsh as she spoke, thick with remembered bitterness. 'Our numbers dwindled, and we began to believe that we had been indeed found wanting. Within a decade, we were hunted almost to extinction. Only through our courage and loyalty to each other did we survive.'

She fell silent for a long while, as if pondering this thought. Kazim waited until he could not refrain from asking, 'What happened then?'

She looked up. 'An accidental discovery: I came upon a dying mage who had been caught unawares by a rival and left for dead. His body was ruined beyond healing and as I bent over him, he died. For an instant, as I was checking to see if he breathed, I thought I glimpsed a tiny puff of luminous smoke rising from his nostrils, and I inadvertently inhaled that vapour. It was his spirit, departing the corpse.' She gestured at the brazier with a curling hand and caused the smoke rising there to twist, a prop to her tale. '*I had inhaled his soul – and gained the gnosis*. And because my fellows were as kindred to me, I shared my discovery, which paved the path to our salvation.'

Kazim stared. Rashid had *never* mentioned anything like this.

'We know now that the ambrosia had not quite worked on us, the so-called Rejects: there had been a flaw in the mix, or maybe some unknown element in ourselves that had retarded the process, leaving us with the *potential* for the gnosis. To gain it fully required a trigger: a soul imbued with the gnosis.'

Kazim's mind raced ahead and began to make connections as Sabele went on, 'My fellow Rejects, desperate to gain the gnosis, followed my lead, but dying magi were not readily available. In desperation, some turned on each other, and to my sorrow, this worked: transformation could also be triggered by absorbing the soul of a Reject. Drinking a human soul *replenished* our powers, but it could not trigger the gnosis. In essence, we had to kill to gain our powers.'

Kazim watched her in sick fascination. *She told me to call her 'Grandmother'.*

'The magi learned of us, and they were appalled. They call us "Dokken", "Souldrinkers", "Shadowmancers", and many other such names. A purge was declared, and the few of us remaining went into hiding. We have been hiding ever since.'

'And you are my great-grandmother?' Kazim asked fearfully.

'Add a few greats, boy,' she told him. 'I fled here when the first windships came, hundreds of years ago.'

Hundreds of years – Ahm have mercy! Kazim forced himself to think, despite the hammering in his chest. He recalled what he'd been told of the magi. 'Then the blood must have dissipated through the generations . . .'

'These things work similarly: you are one-sixteenth blood, so the gnosis in you is thin, but not too thin. You will make a Shadowmancer, if you have the will.'

He gasped and jerked away. 'But I don't,' he choked out, 'I don't want your Shaitan-gifts.' *All I ever wanted was to be was a good man, a happy man, with Ramita beside me.*

'If the children growing in her belly are Meiros', then your woman has the gnosis already.'

'The children are mine!'

'Are you sure?' She smiled indulgently. 'If she had the gnosis, why would she want one who has not?'

'She does not – and she loves me.'

'She is falling under Meiros' spell.'

'Never!'

She looked at him pityingly. 'You think she is unchanged by all she has seen and experienced here? You think, even if she could, she would return to the south? She is his prisoner, until you cut her free.' She held out her hand, palm upward and let flame dance on it, and he found himself watching in fascination, unwillingly wondering what it would be like to be able to perform such miracles – to do it and not be damned. 'Would you not like to pilot your own skiff, boy? Or rain down fire on the infidel? To bestride the world like a prince?'

His mind went back to the joy of soaring above the ground with Molmar, and he recalled the humiliation of being thrashed by Rashid in the arena. *I would never be treated so again. I would be his equal . . .* It was not a dream he could easily reject.

'You say I would have to kill a mage and consume his soul?' he asked, nauseated at the thought.

'You keep on consuming souls to replenish expended energy,' Sabele replied. 'There is something in our condition that retards normal recovery. A mage can regain his powers by rest; we must feed on others.'

'Are – are we—?' Saying 'we' was almost the strangest part of this conversation. 'Are we as strong as the magi?'

Sabele looked at him measuringly. 'Well,' she said, 'that rather depends. Would you know more?'

He looked at her, scarcely able to think. This power she was offering was a dream, a fantasy – but to become a real power in this world, when the times were so perilous, was a Shaitan's bargain that he surely could not afford to decline.

Ramita will understand, he told himself. *I do this to grow stronger, my love, so I may protect you.*

'What must I do?' he asked.

Ramita was alone in her courtyard. Meiros was away, attending yet another emergency meeting at Domus Costruo, and Alyssa Dulayne had taken Justina to a party. Ramita had been largely alone since that night at Southpoint and already it felt like something that had happened years ago to a different person. Only Huriya was left to her, but she was constantly away in the daytime and consumed with her own appetites at night. Ramita could hear the sounds of passion emanating from Huriya's room even now. Jos Klein was intoxicated with the Keshi girl, constantly seeking her out. *She is my sister, but I hardly know her any more.*

She prayed Kazim and Jai were far away, far enough to survive Meiros' wrath, even if things went badly. She had two glimmers of hope: one, that her children truly were Meiros', or if they weren't, that he might forgive her. She rehearsed over and over in her mind how she would beg his forgiveness: her next children would be his, this she would swear; she was so very, very sorry – but she would make it up to him. It sounded pitiful, even in her mind. These were things men did not forgive.

She dined alone on some cheese and bread and a small glass of juice. Olives gave her indigestion this week. Her pregnancy had her appetite rotating in some obscure cycle, so she was never sure what she would be able to eat without having to stagger to the privy. It was the first week of Junesse and the courtyard, a roasting dish during the middle of the day, became bearable only at night. The curfews imposed in the city outside were poorly policed, so the city was noisy after dark, even in their quiet neighbourhood.

Her heart fluttered as a dry voice asked from her doorway, 'My dear, you are still awake?' Antonin Meiros grinned boyishly as he hobbled into the room.

She looked up, feeling a smile return to her face for the first time in several days. 'Husband—' She went to get up, but he kissed her forehead and settled opposite her.

'How are you, Ramita?'

'Well enough. I have some discomfort here,' she said, lightly touching her belly, 'but otherwise I am well. Although I miss my husband,' she scolded lightly.

'I am sorry, my dear. We are trying to get Salim to meet with us, but Rashid cannot get him to agree.'

She remembered the darkly handsome emir with a shudder. 'I don't trust him.'

'Rashid has his uses.' Meiros poured himself some fruit juice. 'His family have been part of the Ordo Costruo from early on; they have much to be grateful to us for. They have remained loyal to the Order through two Crusades. He will be steadfast.' He looked across the table at her. 'I did not come to see you about the woes of the world. I came to see your lovely face and to hear your voice. Tell me, is Justina paying you more attention these days?'

'No – well, a little. She sees me daily, but only to see if I have started to, um, *manifest*.' She steeled herself. 'Husband, is there anything that might prevent this thing happening to me?'

'No. According to the texts, it has always happened,.' He smiled kindly. 'Don't be afraid, my dear. I know you were raised to think of the gnosis as evil, but it isn't; it is just a tool, no more good nor evil than the person wielding it. Your soul is in no danger.'

It was easier to let him think that was what troubled her. She didn't yet have the courage for the real conversation.

'So, may I help you to bed?' he asked, a hint of the lascivious in his words.

She was about to agree when her belly and bowels chose to rebel and she clutched her stomach. 'The only place I need help to go to is the privy! I am sorry, Antonin.'

He looked up at her, startled. 'You used my name?'

She realised it herself only then and she put a hand to her mouth, struck mute. She wasn't precisely sure what this meant, but it felt powerfully significant somehow; he evidently thought so. He tilted her head and kissed her.

'My Ramita,' he breathed.

It felt like some part of her had changed: she had accepted her new life and farewelled the old. *I am sorry, Kazim, wherever you are.* She went to kiss him in return, a kiss of genuine affection, but her body betrayed her. A stomach cramp struck her, making her gasp. 'Please, I must use the privy,' she gasped.

Meiros let her go, an almost foolish look on his face. 'Please, my dear, come to my chambers when you are done, if you feel able. Even if it is just to hold you.'

She nodded, feeling dazed, and staggered into the privy, where she sagged to the ground. Eventually she found the strength to purge herself and crawled out of the foetid little chamber, desiring nothing more than to be clean. There was a small bucket of water left over from the morning.

Huriya should be helping me, she thought irritably. As she washed herself, the cool water began to make her feel better. She found a clean nightdress, then sat in her tiny courtyard for a while, trying to find herself again. *Am I falling for my ancient jadugara?* she asked herself. *Have I forgotten Kazim? Antonin is good to me – better than I deserve.*

Who am I to yearn for love anyway? I am a market-girl – we are coins for our parents to exchange; love does not enter the transaction. It is just a lie we tell ourselves to make it bearable.

Love is simple, the songs said; *love is certain. It sings inside you.* So why was this so complicated? Why all these doubts – why was everything so confusing? Her love for Kazim was simple, but her feelings for Meiros were not. His power and age frightened and repelled, but his gentleness and strength brought comfort. And he *needed* her, it seemed, not just as a mother for children, but as a companion – as a *wife.* And in this frightening new world, she realised she needed him too.

She had tried to do the right thing. She had not eloped with Kazim – how could she? Who on Urte could hide from Antonin Meiros? To flee would have been a death sentence for them both. But *why* had she let Kazim fill her womb? How could she have been so insane? A few moments of bliss, selfishly offered and selfishly taken, had condemned her. There would be a price to pay.

Then I must pay it alone, she decided. *If the children are Meiros', he and I will raise them. If they are Kazim's, I will plead to be allowed to raise them, in captivity if need be. I will beg to be allowed a second chance, and if my husband denies me that, it will be no one's fault but mine.*

There was a movement at the door, a serving boy who ran messages, one of the children of the kitchen staff. 'Madam, there is a man at the gate, asking for you. I cannot find Captain Klein, madam.' He glanced meaningfully at the door to Huriya's rooms.

It would serve them right if I interrupted them . . . She sighed and said,

'I will come,' rising awkwardly. 'My husband is abed and the captain is indisposed.' She clutched her belly, straightened painfully and followed the boy down the stairs.

The courtyard below was silent, and lit by lanterns, little pools of light in the blackness of the darkmoon. The boy with her danced ahead, full of sprightly life. It made her smile to see him and she patted her belly fondly. *I would like a boy-child.* The lanky young guard Morden was on duty with another man, Franck; both waited before the inner gate, the one protected by Meiros' wards. Only a family member or Klein could use the carved handles to admit guests after dark. Ramita glanced down at her acid-etched hand and flexed it slightly. Who could it be?

'The Omali priest is here to see you, madam,' Morden said, jerking a thumb at the viewing slit. 'Something about prayers and candles.' He looked contemptuously amused by it all.

Ramita put her head to the slit and opened it. In the well-lit chamber was a lone man, wrapped in dirty orange robes, his face coated in ash, hunched over a walking stick. But she wasn't fooled for an instant; it was Kazim. She felt her heart slam into her ribs and she clutched her breast.

This is the moment.

She could almost hear Kazim's thoughts: the hope, the determination, the purpose. The boy who loved her had come to take her away. *But now I do not want to go . . .*

She could almost touch his flinty purpose, his determination was as sharp as an arrowhead. It frightened her. Her legs trembled and she almost swooned.

'Madam, are you all right?' Morden gripped her forearm. 'If you are unwell, I can send him away.'

It would be that easy, to make herself non-complicit, to remove herself from the decision. But she owed Kazim more than that. She'd loved him all of her young life. He did not deserve such cowardice.

I must make him go away – he must go – for his own sake he must go!

'It's all right,' she heard herself say, 'I just had a small turn. I will have a few words with him.'

'Is it wise, madam?' Morden wrinkled his nose. 'There is a curfew.'

'He's Omali, Morden,' she heard herself say. 'What does he care for shihads? He's a man of God. See, it is the young chela who has come here before.' She could hear the shakiness in her voice, and marvelled that he could not. She reached out and twisted the handle that enabled the gate to be opened. The familiar tingle of the wards identifying her made her quiver, then the inner gates creaked and sagged slightly as the powers binding the door loosened, allowing the guards to unbar and open them.

'Step through,' Franck told Kazim. 'Put your staff down and raise your hands.'

'It will be only a short conversation, then he will go,' she said firmly, the words meant for Kazim as he stepped through the opened door and put down his staff. He raised his hands.

He's unarmed. What harm can he do? Why is he here?

Morden stepped closer to search him. Unexpectedly, his eyes flashed with gnosis-light as he passed an open hand in Kazim's direction. She had vaguely known Morden had mage-blood, but he'd never used his skills in front of her as he did now, examining Kazim carefully.

'He's unarmed and his intentions are as stated,' he told Franck.

The two guards stepped away and she met Kazim's gaze. Emotion crackled between them. *Please, tell me you are here to say goodbye. Please, let it just be that—*

Franck patted Kazim for weapons himself and then stepped back. 'He's a well-made bastard for a holy man,' the guard observed grudgingly. 'Look at the muscle on him.' He stepped away and glanced at her. 'We cannot admit him further than this without Captain Klein's permission,' he told her.

She shook her head. 'I do not wish him to be allowed further in any case,' she said, her eyes not leaving Kazim's face. *See, I reject you – please go!*

Kazim stared back at her mutely.

'Well, chela?' she asked. Then in Omali she let a little emotion show. 'Kazim, why are you still here?'

'I came for you,' he replied woodenly.

'My place is here,' she told him.

No reaction. Nothing.

Something died inside her – and inside him. A light in his eyes flickered out.

He did not reply but instead bent to his feathered staff as if about to take his leave again. She almost collapsed in relief, but as he straightened, she glimpsed steel among the feathers decorating the top of the staff. He whirled with blinding speed, driving it through Morden's right eye. The young man sagged on the bending shaft of the staff, already dead, but Kazim was still moving; his legs scissored, a kick that broke Franck's jaw before he could cry out. Franck tried to lift his spear, but Kazim blurred inside his guard, plucked the man's dagger from his scabbard and slashed it across his throat. He pinned him against the wall and let him slide down it, almost silent. Beside them, Morden had rolled onto his side, his eye-socket still impaled on the spear-staff.

Ramita fell to her knees in shock at the sudden violence. Kazim turned back to her, a splash of blood across his chest from Morden's death-wound. The child servant beside her backed away, his mouth working towards a scream, but Kazim lunged past her and drove a fist into the boy's face, snapping his head back. The boy bounced and slid across the stone, his head twisted at an unnatural angle. He didn't move.

She opened her own mouth to scream, but Kazim's hand stifled her. 'You will not make a noise,' he said coldly, as if he were made of stone. He kissed her pitilessly, swallowing her whimpering cries. 'Open the gates, Ramita.'

No – no! she screamed inside, but Kazim had grabbed her and was leading her firmly to the gates, his left hand clamped over her mouth. He forced her right hand to the handles and as he worked the gates open dark shapes filed through the security pen and joined them: hard-eyed men, hooded in black. There were six of them, counting Kazim: assassins, come to kill her husband.

Please let this be a nightmare, she prayed hopelessly. *Please, let me wake—*

They moved like shadows, these hollow-eyed killers. One of them turned and looked at her curiously. His face was scarred, she noticed – and then he was bending over the child and straightening the boy's limbs, no emotion showing.

Gesturing silently to each other, the assassins flowed up the stairs. Kazim's arms locked tight about her, holding her up, whispering little endearments in praise of her courage and loyalty as if she were a pet animal that must be calmed. 'Just one more task, my darling, and then we are free of this, free to live and love for ever,' he told her, his arms like shackles about her. He was more muscular than he had ever been, his voice deeper, and terrifying in its implacable purpose.

They swarmed up to the upper terrace where a single lantern lit Huriya, wrapped only in a bloody sheet. She had a satisfied air about her: the afterglow of sex and death. There was a bloody dagger in her hands. She swayed languidly to Kazim and kissed him, the metallic stink of blood all about her. 'The big ape is dead,' she purred. 'He never saw it coming.' She giggled. 'It was better than fucking.'

Ramita felt a great surge of revulsion and the Keshi girl noticed and reached out, stroking Ramita's cheek with a bloody hand. 'Oh, Mita, don't be like that. We're doing this for you.'

Make this stop, she pleaded silently again, wide-eyed with horror.

'Have her open the door,' hissed the scar-faced assassin.

Kazim pulled her against his chest. 'Ramita darling,' he whispered, 'you have to do this one thing: you have to open the inner door. We will do the rest. We can't get to him without you.' She could feel his rising excitement, his tension building towards a climax; the impending death of her husband was pounding through his head. His thoughts were so palpable they made her want to scream. Her very soul revolted at the bloody desires she sensed, and her mind began to rebel.

Parvasi, be with me: they make me their tool. Please, great Goddess, give me strength. Darikha, Mother of Passion, lend me your fire! She walled herself off from Kazim's thoughts, drawing on all that Meiros had shown her of mind-shielding, and drew strength from the silence.

Though it might kill her, there was something she could do. A simple plan she could cling to: *I will bite his hand, and then I will scream, and my husband will do the rest.* She steadied herself and Kazim pushed her towards the security wards while behind her the dark shapes closed in, their weapons poised. Kazim's hand gripped her shoulders. Scarface laid a blade across her path, mutely warning her that there could be no attempt to step inside the door and shut it. She felt all of their thoughts except for Scarface; he was closed and dark, hard like coal. Their murderous auras made her nauseous, but she could also sense their tension and fear – and now she could even see the glittering walls of pale light that protected the Casa, like webs of light patterning the doors before her.

The realisation hit her like a blow: *I am feeling the gnosis – this is the manifestation!* And then: *These children belong to* Antonin! *Oh Gods, what can I do—?*

She could feel the waiting, dormant power around her; in the water, in the stone of the building, in the burning lamps. She could feel it in the people about her, overwhelming her with sensation. But she had no idea how to reach it.

'Just open the door and all will be well,' Kazim whispered.

Scarface gripped her wrist and a dark gritty presence filled her head, as Alyssa's had. She stared into his eyes. *He is one of the magi!*

<*Yes I am, little Lakh.*> His mental touch was hard and invasive and his strange yellow eyes seared into hers. She forced herself to go blank, desperate that her secret not be discovered. He grunted. <*Hmm. I thought for a moment—* > His eyes looked puzzled, then the immediacy of his task distracted him. He reached out, seized her wrist and placed her hand upon the security wards and she felt the acid-burns on her hands work on the lock.

Kazim could barely sense the other Hadishah positioned about the courtyard, silent as shadows. Rashid and Jamil were among them. He didn't know the other three; they were only cold eyes through slitted masks. They held crossbows at the ready. Rashid held a scimitar.

Huriya had sashayed to the side, licking her dagger and looking smugly satisfied. *My sister has become something frightening*, he thought, holding Ramita tight. He could feel her trembling body, sense her inner turmoil. She hadn't wanted to admit him at the gates. That thought burned him, but he told himself, *She's frightened, that is all. She'll get over this, once we're free.*

'Just open the door and all will be well,' he whispered to her, but Jamil didn't wait; though he was looking at her curiously, as if she had just surprised him, he took Ramita's wrist and placed her hand on the security ward.

Her teeth sank into his hand and he recoiled in shock and pain. She screamed something in Rondian and Kazim almost lost his grip. He seized her to him, hard, dragging her away as Jamil whirled and words began to crackle from his mouth.

'Don't hurt her!' Kazim bellowed, shielding Ramita with his own body – then a huge cracking sound shredded the night and the door of Meiros' quarters blasted open, splintering into a hundred shards of carved wood that flew outwards, impaling the crossbow-wielding assassin in front. The Hadishah was torn apart in a gory spray as he was thrown backwards.

A crossbow *thwacked*, launching a bolt into the black passageway, but it disintegrated as it flew. Another Hadishah sprang to the side of the door, raising a blade, and Kazim pulled Ramita away again as Meiros appeared. The assassin beside the door fell to his knees, reversed his dagger and buried it in his own heart, falling sideways like a sack of flour. A second crossbowman fired, but the bolt shattered in blue sparks above Meiros, and then that assassin too was howling, jerking spasmodically as his heart burst. Jamil bellowed a warcry and thrust his sword. The blade struck shields of force and Jamil flew backwards, hammering into the pillars on the far side of the courtyard.

Meiros turned on Kazim and something gripped the inside of his skull with a force like a vice. He cried for Ahm as he fell to his knees, losing his grip on Ramita. Darkness drilled into his mind, tearing his vision apart as he collapsed, screaming.

Then Rashid gestured and Ramita was ripped through the air into his arms. The attack on Kazim ceased instantly as Meiros spun to confront the man holding his wife. The emir pulled off his mask. 'Stop or I'll kill her!' he shouted, and his dagger scored Ramita's throat.

Kazim saw Meiros clearly now, not decrepit, but tall and formidable, clad only in bed-robes, and his face ablaze with fury. For a dreadful second he thought the old man didn't care, that in his rage he would condemn Ramita. Out of the corner of his eyes he saw Jamil trying to stand, but his left leg was buckling. The blade in his own hand spun, aligning with his left breast, and he fought it silently, without hope, knowing only the training he'd absorbed from Rashid was keeping the steel from plunging into his heart.

'No! Husband, no,' Ramita called imploringly, her eyes on the dagger at Kazim's chest. She was on her knees now, Rashid crouched above her, his dagger at the back of her head.

'I will plunge this straight into her brain, Meiros,' Rashid snarled. 'You can't get to me the way you can these others. I can kill her before you get to me, and she and your children will die—'

Kazim's mind was abruptly free and he sobbed in relief as his dagger fell to the marble floor. All about them, the servants were gathering, watching helplessly as this drama played out in front of them. He saw Huriya in the shadows, frozen with terror. *Sister, run*, he thought with all his might.

'Rashid Mubarak,' the old man rasped, 'unhand my wife and I will let you live to stand trial.'

Rashid lifted his head proudly. 'No, Meiros: tonight, you die, or she does.' Rashid poised the tip of the blade at her neck and twisted it, ready to thrust. Kazim almost screamed as her eyes popped and her body went rigid. She clasped her belly, tears streaming silently down her face. 'Choose, Meiros: a few more miserable years before one of us gets to you, or children to bear your name and blood.'

Kazim's eyes flew between these two terrible men, his heart in his mouth.

*

Ramita's knees were grazed, her blood smearing the marble as she
knelt at the feet of Rashid Mubarak. She was pinned and helpless,
his dagger a promise of death, but somehow she could sense the
glacial steel of the two magi's minds: it was like being caught between
two great boulders. But the concealed might of her husband dwarfed
the emir, and they both knew it. Meiros could break him in a few
moments – but in those moments, Ramita and her unborn children
would perish.

<Ramita,> Meiros' dry, gentle voice whispered in her mind.

She quivered in shock to hear him. Intuitively she shaped a return
thought: <Husband, what am I to do?> He heard her, she could sense
the contact. Hope flared unbidden.

<You have found your gnosis, my magnificent wife. I am so proud – but
my dear, you must hide it for now. Bury it deep.> Aloud, he said, 'What
surety will you give me, Rashid, that you will not kill her and the
unborn the moment I am dead?'

<I don't know how to use it,> she wailed inside. <If only it had come
sooner—>

'Why would we do that?' Rashid replied levelly, then suddenly his
voice cracked like a bullwhip, 'Stop that, old man – don't you touch
my mind!' His blade gouged Ramita's skin and blood sprang from
the shallow cut and burned down her neck.

She heard Kazim gasp, and Meiros raised a placating hand. 'I've
stopped – don't harm her.' <I am sorry, my dear girl. I had to try.>

Rashid's face was carved from flint. His next words sounded
rehearsed, his victory speech: 'There is no reason for us to harm
either mother or children. She is an innocent, dragged here against
her will by your misbegotten scheming and perverted lusts. I will
take her under my protection. The children will know their heritage,
and why you had to die. They will bear your name, even as they grow
to hate you and all you did. They will serve Ahm as their talents and
desires dictate. This I also swear.'

Meiros looked down at Ramita, his expression unreadable, but
she could feel his pain. <I am sorry, my child. I see no way out of this.>

<No – please, let them kill me. You can go on and—>

<No, child, what I sought has come about: I have fathered the children I foresaw. The rest is up to you.>

<But—>

<Child, I ruined your life when I married you. I did it to save my creation – perhaps I love it too much, but I saw the great good it did before the Crusades and I did what I did to bring those times again. Please, forgive me.>

<Please, do something – kill him—>

<I can't risk it. Rashid is too quick, too strong – you would be dead before I could intervene. It must be as he says: you or me.> His mental voice was resigned, like a funerary oration. *<My divinations led me to you and to a world made safe. They did not promise that I would live to see it.>*

She felt fresh tears spring to her eyes. *<Please forgive me, for being such a poor wife.>*

<You have been magnificent, my dear: the greatest gift of my elder years. You found it within you to care for an old man, when most would have been revolted and horrified. I love you more dearly than I love anything else, even the Leviathan Bridge. And maybe this way, I can save you both.>

He looked at Rashid calmly and lowered his hands. 'Very well, I accept. You will protect Ramita and our children as if she were your own wife and they your children. Do you accept?'

Rashid smiled triumphantly. 'I accept, old man.' His eyes never left Meiros. 'Kazim, kill him.'

Kazim climbed to his feet and retrieved his dagger. *There can be no pity for the infidel.* And he felt no pity, not for this perverted old goat. It was fitting that he should die in his bed-robes, pathetic, dishonoured. He felt his strength return in body and will.

I have crossed the deserts, survived the raiders. I have trained, I have purified myself. I have deceived him and lain with his wife. I will go down in history as the slayer of Antonin Meiros.

The old man's pale, rheumy eyes turned to him, and focused on him with burning intensity. 'So, you are the Kazim she spoke of. You have come a long way, boy.'

'Shut up, jadugara,' he snarled. He heard Ramita whimper, saw

Rashid stiffen. He felt an urge to rail at Meiros, to berate him for all the ruin his kidnapping of Ramita had wrought – but their lives hung by too thin a thread. There was time for only one taunt, one extra blade to twist. 'The babies in her belly are mine,' he whispered and rammed the dagger up under his chin into his brain. 'She always belonged to me.'

The ancient mage slid to the ground like a pole-axed bull.

He bent over the body. A puff of smoke, bluish-grey, barely visible, formed at the man's open lips and Kazim inhaled. Something entered him, something strong, and he felt his body begin to react. His skin flushed, his muscles quivered and the fires in his heart flared up inside him.

We are not like the magi, Sabele had told him. *The first soul we drink defines our capacity to absorb energy, and therefore our gnostic power. And your first kill will be the greatest mage in history.*

You will be as a god to us.

Someone screamed, a howl of desolate grief that tore at his soul, and he turned and saw it was Ramita, kneeling at Rashid's feet, her face a study in agony. He stared in puzzlement, then went to her – but she looked up at him, and her hatred and despair drove him backwards like a force of nature.

Then something else hit him like a flying wall: the life and memories and powers of an Ascendant mage. They smashed his awareness apart like broken glass.

Antonin Meiros fell, and Ramita's world fell apart. Her grief burst from her like the roar of a tiger. When Kazim looked up, she saw him as a vile rakas-demon, a prince of Shaitan, hideous triumph written across his face, and in that moment all of her love of him turned to hate. She wanted them all dead, for their cold manipulations and stage-managed seductions; for their delight in murder. She hated Huriya for coldly playing with Jos Stein, then slaying him. She hated Kazim, for using her naïveté to destroy all she loved. And above all she hated Rashid, the puppet-master of this bloody shadowplay.

She tried to stand and reach for a fallen weapon, anything to lash out with, even as Kazim stiffened, then collapsed, clutching his skull. But Rashid turned on her and seized her forehead in his hand. 'No you don't, you base-born bitch,' he snarled, and darkness crackled from his palm, searing her forehead with agony, and oblivion blossomed. The world fell away.

36

Shapeshifter

Theurgy Magic

It is the shadowy world of the Theurgist which concerns me. If a man can enslave another mind through Mesmerism, where does that power end? What boundaries are there upon a Spiritualist who can leave his own body to quest through the world? How do we regulate one who can beguile the senses with Illusion? What limits can be placed upon the Mystic when his mind can link with others to impart knowledge and leech power? How can we legislate the Theurgist?

SENATOR FINNIUS LA PIELLE, PALLAS 643

Brochena, Javon, on the continent of Antiopia
Junesse 928
1 month until the Moontide

<*Meiros is DEAD?*> Elena almost lost contact with the mind of the mage she was linked to. Faid was a half-blood Hebb, an Ordo Costruo mage stationed at Krak di Condotiori.

<*Yes, Mistress Anborn.*> Faid's mental voice was shaky, as though he could scarce believe the news he imparted. <*Murdered in his house, with his wife. Their bodies were taken out into the market place and dismembered. The city has gone insane.*>

Elena blinked, her mind working furiously. Antonin Meiros *dead*? It was inconceivable; the man was an Ascendant, one of the original Blessed, the last one still breathing. He'd been with Corineus at the very beginning, six hundred years ago. He was as much part of the landscape as Mount Tigrat.

<Faid, who has taken his place?> she asked, struggling to believe his news.

<No one, Mistress. The Ordo Costruo is holding together under the joint leadership of Magister Cardien and Rashid Mubarak. They have issued a statement saying they will continue Meiros' work. My colleagues and I must return to Hebusalim to attend a special council next week.>

Elena bit her lip. When Faid left Krak, she would be cut off from all news – and it would leave the Krak without the magi who were the main reason it was considered impregnable. The Ordo Costruo contracts to guard the mountain fortress had been in place for sixty years; they were a cornerstone of Javon's security.

<Faid, Cera has sent Lorenzo di Kestria to the Krak. She wants Solinde returned to her.>

She sensed Faid's curiosity. *<When will Seir Lorenzo arrive?>*

<In days. How does Solinde fare?>

<Withdrawn and silent. She is a mystery to us. At times she babbles in Rondian.>

<In Rondian?> Elena bit her lip. *<But she knows no Rondian.>*

She sensed Faid considering. *<As I said, Mistress Anborn: she is a mystery.>*

<Please await Lorenzo before leaving, Faid. Then secure yourself. These are the worst of times.>

She broke the contact and sat staring at the bowl of water, wondering what to make of it all.

'It's hard to believe,' Cera whispered. 'Meiros is really dead?'

Elena had finally managed to speak to Cera again, though it was an enforced meeting, for they were in the blood-tower together. With the day's papers signed, they had been relaxing with a goblet of red wine each, a rich scarlo from Riban. Cera had been distant, but this news had shaken her.

'Everyone dies eventually,' Elena said at last. 'It is a miracle that a man so hated lived as long as he did, Ascendant Mage or not. You must not lose heart, Cera.'

Cera looked at her frostily. 'I have not lost heart.'

'Nor lost your heart,' Elena murmured. 'Cera, why did you accept that offer to marry Salim? Why didn't you confer with your council?'

'Because to delay would have been to insult them and threaten every-thing we've worked for.' Cera bit her lip. The ambassadors had departed, leaving a parting gift: a silver collar, the traditional Amteh adornment for a betrothed noblewoman. It sat about Cera's throat now, chafing her skin. It would be exchanged for one of gold on the wedding day.

'But—'

Cera cut her off with a gesture. 'I must ensure the Nesti survive, that before anything else. Do you understand? That is my only imper-ative.' Cera hugged herself morosely. 'We are foxes in a trap, but this marriage gives us the chance to free ourselves.'

Elena nodded sadly. *But I hoped for more for you. I have heard of the ways of sultans' harems: they are like vipers-nests, full of intrigue and gossip, and you will be the ferang there, the outsider.*

Cera looked sideways at her, her face sly. 'Perhaps after the Crusade Salim will be dead and I can renege on my promise.'

Elena felt a chill at this display of callousness. *It reminds me too much of Gurvon – or how I used to be myself.* She consciously swallowed her doubts and changed the subject. 'I have scryed Lorenzo. He will be back soon with Solinde.'

Cera nodded shortly, not meeting her eyes.

Does she know about my affair with him – is she jealous? Rukka mio, I can't deal with that . . . 'There have been no more murders in the slums,' she reported, changing the subject. 'Our patrols may have made Gurvon pull back.'

'But you haven't found him,' Cera replied, sounding distracted.

'No, I'm sorry. There was never much chance of finding him so easily.' She tried to inject enthusiasm into her voice. 'There are still clues to follow, and a breakthrough we must discuss.'

Cera looked up warily, curious. 'Yes?'

'It's about the murder of Fernando Tolidi. There is a study of gnosis called Necromancy, which concerns speaking with the dead.'

Cera blinked, making the holy sign of Sol, the protection from evil. 'What of it?'

'Would it shock you to hear that I have dug up Tolidi's body and performed a necromantic working, to try and determine who killed him? Spirits often bear psychic traces of the moment of death. I needed to find out if Tolidi did, to lead us to his killer.'

Cera looked troubled. 'You never told me. The priests would condemn this.' She sucked on her upper lip, then leaned forward and whispered, 'Did you learn anything?'

'Not much – a dead soul's recollection of their own demise is usually confusing; it can jump from remembrance into fantasy. I saw a blurred vision of a thin male of pale complexion with red hair. But I also saw Fernando with Solinde, and both this young male and Solinde wore the same nightdress. The more I think about it, the more I'm convinced the strange male and Solinde were one and the same.'

'What?' Cera sat up. 'What do you mean?'

Elena rubbed her chin. 'This is what I think, Cera: remember the divinations we did a few weeks ago in the blood-rooms? Remember the lizard and the coin?'

'You told me that a lizard means a shapeshifter and a coin means corruption.'

'Exactly – but there is another interpretation. There is a notorious shapeshifter who has appeared in the past decade, known simply as "Coin".'

Cera sucked in her breath. 'A shapeshifter? Are you saying–?'

'That the Solinde we sent to the Krak may not really be Solinde? That it might be Coin? Yes, that's what I'm saying.'

Cera's hands went to her mouth. 'Sol et Lune, the things you people do – digging up the dead, shapeshifting . . .' Her voice trailed off, and then, in a deathly whisper, she said, 'Where is the real Solinde?'

Elena hung her head. 'I don't know. Shapeshifters don't like to leave the real person they are mimicking alive.' As Cera glowered at her, her eyes wet, she added, 'I'm so sorry, Cera. It is true, we magi can do dreadful things, I admit that. But everything I do is for you: I swear it.'

Cera looked about to retort with some bitter comment, but then thought better of it. 'When would it have happened?' she asked, brushing at her eyes.

'Probably the day after your father was killed. Remember we were told her behaviour changed that day? We put it down to shock, or perhaps Gurvon's gnosis, but it may be that it was Coin all along.'

'But you tested Solinde before we sent her to the Krak—'

'I did, but if Coin is powerful, I would not have detected his presence – and Coin is reputedly the most able shifter ever known. Morphic-gnosis is very difficult: most cannot change gender, or remain shifted for very long. Coin apparently can do both: he – or she, no one knows – is responsible for the murder of the former Duke of Argundy, which allowed the current Duke to gain the Argundy throne. Coin is a legend among the magi.'

Cera scowled, thinking furiously. 'And Fernando's last vision was of a man in Solinde's nightdress? Did he discover her in another form – is that why Fernando was killed?'

'It fits what we know. It's hard to maintain a shape-change when experiencing heightened pain or pleasure, so maybe Coin inadvertently betrayed themselves to Fernando, and then panicked and killed him to cover their tracks. We know that Gurvon protected Solinde after Fernando's death. Perhaps that was because it was really Coin?'

Cera hugged herself, her face troubled. 'And then you "rescued" Solinde . . .'

'Exactly. We found someone we thought was Solinde the night we raided Brochena. The body was unconscious – but a skilled shifter can maintain a form while asleep. I was amazed she'd survived the tower falling, but a well-shielded and lucky mage could do that. From then on Coin is in our hands and in danger of being unmasked, so she acted antagonistically to get sent away. I used a Chain-rune, which locked Coin into Solinde's form, and suddenly she is helpless in the Krak di Condotiori, a place not even Gurvon could break them out of—'

'And now we're bringing Coin back here.'

'If it is Coin, yes. This is only supposition, Cera, but if it is Coin,

Gurvon will almost certainly try and free her.' Elena frowned, thinking hard. 'Perhaps we can use this to our advantage.'

'How?'

'We could use Coin as bait, to lure Gurvon out. If Solinde is truly Coin, I know ways of detection that no shapeshifter can stand up to. I will unmask her.'

'What about Gyle and his agents?'

'Gurvon will learn Solinde is here: count on it. For now I hope he remains ignorant, or else Lorenzo is in great danger.' She chewed his lip anxiously. 'Once she's here, we'll have maybe half a day before Gurvon finds out. If Solinde really is Coin, he will be forced to act.'

Cera looked increasingly sick, but she lifted her head. 'Then what must we do – surround Solinde with an army?'

'No – they'd just get in my way. A trained group of magi can kill by the hundreds. They'd all die, or be turned against us. I'd be more secure alone: in gnosis, a well-prepared defence can often overmatch the attack. If I can break Coin, then hold out against Gurvon until there is opportunity to display the shapeshifter at court, we can bring the whole nation in behind the shihad, and at that point, Gurvon may as well go home. We will have won.'

Cera looked at her, measuring. 'You can do this?'

Elena smiled grimly. 'I'll have to leave the blood-rooms and prepare for her arrival. I'll seal off the Jade Tower from the rest of the keep and prepare wards for holding Coin. My practise-room is ideal – the only entrance is from below, and I can ward the door to the lower room. If you and Timi stay there and the doors are warded, then no one can enter without your permission or mine.'

'You, Solinde, Timi and me, alone,' Cera repeated dully, her eyes unfocused.

'Exactly! I can't afford to leave you alone away from me while I'm doing the questioning in case Gurvon tries to seize you as leverage.' Elena tried to sound reassuring. 'I'll station Lorenzo with you if you like.'

'You and Lorenzo.' Cera smiled wanly. 'My protectors.'

*

The inner gates thudded open and four huge carthorses towed a prison-wagon into the courtyard. It was Sabbadai, 6 Junesse, and Solinde was back. *If it really is Solinde.*

'Donna Elena!' Lorenzo trotted his horse into the courtyard and her heart leapt, but his smile in return seemed forced. He looked tense and ill-at-ease as he swung down from the saddle. She longed to go to him, but this was too public; the members of the Regency Council were all here, perched about the square, watching with rapt eyes.

Lorenzo bowed formally. 'What are the arrangements?' he asked, his voice clipped with tension.

'Bring her to Jade Tower," Elena told him. She had been preparing it for holding Solinde – or a potent shapeshifter – all week. 'Take her to the threshold only – I have set wards on the door.'

Lorenzo bowed again in acknowledgment and turned as the prisoner's wagon rumbled up to the steps. Elena studied the waiting councillors, wondering if any of them owed secret allegiance to Gurvon. Pita Rosco was joking with Cera. Comte Inveglio stood with Godspeaker Acmed – that was an odd pairing. Don Francesco Perdonello was present, though she couldn't remember inviting him. There was curiosity and hostility directed at the wagon: Solinde had betrayed them all.

The wagon stopped and guards unlocked the doors and pulled out a thin girl in a plain white shift. Her long golden hair was flat and greasy. Solinde's manacles glimmered with power in Elena's gnosis-sight, as did the Chain-rune coiled about her, the one she'd placed upon the princessa herself. Elena stepped forward and the girl's eyes fell on her. They were bruised, as if she had been weeping constantly, and her glare was sullen.

'Welcome back to Brochena, Princessa,' Elena said levelly.

Solinde said nothing, wouldn't meet her eyes.

Cera joined them, looking at her sister distantly. 'Welcome back, sister,' she said quietly. She waited. 'Will you not answer me?'

Solinde stared at her feet, offering no contact or reply.

Cera sighed and turned to Elena. 'You may take her.'

Elena stepped before Solinde and put a hand under her chin and raised it to her eyes. She stared through those eyes, letting the gnosis quest into the princessa's mind. *Fear . . . humiliation . . . anguish . . . sorrow . . .* That was as far as she could go, here. Such surface thoughts might be genuine, or just a mask woven by a trained mind. She would have to break through to establish who or what she faced.

Cera turned and faced the gathering of counsellors. 'Gentlemen, Elena will be dealing with this matter in Jade Tower. No one will be permitted to visit until I have her assurances.' She held up her hand to forestall questions. 'Elena says there is danger. This is her field of expertise. We defer to her.'

Elena grasped Solinde's shoulder. As she started to march her towards the tower she heard footsteps clatter towards her and she looked over her shoulder. 'No, Lorenzo. I must see to this.'

'What is happening?' He glanced up at the darkened tower. 'Why your tower?' His voice sounded unused, as if he'd been silent all the way from the Krak. He moved stiffly, without his normal grace. It must have been a long, hard ride back. 'Will I see you tonight?'

Elena shook her head regretfully. 'Sorry, Lorenzo. Tomorrow,' and she strode on, pulling Solinde along in her wake. She turned to look at him before she shut the door, but she couldn't read his expression. Inside the tower, she locked the door and then activated her wards. Solinde watched, her eyes narrowed. As the web of light faded from normal vision, she turned back to the girl and asked calmly, 'So, Princessa, do I have to carry you up the stairs?'

'Why are you doing this to me?' Solinde demanded.

The voice is right, but the words are wrong. Solinde never spoke like that. 'Upstairs, Solinde. Come!'

On the first-floor landing Elena glanced into the small ante-room. The door to the royal chambers was bolted and already warded, and Cera held the only key, which Elena had attuned to the wardings. Cera and Timi would spend the night in this room, safely within Elena's control.

The top room had been cleaned and Bastido had been pushed next to the wall, where it sat brooding sullenly like a rejected pet.

In the middle of the room was a smoking brazier. A couple of pokers had been left jammed into the coals and the tips were glowing red. There was a pallet bed, but Elena ignored it and led Solinde to the wall. She left the girl's manacles on – they had Faid's bindings on them – and attached them to a chain. Her own Chain-rune still confined her too.

'What are you doing?' the girl asked, her voice quavering as she tugged at her manacles. She began to cry.

'This tower room has been sound-dampened so no one outside can hear you,' Elena said in a deliberately bored voice.

Solinde stopped sobbing as quickly as she had begun.

Elena met her eyes. 'If you are truly Solinde, then I am sorry for putting you through this, but I cannot take any chances with Cera and Timori's lives.' She sighed, this time genuinely weary. 'I have questioned prisoners before. I don't enjoy inflicting pain, but I'll do it if I must.'

'I am Solinde!' The girl looked genuinely frightened, but that proved nothing.

'Perhaps. I will soon find out.' She got out a coin from a pocket and flipped it in front of the girl's face and watched as Solinde's eyes narrowed. Elena smiled mildly, pocketed the coin again and then reached out to touch the girl's forehead. She sent gnosis-energy pulsing through her fingertips and slowly removed her Chain-rune. She watched the girl's reactions carefully, noting the faint relaxing of posture, the tentative flexing of hands, the inwards gaze of the eyes.

Ah – surely I am right?

'So, Princessa.' She half-turned and gestured towards the brazier and flames leapt in response. Elena planted her hands against the wall, either side of Solinde's head, and stared into the girl's eyes. 'This is what I'm going to do. I'm going to take one of those hot pokers you can see there and I'm going to press it to your belly. Your flesh will sear and cook, causing you agony unlike anything you have ever felt. I will use the gnosis to prevent your passing out, so that you feel everything. The pain will trigger responses you cannot control: you will void your bowels and bladder. You will scream like a host of demons. You will lose yourself entirely, and at that moment, I will know if you are truly who you appear to be.'

'You're insane – Cera will have you beheaded!'

Elena gestured, and one of the pokers flew to her hand. *Great Kore, let me be right* . . .

She showed the girl the glowing tip—

— in an instant the princessa's face changed. She issued a throaty snarl as she lunged and snapped with pointed, glistening teeth suddenly inches long. *Breakthrough!* Elena had been half-expecting something of the sort and darted to one side even as a barbed tongue erupted from the girl's mouth and shot at her. It hit her shields and retracted.

The snapping face hissed and snarled impotently, the tongue flailing, as arms and legs suddenly corded with muscle strained against the manacles. The manacles sparked as binding runes prevented the shapeshifter from getting free, although Elena saw her trying desperately, her limbs becoming fluid, though never quite enough for her to pull herself free. The shifter spat in frustrated fury.

Elena spun the poker in her hand. 'Coin, I believe?' She spoke a spell of Negation to disrupt the prisoner's morphic-gnosis, and re-inforced the magical bindings. The shapeshifter's attempts to escape became weaker. Her shift was torn and bloodied by the gore discharged as she tried to alter herself – but she could not get free.

The prisoner subsided into sullen defeat and the muscles of a few seconds before wasted away, revealing a new body: thin, pinched and strangely genderless. Lank red hair was plastered to a bony skull and pallid eyes glittered under delicate brows. Elena swiftly cast a renewed Chain-rune, locking the new form in place: this was the prisoner's real shape, and the last face Fernando Tolidi had seen.

'You are in so much trouble, bitch,' the prisoner whined.

'Not as much as you are.' She held the red-hot poker tip to her prisoner's eyes, close enough for the heat to make her cringe. 'What can I call you?'

'I am Coin,' the shapeshifter conceded, looking away.

Coin, the legendary shapeshifter: male or female, ageless: a perfect affinity with one of the most demanding and exacting of all gnosis studies – the sort of perfect affinity you had to be slightly insane to even possess. Reputedly too expensive to hire, and connected all the way to the top. The *very* top.

'What are you doing here, Coin? How could Gurvon afford you?'

The – girl? boy? woman? man? – scowled contemptuously. 'My patron wished Gyle's mission to succeed. I was a gift to Gyle for the duration of the mission.'

An imperial connection, then. Elena dampened the fear that thought brought and concentrated on her prisoner. Coin might be a master shapeshifter, but appeared emotionally brittle and completely terrified of physical harm, of pain. Elena sighed in relief; she'd been dreading having to torture the truth out of some close-mouthed fanatic. Coin looked willing to speak with little more coercion.

'I need to know everything about you, Coin: who are you, your name, your gender. How old are you, who were your parents – what can you do and not do? And where is the real Solinde?'

'You touch me with that and my patron will carve your soul for all eternity,' Coin hissed, eyeing the glowing poker with terrified bravado.

'That won't help you much, though, will it?' Elena raised the poker and pushed it to within an inch of Coin's belly. 'Knowing it's just you and not Solinde has removed any remorse I might feel – so speak—'

Coin eyed the poker, sweating profusely, trembling in the manacles. Her voice shook. 'My mother will kill you!'

Your mother?

Coin tried to clam up, facing Elena defiantly, but was unable to look away from the glowing metal.

Elena was still loathe to actually harm Coin, but she thought a little humiliation might be all it would take . . .

She reached out and wrenched at the torn shift, which ripped away easily, revealing an emaciated body and unmistakable, if tiny, breasts. Elena blinked, her eyes drawn downwards to a shrunken penis with no scrotum, and the pubic mound beneath it instead strangely slitted.

Great Kore . . .

The shifter was neither male nor female; Coin was both.

A hermaphrodite – no wonder he or she is capable of both genders . . . Sol et Lune! And then, almost unbidden, she found herself feeling a great wash of sympathy: *What must it do to you, a deformed thing with pure-blooded gnosis—*

Elena turned away, shaken. There were freak-shows in Rondelmar where people with birth defects were paraded for entertainment, but this sort of defect on a mage – the implications were horrible.

'Got an eyeful?' Coin sneered defensively. 'Excited, bitch?'

Elena turned back. 'I don't know what to say,' she said honestly.

Coin's face twisted with scorn. 'Oh, really – how *rukking* humane of you.'

Elena wiped her brow, wondering, *What must it be like, to be such a one? But there is too much at stake to feel pity, damn it.* 'Where is Gurvon Gyle?' she asked calmly.

Coin spat at her and Elena hefted the poker, readying herself to use it, when she heard a voice call from outside the door, 'Ella?'

'Wait!' she called, but Cera appeared at the door, holding her key. She froze when she saw the skinny naked body chained to the wall and realised that it wasn't Solinde. Her hand flew to her mouth. '*Sol et Lune!*'

'This is the shapeshifter we hypothesised,' Elena said quietly. 'This is Coin.'

'Then where is Solinde?' Cera asked, as her eyes took in the strange being in the manacles. She shook her head disbelievingly.

'I don't know yet,' Elena said, then added firmly, 'Cera, I really don't think you should watch this.'

Cera looked at her and then at the poker in her hand and backed away. Then she swallowed and folded her arms across her chest. 'I should.'

Elena shook her head. 'No – wait downstairs, please. If we can parade a shifter in front of the Dome-al'Ahm tomorrow, the whole of Javon will rise to shihad and Gurvon's mission to keep Javon out of the war will fail irrevocably – not to mention the secrets this creature must know. It is too late tonight, but tomorrow you can show Coin to the people and they will be yours to command.'

Cera stared at her, clenching and unclenching her fists, her face white. 'Will Gyle try to stop us?'

'If he knows she's here, almost certainly. If he doesn't, all the better!' She felt a bubble of triumph, but suppressed it. There was still the night to survive. 'Are the men-at-arms in position?'

Cera nodded. 'The courtyard is full of Nesti fighting men; all the entrances are sealed.' She dangled the key. 'Only I can admit anyone now.'

Elena nodded. 'And Lorenzo?'

'He's downstairs.' Cera's eyes narrowed slightly. 'Elena, are you and he more than friends?'

Elena glanced at her, unsure why this question had come up. It had the feeling of a test . . . 'This isn't the time or the place, Cera. We are colleagues, working to protect you and Timi.'

'Really?' Cera asked, her voice hinting at doubt.

Elena closed her eyes. *I have no time for this.* She opened them again and looked at Cera. *I'll tell her the full truth later.* 'Please Cera, I must question this creature now.'

Cera looked at Coin. 'It would have been better had Corineus never lived,' she said bleakly.

Elena bowed her head. 'Sometimes I agree,' she admitted.

Cera backed away with a distraught look and was gone.

Elena watched her leave, troubled by the exchange. *I've put so much on her – too much. She is only eighteen, for Kore's sake. But this will be over tomorrow. Once Javon is irrevocably tied to the shihad, the game is over, and nothing Gurvon can do will make any difference. He will be forced to concede and leave – and then I will leave too, so that any revenge is directed solely at me.*

She turned back to the hermaphrodite, fighting her sympathy for this strange creature. 'All right, Coin, it's time to talk.'

The shifter eyed the poker fearfully, tears in its eyes, and whispered, 'If you don't hurt me, I will secure your safety. My patron can protect you.'

'Really?' Elena replaced the poker in the brazier and put her hands on hips. 'All right then, I will allow you the chance to be honest with me. Tell me: who is this patron?'

'Mater-Imperia Lucia,' Coin said. 'She's my mother.'

Elena sat on the floor, her back against the wall, staring at the dying brazier. Coin, chained to the wall opposite, slumbered uncomfortably. She had draped blankets over the hermaphrodite against the cold, and to give her back a shred of dignity.

Great Kore, this is Mater-Imperia's child, she thought again, still struggling to take everything in. Coin – initially named Yvette, despite the non-gender – was a secret child, known to only a discreet few. Most likely she was a deformed freak because she'd been conceived of incest: her father was Lucia's now-dead brother Henri Fasterius; this family shame had been hidden deep. But Coin was a mage of huge but very specialised power, too valuable to simply dispose of.

Elena had been right: Coin had supplanted Solinde, but lost control during sex with Fernando Tolidi, and killed him to preserve her secret. Coin claimed to have no idea whether the real Solinde was alive or dead, nor what Gurvon's plans were. No wonder, having been effectively removed from the game. *But now . . . what a bargaining chip! In the right hands in Pallas, this piece of information could bring down the Fasterius-Sacrecour dynasty.*

Elena's mind reeled as she explored the possibilities. The night crawled past. She had bricked up the windows of the tower to prevent any Air-magi entering, and had warded the entire stonework, to prevent someone simply bombarding it. The doorways were protected with wards and bindings and gnostic traps, so right now, Jade Tower was the most impregnable place in Brochena. But who knew what resources Gurvon had?

Hours passed. She sensed the descent of the moon and the distant throb of power that was the approaching sunrise; dawn was coming, and still the enemy had made no move. *Perhaps Gurvon doesn't know Coin is here after all? Perhaps I really am a step ahead this time . . .*

Footsteps climbed the stairs outside and turned the door handle and Elena stood and strode to the door. 'Cera?'

The door opened. It wasn't Cera. A robed figure faced her, bearing the iron cross-staff of an Inquisition Grandmaster. The bland-faced man was expressionless as he took stock of the room, not moving his head or his eyes, which he kept focused on her.

A Grandmaster, and therefore an Ascendant – but I'd have felt it if he broke my wards . . . so someone let him in . . .

Always have a plan – but how could I plan for this?

The Grandmaster gestured with a finger and a wave of force threw her against the walls of the cell. She twisted in midair and struck feet-first. Beside her, Coin too was slammed against the brickwork, screaming soundlessly, helpless within the Chain-rune.

Elena kicked off the walls and somersaulted to the centre of the room, then, leaving an image of herself there, she blurred left and fired off an energy-bolt whilst triggering the six crossbows she had hung from wires attached to the ceiling. Each crossbow turned and tracked the Inquisitor as he lifted his staff, ignoring her illusion and shielding her gnostic-bolt effortlessly.

He slammed another pulse of force at her, hammering her against the wall again and she hit hard, her lungs emptying in a bellow of pain. Something cracked in her ribcage. Then a wave of fire washed towards her as she struggled back to her feet and she flew sideways. The blast of heat ripped past her shoulder and charred bricks in one of the blocked windows.

The six crossbows discharged at once, hammering impotently into his shields, but before she could trigger them to reload he blasted them with flames, snapping bowstrings and setting fire to the wooden stocks. Elena flowed on, circling faster, her blade in hand. More fire washed through another illusion she spun, roasting empty air. She cloaked her form in darkness and went at him.

Let's see if you know how to fight—

But she never got close; he turned straight towards her, piercing her cloaking spell so effortlessly she realised that he'd been tracking her all along. He raised an open-palmed hand and clenched it shut and the air about her congealed, gripping her as if in a giant fist, then it snatched her up and hammered her head-first into the ceiling.

Plaster and wood splintered about her shields, and she flailed about desperately, but she couldn't gain purchase – then she was mashed feet-first into the stone floor before she could realign her shields. Her right ankle shattered in a burst of white-hot agony that jolted through her. The sword flew from her hand as she splattered against the floor like a squashed bug.

She fought for air through a mist of pain as the Ascendant, his face now showing utter contempt, moved his right hand again, this time picking her up and flinging her at the far wall. Her left shoulder-blade cracked as she battered into the stone. Her head struck hard and the room dissolved in stars for a few seconds as she flopped helplessly, still trying to breathe. Above her, Coin watched with a gloating smile as the Inquisitor walked towards her leisurely, as if she were no more threat than a dormouse, and never had been.

One last try . . .

She triggered the release of the Chain-rune on Coin—

—and *leapt*—

—not with her body, so badly broken, but with her soul—

Abruptly her perspective changed: she was hanging from the wall on gnosis-bound manacles, naked, in a strange body, and staring down at the blanket on the floor, which had been blasted away by the Inquisitor's Air-gnosis. The blanket was lying beside a motionless body: Elena's own. She felt Coin's panic at her intrusion, trying to resist, but she was overmatched by Elena's desperation and experience.

The Inquisitor – Coin knew him as Fraxis Targon – turned towards Coin as he saw Elena Anborn's body go limp. He lifted his hand and the bindings on her wrists fell away. His eyes finally showed an emotion: concern, for the child of Mater-Imperia Lucia. 'Yvette,' he said, bending to pick up the fallen blanket to cover the prisoner.

Got you.

Elena stole control of Coin's body from its owner just long enough to turn Coin's right hand into a multi-taloned claw that she drove into the Inquisitor's chest. He stared, goggle-eyed, into her face as the claw burst through skin and sinew between his ribs to grasp the pumping muscle beneath.

She wrenched.

The still-beating heart came out in the gore-soaked talon as the Inquisitor crumpled, disbelief and horror etched into his face as his fingers clawed for life, his eyes turning molten as he tried to seize his own heart from Coin's hands. Coin roared inside her own head, fighting for control with renewed intensity.

This time Elena didn't resist . . .

She let go and in an eye-blink was back in her own pain-racked body, staring up from the floor as Fraxis Targon blasted lightning from one flailing hand into the unshielded face of Mater-Imperia's freakish child. The hermaphrodite's scream vanished beneath an explosive crack of blinding light.

The Grandmaster sought his squirming heart, but missed as the gore-soaked organ slid from Coin's hands and flopped wetly to the floor. Targon struck the ground beside it, both hands going to the hole in his chest, and Coin fell beside him, spasming and jerking, writhing like a worm in water before falling still.

The Inquisitor's face rolled sideways, the eyes staring glassily at Elena. She smiled grimly back. A mage could survive much, but not the loss of heart or head.

Got. You. Bastard . . .

Then the awareness of her own battered body kicked in, the pain a wave of fiery darkness that rolled over her and pulled her down into oblivion.

Footsteps. She lifted her head, dimly aware. *Lorenzo . . . Thank God!*

He hurried to her side, bending over her, and she reached out with her gnosis to caress his familiar mind.

And encountered someone else.

No!

'By the Kore, you live!' the mage in Lorenzo's body said in Rondian, looking at the ruined bodies of Fraxis Targon and Coin. He exhaled in wonder. 'Unbelievable!'

No – not after all I've endured!

'Lorenzo' drew his dagger. It flashed silver as he stroked it, right to left, cutting her throat. She flailed weakly, staring at the gushing blood that was spraying over his chest and face as he held her down. Her hands flew to her neck as her legs spasmed, her hips jerking uncontrollably, her mind screaming *<Cera – Cera!>*

'Elena Anborn,' laughed 'Lorenzo' cruelly, 'you were so close and yet so wrong.' He caressed her cheek. 'We were waiting for your lover as he rode back from the Krak, Gurvon and I. Can you guess who I am?' He laughed and opened his mouth, and the head of a necromantic scarab bulged from his mouth and vanished inside again. 'Yes, it is I: Rutt Sordell.'

She threw all that remained to her into trying to stem the flow of blood from her open throat, to sucking air through the severed windpipe, but Sordell laughed and jerked her hands away from the wound, spraying fresh blood as she wheezed and bubbled her last breath away. 'No, no healing allowed. It's time to die, Ella. I'm sick of playing second fiddle to you. Gurvon made you his number two by dint of your whoring, but I was always the better mage.'

<Gurvon!>

'No you don't!' Sordell scowled, his presence lending a hideous malice to Lorenzo's face. 'You're not going to get the chance to beg his mercy. He's going to find you dead, with no regrets.'

He wiped his blade on her thigh, stood up and stomped his foot down into her belly, and her healing-gnosis fell apart in another burst of pain.

'Farewell, Elena. You can die now.'

37

Beneath the Surface

General Leroi Robler

Leroi Robler was already old in 909 when his country summoned him to war, but he was a veteran of the First Crusade, and he had the respect of his men. That respect became adoration after victory upon victory against the much larger armies of Rondelmar in the Noros Revolt. Unbeaten in the field, General Robler was the banner of Noros, and only when he laid down his blade did his country surrender.

MAGNUS GRAYNE, THE GLORIOUS REVOLUTION, 915

Norostein, Noros, on the continent of Yuros
Junesse 928
1 month until the Moontide

Alaron bellowed in fright as Muhren lurched out of the torrent of fire, his shields flickering, Ramon convulsing in his arms. Langstrit raised his hands and shouted, and chains of emerald light flared around him, then shattered with a deafening roar that any mage would have felt ten miles away. Alaron staggered from the force of it, but he stumbled forward to try and reach Ramon, Cym beside him. Muhren sealed off the hatch with a warding of blue light, even as it started to shake from the blasts striking it.

Cym pulled Ramon, choking for breath, from Muhren's arms and shouted at him to lie still, to *just hold on*. Alaron offered up his own gnosis-energy to Cym, to to aid her healing-gnosis, trying to let his power flow cleanly. Desperation lent him clarity, and he cradled Ramon, trying not to gag on the seared meat smell as he stared at the feathered bolt jutting from his best friend's belly, and the charred skin around it. *Breathe, Ramon, just breathe.* He felt Ramon convulsing faintly, his heartbeat erratic.

Muhren stood over them, straining to keep his barrier on the hatch intact. The pulsing light and flaring about the warding showed the forces he was fighting, but his strength was buying them precious seconds. Jarius Langstrit eased Alaron to one side. 'Lad, let me.' The old man gently laid Ramon on the stone and raised his hands, which began to drip pearls of liquid energy: Ascendant power, unchained: he'd broken from the Chain-rune that bound him. The bloody crossbow bolt disintegrated and liquid light poured into the wounds, soothing the seared skin. At last Ramon went limp, groaning, and Langstrit cocooned him in a web of gnosis, shields and wards.

The general turned to Alaron. 'Lad, we have to go.'

'Ramon's still alive – we have to take him!'

Langstrit's gaze was patient, despite the urgency. Behind him, Muhren was pulling Cym to her feet, his eyes on the warded hatch. 'You can't help him now. He will live, if he suffers no further harm, but I can do no more. But he cannot be moved, and we must go, or Vult will have us all. You can stay if you want, or you can come with us and fight. I'm sorry.'

Alaron flinched from that intense stare, looked helplessly at Ramon. 'But we can't leave him for Vult—'

'If we all move, Vult will follow us. If we triumph, we will return for him. But if even one of us stays, both will be taken.'

'My father said that you would never leave a wounded man on the field!'

Langstrit winced. 'That's just ballads and poetry, boy. In war, all choices are evil.'

Above them the ground shook and dust and small pebbles fell from the ceiling. 'Sir, we *must* go,' Muhren shouted from beneath the hatch. His voice was strained as his hands wove new shields. Coruscating light boiled above, casting garish hues about the cellar. 'There are at least four magi up there.'

Cym grasped his hand. 'Alaron, *come on.*' Her face was as hard as diamonds. 'Ramon is out. Are you with us or not?'

He snatched his hand away, feeling torn in two. *A true hero would know what to do: he would stay with his friend, if that was right – or he would see out this quest to the bitter end, if that was right. But he would know.* 'I don't know—' he started.

'*Rukka mio*, Alaron – *decide*,' Cym shouted.

The floor shook again and Muhren cried out. Langstrit put a hand on Cym and Alaron's shoulders. 'Here's what we're going to do. I'm going to use Earth-gnosis to get out of here. I'll draw Vult away to the south – he'll believe that I'm making a break for where I've hidden the Scytale, and he'll follow. You two stay with Jeris and retrieve the Scytale. We'll meet in Bossis next week, at the Blackwater Chapel. Don't wait longer than a week, understood?'

Cym nodded, her eyes boring into Alaron. 'Yes!' she snapped, then to Alaron, 'Let's go!'

Alaron looked at the cocoons of light about Ramon and then met her ferocious gaze. 'Okay,' he said at last.

Langstrit looked at him sympathetically. 'Go with Jeris. Farewell!'

Then his face hardened and he gathered his powers. The air about him swirled until he was at the eye of a tiny storm. He looked at Muhren and grinned, then thrust his left hand upwards and his right hand sideways. A concussive force flew from either hand and the general drove upwards, soaring through the earth as if it were paper. The burst of energy as the ground ripped dizzied them, and they heard the screams of at least three men. Then the general was gone, his presence receding in a blaze of gnosis like a comet.

Muhren pointed to the northern wall, where Langstrit's right hand had blasted a hole into another chamber beyond, and cried, 'This way – come on!'

Cym gripped Alaron's hand and yanked him after her, but he looked back at Ramon and whispered a prayer, he had no idea to whom: *Be safe. Be safe. Please, be safe.*

Muhren closed the hole behind them with a pained effort, in stark contrast to the Ascendant general's effortless explosion of might. He might be a Hero of the Revolt, but he was only a half-blood – *And we're probably going up against pure-bloods,* Alaron thought fearfully.

Gnosis-light glowed in Muhren's left hand, illuminating the chamber: a small cellar full of broken barrels, generously festooned with spider-webs. The captain spotted stairs in the corner and stormed up them. He burst the locks of the door at the top and they followed him into the house, ignoring the frightened cries of the owners as they thundered out the back door and into a yard.

Muhren spoke into their minds as they vaulted the low fence and sprinted down an alleyway. *<Vult won't have too many with him, because he won't want to share the prize. Let's hope they all went after Jari. Come on!>*

Movement drew his eye and Alaron glanced over his shoulder, but it was gone before he could react. They ran down another alley and into a small square lit by the half-moon, their feet thudding on the cobbles as they flew across the open space. Then a crossbow sounded, and a bolt flew past Cym's shoulder. Muhren threw a gnosis-bolt down the alley behind them and was rewarded with a shriek. He pointed towards a street opposite and cried, 'Run!'

They ran.

When Norostein Council extended the reservoir at the western end of Lake Tucerle, they botched the job – or deliberately got it wrong, depending upon who you believed. One spring morning in 887, seventy rickety buildings on the northwest tip of the lake were swept away when the flood-banks gave way under the first flush of the thaw through the newest aqueduct. More than two hundred people lost their lives. An error in the peak-flow calculations was blamed, though the engineers were not fired, nor even reprimanded. It was just coincidence that the council had tried to evict those same tenants and had been blocked by the courts. Despite the rumours of conspiracy, the council finally had their extended reservoir, and new flood-banks were established to contain it. When the water was particularly clear, anyone standing on those flood-banks could see the decaying buildings below.

Alaron and Cym ran, panting, to the edge of the lake and almost collapsed. Their gasping breaths rose like clouds. Muhren joined them, far less distressed by the mile-long run. They had paused only once, when they ran into a Watch patrol, but Muhren had sent them off with a cock-and-bull story about robbers in Old Town.

Now the tenth bell of night chimed through the city. The half-moon was westering, its face beginning to turn pink, and the eastern sky was softening towards dawn. The flood-bank was capped by a promenade, complete with a bronze statue of Jarius Langstrit himself, posed as he'd been in the Revolt: shouting orders whilst pointing with his sword.

Cym patted it as if for luck. 'Is this where we go in?' she asked, peering at the black water. It radiated cold. Her face was all fierce purpose and she frightened Alaron right now; her almost callous dismissal of Ramon's plight bothered him. *Only the prize matters to her now.*

'It is as good a place as any,' Muhren replied, looking up at the statue of Langstrit. Alaron wondered if the general still lived. He was an Ascendant, but he was old and outnumbered.

Cym touched Muhren's arm: shadowy shapes as large as ponies had emerged from the alleys, dark things that reflected the moon-light as they stalked across the green towards them. Alaron gulped as their forms became clear.

There were five of them, moving with jerks and bounds. They were shaped like hounds, but with carapaced bodies, each with six legs. The heads seemed to be pure insect, except for the inches-long teeth in their maws. Instead of tails, some kind of stinger rose from their hindquarters and swayed like bobbing bulbs above their heads. The head of each was about chest-height. They had probably three times the bulk of a man.

'Constructs,' Muhren cursed, and Alaron scowled; animagus constructs were warped products of nature and you couldn't banish them as you could a spirit. You had to kill them. 'Fyrell's work, I warrant,' Muhren added, edging his blade with gnosis-light. 'Get behind me.'

One had advanced much faster than the rest and Muhren strode forward to meet it. It emitted a shrieking sound, and the rest responded by surging into an awkward gait, rearing up so that their forelegs – long, jointed limbs with sharp, raking claws – were free to attack.

Alaron and Cym shivered and she whispered a prayer.

'Go, you two,' yelled Muhren, blurring into motion, 'go – now!'

Alaron's jaw dropped as the watchman thrust out a hand and a curtain of fire rippled across the wet turf and engulfed the charging creatures. For a moment he thought it might have stopped them as two went down in the blaze, emitting a high-pitched squeal that tore at his eardrums, but one had managed to leap the fiery barrier and now it skidded towards them on the wet turf. It snapped at Muhren, but his form blurred with the shadows. The construct's mandibles clashed on empty air and it wrenched its head about in frustrated fury. Then it spied Alaron and its eyes lit up.

Muhren lunged out of the darkness. He stabbed his sword into the creature's side and twisted; dark blood sprayed and it sagged sideways, an unearthly shriek rending the night. Then the remaining two creatures leapt the fire barrier and charged. One went for Muhren; the other headed straight for Alaron.

'Into the water!' Muhren's cry was frantic, and then he was rolling away from a stabbing tail-sting. The construct followed his roll, landing on him, and they heard him cry out. He stabbed upwards into its open mouth and the thing staggered, but its tail whipped over and punched its deadly venom onto Muhren's chest before it toppled sideways.

An instant later, the other charging beast had reached Alaron.

Come on, you're supposed to be able to do this, he snarled at himself, hurling up a Barrier-rune. He threw everything he could muster into it, but he knew he'd screwed it up even before the creature came straight through it. He desperately flung himself aside, feeling the stinger as it whipped past his thigh and stabbed the earth. He rolled and thrust blindly, in case it had followed his movement, but it hadn't: it had careered straight onwards and was leaping at Cym, who was floating a foot above the flood-bank.

'Cym!' he screamed in horror.

The thing soared, its jaws snapping, its claws reaching, and she blurred away to the left – revealing the statue behind her, its bronze sword extended. The creature's headlong leap ended in a sickening thud as it impaled itself upon the outstretched bronze weapon. The blade punched through the creature's chest and came out its back. Black blood spurted as the creature thrashed weakly, then went limp.

<*Well struck, General!*> Alaron heard Cym exult.

Alaron looked back for Muhren, who was crawling to his feet, his battered breastplate covered in noisome fluids, his breathing laboured. 'Muhren,' he asked, 'did it—? Are you—?'

'Good Noros steel,' the watchman panted, slapping at his dented breastplate. 'But I'll need a blacksmith.' He turned and sent a further torrent of fire into the two burning creatures, which made them squeal like pigs and thrash about wildly before they went rigid and curled up like dead flies. 'Are you both all right?'

Cym nodded. 'The general got that one,' she remarked of the one impaled on the statue.

'I hope the real Jari is faring as well,' Muhren panted. 'Now it's time for you to do as you're told. Get into the bloody water and find that thing. I'll keep anything from coming for you.'

'Come with us,' Alaron urged, 'while there's time.'

'There is no time,' he said grimly and pointed back across the green where the creatures had come from. A man walked towards them: Darius Fyrell. The Arcanum Magister clicked his fingers and the two burning construct corpses suddenly stood in a flux of purple gnosis-light, their eyes glowing as they sought Muhren.

'Now *run*,' Muhren shouted.

Alaron saw the burning gnosis-constructs stumble erect, violet necromantic-gnosis spilling from their eyes, and felt a sickening hopelessness. Cym gripped his shoulder. 'Stand still,' she hissed and clapped a hand over his mouth and nose. He felt fluid fill both and nearly screamed before he realised what she was doing. *Water-breathing gnosis* . . . He gasped, and nearly choked. *Rukka*, he thought, *I've got to breathe water now, or I'll drown up here!* He ran desperately towards the top of the flood-bank and dived off the edge into the black water. Even as he plunged through the water, he heard another splash and he opened his eyes to see a pale shape dart past him in a swirl of bubbles. Gnosis-light flared, revealing Cym kicking off her shoes and billowing skirt before plunging downwards into the darkness.

Good idea! His own boots and clothes felt impossibly heavy. He fought his way free of the clothing and footwear, and managed to loop his belt, the sword still attached, over his shoulder. He'd not yet taken a breath, but he could delay it no longer and sucked in water, fearing the worst. But Cym's spell worked, and all that hit the back of his throat was air.

Thanks and praise! He winced a little as the cold water filled his mouth and became air: it felt uncanny, but it was endurable. He created a gnosis-light before him, like a will o' the wisp, and sent it ahead, lighting the way down into the depths of the lake.

The sword's weight helped pull him downwards and he soon caught up with Cym. Her legs were pale in the dark water and her long black hair and white blouse rippled as she swam. She too had a gnosis-light bobbing before her. As they descended, fish darted aside in silvery flashes. A dark bulk loomed out of the depths, the roof of a drowned hovel. Cym flowed past it into what would have been an alley. <*This way!*> she whispered into his mind.

Alaron glanced back up at the shimmering surface far above, trying to quell his fear. *How long have we got? Can Muhren hold out against Fyrell?*

Belonius Vult's moneyed friends liked to talk about 'risk-free investments', but Vult knew such things did not exist. There was risk in all things, and the bigger the gain, the bigger that risk.

He could live with that. You picked your battles, avoided foolish fights like Lukhazan and went for the jugular when the odds were tilted in your favour. He had never flinched in the face of danger, not when there were worthwhile gains to be had. They were always *calculated* risks, certainly – unknown risks were for fools dazzled by the prize.

But this is for the greatest prize of all.

Langstrit had erupted from the earth and soared into the skies like burning pitch hurled by a siege-engine. Fortunately, Vult had anticipated the potential for a chase; he had a skiff ready for just such an event. He gestured for Besko to follow him, leaving Fyrell and his entourage to mop up the others. A young pilot-mage crouched beside the tiller, his eyes eager. Vult leapt in beside him with gnosis-assisted grace, Besko clambered in behind him, then they lifted and caught the wind. In seconds they were soaring above Turm Zauberin, over the south wall and towards the Alps.

Their quarry flew before them, his arms spread like a bird, but they were gaining on him. Flying with just the gnosis was hard, while the skiff took almost no energy and travelled faster. *We will catch you soon, Langstrit,* Vult thought. *You can't keep that up for long, Ascendant or not.*

He thought about who they faced: *An Ascendant, ill-equipped and unused to exerting his powers –he's already burning gnosis at a dangerous level. He's an old man, despite his power, and frail after all those years we had him under lock and key.*

'Where is he going?' Eli Besko panted.

Vult masked his disdain for the fat popinjay; Besko knew what was at stake, of course – that was unavoidable. But Vult had no intention that Besko should ever survive their victory. He wished for an instant that Gurvon Gyle was here, but that was a dangerous wish – with Gurvon present, he'd have to watch his back. At least Besko's treacheries were containable.

'There are two possibilities, Eli: one, that he has abandoned his accomplices and is running straight for the prize. Two; he seeks to divert us, and his accomplices are going for the prize.'

'The former, surely,' Besko said instantly. 'The stakes are too high to risk anything else.'

'Perhaps – but it is in his nature to trust his underlings, and he is already an Ascendant. He can afford to run the other way. Worst case, he will still be what he is, an Ascendant mage. The second option cannot be ignored.'

Besko frowned, digesting the idea that Langstrit might have trust-worthy accomplices, when Vult might feel that he himself did not. 'You can trust me absolutely, Governor,' he responded, tellingly.

Really? We'll see . . . 'That's excellent news, Eli, but we are considering Langstrit: his character would lead one to believe that option two is the more likely, and that would mean Muhren and his young friends are the people we should be following. However, you will notice that I still elected to follow Langstrit south.'

Besko thought it through. 'The risk of letting him go is too great. If he's really the one going for the Scytale we'll never get it back if we let him go. If his accomplices are the real hunters, Fyrell will destroy them; or we can return to their trail as soon as Fyrell confirms that fact.'

'Correct, Eli: Darius Fyrell is more than a match for Muhren, and Mercer and his friends are worthless. No, the real challenge is ours: how do we deal with Jarius Langstrit?'

Besko swallowed, reflecting on his own narrow escape from annihilation when Langstrit fire-blasted the street as he flew up through the stone. 'He might not even have a periapt attuned.'

'True, but we cannot count on that. So what plan have you formed to take him down, Besko?'

Besko grimaced, clearly unused to thinking so hard. 'Uh, he is a Thaumaturge, lord. His greatest strengths are the elements, but he is weak against mental attacks.'

'Indeed.' Vult sent his mind outwards, following that blaze of energy ahead. 'And old, Eli: he is old. Conserve your powers, when the battle comes; remember, it is more economical to defend than to attack. We harry him, we wear him down. And if Fyrell sends confirmation that Muhren should be our target, then we break off immediately.'

Eli hissed suspiciously, 'What if Fyrell betrays us, lord?'

'Then we kill him. Do not fear, Eli. He won't become Ascendant the moment he touches the thing – that's a myth. I have spoken with Ascendants. The process takes hours. We can afford to be second to the Scytale, as long as we are not overly delayed.'

Vult watched Besko wondering just how secure his own position was. *Wonder all you like, Eli; you won't see my blow coming.* Returning his attention to Langstrit, he noted the man was slowing. Flying-gnosis was very energy-hungry, and they had been gaining on him all the time, their pilot working with dogged skill. He smiled to himself. *It will be soon.*

Jarius Langstrit saw the windskiff clear the ridge behind him with a sinking heart. He could fly no further without destroying his own ability to fight when caught. He chose a rough gully where he might be able to use the terrain, and prepared to make his stand. He had barely thirty seconds to prepare. The slope was tussocky grass, studded with boulders. Part of his mind was tracking Muhren; the watchman was still running as the tenth night-bell rang miles away in the city, still audible here in the thin air of the alpine foothills. He glanced to his right, where the sun would rise within the hour.

So, old man, ready for one more battle?

Not really, was the answer. He hadn't had time to attune to the periapt Muhren had slipped him, so every spell was costing thrice the energy it should. And pain accompanied every casting, a constriction of the chest, a hollowing of his gut that he didn't like. He was badly out of practise – his spells were overdone, sloppy – and that could cost him everything. He was sodden with sweat and shaking in the cold air. Standing was an effort, and the fight had barely begun.

He consoled himself that if someone had come to his cell one of those nights after Vult's questioning and offered him a chance to fight, he'd have taken it. He'd lost so much of himself, and so much *time*: eighteen years! The slow release of his memories from that crystal had been like waking up from a long, half-recalled dream. But that desperate scheme hatched so many years ago had come through in the end. He was himself again, and the goal for which he'd sacrificed himself was close.

But first he had to deal with his pursuers, though he felt frail, frighteningly weak. He watched the skiff glide closer. There were three men aboard, and one of them was definitely Belonius Vult.

Let's see what I can do . . . He summoned Air-gnosis and sent it in a vicious gust that caught the skiff and hurled it to the rocks below. Evidently Vult had underestimated his reach, as there was no counter or ward raised against the strike. Two men spun from the craft as it fell, but the other clung on as the skiff slammed into the rocky slope and splintered. A shout was cut off instantly and he felt momentary guilt, but he reminded himself that Vult didn't recruit innocents. *One down.*

He sent a ball of flame fully one hundred yards, far beyond the range a non-Ascendant could attain, and engulfed the shattered skiff in fire. *That's your wings clipped, Bel.* But they would have noted his position now.

He moved, hobbling awkwardly, sucking in great mouthfuls of the thin mountain air, his lungs struggling with the altitude. His heart was tight in his chest. *Who's with you, Vult? Someone I know?*

A flicker of movement to the left caught his eye: he blasted with Fire-gnosis, but only succeeded in scorching a patch of dewy grass. *An illusion . . . it was the other mage: not Vult.* Illusion had never been Vult's affinity, despite people's impressions of him. Vult was an absolute realist, a pragmatist who liked to know all the facts, then manipulate them. So it was Vult's companion he faced.

If you want to play with illusions, stranger, try this. He sent an image of himself walking to the ridge-line, while he himself circled in the shadows. He made his illusory alter ego top the ridge and cautiously scan the gully. *Come on, have a go!* He waited eagerly for a bolt to flash from the darkness and reveal the hiding-place of his foe, but nothing came.

So it's to be a stalking game. Damn. I don't have the stamina for that.

He made his illusory form crouch, moved it out of sight, then let it fade to conserve energy. He felt the tentative touch of a mind, hunting his. *That's more what I expected, Belonius: a little Theurgy.* He clamped down his aura, hiding from that questing touch, and clambered towards a cluster of broken boulders. Vult's probing nagged at him, forcing him to strengthen his mind-wards. His control was draining without a periapt. He shuddered in the frigid air, each swallow chilling him. His chest felt tight, his heartbeat too rapid. *It's too damn cold here . . . too hard to breathe.*

His tenuous link with Muhren flared suddenly: the watch captain was fighting someone or something, fighting hard. *Damn . . . Kore be with you, Jeris – Kore be with you all!* He would not regret the decision to separate: *if we'd fought in that street we'd all be dead. If I'd gone for the Scytale, I'd still have Vult on my arse. We did the right thing. Just let me live through this . . .*

He topped the rise, sensed a movement and blazed flame at it, and something small squealed and died in the hiss and crackle of burning wet grass. A rabbit. *Damned waste – stupid!*

Blue fire flared from along the ridgeline, struck his shields and deflected away. He fired back at a dim shape walking towards him, and it vanished as the fire struck. Another damned illusion – it was too hard to tell in this pre-dawn dark. *Damn this, I'm jumping at shadows and taunts!*

Muhren's hurt. He sensed the flare of pain and clenched his fists in helpless fury. *I should have stayed with him.* He felt his heart pounding over-fast, his blood pumping. *I should be back at the lake – damn this—* He ran back the way he had come, burst around a boulder and ran straight into Eli Besko.

So it's you, you arse-licker!

The fat man squealed, erecting panicky shields in time to deflect Langstrit's bolt of energy, and they staggered to a halt mere feet apart. Langstrit had raised his hands to pour flame into the man when Besko did something completely unexpected: he leapt at him, and his sheer bulk battered through the general's shields and smashed him backwards into a boulder. Air belched from his lungs and his head crunched wetly against the jagged stone. He was wrenched back and hammered into the stone again as Besko shouted something. His face was maniacal. Langstrit's vision dimmed, his chest felt about to burst and for an instant he was teetering on the edge of darkness. Then he snarled and roared flame from his mouth as if he were a dragon of Schlessen legend.

Besko screamed as his face melted, sinking to his knees as he went up like a torch, but Langstrit felt no pity. He could feel the pulpy wetness at the back of his skull and a throbbing pain in his chest that overwhelmed him. He fell to the ground, the pain in his chest ripping him apart. His left hand pawed impotently at his breast—

My heart! He managed a sob. His mind was clogged, his senses all astray. He saw Besko topple forward, flames licking at his body, and tried to focus beyond the agony in his breast. *Two down . . .*

But I'm rukked as well—

He tried to stand again, but that pain had become unendurable. He fell back, his mouth sucking like a beached fish, and he tried to feed himself oxygen through Air-gnosis, but the exertion made his heart pulse even more frenetically. He clawed the earth desperately. *You're having a heart attack, you old fool. Lie still and think!*

He could feel Vult, making careful little forays, measuring his strength, assessing his weakness.

<Come and get it, Belonius!>

His foe didn't reply, but a faint greenish cloud washed down the slope. *Smoke? Poison?* Langstrit pushed it away, and his heart thumped harder, harder. *No, I won't go out like this—*

More green smoke washed down the slope: poisonous vapours. *A cautious and clever attack, easier to launch than to counter.* Somewhere in Norostein he felt Muhren take a savage wound, as if the blow had been inflicted upon his own flesh. But worse was the tearing thunder in his own chest, a wrenching that felt like being physically torn in two . . . He shook uncontrollably while the morning sky turned to midnight, desperately holding his last reserves inside, praying for one final chance.

Somewhere up the slope, booted feet came ever closer.

One last chance . . .

Alaron swam frantically after Cym, fear of being left behind driving him faster. The girl's face was concentrated and fierce as she glanced back, then plunged through a crossroads into another drowned alley. *<Do you know where you're going?>*

<Of course I know where I'm bloody well going – unlike you, I was listening when the general gave us directions.*>* Her voice was caustic in his mind. *<You're a babe in the woods, Alaron.>* She frog-kicked away into the gloom.

<What's got into you? Ramon may be dying back there—>

<You heard the general: Ramon can't be helped further. It's the future of the entire world I'm more interested in right now.>

Alaron looked up anxiously: something was silhouetted briefly against the shimmery silver sky that was the surface of the reservoir. *<Cym – someone's in the water with us.>*

<Rukka – watch it, we're nearly there . . . I think this is it.>

He worked his way to her side, panting out huge pearly bubbles, and reslung the sword belt.

She turned to face him, her face wide-eyed and urgent. *<Look at this.>* Her gnosis-light darted ahead, illuminating the smashed remnants of a stone plinth. A statue lay fallen at its feet, grimed in green algae; around it pale waterweed swayed in the sluggish currents of the lake.

<Are you sure that's it?>

<Of course.> Cym gripped the plinth with one hand and scuffed away the algae. *<The Scytale should be inside the plinth. Do your thing, Earth-mage.>*

He was suddenly overwhelmed. *<This is really it?>*

<Rukka mio, just get on with it.>

He kicked his way through the icy water, fighting the cold with gnosis-heat, and gripped the plinth. Earth-gnosis: something he could do. The drowned buildings were black silhouettes, the surface silver. There were no fish here. Maybe they'd scared them away – or someone else had. *<Here goes.>*

He reached out with Earth-gnosis, though it wasn't easy beneath the water, and plunged his hand slowly into the stone plinth, one inch, two inches, three, four, until his fingers popped through the stonework into a tiny chamber beneath. As he touched a cold metal cylinder his heart double-thumped and almost stopped. He lifted it free. *<I've got it!>*

She thrust out a hand. <*I'll take it, I'm the faster swimmer.*> He wrenched it away and faced her. Her eyes flared, then slitted, and he felt the cold water bite his soul. Something ugly moved behind her gaze, though her mental voice remained calm and reasonable. <*Alaron, I'll take it. Be sensible: you can't even breathe down here.*>

<*Is that a threat?*> he sent, shocked.

She stared at him, anger flickering across her face. <*No, it's not a threat – it's logic, damnit. Why won't you let me have it?*>

<*Yes,*> cackled Gron Koll into both of their minds, <*why won't you let her have it, Mercer? After all, you're the one who* can't breathe *down here . . .* >

38

Not Dead

Hermetic: Healing

Healing is surely the most blessed of the Gnostic Arts, yet so many scorn it as unmanly – until the day they take a wound!

SIMONE DE ROOP, ARGUNDY 793

It is better to die than to suffer the accursed touch of Shaitan upon thy flesh

BRANDED SCRIPT UPON THE BELLIES OF
CRUCIFIED HEALER-NUNS OF THE ORDO JUSTINIA,
LEFT BY HADISHAH ASSASSINS IN 908

Brochena, Javon, on the continent of Antiopia
Junesse 928
1 month until the Moontide

She wasn't dead. Yet. This one thought rose from Elena's mind, above even the desperate attempt to restart her healing, as Sordell stood over her, watching her shudder towards oblivion. It was primal: the need for survival entwined with the urge to strike back.

<Bastido! Cinque!>

On Sordell's right, Bastido creaked into life and a faint sound warned Sordell, and he spun, somehow blocking the wooden stave that thrust for his midriff. But Rutt Sordell had never been a warrior and in his alarm he put all his shielding there, leaving him naked to the other blows. The chain-flail lashed his face, making him reel drunkenly, then the mace smashed into his temple from the other direction and his body left the ground, spiralling sideways, and blood sprayed, arcing across the chamber as he struck the wall in a pulverising crunch. His skull left a wet stain as it slid down the stone. He landed on his back, his head propped slightly. His face was slack and devoid of awareness. It had taken perhaps half a second.

Then she realised what she'd done. *Lorenzo!* Blood began to pump from his broken skull. *No!*

She reflexively flooded her own throat-wound with healing-gnosis, all that was left to her, sucking air into the wound, then sealing it. She vomited blood, gulped down oxygen, and her vision came and went. All she could do was lie there, staring at the other three bodies.

Gurvon had laughed when he found the deadliest killer in the Grey Foxes was also a healer. *It makes me tough to kill*, she had boasted in return. *I just keep coming back.*

<*Bastido, enough,*> she told the fighting-machine and it went still again, almost smirking. She had nothing left now. All she could do was crawl. So she crawled.

She began to pull herself along the floor, first to Lorenzo, though she knew already she was too late. His mouth fell open and a black scarab the size of a fist scuttled out and away, seeking the shadows. Sordell, gone again.

I killed Lori . . . Damn this! <*Cera!*>

No one came.

I've got to get help, or I'm dead. She groaned and jack-knifed her way across the floor to the head of the spiral stairs. Her legs were still too far gone to stand. She began to crawl down, head first, her mind churning as she went, barely holding spirit and body together.

<*Cera!*>

Every movement threatened to rip her open again. Her ankle was pure Hel, her shoulder-blades grated and her throat was a line of fire despite all her efforts. She kept coughing up blood, unable to get a clean breath, but she went on, contorting her way through the maze of pain, slipping in and out of consciousness, not rational – but not dead either.

Somehow she reached the landing and kicked at the door. <*Cera! Someone!*>

The door opened, and someone knelt over her. She knew it was Cera just from the smell of her.

'Oh, Ella,' she breathed, 'you weren't supposed to live.' Her face was stricken, but her tones were measured. 'I am sorry, but you were the leg the fox had to gnaw off to escape the trap. I'm truly sorry. I made a deal. Our lives for yours.'

Elena let the world fall away.

She woke on a linen-draped bed, half-naked beneath a sheet, swathed in bandages. Her neck was encased in cloth, as were her shoulder and ankle. Chains clamped down her arms and legs. It was a battle to breath, a war against all the pain and the crushing weight of failure. She tried to reach out with the gnosis and got nothing at all. *I've been Chained.*

The door opened. She did not need to look to know who it was.

'Hello, Elena,' said Gurvon Gyle, sitting on the bed. 'I swear, you're harder to eradicate than a cockroach.' He removed the sheet. She writhed, but the chains held. Her former lover studied her body coldly, then met her eyes. 'I wondered if I would still feel any desire for you, despite everything. But I feel nothing at all.'

She walled up her mind, though the Chain-rune left her with limited defences, but Gyle did not attack her with the gnosis; he employed words instead.

'You never stood a chance, Elena. The attacker has all the choices. The defender can only react. Your little protégée came to realise that.' He smiled faintly. 'Thank you for ridding me of Targon – though the emperor will not be pleased.'

'I hope he dismembers you for it,' she rasped, startled by the hideous sound of her own voice.

'Don't try to speak, Elena,' Gyle warned. 'The throat wound is still raw.'

She coughed up blood and spat it at him, missing by some distance.

Gyle stroked her brow thoughtfully. 'You trained your little princessa well, Elena. When the moment of truth came, she knew how to cut her losses. Ironic, isn't it? The one who taught her how to be rational and self-serving became the pawn she sacrificed.'

'Go to Hel, Gurvon,' she grated.

'While Mara led you a dance, chasing shadows in the canals, I was working on the princessa, poisoning her mind against you and the Kestrians. When you obligingly started screwing Lorenzo, it was the final proof she needed; from then on you were doomed. She herself sent Lorenzo into the trap we laid on his way back from the Krak. I was waiting for him.'

She cringed at the remembrance of Lorenzo. *He loved me, and it got him killed. I saw Cera change – I should have known—*

'Oh, don't be too hard on yourself, Elena,' Gyle said mockingly. 'You've done magnificently, if wrecking my plans is a criteria for magnificence. It couldn't last, though. You got lucky, locking up Coin without realising who she was, but that only bought you time.'

Gyle paused, as a huge black scarab beetle crawled out of his pocket. He smiled thinly. 'Rutt also says "hello".' The scarab ran down his arm onto her belly.

She felt a wave of desperate fear. *'Get it off me!'*

Gyle smiled as the scarab crawled up her body, its feet sharp on her skin. She writhed, trying to throw it off, but the chains held her in place.

'Please, Gurvon!!' she begged, truly terrified now.

The beetle paused on her left breast and its pincers teased her nipple. She screamed, *'Please, Gurvon!'*

'The thing is, Elena, I've got a severe manpower shortage now – and there is so much to do to complete this coup.'

She shook her head mutely as the scarab crawled onto her collarbone.

'Make no mistake, Elena: you and I are mortal enemies now. You betrayed me, and I can never forgive that. But I'm a practical man, and I can even bear to see you on your feet again, provided you're under my control.' His face became bleak. 'I'd like to kill you, but Javon needs to see that its heroic Queen's Champion is alive and well; that will reassure them when Cera starts making overtures to the Gorgio and suing for peace.' He raised his arm and the scarab of Rutt Sordell crawled onto the back of his hand. 'And of course, Rutt needs a new body.'

She clamped her jaws shut. <*No!*>

He grasped her jaw and nose with deft hands and pulled open her mouth. The scarab slithered down his hand and onto her cheek. 'Of course, Rutt would prefer a male body, but beggars can't be choosers, can they? If he wants a body capable of gnosis, it will have to be yours.'

<*Please, Gurvon, no!*>

Gyle's eyes hardened. 'You know, if you hadn't screwed that Kestrian, not only would Cera have retained her friendship towards you, but I might have felt some sympathy now. But I feel nothing at all any more. Goodbye for ever, Elena.'

The head of Sordell's necromantic scarab peered into her right eye, feelers waving, mandibles working feverishly. Then it turned and crawled inside her mouth.

There was a sharp pain and a hideous burrowing sensation in her palate.

Then nothing at all.

39

Mountains at Dawn

Jarius Langstrit

Jarius Langstrit was Argundian, a gruff career soldier who late in life found himself at the head of a legion in Noros. Two years in the Revolt elevated him to the status of legend in that country. But after the war he vanished and was never seen again. When asked during the Revolt why an Argundian would fight for Noros, he said, 'There is no place I love more. If the mountains of Noros are my last sight, then I will die content.'

CHRONICLES OF NOROS, 923

Norostein, Noros, on the continent of Yuros
Junesse 928
1 month until the Moontide

Alaron didn't pause to look around; he took a deep breath and kicked for the surface, gripping the cylinder of the Scytale in his hand. With the other hand he cast off his sword so that he could ascend faster. Below him he glimpsed Cym whirling, seeking a target. *She's barely trained*, he thought, but then he felt Koll's first attack, a negation of the water-breathing spell Cym had given him, while he was still dozens of yards below the surface. His next breath had to be of air, or he was dead.

He kicked for the surface in blind panic as a bolt of blue fire smashed through his shields, scorching his left thigh. He could have screamed, lost his air and died, but he didn't – maybe it was all the blows that had been rained upon him in the practise-yards, inuring him to pain. He contorted in agony, but he kicked on. More bolts flashed below, but no more were directed at him. The silvery surface was almost in reach—

—and then he was exploding through it, gasping in the freezing air. A dark shape loomed: the statue of the King of Noros the council had set in the middle of the reservoir. He splashed towards it, and the next burst of gnosis-fire from below caught him in the belly. He shrieked and almost dropped the cylinder.

Shields, shields! He summoned Air-gnosis and rose clear of the water, a clumsy flight that pitched him at the foot of the statue of King Phylios III. He heaved himself to his knees. The waters about him grew menacingly still and he could hear shouting from the flood-banks a hundred yards away. He prayed Muhren was winning, then he heard a *plop!* in the water ten yards to his left and all thoughts of what might be happening ashore fled.

Cym bobbed to the surface, face-down, in a cloud of black hair. A knife protruded from her back and as she surfaced blood bloomed over her back like an opening flower. All rationality disintegrated, he dropped the Scytale cylinder and leapt into the air, swooping towards the stricken girl. He heaved Cym from the water with gnosis alone and she rose in a cascade of dark fluids, her body limp. <*No!*> he screamed into her mind as he caught her in midair, <*Cym, please wake up – I can't heal you! You have to wake up—*>

He started to take her back to the statue, and stopped dead, all hope dying.

Gron Koll stood beside the statue, black hair plastered over his sallow face. He bowed mockingly. 'Thanks for bringing me this,' he purred, stroking the cylinder.

'I don't care about that,' Alaron pleaded. 'Just let me save Cym.'

Gron Koll sniggered. 'You've got nothing to bargain with.' He raised a hand, gnosis-fire licking his fingers.

A torrent of flame lit the surface of the lake.

Belonius Vult edged cautiously towards Langstrit, who was moving with painful slowness some twenty yards down the slope. Beside him was the charred corpse of Eli Besko. *That saves me the trouble, I guess.*

He peered with a seer's eyes at the old man. *Oh dear, you are in a dire way, aren't you, Jari? But not dead yet.* He paused. He knew Langstrit; even now, there were risks . . . *And you've already done more than enough damage . . .* The skiff was destroyed and its pilot slain. It would be a slow journey home under his own power.

And the Scytale isn't here, that is clear now. I need to get back, before Fyrell gets ideas above his station. But first you must die, old man. Eighteen years of your riddles was far too long.

He assessed Langstrit's remaining physical and psychic strength, then struck, a threefold attack: a cloud of gas for poison; a mental attack, and an Air-gnosis-assisted leap to drive his staff into the man's chest. What did Gurvon Gyle like to say? '*A short fight is a good fight.*'

Langstrit saw the blur of movement and the billowing gas and with his last strength rose to his knees, pushing outwards with Air-gnosis. *Ha – didn't think that one through, did you, Bel? Two attacks that could be countered with one parry. You always were a desk-mage.* He rose to his feet unsteadily, clutching his heart, feeling it drumming furiously inside. *You're not going to make it, old man, but you can take this prick with you . . .*

Then his link to Muhren went dead: utterly, absolutely severed.

No! <Jeris? Answer me!> But there was nothing – and Belonius Vult rose in front of him with a face like vengeance.

No – Jeris!

Evidently Vult had some connection to Fyrell, for his head was cocked, listening. 'It's all been for nothing, old man,' he purred.

'Not if I take you down, you worm,' Langstrit spat, and Vult came at him as his final strength faded. It felt as if he was wading through water. Vult tipped his blade aside, then drove his stave at him, hammering his shields and knocking him backwards. He slashed as he stumbled, but he couldn't control his blows. Then the iron-heeled staff was battering him again, once, twice, with energy crackling along it, too much for him now. Wood and iron smashed into his ribs and something tore inside his left breast as his ribs broke. He couldn't breathe. He felt his legs give way and then Vult, his usual smooth mask warped with bestial anger, smashed the staff into his chest again, right over his heart, and he felt it burst. He fell backwards, the sky filling his eyes. *I've failed. It was all for nothing.*

Above him, the sunlight kissed the snowy heights with the faintest rose-pink and gold: remote, heartrending beauty – the reason he had come here from fair Argundy, the reason he had fought for this land. *A fitting last sight,* he remembered telling someone once, *beautiful – and out of reach.*

Alaron was too tired to react; he hovered above the waters holding Cym to him protectively and waited to die. He saw Koll's glee as he summoned energy for the fatal strike—

—but Koll's gnosis-fires disintegrated before they reached him.

'*Get away from my son!*' Tesla Anborn flowed out of the shadows, clad in red battle-mage robes, her ravaged face bared, her empty eye-sockets gleaming with pale gnosis-fire. Her ruined hands were raised in an inwards-reaching gesture as she defused Koll's fires.

Gron Koll snarled and blasted at her, but she batted it aside and struck back with a whip-crack of lightning that made Koll's shields flare and crackle. His body jerked and he yowled and dropped the cylinder.

Tesla struck again, no subtlety, just a torrent of fire hurled at the young mage. Koll raised shields laced with water and the fires burst over them in a hiss, and scalding steam billowed, blinding all sight. Koll shrieked, the most harrowing cry Alaron had ever heard, and fell over the cylinder.

His mother swooped towards Alaron, laid a hand on the knife in Cym's back and pulled it. The weapon came free and she thrust it into her belt, then laid her hand on the wound, sealing it with a searing flame that made Cym cry out, almost twisting from Alaron's grasp.

Tesla placed a clawed talon on his shoulder and drew him with her as they swept across the waves to the statue. <*Don't let her get hurt again. Come!*>

Gron Koll lay convulsing on the ground below the statue, inches from the water's edge. He had been scalded by the steam where his water-shield had met Tesla's fire – a water-shield was an effective defence against fire, unless the attacker was more skilled. In that case, it was supreme folly. Koll had been hugely overmatched; every inch of exposed skin was blistered and broken, revealing scarlet under-layers raw and weeping with seams of white fluids.

Alaron looked towards the flood-bank. <*Muhren—?*>

Tesla snorted dismissively. 'The valiant Watch Captain Muhren is more or less alive. He seemed to think he could take on Darius Fyrell head-to-head and win.'

'Is he—? What happened?'

'He was losing. Then some of his watchmen came and got killed trying to defend him. Then I came. Fyrell wasn't expecting *me*.'

'Is he dead?'

'Fyrell is a Necromancer, dear. They're like head-lice – those bastards can survive almost anything. But you won't be hearing from him for a while.' There was a touch of satisfaction in her voice. 'Did you and your friends really think you could keep all your little conspiracies from me, boy? Did you think I was deaf and stupid as well as blind?' She glanced down at Gron Koll. 'This was one of those slimes you schooled with, yes?'

Alaron looked down, nauseated by the agony of his old rival.

Tesla appeared to have no such qualms. 'Good. Then let him suffer a little longer.' She picked up the cylinder. 'So this is it?'

He tried to push the sight of Koll from his mind. Cym gave a faint sigh and he lowered her to the ground. *Cym, please be all right!*

Tesla stroked the cylinder. 'The Scytale of Corineus. So this was what it was all about, back in 909 . . . All that patriotism and speechi-fying that got half our menfolk killed. Stolen, lost and now found.' Her empty sockets blazed with some emotion and her shoulders shook, but her voice was its usual raven's croak when she spoke again. 'What do you think you're going to do with it, son?'

'I don't care any more. Ma, I have to go. Ramon—'

'Was still breathing. I got to him about a minute after you left. I did enough.' She brandished the Scytale. 'You might not care what happens to this thing, but the rest of the world does. The fate of nations, Alaron: that's what this thing is. What did old Jari have planned?'

'A new Order, dedicated to peace.'

'Really? How sweet.' She suddenly sucked in a distressed breath and staggered slightly.

'Ma!' He grabbed at her. 'What's wrong? Are you hurt?'

She shook her head. 'I'll tell you later. Come on, we've got to go now. Jeris Muhren is with his men; they'll look to him. I know a safe place nearby.' She handed Alaron the knife she had pulled from Cym's back. 'I'll look after the girl, Alaron. You deal with that little prick in the mud over there.'

He stared at her as she wafted her hand to lift Cym and began flowing away across the dappled waves. Someone called across the waters: a watchman. Tesla ignored the man.

He walked back to Gron Koll. He was lying totally still, his breathing laboured and shallow. His eyes flickered at Alaron. *<Please – mercy—>*

What is mercy? To spare an enemy so he can come after you?

A memory of Auntie Elena, when he was much younger: *If you pick up a weapon, you must be ready to kill with it – that's what they tell us at weapons-training, Alaron. But the thing is, for a mage, our whole being is a weapon. Even healing-gnosis can be used to kill . . . We pick up our powers and use them every day. We are killers by nature.*

It had sounded wrong then. *Aren't we shields too,* he had replied, *don't we protect people too?*

She had looked at him thoughtfully. *Perhaps we are, boy,* she'd said. The next day she'd left for Javon. That was the last time he'd seen her.

Now Alaron steeled himself and forced his eyes to take in the ruined youth, his gorge rising as he looked at the bones exposed where the skin and sinew and flesh had been boiled away. He realised that there was only one mercy he could give. He knelt and placed the blade on Koll's chest. *This is mercy.*

As he pushed it into Koll's chest, Koll wheezed, '*Fuck . . . you . . . Mercer—*' Then his eyes went misty and lost focus. His head fell back and his features went slack, empty.

Alaron knelt over him, his emotions churning as hard as his belly, and then he straightened. Dawn kissed the mountains and shafts of light burst across the sky. He turned his face from what he'd done and took to the air, skimming across the water in his mother's wake.

Belonius Vult stumbled down the slope, shouting with the remainder of his gnosis for some kind of response: *<Fyrell – Fyrell, answer me! Koll – where are you? Answer me!>* He stumbled again, rolled down a slick, grassy slope, barking his shins, and slammed his ankle against something, making him cry out. He stopped then, clutched his bloodied knees and for an instant felt like a small boy, before his gnosis had developed, when he was just the runt of the nursery, his elder brother's prey.

He stifled a groan. *Fool: rest, recover – Langstrit is dead, Fyrell and Koll are either dead or not answering and exhausting yourself won't change that. Rest for an hour or two. You will still triumph: when you want something enough, the whole universe conspires to aid you. The Scytale will be yours.*

You are still governor. You are still Magister. There are no enemies here.

But no fresh energy rose inside him. He'd reached his limits, softened by nearly two decades of ease and luxury. *It won't matter. A few minutes' rest. A few minutes of sleep.*

Sleep; Alaron craved it more than anything else as he carried Cym through the waking streets, his mother clutching his shoulder, her gnosis exhausted, once more a helpless blind woman. Occasional people stared, but no one approached, not even Watchmen, daunted perhaps by Tesla's battle-mage robes and blasted countenance.

She guided him to a side-street and down a filthy flight of stairs. A furtive man with white whiskers kissed his mother's hand and led them to a rough wooden door. 'And this is young Alaron?' he murmured reverently. 'I served your Aunt Elena in the Revolt, so I did. Pars Logan, I am. You remember me to your aunt if you see her.' He took Tesla's arm. 'Come this way, milady.'

Logan led them down many stairs, deep beneath the earth, where they'd be safe from scrying. Cym was ashen-faced and breathing shallowly; Tesla was tottering on her feet by the time they reached the room, where a woman, Logan's wife, was watching over an occupied bed. Alaron almost burst into tears when he saw that the occupant was Ramon. He carried Cym to the other bed, then sagged against it, his knees turning to jelly.

Ramon's breath was laboured, but his burns were already half-healed from Langstrit's earlier aid. Alaron whispered thanks, wondering where the old man was.

Cym clutched his hand when he bent over her, her eyes flickering open, wide and frightened. 'Alaron?'

'It's me. You're okay.' Stinging tears welled from his eyes.

'Where is it,' she whispered, 'the Scytale?'

'Ma has it,' he whispered back. 'It's okay, we're safe.'

'What about Muhren? And the general?'

'Muhren's alive, but not here.' He swallowed. 'We don't know about the general.' He glanced at the other bed. 'Ramon's here. He's healing up.'

'Good thing you've got a mother to haul our asses out of the fire, eh?' Cym murmured, and Alaron nodded mutely. 'Go to her. Let me sleep.'

He bent down and pressed his lips to hers and she started to turn away, as usual, then stopped resisting. She tasted tart and cool, and he wished he could freeze this moment for ever. 'I love you,' he whispered.

Her eyebrows twitched. 'Idiot. Piss off.' She smiled sadly, nothing but sympathy in her eyes.

He turned away to hide his face from hers, brushing away tears. *I love her and she feels only pity.* He felt his heart crumble inside his chest. 'You rest,' he whispered huskily, and stumbled away.

He found his mother in a small room at the end of the hall, in one of two armchairs beside a fireplace. Pars Logan had lit the fire and left them a goblet of red wine each. Tesla turned at the sound of his feet, cringing as she did when her gnosis was not engaged. The Scytale cylinder lay in her lap, unopened.

He kissed her forehead, fell to his knees and hugged her. 'Thank you, Ma.'

She snorted slightly. 'It's what mothers do, isn't it? Clear up their children's messes.'

'Where's Da?'

'Stuck in a ten-mile swamp on the Verelon Road with all of our worldly goods. Idiot man.' She stroked Alaron's head. 'Idiot son. Lucky for you I'm not dead yet.'

He remembered her earlier faltering. 'Are you all right, Ma?'

She gave a small sigh. 'I'm still alive, Alaron – but not for much longer. I have a cancer, you see. It would have killed a non-mage, years ago, and most of my strength has gone into fighting it.' She grimaced. 'I've got a few weeks, maybe. That's all.'

'I'm sorry we dragged you into this. You should have saved your strength.'

'Nonsense. I've always wanted to give that shit Fyrell a good kicking. A shame Vult wasn't there too. I'd have given him something to think about, pure-blood or not. You don't mess with an Anborn.' Her voice held all the bitter combativeness he remembered. She touched his face. 'Life is struggle, Alaron. You have to be strong and fight for what is yours.' She brandished the Scytale. 'Right now, that includes this.'

He nodded mutely and Tesla stroked his face with her ruined fingers, reading the shape of his nose, his mouth, his chin. 'You know, I've never seen you in the flesh, only with the gnosis, and that's not the same as real sight.' She gripped the back of his head and pulled him to her neck, pinioned him to her. 'I could have been a better mother, I suppose, but it's not easy, being a burnt-out wreckage like this. In the end I gave up. It was hard on you and your father. I'm sorry for that.'

He gripped her thin body and wept. 'I love you, Ma.'

She grunted thickly. 'I know, boy. Go and sleep, now. I'll still be here in the morning.' She kissed his forehead with cold lips and he felt her mind brush roughly against his: <Goodnight, son. I'm proud of you.>

At the door he half-turned, but she was stroking the Scytale, lost in reverie. Logan was outside the door. He led Alaron to another spartan chamber with a mattress in the corner. He staggered forward and collapsed onto it. All of the terror and adrenalin ebbed away. It was all too much.

Pars Logan shook him awake, countless hours later, murmuring, 'Young master, you better come. It's your mother.'

Alaron stumbled up from the mattress. 'What time is it? What's happened?'

'Almost midday, lad.' Logan led him back to the lounge, where Tesla was still huddled in the big armchair.

Alaron waited for her to turn her head, for her sightless eyes to pin him down. But she didn't move.

'I came in to check on her,' Pars whispered, 'but she wasn't breathing.'

Alaron swallowed a sob, tiptoeing to her side as if scared to wake her. Her hand was cold, the scarred face slack and unmoving. Her face was uncharacteristically calm. *She used all that she had to save me and it killed her.* He dropped to his knees and hugged her cold body to him, fighting the welling grief.

Her taloned hands were gripping the blanket tight. His eyes fell to her lap and then cast about the room. The cylinder containing the Scytale of Corineus was gone. His heart pounded.

Pars Logan handed him an envelope. 'This was on the mantle, young master. It's got your name on it.'

Cym's writing. Alaron tore it open.

Dear Alaron

Do not think the worst of me. Your mother was dead when I found her. I would never have wished her ill. She told me one night when I was tending her that she ought to be dead already. My deepest sorrow for your loss.

I can never repay you and Ramon for your kindness. You risked your futures to teach me. You are my heroes.

The Scytale – yes, I have taken it. I couldn't just hide here until Vult returned to take it from us. I had to act. I'm sorry.

I've never told you about my mother. I will now, so that you know that my decision is the right one. Her name is Justina, and my grandfather, the true and rightful owner of the Scytale of Corineus, is Antonin Meiros. My father and mother were lovers one summer. She never wanted a child, so Father took me away.

I know you have spent most of the last seven years in love with me. Perhaps I love you back, but not in the way you want. Maybe when this is all done, we'll see one another again, free from danger. How we will laugh! But until then, please don't hate me and please don't try to find me.

Show this letter to Ramon. Tell the little sneak that I love him too, in the same way I love you: as a brother.

Be safe,

Cymbellea Meiros de Regia

He looked at Pars Logan. 'She gone, isn't she? The Rimoni girl.'

Pars hung his head. 'I'm sorry lad. She must move like a ghost. Like a moonbeam.'

'Like a moonbeam,' Alaron echoed bleakly.

EPILOGUE

Endings are Beginnings

Destiny

The greatest lesson of the art of divination is that there is no such thing as destiny. Some futures can seem crushingly inevitable, but they are not certain until the moment they occur. I find this a source of great hope.

ANTONIN MEIROS, 904 (YEAR OF THE FIRST CRUSADE)

Hebusalim, on the continent of Antiopia
Junesse 928
1 month until the Moontide

'I hate you,' Ramita hissed at Kazim. 'I will hate you for ever.'

There was some horrible power inside him now, something she could almost see. He had killed her husband and then he'd done something horrible that made him flare up with some ugly energy she could almost touch. She had almost lost control then, almost betrayed herself and her fledgling powers, until Rashid had snuffed her consciousness out like a candle. Oblivion was a blessing: only when she was completely unconscious could she escape the dreadful image of her husband as he fell. It replayed over and over whenever she shut her eyes. *Antonin, husband . . .*

His hand touched her cheek and she woke—

But it was Rashid Mubarak, sitting beside her on a bed. She stiffened in dread.

'So, you are awake at last,' the emir said softly. He reached out to caress her face again and she flinched from him. 'You should rejoice.

You have been freed from your unwanted marriage. Your dishonour has been made good, delivered by the hand of the young man who crossed the continent to rescue you. It is quite the epic tale.' He sighed regretfully. 'But I fear just now that you don't appreciate it. The trauma is too much for you. And no doubt you have been bewitched by some Shaitanic evil, the sort of foul magic Meiros employs when he couples with young girls like you.'

'Go to Hel,' she whispered, despite her terror. '*Murderer.*'

He leaned over her. 'He has poisoned your mind, Ramita. You have become his creature. But there is hope for you. We can save you.' He stroked her hair. 'What happens to you next depends upon whose children you carry. If you bear Kazim's child, then he shall have you to wife. But if those are Meiros' children you bear, then I shall have you to wife myself, as you will gain the gnosis through bearing his babies.' He bent closer. 'Does this please you?'

She spat in his face.

He wiped her spittle away and stood. 'You will not do that again.' With a sudden crack he backhanded her across the face and her vision swam. 'You will obey me, or every one of your family in Baranasi will be put to death.'

She cowered, her resistance shaken by his sudden brutality. He bent over her, his expression baffled and angry. 'Why *you*, girl? Why a Lakh, and why *you*? How could he think children who will not play a part for decades could affect this shihad?'

Rashid spat on the floor and shook his head. 'He told you nothing?' he demanded, and when she shook her head he spat again. 'Fertility – was that all it was?' He squeezed her cheeks between fingers and thumb, hurting her. 'Well, you're certainly fertile – just to the wrong man. Or perhaps not. Time will tell.' He whirled and stalked out in a swirl of rich clothing and glittering gems.

Hebusalim, Antiopia
Junesse 928
1 month until the Moontide

Jai looked him in the eye. 'Kazim, please come home.'

Kazim scowled and drank another mouthful. His senses were blurred from the alcohol, but it felt pleasant. This Hebusalim fenni-house was one the warriors frequented. Jamil and Haroun were with him – but Jai had found them and was begging him to leave.

Jai did not seem to realise that the Kazim Makani he knew did not exist any more.

I am a Souldrinker. I have the gnosis. I am a murderer.

He shook his head irritably. 'No, Jai. This is my place, here with the shihad.' He jabbed a finger at him. 'It is you who should go home, Jai. This is not a place for you.'

'Please, brother,' Jai said, more insistently. 'Please! Ramita is gone. Huriya is gone. The world is going mad. Please, come back with me to Baranasi.'

Kazim stood. 'No, Jai, I do not belong there now. This is my place.'

Jai stood also, tears running down his cheeks. 'Brother – *please*,' he said in a broken voice, 'all our lives we have done everything together. We are half of one soul: you have always told me this. Let us leave this accursed place and go home, please. We belong together.'

Kazim stepped forward, hugged Jai, then pushed him away gently, and tried not to see as Jai's face collapsed. When he turned away, he moved like an old man.

When he was gone, Jamil put a hand on his shoulder. 'Jai is weak,' he said. 'He would not survive the battles we will face.'

Haroun agreed. 'Jai is no warrior.'

So true. 'I will pray he gets home safely,' Kazim said. He wished hard that it would be so, could almost picture Jai embracing his mother in Baranasi. Then he became melancholy again, thinking of Ramita. *What more does she want of me? I freed her. She bears my children. Why won't she see me?*

Though in his heart he thought he knew.

Jamil broke into his thoughts. 'How goes your training?' The Hadishah warrior was warier of Kazim now, according him greater respect and caution.

For you are a mage and I am a Souldrinker . . . But we are still brothers-in-arms, Jamil. You are still my friend. 'Sabele says it will take years to fully master the gnosis,' he replied, though in truth it was coming naturally to him, this Shaitan-magic. Fragments of Antonin Meiros' memories had clung to the energy he'd absorbed, and he found he could manipulate the raw energies almost instinctively, though they frightened him. The more esoteric abilities were locked away, but Sabele said he would learn them swiftly. If he had the stomach for it.

'And you truly have his strength now?' Jamil asked, his pupils slightly dilated.

Kazim nodded shortly. 'We attain the strength of the strongest mage we soul-drink,' he said, repeating what Sabele had told him. 'I have Ascendant-level power now.'

Jamil whistled. 'Then I am no longer your sparring partner, my brother.'

Kazim grunted, a half-smile, but he could not regain his cheer. This new strength frightened him. Worse still, he'd glimpsed emotions and desires before Meiros ceased to exist. He'd tasted the nature of the man, and realised that he'd not been what he expected at all: *Antonin Meiros was not Shaitan incarnate. He was a man, a good man, who meant well. And he loved Ramita, as much as I, maybe even more – because I treated her as a prize and he treated her as a woman.*

The memory of what he'd done, and the hatred and horror on Ramita's face as she watched, were slowly destroying him. The two guardsmen; the young boy, innocent and undeserved – but above all, Meiros himself. He could not sleep unless drunk. Yet Sabele and Rashid expected him to take pride in the blood he'd spilled. *I thought I was a killer, but I'm not . . .*

'What of Huriya?' Jamil asked, his voice hungry.

Kazim scowled. *Klein was a half-blood, despite his brutish looks. And she throws herself into Sabele's training; she doesn't fight it as I do. She is as corrupt as Sabele.* 'She is a born jadugara,' he muttered. 'She excels.'

'I have asked to mate with her,' Jamil said seriously. 'With your permission? And Rashid's, of course.'

'None of us can do anything without his permission, can we?' he snarled. 'I don't give a shit about Huriya. Do what you want. I never want to see her again.'

Norostein, Noros, on the continent of Yuros
Junesse 928
1 month until the Moontide

Jeris Muhren sat across the table from Alaron, heavily bandaged, his face like a beaten pugilist. Even his eyes looked defeated, tired and full of sadness. Ramon was with them, though he was still groggy. It had been three days since Cym left, and Alaron had only just regained enough strength to move.

'So the general is dead, then?' Alaron said.

Muhren nodded heavily. 'Yes. My men took a windskiff out to the slopes. They found Big Jari's body. There were two other men – Eli Besko was one, but the other was too burned to identify.'

'What about Vult?'

'He's here in Norostein.'

Alaron's heart sank. 'Then we've lost. He'll find us, work out Cym has it, then he'll hunt her down.' He buried his hands in his head. 'It's all been for nothing – worse than that. If we hadn't gone after the Scytale, it would never have been found. I led him to it, as he always knew I would.'

Muhren shook his head. 'It's not so bleak as all that, Alaron. You see, I've arrested Belonius Vult.'

Alaron stared while Ramon started grinning painfully.

Muhren chuckled at their faces. 'I used the letter you recovered from Vult's records to obtain a royal warrant to search his premises. We smashed the panels of his trophy room – there was some damage to the contents because of his traps, but we salvaged enough material to blackmail most of Norostein and half the court at Pallas. So I obtained an arrest warrant and surprised him with plenty of Arcanum support on the outskirts of the city. He was still exhausted from fighting the general. He didn't even resist. He's under Rune of the Chain in his own dungeons right now.'

'Thank you,' Alaron said, dazedly. 'You're my hero.' Ramon nodded fervent agreement.

'Well, that makes a change. Anyway, my arse is on the line too,' Muhren remarked lightly. 'We won't be able to keep him locked away for long. Pallas will claim jurisdiction and send Inquisitors. I've bought us some time, that's all.'

'If he tells them—' Alaron choked.

'I rather suspect he may have an unfortunate accident whilst in the cells,' Muhren replied grimly.

Alaron swallowed, then growled fiercely, 'Couldn't happen to a better person.'

Muhren ran his fingers through his hair. 'It will mean the end of my career too.' He sighed regretfully, then shook his mane. 'So, what will you lads do?'

'Sleep,' Ramon said morosely. 'It's going to take me days before I'm mobile again.' He looked apologetically at Alaron. 'Then I guess I have to join my legion or I'll be up for arrest too. I'd stay if I could, but I can't see how I can without bringing the military down on top of us.'

'It's the only way,' Alaron agreed. 'If you don't go, if a mage became a deserter, the Inquisition gets involved.' He looked at Muhren. 'Do you think it's safe for Ramon to join his legion?'

'Vult wasn't working through official channels. I believe he'll be in the clear.'

'Is Fyrell dead?'

Muhren shrugged. 'I don't think so – but he can't afford to come forward either. The Inquisitors would flay him.'

'Then that's that,' Ramon said. 'Keep me posted, Al. I'll slip away and help you if I can.'

'And you, Master Mercer?' Muhren asked.

Alaron looked him in the eye. 'I'm going after her.'

Muhren didn't look surprised. 'With what intention?'

'I don't know. I just feel I ought to.'

The watchman sighed, 'Ah, young love.'

'No, sir, it's not that,' Alaron said firmly. 'She doesn't love me – she never has. It was always all one way, all on my part, and I think I knew that deep down. But she is my friend, and she's going into danger, so I think I must help her.'

'Well spoken, lad,' Muhren said. 'You're becoming a man – a good man, like your father, I deem.'

Alaron gripped the captain's hand. 'Thank you, sir.'

'Don't thank me, Alaron. Get the Scytale back.' Muhren frowned. 'Or at least, make sure it ends up in good hands.'

Brochena, Javon, on the continent of Antiopia
Junesse 928
1 month until the Moontide

Gurvon Gyle conjured the image of the Mater-Imperia's crest and submitted his identity codes. He held a relay-stave, which sent his call questing out powerfully. The request for contact was answered immediately. Lucia Fasterius-Sacrecour's serene visage manifested in the smoke of his brazier.

<*Magister Gyle? To what do I owe this unexpected pleasure?*> She didn't sound pleased at all.

<*Good news, Majesty. Javon belongs to us. Cera Nesti has capitulated and allowed my agents to take over control. She will remain the figurehead until it suits us to install the Dorobon. In the meantime, Javon will definitely not aid the shihad. The people do not suspect her; in fact, they have not even noticed the coup. We are about to announce a truce with the Gorgio. The populace will be troubled, but where Cera goes, they will follow.*>

Lucia's motherly face crinkled and grew larger, as if she was leaning closer to his own image. Her mouth curved into a satisfied smirk. <*Excellent news indeed, Magister. You have done well. I am . . . most pleased.*>

He smiled slightly, but knew enough not to relax. The rest wasn't going to go down so well . . .

She leaned even closer and purred at him, <Is Coin enjoying being a princess?>

<Coin is dead, Majesty,> he answered flatly.

Lucia blinked twice at the news of her daughter's death – Coin had confided little, but he'd made that connection quickly enough; he'd been prepared for anger, maybe even some grief, but Lucia merely shrugged. <I understood Coin would replace Cera Nesti?> she said, apparently more concerned that their plans might be disrupted than for the loss of the shifter.

<Cera herself is reconciled to our cause. And I have plenty of leverage over her.>

<Destroy the body of my daughter, Gyle. Burn it.>

<As you command, Majesty.>

The Empress' expression relaxed. <Well, Magister, you are redeemed, albeit late in the game. Still, you're doing better than your friend Vult. He has got himself arrested, can you believe?>

He's what? <This is news to me, Majesty.>

<Some local guardsman has apparently persuaded the Norostein crown to lay corruption charges. I'm sending Inquisitors to get to the bottom of it. It's quite amusing, in its way, but it doesn't come at a convenient time. In fact, it is suspiciously inconvenient. What do you think?>

He licked his lips, stunned for a moment. Belonius Vult, arrested? It was too bizarre to comprehend. He stopped himself speculating, settled for a cautious response. <He has many enemies, Majesty.>

<Indeed? You shock me.> She chuckled wryly, then her eyes narrowed. <The Crusade is about to march, Magister. You've cut it fine, but your news is most opportune.>

He gave a small bow. She smiled warmly, but then her face changed from her warm-hearted 'Mother of the Nation' mask to a darker persona. <And the Anborn bitch? You will send her to me.>

<I cannot, Majesty. I have possessed her with the scarab of my lieutenant, Rutt Sordell.>

Her face contorted. <That was not my wish, Magister.>

<It became necessary, Majesty. I need Sordell in a body capable of gnosis.>

<Then find him another. I want that woman.> Her face tilted and she bared her teeth. <Where is Fraxis Targon?>

<He's dead.>

She recoiled in amazement. <How?>

<I killed him,> Gyle lied. <He was beginning to annoy me.>

As he'd hoped, Lucia was stunned. <You killed an Inquisitor, an Ascendant, because he annoyed you?>

<Yes, Mater-Imperia.> The pure joy of watching Mater-Imperia's mouth goldfish was something he would carry to his grave. <Now, Majesty, we need to reach a new deal over the control of Javon, with a more appropriate fee.>

Northpoint, Pontus
1 Julsep 928
Day One of the Moontide

Kaltus Koron watched his enemy with hooded eyes. Bluff, robust and relentlessly energetic, Echor Borodium, Duke of Argundy, sat his chestnut horse twenty feet away, surrounded by long-haired Argundian guards. All about him were the generals and legion commanders, ranks of old warriors and swarms of magi: the military wisdom of an empire, gazing out at the line of stone sixty yards wide and three hundred miles long, stretching before them, carving a path through the sea.

The tide was visibly rising, battering against the massive flanks of the Bridge, gurgling and gushing beneath the arches in white churning maelstroms. Fresh spray erupted with every crashing concussion of water on stone. Behind and above, Northpoint towered, impossibly tall. The beacon at its top beamed vivid white. It was said to be visible for almost one hundred miles over the ocean. The pounding of the sea was awe-inspiring, enough to make the very earth quiver like jelly.

Another wave almost broke over the rim of the Bridge, and spray cascaded in a mighty cloud.

Korion glanced along the line to where an Ordo Costruo mage – one of the Northpoint magi who had betrayed Meiros and allowed the First Crusade onto the Leviathan Bridge – took a sighting along a sextant, then conferred with Duke Echor. This wave had been higher than the seven before, yet it had not covered the whole of the Bridge. Korion found himself smiling. It was high tide and the bridge remained out of the water. Someone cheered and it was taken up all down the line, young men and greybeards alike whooping like children.

Echor shook the hand of the Ordo Costruo man and then turned his horse to face the generals. 'Gentlemen,' he called, 'it is high tide and the Leviathan Bridge stands clear of the waves. The Moontide has begun!'

THE END OF BOOK ONE OF THE MOONTIDE

Acknowledgements

First and foremost a big thank you to Jo Fletcher, JFB and Quercus for believing in this series, and their expertise and eye for detail in making it the best it can be.

Also my immense gratitude to my agent Heather Adams for opening the doors for this series, and her invaluable feedback on earlier drafts.

Thanks also to the test readers on this one (a much bigger task than usual!): my wife Kerry Greig and my friend Paul Linton, who have each left their imprint on it. Also Tanuva 'Sister Tina' Majumdar for her guidance on Indian and in particular Bengali wedding rituals (all inaccuracies are either deliberate or down to my mistakes!).

Thanks also to Emily Faccini for the cool maps and to Patrick Carpenter, Jem Butcher and Paul Young for the cover art.